"Politics, science and rom [barcode] S0-ADF-921
fast-paced story that increases readers' understanding of the
complex Eubian empire. Asaro surpasses her usual outstand-
ing characterization, giving key players extraordinary depth
and revelation."   —*Romantic Times* on *The Moon's Shadow*

Tor Books by Catherine Asaro

THE SAGA OF THE SKOLIAN EMPIRE
Primary Inversion
Catch the Lightning
The Last Hawk
The Radiant Seas
Ascendant Sun
The Quantum Rose
Spherical Harmonic
The Moon's Shadow
Skyfall (forthcoming)

The
Moon's
Shadow

Catherine
Asaro

A TOM DOHERTY ASSOCIATES BOOK
NEW YORK

This is a work of fiction. All the characters and events portrayed in this book are products of the author's imagination or are used fictitiously.

THE MOON'S SHADOW

Copyright © 2003 by Catherine Asaro

Edited by James Minz

A Tor Book
Published by Tom Doherty Associates, LLC
175 Fifth Avenue
New York, NY 10010

www.tor.com

Tor® is a registered trademark of Tom Doherty Associates, LLC.

ISBN 0-765-34324-X
Library of Congress Catalog Card Number: 2002075661

First Edition: March 2003
First mass market edition: March 2004

Printed in the United States of America

0 9 8 7 6 5 4 3 2 1

To my aunt and uncle,
Marie and Jack Scudder,

with love

Acknowledgments

I would like to express my gratitude to the readers who gave me input on *The Moon's Shadow*. Their comments greatly helped the book. Any errors that remain are mine alone.

To Aly Parsons, Jeri Smith-Ready, Michael La Violette, and Trisha Schwaab for their thorough readings; and to Aly's Writing Group, for critiquing specific scenes: Aly Parsons, Simcha Kuritzky, Connie Warner, Al Carroll, Michael La Violette, George Williams, and J. G. Huckenpöler.

A special thanks to my editor, Jim Minz, for his insights and suggestions; to my publisher, Tom Doherty, and to all the fine people at Tor and St. Martin's Press who made this book possible; to my excellent agent, Eleanor Wood, of Spectrum Literary Agency; to Binnie Braustein for her enthusiasm and hard work on my behalf; and to Nancy Amis and her son Peter for their wonderful hospitality.

A most heartfelt thanks to the shining lights of my life, my husband, John Kendall Cannizzo, and my daughter, Cathy, whose constant love and support make it all worthwhile.

Contents

Part Three: Penumbra

PART ONE

Penumbra

1

Throne

In his seventeenth year of life, Jai gained an empire and lost everything he valued.

Stately buildings faced a plaza tiled in white and gray stone. Clouds hung low in the sky, their drizzle saturating the air. Evening had come, a time when the heat of the sixty-two-hour day on the world Delos cooled enough to make the temperature tolerable for its human colonists.

Two young men walked across the plaza, coming from the embassy of the Allied Worlds of Earth. One wore simple clothes, a sweater and trousers. The other had on elegant garb with a severe cut, the cloth as black as shadows. Even in the misty air, his black hair glittered.

On the other side of the plaza, the embassy of the Eubian Concord stood in grandeur, large and solid, with many columns. Six men descended its stairs. Four were strongly built and moved like machines, their uniforms black and their eyes the color of rust. They were guarding the other two men. The larger of the two, taller even than the looming guards, had a shock of glittering white hair and a commanding presence. His patrician features and red eyes identified him as a High-ton Aristo, a member of the most powerful, the wealthiest, and possibly the most hated ruling caste ever known to humanity.

The other man had his wrists locked behind his back in slave restraints. The prisoner moved stiffly, his chin thrust out but his eyes glazed. A gust stirred his wine-red hair around his handsome face. A diamond collar circled his neck and diamond guards glinted on his wrists and ankles. His white shirt, costly and impractical, was tucked into his dark pants. He walked barefoot.

The groups approached each other.

The two youths from the Allied Embassy stopped in the center of the plaza. The one in black clothes was tall, with broad shoulders and an athletic build. His features very much resembled those of the Highton man with the glittering white hair and were subtly echoed in the faces of the four guards.

The prisoner bore no resemblance to him . . .

At least not at first glance.

Jai Rockworth waited with his friend, Mik Fresnel, as the group of Eubians crossed the plaza to them. A deep-seated fear within Jai urged him to run, but he forced himself to remain still. He now wished he had brought more people. Had he been naive, assuming the Eubians would treat this exchange with honor? Given the number of armed guards in their group, he would have little recourse if they decided to take him without relinquishing their prisoner. But it was too late for second thoughts. If he didn't go through with this now, he might never find the courage to try again.

He recognized the white-haired man in the center of the Eubian group: Corbal Xir. Jai had seen him on countless news broadcasts. As a cousin of the late emperor, Xir stood close to the Carnelian Throne of Eube. The emperor, Jaibriol the Second, had died without a known heir, and many expected Xir to claim the title. The ruby color of Corbal Xir's eyes disturbed Jai—for it exactly matched his own. During the last two years, Jai had hidden his with brown lenses. Xir showed no such compunction about revealing his Aristo genetics.

Jai felt as if a band were constricting around his chest. He had no idea how to deal with a man like Xir. The Eubian group halted a few paces in front of him. The man in slave restraints stood with a numb expression, watching Jai with no hint of recognition. But Jai knew his face. Eldrin Valdoria. Prince Eldrin.

His uncle.

If I could free you from your pain by taking it into myself, Jai thought, *I would.* Nothing he could do would change what his uncle had already suffered, but he could see to it that Eldrin endured no more. He tried not to think that it would take so little, so terrifyingly little, for him to end up exactly like his uncle.

Xir spoke to Jai in the language of the Highton Aristos, his voice a rumble of authority. "I propose a simultaneous exchange. You and Prince Eldrin walk forward at the same time."

"Very well," Jai answered in flawless Highton. But when he turned to Mik, he switched to English. "Thank you for coming." He wanted to say so much more, but he couldn't take the risk.

Mik glanced uneasily at the Eubians. When he gave Jai a questioning look, Jai shook his head, fearing Mik would ask for an explanation Jai could never provide. But Mik just offered his hand. Jai shook it with a gratitude he didn't dare show, and also with sorrow, knowing he was saying goodbye to his friend forever.

"I'm not sure what you're doing," Mik said quietly. "But I will remember what you said."

Jai wished he could say more: *Never forget. No matter what you hear of me from this day on, remember the Jai you knew.* But Mik couldn't hear his thoughts, and Jai could say nothing in front of the Eubians. He nodded to Mik, his throat tight. Then he composed his face into a mask of Highton arrogance and faced Corbal Xir. Jai had barricaded his telepath's mind, turning it into a mental fortress, and so he received nothing from the Eubians, no sense of their emotions or thoughts.

Prince Eldrin was staring at him—and suddenly Jai *felt* his uncle's mind. Recognition went through him like a jolt of electricity: Eldrin was also a telepath. Even having known it ahead of time, Jai was still startled by the strength of his uncle's mind. Either Jai was more attuned to him than to the Aristos, who had no ability as psions, or else his uncle's mental barriers had slipped. Whatever the reason, the impact of Eldrin's emotions staggered Jai. He knew the other man's confusion and anguish as if it were his own. Another realization hit him: until this moment, Eldrin had known nothing about the exchange. The shock of realizing his captors intended to trade him had caused Eldrin's barriers to slip.

When Jai spoke to Eldrin, he made himself show a calm he didn't come close to feeling. "Shall we begin?"

"Yes." The prince's voice rasped with laryngitis so severe he had trouble speaking.

The raw sound of his uncle's voice shook Jai. He feared to learn what had injured Eldrin's vocal cords. Screams left scars that could haunt a man.

He and Eldrin walked forward. When they reached each other, Jai wanted to stop, to ask Eldrin the questions surging within him, to offer reassurance, to beg forgiveness for the life Jai was embarking on. But he could do nothing, show no hint of his roiling emotions. They passed in silence, Eldrin going to the Allieds and Jai to the Eubians.

Jai stopped when he reached Corbal Xir. The older man nodded in acknowledgment, though of what, Jai didn't know. A chill went through him at the soulless intensity of Xir's gaze. Jai returned his nod, then turned to see Eldrin reach Mik. As the prince halted, he looked back. For an instant he and Jai stared at each other. In that moment, even the mist seemed to wait. Would Eldrin ask *why*? Would he curse his captors?

The moment passed, and Jai no longer felt his uncle's emotions. Eldrin's mental barriers had come up again. Jai didn't think his uncle even realized they had slipped.

The Eubians closed around Jai in a tight formation and

swept him away, headed for their embassy. Jai set his shoulders and faced his future, though dread haunted him.

So it was that Jai Rockworth—also known as Jaibriol the Third—claimed his place as emperor of Eube, the largest empire in the history of humanity.

2

Advent

A portico with a high arch formed the entrance of the Eubian
Embassy. As Jai entered the building, a muscle in his
cheek twitched. The four guards loomed around him, bulky
and silent, arms swinging precisely at their sides, their faces
hard. He found it difficult to absorb the enormity of it, that
he walked with Lord Corbal Xir, one of the most feared men
in settled space. When the great doors of the embassy thundered shut behind them, Jai felt as if he were trapped in a
mausoleum. Jai Rockworth had died; from this day on he
was Jaibriol III.

He protected his mind, strenghtening his mental shields
until no trace of his telepathic ability could leak to the Traders with him. No, the *Eubians*. He had to remember; Eubians
never referred to themselves as Traders. That name came
from the people of the Skolian Imperialate, who abhorred the
Eubians for basing their economy on a slave trade. For the
rest of his life, Jai would have to maintain his defenses; he
could never weaken, neither in his behavior nor his mental
protections, lest it reveal that he who dared claim the Carnelian Throne was a slave. A provider.

Nausea surged in Jai and he nearly lost his composure.
More than any other reason, Aristos were hated because they
used providers to transcend. Providers were empaths and te-

lepaths; Aristos were anti-empaths. An Aristo could pick up the physical or emotional anguish of a psion, but instead of registering it as pain, the Aristo felt pleasure. The stronger a psion, the more transcendence he or she "provided" the Aristo. Craving the experience with a need that verged on obsession, Aristos made psions into the slaves they called "providers." Their pitiless culture allowed no exceptions; all empaths and telepaths were providers.

Jai knew he would have to protect his mind every day for the rest of his life. The immensity of it was more than he could absorb. If he slipped even once, revealing he was a psion, his life would become hell.

And yet—his claim to the throne was genuine.

To gain his title he had sent Corbal Xir a lock of his hair. Its DNA would show him as the true son of Jaibriol II, the previous emperor of Eube, who had died less than two months ago. The Eubians would undoubtedly check and double-check his DNA, but Jai knew they would find the proof they needed. His great-great-grandfather, Eube Qox, had founded the Eubian Concord and been its first emperor. Eube had been an Aristo of course, a Highton in fact, part of the highest Aristo caste. Only a Highton could be emperor. Jai's great-grandfather, Jaibriol I, had also been a Highton Aristo, as had been Jai's grandfather, Ur Qox.

Or so everyone believed.

Only Jai knew the truth: his great-grandfather had bred psi traits into the imperial line. A powerful enough psion could use ancient technology that survived from the long-dead Ruby Empire, technology the modern age couldn't reproduce—or defend against. But no Aristo could be a psion; the traits, considered a debilitating weakness, weren't part of the Aristo gene pool. The genes that created a psion were recessive, which meant *both* parents had to contribute them to their child for the abilities to manifest.

Jaibriol I had sired a son with one of his providers and forced his empress to acknowledge the child as her own, making the boy heir to the throne. It was an unspeakable abomination by Highton standards, but the emperor had been fanatically hungry for the power of the ancient Ruby machines.

The boy, Ur Qox, had been Jai's grandfather. Ur had the psi genes only from his mother, so he wasn't a psion. But he too fathered a child on one of his providers—and that son, Jaibriol II, had been a Ruby telepath, the most powerful of all psions. He possessed the mental power to use the ancient machines, which would have made it possible for him to conquer human-settled space. Through him, the Aristos could have subjugated all humanity.

Jaibriol II had other ideas. He had fled his heritage, appalled by its brutality, and secretly married another Ruby psion, a warrior queen of the Skolian Imperialate, Eube's greatest enemy. Her name had been Soz Valdoria.

Jai's mother.

So Jai had been born a Ruby telepath, the first child of Jaibriol II and Soz Valdoria. No one knew his mother and father had hidden in exile for fifteen years. But ESComm, the Eubian military, had finally found Jai's father and torn him away from his idyllic life, never realizing he had a family. In secret, Jai's mother had left her children on Earth, to protect them. Then she had launched the Radiance War—a shattering conflict that brought two star-spanning empires to their knees—all to rescue her husband from his own people.

Jai's parents had died in that war.

One consolation remained to Jai, the knowledge that his mother and father had been reunited in an escape shuttle before a missile exploded it. They had died together. He struggled against the hotness in his eyes. The grief was too great; he had never been able to weep for their loss. He feared if he started, he would never stop.

His parents had dreamed of a time when Eube and Skolia would know peace. Somehow, some way, he would turn that dream into reality. He would find a way to ensure that the two people who had gifted him with their unconditional love hadn't died in vain.

Drizzle misted over Eldrin, dampening his clothes and hair. His body ached from his last "chat" with his interrogators. He stared dully after the Traders as they walked toward their embassy, two Highton Aristos surrounded by four guards. He wondered what game of cruelty they were playing with him this time.

The unfamiliar youth who had stayed here in the plaza spoke to Eldrin in stilted Highton, his accent almost too thick to understand. "Cold you are? We go back."

Eldrin narrowed his gaze. The youth looked about eighteen, average in height, a bit shorter than Eldrin, with brown hair and eyes, and a friendly face. If Eldrin hadn't known better, he would have mistaken his new tormentor for a schoolboy from Earth.

The youth glanced at Eldrin's bound arms, then raised his gaze quickly, as if he didn't want to look. "Like you to make your arms free?" he asked.

Eldrin stepped back, his head jerking. What new tricks had they devised? His jaw clenched so hard, he felt tendons stand out in his neck.

"Okay, we don't have to do that," the boy said in English, more to himself than Eldrin. In his terrible Highton, he added, "Go we to Allied Embassy." He indicated a building. "Embassy. Allied Worlds. Earth. You come with me, yes?"

They picked a good actor. Eldrin readied himself to fight or run. Realistically, he knew he would lose either way; he could do little with his hands locked behind his back. But he had to try. He couldn't let them break him.

"Come, yes?" the boy repeated. "We remove restraints."

Eldrin had intended to stay silent, but he couldn't keep his hatred inside. "Go rot in a Tazorli whorehouse." He spoke in Skolian Flag, a language of his own people. He would never willingly use Highton, not if they tortured him for a hundred years.

The youth's eyes widened. He switched into Flag. "I'm not a Eubian, I swear it." He spoke the Skolian much better than Highton. "You are free now, in the territory of the Allied Worlds of Earth. We offer you protection."

Eldrin said nothing.

The boy tried again. "My name is Mik Fresnel. I'm a volunteer with the Dawn Corps. We're a group from Earth helping with rescue and relocation operations now that the war is over."

"Mik" looked so earnest, he could have fueled a spaceship on his sincerity. Eldrin saw their game now: convince him that he was free, that the fighting had ended, let him taste it, believe it, revel in it—and then send him back to interrogation.

After another silence, Mik said, "It's warmer in the embassy." His lopsided smile would have been charming had it been genuine. "The dining room has some pretty good soup."

Eldrin tried not to imagine the soup. Cold was seeping into his body, weakening the emotional numbness he held around himself like a shield. His arms and wrists throbbed. He had been shackled during the trip he and Corbal had taken through space, or wherever, to reach this place. At least Corbal hadn't ordered any other restraints beyond what basic security required. Strange that only Eldrin's interrogators inflicted pain, never Corbal.

Eldrin struggled to suppress his memories of what he had endured from the intelligence officers in ESComm, Eubian Space Command. He hoped the bastards rotted in hell. They could have questioned him without savagery. Humane methods existed, but they had chosen otherwise.

He had expected even worse from Corbal Xir, a Highton lord high in the Aristo caste system. Corbal could have done whatever he wanted to Eldrin, yet he had held back. Had Eldrin been more gullible, he might have believed Corbal was showing compassion. But it was impossible.

Rain continued to soak his clothes. His feet had become so cold he could barely feel his toes. Muscle tremors shook his body.

"Please," Mik coaxed. "We can help you." For some reason he looked upset. "Let us help."

"Liar." Eldrin's voice rasped. So cold. He was so cold.

"No one will touch you without your consent." Mik stepped away, toward the purported Allied Embassy. "You have my word."

Eldrin didn't want to go with him. He had to resist. But he couldn't keep the image of steaming soup out of his mind. Almost against his will, he moved toward the embassy.

Mik gave him an encouraging smile. He continued to walk, looking back at Eldrin, his expression offering unspoken assurances. So Eldrin limped after him. A drop of rain coalesced in his eye and ran down his face. It had to be rain. He refused to weep.

Mik led him around the side of the supposed Allied Embassy. But when they reached a recessed entrance, Eldrin froze. A soldier in fatigues guarded the door, a burly man standing ramrod straight with a laser carbine gripped in both hands.

"No." Eldrin despised the edge of panic in his voice. He jerked back and stumbled on the slick flagstones. Unable to regain his balance, he dropped to one knee. Agony flared through his leg, and he bit the inside of his mouth to keep from groaning.

Mik was speaking gibberish in that damnable soothing voice of his. Eldrin bent his head and shut out the words. He willed his body to be impervious, trying to believe it would work today, unlike all the other days. Even knowing they would soon pull him to his feet and take him away, he couldn't give in, couldn't let them see him weaken.

After a time, his mind began to clear. Focusing outward, he saw Mik a few feet away, also kneeling, his forehead creased with concern. Behind Mik, the soldier was still by the column, but he had lowered his gun and taken a less threatening stance. He looked troubled rather than implacable.

"Are you all right?" Mik asked.

Eldrin said nothing. He rose slowly, his battered muscles protesting the effort. Mik also stood, looking solicitous. The kid could have won an acting award. If he was a kid. For all Eldrin knew, the Traders had biosculpted one of their special operations officers to pass as an Earth boy.

Mik indicated the soldier. "Lieutenant Parkins won't hurt you. No one will." He spoke carefully. "We understand what you are."

"And what is that?" Eldrin could barely speak, his throat hurt so much. "Scum, according to your Aristo owners?"

"I'm not a Trader. I swear it to you. I'm an Earth citizen. You're on Allied territory." Awkward now, Mik added, "You're no longer a provider."

Eldrin sneered at him. "A provider? How could you know? I never told you."

"Your collar." An unstated horror lurked in Mik's gaze. "Only a provider would have one made from diamonds."

Eldrin would have touched the collar around his neck if his hands had been free. An Allied citizen might have guessed that he was a provider from his rich garb and restraints. More likely, "Mik" already knew. Although Eldrin couldn't pick up anything from the youth's thoughts, that meant nothing. Eldrin's mind was bruised. While interrogating him, his tormentors had transcended, and the anti-empathic link they had forced on him, using his pain for their pleasure, had wounded his mind.

Yet he couldn't quell the traitorous hope stirring within him. Watching Mik and the soldier, he limped across the flagstones. The ground felt like a furnace; the soles of his feet could no longer distinguish hot and cold.

Mik ushered him through the doorway, placing himself between Eldrin and the taciturn lieutenant, who persisted in looking worried. Inside the embassy, they followed corridors of rose-hued marble veined in gold, with ceilings that arched high above their heads. Every now and then they passed a statue in a wall niche.

When Mik stopped at a door bordered by friezes, Eldrin

stayed back. He could feel his feet a little now, perhaps enough to run. But to where?

Mik held open the door. "Would you like to come in? You can rest."

Eldrin meant to refuse; instead he found himself saying, "The soup . . . ?" Images came to him, hot and savory.

"I'll have someone bring dinner." Another emotion showed now in Mik. Dismay? It made no sense to Eldrin.

Wary, full of mistrust, Eldrin entered the foyer inside. White walls surrounded him, with abstract holo-art in swirls of soft color. As he walked into a hallway beyond the foyer, his toes sunk into a bone-white carpet. Just that slight relief was too much to bear. This was an excruciatingly effective torture; even knowing what they intended, he would weep when they took this away.

The hall ended in a living room with white walls and more of the soothing holo-art. The opposite wall consisted of a floor-to-ceiling window; beyond it, outside, paths circled gardens planted with purple blossoms. In the central flowerbed, bushes sculpted like ships sailed a sea of blue-green foliage, their bases foamed with white flowers. The beauty of the scene lied, promising peace instead of misery.

A click came from the right. Eldrin spun around, tensing to defend himself. Mik was bending over a console by the wall, but when Eldrin moved, Mik glanced at him. Eldrin didn't know how his expression appeared, but however it looked, it caused Mik to stop what he was doing and straighten up.

"I'm just contacting the dining room," Mik said. "That's all."

Eldrin wished he could fold his arms across his chest for protection against the cold. It didn't matter that the air was warm; the chill came from inside him. He fought down his nausea.

When Eldrin said nothing, Mik went to work on the console again, but slowly, letting Eldrin see his every move. The boy appeared to do what he claimed, ordering food, but Eldrin had no doubt the ever-so-trusty Mik also notified his superiors that their prisoner had arrived. Their security would be monitoring this room.

Mik turned to Eldrin, then hesitated, seeming uncertain. He motioned at a sofa across the room. "Would you like to sit?"

Gods, yes. But Eldrin stayed put.

"Sir?" Mik gestured, offering the couch.

Eldrin wanted to refuse, but he knew they would play this game however they wished regardless of what he chose. He walked to the couch, more in defiance of his fear than in acceptance of Mik's invitation. He expected an attack from behind, but he reached the sofa unharmed. He sat on one end, lowering his body with care, ready to jump up if he had to defend himself.

Eldrin wondered when Corbal would arrive. The Xir lord often joined him for dinner, lavishing feasts on his exotic new provider. He treated Eldrin well, but as if Eldrin were a treasured art object rather than a human being. Except a collector wouldn't touch a work of art for fear of causing damage. Corbal had no such compunctions.

Eldrin shut away that thought. Safer to wonder who owned Mik. Although the youth wore no restraints, he had to have an Aristo owner. Of all the billions of Eubians spread across the Eubian empire, none was free except those in the three Aristo castes—Hightons, Diamonds, and Silicates—and they numbered no more than a few thousand. Most Eubian slaves were taskmakers and lived comfortable lives, some even rising to a certain amount of authority and wealth. Over a trillion taskmakers existed; with so many owned by so few Aristos, they had to have enough autonomy to run their own lives and maintain the riches and power of their owners.

Providers were different. As psions, they were rare almost to extinction and difficult to create in genetics labs. As a result, only a few thousand existed, most of them conceived naturally. Eldrin grimaced. He didn't want his "elite" standing. Providers had no status, no possessions, and no autonomy.

He thought of the Aristo who had switched places with him in the plaza. The exchange baffled Eldrin. Apparently they expected him to believe they had traded him to the Allieds for some Highton youth. Did Corbal really think he was that stupid? No trade in the universe was worth giving up Eldrin Valdoria, their captive Skolian prince. The Traders knew it. The Allieds knew it. Eldrin knew it. Even if Corbal had agreed to such a trade for some bizarre reason, the Allieds wouldn't have sent two teenage boys to do it. What did Corbal hope to achieve with this charade? It was almost strange enough to believe it was real.

No. He couldn't weaken. They wanted him to believe, but he wouldn't be fooled. He couldn't bear the pain of having his hope crushed.

Eldrin drew his feet up on the couch, pulling his knees to his chest, his limbs shaking from his inner chill, a coldness that had begun the night of his capture. He wasn't sure how long he had been a prisoner—a month, maybe even two.

A rustle drew his attention. Mik was standing in front of him, holding a thermal quilt. Eldrin thought the boy had spoken, but he wasn't sure.

"What?" Eldrin asked hoarsely.

Mik offered the quilt. "You were shivering."

"Cold."

Mik tucked the blanket around him. Unexpected warmth spread over Eldrin like a benediction.

"Do you mind if I ask your name?" Mik asked.

"Who is he?" Eldrin whispered.

"He?"

The Aristo in the exchange, Eldrin wanted to say. But he didn't speak. His throat hurt too much.

Mik pushed his hand through his hair. "Can you tell me about yourself? I need to notify my superiors."

"You already did." Eldrin could barely manage the words.

"They do know you're here," Mik admitted. "But no one will approach you without your permission."

Eldrin shook his head. He knew he should stay alert, but he was so tired . . .

So tired . . .

Voices made Eldrin stir. Had he slept? He was lying with his head on the armrest, his body pulled into a ball, his hands clenching the quilt in front of his body.

Across the room, Mik stood talking to a woman with white hair and a dark-haired man. Two guards were posted where the hallway met the living room. Sweat broke out on Eldrin's forehead. These newcomers wore civilian clothes, but he knew military officers when he saw them.

Mik was speaking in a low voice. He seemed flustered now, confused, worried. "I assumed Jay was carrying out orders. It never occurred to me he would arrange a trade on his own, without telling anyone."

"You're sure the trade was consensual?" the woman asked.

The dark-haired man spoke. "We've contacted the Eubian Embassy. They don't say much, but it's clear Jay isn't coming back."

"You lied," Eldrin whispered.

No one in Mik's group heard, but one of the guards by the hall glanced at Eldrin. Then the man turned to Mik's group. "Major Armstead, I think our guest is awake."

As they all turned to look, Eldrin sat up, slow and stiff, pulling the quilt around himself, though his shirt offered plenty of warmth. Then it hit him: his arms were free. Mik had said no one would touch him without his consent, yet someone had removed the restraints. They had also treated his injuries; his lacerations no longer bled, and his welts had faded. For all that Mik's claim had been false, Eldrin was grateful they had eased his discomfort.

Grateful? His anger sparked. They extorted his emotions so easily, offering freedom from the pain if he would just talk. But he could tell them nothing. Even if the agony became unbearable and he screamed with the effort to speak, he could reveal nothing they would find useful. The Skolian military had put traps in his brain. If he weakened, those traps would disrupt his neural connections, erasing memories. Even knowing it was necessary, he hated that he would forget his family, his wife, his son . . .

"Sir?"

Eldrin focused outward. Mik was sitting on the table in front of the couch. A hearty aroma tickled Eldrin's nose; behind Mik, a tray waited with a steaming bowl of soup. Eldrin's mouth watered.

"Would you like to eat?" Mik asked.

Eldrin nodded, letting the quilt fall to his waist. He wanted to clench it around himself like a shield, but he refused to let his fear show. He regarded Mik with cool reserve.

The youth offered the tray. Eldrin balanced it on his lap, aware of everyone watching him. Then he ate. The soup warmed his throat, a balm to his ravaged vocal cords. His hope flared. Perhaps someday he could sing again. He might never regain his full voice, but he would have his music.

Sing for whom? Corbal? He would die first.

After he finished the soup, he drank the wine, grateful for its numbing effect. Then he slid the tray back on the table.

The two people with Mik had, surprisingly, stayed across the room. A realization came to Eldrin: the guard had called the woman "Major Armstead." Only an Aristo, or a task-maker with significant Aristo heritage, could become such a highly ranked military officer. This major, however, had blue eyes with no hint of red, and her face showed no sign of Aristo blood.

He steeled himself against hope. They had done this to him before, when they claimed they had his son and would let Eldrin see him. He had rejoiced to know his son lived—until they revealed it was a lie. He had died inside then. He couldn't let them do that to him again. Never again.

Mik was waiting. When Eldrin focused on him, the youth said, "Colonel Yamada would like to speak with you."

"Who is Colonel Yamada?" Although Eldrin's voice was ragged, it didn't hurt as much now.

Mik indicated the officer next to Major Armstead, a man with dark eyes, a smooth, golden complexion, and an aura of authority. He didn't resemble an Aristo, and his mind lacked the hard edge of an ESComm officer. In fact, Eldrin sensed no deception in any of these people. He shook his head. This couldn't be true. The Eubians would never trade him, not even for another Highton.

After a moment, Mik said, "Would you prefer if we came back later?"

"What does Colonel Yamada want with me?" Eldrin asked.

"Your name, for a start." Mik sounded friendly.

Eldrin just looked at him. And then? Information about his family? Not only was Eldrin the consort of the Ruby Pharaoh, he was also, through his mother, in line for the Ruby Throne itself.

Mik tried again. "Can we do anything for you?"

The question confused Eldrin. They never asked what he wanted. It had to be a trick. He could call their bluff. "I would like to sleep."

Mik indicated a door in the hallway. "The bedroom is in there. If you need anything, you can use the console."

Eldrin inclined his head, his gesture contained and guarded. "All right."

Unexpectedly, everyone left, true to Mik's word. After a moment, Eldrin went to the door in the hallway. It opened onto a comfortable room with a holobook rack on one wall and a bed with a blue quilt against another. Puzzled, Eldrin went back out to the foyer and tried the front door. To his surprise, it opened. The two guards were outside, and one nodded to him. It was too strange. At a loss, Eldrin stepped outside and waited. Incredibly, neither guard objected. He walked down the hall and they came with him; when he stopped, so did they.

"Can we escort you anywhere?" one asked.

Their behavior bewildered him, so much that he couldn't answer. The Traders had never let him leave his room. In truth, he had little wish to go anywhere; what he really wanted was the sleep his tormentors had denied him for days.

Probing their behavior now, Eldrin returned to his suite. The guards came, too, and took up their posts outside. Finally convinced they intended nothing dire, he went back into the suite to the bedroom, where he collapsed on the bed.

Eldrin's last thoughts, as he fell asleep, were of Dehya, her dark hair flowing. Dehya. Dyhianna Selei. The Ruby Pharaoh.

His wife.

They had told him she died.

3

The Gilded Cage

Corbal Xir poured the wine. It flowed into the crystal goblets, sparkling like rubies.

He offered Jai a drink. "It is from my vineyards, Your Highness." He said the title easily, as if he had addressed Jai that way for years.

At a loss, Jai took the goblet. His inclination was to thank Corbal, but he had no idea how an Aristo would respond. So he said nothing. He had been in the embassy for only a few minutes and already he felt as if he were treading water in an ocean where he could all too easily drown.

The room disoriented him. It was circular rather than square. Plush red upholstery covered its walls, and gold shone everywhere, from the moldings that bordered the ceiling to the onion-shaped arches above the doorways. Crystal sparkled on the chandelier, and the black lacquered tables gleamed. It all made him feel suffocated.

He and Corbal were nominally alone; their guards had stayed outside. But Corbal surely had security watching the room. Jai was clenching the stem of his goblet so hard, his hand ached. He felt so far out of his league, he had no idea where to begin.

Corbal raised his drink, his smile as smooth as glass. "To your health."

Jai just nodded, afraid to drink. Corbal took a long swallow, then lowered his goblet. He glanced at Jai's glass with concern. "Does the wine not please you?"

"Yes, certainly." Jai waited longer, but Corbal showed no distress. Relieved, Jai lifted his own goblet.

Corbal caught the glass just before the wine touched Jai's lips. Without a word, he pulled away the goblet.

Jai stiffened. "What are you doing?"

Disappointment showed on the older man's face, though whether it was real or planned, Jai couldn't tell.

"Come," Corbal said.

He took Jai to an antique stand by the wall. A gold cage hung from a hook at its top, and inside a bird fluffed red feathers. Corbal opened the cage and set Jai's goblet inside.

The bird chirped. It dipped its translucent beak into the goblet, sipping the wine, and gave an appreciative trill. Just as Jai smiled, the bird went silent. Swaying on the perch, it tilted its head. With a harsh cry, it toppled off the perch and hit the bottom of the cage with a thud.

Jai stared at the bird, then at the wine in his goblet next to it. Without a word, he reached into the cage and picked up the bird. It lay inert in his palm. Dead.

"Gods," Jai whispered.

Corbal took Jai's glass and went to a pearly oval set into the wall, what Jai had thought was part of the decor. When Corbal opened the panel, Jai realized it was a disposal unit. Corbal dropped in the goblet, and the hum of its disintegration filled the room.

Jai felt ill. "You poisoned the wine."

Corbal slowly turned, his face and manner cool. "It's possible. Or perhaps I put poison in your glass or an antidote in mine. Maybe I have internal systems that neutralize unwanted chemicals. Or the bird might be sensitive in ways we aren't." He leaned against a darkwood desk that reflected the chandelier in its polished surface. Then he took a long swallow of his own wine.

Jai set the bird in the cage. His heart was racing, but he

made himself speak without losing his cool. "You won't kill me."

"No?" Corbal smiled pleasantly. "And why is that?"

"You gave away Prince Eldrin. The greatest prize Eube ever attained, and you let him go." Somehow he kept his fear out of his voice. "No trade in the universe is worth that crime—except one. The Emperor of Eube." He prayed he was right. "Fail to produce me, and the other Hightons will obliterate you."

Xir sighed. "You are so painfully innocent."

Jai gave a short laugh, hoping Corbal couldn't see the fear it hid. "So I turn to the wisdom of my mentor, the mighty Lord Xir? I don't think so, Uncle."

"Actually, we are cousins." Corbal paused much the way Jai's mother had often done when she accessed her internal computer. "Your first cousin, twice removed. I was your grandfather's first cousin."

Like a sharp pain, Jai longed for the family he would never see again. He could never admit that the girl and two boys who had been foster children with him on Earth were actually his younger sister and brothers. He had no friends here, no one he could trust, nowhere he could turn. He fought the foolish, lonely part of him that wanted Corbal to fill the gap left by the loss of his family, friends, and the life he had known.

Xir finished his wine. Then he smiled, his face as cold as his ruby gaze. "Welcome to Eube, Your Highness."

The words sounded like a curse.

Lady Tarquine Iquar, the Finance Minister of Eube, appreciated the hospitality offered to her and the other bidders invited to the auction. Admiral Taratus, the seller, had provided a sumptuous dinner for the bidders. The dining chamber had the octagonal shape he seemed to favor, with gold walls and a domed ceiling tiled by platinum mosaics. An airbed stood discreetly in one corner.

Three other Hightons sat at the low dinner table with Tarquine. They reclined in loungers, two other women and a man in the uniform of an ESComm general. Tarquine sipped wine from her goblet. As the Highton Minister of Finance, she advised the emperor on the economy. Although she kept her appearance at a healthy and vibrant forty years old, she had lived 104 years.

The chamber contained one other person, the provider on auction. At the moment, he was sitting on the floor by another of the Highton women. Tarquine studied the man. He was an unparalleled item, no doubt. Tall and well built, with long legs, a muscular physique, and an athletic grace, he compelled attention. The age lines around his eyes and the maturity of his features added to his allure; this was no untried youth or body-sculpted mannequin.

But this provider had more to him than his beauty. Although his hair and eyes appeared light brown, Tarquine knew otherwise. He had bought some cheap genetic tattoo job that changed his coloring; reverse the tattoo, and he would shimmer gold, his hair, his skin, even his eyes.

Yes, she knew. Only she had recognized him. He was supposedly a Skolian psion Admiral Taratus had captured illegally, with his pirates, but that barely touched the truth. Tarquine believed him to be Kelricson Valdoria Skolia, a Ruby prince killed in battle eighteen years ago. He looked remarkably fetching for a dead man. Here he was, a long lost heir of Imperial Skolia, kidnapped by pirates barely two months after the end of the war and put up for auction.

Fascinating.

Tarquine took a sip of wine, listening as the others questioned Kelric. He answered in one-word sentences, with no attempt to hide how much he hated the auction. His resistance attracted her.

It didn't surprise Tarquine that no one else recognized Kelric. He had been in the news only briefly, thirty-five years ago, when he had wed a Skolian noblewoman, and then again when she had died two years later. But Tarquine had never forgotten the gold prince of those newscasts, because she had so greatly coveted him. He looked older now, experienced, his physique more heavily muscled than the leggy youth from over three decades ago. When Taratus had sent holos of the provider he had to auction, she hadn't been certain it was Kelric. But now, seeing him in person, she had no doubt. Fortunately, Taratus would keep this auction quiet, given his questionable methods.

Of course she wouldn't reveal his identity. If ESComm learned that Eube had another Ruby prince, they would take him for interrogation. She couldn't allow that—because no matter how much it cost, she intended to own Kelric Valdoria.

Corbal Xir wasted no time taking Jai to the capital planet of Eube. They arrived only a few days after they met on Delos. Jai's great-great-grandfather, Eube Qox, had named this world Eube's Glory. Eube had redesigned its solar system to please himself: he terraformed Glory to fit his taste, destroyed several planets he didn't like, and removed an asteroid belt that annoyed him. It gave Jai a window into his progenitor's mind, offering whole new insights into the word "megalomania."

Over a century and a half ago, Eube had comissioned the construction of a mansion for his sister Ilina on her marriage to a Lord Xir. Corbal was Ilina's son. Jai found it hard to absorb that his cousin had been born 132 years ago. It made Jai acutely aware he was only seventeen, terminally young and inexperienced.

Corbal had brought him here to the Xir mansion after their arrival on Glory. It relieved Jai; he didn't want to see the Qox palace yet. His palace. His mother's forces had left it in ruins. She had come for his father, but both of them had died trying to escape. Jai wasn't ready to face so many reminders of what he had lost.

He went out onto a balcony and rested his hands on the rail, a bar of platinum engraved with abstract tessellations. This rail alone was worth more than everything his family had owned in their exile. He would have traded a thousand such bars to have back that simple life.

A spectacular landscape spread out below this high mountainside that served as home for the Xir mansion. In the distance, across a valley, the Jaizire Mountains sheered into the sky, shrouded in mist. Primordial forest tangled on their slopes and carpeted the lowlands. Jai inhaled the cold, thin air, adjusting to its strange scent.

"A striking view," a voice said.

Startled, Jai looked around. Corbal had joined him, elegant and imposing in his dark clothes.

"Indeed," Jai said. Corbal often used the word, though it meant nothing as far as Jai could tell. Right now, it was conveniently vague.

His cousin motioned at the valley. "This is my land. You own the Jaizire Mountains and everything beyond them."

Jai stared at him. He *owned* that landscape? Surely he had misheard.

"You will need to visit the palace now and then," Corbal continued as if his new sentence was a perfectly logical continuation of the last. "Make appearances to your staff."

Corbal's conversation disoriented Jai; his cousin talked in circles, twists, and turns. Nor could he sense Corbal's mind that well. Aristos didn't project their emotions as strongly as psions, and Jai had fortified his mental barriers so much that he had trouble now picking up more than bits and pieces from anyone.

He spoke with caution. "I will need more than brief appearances to do my job."

"Perhaps."

Jai waited, hoping for clarification, but Corbal said no more. Jai had wearied of trying to untangle Corbal's speech. So he looked out at his mountains.

"You haven't asked about your providers," Corbal said.

Jai felt as if Corbal had kicked him in the gut. "I have no providers." The idea made him sick.

"Of course you do. You inherited everything your father

owned, billions of taskmakers and dozens of providers."

Jai swung around to him, staring. *Billions?* He couldn't imagine it. Nor would he ever believe his father had kept providers. It was impossible.

Corbal was studying his face. "You own several hundred worlds, including everything and everyone on them."

The idea revolted Jai. Knowing any remark he made would come out inadvisably hostile, he said nothing.

"Perhaps you would like a provider this evening?" Corbal asked pleasantly. "I would be happy to offer you your choice of mine."

Jai was aghast, or so he told himself. Appalled. Ah, hell. Corbal had just offered him his pick of among the most desirable pleasure slaves in an empire. It would take a saint not to respond, and Jai was no saint.

His cousin smiled. "Take any girl. As many as you like, as often as you like, for as long as you like."

Jai's face was burning. "That's, uh, generous of you."

Corbal indicated the glass doors leading into the living room. "Come. Look at my stock. See if any pleases you."

Stock? The word hit Jai like ice water. His anticipation turned to disgust. "Maybe later." His body had other ideas, but he pushed away the thought, angry at himself. If Corbal thought he could control his young cousin with pleasure girls, he was mistaken. It was hard to stop thinking about them, though.

Corbal laughed. "Saints, but you're young."

Was he that easy to read? "I've no idea what you mean."

His cousin leaned against the rail. "You lived in seclusion all your life, with your mother, yes?"

"That's right."

"Your Aristo mother."

"Yes." Jai's pulse jumped at the lie.

"And there?"

"Pardon me?"

"Always, Your Highness."

Gods. Conversing with Corbal was maddening. "What did you mean, 'And there'?"

"Where did you live?"

Sweat broke out on Jai's forehead. "I don't know."

"Interesting," Corbal murmured, "that you lived there but didn't know where it was."

"Only my mother needed to know the planet's location."

Corbal studied his fingernails. "Odd that we have no record of this woman."

Jai restrained himself from wiping his sweating palms on his shirt. "My father wanted to protect me from assassins. So he hid both my mother and me and told no one about us. Even I didn't know all the details."

Corbal exhaled. "The hell of it is, that makes sense."

Personally Jai thought it made his father sound like a paranoid lunatic. But maybe Aristos found such behavior logical.

"Of course," Corbal added, "it makes just as much sense that you are an impostor."

"You've analyzed my DNA." Jai had no doubt Corbal was having that analysis verified. His cousin could have easily stolen a sample of Jai's tissues during the past few days. Jai wasn't worried. His genes offered the necessary proof. Before contacting Corbal, he had also bought an expensive genetic tattoo that made him appear more Highton.

Corbal waved his hand. "Oh, I've no doubt you're the son of Jaibriol the Second. But you have no proof he married your mother."

Jai scowled. "My birth is legitimate."

"Can you prove it?"

He could, in fact; their marriage was recorded on Earth. But he doubted it would do him any good to prove his father had married the Skolian Imperator. So he summoned up the most arrogant bearing he could manage. "I find your implication offensive."

Corbal looked amused. "That may be. But nevertheless, you have no proof of your legitimacy."

Jai shrugged. They both knew Corbal had to produce an emperor after giving up Prince Eldrin.

Corbal sighed. "I suppose proof can be supplied. An impeccable Highton woman, young and beautiful, though of course we Hightons are all uncommonly pleasing to the eye."

Modest, too, Jai thought.

"It should of course be possible to find your father's records of the marriage," Corbal added.

"Of course." Good gods. It sounded like Corbal had offered to falsify records proving Jai's mother had been an empress. It was a crime punishable by execution. Then again, if Corbal didn't produce an emperor he could also end up dead. The more important question was why he had accepted Jai as the emperor in the first place. Even after only a few days with the Xir lord, Jai had no doubt about one thing; if he just came out and asked why, Corbal wouldn't give him a straight answer.

"You look like him, you know," Corbal said.

"My father?"

Corbal nodded. "You have his face. His build. You even sound like him. Except—" He let the word hang.

"Yes?" Jai asked.

His cousin tilted his head as if searching for words, though Jai suspected he knew exactly which ones he wanted.

"You're *more*," Corbal said. "Taller, stronger, broader in the shoulders, more hale. You have an intensity he lacked."

Jai spoke quietly. "He was more than I will ever be. I can only hope I am worthy of his example."

Corbal snorted. "I hope not. He is dead."

"Everyone dies."

"Follow your father's example," Corbal said, "and so will you—long before your time."

4

Carnelian Throne

Jai waited with his bodyguards in a lobby of the Qox palace, outside the Hall of Circles. It was too much; he felt like a desiccated sponge submerged in water, at first too dry to take in liquid, then gradually soaking in the full import of this place. His father, grandfather, and great-grandfather had been born in this palace. His mother had come for his father here and destroyed half the palace in the process. The weight of its history pressed on him as if it could mold him into an Aristo by its sheer gravity.

The half-ruined palace had once been a spectacular work of architecture. This wing remained intact, with its high arches, though cracks showed on one wall. Black and gold diamonds tiled the floor, and columns graced the airy space. The walls were made from a blend of gold and snow-marble created atom-by-atom by specialized nanobots.

Four men waited with Jai, all in the midnight uniforms of Razers, the secret police that served the emperor. Jai didn't understand their status; gunmetal collars circled their necks, indicating he owned them, yet they seemed more his jailers than his bodyguards. The captain of the four stood silent, his posture alert, his face neutral. The red tint of his coppery eyes gave witness to his heritage; either his mother or father had been an Aristo, the only Eubians with red eyes. His other parent would have been a slave, possibly a taskmaker but more likely a provider.

The Razers disturbed Jai. Their minds exerted a mental pressure he thought would crush him if his defenses weakened. He would have sweated, but this morning his protocol aides had injected him with temporary nanobots that controlled his perspiration. It kept him dry, but it didn't calm him down. He wasn't ready. These past five days that he had spent at Corbal's mansion, learning about Eube, were nowhere near enough to prepare him for what lay ahead.

Lights blinked on the captain's gauntlet. He spoke into its comm, and a low hum came from the doors. As they swung inward, opening into the Hall of Circles, Jai felt as if he were on a wild ride, unable to stop as he plunged toward disaster. Determined to hide his fear, he set his shoulders and entered the Hall.

Impressions hit him like an avalanche. Rank upon rank of Aristos filled the Hall, sitting on high-backed benches, hundreds of them, all in glittering black: Hightons, who controlled the government and military; Diamonds, who managed commerce and production; and Silicates, who produced the means of pleasure, including providers. Every one of them had ruby eyes, shimmering black hair, and perfect, cold faces.

Show no hesitation. Jai repeated the words in his mind like a mantra. He strode down an aisle toward the dais in the center of the Hall. Corbal waited there, his expression triumphant. He stood with one hand resting on an arm of the Carnelian Throne, a large snow-diamond chair inlaid with red gems. Jai knew the script; just before he had entered, Corbal had dropped his bombshell: *I present to you, His Honor, Jaibriol Qox the Third, Emperor of Eube.*

Every Aristo in the Hall was staring at Jai. Their shock vibrated against his mind, so great it penetrated his barriers. It was a nightmare. They exerted a pressure far worse than what he experienced with the Razers; this many Aristos in one place were like a black hole ready to suck him in and crush him into nothing.

Somehow he kept walking. As he climbed the dais, Corbal watched him, his gaze like a ruby laser. When Jai reached the throne, he turned to face the assembled Aristos.

And he spoke.

His voice rolled out, amplified by the extraordinary acoustics of the Hall. "In honor of my father's memory, I accept the Carnelian Throne."

His audience murmured. The suspicion and hostility he expected were there, but another emotion also came through, strong and sharp—and unexpected. *Hope?* They seemed to lean forward, though no one actually moved.

Jai made himself start the speech Corbal's staff had prepared. "Eube in her magnificence will attain ever more lofty heights, a glory greater than ever before known in our illustrious empire." It sounded as pompous now as it had the first time he had read it. But his voice rolled out exactly as the protocol aides had predicted when they rhapsodized over his "incomparable resonance." It startled him; he hadn't realized how deep his voice had become this last year.

"We will triumph!" he continued, feeling like an idiot. "We will bring ever greater splendor to the exalted memory of our ancestors."

Pah. He couldn't believe anyone thought this would inspire people. Aristo logic was more alien to him than the chlorophyll-based animal life on Prism, the exile world where he had grown up with his family. Right now Eube needed vitality and energy, not overblown platitudes.

With sudden resolve, Jai dropped the speech and spoke his own words. "The wounds of this war *will* heal. We have survived. Our strength will return."

The mood of his audience shifted: he had startled them. He went on, using his own words, terrified of these people and their crushing minds. Incredibly, he seemed to mesmerize them. Even through his barriers, he felt their confidence building. Three times during his speech, they chimed the small cymbals they wore on their fingers, showing approval.

And he despised himself for giving hope to a people who inflicted such atrocities on humanity.

Tarquine Iquar, the Highton Finance Minister, reclined in the banquet hall on her space habitat. Most of the Diamond Aristos who had attended her feast were also sprawled nearby, watching a news-holo projected on the wall. The recording came from Eube's Glory, many light-years away. After the collapse of the interstellar webs during the war, the only way to carry news was by starship, which meant it could take weeks, even months to cross interstellar space. This broadcast had been made two days ago, yet she was seeing it only a few days after receiving the news of Prince Eldrin's capture, which had happened nearly two months ago. But she understood why this news had traveled so much faster.

Eube, it seemed, had an emperor.

Jaibriol III. How terribly convenient. Tarquine had to admit, his charisma filled the screen. Even by the exacting standards of Aristos, he was uncommonly handsome. His voice resonated, full timbred and deep. Sensual. His self-possession was remarkable in one so young, and he chose his words far better than the inane propaganda produced by government speech hacks, which suggested he had intelligence. For all his impressive qualities, though, she doubted this man-child would rule. Corbal Xir would control him: the power would be Xir rather than Qox.

Tarquine frowned. As Finance Minister, she sat within the emperor's highest circle of advisers. She had spent decades building her political position. A new emperor would bring change. Her family, the Iquar bloodline, had no current feud with the Xir bloodline, but neither did they have strong ties. Corbal might seek to replace her with someone the crafty old lord thought he could control.

She studied Corbal, who remained on the dais as the boy spoke. As the oldest living Eubian, Corbal had dealt in Aristo politics longer than anyone else alive. But Tarquine had spent over eight decades breathing the rarified atmosphere of Highton intrigue herself. If Corbal thought he could trifle with her, he would soon discover otherwise.

She wondered at his white hair. Many Aristos would do away with that sign of age, believing it marred their Highton perfection. But others thought the white accented Corbal's authoritative presence. Tarquine took a tendril of her own hair and wound it around her finger. White threaded the black. Although she had considered having it treated, she had decided to leave it for now, to augment her aura of experience, a reminder that she was no untried youth but a force to deal with. Or so she let others believe. And it was true. But her hair hadn't turned white because of age.

Had Corbal's whitened for the same reason as hers? She would probably never know; if he was hiding a secret as dire as her own, he would certainly never reveal it to her.

Tarquine looked around at her guests. Most were watching the broadcast, but a few had remained in alcoves or shadowed corners, enjoying themselves with the providers she had made available tonight. An atmosphere of sensuality overlaid the dimly lit banquet hall as the night receded into its latest hours. If not for the broadcast, most everyone would have been asleep by now.

She was the only Highton present; her guests were all Diamonds. As the caste involved with commerce, they were intimately tied to the economy; as Finance Minister, it behooved her to maintain profitable relations with them—and to keep abreast of whatever schemes they hatched.

Tarquine was sitting next to Kiv Janq. Sleek black hair swept back from Kiv's forehead, accenting the icy severity of her features. The Janq Line owned one of the largest Eubian banks and had great influence over the flow of credit throughout Eube.

When she noticed Tarquine watching her, the banker curved her lips in a cool smile. "So. The emperor had an heir after all."

"Apparently so," Tarquine said.

"A delectable young piece, eh?"

Tarquine held back her laugh. "I would hardly presume to call our esteemed emperor a 'delectable young piece.' " In truth, though, Kiv had it right. Eligible young Highton women would soon be throwing themselves at this scrumptious boy, seeking to become empress. It promised to be immensely entertaining.

Corbal Xir would undoubtedly sidetrack the young emperor with the flower of Eubian femininity. The more time Jaibriol III spent distracted by their charms, the more freedom Corbal would have to scheme. Tarquine considered the idea. Amorous pursuits might keep Jaibriol III's attention away from finances as well. The last thing she needed was an emperor who paid attention to what she was doing. She could think of a few charming young Iquar women with political acumen. Perhaps she would send them his way and see what they could learn while they kept him diverted.

Tarquine knew the game well. In her youth, she had fended off many ambitious Highton men bent on becoming consort to the heir of the Iquar bloodline. After she had come into her title as the head of her line, she had done her duty and accepted an arranged marriage. It had been worse than prickle-heat in the summer. She had soon sent her esteemed husband away, much to their mutual relief, and they had divorced several years later. So it was that she had no legitimate offspring. No heirs.

She did have several children whose fathers had been her pleasure slaves. Although she had given her progeny wealth, status, and education, none could inherit her title. Long ago, she had frozen some of her eggs but she had no interest in conceiving any more children. Nor did she desire to let a cold Highton man share her title and her bed. Pah. Never again would she tie herself down that way. When she died, her title would go to her younger brother, Barthol Iquar.

Tarquine looked down the length of her banquet hall. On the raised area at the far end, Kelric was sitting on the top step, watching the broadcast. He had put his clothes back on, his gold shirt and leggings, but he was barefoot. She hadn't given him shoes. Walking wasn't what she had in mind for him. A slow smile curved her lips. Why waste her life in a chilly Highton marriage? Far better to enjoy the charms of her incomparable provider, a pleasure slave worth every one of the unprecedented fourteen million she had paid for him.

Her Ruby prince—and no one suspected. *No one.* Even his own people believed him dead. Who would have thought he would show up after eighteen years? In the few days she had owned him, he had kept his past to himself, but she would learn where he had been all those years. She had plenty of time. He would be hers for the rest of his life.

Ironically, Kelric threatened everything she valued. He was too strong a telepath; he had learned her secret. But he would never reveal it. He didn't dare, for it meant she would no longer own him. He would go to another Aristo, who would force him to provide by torturing him. Yes, Kelric knew her secret—and so he knew that as long as he remained silent, he would never have to endure transcendence.

Fifteen years ago, Tarquine had used telepresence to operate on her own brain, in secret. It had taken years of planning, but when she finally tried the operation, it had succeeded. The only outward change was the whitening of her hair. The real alteration remained unseen—she could no longer transcend.

By Aristo standards, that made her abnormal, sick, a pariah. If the truth became known, she would lose her title, lands, wealth, possibly even her life. She had done it anyway. She couldn't have lived with herself otherwise, for she didn't think she could have resisted the temptation to transcend as long as it remained possible. The experience was too intense. So she had ensured she could never do it again—for she had gradually, in her later years, developed a new, unexpected trait.

Compassion.

However, Tarquine remained a Highton in all other ways. The exhilaration of ambition, the challenge of gaining power, the gratification of using it—she relished it all. She thrived on the excitement of accruing wealth in ever more creative ways. She had no intention of letting this inconvenient new emperor interfere with her plans to dominate the political structure of Eube.

If he tried, Jaibriol III would discover he had a formidable enemy.

5

Sunrise

Corbal Xir was an impostor.

Lying in his opulent bed with its ornate posts and tasseled canopy, Jai brooded. The minds of Aristos were like an immense weight pressing on his mind. It exhausted him to maintain his barriers every moment, never relaxing except at times like this, when he was alone.

Corbal caused no pressure.

Jai didn't understand how his cousin could be so unlike other Aristos. Didn't they notice he was different? Maybe only a psion could sense the lack of threat. Corbal acted like an Aristo, owned worlds, had providers, and looked Highton, except for his white hair.

Strange, that. White hair. Aristos were fanatics about their supposed "perfection." Taken altogether, they were like a huge machine with identical parts, each Aristo icily designed in their unforgiving ideal of beauty. It had no appeal to Jai, but they considered their homogeneity inviolate. He understood why Corbal had chosen to interrupt it; his cousin's white hair accentuated his authority. But Jai felt what the Aristos would never know: Corbal wasn't like them. It made Jai wonder.

A rustle came out of the darkness.

Jai sat bolt upright in bed. "Who is that?"

Another rustle. He sensed the mind of a psion. Alarmed, he strengthened his mental barriers. "Lumos on," he said.

The lights came up, revealing his bedchamber. It made him dizzy. The gold and sapphire furnishings sparkled. Gold hangings adorned the walls, and ivory friezes bordered the horseshoe arches. The room's antique quality spoke of more than his wealth, it was also a testament to his power that no holo-ads adorned the furniture or trim. He had the authority to prevent the planetary network from marring the privacy of his rooms. But the decor wasn't what riveted his attention. No, a far more natural beauty caught him. A girl.

She stood across the room, an impossible vision. Jai flushed, suddenly remembering he wore nothing except a dark nightshirt he had found in the bureau. The girl's negligee drifted around her thighs, barely veiling her spectacular curves. Her breasts strained against the gauze, the enlarged nipples erect. Her hair glimmered like the proverbial spun gold, but soft and pliant, pouring around her body. And her *eyes*. They were huge, bluer than the sky on Earth and framed by gold lashes. A rosy blush touched her cheeks, and she averted her gaze with virginal shyness.

"Who are you?" Jai stuttered.

"My honor at your presence, Your Glorious Highness." Her voice was a blend of innocence and sultry promise.

Sweat broke out on Jai's brow. "Why are you here?"

"Lord Xir sent me." She looked up. "As a present, to welcome you to the palace."

"You're his pleasure girl."

"Tonight, I am yours."

Oh, Lord.

"Would you like me to come over?" she asked.

"Yes," he managed, forgetting any reasons he might have had about refusing providers.

She walked forward, her negligee molding to her breasts, her slim waist, her hips, and thighs. Jai couldn't stop staring. She climbed onto his air-bed and knelt next to him, her hair brushing his arms. He could barely think.

"You're so pretty." Jai winced as soon as he spoke the words. He sounded as nervous as he felt.

Her smile warmed her face. "You are kind to say so, especially when you are a man of such magnificent form."

Even knowing she was supposed to compliment him, Jai wanted to believe every word. Mesmerized, he ran his finger along her lower lip, tracing its curve. She shyly laid her hand on his shoulder, then slid it down his chest. He knew he should hold back, find the hidden thorns on this gift, but he didn't want to be sensible now.

"So strong," she murmured, moving closer. "Hold me."

With a sigh, he pulled her into his arms. Her mouth was so close when she turned up her pretty face that he couldn't help but bring his lips to hers. It wasn't his first kiss; there had been a few times during his two years on Earth, though he had never gone any further. But it had never been like this. The provider melted against him, warm and pliant, her mouth opening under his.

With care, Jai laid her on her back, pulling down the covers so she sank into the downy sheets. Then he stretched out on top of her, and filled his hands with her breasts. Being emperor of Eube suddenly seemed less daunting. It had a lot more going for it than he had thought.

Then he saw the images in her mind.

Her telepath's mind magnified their violent impact. She had lain this way with a select few of Corbal's guests, and had suffered at their hands. Their brutality went beyond Jai's ability to comprehend. She pretended to want him, but fear saturated her thoughts. She expected the same agony from him—no, worse, because he was the emperor.

"Gods, no." Jai sat up, his desire transformed into horror. "I could never—" Too late, he stopped, realizing his words would give him away.

If she understood what he had just revealed, she gave no hint. "Have I displeased you?" She sat up quickly and laid her hands against his chest, toying with the fastenings on his nightshirt. Her delicate fragrance drew him.

Jai caught her hands. Her fear intensified, and he longed to say *I won't hurt you.* Her fear made him want to hit someone. Even having known what it meant to be an Aristo, he had never really understood. It was beyond his ability to comprehend how they could consider themselves exalted when they committed such violence against people they were supposed to love.

She had no mental defenses. None. No one had taught her to protect herself. It sickened him to realize why; it made her more vulnerable to the link that formed between an Aristo and a provider. Aristos had a cavity where their capacity for compassion should have been, a void in their souls.

Alarm sparked in the girl's mind. "Please forgive me if I have disappointed you."

"No! You haven't. You're perfect." He took her hands in his. "I just—uh—took a vow."

"A vow?"

He tried to think of an intelligent follow-up to that panicked remark. Given Aristo culture, she was hardly going to believe a vow of celibacy.

Then her mind prodded his.

Ah, hell. She was trying to probe his thoughts. Corbal had sent her to *spy* on him. Pah. Maybe Corbal was the one he should sock.

"A vow?" she repeated.

"That's right. To protect myself." Jai raised his voice. "You hear, Corbal?" He had no doubt his cousin could monitor this room. "Sending pretty spies won't work. I'm not that stupid." He hoped Corbal really was listening; otherwise he would look like an idiot, telling the room he wasn't stupid.

The girl tensed, gripping his fingers. He spoke to her in a gentler voice. "Don't be afraid of me. Lord Xir made a mistake, that's all."

Doubt leaked from her mind. Then he felt another of her emotions—and it scared the hell out of him. Recognition. Just as he could feel her psion's mind, so she could do the same with him. She didn't understand yet, but she might soon. His parents had given him extensive training in using his abilities, and he had a greater mental strength than the provider, so it was easier for him to detect her than the reverse. But a faint suspicion glimmered in her thoughts.

Jai exhaled. "The hour is late."

"Do you wish me to go?"

"I think so." He had to force out the words.

She slid off the bed and padded across the room, her shift clinging to her body. He so wished she could stay. What a bizarre life this was, that he had to worry about being discovered as a kindhearted man.

After she left, he lay down, even more aware of his loneliness. It wasn't only sensual; he missed his family, too. For the first fourteen years of his life, they had been the only people he knew. Now they were gone. He had lost a part of himself.

Lisi, his sister, was almost fifteen, bright and quick, with her teasing humor. Ten-year-old Vitar had always shouted with delight when Jai swung him around. Del-Kelric wasn't even five. Their mother had left them in the care of Admiral Seth Rockworth on Earth, trusting him because he had once been married to her aunt.

Jai had searched the nets for news about his siblings, but found nothing. He knew they would go into hiding when they learned he had become emperor. He dared investigate no further, lest he draw attention to them, risking their freedom and raising questions about his own parentage.

Jai grieved, knowing he could never see them again.

Corbal sat in his dimly lit study, relaxed in his smartchair, his hands folded around a crystal tumbler. He took a swallow of brandy and let it warm his throat.

A door opened across the room. His bodyguards had let him know who was coming, but he said nothing, just stared into space, sipping his drink.

Bare feet padded on the floor. Then she came into view, Sunrise, his favorite provider. She dropped to her knees in front of his chair, between his thighs, and bowed her head. "I am sorry," she whispered. "Please forgive me."

Corbal took another swallow. "All right." He wasn't displeased; she had done her best. He could never be angry with her anyway.

Her relief at his response showed in the relaxing of her shoulders. He set his tumbler on the arm of his chair, which adjusted to secure the glass. He ruffled Sunrise's hair, enjoying its glossy texture. Pressing his legs against her body, he savored the flex of his muscles against her curves. One-hundred-thirty-two years old and he had a better physique than men in their thirties.

"So." He reclined in his chair. "Our prudish emperor talks to the air."

"He is intelligent."

"Is he now?"

"Not as intelligent as you," she added quickly. "Your wisdom is matchless."

"Hardly," Corbal said. She would tell him he was the greatest genius alive if she thought he wanted to hear it. She might even believe what she said. Such traits had been bred into her; she came from a line of providers designed for devotion, submission, and affection. It was why he liked her so much.

Jaibriol was a fool to send her away. Not that Corbal minded. It meant he had Sunrise tonight. And he did like her. Although she was his best spy, it had become harder and harder to offer her to other Hightons. He wanted her for himself, only for himself—and he hated that they hurt her.

Careful. Love made a person vulnerable, which was, of course, unacceptable. He had enough to worry about, like the new emperor. He had suspected the boy's intelligence from the start. Jaibriol had contacted him with what looked, at first glance, like a crude claim of Xir heredity. His true message had been cleverly hidden within the message.

After watching the boy these past days, Corbal thought Jaibriol would comport himself as emperor better than his father. That wasn't saying much; the father had lived in seclusion during the two years of his reign. The previous emperor would have been better suited to domestic life than to ruling Eube. The son clearly had more to work with. Maybe too much; the boy was proving unpredictable.

Corbal knew he had to watch himself with Jaibriol, lest the boy discover his Xir cousin no longer transcended. Corbal had no intention of changing any other aspect of his life; being one of the most powerful and wealthy men alive suited him just fine. But he had no wish to hurt Sunrise. Providers were pleasure slaves in every sense of the word; that he had stopped transcending didn't alter his enjoyment of her sensual charms.

To change his brain, Corbal had needed to learn why he transcended, including how his genetics related to those of psions. It gave him knowledge possessed by few others—and so he had recognized the anomalies in Jaibriol's DNA.

The emperor was a psion.

Jaibriol had hidden the evidence well; Corbal would never have noticed if he hadn't already conducted forbidden research when he investigated his own genetics. Jaibriol III was without doubt the son of Jaibriol II, yet he was also a telepath and empath. It was impossible.

Compelled to understand, Corbal had tried ever more obscure tests on Jai's DNA, going far beyond those necessary to verify the boy's paternity. Then he had cracked open the records of past emperors. It had taken an immense amount of work, and he couldn't have managed without the intelligence networks he had been developing for over a century, but he had finally uncovered the truth.

Eube Qox had been full Highton.

Jaibriol I had been full Highton.

Ur Qox had been half Highton.

Jaibriol II had been one-fourth.

Jaibriol III was one-eighth.

The Qox dynasty had bred itself a Ruby psion. Corbal even understood why. Centuries ago the Skolians had found three Locks, ancient machines that had survived for five millennia after the fall of the Ruby Empire. Modern science couldn't replicate the Locks. However, Ruby psions could use them to create a computer web in Kyle space, a universe outside of spacetime. The physical laws of spacetime had no meaning in Kyle space, making it possible to bypass the limitations of light speed—which allowed instantaneous communication across interstellar distances.

Skolians often called the network the "psiberweb." The name annoyed Corbal. Psions were providers. It was like saying "providerweb." He preferred the designation "Kyle web." Regardless of what they called it, the web gave Skolians a great advantage over Eube. Their communications sailed; Eube's trudged.

To operate, a Lock needed a Key—a Ruby psion. During the Radiance War, ESComm had stolen a Lock and captured Eldrin Valdoria, a Ruby prince. With both a Lock and Key, they could have built their own Kyle web. Corbal knew many Hightons condemned him for giving up Eldrin, even though they gained an emperor in return. Only Corbal knew that Jaibriol offered an even better solution. The pieces fit together, like a jigsaw puzzle.

The Kyle webs protected the Skolians.

A Triad of Ruby Keys powered the webs.

The Radiance War had decimated the Ruby Dynasty.

Soz Valdoria, the Imperator, had died. A Key.

Dyhianna Selei, the Ruby Pharaoh, had died. A Key.

Two vacancies now existed in the Triad.

A new Ruby Key could join the Triad using a Lock.

Eube had a Lock.

The emperor of Eube was a Ruby Key.

The beauty of it gratified Corbal. Jaibriol could join the Triad. Although they could have used Eldrin to power a Kyle web, Corbal doubted they could have forced him into the Triad. Jaibriol was another story. As the emperor of Eube, he had motivation to do what Eldrin would have resisted with all his might. If Corbal had unlimited access to a Kyle web and the Triad, he might even collapse the power structure of Skolia without going to war. He doubted the restless young emperor could resist the allure of conquest on an interstellar scale.

Closing his eyes, Corbal waved to Sunrise, a gesture she knew well. She unfastened his trousers and took him into her mouth exactly as he liked. He exhaled, his tension easing. He enjoyed his retirement. He enjoyed Sunrise. He had enjoyed Eldrin. He had hated giving up the Ruby Prince, but he hated it even more when ESComm interrogated Eldrin. Damn inconvenient, this business of remorse.

Corbal was tired of wars. He wanted Skolia conquered, yes, but without fighting. Perhaps he was a fool, to let a provider sit on the Carnelian Throne. He could have been emperor himself. But his age had given him plenty of time to contemplate the job; it was an imperial pain. He had no wish to be emperor. Let Jaibriol have the high profile; Corbal would rule from behind the throne. Through Jaibriol, he would control the Triad; through the Triad, he would control the webs; through the webs, he could manipulate interstellar civilization. Eventually he would dominate all humanity.

To achieve his ends, he needed only to control an inexperienced boy.

6

Heredity

Prince Eldrin stood at the glass wall of his room. Outside, the garden drowsed in the sun, unaffected by the heat of the long day. This view had never changed in the four days he had been here at the so-called Allied Embassy on the planet Delos, where the Traders had purportedly exchanged him for an Aristo. His routine never changed; in the morning, they brought him breakfast, later they came with lunch, and in the evening they brought dinner. Always they were solicitous. Always they plied him for information.

Eldrin revealed nothing. He waited for the game to end, but it continued, and the seeds of hope had grown despite his struggle to stop them. Could this be an Allied embassy? It was still a prison, but far preferable to Eube. He rather liked the Allieds, or he had before today, when they had brought The Message: *You have a visitor.*

Was it Corbal? ESComm? Other Aristos? He clenched his fist and stared at the garden. He would rather die than return to the interrogation room.

When the door of his suite opened, he didn't move. Steps sounded in the hallway, muffled on the carpet. Even when his visitors entered the living room, he remained at the window. The gardens beckoned with their unattainable freedom.

A woman's voice came to him in a stunned whisper.

"Eldrin."

No. *No.* Of all the torments they could have inflicted, this was the cruelest. He turned slowly, unwilling to see her but unable to stop himself.

She stood across the room, surrounded by officers, both Allied and Skolian. Small and slender, she resembled a waif more than an interstellar potentate. Her glossy black hair hung down her back, thick and healthy, streaked with gray. Her eyes, a clear green, seemed too big for her face. They had more lines at the corners than before, and he didn't remember those dark circles under them.

This impostor isn't a true match. She had to be an impostor. He couldn't believe otherwise. She couldn't be a prisoner, too. It couldn't be her.

It couldn't be his wife.

"Eldrin?" Her husky voice was painfully familiar. "Don't you recognize me?"

Unable to bear her presence, Eldrin turned back to the window, knowing if he looked at her any longer, he would shatter. The Traders had captured him when their commandos broke through to the habitat where he lived with Dehya. Eldrin and Dehya had fled with their son while their bodyguards fought the intruders. In the end, Eldrin had sacrificed himself, blocking the commandos so Dehya and their son could escape. But he had never known if those two people he loved had made it away.

The Traders had claimed his family died.

As much as Eldrin had denied their words, pain had shredded his heart. He couldn't bear this hope. It was killing him.

She came to stand with him. Together, they gazed out the window. Blue-tinged light slanted across the gardens outside.

His mind refused to accept her presence. She spoke and he answered, their words constrained, but he couldn't hear. Hope was jagged glass that gouged his heart.

Gradually he became aware of a change. It spread over his mind. Warmth.

No.

An impostor could falsify a great deal—face, build, voice, mannerisms—but nothing could counterfeit what he felt now from the woman at his side. He had shared his mind with her for most of his life, through decades of marriage. She was dropping her defenses, leaving her mind vulnerable. His thoughts blended with hers, responding by instinct before he could stop himself.

He could take it no longer. He turned and spoke hoarsely. "Dehya?"

Her voice caught. "Welcome home, Dryni."

Moisture gathered in his eyes. "It was for nothing."

"What do you mean?"

"I thought—I thought you and Taquinil escaped."

"We did." She said more, but he couldn't hear. Her mind overwhelmed everything else. The Traders had raised falsehood to a fine art, but he could feel the lies in their minds. Dehya had none: she spoke the truth. It filled his thoughts and flowed into his heart.

Eldrin embraced her then, holding her as if she would break. She slid her arms around him, her cheek against his chest. As he bent his head over hers, a tear slid down his face and dropped onto her hair.

Finally he let himself hope.

Seated behind his desk, Corbal peered at Jai over his spectacles. "Normally you wouldn't be asked to deal with such a matter. But this case is unusual."

Jai didn't believe for one instant that Corbal needed reading glasses. His cousin undoubtedly had perfect vision. By easing his mental barriers, Jai picked up enough from Corbal to know the spectacles were supposed to create a scholarly aspect that would inspire Jai to trust his cousin. It didn't work. Everything about Corbal made Jai tense, including this office, with its steel-diamond desk, silver walls, and steel-hued carpet.

Jai sat in a chair near the desk. "Tell me more about the case."

Corbal paused at the blunt question. Jai was beginning to realize that in many situations, direct speech between Aristos was considered an insult. He wondered how his advisers expected him to benefit from their advice when he couldn't figure out what the blazes they were saying.

Corbal, however, could use more direct speech without giving offense because he and Jai were kin. "The problem," Corbal said, "concerns two of your more vital people. The man is Azar Taratus, an admiral and also the younger brother of Kryx Taratus, one of the Joint Commanders of ESComm. The woman is Tarquine Iquar, the Finance Minister. Her niece was your grandmother."

Jai stared at him. "Vital" hardly began to describe them. Tarquine Iquar had formidable authority among his advisers, and she used her power like a honed knife. Few dared cross her. Azar Taratus was one of ESComm's renowned war leaders, or perhaps notorious was a better word. He had survived the Radiance War by breaking just about every law in the Halstaad Code, which was meant to define civilized behavior during wartime.

With foreboding, Jai said, "Go on."

Corbal removed his glasses. "Minister Iquar claims Admiral Taratus cheated her."

"That's it?"

"That's it."

Surely they didn't expect the emperor to settle private arguments. "Why bring it to me?"

"An apt question, Your Highness."

Jai waited. Then, exasperated, he said, "Perhaps you have an apt answer."

Corbal could have taken offense, but he chose otherwise. "Admiral Taratus sold Minister Iquar a provider. She paid fourteen million for the man."

Jai barely kept from choking. *Fourteen million?* That could feed the entire population of some planets.

Watching him, Corbal added, "A large amount indeed."

Jai flushed. He had to learn better control over his face.

"It sounds like a matter for the insurance bureaus." He couldn't believe the Aristos had an entire industry devoted to insuring providers.

"Minister Iquar has contacted them," Corbal said.

"And?"

Corbal's eyes glinted. "Apparently Taratus neglected to tell her this provider was dying."

"What, he didn't think she would *notice*?"

Corbal rested his elbows on the arms of his chair and steepled his fingers. "He probably expected her to make a deal with him. If she lied to the bureaus about how much she paid for the provider, reporting a much lower price, she wouldn't have to pay much for the insurance."

Jai had seen the criminally exorbitant fee scale used by the insurance bureaus. "I understand the advantage to her if she lies. But why would Taratus?"

"Then he wouldn't have to pay much tax on the sale."

Jai could see where this was going. "So when she found out Taratus cheated her, she would have no recourse, because she had claimed she paid almost nothing for the provider. If she admitted she lied, she could be convicted of fraud."

"Exactly."

"But it didn't work?"

Amusement showed on Corbal's face. "Minister Iquar reported the full fourteen million to the insurance bureau. Then she sued the holy hell out of Taratus."

Jai frowned. "And just when, in all this, did someone send the fellow to the doctor?"

"I'm afraid that wasn't possible." Beneath his reserve, Corbal was positively gleeful.

"Why not? Doesn't Minister Iquar have doctors?"

"Certainly."

"But?"

"Well, you see, it seems the provider escaped."

Good for him. Jai didn't see how the the man could have managed it, though. "Did Minister Iquar let him go?"

"Of course not. He managed on his own."

"How?"

"Apparently he was a Jagernaut."

That Jai understood; his mother had been a Jagernaut, a Skolian military officer in the elite corps of psions whose ability to link their minds to their ships gave them an immense advantage in battle. They also lived with the danger of what had befallen this man, that they might be captured and sold as providers. The thought made him ill.

Jai strove to hide his disquiet. "Did ESComm question the Jagernaut before he escaped?"

Corbal shrugged. "The fellow had been missing for nearly two decades. His knowledge and internal systems were too far out of date to provide useful data." His amusement faded. "Still, it was sloppy of Admiral Taratus not to question him more thoroughly."

"Why didn't he?" Although Jai was glad the Jagernaut had benefited from Taratus's negligence, it surprised him the admiral had overlooked such a detail.

"Taratus claims it wasn't worth the trouble. He wanted the man in good shape for the auction."

"Do you believe him?"

"It isn't unreasonable."

"But do you believe him?"

Irritation flashed on Corbal's face. "I think our dear admiral wanted to unload the man fast, before his appallingly bad health became obvious."

"It sounds like a mess." Jai could hardly admit he supported the Skolian escaping. "But I don't see why the courts can't take care of it."

"Well, you see, we have a bit more of a problem."

Jai regarded him uneasily. "More?"

Corbal leaned forward. "To escape, this dying provider just walked to a launch bay of Minister Iquar's space habitat and stole a shuttle."

"Wasn't anyone watching him?"

"They were watching the news-holo of your speech when you became emperor." Corbal smirked. "Minister Iquar says this provider of hers was also watching the speech. The next time she checked, he was gone."

It still made no sense to Jai. "Her habitat must have security systems that could have stopped him."

"Indeed it does. State-of-the-art, designed by ESComm."

"The military? I thought her habitat was civilian."

"It is."

"But then why—"

"Apparently," Corbal said, "your military and finance advisers have, shall we say, ties that are a bit too close."

Jai had no clue how to unravel the conflicting intrigues here. He stuck to the obvious. "How did the provider escape?"

"It seems that he somehow shoved his mind into the computer networks and shredded the security throughout the habitat."

Jai had learned enough about ESComm to know what Corbal described couldn't happen. "That's impossible."

"Indeed." Corbal couldn't contain his glee any longer. "Astonishing, isn't it? This man pulverized Minister Iquar's system and *pfifft*—he was gone. It is one of the worst security breaches in history. And *one* provider managed it, without a single weapon."

"It's incredible." Jai could see why this had reached the highest levels of the government and military. Unfortunately, he had no clue what to do. "Is ESComm working on it?"

"Yes. Also the Ministry of Intelligence."

Jai squinted at him. The Intelligence Minister, Azile Xir, was Corbal's son. The chronicles of Azile's rise to power showed an impeccable record. Too perfect, in fact. Jai had found traces of less-than-impeccable deletions in the files. Having one's father next in line for the throne had its advantages.

What to do? Jai felt as if *I'm lost!* was emblazoned on his forehead. Trying to project confidence, he leaned one elbow on the arm of his chair, copying his posture from portraits he had seen of his great-grandfather. The pose felt more natural than he wanted to admit.

"What Minister Iquar and Admiral Taratus need is a judge and court," he said. "Not me."

Corbal studied Jai as if sizing him up. "Your Finance Minister is set against one of your top admirals in a matter that involves a severe breach of security, and a phenomenally expensive provider with too much military knowledge is gone. This isn't the time to distance yourself, particularly not from Tarquine Iquar. She has too damn much power, and she isn't likely to ally herself with us."

Interesting. Apparently Corbal didn't much like the Finance Minister. "Why wouldn't she?"

"She covets the influence of the Xir Line."

Hah! So Corbal didn't like the competition. That could be useful. "What do you suggest I do?"

A gleam came into Corbal's eyes. "I think it is time Minister Iquar and Admiral Taratus paid their respects to our new emperor."

The four of them met in the ivory and gold sitting room of the palace: Jai, Corbal, Minister Iquar, and Admiral Taratus. They sat in wing chairs around an octagonal table, and Jai's bodyguards took up posts around the walls.

Jai was surprised to find that even with three Aristos at close range, he could bear their minds enough to control his anxiety, at least for a short time. Actually, they were two Aristo minds; he had given up trying to detect Corbal. Iquar and Taratus affected him as a single force he couldn't separate.

He listened as Corbal went through the formalities required before the minister and admiral could address their emperor. Jai wondered how Hightons ever got anything done when they spent so much time giving honorifics. As he waited, he thought back to the files on Iquar and Taratus. Both were wealthy and powerful even by Highton standards, and well on in years, Taratus in his eighties and Iquar over a century. The sheer length of their lives intimidated him. How could he, at seventeen, hope to deal with these people?

He distrusted Taratus immediately. The admiral looked the perfect aristocrat, but he had the mind of a master thief. His hair was pure glittering black, unbroken by a single strand of gray. He had a narrow face and hooked nose, and his eyes were a darker red than Jai's. He seemed to assess everything around him, missing no details.

Tarquine Iquar was another matter. Jai couldn't stop looking at her. To say she was a striking woman was akin to saying the Eubian empire was sort of impressive. Her high cheekbones and aquiline nose gave her an austere beauty that had matured into honed elegance. Her snow-marble skin had no flaw. Long and lean, she was almost his height. She was mesmerizing, and she intimidated the hell out of him.

Technically, he and Tarquine were kin; she was the aunt of his grandmother, the late empress dowager, which made Tarquine his great-great-aunt. But the empress hadn't really been the mother of Jai's father, so Jai had no blood relation to Tarquine, though only he knew. But the red of her eyes matched his, suggesting they did have mutual ancestors; it wasn't a common shade, except in the Qox Line.

Tarquine had the usual Aristo hair, with one difference: white threaded the glittering mane that brushed her shoulders. It added to her mystique. She distracted Jai, disrupting his concentration.

Corbal turned to him. "Minister Iquar and Admiral Taratus request the honor of your acknowledgment."

Jai wondered what they would do if he said "no" after that interminable introduction. "It is given."

Tarquine spoke. "You honor the Line of Iquar, Your Esteemed Highness."

Jai inclined his head as his protocol people had taught him. He wished everyone wouldn't address him with so many titles. He also hoped Tarquine couldn't tell how much she flustered him.

Taratus spoke. "You honor the Line of Taratus, Your Esteemed Highness."

Jai nodded again. He couldn't imagine having to go

through this every time he met a Highton for the first time. The seclusion Corbal wanted to impose on him looked more inviting all the time.

Finally they got down to business. Jai wanted to ask about the situation, but of course he couldn't be direct. Unfortunately, he had about as much proficiency in the intricacies of Highton speech as a brick. He made a stab at it anyway. "I've noticed a remarkable amount of credit flowing lately."

Taratus nodded as if accepting a compliment. "More to the glory of trade."

"Indeed." Tarquine spoke dryly, her voice deep and husky. "One would certainly prefer such a glorious trade to, say, fraud."

The admiral sat in a relaxed posture, surveying her as if he were a sage and she a callow youth. Given that she was twenty years his senior, it had less effect than it would have had on someone less imposing.

"Perhaps 'glory' is an inadequate word," Taratus said. " 'Astonishing.' There is a word for you. It describes many things, even, say, escapes by a supposedly dying man."

She looked unimpressed. "Many words come to mind, Admiral. Like 'swindle.' "

" 'Security.' " Taratus smirked. "Or a lack thereof."

Jai couldn't see what they hoped to accomplish with this dissembling. But if he came straight to the point, it would diminish him in their view. So he tried an oblique angle. "You must be a much-beloved patron of the arts, Minister Iquar."

Tarquine tilted her head, a sultry curiosity leaking from her mind. "I've always appreciated aesthetic compositions, Your Highness."

A blush heated Jai's face. She was looking at him as if he were the aesthetic composition. He stumbled over his words. "Fourteen million worth of art."

Her smile soured. "Fourteen million of dying art."

"An unusual acquisition," Jai managed.

"Perhaps that is the current fad right now," Taratus said,

too smoothly, like acid eroding a surface. "Death. Change. Escape."

She gave him a bored look. "Have you ever noticed, my dear admiral, how often auctioneers are themselves something of a fad? Popular one day, vanished the next."

Jai winced. What did she imply, that someone would assassinate Taratus? He wished Corbal would jump in and give him some guidance. His cousin, however, was sitting back, listening with interest.

The admiral regarded Tarquine blandly. "I do realize the vigor and energy of youth can be wearing on our more elderly citizens."

"Youth is often a euphemism for inexperience," Tarquine murmured. She glanced at Jai.

Good grief. Had she just insinuated he was immature? This meeting was going nowhere; so far all they had done was insult one another.

Like an optical illusion, Jai's perception shifted. The conversation had no point; how they spoke was what mattered. This was his chance to take the measure of the minister and admiral, and for them to assess him. He wondered if it even mattered whether or not their discussion made sense.

"Words are like the poles on a planet," he said. "North and South. Immature and mature. Vigor and serenity." Let them figure out his meaning. He didn't know himself, but what the hell.

"Indeed," Tarquine said.

Taratus scratched his chin. "So they are."

"Transcendence and compassion," Jai said.

As soon as Corbal stiffened, Jai knew he had made a mistake. He wasn't sure what, though.

"An Aristo," Taratus said, "can show no greater compassion than to elevate a provider through transcendence."

Bile rose in Jai's throat. He wondered how Taratus would like it if someone "elevated" him that way.

Although Corbal spoke casually, his laser-like focus never left Jai. "An interesting juxtaposition of words. It inspires provocative pairings." He paused. "Eube and Imperialate. Qox and Ruby."

Jai froze. Was it coincidence Corbal paired Qox and Ruby? He answered with a nonchalance he hoped hid his alarm. "I hadn't realized you had such a liking for opposition."

"Qox and Ruby?" Minister Iquar snorted. "Hardly the most innovative opposition."

Jai tried to relax. She had taken Corbal's comparison at face value. Qox and Ruby: they were the ultimate opposed pair, but she was right, that made them a cliché. He wanted to believe Corbal had simply tired of the verbal parrying, but he couldn't stop worrying. Did his cousin suspect the truth, that Jai was both Qox and Ruby? Perhaps he ought to send Taratus and Iquar away before Corbal said too much.

Shifting his weight, Jai tried to communicate dismissal. To his surprise, it worked; Corbal began the process of letting the minister and admiral leave. On the surface, the Xir lord seemed no different, smooth in action and word.

Jai just hoped he hadn't revealed himself.

Standing in his office, Corbal poured red wine into two goblets and gave one to Jai. "To your health."

Jai didn't drink. "To my health."

Corbal sipped his wine. "And to your father's honored memory."

"Of course."

"And your mother's, may she rest in peace."

Sweat broke out on Jai's forehead. *Stay calm.* He shouldn't have let Corbal send away the Razers. They were supposed to guard both Jai and Corbal, but Jai wondered who would protect him from Corbal. Could his cousin shield this room even against the emperor's security? Corbal had a formidable security network, including his son, Azile Xir, the Intelligence Minister.

Corbal lifted his glass to the light. "Lovely, isn't it? Like liquid rubies."

Panic constricted Jai's chest. The word "ruby" could be coincidence. *Let it be coincidence.*

"Or blood." Corbal took another sip. "Rubies and blood."

Jai relaxed his barriers enough to probe the surface of Corbal's mind, but if his cousin knew the truth, he hid it well. Jai wished he could find out how much Corbal had guessed about his parentage. He feared to push too hard, lest he make Corbal suspicious. He also hesitated to lower his defenses any further. Hightons could sense the link they made with a provider. He didn't know if Corbal had that ability, given his differences from other Aristos, but if he did, Jai might reveal himself in the process of trying to discover what Corbal knew.

Jai spoke casually, though inside he was as tight as a coil. "Rubies and blood? That sounds unpleasant."

"Rubies. Transcendence. Compassion." Corbal took another swallow of wine. "Or should I say an abnormality of compassion. And one of parentage. Distasteful topics, don't you think? Unpleasant enough that I should hope not to speak of them again."

Jai hesitated. He was only just learning to interpret Highton speech, so he couldn't be sure, but it sounded like Corbal was offering a bargain; he would remain silent about Jai's questionable parentage if Jai would remain silent about Corbal's lack of transcendence.

Jai spoke with care. "Yes. I agree."

"Good." Corbal tapped his finger against the rim of his goblet. The hue of its wine matched the clear, crystalline red of his eyes. "Think of it as insurance."

"Against what?"

"Perdition, perhaps." Corbal softly added, "Shall we spend eternity in a hell of our ancestors' making? At the least, we should make our own hells."

Jai shivered. "I prefer none at all."

"So would we all," Coral murmured.

Jai feared his had only begun.

7

Fugitive

Jai recognized the man in the holo.

He viewed the recording by himself, or as alone as he could be given that Security monitored him all the time. He thought he and Corbal had come to an agreement to guard each other's secrets, but their verbal skirmish made him uneasy. He decided to keep his Razers in the room from now on. They stood by the walls and Jai sat in a wing chair, far enough from them to ease the pressure of their minds. He had the holostage replay the report about the provider who had caused such an uproar.

Jai knew the man.

At first it surprised him that no one had identified the provider. But then Jai realized he had seen images of this man available to no other Eubian. Jai's mother had kept those holos in a family album, one of the few personal items she had taken into exile. The man was her brother, Kelric Valdoria. Jai's youngest brother had been named for him: Del-Kelric, which meant, "in honor of Kelric"—because Kelric had died over eighteen years ago.

Jai rubbed his eyes. This situation grew ever more bizarre. He couldn't be certain this was his uncle Kelric. The provider certainly looked older than the man in his mother's album. Kelric had also had gold skin, hair, and eyes, whereas this man had brown hair and eyes, and tan skin. Gold highlights showed in his hair, though, and his irises had a metallic glint. Could it be his uncle, or was that only wishful thinking on his part?

Another puzzle tugged at Jai; he wasn't sure, but he thought he had met this man recently. When Jai had been a Dawn Corps volunteer on the planet Edgewhirl, a man had come into his office, a refugee searching for his family. Jai could have sworn this was the same person.

Jai touched a panel on the arm of the chair. "Attend."

"Tomjolt here," a voice answered.

Jai jerked, then schooled his face to impassivity; he couldn't afford behavior that might make people notice him. He could get away with some "eccentricity" because everyone knew he had grown up in isolation, but he kept as low a profile as possible.

It had shaken Jai deeply to discover that the emperor's personal EI, or Evolving Intelligence, answered to "Tomjolt." His father had named it. Jai suspected he was the only one who understood its significance. Tomjolts were animals on the world Prism, where Jai's family had lived in exile. The symbolism gave Jai a grim satisfaction; a tomjolt was the top predator in the food chain there. His father must have christened this EI in defiance, after he had been ripped away from his family and forced to become a puppet emperor.

"May I help you?" Tomjolt asked.

Jai shook himself out of his reverie. "Yes. What is the latest news on the provider who escaped from Minister Iquar?"

"ESComm is increasing the search volume in the region where he is believed likely to cross into Skolian space."

Jai frowned. Nothing about this had been in the report sent to him a few hours ago by Azile Xir, the Intelligence Minister. "And what region might that be?"

Tomjolt described the Skolian border territory that had been closest to Minister Iquar's habitat at the time Kelric escaped. It seemed unlikely he could evade capture; the searchers would detect his ship as soon as it dropped into normal space. Had the fugitive been anyone else, Jai would have assumed, like ESComm, that he would run for home. But Kelric was a Jagernaut; he probably knew how ESComm would search. Even if he had the foresight not to head for the border, though, he had very few choices, given how little fuel his stolen ship carried.

"Have they found any trace of him yet?" Jai asked.

"None." The EI's blunt response was a welcome change. Jai wondered if other Hightons programmed their computers to speak plainly.

"Show me the volume of space where Minister Iquar's habitat was when her provider escaped," Jai said.

"Done."

A holomap appeared, rotating to display different views of space. According to the glyphs scrolling below the image, a few Eubian settlements were within range of Kelric's ship, but none he could safely approach. Removing slave restraints wasn't easy, given how they linked to the nervous system. Anyone Kelric contacted would recognize him as a provider and take him into custody. He might find an empty asteroid or rogue world, but his food and air wouldn't last long.

Jai studied the maps. Kelric could also reach several military bases, including the one where ESComm was keeping the stolen Lock. That would do him no good, either, though. As a Jagernaut, he might possibly escape from such a base, but entering one would be crazy, especially the one with the Lock, given how ESComm could use his mind if they caught him.

Jai pushed his hand through his hair. He wished he knew if the fugitive really was Kelric. Would he act as ESComm expected? They didn't know Kelric was a Ruby Key. In that, Jai had an advantage, being a Key himself. He tried to imagine how he would act if he were a prisoner of ESComm. Thoughts of Corbal came to mind; if his cousin suspected Jai was a Key, his willingness to trade Eldrin made a lot of sense. But if he believed Jai would use the Lock to conquer Skolia and enslave his own family, the Ruby Dynasty, Corbal was out of his allegedly esteemed mind. Jai would do anything to avoid such a fate, even take his own life.

And Kelric?

Suddenly Jai knew what his uncle had done.

Some called Admiral Xirad Kaliga a shadow. His black uniform had no ornamentation, medals, sash, or piping, nothing except the red braid on his cuffs that denoted his rank. Gaunt of feature and narrow in the face, he appeared—at first glance—ordinary. But that fooled no one who knew him. Few could match his razor-sharp intellect; none could claim his combination of exalted bloodlines, family influence, education, and cold-blooded military brilliance.

Kaliga spoke little and listened well. He had infinite patience for his own intrigues and none for those of people he considered fools. As one of the two Joint Commanders of ESComm, he had earned the gratitude of the Aristos, who wished to conquer human-settled space, and the dread of the Skolians, who sought to staunch the near-fatal wound his armies had dealt their civilization.

Kaliga considered himself an efficient man, punctual, and generous, too, perhaps to a fault. On his home world, he donated to local schools. He brought his spoiled young bride gifts when appropriate and resisted the impulse to gag her when she prattled. He prided himself on his dedication to his job and his integrity in performing it to the best of his ability, indeed, to the best of anyone's ability. That his job had, over the decades, involved ordering the deaths of billions of people didn't factor into his assessment of his character.

Kaliga walked through the gardens in the space station where he lived. The habitat was one within a collection of mutually orbiting stations that made up the Sphinx Sector Rim Base. Bodyguards accompanied him, forming a bulwark; any taskmakers who saw them quickly withdrew.

Today, Kaliga had company: Lord Jaibriol Raziquon, a

lanky man with a sardonic lift to his mouth. His gray trousers and silver-blue shirt were impeccably cut. Like many Highton men, he had been named for a Qox emperor, either Jaibriol I or Jaibriol II, Kaliga didn't know which. Now that a Jaibriol III had turned up, Eube would probably be inundated with Jaibriols. Xirad Kaliga had never cared for the name. He preferred sharp words that hit with a solid sound. Like Xirad.

Raziquon had no formal position in either the military or civilian command on the station. He was simply a private citizen. It made his intelligence work for Kaliga all the more useful, because he operated outside established hierarchies. However, it also made him harder to control. No chain of command checked Raziquon; he did as he pleased. Although Kaliga found him useful, he didn't trust him.

They strolled down a path between two manicured lawns. This residential area was in the wheel of the station; in the distance, a spoke rose like a huge pillar from the ground to the "sky" far overhead.

"My Line honors the new emperor," Raziquon said. "We esteem his honored presence."

Kaliga almost snorted. Raziquon esteemed no one but himself. "The Line of Raziquon has always been loyal to the Qox Dynasty."

Raziquon inclined his head. "We value our ties with the imperial house."

"As do we all." Right now Kaliga valued Raziquon's ties more than his own. Kaliga interacted with the imperial court as a military officer, but Raziquon moved in those circles socially. He was well placed to gather intelligence on this new boy-emperor.

Kaliga wanted to know what Corbal was plotting. The Xir lord could have kept both Eldrin and the throne for himself. Not that Kaliga believed Corbal would let Jaibriol rule; the cagey lord would control the emperor from the shadows, much as Kaliga cloaked his influence by appearing nondescript.

Kaliga spoke dryly. "I imagine the Line of Xir also values its ties to the imperial Line."

Amusement glinted in Raziquon's eyes. "One would think dear Corbal had a penchant for politics." He laughed. "And for providers, eh? Pretty girls with yellow hair and big blue eyes."

That caught Kaliga's attention. "Penchants have uses."

"Let's just say, he might do anything to protect the dawn." Raziquon flicked his hand to indicate his last word referred to his previous sentence.

So. Corbal had a weakness, a provider named for the dawn. Although Kaliga had never seen Corbal show one mote of sentimentality, he had heard rumors of doting behavior. Could the powerhouse of the Xir bloodline be losing his edge? Kaliga doubted it. Corbal was as sharp as a man in the vigor of youth. But if he cared for this provider, it offered possibilities; a Highton who let improper affection enter into his life became vulnerable.

"It would be interesting," Kaliga remarked, "to see how Lord Xir would react if the sun ceased to rise."

Cruelty edged Raziquon's smile. "She might rise for another, eh? Sweet tears."

Kaliga thought of his own providers. Through them, he attained heights of transcendence that lesser beings could never know. Providers, despite their beauty, or perhaps because of it, were at the bottom of the human hierarchy. He had heard it argued that they didn't even deserve the notice of Aristos. Kaliga honored his with attention, letting them earn elevation by providing for him.

Raziquon's implication troubled him. It was true that if Raziquon stole the girl, she could make a useful lever against Corbal. But such a theft was a tricky proposition. Providers were costly. Stealing one was serious business, both because of the wealth involved and because of the insult it did to another Aristo.

Taskmakers cost nothing, of course; everyone who lived on the worlds an Aristo owned belonged to that Aristo. Yet even with taskmakers, the fines were steep for tampering with their populations. It had to be that way; the economy would falter if trade protocols broke down. Providers could cost millions. If Raziquon took this girl and was caught, Kaliga's association with him could prove damaging.

"Tears may be sweet when they come from a provider," Kaliga said. "They are less so from a convicted thief."

Darkness lurked behind Raziquon's mocking gaze. "That assumes the thief is caught."

"Such a bandit must be circumspect."

"Of course."

Kaliga nodded, understanding Raziquon's unspoken assurances. He would use the necessary caution.

They continued their walk, discussing other matters, avoiding any more mention of the dawn. Eventually they parted and Kaliga continued on with his bodyguards. Gardens bloomed on either side of the path, part of a park that extended the width of the wheel rim, several hundred meters. After that, the land sloped into terraced hills, where droop-willows shaded houses that resembled small pagodas but were far stronger than their delicate appearance suggested.

Although he could have ridden a magrail home, he walked for the exercise. He was at his prime, only seventy, and he intended to stay healthy for a long time. He had two goals in life: to make ESComm invincible and to conquer the Skolian Imperialate. He gave his loyalty to the Qox Dynasty, but that assumed the emperor acted in the best interest of the empire. Or perhaps he should say the Xir Dynasty; Corbal would soon have the young emperor so distracted with providers, drugs, and debauchery, the boy wouldn't notice he wasn't running anything.

Kaliga walked through the droop-willows that sheltered his house. On the station, no one worried about weather; it was always perfect. With neither rain nor wind to bother it, the house had many open doorways and windows, even walls that slid aside. The parchment-wood used to construct the house had cost ESComm a great deal; tree growth was controlled on the habitat to avoid draining resources.

After leaving a package for his wife in the living room, Kaliga paced down the central hallway, lost in thought. He disliked the way Raziquon's mind worked. Although stealing Corbal Xir's favored provider had appeal, it was a subversive proposition. It would have been more palatable if Raziquon had a job or family he valued, something Kaliga could use to control him. But the man lived off his wealth and did nothing useful. In that sense, he was like Corbal. At least Xir presided over the shipping empire he had built, some of it legal, but most of it based on the spoils of his pirate fleets, which of course he claimed didn't exist.

A shrill voice intruded on his thoughts. "Hightons *always* buy their spouses slaves. Why should he be different? It isn't like you're a person or anything. If he ever caught me with another Aristo, *well,* that would be different. He would have me executed."

Kaliga winced. Arranged marriages had their drawbacks. If his alliance with his wife's family hadn't been so useful, he would have sent her back to them. He stopped at a doorway on the hall. Inside, across the room, his wife was kneeling in a clutter of pillows. Her filmy robe revealed tantalizing glimpses of her curvaceous body, and rubies studded the hair piled on her head, reminding him why he enjoyed seeing her when she kept her mouth shut. But today her lovely face was set in a pout and she was facing a stranger, a gold-skinned man sitting on the floor in front of her.

Kaliga frowned. "Xirene, what are you talking about?"

His wife scrambled to her feet. She ran to him and threw her hand over her heart. "Why, Xiri? *Why?* Do I make you so unhappy?"

Kaliga wearily rubbed the bridge of his nose with his thumb and forefinger. "What is it now, Xirene?"

"I won't go away. You can't do this to me."

Skolia be damned. "Do what?"

She waved at the gold man. "Isn't that why you bought

me this provider? So I wouldn't complain as much when you sent me away?"

"I'm not sending you anywhere." He took her hands, pointedly ignoring the stranger. "Why would I do such a thing?" Why indeed. The prospect had appeal. Whenever he looked at her body and face, though, he tended to forget that he wanted to send her away.

Xirene pouted. "You're always upset with me, love."

"I'm not upset with you."

"You *ignore* me." With a flourish, she whipped her hands out of his.

I don't have time for this. "Xirene, I don't even remember ordering this provider. I will check with my steward tomorrow. But I've no intention of sending you anywhere."

Her smile transformed her face from petulant to radiant. "I'm so glad to hear that. I don't want to go away. I really do like you, you know."

Kaliga sighed. Almost against his will, he drew her into his arms and tilted her face to his. Ignoring the overmuscled provider, he kissed his wife. She needed no steroid-packed provider. He might have less bulk and greater age than the young bucks she could have married, had she been given a choice, but he was her husband. Someone had sent the provider as an insult, implying Kaliga couldn't keep his young wife satisfied. When he found out who had done it, his retaliation would be swift and subtle.

Kaliga sent his wife off to the living room, where he had left her a gift. Mollified, she gave him a bright smile and swept out of the room.

Kaliga turned to the provider. "Get up."

As the man stood, Kaliga's anger hardened. The slave towered over him. He wore gold trousers and shirt, nothing blatant, but fitted to showcase his magnificent physique. Even more galling, age lines showed around his eyes and gray streaked his hair. He obviously hadn't been sculpted; he came by his looks naturally, an appearance Kaliga could never match even with modification.

Strangely enough, the provider had been subjected to some cheap genetic tattoo that was either wearing off or had been reversed. His brown hair was turning a metallic gold, and his eyes and skin had a gold shimmer. It didn't surprise Kaliga; many providers resembled precious metals or gems. But the shoddy tattoo job was another insult. He would find out who had done this, and when he did, they would pay.

"Who sent you?" he asked.

The provider looked at him blankly. "Don't know, sir. I'm sorry." He had an unusually deep voice.

"You're sorry." Kaliga would see to it that whoever had sent him was more than sorry. "Where are you from?"

"I don't know that either, sir."

"Why not?"

"I don't understand those things."

The man's responses were off in some way, but Kaliga wasn't sure how. He wondered if the fellow was faking a vacuous personality to protect himself from questions. But a provider could never have the cunning for such a deception. Far more likely, the man had been deliberately chosen for his limited intellect. Kaliga didn't miss the implied taunt: *he needs no mind to satisfy your neglected wife.* He made a conscious effort not to grit his teeth. "What did they do, take your brain out?"

"No sir. I don't know."

Kaliga had no intention of letting this insult remain in his home. He snapped out an order. "You will work on the rim crew." Then he left.

As Kaliga walked to his office, he contacted his aide about the rim-walk crew. Like the robots that maintained the station, rim-walkers did upkeep. Robots had higher status, though, because they were more durable and less emotional.

Then Kaliga told his intelligence people to find out who had mailed this provider to his wife. After he had the man killed, he would send the body back to the true owner, cheap tattoo job and all.

8

Lock's End

Jai told no one his plans. He summoned his aide, Robert Muzeson, before the sun rose on Glory's sixteen-hour day. He chose Robert for two reasons: the aide had no direct relation to Corbal Xir, and his mind didn't create any mental pressure on Jai. Robert, however, insisted on summoning Jai's Razers. Jai balked at first, but he finally gave in, knowing that if he didn't choose his battles wisely, he would exhaust himself fighting everything.

So it was that two hours before the sun rose, Jai left Glory and headed to the Sphinx Sector military base where ESComm kept the Lock they had stolen from the Skolians.

The stations of Sphinx Sector Rim Base orbited one another in complex trajectories that covered an immense region of empty space. "Empty," of course, was relative; interstellar dust, high-energy particles, radiation, and asteroids regularly visited the neighborhood.

The Lock orbited near the center of the SSRB. Only a select few of ESComm's highest officers had clearance to enter the space station. Jai was irked to discover that even he had trouble securing permission on such short notice. He didn't try threats; instead, he bestowed gifts on those who cooperated with him, everything from expensive baubles to implied promises of imperial favors.

Jai didn't know what to expect. He had no experience with space stations. He had read about them during the journey to the SSRB, between his bouts of space sickness, so he understood that larger stations supported biospheres with plants and animals, and crews that numbered in the millions. The Lock was apparently much smaller, purely utilitarian, with no biosphere, only machinery and metal.

Colonel Vatrix Muze, the ranking officer on the Lock, took Jai on a tour. As it turned out, Muze had kinship ties to both Jai and Robert. The colonel was the grandson of High Judge Calope Muze, who was a niece of Eube Qox, and Calope's son had sired Robert's mother on a provider. Jai realized even he and Robert were related, through Calope. It was no wonder Aristo introductions included a recitation of ancestors, given their labyrinthine kinship bonds.

Jai couldn't fathom why Hightons so adamantly believed inbreeding strengthened them. True, most of the deleterious recessives had been purged from their DNA, but that didn't stop them from stagnating. They needed new genes, which they would never get if they insisted on marrying each other all the time. There weren't even that many Highton bloodlines. So far he knew of only eleven: Qox, Xir, Muze, Iquar, Kaliga, Taratus, Vitrex, Raziquon, Haquail, Kayzar, and Quaelen.

Colonel Muze escorted them through command centers which all looked the same to Jai, just chambers with dormant consoles that would sleep until a Key activated the Lock. But for all that ESComm believed the Lock slumbered, Jai felt its mind even through his barriers and the pressure of Colonel Muze's Aristo mind.

The Lock was alive. Its sentience tugged at him, just barely awake. It wasn't life he understood; its intelligence felt alien.

But it recognized its Key.

————

=They've shown us nothing,= Jai wrote to Robert on his palm-mesh. =Just inoperative consoles.=

Robert had swept the office for monitors, and dismantled several, but Jai doubted they had found everything. Instead of speaking, he passed his mesh to Robert. That didn't guarantee privacy either, but it would help. Jai wondered just how paranoid he would become, living among the Aristos.

They were sitting at a table in Jai's suite on the space station. Robert wrote on the mesh, =Some command stations must work; otherwise this station wouldn't operate at all.=

=I want to see the Lock,= Jai wrote.

Robert's forehead creased. =This is it.=

=We haven't seen the actual Lock.=

=You mean the singularity in spacetime?=

=Yes.=

Robert blanched. =It will suck us away. Take our souls.=

It wasn't the first time Jai had heard a Eubian express superstition about the Lock. He didn't miss the irony, that Aristos felt soulless to psions, yet Eubians feared the Lock that protected Skolians would suck away their souls.

=It can't affect you unless you walk into it,= Jai wrote. =Even then, only a psion would feel anything.=

Robert stiffened. =I am a taskmaker.=

Damn. Jai knew he had blundered. He had lived most of his life surrounded by psions. It wasn't until he had gone to live with Seth Rockworth on Earth that he realized most people weren't empaths or telepaths. Although he had kept his abilities to himself, he considered them a benefit, traits he greatly valued.

Eubians didn't share that opinion. They saw psions as inferior. Weak. Although most providers lived in a luxury few taskmakers could ever attain, they were at the bottom of Eubian social hierarchies. In contrast, Robert was close to the top. If Jai implied he was a provider, it would be a grave insult.

=You are a lord among taskmakers,= Jai wrote. =You are my respected aide.=

Robert lifted his head. =It is my honor.=

=I will go into the Lock alone. As a Highton, I'm immune to its effects.= Jai had wanted an excuse to dump his guards, and Robert's superstition gave him an opening. =You and the guards will wait outside.=

Robert took the mesh from Jai. =I would give my life rather than let you risk entering the Lock alone.=

=I won't enter. Just view it.= Although he could use the Lock to join the Triad, it would be about as smart as shooting himself with a laser carbine. Command centers all over the station would come to life. Not only would it give him away as a Ruby psion, but he would also be handing the Hightons a Key who was already in the Triad.

Jai had come here only to find Kelric. His uncle was the one who should join the Triad; Kelric had the experience, maturity, and background to rule as Imperator, the military commander of the Skolian Imperialate. Jai's mother had been Imperator before she died, but no one held the position now.

The other two Triad members were Jai's grandfather and Jai's great-aunt, the Ruby Pharaoh. His grandfather was in custody on Earth; their military refused to release him for fear the Ruby Dynasty would build another psiberweb and go back to war with Eube, throwing world-slagging armies at each other until they destroyed civilization. In his darker moments, Jai wondered if the people of Earth weren't right.

ESComm claimed that Dyhianna Selei, the Ruby Pharaoh, had died when they captured her husband, Prince Eldrin, but Jai had his doubts. If they had killed her, they would have trumpeted it across interstellar space. That they were so quiet made Jai suspect they didn't know what had happened to her. But if she had escaped, why didn't she reveal herself? The silence unnerved him. The Skolians were demoralized; her appearance now could reenergize her people much as Corbal claimed Jai had done for the Eubians. So where was she?

Jai exhaled. Perhaps the Ruby Dynasty truly was broken, with only his grandfather in the Triad. Jai had found no hint of his uncle Kelric here. It disheartened him: he had been so certain. The escaped provider was probably someone else, a man who just happened to resemble the uncle Jai had seen only in holos. It was stupid to hope. Kelric Valdoria had been dead for eighteen years.

Regardless, Jai wanted to visit the Lock. He felt compelled, an impulse that had grown as the day passed.

Robert wrote on his mesh. =You must take an active comm into the Lock. And we will monitor you. If anything goes wrong, we will be ready.=

Jai didn't want them monitoring him; it would limit his actions. But it was probably the best he could do. If he kept insisting on privacy, it would arouse suspicion. Relaxing his barriers, he concentrated on Robert. His aide genuinely believed only a Highton could enter the Lock without being destroyed. But if Robert thought Jai was in danger, he would go in anyway, even believing he risked his soul.

=You honor me with your fealty,= Jai wrote.

Robert looked pleased. =We should go now, during the night shift.=

Smart man. =Yes. We are less likely to encounter obstacles.=

Robert understood exactly what "obstacles" Jai meant. =I can hide us from ESComm Security.=

Jai grinned. =Good.=

The only entrance to the Lock was through an ancient airlock. Unlike modern airlocks, which were permeable membranes that clung to a person as they stepped through, this one consisted of two solid hatches. Jai waited with Robert next to it while two of his Razers used their gauntlets to check the monitors inside his body. His other two bodyguards opened the outer hatch of the airlock. Jai wondered why the Lock chamber needed it. An extra safeguard, perhaps, in case this section of the station ever became cut off from the rest. Psions strong enough to use the Lock had always been rare and well protected.

After he stepped through the hatchway, his guards shut the hatch, closing him into a metal antechamber. He tried the inner hatch, straining to turn its circular handle, but nothing happened. He tried pulling it the other way.

Nothing.

Jai frowned. Could he even enter?

Come.

Jai froze. He felt the thought as a sense of meaning rather than an actual word.

I know you, Jai answered. It was true. The sentience had been trying to contact him since he boarded the station.

No answer.

Jai tried again. **How do I enter?**

I will veil you.

Veil? **I don't understand.**

An impression formed in his mind, neither words nor images, but he understood. The Lock would disguise his actions within its chamber so the guards monitoring him would know nothing of what transpired.

How do I open the hatch? Jai asked. When no response came, he tried again. **May I enter?**

The handle turned and the hatch swung open.

Taking a deep breath, Jai stepped through the hatchway into an octagonal chamber about twenty paces wide. The dark shapes of consoles hulked in the gloom, but across from him, a corridor sparkled, shedding the only light. Its path arrowed straight back until it became a point in the infinite distance. That had to be an illusion; it couldn't go on forever within a finite space station. The corridor had no walls; transparent columns delineated it, each filled with clockwork mechanisms that looked as if they were made from precious metals and ebony. Lights spiraled within the columns, racing around and around, hypnotic.

Jai didn't know how long he stood enthralled. Gradually he became aware of the chamber around him. He could just make out the dormant consoles against its walls. A dais rose to his left, and a great chair stood there. Its armrests were rectangular blocks threaded with conduits, glistening with trapped light. Equipment embedded the backrest, a slab of metal several meters high and half a meter thick. Blocky and solid, the shadowed chair stood like an empty throne.

He walked to the dais, inexorably drawn. The pulse of the chamber rumbled through him like a heartbeat.

Jai went to the chair. It adjusted to his weight as he sat down. Looking out, he saw a console on the opposite wall, indistinct in the shadows.

A man was working there.

Jai froze. He knew that man. Few had such great height or massive build. Even in the dim light, his skin and hair glinted.

Kelric? Jai formed the word in his mind. The man remained absorbed in his work. Even knowing he was there, Jai could barely see him.

Jai didn't know how long he sat without moving. Then a man's thought reverberated in his mind, ragged and harsh, raw with power. **Suspend.**

The Lock answered: **Done.**

And it died. The heartbeat vanished; the luminous corridor went dark; the sentience ceased. Jai suddenly felt bereft.

The man left the console then and walked to the darkened corridor. He paused at its entrance, glancing back—

And looked straight at Jai.

9

The Promise

The man's aura of power was tangible, evoking the myths of Ruby gods from five millennia ago. Jai was so startled, he nearly forgot his role as emperor. He had to catch himself from responding like an astonished boy.

Jai summoned up his most aloof Highton tone. "Are you done staring at me?"

The man stood motionless, his face unreadable. "How did you get in here?"

"I should ask that question of you." Jai leaned his elbow on the arm of his chair, copying his grandfather's regal pose. "You were intent on your work. Killing the Lock, I gather."

Recognition flared in the man's gaze. "You're the one who spoke in the broadcast from the emperor's palace."

"You saw the broadcast?"

"From a distance." With a quiet certainty, he said "I know you."

Jai wished he had some of those nanomeds that controlled his sweat now. Did this man remember him from Edge-whirl—or did he recognize a deeper kinship? Even if this was his uncle, Jai couldn't reveal himself. The Ruby Dynasty was about as likely to welcome a Highton into their midst as they were to eat machine parts. Nor did Jai have any reason to believe they would protect his secret.

He schooled his face into what he hoped was a convincing Highton arrogance. "I should think all settled space knows me by now."

Kelric spoke in a low voice. "You're a Qox."

Although Jai laughed, it felt hollow. "Not *a* Qox. *The* Qox."

It was a long moment before Kelric answered. "The emperor's heir." He had remarkable composure given his situation.

Jai thought of Corbal's intent to make him a puppet emperor and his anger sparked. "I am no heir. I rule Eube. As Jaibriol the Third."

"Jaibriol the Second had no heir."

"Of course he did. Me."

Kelric studied him with an unsettling concentration. "I know you from somewhere."

Worried now, Jai tried to redirect him. "Perhaps you were dazzled by your time in the Lock, Lord Skolia." Too late, he realized what he had said. *Lord Skolia.* His subconscious had recognized the truth; Kelric had already joined the Triad, becoming Imperator.

Kelric's realization was so sharp, it pierced Jai's mental barriers. "You're Jay Rockworth. The Dawn Corps volunteer on Edgewhirl."

Jai waved his hand, hoping it looked like a convincing dismissal. "This was all in the broadcast."

"That you were with the Allieds?"

"That my parents hid me on Earth. The Allieds discovered it and traded me to Eube." Faced with this man who might be his uncle and the Skolian Imperator, Jai couldn't maintain his cold veneer. With wonder, he added, "I had no idea who you were, that day on Edgewhirl."

Kelric exhaled. "Nor I, for you."

Jai hesitated, afraid to discover his hopes were wrong. But he made himself ask. "Which one are you?"

"Which one?"

"In the Ruby Dynasty." Jai held his breath.

Then the man said, "Kelricson Valdoria."

Tears stung Jai's eyes. Memories of his little brother flooded his mind, stirring his loneliness. "Del-Kelric."

When Kelric's recognition of the name jumped in his mind, Jai wanted to kick himself. He *had* to be more careful. He strove to recover his Highton tone. "Where did you come from? You've been dead for years."

Kelric evaded the question. "Why were you with the Dawn Corps? It makes no sense. You expressed sympathy for the Ruby Dynasty."

Jai shrugged. "Perhaps you remember what you wish."

"No. And you look familiar. I don't know why. But I *know* you."

Jai longed to reveal himself, to seek the solace of his kinship with this man. He didn't dare. But he could help his uncle escape. He stepped down from the throne and walked to Kelric. Laying his hands on the rail separating them, he regarded his uncle steadily. "Go. Now. While you can."

"You would let me go?"

"Yes."

"Why?"

Sorrow tugged at Jai. If anyone could help him ensure his parents hadn't died in vain, it was Kelric. His hopes, fears, and longing all mixed into his voice. "Meet me at the peace table."

"You want me to believe you wish peace, when you have a Lock and two Keys?"

Jai tilted his head. "What Lock? It no longer works. We had one Key. We gave him back."

Kelric waited. Then he said, "Gave who back?"

"Your brother. Eldrin Valdoria."

Kelric stiffened. "Don't lie to me, Highton."

"Why would I lie?"

"It's what you Hightons do. Lie, manipulate, cheat."

He heard the pain that underlay his uncle's anger and knew Kelric had suffered his own trials. *Would that I could tell you the truth.* Jai hurt so much, surrounded by Aristos, cut off from his former life, unable to confide in anyone. He struggled to maintain his crumbling Aristo facade. "I've little interest in your imagined list of Highton ills."

Kelric spoke slowly. "Eube would never give its Key to the Allieds. Not when you finally had a Lock. Nothing is worth it."

"Not even me?"

Kelric went very still. "You, for Eldrin?"

"Yes." Jai could sense his uncle's mind better now; Kelric wanted to believe his brother was in the custody of the Allied Worlds, but his hope fought with his conviction that the Aristos would never trade their Ruby psion.

"You are right," Jai added dryly, thinking of his dismal showing as emperor. "It wasn't a universally popular decision. But it is done. I am emperor and your brother is an Allied prisoner."

Although Kelric controlled his expressions, Jai was picking up more from his uncle, including Kelric's innate decency and stoicism. The older man's sorrow for the family he had lost also filled his mind. He didn't believe Eldrin was free; he thought Jai was taunting him while Razers waited to take him prisoner.

Troubled, Jai said, "I am alone."

Kelric froze. "Why did you say that?"

Jai silently swore. He had become so caught up in their exchange, he hadn't realized he was responding to his uncle's thoughts. "You didn't wonder if I had guards? I find that hard to believe."

Kelric didn't hide his disbelief. "And you just happened to come in—alone—when I was here."

"Ah, well." Jai realized he could only stretch the truth so far. "It would be a great coincidence, yes? But I knew you were here."

"How?"

"Perhaps you could say I felt it."

"Perhaps. I don't believe it."

"I suppose not." Jai rubbed his chin, trying to think of

another excuse. "I detected your entrance in the station web." He felt as if time were rushing past them. The longer they spent here, the greater the chance his guards would come for him and find Kelric. "Imperator Skolia, meet me when we can discuss peace."

"Why should I believe you want this?"

"Ask for something I can grant as proof of my intent."

Kelric paused, thinking. Then he said, "There is a man. A Skolian. Jafe Maccar, captain of the *Corona.*" Anger sparked in Kelric's mind. "After a battle at the space station Chrysalis, Maccar was sentenced to ten years in an ESComm prison. Unjustly." His forthright gaze became a challenge. "Pardon him."

Jai knew nothing about Maccar or why ESComm had sent him to prison. Nor did he know if he wielded enough authority to make a pardon stick. It would certainly alienate ESComm. But he could admit none of that to Kelric, so he said only, "I will consider it."

Kelric's expression clearly said he expected Jai to do nothing. It bothered Jai that his uncle thought his offer was false. He motioned upward, a well-known gesture meant to include all Eube. "It's like a great thundering machine I hold by the barest thread. If I am to find a road to peace, I need your help."

Kelric stared at him for a long moment. Gradually his wariness changed, becoming a quiet incredulity. Then he spoke in a low voice. "You're a telepath."

Jai stiffened. "No. I am what you see. Qox."

"At what price?" Kelric asked. "What must you suffer to hide the truth?"

Jai couldn't answer. It would cost him too much. Instead he said, "Was anyone here when I came into the Lock? I never saw him."

His uncle answered with an unbearable compassion. "Gods help you, son."

"Go." Jai felt as if he were breaking inside. "Now. While you can."

Kelric stepped into the darkened corridor. He started to walk, his back to Jai, his steps measured, as if he expected an attack.

"Lord Skolia," Jai said.

Kelric turned back, poised and tense. "Yes?"

"If you make it to Earth—" Jai lifted his hand as if to reach out to Kelric. Then he caught himself and lowered his arm. "Go see Admiral Seth Rockworth."

The older man paused. "I will go."

Then the Imperator continued down the corridor. As he strode along that avenue of the ages, Jai thought:

Gods' speed, my uncle.

On Jai's second day at the Lock, Colonel Muze took him to visit its operational command center. Officers crewed the consoles and lights flickered everywhere. Jai stood flanked by Muze and Robert, his hands clasped behind his back, watching a holoscreen that curved around the forward bulkhead showing the panorama of space. Stars glittered in a multitude of colors, and spumes of interstellar dust glowed, moving out of view as the station rotated. In the distance, another space station came into view.

"Such beauty," Jai murmured.

"Beauty worth securing." Muze paused. "I hope you found the security in the Lock to your approval last night."

Jai inwardly swore. So. They knew about his visit. "It appeared adequate."

"Adequate offers the opportunity for improvement."

Jai couldn't tell whether the colonel suspected him of treason or feared Jai had found his command lacking. In Muze's presence, he had to fortify his barriers so much, his thoughts felt muffled. Rather than risk implicating himself, he said nothing. Stars wheeled past on the holoscreens.

A young lieutenant approached them and went down on one knee to Jai.

Embarrassed, Jai said, "Please rise."

The lieutenant stood, his gaze averted. "You give me great

honor by your presence, Esteemed Highness."

Jai reddened. He couldn't believe it when they said such things. Fortunately Muze saved him from having to think of a response. "You have a report?" the colonel asked.

The lieutenant saluted. "Yes, sir. A frigate is approaching the Lock."

Muze frowned. "Does it have clearance?"

"Yes, sir."

"Who is it?" Jai asked.

The lieutenant averted his gaze again. Jai wished they wouldn't do that. Taskmakers weren't required to look down, but they often did anyway. Many believed the nonsense promulgated by Highton propaganda, that the emperor was, if not an actual deity, then close to one.

From his parents, Jai had learned about the pantheon of gods and saints worshipped by the ancient peoples of the Ruby Empire, and by some Skolians and Eubians even in this modern age. His parents had also told him about the religions of her father's people. On Earth, Seth had introduced him to Christianity. After all that, it embarrassed him to have the Eubians treat him this way. He didn't know how to respond, so he "solved" the problem by not reacting. Not only did it make no difference, his remote behavior seemed expected.

"We have a visitor, Your Highness," the lieutenant said. "Corbal Xir, High Lord of the Xir Line."

Ah, hell. His escape from his cousin had just ended.

10

Silver

Too many Aristos came to dinner.

Admiral Xirad Kaliga, Joint Commander of ESComm, hosted the affair in his home to welcome Jai and Corbal to Sphinx Sector Rim Base. He invited the local Aristo aristocracy. His child-bride, Xirene, presided over the festivities, unceasing in her chatter.

Reclining at the high table, Jai felt so far out of his depth, he wondered that he didn't drown. Xirene was the only person even close to his age, and she had years of experience in Eubian society. Even with his barriers at top strength, his mind reeled under the onslaught of so many Aristos. Their minds weighed on him until he thought his head would burst from the pressure.

The excruciating day never seemed to end. At least no one else mentioned his visit to the Lock. Jai prayed they hadn't captured Kelric. If they had, they should have told him, but he didn't know if they would. Maybe they were toying with the emperor they would soon accuse of treason. Or maybe they had no idea Kelric had been there. With his barriers up, Jai couldn't discern if the Aristos even knew the Lock had died. It seemed impossible they could be oblivious to such a dramatic change, yet either no one had noticed or else they were more adept at pretense than he realized. For all he knew, they had been grilling him all day, in their convoluted discourse, and he just hadn't known.

Twelve people sat at the high table: Corbal Xir; Xirad Kaliga and his wife Xirene; Jaibriol Raziquon, high lord of the Raziquon Line; and other Aristos Jai couldn't remember. It overwhelmed him. He didn't see how he could survive as the emperor if he couldn't even make it through one dinner.

Providers served the food and poured wine. A pleasure girl leaned over to fill his goblet. Jai tried not to stare, but he couldn't stop. Silver hair floated around her face in glossy curls. She had silver eyes too. Her skin was flawless, almost translucent, with a rosy blush. She wore nothing but a silver G-string, silver collar, silver wrist and ankle cuffs, a silver chain low on her hips, and silver rings circling her nipples. He couldn't figure out how her incredible breasts stayed up that way with no support.

The girl straightened gracefully, holding the carafe. As she turned to a table behind her, Jai had an agreeable view of her backside. When she bent over the table, he had to struggle to keep his hands to himself.

"You," a harsh voice said. "Silver hair."

The provider froze. Then she turned to the table. Irked, Jai looked to see who had disturbed his appreciation of the girl. It was the man with his own name, Jaibriol Raziquon, who, as far as Jai could tell, did nothing but live as hedonistic a life as possible, soaking in his own riches and that of his similarly wealthy companions.

Raziquon was watching the silver girl with malice. "What, do you plot against His Magnificent Highness?"

Spots of red flushed her cheeks. "I—I don't know what you mean."

Neither do I, Jai thought. What was Raziquon about?

Unexpectedly, Corbal answered. Reclining in a lounger on Jai's left, he spoke coldly to the girl. "Perhaps you put an extra draught in his Highness's drink, eh?"

Her face paled. "Never, most esteemed sir. Never, I swear

it. I swear." She dropped to her knees next to Jai and bowed her head. "Please," she whispered.

What the hell? It mortified Jai to have her kneel that way. She was a strong enough psion that he caught hints of her mind even through his defenses. She had no intention of causing harm; she had been distracted by how pleasing she found his appearance and had forgotten to give his drink to his food testers. He was one of the few Hightons who had no internal systems to protect him against poison; he had resisted them, disquieted by the idea of more implants in his body, but now he had second thoughts.

As the girl trembled, Jai started to offer his hand to help her stand. He would have enjoyed knowing she thought him handsome if Raziquon hadn't ruined it by bullying her over the wine. He knew Corbal was staring at him, trying to attract his attention, and Jai was sure his cousin wanted him to ignore the provider, but he didn't care. He wasn't going to leave her shaking on the floor.

"We will give you a chance at redemption, provider." Raziquon's eagerness drew everyone's attention before they noticed Jai's unusual behavior. Cruelty edged the lord's voice. "You may drink the wine yourself."

Jai frowned. He hadn't liked Raziquon from the start and he had no intention of letting any Highton give orders for him, let alone this one. He raised an eyebrow. "You would speak for me, Lord Raziquon?" He leaned back in his lounger. "Perhaps *you* should drink it."

The other Aristos, who had been watching with amusement, suddenly stopped smiling. A woman at the end of the table abruptly set down her goblet, and the man next to Raziquon, an elder lord of the Blue-Point Diamond Line, moved discreetly, putting more space between Raziquon and himself.

Concentrating, Jai tried to probe Raziquon's mind. His head throbbed, and he couldn't lower his barriers among so many Hightons, so his impressions were muffled. But he did pick up a bit, enough to sense that the other man genuinely feared the wine did carry a poison, one that even the protections in his body might not neutralize. Stunned, Jai realized he might have just condemned Raziquon to death. He couldn't back down; it could be a potentially deadly admission of weakness.

Raziquon reached slowly across the table and picked up Jai's goblet. Then he took a swallow. Watching him, Jai felt ill, remembering the bird in Corbal's office.

After a moment, Raziquon set the goblet on the table. His expression had a hard edge now, one directed toward Eube's emperor.

Jai wished he could end this dinner. But he had no choice. He spoke lazily to Raziquon. "You look well." It relieved him more than he would ever admit. The longer Raziquon continued to look that way, the less likely it was that the wine had been poisoned.

Raziquon answered with cold formality. "Thank you, Your Highness."

The other Aristos at the table remained silent, their faces guarded. Jai sensed they were waiting to see what he would do about the provider. He had no idea. As much as he resented his dependence on Corbal, he needed his cousin's crafty experience. Jai turned to him. "Perhaps you have a suggestion for this lovely silver girl, Cousin."

Corbal was impassive. "I would never presume to speak for Your Highness."

Jai waved his hand. "I give you leave. Entertain me."

Corbal spoke quietly. "Perhaps she needs to provide for the emperor she would betray."

Damn. He should have seen that coming. They expected him to appease their merciless conception of right and wrong, to make her suffer for their entertainment. Even through his barriers, he felt the girl's terror. She wondered if she would survive the night. It horrified him.

Jai felt drained, unable to keep this up. Good and evil were backward here. He had been a fool to think he could bring peace to Eube and Skolia; he would be lucky to stay alive.

Someday he could end up kneeling as the provider did now, his life made into hell.

Corbal spoke to a server. "Clear the table."

At first Jai didn't understand. Then he realized Corbal wanted the table cleared for whatever they intended to do to the provider. As servers removed the remnants of the meal, Jai clenched his jaw. He had requested an opinion, nothing more. He didn't know how to avoid alienating his so-called peers, but he had no intention of letting them torture the silver girl.

In a lounger on Jai's other side, Xirene Kaliga sighed. Distracted, he turned to her, and she gave him a sympathetic look. "These providers," she said. "They are so inept. I mean, really, not testing your wine, I *never* heard of such foolishness. Have you? I never have. Not even when my friend Zarla—well, you don't know Zarla, she wasn't invited tonight—but I tell you, never have I seen such a silly mistake." She flipped her hand at toward the silver girl. "I mean, *really*. I *never*."

Jai stared at her, awed by her ability to produce so many words and say so little. He had no idea how to answer, but it didn't matter. Xirene continued on, oblivious to the aghast stare of her husband, the admiral.

"When I have problems with my providers," she confided to Jai, "I send them to bed without their dinner." She laughed as if she had made a hilarious joke.

Admiral Kaliga rubbed his eyes. "Xirene."

Jai had had enough. He motioned to one of his Razers, who stood by the wall, looming and silent. The man came to the table and bowed. Technically, Razers were supposed to kneel like everyone else who wasn't an Aristo, but Jai had one trait in common with his Qox predecessors; he preferred his bodyguards at their most alert, not on their knees.

Jai indicated the silver girl. "Take her to my rooms."

The Razer nodded. When he touched the girl, she rose, her gaze averted, and went with the guard, walking so softly, she made no sound. Jai turned back to the table to see Kaliga watching his wife with a sour look.

"What?" Xirene pouted at her husband. "It's not my fault she's gone. You spend too much time with her anyway." She didn't seem the least embarrassed to have revealed an intimate detail of her husband's life to half the Aristo population of the SSRB.

Jai suppressed his smile. Who would have thought it, that the notorious Xirad Kaliga, Joint Commander of the greatest military ever known, couldn't handle his teenage bride? So this was one of the Highton marriages arranged to maintain the "everlasting glory" of Eube. No wonder the Aristos had so many problems.

He became aware of Raziquon watching him, his gaze like ice. Even through his mental defenses, Jai caught the lord's vivid thought: his internal systems had determined that the wine wasn't poisoned. Jai lifted his controversial goblet and took a long swallow of the wine. For all its superb quality, it might as well have been engine fuel for all that he enjoyed the taste.

The other Aristos followed his lead and drank, their decided lack of enthusiasm evident only in their minds, but intense enough from so many of them that it came through his fortified shields. When Kaliga said, "To the continued health of His Esteemed Magnificence," Jai felt his sarcasm.

I'm in trouble, Jai thought.

"I can't decide whether you are phenomenally clever," Corbal said, "or phenomenally stupid."

Jai lay back in a pile of pillows on the floor of the study, an unfurnished room with sliding screens for walls, an ivory carpet, and an antique lamp in the corner. He and Corbal had retired here after dinner, though to Jai it felt more like an escape. Corbal's people declared the room clean of monitors. Although Jai had reasonable faith in their ability to clean them out, he could never be sure.

Sprawled among the pillows, he stretched his legs across the carpet. "That dinner was interminable."

Corbal slid open a screen and stood gazing out at the garden outside, where a bridge arched over a burbling creek. Even the murmur of water didn't soothe Jai.

"You antagonized Kaliga's guests," Corbal said.

"Those people have problems."

Corbal glanced at him. "By their standards, you are the one with problems."

Jai closed his eyes. "I don't care."

"You should."

"I'm too tired to care."

"You made an enemy of Raziquon."

"That statement implies people exist who aren't his enemy." Jai opened his eyes. "That viper actually has friends?"

Corbal frowned. "It would behoove an emperor to act with less sarcasm."

Jai thought of what Kaliga's guests had wanted to do to the silver girl. "It would behoove your peers to act more like human beings."

"Jaibriol." Corbal exhaled. "You must adapt better than this."

"Well, you're certainly direct tonight." It was a relief; the circuitous discourse that Hightons favored gave him a headache.

"If it takes rudeness on my part to make you conform," Corbal said, "so be it."

"Maybe I shouldn't conform."

Corbal scowled at him. "You sulk like a teenage boy."

"What a coincidence. I am a teenage boy."

"You don't have that luxury."

Jai crossed his arms. "Then let me make my own decisions."

"Such as sneaking off to the Lock?"

So. They finally came down to the real reason for Corbal's visit. Maybe he shouldn't wish for directness after all. As long as Corbal kept his inquiries oblique, Jai could obliquely evade them. Dryly he said, "It would behoove the emperor's relatives not to spy on the emperor."

"Don't be crass, Jaibriol."

"What, now I'm just Jaibriol? No 'Your Everlastingly Marvelosio Magnificence'?"

Corbal walked over to him. Although he knelt on one knee, his pose had no trace of humility. "You are going to get yourself killed."

Jai met his gaze. "By whom? Raziquon? Or you?"

"Without me, you wouldn't survive two days."

"And with you?" Jai tried to maintain his veneer of unconcern, but his facade was cracking. "If I'm lucky, I'll make it three days." He despised himself for the fear and loneliness he heard in his voice.

Corbal sat down, one leg bent, his elbow resting on his knee. "Did you really think coming to the Lock would help?"

Jai sat up, uneasy with Corbal's greater height. He hated not knowing how much the older man had guessed about him. He caught only vague impressions from Corbal's guarded mind, and he couldn't delve any deeper without collapsing his own mental defenses. Nor did it work when he tried to draw Corbal into a conversation that might make the Xir lord let slip information. His cousin was too crafty and too adept at deciphering nuances of gesture, word, and expression. Jai could end up revealing himself to Corbal instead of the reverse.

"The Lock didn't look like much," Jai said.

"According to Colonel Muze, you didn't look at much."

"There wasn't much to see."

Corbal studied his face. "One might find it hard to observe anything if one sits in a chair the whole time."

That gave Jai pause. It sounded like the monitors had registered nothing except him sitting. He wondered why the Lock would hide his conversation with Kelric. Easy answer: it wanted to protect its Keys. But its sentience was too alien to fathom; it might find no significance in human motivations. Even more eerie, the Lock had died while he was in the chamber, but its protection had apparently extended beyond its demise.

The people here seemed oblivious to the change in the space station. Perhaps only an empath or telepath could detect that sense of *ending*. The stronger psions among their providers might have sensed the Lock's sentience, and its end, but they seemed too traumatized to respond beyond the limited sphere of their existence.

Corbal's lover, Sunrise, was unique as far as Jai had seen; much less withdrawn than other providers, she could operate beyond the strictures of her constrained life. No wonder Corbal used her as a spy. Other Hightons could learn a lesson from him, though Jai doubted they would acknowledge it, and not only because they were too arrogant to admit they might be wrong about the inability of providers to think. For them, letting a provider develop self-worth was dangerous.

Corbal was waiting for Jai to answer his implicit question—why Jai had just sat in the chair. Jai said nothing; he had discovered silence could prod Aristos to speak, as if they couldn't bear a hole in the webs of discourse they wove around themselves.

"I've heard it said that sons are their fathers reborn," Corbal finally said. "I'm not so sure that is true."

Jai knew Corbal meant the previous emperor, Jai's father. He evaded the implication by turning it around. "You doubt your rebirth in your sons?"

Corbal actually smiled. "Gods help Eube, should that ever happen. One of me is enough."

"You think so?"

"Indeed."

Pah. Jai was heartily sick of that word. "Do you know, Cousin, if one could put a price on a word—say, 'indeed'— we Hightons would be unbearably wealthy."

To his unmitigated surprise, Corbal laughed. "Some might say we already are."

Jai blinked. Corbal had a sense of humor. Although it

wasn't exactly the star-exploding discovery of all time, it did surprise him.

With his elbow on his knee, Corbal propped his chin on his fist. "You found the Lock dull, eh?"

Jai suspected Corbal's friendly display was meant to relax him, so he would confide more about his experience. He decided to play along, probing for information.

"It bored me," Jai said. "Nothing works."

"What did you expect it to do?"

Good question. "You've often been on the bridge of a ship. Lights glow. Voices hum. Levers move."

Corbal shrugged. "Only when the ship is in operation. Leave it inactive, and it has no use for glows, hums, or motion."

Jai thought of how ESComm had wrested the Lock from the Skolians. "Unless thieves steal it for their own use."

"Indeed." Corbal's mouth quirked up. "If you will allow the word."

Good Lord—another joke. Jai smiled slightly. "I will indeed."

A strange look passed over Corbal's face, then vanished. Longing? Jai caught a surge of emotion from Corbal, one the Xir lord smothered as soon as it emerged: longing and loneliness. For all his children, peers, lovers, and heirs, Corbal was lonely for a family. His moment of humor with Jai gave him just a glimpse of what he lacked.

No hint of Corbal's thoughts showed in his manner. He continued to study Jai. "Perhaps the thieves need someone to wake up the ship."

That sounded like ESComm didn't know the Lock had been active earlier today. Perhaps Kelric had awoken it when he joined the Triad. Jai was certain, though, that Kelric had later killed or otherwise ended the Lock, ensuring the Aristos couldn't use it. And the Lock had let him. Whatever its wishes, they apparently didn't include serving Eube.

"Perhaps the ship will never wake again," Jai said.

Corbal's gaze narrowed. "That would be a great sorrow."

Jai didn't answer. It wasn't a power play this time; he didn't know what to say. Fatigue wore on him. He had left the palace many hours ago and hadn't slept since. Stretching out in the cushions, he closed his eyes.

Corbal spoke, but Jai couldn't concentrate. His mind drifted in the hazy state just before sleep. Someone laid a blanket over him, but it was a few moments before Jai drowsily opened his eyes. Corbal was sitting in a corner of the room, beneath the lamp, reading a holobook.

Jai's lashes drooped . . .

Slowly waking, Jai lay among the cushions, warm beneath the blanket. Darkness had fallen outside, beyond the parchment-like screens. He rolled onto his back and stared at the ceiling, his contentment fading as he remembered dinner.

Groggy, he climbed to his feet, letting the blanket fall to the floor. He was alone now. Out in the hall, he found two of his bodyguards. They escorted him to his guest suite and accompanied him inside, but when they tried to follow him into the bedroom, Jai balked. Neither guard seemed surprised. They took up posts outside the room.

Relieved, Jai entered his bedroom and closed the screen quietly, caught by the hushed sense of the late hour. The night was synthetic; it came when the light panels in the "sky" darkened and slid back, letting starlight flood the residential areas of the habitat.

A dim lamp glowed in one corner, an orb on an antique stand. Jai stripped down to the stylized loincloth Highton men wore under their clothes and crawled into his bed, a far less ostentatious affair than the one in his room at the palace. He appreciated the elegance of this simple, airy house.

Jai stretched—and nearly jumped out of bed. He wasn't alone. The silver provider lay sleeping near him, on top of the covers. He froze, his hand clutched on the thermal blanket he had been pulling over himself. With a sigh, the girl rolled toward him, onto her side.

Good gods. He had a full view of her now, with no one to intrude on his appreciation. A spectacular view. She had a tiny waist and well-rounded hips, and her thighs were full and smooth. He imagined how they would feel with his hips between them, and sweat broke out on his forehead. And her *breasts*. He couldn't figure out how her nipples stayed erect. The silver rings around them accentuated their size. He wanted to say sweet words to her, but he couldn't think of anything that wouldn't sound clumsy, besides which, she was asleep.

No wonder the Razers hadn't argued when he told them to stay outside. Jai had told them to bring her here so no one would hurt her, but he knew what everyone thought. Although Kaliga could have objected, Jai doubted the admiral would deny the emperor such "hospitality" for the night.

Jai knew he shouldn't wake her. Kaliga would surely question her tomorrow; whatever she discovered tonight, the admiral would soon learn. She couldn't detect anomalies about Jai if she slept the whole night. Kaliga might wonder about the imperial libido, or lack thereof, but he wasn't likely to suspect Jai was a psion.

But he wanted to touch her. He struggled to distract himself. He had barely even held a girl, let alone slept with one. During his years in exile, he had naively assumed he would leave Prism, find a wife, bring her back, and love her the way his parents had loved each other. Then ESComm had ripped his father away, and Jai's mother had hidden her children on Earth. Jai had never really recovered from the shock of his immersion into human culture. Shy and reserved, he had kept to himself, unable to forget that entire civilizations considered his father a despot and his mother a dictator. They had taught him everything he knew about honor and decency, yet the rest of humanity reviled them.

Jai knew the truth now: he would never have what they had shared. His marriage would be a chilly union with whatever Highton woman became his empress. It would have to be a visitation marriage; he couldn't share his life with a lover whose very presence crushed his mind. Refusing to live with her would make him look even more eccentric, but it was better than her discovering that his purportedly Esteemed Highness was a psion.

Who else could he love but a provider? Yet that way courted disaster, for she could sense his differences. Nor would he ever truly know, even as an empath, if she really loved him or was only acting as she had been bred and trained to behave. For all that he wanted her, she made him feel vulnerable, as if she could hurt him, not through any wish of hers, but because he felt raw in her presence, uncertain. But Jai craved affection, and here was the silver girl, warm and sensual in her sleep.

Jai slid over to the girl. Then he stopped, afraid she would scream if she awoke to find a man she barely knew leaning over her. He had to remind himself this was his bed. After a moment, he cupped his hand around her breast and slid his thumb over her nipple. When she flinched in her sleep, he froze, afraid he had hurt her. He suddenly hated Kaliga, knowing the Aristo could do whatever he wanted to this girl. Strongly empathic, Jai couldn't separate his desire for the silver girl from his emotions; he wanted to protect her, to wrest her away from Kaliga.

As he caressed her breasts, she rolled onto her back and sighed. Her fragrance made him lightheaded. Aristos heightened the pheromones a provider exuded to intensify the sexual experience, but he hadn't expected the effect to be so intense. As a psion, she would also produce chemicals targeted for other psions. For him. It was nature's compensation for the fatal recessives associated with the mutations that created psions; their low birth rate was offset by how diligently their pheromones stirreded them to reproduce.

Jai bit his lip, fighting his need for her. He ought to roll away. Another sobering thought came to him: he had no wish to impregnate this girl. If she bore him children, they would be powerful psions, a dead giveaway he wasn't pure Highton. And it horrified him to think his children would be slaves.

What if he couldn't protect them? He would have to sire an heir on his empress, but that child would be more than half Highton. His heir would transcend. He couldn't bear knowing his legitimate children would threaten him just by existing, even if they never knew the truth about him, and no matter how much he loved them.

Then it occurred to him that Kaliga probably took steps to ensure she didn't become pregnant. Corbal certainly did with Sunrise. Jai was starved for affection, mourning the loss of his family, and here lay the silver girl, tousled and inviting. He couldn't give her up for tonight.

Stretching out on the bed, Jai pulled her into his arms. She stirred, her eyelashes fluttering, her breath warm against his chest. Not wanting to alarm her, he only pressed his lips against her forehead, restraining himself.

She nestled against him. "My honor at your company, Your Highness."

Encouraged, he slid his hand down to the silver triangle of her G-string. It crinkled under his touch—and disintegrated. Startled, he looked down; it had turned into glitter that dusted her thighs, sparkling in the dim light.

"That's pretty." He traced his finger through the glitter. Her skin felt smooth, like satin.

The girl laughed softly. She moved her hips against him with a curious mixture of innocence and temptation, as if she had no idea of the effect it had on him. But when she kissed his dark-haired chest, he stopped stroking her, mortified. He had read on a mesh site selling hair-removal tech that such body hair disgusted women. The holos had shown impossibly well-muscled men with perfectly smooth chests. The vendor had apparently done a good business.

The girl was watching his face, her head tilted as if she were listening to a distant conversation. Then she ran her hand through the hair on his chest. "Such a man," she murmured. "So strong. So sexy." Sleepy desire flowed from her mind and rolled over him.

Knowing she wanted him so much was even more arousing than the manufactured pheromones or her vanishing clothes. He held her tight against his body and kissed her hungrily. She felt incredible in his arms, and she seemed to sense how he wanted to be touched before he knew himself. He tried to hold back, afraid he would lose control and hurt her.

Finally he could take no more. Groaning, he rolled the girl on her back and covered her with his body. He reached to remove his loincloth, only to find it was already gone. The girl felt right. He wanted to whisper endearments, but he feared to sound foolish. Her mind was a sensual haze of arousal, so much so that he wondered if she had been drugged with aphrodisiacs. He pushed away the thought, needing her too much to believe synthetics produced her loving response.

So Jai held her and kissed her and moved with her in a rhythm more dreamlike than real. In the heady rush of his hunger, he whispered, "I love you, beautiful silver girl."

"And I you," she murmured.

Jai took her with tears on his face, knowing this charade was the closest he would ever come to love. Then he could no longer think at all. His body turned into a nova and he lost control in a burst of sensation.

Sometime later Jai became aware he was lying with the girl. When he lifted his head, she dimpled. "Such sweetness, Your Highness."

Jai reddened. "Sweet" wasn't how he wanted his first lover to think of him. Other words came to mind: powerful, masculine, virile. Somehow, though, "sweet" was all right from this silver girl.

Shifting his weight off her, he pulled up the quilt, cocooning them in its downy nest. It was like submerging into clouds. The girl closed her eyes, her lashes long and glimmering. He felt her satisfaction, and was gratified that he had given her enjoyment. He gathered her close. "I wish you could stay with me."

She fitted her body against his side and laid her head on his shoulder. "You are kind."

Kind. He winced, remembering how he had so passionately sworn his love. What an idiot. Yet even now, he could say it again. He wondered how he would respond when her pheromones were no longer influencing him. Well, what did it matter? She felt good and he liked her. That was enough.

"Maybe you could come home with me," he said.

"Your Highness honors me."

He could tell she didn't believe he would take her anywhere. Such declarations from Hightons were easily made and easily forgotten. Her mind gave no hint that she suspected the truth; unlike Sunrise, Corbal's lover, this girl couldn't imagine anomalies. The idea that the emperor might be a psion was too strange for her to conceive.

But she did think him handsome. He grinned. Then he said, "Jai."

Her lips curved. "Jai? What is that?"

"My name."

"It is a very fine name. Strong and vigorous."

He laughed at the idea of his nickname being vigorous. "You can call me Jai."

"Yes, Your Esteemed Glory."

Ah, well. Give it time. He could think of worse things than being called Your Esteemed Glory by his first lover.

Jai was almost asleep when she spoke again. "Thank you for sparing me at dinner tonight. I swear I would never try to harm you."

"I know." He yawned. "You seemed distracted."

"I was awed by your splendid presence."

Jai sighed. "You don't have to say that."

"It is my great honor to tell you the truth."

He knew all too well that it wasn't the truth. "What is your name?"

She slid her palm across his chest. "Silver."

Well, that was no surprise. "Do you like it?"

Her hand paused. "Like it?"

"Your name."

After a moment, she said, "Yes. I like it."

"Then I will call you Silver."

"Thank you, Your Highness."

"Jai."

Mischief shaded her voice. "Yes, Your Jainess."

"Silver!"

She laughed against his chest. "Jai."

Smiling, he pulled her close.

So the emperor slept, and for the first time since coming to Eube, he had no nightmares.

11

Loss

ESComm had become a threat.

Corbal sat in his chair, brooding. He had left Jaibriol asleep in the study down the hall, but his monitors indicated the boy had retired to his own suite. Jaibriol's jaunt here to the Sphinx Sector Rim Base disturbed Corbal; the new emperor was proving harder to keep an eye on than Corbal had expected. What had Jaibriol thought to gain from sneaking off to the Lock and sitting in its chair?

Corbal had seen the disheartening records; nothing in the Lock had operated since ESComm had taken it from the Skolians. The ancient station was either dormant or dead. Jaibriol claimed it couldn't awake, but Corbal wasn't ready to believe him.

Jaibriol. A conundrum. As much as his behavior at dinner tonight had aggravated Corbal, he had to admit he rather enjoyed the boy's audacity. But without ESComm support, Jaibriol could accomplish nothing—and Xirad Kaliga was ESComm. Only General Kryx Taratus, the other Joint Commander, had as much power within the military. General Taratus was the older brother of Azar Taratus, the idiot who had cheated Finance Minister Tarquine by selling her a dying provider for fourteen million credits.

Corbal grimaced. The current political landscape was a

disaster. Taratus and Iquar were embroiled in a morass of lawsuits. Not only did Iquar want her fourteen million back, she had sued Taratus for punitive damages, both for his actions and because the provider had escaped. Taratus had countersued, claiming harassment, saying it was her problem if she couldn't keep her provider, and that she had already filed an insurance claim for the money.

The insurance bureaus had taken action against both of them, Iquar because the security on her habitat supposedly hadn't fulfilled the requirements specified on her policy, and Taratus for fraud. In response, Iquar had filed an absurd claim against the bureaus for what she asserted was a retroactive change in their policy. Further, she wanted them to pay for the other systems on her habitat that had been damaged during the provider's escape, and for the shuttle he had stolen.

As if that wasn't enough, Taratus had taken additional action, claiming Iquar's intelligence systems had spied on him during the auction, compromising ESComm security. ESComm responded with an investigation of Taratus, wanting to know why he was using ESComm resources in a private auction. They were also pursuing action against Iquar for the failure of her security. And she had counterfiled against ESComm, for gods' sake, claiming the failure was their fault because they designed the systems on her purportedly civilian habitat.

The whole business reeked. General Taratus would almost certainly align with his brother Azar. If Xirad Kaliga, the other Joint Commander, also sided with them, it would set ESComm against the Finance Ministry, putting the military in opposition to the people who controlled the flow of wealth through Eube. It could destabilize the stumbling economy, which had suffered during the war, particularly the Platinum Sectors. On the other hand, if Kaliga opposed Taratus, it would create a schism within ESComm, weakening the military, which the war had also decimated.

It was a hellacious mess.

Azar Taratus and Minister Iquar were both bringing their

formidable resources and political clout to bear in the chaos created by Taratus's hoax. The hell of it was, his actions made sense. Had Iquar been anyone else, she probably would have done what he expected, paying the fourteen million off the record and reporting a negligible price to the bureaus. Taratus would have paid taxes only on that amount, the two of them cheating both the tax and insurance collectors. Then when Iquar discovered Taratus had sold her a dying provider, what could she have done? Had she reported only a minimal price to the insurance bureaus, it would have appeared as if she received exactly what she paid for.

Why Tarquine Iquar had reported the full price, Corbal had no idea. Perhaps she knew the provider was sick but wanted him anyway. Or maybe she was too savvy to trust Taratus. Whatever the reason, she had incontrovertible proof that Taratus had committed a mammoth fraud. The bureaus had charged her an obscene amount to insure the provider—and now they had to pay up for his loss. Taratus had a monstrous tax bill. Given the immense wealth and far-reaching security considerations involved, it was no wonder everyone was suing everyone else up, down, backward, and around the sun.

Corbal blew out a gust of air. He saw no good solution. No matter what the courts ruled, it would create schisms in the structures of Highton power. He felt as if he were watching a magrail train hurtle down a mountain, out of control, and nothing he could do would stop the crash. Because he knew what was going to happen.

Yes, he knew exactly what.

They were going to drop the whole mess into Jaibriol's lap.

The whisper of a sliding screen awoke Sunrise. "Come to bed, love," she murmured. "Do your worrying tomorrow."

Corbal didn't answer. He crossed the room quietly, with consideration for the late hour. In her younger days, Sunrise hadn't believed Aristos like him existed. But it was true. He was gentle. She had heard, through palace gossip, of one other: High Judge Calope Muze, Corbal's first cousin and second in line for the Carnelian Throne. Sunrise had even wondered about the emperor. She had only been with him a few moments that night, and he had guarded his mind, but she had felt an odd sense of recognition. Perhaps something in the Qox line made them different from other Aristos.

Another rustle came from across the room. She rolled over in the billowy covers. "Cori? Are you—"

A hand clamped over her mouth. It happened so fast, she had no time to breathe. No! *Who was this?* An air-syringe hissed against her neck, bringing darkness . . .

Corbal gave a long stretch as he stood up, working out kinks in his muscles. He felt stiff more and more often now. For all that the nanomeds in his body delayed his aging, they couldn't stop it. The years were beginning to take a toll.

He headed for bed, seeking the comfort of Sunrise's arms. A century ago, Corbal had done his duty, married a Highton woman and sired heirs. He and his wife had lived together for twenty-five chilly years. When she had passed away, he had given her a magnificent burial. He never again had to marry, never again had to live in the vacuum of a cold Highton union. Now he wanted Sunrise.

It was dark in the bedroom, but a breeze wafted across his face. A wall screen was open, letting starlight into the room. Odd that Sunrise would leave it that way. She didn't like to sleep in open areas. It made her feel vulnerable.

"Suni?" Sitting on the bed, Corbal reached for her. But no one lay there; the covers were piled in a heap. Puzzled, he said, "Lumos on."

The lights activated—revealing an empty room. Corbal frowned. Sunrise wouldn't just leave. He went to the open screen and peered into the night. "Lumos outside."

Lights came up in the garden, bathing the flowerbeds in soft colors. It was very lovely and very empty.

He made a thorough search of the slumbering house and

gardens, aided by several Razers. By the time they had verified she was neither inside nor out, his bewilderment had turned to anger. Sunrise wouldn't disappear. Someone had taken her. But how? According to the monitors, no one had come in the room. She had gone to bed and stayed there.

Corbal expected Xirad Kaliga to be asleep, but he found the admiral in a console room, with two bodyguards and a slew of aides. A guard searched Corbal before letting him enter. Kaliga was leaning over a console, talking in staccato bursts to someone on the comm. Corbal didn't like it; ESComm's Joint Commander looked as if he hadn't slept at all.

As the guard escorted Corbal to the console, Kaliga glanced up and nodded formally. "The hospitality of my household is at your service, Lord Xir."

Corbal understood the unstated question: Why was he wandering around the house late at night instead of enjoying the charms of his concubine?

"We appreciate your hospitality," Corbal answered. He doubted Kaliga missed his implication; a satisfied guest would offer more praise than "appreciate."

Kaliga motioned an aide over to the console. "Lord Xir, perhaps you would join me for a late-night refreshment? One of my ships brought in an unusually fine liqueur."

Corbal nodded, relieved. "It would be my pleasure."

As they left the console room, Corbal said, "Your household is admirable in its work ethic." In other words, why the blazes was everyone working at this hour?

"Rumors, my friend." Kaliga rolled his left shoulder slightly, indicating concern. "They sprout everywhere."

"Tales and truth are not necessarily the same."

"No, not necessarily." Kaliga said no more.

Corbal fell silent. He wanted to press the matter of Sunrise, but whatever troubled the admiral clearly had greater import, at least to ESComm and the empire. He discovered that right now he didn't care a whit about the welfare of Eube.

It wasn't until they were inside Kaliga's study, with their

guards outside, that the admiral spoke again. "It appears the Ruby Dynasty also works long hours."

Corbal inwardly swore. Eube had enough problems without the Skolians creating yet another of the never-ending crises they precipitated simply by their onerous existence. "The Ruby Dynasty would do well to rest. It might improve their ability to think."

Kaliga laughed dryly, with fatigue. He went to a table and poured goblets of a turquoise-hued liquid, then handed one to his guest. As Corbal swallowed, nanomeds in his lips and saliva checked the liqueur; then bioconduits in his body shunted it to a holding area, where other meds analyzed the liquid. After his security systems finished their checks, they released the liqueur. He barely noticed the pause before it continued down his throat.

He raised the goblet to Kaliga. "A fine choice."

The admiral nodded, obviously preoccupied, and motioned Corbal to a sofa, then sunk into a wing chair himself.

Corbal settled in his chair. He was tired enough to wish he could just come out and say, *What happened with the Ruby Dynasty?*

Kaliga took a swallow of liqueur. "It has a punch, eh?"

"Is it from Emerald Sector?" In truth, Emerald wasn't known for its liqueurs. However, "punch" could refer to whatever Kaliga had learned about the Ruby Dynasty, and ESComm had major command centers in Emerald Sector.

Kaliga considered him. "So it does. It just came in tonight." He set his goblet on a table and leaned back, closing his eyes. "A long night."

Corbal wanted to groan with the delay. "Longer yet, if one has to deal with Ruby Dynasty machinations."

"Or rumors of such."

"Rumors often fall apart under scrutiny."

The admiral lifted his head. "Unfortunately, some become even more odious."

Corbal tried not to grit his teeth. Sunrise could be dying

while they sat chatting about the infernal Skolians. "What isn't odious about the Ruby Dynasty?"

Kaliga regarded him steadily. "Their deaths."

Corbal paused in raising his goblet. Then he lowered it. "I take it no more of them have died, then?"

"Even worse." Kaliga's expression soured. "They have an uncanny ability to show up alive after we eliminate them."

Skolia be damned. "One more is always too many."

"One implies a single occurrence. It seems we are infested with them."

Corbal's grip on his goblet tightened. Did they suspect Jaibriol? Surely not. Corbal had destroyed the evidence. It wouldn't surprise him if ESComm had stolen genetic material from Jaibriol for more analyses, but they would find only that the boy's DNA came from his father. Corbal had arranged proof of a Highton mother who had passed away. He kept his suspicions about Jaibriol's real mother to himself; Soz Valdoria, the Skolian Imperator, was dead now, blown to plasma, along with her inconvenient DNA.

Corbal suddenly tensed. Could Kaliga's remarks refer to the late Imperator? Had she arisen from the dead? *Good gods.* "Infested by whom?" he asked.

At the blunt question, Kaliga raised an eyebrow. "I apologize if the nocturnal activity in my home has disturbed your sleep, Lord Xir."

Corbal held back his grimace. Kaliga had good cause for the rebuke, and he was courteous enough to imply Corbal's bluntness came from fatigue rather than an intended insult.

"Your hospitality is unsurpassed," Corbal said. "Even the dawn avails herself of its freedom." He had no doubt that Kaliga knew perfectly well providers didn't up and avail themselves of freedom.

"An intriguing concept," Kaliga mused, "that the sun would rise on a space station."

"It honors your home that such a remarkable occurrence should happen here."

Kaliga leaned forward. "I will relay your compliments to my security people immediately."

Kaliga's implicit promise to take immediate action in finding Sunrise relieved Corbal. While Kaliga contacted his security, Corbal checked with his own people. No sign of Sunrise had surfaced. His unease deepened; a provider couldn't vanish from the home of Xirad Kaliga. Someone must have taken her, which meant they had penetrated security and slipped away without a trace. That implied a betrayal at high levels.

Kaliga met Corbal's questioning look. "It seems it will be longer than we thought until the dawn arrives."

So the admiral's people claimed they knew nothing. Corbal didn't like it. "The dawn always arrives. Nothing can stop it."

"Rest assured, Lord Xir, we will do everything possible to make that true."

Corbal nodded. It wouldn't help Sunrise for him to dash about like an untried youth, but he loathed just sitting here. Where was she? If someone harmed her, he would see that the perpetrator suffered, long and hard.

He narrowed his gaze at Kaliga. The admiral had the means and opportunity to arrange a kidnapping. He would be a fool to do it in his own home, and Xirad Kaliga was no fool. Even so. If Kaliga didn't produce her soon, he could find himself embroiled in a legal tangle with the emperor's cousin.

Kaliga pushed his hand across his buzz-cut hair. "It has been a long night."

"A night of Rubies," Corbal said.

"Rubies," Kaliga muttered. "Thrones. Pharaohs."

Hell and damnation. Dyhianna Selei, the Ruby Pharaoh, had died during the war. That was how ESComm had captured Eldrin, her consort; he had sacrificed himself so she and their son could escape. The ESComm commandos who made the capture reported that she committed suicide by jumping into one of the Locks, but no one really knew what would happen if a human being fell into an operational Lock, which was a singularity in spacetime.

"I wouldn't have thought the Pharaoh had such resilience," Corbal said. "She looked weak."

"Perhaps." Kaliga sounded tired. "The loss of the Kyle webs makes it difficult to gather information. My ships bring messages, but that takes time. One rumor says the Pharaoh is dead, another says she is missing, yet another says she lives."

"Such stories show creativity." Or so Corbal hoped.

Kaliga's gaze hardened. "Another says Eldrin Valdoria, her consort, has been reunited with his Pharaoh wife."

At the prospect of the Ruby Dynasty retrenching, Corbal silently went through his arsenal of profanity. Even worse, he was the one who had released Eldrin. "Xirad, your liqueurs are unsurpassed. Perhaps you have one that is even stronger."

"Indeed." Kaliga grimaced. "For both of us."

This time, the admiral poured whiskey. As they drank, Corbal brooded. If Eldrin was reunited with his wife, it would lift morale among their people. The awe that the Skolians held for the Ruby Dynasty baffled Corbal. Weak and uncontrolled, the Ruby psions created havoc. They were *providers*, for saints' sake. As long as they promulgated their notions of freedom for taskmakers and providers, they corrupted human life.

And Jaibriol? The boy's naiveté and inherent weakness as a psion should have made him malleable; instead, he caused no end of trouble. Corbal also had other concerns. Hightons reacted to providers. So far Jaibriol had hidden his telepath's mind, but it would only take one mistake to reveal him. An unwelcome realization came to Corbal: Jaibriol's well-being mattered to him. He didn't want to care; it made him vulnerable. Nevertheless, apparently he did.

Then he had an even more disturbing thought, scandalous, preposterous. Yet there it was: given time and guidance, Jaibriol might make a better emperor than a true Highton.

Raziquon leaned over the girl manacled to his interrogation bench. "The procedure is simple. I ask questions. You answer. If you refuse, I will, shall we say, encourage you to speak."

Sunrise shook her head, her eyes wide with fear.

"Oh, I understand," Raziquon said. "You are loyal to Lord Xir. You have neural implants that prevent you from telling me about him, that may even erase your memories if I push too hard, hmmm?" A smile spread across his face. "But you see, no method is one hundred percent effective. You will tell me what I want to know. Eventually." He touched her breast. She truly was a beauty; she must have cost Corbal millions. He hoped the old man had good insurance for her. "Yes, eventually you will reveal all his secrets."

Raziquon had no personal animosity for Corbal, at least no more than he had for anyone else. His antipathy came from the danger Corbal posed to the Aristo way of life. Most considered the Xir lord's behavior toward this provider no more than eccentricity, but Raziquon knew better. If Xir took a moderate hand with Sunrise, other providers might come to expect the same. What then? Providers agitating for change? It was absurd. Dangerous. Xir would probably argue that they were incapable of agitation, but he was a fool to take risks.

Eube was the largest empire created by humanity, its population two trillion strong, taskmakers mainly, governed by a few thousand Aristos. It didn't take a genius to see that each Aristo held sway over far more people than he or she could individually control. Fear and punishment weren't sufficient motivators to manage groups that large. However, a contented populace rarely started a revolution.

Those taskmakers who lived acceptable lives were rewarded; those who disobeyed were punished. If their defiance became serious, they were eliminated, on a planetwide scale if necessary. The slagged remains of several worlds served testament to that fact. But no sane Aristo wanted genocide. Taskmakers formed the backbone of civilization; keeping them happy was far preferable to killing them.

Providers were another story. Only a few thousand existed. Their sole purpose in life was to please their owners. Their happiness made no difference; in fact, it benefited Aristos for them to be unhappy. Besides, their suffering elevated them.

If providers began to demand contentment and self-determination, it would create chaos. From there, how far to the decadence of the Skolian Imperialate, where providers roamed uncontrolled, and even worse, presumed to positions of authority? An upsurge of immorality among Eubian providers could destabilize the social structure of Eube. And if providers aspired to freedom, would taskmakers be far behind? A specter lurked in every Aristo's mind, the remote but not impossible chance that one day the taskmakers would rise against them, not a world, not a star system, but all of them, billions, trillions. Nothing could stop the fall of Eube then. Civilization would collapse.

Corbal Xir's "eccentricity" threatened the very fabric of Eubian society. And Xir stood closest to the throne, far more astute in the ways of power than the emperor himself.

Raziquon leaned over the bench, his gaze hard on the girl. *Mines,* he thought. *Platinum mines.*

Then he went to work, "encouraging" Sunrise to divulge the secrets of Lord Corbal Xir, arguably the most powerful man alive.

12

Betrayal

You're taking Lord Xir into custody?" Bewildered, Jai stood in the entrance to the console room and looked from Kaliga to Corbal. None of Kaliga's busy staff in the room had realized Jai had arrived.

"Why?" Jai asked Kaliga, his voice low. It was early morning, but neither the admiral nor Corbal looked as if they had slept.

"A good question." Corbal's anger was sharp enough to pierce Jai's mental barriers.

Guards surrounded them. Four were Jai's Razers, who had accompanied him as he wandered through the house, looking for breakfast, his heart content and his thoughts full of Silver, who was sleeping in his bed right now. Instead of food, he had stumbled into the console room and what felt like a surreal play, where he found himself onstage with no script.

Kaliga spoke coldly to Corbal. "I've just returned from meeting with my security chief. Apparently the dawn comes and goes of its own accord."

Jai stared at the admiral. What the blazes did the dawn have to do with anything?

Corbal, however, obviously knew what Kaliga meant. His voice hardened. "And apparently preposterous ideas come and go of their own accord within ESComm now."

At a nearby console, a major spoke, a man intent on his holoscreens. "Admiral Kaliga, we've another scout ship coming in. I'm getting a transmission."

Kaliga went over to the console. "Any verification?"

The man scanned his screens. "It's ESComm—been on reconnaissance—got it, sir!" He looked up, his face flushed. "We have verification. The Ruby Pharaoh was seen alive on Delos."

Jai felt as if the ground dropped beneath him. Alive? His aunt was *alive*? Good Lord, how long had they suspected? That no one had bothered to notify the emperor gave him an all too clear idea of how they viewed his role.

"Hell and damnation," Kaliga said.

Corbal stepped over to the console. "Where is she now?"

Kaliga spoke sharply. "Major, do not answer that. Until further notice, Lord Xir is in custody."

Sweat broke out on Jai's forehead. Why were they arresting Corbal? "What are—"

Corbal shook his head at Jai, cautioning silence. The major glanced coolly in Jai's direction—and froze, his eyes widening. Immediately, he went down on one knee. People around him looked up, saw Jai, and followed suit, their reaction spreading like a wave. As Jai watched, dumbfounded, every taskmaker in the crowded room knelt to him.

As Hightons, Corbal and Kaliga remained standing, as did the guards, both Jai's four Razers and Kaliga's four men. The admiral motioned to his guards, and they fell into formation around Corbal.

"Wait." Jai struggled to contain his alarm. They couldn't take Corbal. Without his cousin, Jai would be lost.

Kaliga bowed to Jai. "Our good morn to Your Highness."

"Admiral." Confused by the out-of-place greeting, Jai barely managed a nod. The commotion in the room disoriented him, as consoles continued to spill out data and voices. While everyone knelt and Kaliga paid him courtesies, valuable facts, figures, and images scrolled by on consoles. But Jai had no clue how to tell everyone—without being direct—

that they could return to work. Although technically he could speak plainly to ESComm officers who weren't Aristos, the ones here had high enough rank to make it an insult. But if he spoke to someone of a lower rank instead of the top officers, that would also be an insult.

Jai fell back on Highton clichés. "A fine morn," he told Kaliga. "Your staff does it great honor."

Kaliga bowed. "Thank you, Your Highness."

That hadn't helped any. They all continued to kneel. Corbal was frowning, trying to communicate something. Jai concentrated on his mind. Something about moving his hand. Guessing, Jai waved his hand at the major who had first knelt. Although the man had his eyes downcast, he apparently saw, because he immediately stood and bowed to Jai. Then he returned to work, followed by everyone else.

Jai made a conscious effort to restrain his exhale of relief. His reprieve didn't last long. Kaliga's guards were escorting Corbal into the hall. Just as Jai opened his mouth to protest, Kaliga said, "Please accept my apologies, Your Highness, for the disorder." At the same instant, an aide said, "Admiral Kaliga, we have an emerg—" She broke off when she realized he was addressing Jai.

Jai wanted to call *Stop!* Everything was happening too fast. He spoke to the guards taking Corbal out of the room. "Leave him here."

The men froze, their gazes shifting from Jai to Kaliga.

Admiral Kaliga addressed Jai with a deference that had an edge despite the outward courtesy. "Would you care to take breakfast in my private dining room, Your Highness? We have delicacies imported from Taimarsia. It would be my honor to entertain your glorious presence."

Jai barely held back his irate retort. How could Kaliga talk about breakfast while he was arresting Corbal and the console room hummed with activity that demanded attention? Jai was about to refuse when he caught Corbal's glare. The older man shook his head. Pah. Corbal *wanted* him to go eat. Highton customs would never make sense to Jai.

Fuming, but hiding it, Jai nodded to Kaliga. "It would be my pleasure to join you for the morn's repast."

Kaliga bowed, formal and restrained. As he ushered Jai out of the room, guards took Corbal the other way, down the hall, out of sight.

The delicacies from Taimarsia were spiky sea creatures Jai could barely look at, let alone eat. They had tentacles. He sipped his wine, so Kaliga did the same, leaving his food untouched. Jai would have rather had juice for breakfast, but he understood Highton customs enough now to know he would look childish if he requested it. He had a sense that Kaliga actually liked the monstrosities on his plate. Jai knew the admiral wouldn't eat unless the emperor did, but he just couldn't bring himself to force down the creatures.

They talked in loops. Kaliga's elliptical conversation gave Jai a headache. Nor did it help him find out why ESComm had imprisoned Corbal. Frustrated, he even tried to discover out what Kaliga knew about Jafe Maccar, the Skolian captain ESComm had imprisoned, the man Kelric wanted him to pardon. With a prodigious skill at misdirection, Kaliga avoided telling him anything at all, let alone something useful.

Finally Jai said, "Admiral Kaliga, I have appreciated your hospitality, but I find myself puzzled."

Kaliga raised an eyebrow. "Indeed."

Jai thought he would strangle the next person who said *Indeed*. "Yes. Also troubled."

"It would honor the Line of Kaliga if Your Imperial Magnificence would allow us to ease any troubles you have encountered."

Jai couldn't tell if Kaliga was serious or mocking him with the "Imperial Magnificence" bit. "I have noticed that the Line of Kaliga has taken a security interest in the Line of Xir."

Kaliga relaxed in his chair, appearing sociable. From his mind, though, Jai could tell he was irritated. "One might think the Line of Xir has taken liberties."

Jai made a conscious effort not to grit his teeth. "One might also think I have no idea what that means."

A muscle in Kaliga's cheek jerked. "It means he committed treason."

Jai froze. Treason? Impossible. Even through his barriers, he felt the admiral's annoyance. Angered by Jai's clumsy Highton discourse, Kaliga had deliberately given a direct answer, a great insult among Aristos, but he assumed Jai had neither the savvy nor intelligence to know.

Jai didn't miss the irony; had he truly been a naive Highton boy from a sheltered background, he probably would have missed the gravity of Kaliga's offense. But because he was exactly what Kaliga suggested with his direct speech—a psion—he recognized the admiral's intent.

"Treason against Eube?" Jai asked coolly. "Or against the courtesy a Highton might expect at, say, breakfast?"

Shock jumped in Kaliga's mind that Jai understood the insult. He spoke fast. "Your revered presence deserves the greatest courtesy, Your Glorious Highness."

Jai pushed back his chair. "We appreciate your esteem. We are especially pleased at the opportunity to visit Lord Xir."

Kaliga obviously wanted to deny him the visit. But he rose to his feet, apparently choosing to avoid the risk of compounding the offense he had given. "Certainly, Your Highness."

It took an order from Jai to clear Kaliga's guards out of Corbal's study, where security had confined the Xir lord. Not that anyone believed sending them away would give Jai and Corbal privacy; with Corbal under arrest, Jai's people could no longer scan the rooms for monitors.

"You mean Sunrise?" Jai stared at Corbal, certain he had misunderstood. Sunrise would never steal security files from Kaliga. "She isn't capable of betraying your trust."

Corbal paced the room. "ESComm agrees with you."

Ah, hell. No wonder they had arrested Corbal; they believed he had put Sunrise up to the theft. "I thought the monitors showed her in your room the whole night."

His cousin stopped pacing and scowled at him. "Our most honored admiral believes my own people bestowed their skills on those monitors to 'improve' the recording."

It sounded like they had accused Corbal of altering records to protect Sunrise while she stole from Kaliga. Jai wanted to question him, but he wasn't certain how to proceed. Although Corbal often spoke more plainly with him without meaning insult, Jai didn't have a good feel for when direct speech was or wasn't appropriate among kin.

"Admiral Kaliga is a man of intelligence," Jai said. "He can work wonders in many media." It wasn't the most subtle point, given how close it came to an accusation that Kaliga had forged the record, but it would do.

Corbal began to pace again. "I have been impressed by the elegant dinners set by the Kaliga Line. Many other Hightons share my admiration. Just look at the caliber of the guests who dined here last night."

"A fine company." In truth, Jai had thought them detestable. But Corbal was right. Kaliga wasn't the only suspect.

Corbal stopped in front of Jai, thoughtful. "Our esteemed host has high connections. Few others have the intellect to achieve his accomplishments."

Jai nodded. In other words, few of the dinner guests had the access and ability for such an audacious theft. Unfortunately, that helped implicate Corbal, who *did* have both. Admiral Kaliga had the best access, but he was too smart to plan such an outrage in his own home—unless he expected everyone to make exactly that assumption.

Jai didn't think Corbal had done it; he sensed no deception in his cousin's mind, and he knew Corbal would never endanger Sunrise. But if not him, then who? And why frame Corbal? Given his power and wealth, and his own son's position as Intelligence Minister, it wasn't likely ESComm could make a successful case against him.

Although Jai had heard of no conflict between the Kaliga

and Xir Lines, that said little, given the incomprehensible tangle of Highton interactions. For all he knew, Corbal and Kaliga were mortal enemies. Perhaps Kaliga wanted to discredit Xir. But Jai found it hard to believe Kaliga would arrange such a crime; it was too extreme, especially given the current disaster with Minister Iquar and Admiral Taratus over Kelric's disappearance.

Jai left Corbal's rooms more uncertain than before. Surrounded by Razers, he went out to the gardens and paced down the paths. He would have to return to Glory without Corbal. As much as he had chafed at Corbal's scrutiny, he had more independence now than he could handle. He *needed* his cousin; without him, he was lost.

As emperor, surely he could obtain Corbal's release. The problem was, he didn't know how, and if he stumbled in this, he could antagonize ESComm. He didn't trust anyone enough to ask. Corbal had mentioned his cousin, High Judge Calope Muze, several times, but Jai didn't see why he should have confidence in her over any other Highton. He felt more inclined to seek out Corbal's son, Azile.

Dispirited, he sat on a bench by a lake and stared into the water. Life glimmered in its depths, ribbons flickering here and there.

Jai looked up at one of his Razers, who stood under the overhang of a nearby droop-willow. The man bowed. "May I serve Your Highness?"

Jai motioned him over. As the Razer approached, Jai stood up, feeling vulnerable next to his towering bodyguard. "Is the silver girl still in my suite?"

"I will check, sir." Using his gauntlet comm, the Razer conferred with guards in the house. Then he said, "She is in her own suite, Your Highness. Housekeeping took her back this morning."

Housekeeping. Jai hated it when they spoke that way, as if Silver were furniture to be dusted. She had been his first lover, sweet and sensual; in her arms, he had felt like a real emperor instead of a bumbling youth. He started to tell the

Razer to show him to her suite, then realized it would be awkward, even scandalous, if the emperor attended a provider. So he said, "Please bring her here."

His guard bowed. "Yes, Your Highness." He headed to the house, leaving Jai with the other Razers.

Sitting on the bench again, Jai gazed across the lake to the far shore, where droop-willows were reflected in the water. He wished the tranquil scene could settle his troubled heart.

Silver soon appeared, walking along the lake with his Razer, her blue drapes fluttering around her body. When she saw him, her face suffused with pleasure. Jai rose to his feet and she came to him, her cheeks touched by a rosy blush.

Then, to Jai's dismay, she knelt. He didn't know which was worse; having them treat him this way or fearing he would someday come to expect it.

He touched her shoulder. "Please stand, Silver."

She rose and smiled, her face aglow. "My pleasure at your presence, Most Honored Highness."

"Jai," he murmured.

"Jai." She spoke so only he could hear.

He took her hands. "Thank you."

Confusion washed across her face. "You are most welcome."

Jai wanted to explain his gratitude, but what could he say? *Thank you for making my first time with a woman such a gift. Thank you for being an island of serenity in a turbulent ocean.*

Silver's gaze softened as if he had spoken aloud. She raised his hands and pressed her lips against his knuckles. With a sigh, Jai pulled her close, filling his arms with her soft curves.

"Come home with me," he said against her hair. "To my palace on Glory, in the Jaizire Mountains."

She drew back enough to look up at him, regret dimming her luminous gaze. "It would be an incredible honor."

"Why are you so sad?" He spoke in a low voice, aware of his Razers under the trees. "Would leaving here give you sorrow? I won't take you away if you want to stay."

"I have only joy at the thought of pleasing you." Her smile was tremulous.

Sensitized to her empath's mind, Jai picked up her mood through his defenses; Kaliga would never let her leave. If Jai pushed enough, he could force the admiral to let her go; few Hightons would deny the emperor. But Silver would come to him at the price of what little goodwill he had left with the Line of Kaliga.

"Fare you well, dear Jai." Silver touched his cheek. "You deserve the best of life's intangibles, those gifts that wealth and power can never measure."

Jai swallowed, wondering if Kaliga had any clue his provider was so articulate. In revealing herself to him, Silver had given him one of those intangible gifts.

He kissed her for the last time, holding her as if she were a fading light within an encroaching darkness.

13

Tribunal

No ornamentation adorned the marble walls of the High Judge's courtroom. Its austerity surprised Jai, given the rich decor everywhere else in his palace. He did see one similarity: this room had an octagonal shape. He couldn't recall seeing a square room anywhere in the palace. They were all round or octagonal. Here, the judge's bench stood along one wall, and octagonal tables were arrayed before it. The courtroom was too small to hold an audience.

Tarquine Iquar sat with her counsel at one table. Tall and composed, she fascinated Jai, with her aquiline beauty and aura of power. Azar Taratus and his people had another table. Sprawled in his chair, the lanky Taratus watched the room with a sardonic gaze. Legal aces from ESComm occupied two tables, and agents from the insurance bureaus took up two others. Razers stood posted around the walls. Jai sat at a table on a dais to the left of the judge's bench. Several members of his staff sat with him, including one Highton— Azile Xir, his Minister of Intelligence. Jai barely knew any of them, except for his aide, Robert Muzeson.

The hum of voices filled the courtroom as the various parties conferred. Jai just watched, his head throbbing from the presence of so many Aristos. It was excruciating; the proceedings hadn't even started and already he longed for them to be done.

A door opened behind the bench, and High Judge Calope Muze entered, wearing the gray robes of her office. Everyone except Jai rose to their feet. As tall as Corbal, her cousin, she stood behind her high bench, surveying the court. She bowed deeply to Jai, her white head inclined. It made him acutely self-conscious to receive such deference from someone so many decades his elder.

After Jai nodded to her, Calope sat in her high-backed judge's chair, and everyone else in the room resumed their seats. Calope was the only other Aristo that Jai had seen besides Corbal who had white hair. As High Judge, she oversaw the Eubian courts and served as chief justice in the Qox palace, giving her a status equivalent to that of Jai's ministers.

An obsidian mallet lay on the bench next to a small gong with a gold octagonal disk. Judge Muze tapped the gong, sending a clear note throughout the chamber. So the proceedings began.

And went on.

And on.

And on . . .

If Jai hadn't sat through every excruciating minute, he wouldn't have believed a hearing could be so interminable. He listened to each side present its purportedly noble cause and accuse everyone else of perfidy. Although the circuitous arguments weren't quite as abstruse as Highton social discourse, it took forever for anyone to make a point.

Jai's head ached. Even with his table set apart from the others, their minds pressed on him, crushing. Having Azile Xir at his side multiplied the effect; Corbal might not transcend, but his son did. Jai was exhausted before the hearing even started. He would go catatonic with this much exposure to Aristos. Much as he wanted to be here in person, to pick up mental undercurrents, he was beginning to think he would have no choice but to retreat to his private rooms and set up a virtual link to this hall. It would let him attend the rest of the sessions as a VR simulacrum.

Listening to another endless speech, Jai grimaced. He would go catatonic all right—from boredom. If Hightons approached all official matters this way, he didn't see how the government managed to function. They ought to throw Taratus in prison and be done with it. ESComm should concentrate on fixing the hole in their security that this mess had revealed. And the bureaus owed Tarquine Iquar. She had met their exorbitant fees; now it was time for them to pay up.

He wondered how they would all feel when they discovered her escaped "property" was a Ruby prince who had ascended to the Skolian Triad. As far as he knew, ESComm had found no trace of Kelric yet. It gave Jai hope that his uncle had escaped.

Jai wished he could have told Kelric why he valued their meeting. But his dream of peace between Eube and Skolia seemed more distant every ceaseless minute he spent among the Hightons. The more he learned during these proceedings about Kelric's failing health, the more it astounded him that his uncle had even reached the Lock. It was harder and harder to believe Kelric would live long enough to assume his place as Imperator.

When Judge Muze finally called a recess, Jai could have wept with relief. He stood, and everyone else in the chamber followed suit. With a nod to the High Judge, he gave his sanction to end the session.

As Jai's retinue prepared to leave, his gaze went to Minister Iquar. She moved with a feline grace, her sleek curves discreet but visible in the starkly conservative black jumpsuit she wore. When she caught him staring, she didn't look the least intimidated. Her lips curved and she quirked an eyebrow. Mortified, Jai inclined his head, struggling for that chilly Highton indifference. Then his retinue swept him out of the chamber, using the door behind the bench, giving him the privacy available to only one other person, the High Judge.

Calope was already in the small antechamber. She bowed to Jai. "My honor at your presence, Your Esteemed Highness."

Relieved to escape the pressure of the Hightons in the courtroom, he gave a friendlier nod than usual. "It pleases me to meet you, Cousin."

Her smile was reserved, but he sensed no hostility. He spoke briefly with her, and was surprised to enjoy the moment. It wasn't until he had taken his leave that he realized why her presence hadn't bothered him.

Her mind exerted no mental pressure against his.

Jai stood in his darkened study watching the holostage, where a recording of the hearings was playing. It was hard to believe they had begun only this morning; he felt as drained as if they had been going for weeks. He couldn't stop staring at Tarquine Iquar. All that power and menace. She was like a black puma, smooth and muscled, sleek and deadly. He ran his finger around the collar of his high-necked tunic, wiping the sweat from his neck.

Pah. Jai tried to clear his mind. He jumped ahead to another section of the recording where Tarquine was only in the background. During the hearing, the speeches had seemed tangled in snarls, but now that he could concentrate, he realized they had a surprising coherence. The Iquar legal team was inexorable; Taratus's people were brazenly confident; ESComm put on a virtuoso display of misdirection; and the insurance bureaus were geniuses at obfuscation.

Jai was beginning to understand their speech. He had thought he was fluent in Highton, but he realized now that his knowledge only skimmed its surface. Hightons spoke in more than one dimension; the structure, cadence, and tangents conveyed as much as the words themselves. Gestures and posture were integral to the language, and Hightons also said a great deal with what they left unspoken. Ironically, the very thing that made it hard for him to bear the presence of Aristos—his telepath's mind—also gave him some facility in Highton, letting him discern hidden meanings he wouldn't have picked up otherwise.

Calope Muze surprised him. Beyond her cool reserve, he saw wisdom. Perhaps that shouldn't surprise him; Eube would never have thrived so well if Aristos weren't so thoroughly adept at running their empire. He had seen brutality and vicious pride among them, but also intelligence, artistic genius, and insight. Yet that only made him feel worse. He had assumed their cruelty was instinctual, a genetic trait they could no more change than they could stop breathing. If they could choose otherwise, it made their brutality that much harder to bear.

The wall comm next to him buzzed. Jai flicked his finger through the receive holo. "Yes?"

Tomjolt, his personal EI, answered. "Your Highness, Azile Xir requests permission to speak with you."

"Put him on audio." Jai knew his facial expressions and body language gave away clues about his thoughts. He tried to mask his reactions, but he had little experience guarding himself that way, whereas Hightons had raised the process to an art form, both in hiding the hints their own behavior gave about their thoughts and in reading those clues in others.

Azile's deep voice came out of the comm. "I most humbly thank Your Esteemed Highness for granting this audience to the Ministry of Intelligence."

When Jai had first come to Glory, a few weeks ago, he would have assumed the greeting was meant only to stroke his ego. He still thought it had a measure of that, but he realized now the phrasing was itself a message. What it meant, he wasn't sure, but the reference to the Intelligence Ministry implied a problem had come up with security.

"The Line of Qox appreciates your ministry," Jai said.

"I thank you," Azile said. "Your office is known for its generosity."

Generosity? Hardly. Maybe he ought to speak to Azile on a comm channel that couldn't be monitored. Unfortunately, that eliminated every channel in the Eubian Concord. But Jai thought his private study, in his own palace, was probably more secure than a comm line.

"Have you ever tasted Taimarsian wine, Minister Xir?" he asked. "I've a fine vintage here. Perhaps you might attend me this afternoon, at sixth hour." The hearings wouldn't resume again until tomorrow. In this season, nights in the Jaizire Mountains lasted six hours, which meant daylight lasted ten. The people on Glory counted hours from sunrise; today, sixth hour came in early afternoon. Jai thought it made timekeeping absurdly complicated, given that they had to recalculate the time every day. Then again, maybe that was why Aristos liked it.

"Your Highness is most gracious," Azile said. "It would be my great honor to attend you."

"Very well." Jai thought Azile sounded wary, but he couldn't be sure. As much as it relieved him to be isolated from other Aristos, it limited his ability to discern their thoughts—and his well-being, freedom, even his life, depended on how well he could gauge their intent.

Azile barely touched his wine. The minister's agitation was strong enough for Jai to sense even through his barriers.

"ESComm is admirable in their attention to detail," Azile said. He was standing by a window, facing Jai, his glass in his hand. Beyond him, in the bleached evening sky, the crescents of several moons glowed. "My father has always commented on their steadfast dedication to their work."

To our misfortune, Jai thought. Right now Azile's father was the object that dedication. "Your father has always been a man of great intelligence." He hoped Azile understood his question: Had ESComm's intelligence people found any evidence linking Corbal to the security break at Kaliga's home?

"He has long valued persistence," Azile said. "It was a trait witnessed by every dawn."

The dawn. Azile had to mean Sunrise. His use of the past tense made Jai think they hadn't found any leads in her disappearance. Mercifully, he found no indication of her death in Azile's mind. He couldn't lower his barriers around Azile, but surely if she had died, the minister would be grieving deeply enough that Jai would feel it through his defenses. Azile liked Sunrise, maybe even more than he liked his own Highton mother. Jai didn't know if Aristos could love, but if they did, he thought Corbal and Azile both loved Sunrise, each in his own way.

It had to be maddening for Corbal, unable to help in the search. Technically, ESComm hadn't imprisoned him; incarcerating a Highton was almost never done. They detained him in an opulent mansion owned by the military while they investigated the situation. Corbal could neither leave nor have visitors, except ESComm officers, but he otherwise lived in luxury. Jai could have seen him if he wanted, but it was impractical to the point of impossibility; ESComm had taken him to another planet and Jai had far more duties here on Glory than he could handle.

Jai didn't understand what Azile meant by every dawn having witnessed Corbal's persistence. Perhaps Sunrise had mentioned his tenacity, or maybe she had seen something she shouldn't have. How that connected to her abduction, he had no idea, but he could tell Azile feared for her life. Jai couldn't bear to think of her being hurt, and he wanted Azile to know the investigation would remain a top priority.

"Minister Xir," he said. "Please be assured we will do our best to ensure that the joy of the new day isn't lost. I will see to it myself."

Azile studied him, so closely that Jai wondered if he had said more than he intended. Then the minister bowed. "You are most wise and generous, Your Esteemed Highness."

Most wise? If there was any adjective Aristos didn't associate with him, it was wisdom. Jai hoped he hadn't just promised more than he could deliver. Perhaps he ought to quit trying to talk like a Highton, before he landed himself in trouble. He wished he could consult Corbal, the only Aristo who would speak with him in a comprehensible manner.

Not that he trusted Corbal either, but at least they had the same goal: Jai's survival.

Corbal, however, could no longer help him.

The pressure felt as if it were driving broken glass into his temples. It was the only way Jai could describe the minds of the Aristos in the courtroom. They felt even worse than yesterday, when the hearings had begun. His mental defenses were weakening under the strain.

He vehemently wished he had followed through on his idea to attend the hearings using a VR set up in his private rooms. He had returned here because the insights he gained as a psion could prove invaluable, and he only sensed the moods or thoughts of people when he was near them, unblocked by walls or other barriers. But now his decision seemed crazy. Nothing was worth this misery.

Jai struggled to concentrate. The insurance bureaus were arguing that they owed Tarquine Iquar nothing. To an extent, they had a point; if she won against Taratus, he would owe her the balance between the true worth of the provider and the fourteen million. Given that Kelric had been dying, his price should have been a small fraction of what Tarquine paid.

However, the bureaus also claimed Tarquine had lost her provider due to negligence, besides which, she had sued Taratus for punitive damages. If she won, she would end up with far more than the fourteen million renormalized credits she paid in the first place, so they insisted they shouldn't even have to refund her insurance fees.

Their blithe refusal to acknowledge any responsibility amazed Jai. He also wanted to laugh every time he heard "renormalized." The word came from quantum field theory. Basically it meant turning an infinite quantity into a finite one. It said a great deal about economic inflation in the Eubian Concord, that they had to "renormalize" their money.

Tarquine's legal team claimed the bureaus had violated her rights by forcing her to pay their fees before she could verify the health of her provider. Even worse, they said, she had lost an immense amount of interest while the bureaus kept her credits, and continued to do so as long as they refused to honor their contract. For good measure, they even accused the bureaus of setting criminally high fees and exhorted the High Judge to investigate them.

Objections multiplied. Taratus's people weighed in, declaring he had been convicted of no crime. ESComm objected to the demand made by the bureaus that Tarquine turn over details of her security system, which had been designed by the military. Calope Muze reminded everyone that the fee schedule of the bureaus was not on trial.

The debate dragged on. ESComm made veiled threats at every turn. The bureaus threw every metaphorical wrench imaginable into proceedings. If it was this bad now, Jai dreaded the chaos that would explode when they discovered the truth about Kelric.

The main players, Tarquine Iquar and Azar Taratus, rarely spoke. The few times Tarquine addressed the court, she was terrifyingly articulate. Jai hoped he never faced her in any proceeding. She would shred him. He tried to stop noticing her: he didn't see her hawk-like beauty; he wasn't aware of her lean body; he didn't find her mesmerizing. He noticed none of it, none at all.

His head hurt so damn much. The onslaught of their Aristo minds came with so much force, he caught valuable impressions even without lowering his barriers. Taratus expected to lose on the fraud charge. Despite his outward nonchalance, he feared ESComm would strip him of his rank. ESComm was irate, at the bureaus for trying to compromise military security and at Taratus for getting caught. The bureaus were determined to do whatever necessary, no matter how sleazy, to avoid paying Tarquine.

Jai's mind reeled. Pressing the heels of his hands against his temples, he groaned. He could no longer hear the speakers in the courtroom.

"Your Highness?" Azile's voice pierced the roar in his ears—no, in his mind—so much pain—

Jai stood up, knocking over his chair. The colonel giving testimony stopped and turned with a start. Everyone else in the room rose, including the High Judge. Jai stared at them. He caught an image of himself in Tarquine's mind, a tall youth with his eyes wild, his body tensed and partially bent over. He looked half-crazed.

Jai could endure no more. With excruciating care, he walked off the dais and went to the private exit behind Calope's bench.

Then he escaped the courtroom.

The stone bench where Jai sat curved around the secluded antechamber behind the courtroom. With his feet planted wide, he rested his elbows on his knees and put his forehead on the heels of his hands. He didn't see whoever opened and then closed the door, but he heard breathing. It couldn't be Azile; Jai would have recognized his mind. His Razers affected him, too, though they were only half Aristo, so the effect wasn't as pronounced. He felt nothing now.

Jai raised his head and saw Calope Muze standing by the door. She bowed to him. "Please accept my apologies for disturbing your contemplation, Your Highness."

Contemplation. That was certainly a polite way to put it. He indicated the bench against the opposite wall, a few paces away. "Join me, please." He wanted to send her away, but isolating himself now would only worsen his reputation for bizarre behavior.

Calope settled on the bench. "I am amazed at the variety of atmospheric conditions humans can tolerate on different worlds."

Jai knew she was trying to offer him an excuse for his "attack." The atmosphere on Glory wasn't unusual, given that the world had been terraformed for humans, but a difficulty in breathing was the best excuse for his behavior he could think of right now.

"Your Highness impresses with his ability to adapt to our world," she added.

"Thank you." Jai's head was clearing now that the pressure from the Hightons had receded, muted by distance and the marble walls. He focused on Calope and even relaxed his barriers, but he still felt no pressure. Just like Corbal. Jai wished he knew why they didn't affect him. Calope and Corbal had three attributes in common: white hair, advanced age, and Qox heredity.

"Your handling of the hearings invites respect," he said.

Calope inclined her head. "You honor me."

Jai hesitated to say more. He suspected he had stumbled in his talk with Azile about Sunrise. The Intelligence Minister remained maddeningly vague on the subject. Jai didn't even want to imagine what he could end up saying if he conversed with the judge.

With his barriers relaxed, he felt Calope's curiosity: he intrigued her. She thought of him as a beautiful enigma begging to be solved. Jai winced. The only person who truly saw him as an emperor was Silver. He wished he could go home to her at night, but Kaliga had turned down his offers for the girl. Although the admiral used great courtesy, he showed no sign of relenting. Jai didn't blame him. Silver was a miracle. As much as Kaliga didn't deserve her, Jai couldn't imagine anyone in his right mind giving her up.

More impressions came to him from Calope; she liked him despite his oddities, but she expected him to retreat into seclusion, as his father had before him. She wondered if inbreeding had made the Qox Line mentally fragile.

Inbreeding. He wanted to laugh. *If only you knew.* Aloud he said, "You bring a mark of distinction to these difficult proceedings." It was the closest he could come to saying what he really meant: *It's a wretched muddle in there.*

Calope smiled dryly. "I'm afraid any mark would be distinct within such confusion."

Was that a Highton joke? Startled, Jai smiled.

Calope blinked, her emotions clear; she found his smile

guileless, a quality she had never expected to associate with a Qox emperor. Jai inwardly groaned. No one took him seriously. He stood up slowly. His headache had receded enough that he thought he could return to the hearings.

Calope rose as well and opened the door, then followed him into the courtroom. The legal teams were all conferring, each group using sound-shrouds to keep their adversaries from eavesdropping. Everyone stopped and stood when Jai entered. As he sat at the table on the dais, Calope took her chair behind her bench. Jai offered no explanation for his departure and no one dared ask.

After the usual formalities, Calope resumed the hearing. As Taratus's people wound up to their previous argumentative pitch, Azile spoke to Jai in a low voice. "It is gratifying to see Your Highness in good health."

Jai wanted to say, *I feel like someone hit me in the head with a stardock crane.* But he nodded and kept his mouth shut. Perhaps he could make Imperial Silence a new fad.

The legal counsels continued to perform remarkable feats of indecipherable verbosity. At one point, someone actually said, "It is our contention that the contrary prediction of safeguards as established by the forward-leaning claims in document four-seven-three-nine-two, presented by my most honored colleagues in EFC, pursuant to the final decision of the back stripes did in fact alter." Jai hadn't a clue what the fellow meant.

Why anyone would aspire to imperial sovereignty, Jai couldn't imagine. If this was typical of a day on the job, his relatives could have it. Pleasure girls excepted, it was a singularly unpleasant occupation.

He could see why Kaliga and his cronies assumed it would be easy to distract him with providers, drugs, and other numbing pursuits, while his elders ran his empire. He longed for Silver. He could have any of the providers he had inherited, and he had no doubt they were just as beautiful. But he didn't want some other woman. He wanted her. Unlike the

Aristos, he couldn't switch his affections as casually as he changed clothes.

"So it is with great expectation," Taratus's counsel continued, "that we come before you, most esteemed High Judge Muze, to partake of your wisdom in this matter of spurious accusations."

Jai blinked. Were they finally going to stop talking and partake of some wisdom? It was about time.

Calope nodded. Her hair glittered like white crystals in the diffuse light. "Counsels please stand."

Relief swept over Jai. Not only had they quit pontificating, but Calope had spoken a sentence he could understand. Curious, he waited to see what came next.

Everyone at the tables below rose to their feet. Calope spoke to the Hightons arrayed before her. "The Court of Qox accepts your words. The record is complete." Now she rose, too, and turned to Jai. "It is with the utmost reverence that we honor your decision, Most Sagacious Majesty."

Jai froze. *What* decision? And since when had he become a "Sagacious Majesty"? Corbal had gone over in detail what was expected from him at the hearings. These opening arguments were only the start. Rebuttals and examinations could go on for months, even years. None of it had included Calope Muze asking his sagacious self for a decision.

Jai glanced at Azile Xir. The Intelligence Minister nodded with respect—and gratitude.

Gratitude.

Ah, hell. Jai made himself drop his barriers, so he could verify what he feared, reading the truth from Azile. Comprehension hit him even worse than the impact of the Aristo minds. He hadn't just blundered when he spoke with Azile about Sunrise, saying he would see to the matter himself.

He had promised that he, Jaibriol III, would render the verdict in these hearings.

I'm dead, Jai thought.

14

Verdict

Panic surged in Jai and his mind reeled. They were all waiting for him to speak. What did he do now? With the perfect vision of hindsight, he realized Azile had been waiting for exactly the opening Jai had given him. The minister had deliberately chosen to interpret Jai's comment in a broader context than Jai had intended, and Jai had been too naive to stop it from happening.

He tried to intensify his barriers, but he couldn't do it right with so many emotions pouring in on him and so much pressure from the Hightons. He had to get out ·of here, talk to someone, find out how to respond. But he had no one to confide in. *No one*. If he showed any weakness, the Aristos would devour him like Earth's legendary piranhas.

The silence stretched out like a band pulled too tight. He felt everyone's disquiet, all wondering why their untried and perhaps unstable emperor didn't respond.

Jai took a shaky breath. Then he rose, followed by the others at his table. He had trouble sorting out the emotions bombarding him, but Calope's came through strongly; if he left the chamber now, it would be tantamount to dismissing the case. The result would be unmitigated disaster: Taratus would go free, the bureaus would escape paying, ESComm would be left hanging, and Tarquine Iquar would recoup none of her losses.

After the emperor, the three most powerful civilians in Eube were the Ministers of Finance, Trade, and Intelligence. With her influence, Tarquine could cause a major economic crisis if she chose to do so. Jai had no doubt she was fully capable of doing it. If he walked away from this, he would set appalling precedents in the criminal, military, and economic sectors, and possibly precipitate an interstellar catastrophe.

Jai fought down his panic. He had to say something. Although he had an idea what to do in some of the cases, he was lost for how to phrase his decisions. He had nothing resembling the fluency in Highton he needed, but if he answered plainly, it would be an insult so deep, gods only knew what would happen. Maybe someone would assassinate him and put him out of his misery.

Until now, his lack of experience had been a shield. No one had taken him seriously enough to consider him a danger. But no matter what he did now, he would make potent enemies. And whatever he decided would directly impact Corbal. Sunrise's situation had too many similarities to what had happened with Kelric. No wonder Azile had been so grateful; Jai had practically promised to render a verdict that benefited Corbal. If he didn't follow through with what Azile expected, he would alienate the Intelligence Ministry.

At the table below, Taratus shifted his weight. Jai felt everyone's concern growing as their emperor's silence continued. They had to realize his quandary. Most of them knew he didn't speak Highton well. His strange behavior heightened their concern. Conformity meant everything to Aristos; they feared he would cause a crisis, become unhinged, even destabilize the government with his erratic behavior.

Desperate, Jai turned to his aide, Robert Muzeson, who stood at the end of the table. Beyond him, Jai could see the waiting Hightons.

Jai spoke carefully. "It is well known that as the emperor's heir, I was in seclusion for most of my life."

Robert stared at him with undisguised shock. That Jai addressed him now, instead of the Hightons, was so anomalous, it verged on deadly. He looked petrified.

Anger came from the Aristos—and curiosity. Jai had startled them. Still talking to Robert, Jai said, "As such, I have less facility with the perfected discourse of the Highton language than needed for a proceeding this sensitive."

Robert's rigid posture suddenly eased, as he understood. He met Jai's gaze squarely so it would be obvious the emperor was speaking to him, a taskmaker. Jai could then use plain language without—he hoped—giving insult.

Here goes, Jai thought. "I will leave my most esteemed High Judge to implement my decisions." Given the bare bones of his decisions, she would know far better than he how to implement them. Jai had no time to weigh consequences; the best he could do was start with the easiest case, giving him space to think. "In the matter of security, Eubian Space Command shall not be required to release any confidential documents to any bureau that doesn't have a direct need to know. I also charge ESComm with determining what caused the security lapse on Minister Iquar's habitat and ensuring that no such lapse occurs again."

That created no stir, except for relief from the ESComm officers. No one expected that the military would give out classified information. Had Jai commanded them to, he would have no doubt found himself mired in bureaucratic resistance. As for the investigation, they were already doing one.

Jai continued. "In the case brought by Minister Iquar against Admiral Taratus, I rule thus: Admiral Taratus will repay Minister Iquar her purchase price of the provider minus whatever the insurance bureaus estimate as his true value."

Triumph came from Tarquine, anger from Taratus, and cautious approval from Calope Muze. Jai didn't think he had made any drastic mistakes so far, but the punitive damages

Tarquine wanted would be more difficult. Although high, the amount wasn't unreasonable given the magnitude of Taratus's fraud. Reasonable, yes—until it became known that the "overpriced" provider was a Ruby prince, the *Imperator,* for saints' sake. Jai hated that Hightons so cavalierly put a price on human beings, but regardless of what he thought, the military ruler of Skolia would be well worth fourteen million to them.

Jai knew he was about to make an enemy of someone he really, really didn't want to antagonize. But if he didn't do this, the eventual consequences could be even worse. Steeling himself, he said, "I award no punitive damages to Minister Iquar."

An explosion of breath came from someone. Surprise washed over Jai from the assembled Hightons, and Judge Muze frowned. Wicked glee flashed in Taratus's eyes. Tarquine met Jai's gaze with a hard stare, like ice, unforgiving and promising vengeance.

Damn.

Jai didn't try to explain, afraid to tangle himself into more trouble. If Kelric's identity became known, Minister Iquar's case against Taratus would disintegrate. Although it would infuriate Taratus that he had been forced to repay her the fourteen million, that ruling would probably hold, given the way he had cheated her. But if Jai awarded her additional damages, it would be too much when the admiral discovered the truth about the "worthless" provider. The situation could explode.

Jai forced himself to go on, speaking to Robert, though he could see everyone in the chamber. "In regards to the insurance claims: since Minister Iquar will receive repayment from Admiral Taratus, the bureaus are responsible only for the value of the provider determined by a reevaluation based on the records of his health made available to this court."

Someone gasped, an aide maybe, Jai wasn't certain. If Tarquine could have killed with her laser-like stare, Jai knew he would be dead. Sweat broke out on his brow. She, more than the others, was the one he feared. And she might as well have come out and said, *You're ashes now.*

Not unexpectedly, the insurance people looked pleased, self-satisfied even. Taratus was smug, more from knowing that Tarquine, his foe, had been outmaneuvered than because he cared what the bureaus paid her.

Jai's anger smoldered. They were too full of themselves. He spoke quietly. "I make two stipulations. The first: the insurance carrier will recalculate the fee it charged to cover the provider, setting a new fee based on the updated appraisal of his worth. They will reimburse Minister Iquar for the difference between that fee and the higher one she has already paid, plus interest." He paused. "In addition, I may, at any time, order an independent evaluation of the provider. If it proves him worth more than the lower value set by the bureaus, they will pay Minister Iquar double the difference between their assessment and the independent appraisal."

That elicited little reaction. The fee the bureaus would have to repay Tarquine, although large, was nothing compared to the fourteen million they would have had to pay if Jai had ruled in her favor. And no one could evaluate a missing provider. Even if they found him, it was unlikely any reevaluation would place the worth of a dying man higher than that determined from his health records.

Just wait, Jai thought. *Just wait.*

Tarquine's hostility was palpable. Jai wished he could brush the back of his hand across his forehead, wiping away the sweat. To Robert, he said, "In the matter of Admiral Azar Taratus—" Then he stopped, flooded with animosity from the admiral. It didn't show on Taratus's face; he hid his emotions behind an icy Highton veneer. Just once Jai wished he could tell them, *You can't fool me. I know the deceptions in your minds.*

Jai took a breath. "I find Admiral Azar Taratus guilty of fraud and the misuse of ESComm resources. His sentence will be—" He pulled straight from Taratus's mind the sentence that the admiral had feared to receive. "A fine of one million credits and a suspension from ESComm for a period of time determined by Judge Muze."

A harsh chiming filled the chamber. Struggling to handle the avalanche of emotions in the courtroom, Jai was too distracted at first to register the source of the sound. Then he remembered: Aristos made their opinions known, not with words, but with finger cymbals worn on the thumb and index finger during formal assemblies. He wasn't sure what they were expressing now, but it wasn't happy. Taratus had clenched his fist at his side.

Jai felt as if a mountain were collapsing on him. Judge Muze had a strange expression, as if she saw it thundering down but didn't know how to stop it. Her thoughts came to him: although she respected many of his decisions, she also believed he had just undermined his reign, probably beyond repair. He had no idea how many unwritten rules of custom and favor he had broken. Worse, he had made an enemy of his Finance Minister, who wielded far more influence than he, regardless of his title. Tarquine had spent decades building her power base, and now she would turn it against him.

Jai felt sick. *Corbal, I need you.* But he had no ally. He had to keep going, sinking into the hole he had dug for himself while the world buried him. He looked out over the courtroom, and Tarquine met his gaze with undisguised enmity. He stared back, taking in her terrifying and glorious fury. Again he saw the white at her temples. White hair, advanced age, and Qox heredity: after Corbal and Calope, Tarquine was the only other Aristo he knew with those three traits.

She terrified him.

She mesmerized him.

Jai turned back to Robert. "I have one more verdict."

Everyone froze. He had ruled on all the cases; what further damage could he do now?

Even Jai didn't know what he intended until the words came out of his mouth: "Tarquine Iquar shall become my consort—the empress of Eube."

PART TWO

Umbra

15

Betrothal

The cacophony of finger cymbals in the courtroom hurt Jai's ears. Only Tarquine hadn't moved. She stared at him, finally losing her cool, her icy expression turning into incredulity.

Calope Muze grabbed her mallet and banged the gong. "Enough!"

The cymbals silenced, but shock from the Aristos filled the room like smoke, so thick that Jai found it astounding none of the others felt it. He was suffocating. Maybe it would asphyxiate him right here, saving him from his lunacy, for surely he must have gone insane.

And yet—even if he could have retracted his words, he would have let them stand. If he was wrong about Tarquine, he had just condemned himself to one hell of a marriage, but he had expected that anyway. If he was right, he had chosen one of the only Highton women whose presence he could endure without pain. And she brought with her an incredible power base. Not that marrying him meant she would turn that formidable political machine to his advantage, but at least it might motivate her not to pulverize him.

The sunset flamed, visible through a window in Jai's office. Silhouetted against the fire, Azile stood facing him. The last person Jai wanted to talk to now was Azile, whom he barely knew, besides which, his head already throbbed from too many Hightons. But Azile refused to be put off.

"Eube has venerable, well-established traditions," Azile said. "Traditions don't form without reason."

Jai paced his office, back and forth past Robert, who was standing by the door. He knew Azile's point: emperors didn't marry ministers. He was supposed to choose his wife from among the most beautiful of Highton maidenhood, name one of the fourteen moons for her, and bring her out to look aesthetic at balls and galas.

The hell with it. No law forbade him from marrying his Finance Minister. Jai didn't want a lovely young thing for his empress. His mother had been a Jagernaut, a cybernetic warrior, as deadly as a puma protecting her brood, and later she had become the Imperator of Skolia, military ruler of an empire. For the first fourteen years of his life, she had been his sole model for an adult woman. He couldn't imagine his empress as a marginalized Highton girl whose primary purpose was to look decorative.

Jai stopped in front of Azile. "Traditions are created so new generations can rebel against them."

The minister snorted. "New generations exist because the previous generations gave birth to them."

Jai understood *that* implication. Tarquine, who was over a century old, would have to give him an heir. "It is astonishing what modern medicine can accomplish. Store enough eggs, and woman can have a child at most any age."

Azile scowled, probably as much for the bluntness of Jai's response as for its content, but before he could answer, the door comm buzzed.

Robert touched the panel. "Muzeson here."

The voice a guard came out of the comm. "Minister Iquar has arrived, sir, as summoned."

Jai swore under his breath. Had they told her that he "summoned" her? He had made a point of saying, "request that she attend him." Just what he needed, to further aggravate

Tarquine by having her think he was ordering her around.

Robert glanced at Jai. "Your Highness?"

Sweat broke out on Jai's forehead. "Yes. Bring her in."

Robert bowed, his face neutral, though his thoughts were anything but. He believed his emperor had either gone mad or had a death wish.

As Robert left, Jai dismissed his bodyguards. Then he turned to Azile. "I find myself anticipating what my betrothed will say to me in private."

Azile gave him a dry smile. "You are a brave man."

Right. He was practically hyperventilating.

As Azile took his leave, Robert returned. He bowed to the departing Intelligence Minister, then to Jai. "Your betrothed awaits, Your Highness."

"You may escort her in."

After Robert withdrew, Jai went to the window and stared at the darkening sunset. Night came fast. When he heard a rustle behind him, his stomach clenched. He half expected to feel a laser slice into his back. Slowly he turned around. Tarquine was standing by the closed door, watching him. He was suddenly aware of her height, as tall as him. Danger and sensuality filled the room, and he didn't know which unsettled him more.

Tarquine bowed and languidly straightened. Then she spoke in a voice like whiskey, dark and potent. "My honor at Your Most Unpredictable Presence."

Good gods, another Highton joke. "My greetings, Minister Iquar."

She emanated a blend of emotions: puzzlement, anger, curiosity, conjecture. When he realized her speculations included his clothes, or their potential absence, his face heated.

More than what he sensed, though, he responded to what he *didn't* pick up from her. He had been right. Her mind exerted no pressure. He could bear her presence. The relief hit him so hard, he started to close his eyes. He caught himself, but he couldn't stop his audible exhale.

She considered him. "I must admit, I've never been be-trothed as part of an insurance settlement."

Her remark sounded odd, though Jai wasn't sure why. "I've never been betrothed at all."

Dryly she said, "Usually one inquires about the bride's willingness before announcing the hallowed event."

Jai finally realized what sounded strange. She was speaking directly, yet he detected no intent to insult him, neither in her body language nor her mind.

He smiled. "I haven't participated in too many hallowed events."

"This makes a rather inauspicious start, then."

A flutter tickled his throat, as it often did when he was nervous. He crossed the room, never taking his gaze off her face, and stopped in front of her, his eyes level with hers. He could smell her now, an astringent soap fragrance mixed with her own natural scent. He spoke in a low voice. "I would differ on that estimation, Minister Iquar. I don't find it inauspicious at all."

Her eyes closed halfway, like a cat contemplating a bird. "Indeed."

He didn't know whether to run or hide. Instead he chose an even more lunatic course. Closing his hand around her upper arm, he pulled her forward—and kissed her.

Jai expected her to resist. Instead she slid her hand around his neck, and a jolt went through him, like electricity. It astonished him to feel her muscled curves against his body, giving him that reeling sensation of finding the impossible within reach. He had wanted to do this since the first time he had met her, though he only now admitted it to himself. Vertigo shook him. She represented everything he hated, but as intense as the responses were that she evoked in him, they definitely weren't hate.

An unwelcome thought cooled his heat. *Kelric.* Jealousy surged through him as he imagined Tarquine with his uncle. The matured Imperator of an empire had far more to offer than an untried youth. Angry at himself, Jai suppressed the images of Tarquine and Kelric that intruded on his thoughts.

Without warning, she stepped away. Jai reached for her, but then he froze. She was watching him with a look that, had he been prey and she a hunter, would have petrified him.

"So," she murmured. "You want an empress."

He lowered his arm. "I already have one."

"Do you now?" Her gaze didn't soften. "You made many enemies today. Enemies you don't want."

"Including you?"

"Perhaps."

He quirked his eyebrow. "You don't know?"

"This empress isn't your type."

"Whose type are you?"

Her gaze turned sultry. "One out of your league."

"I'm the emperor. No one is out of my league."

Amusement flickered on her face. "Your boundless humility certainly knows no league."

The conversation made Jai feel as if he were in a boat hurtling over a waterfall, out of control, both exhilarated and terrified. "Such reverence for your emperor."

Her gaze darkened. "Your grandfather made my niece his child-bride, and she spent her life subordinated to his whims. Now you aspire to be my child-groom. For what? An easy road to power? Think again. You need a mother figure? Don't make me laugh. A compliant shadow? Then you are deluded."

Her words sliced the air, but they only made him want her more. "I've no interest in ease, mothers, or compliance. I want Tarquine Iquar."

"Plainly put, Your Highness."

In other words, an insult. Yet he sensed no offense from her. Far from it. Her mood was clear: he fascinated her.

"You began the plain language," he said.

"Not I."

"Then who?"

"I offered no betrothal."

"A betrothal is an insult?"

She laughed. "Well, that depends."

"On what?"

Her sensual voice deepened. "A betrothal, my innocent, is an invitation to intimacy."

Jai would have winced at her evocation of his innocence, except her other words caught his attention. Was she saying that in sexual intimacy, Hightons spoke plainly? She had used direct language since she entered his office. She invited his touch even as she challenged him, spurned his advances even as she seduced him. Jai had never met anyone like her, which wasn't unusual given his life, but he had no doubt she was unique.

His thoughts were knotting into snarls, his convictions of right and wrong turned backward and upside down until nothing made sense. None of it stopped him from drawing Tarquine toward him and pressing her body against his. He sought her mouth hungrily. Embracing her power, her menace—it excited him more than he would have thought possible.

So he fell hard, into a darkness of his own making.

Roca Skolia, sister and heir to the Ruby Pharaoh, served as the Foreign Affairs Councilor for the Skolian Assembly. It made her a top adviser to the First Councilor, who served as the elected leader of the Skolian Imperialate and shared power with the Ruby Pharaoh. As a member of the Assembly's inner circle, Roca wielded a great deal of authority herself. For the past two years, however, she had been denied access to her power.

Now she lay in bed, staring at the canopy overhead. Her husband Eldrinson slept fitfully next to her. Age wore on him, like weather eroding granite that had been solid for ages.

Fate had been cruel.

From the moment of her conception, Roca had been infused with nanomeds from her mother's body, including species designed to repair her cells and delay aging. She still had them. Roca would enjoy a youth that few people could claim in one lifetime, let alone the centuries she would live.

Not so for her husband. He had been eighteen when she met him, his growth finished, his body formed. He had started the age-delaying treatments then, and it had helped give him a long life, close to a century, but his body was failing now. Silver streaked his hair. His walk had slowed, hobbled with a limp. Arthritis plagued him, despite the best efforts of his doctors. The lower gravity on Earth helped, as compared to his native world, but nothing could stop the decline of his years. So Roca grieved, her tears gathering.

She brushed her hand across her eyes, angry at herself. Her husband still lived, warm at her side. Dwelling on his death was morbid. She didn't know how much time he had left, whether it was months or weeks, but for now they had each other. She wanted to give him happiness in these last days, not tears.

Roca kissed his cheek, savoring his warmth. But with all the trouble he had sleeping lately, she didn't want to wake him. So she rose from bed and pulled on a robe over her floor-length nightgown. Padding in her bare feet, she crossed to a bureau against the wall. Her holo-album stood there, a cube glimmering with rainbow shimmers.

She rubbed an edge of the cube. It came alive, bringing up memories she treasured. The image formed of a golden-haired youth in the black leathers of a Jagernaut. He stood by a Jag starfighter, grinning. It was hard to believe this young officer had later become Imperator, a rock-hard leader who had commanded Imperial Space Command for decades. Feared and admired by his supporters and enemies alike, Kurj Skolia, her son from her previous marriage, had built the military into the mighty force that made Skolia an inter-stellar power.

Many had called him a military dictator, the true ruler of Skolia rather than the Assembly. Roca disagreed. Yes, he had been hard. But he had also been fair, and dedicated to the Skolian people. Three years ago, at the age of 105, he had died in an ESComm ambush. Roca swallowed, fighting the hotness in her eyes. *Kurj, my son.* To her, he would always be the shining young man in this holo, full of hope and dreams.

Roca's vision blurred. She flipped the cube around and a new holo formed, a handsome child with bronze hair and violet eyes. Althor. Her third child. He had also become a Jagernaut—and he too had died, a casualty of war. Her eyes burning, Roca fumbled the cube around. A girl appeared, her head thrown back in laughter, her eyes full of mischief. Sauscony. Soz. She had been Roca's seventh child, a storm, a force of nature who had grown into a formidable woman. At Kurj's death, she had become Imperator. It was Soz who led Skolia into the Radiance War, Soz who brought two empires to their knees—and Soz who died in combat.

Roca couldn't bear to look at that young face, the happy child with no idea of the hells she would face as an adult. Her hand shook as she turned the cube—and again her heart broke. A six-year-old boy smiled in this holo, his face luminous. Her golden child. Her youngest.

Kelric.

He had been the sweetest natured of her children, loving and affectionate. He had grown into the largest, towering over his siblings, a taciturn giant, muscled and powerful. And one day he too had gone off to war, wearing the uniform of a Jagernaut. She had lost him first, eighteen years ago, his ship attacked in the cold, lonely reaches of space.

Tears ran down Roca's face. She tried to rub the edge of the cube, to stop the memories, but she couldn't find the switch. Kelric smiled at her across the years, the little boy who laughed so easily and loved so deeply.

"My children," she whispered. To have outlived them was more than she could bear. Soon their father would join them. Roca grieved soundlessly. With shaking hands, she put the cube down.

Unable to remain still with her memories, Roca walked into the living room, where gusts of wind stirred the curtains on the glass doors across from her. She went to pull them open, letting in the wind. It whipped back her hair, throwing it around her shoulders, arms, and hips. Her floor-length robe blew open and billowed out behind her, and the layers of her nightgown fluttered. Even with heat threads weaving through her clothes, she felt the chill of the Scandinavian night.

Roca walked onto the balcony of the house where she and Eldrinson had lived these past two years. The Allied United Centre spread out below, one of many Centres established on Earth to study the effects of uniting Earth's many nations under one world government. Located in Sweden, this one was hidden in a remote wilderness, surrounded in every direction by snow and trees. It was here the Allied military held their Ruby Dynasty captives.

Roca couldn't deny the Allieds treated them well, with an elegant home and every amenity. But it didn't change the fact that she and Eldrinson were prisoners. Whatever happened to them affected the interstellar balance of power.

Three civilizations reigned: the Eubian Concord, the Skolian Imperialate, and the Allied Worlds of Earth. Eube and Skolia were giants, more militaristic than the Allieds. In a treaty with Skolia, the Allieds had agreed to provide sanctuary to the Ruby Dynasty during wartime. But after this last war had ended with no winner, crippling both Eube and Skolia, the Allieds refused to free their "guests." They feared, perhaps rightly so, that if the Ruby Dynasty regained power, the star-spanning devastation would resume.

Roca gazed at the forest, wishing its wild beauty could ease her pain. A few lampposts glowed among the trees. She didn't know why she felt so restless. She kept thinking of Kelric, her youngest—her first child to die. A tear ran down her face. She walked along the balcony to a staircase. Going down the stairs, she picked up her pace. Her heart beat fast, in time with the slap of her bare feet on the stone steps.

An AUC lieutenant was waiting at the bottom, crisp in his khaki uniform, a carbine in his hands. She had no doubt a monitor had detected her activity and told security to find out why she was stirring at this late hour. His presence didn't intimidate Roca. She set out on a path through the rustic buildings and the soldier followed. He spoke into his comm, his voice low. Whatever orders he received apparently didn't include taking her back to the house. He simply kept pace with her, a discreet distance away. Another soldier joined him, both of them accompanying her on her walk to—

To where?

Roca wasn't sure, but she had to keep going.

A drum beat within her.

A drum.

Stronger now.

Recognition.

Recognition of—what?

She began to run. Three soldiers were jogging with her now, but no one tried to stop her. A strange urgency drove her, undeniable. Lengthening her stride, she ran up a long hill. At the top, she crossed a wooden bridge high above a river that roared in a cataract. She kept running.

Feet pounding.

Pounding to a drum.

The beat of a drum.

Beyond the bridge, Roca ran down a slope, barely feeling the icy grass beneath her feet. She kept going, driven toward the visitor's center. Why? The long building stretched before her, surrounded by snowy trees. A raised walkway with an arched roof led to its nearest entrance, like a pier. Roca ran toward it, her heart pounding, her breath condensing in the air. In her mind, she called to her husband, reaching to Eldrinson through a link so strong, it defied the distance limitations nature put on telepaths.

Eldri, wake. Eldri, come.

She felt his mind stir, felt his answering awareness. He would come, striding in the forgiving gravity of Earth.

Roca took the stairs to the raised walkway two at a time. She ran down the pier, the soldiers jogging with her. As she approached the entrance of the visitor's center, she slowed to a walk, then stopped before the double doors.

The drum beat within her.

No. Not a drumbeat.

A heart.

The heart of the sun.

Roca grasped wooden handles and heaved the doors open. The wind whipped back her robe and her hair. Holding the doors wide, bracing herself against them, she stared into the lobby beyond. A man stood in its center, his golden gaze heartbreakingly familiar, though in that moment she knew he had gone blind, that his eyes could no longer see her.

But his mind knew.

His mind saw.

He had changed. Gray streaked his metallic gold hair, and lines added years to his face. He had aged decades since she had last seen him. She could only guess what hells he had gone through to reach Earth. He stood now only through the strength of his indomitable will.

But he was alive.

Roca ran across the lobby and flung her arms around him. With infinite care, he took her into the powerful arms that could crush a man twice her size. Her head barely reached his shoulder. As tears poured down her face, she repeated his name over and over, sobs catching in her throat. He was crying as well, in silence.

Hoshma, he thought. *Hoshma, I've come home.*

Roca's stunned, astonished joy filled her heart. *Welcome home, my son. Welcome home, Kelric.*

16

Lost Dreams

It was one hell of a job.

Jai's daily routine alternately riveted him and bored him stiff. When he had lived in exile, his parents had educated him with the help of computers; on Earth, he had spent two years in an American high school. He had mostly enjoyed those studies, but learning to run an empire was nowhere near as easy.

He sat at his desk, inundated with data. Star holomaps rotated to his right. He had rolled out the film of a mesh screen, and holographic glyphs scrolled above its surface as a comp feed taught him about trade revenues. On his left, an aide was stacking memory cubes for him to review. Another aide was speaking into a comm across the room, while two others worked at a table. Jai had chosen these aides for their lack of Aristo traits; their minds didn't bother him.

Jai rubbed his eyes. He couldn't absorb all this. As much as he hated the thought, he needed a biochip in his brain. It was the only way he could learn everything he had to know and keep up with the information he had to process every day.

Darkness lurked at the edges of his mind. ESComm had Corbal in custody, and Corbal knew Jai wasn't a full Highton. Every time Jai received a military communication, his heart raced, until it became clear no one had discovered his secret.

His comm buzzed. He jerked, then flicked the receive holicon. "Yes?"

Robert answered. "Your Highness, we are receiving a transmission from the Embassy of the Allied Worlds on Delos."

"Delos? You mean the Allied planet?" He had traded himself for Eldrin there.

"Yes, Your Highness," Robert said.

"Very well. Relay the communication."

A starship had carried the message to Glory. The communication was short and direct, which would have been unpardonable, except that it came from an Allied citizen, which in the uncompromising Aristo view of the universe meant a slave. Direct speech from taskmakers or providers didn't bother Aristos in the least: it was expected.

What delayed Jai's response had nothing to do with the brevity of the Allied message. Many protocols had to be observed before he could answer. He had to do this right; it was too important to fumble. His Ministers of Foreign Affairs, Protocol, and Intelligence joined him, along with a protocol officer from the Foreign Affairs Ministry and a foreign affairs officer from the Protocol Ministry. Jai sometimes thought he would need a doctorate just to keep track of who did what on his staff.

His advisers helped him compose a reply. He kept it simple, though he obfuscated enough to make it authentic as a Highton message. Night had fallen by the time he transmitted it to the ship in orbit, which would carry it to Delos. From there, the Allied authorities would send it on to Earth. It could be weeks before it reached its final destination, but when it did, a new era in interstellar relations would begin.

So Jai acknowledged the agreement made by the Allieds to mediate the peace talks between Eube and Skolia.

Jai walked to his rooms, lost in thought, accompanied by his bodyguards and Robert. He had been up for two days now, thirty-two hours. His fatigue made it hard to concentrate, and his thoughts wandered.

"Shall I have your dinner sent up?" Robert asked.

"No, thank you." Jai rubbed his eyes. "A pot of kava would be good, though."

Robert bowed as they stopped outside the anteroom to Jai's suite. "I will see to it, sir."

"I appreciate it."

After Robert left, Jai went through the antechamber into his bedroom. The part of the suite where he entered was four times the size of the room he had shared with his brothers on Prism, and this was only the sitting area. Far across the suite, his canopied bed stood on a dais. The nook to its left had recessed window alcoves, elegant wing chairs, and a love seat. To the right of the dais, an arch led into the bathing room, with its pool and fountains. The suite gleamed, from its gilt and ivory decor to the tiered chandeliers.

Jai sank gratefully into a smartchair, and it adjusted to make him comfortable. His Razers took up posts at the walls with no need for orders. Jai wondered if they would even take his orders if he went beyond simple requests, like that time he had had them wait outside his office while he spoke with Tarquine.

He exhaled. Tarquine. Although it had been two days since he announced his decision to wed her, he had barely even had time to ponder his bride-to-be, let alone speak to her. He had the proverbial tiger by the tail and feared to let go, lest she turn on him and metaphorically rip out his throat.

A voice said, "Your kava, sir."

Jai looked up to see one of his Razers in the entrance of the suite. With a tired nod, Jai said, "Have Robert bring it in."

The Razer bowed and departed, taking the pressure of his half-Aristo mind with him. Jai sent the other three guards out, too, though he knew they wouldn't really leave. One would stay in the antechamber and the others would take up posts around his suite. At least their distance eased the pressure on his mind.

He stretched out his legs and leaned his head against the back of the chair, closing his eyes. The blissful heaviness of sleep settled over him.

A rustle brought him awake. Lifting his head, he saw Robert in the entrance. His aide held a tray with a white pot and several sparkling diamond-china cups, each gilded in gold.

"Come in." Jai sat forward.

Robert entered and set the tray on the table by Jai's chair. "Would your Highness like his bed prepared?"

Jai reddened. "That won't be necessary." Having his household staff "prepare" his bed had turned out to mean bringing him a provider. They seemed to find his celibacy strange. With so much emphasis on heredity and inheritance, the penalty for adultery among Hightons was death, in law if not always in practice. Supposedly, no one cared if Aristos played with their providers, but Jai didn't see it that way. Besides, he had no intention of risking his betrothed's wrath. He would rather face a nuclear reactor gone critical than an angry Tarquine. The only provider he wanted anyway was Silver, and he couldn't have her.

Jai picked up a cup of steaming kava and took a swallow, then sighed as the rich beverage warmed his throat. He motioned Robert to a nearby chair. "Any news on the ESComm investigation into Minister Iquar's habitat?"

Robert took his seat, then slid a mesh rod out of a sheath in his sleeve and unrolled it in his lap. Holicons formed over the screen, the holographic icons that specified functions of the comp. Robert flicked his finger through one, then read from his screen. "They've filed a report with the Intelligence Ministry."

"Have someone send me a summary."

Robert made a notation on his comp. "You will have it tomorrow morning, sir."

"Good." Jai took another swallow of kava. "What is happening with Corbal Xir?"

Robert checked his comp, then frowned. "Nothing, it seems. Both our people and ESComm are still examining the records of the provider stealing files from Admiral Kaliga."

It didn't sound promising. "Any indication the records were falsified?"

"Not yet." Robert gave him an apologetic look.

Damn. Azile was pressuring him to free Corbal, but Jai knew if he simply ordered ESComm to do it, they would resist. He had neither the authority nor the savvy to bend them to his will. Saints knew, he could use Corbal's advice now.

"Any progress in finding Sunrise?" he asked.

"None, Your Highness." Robert didn't hide his regret. "I'm sorry."

Jai nodded, feeling heavy. If Sunrise really had stolen the files, he could hope she traded them to an Allied or Skolian agent in return for her freedom. If she had done it for another Aristo—no, he couldn't believe she would betray Corbal that way. Besides, it made no sense; another Aristo would treat her with a brutality Corbal had foresworn. Of course, she might have been working for Corbal exactly as ESComm suspected. If so, Jai fervently hoped his cousin had made sure she didn't come to harm.

Unfortunately, the worst scenario he could imagine was also the most likely, that someone had kidnapped her. It would have to be someone high in ESComm. The thought of what they would do to her haunted Jai.

He set down his kava. "I would like updates every morning on the search. If any breakthrough occurs, let me know immediately."

Robert made a note on his screen. "I'll see to it myself, Your Highness."

"Thank you, Robert."

Pleased surprise came from his aide, though outwardly Robert showed only his usual calm efficiency. It puzzled Jai.

He saw no reason why his comments should surprise or gratify his aide.

Robert scanned his schedule. "You have a meeting tomorrow with representatives from the insurance bureaus."

Jai didn't relish facing them. "Are they arranging the repayment to Minister Iquar?"

"It appears so." Robert studied his screen. "Her status creates complications."

"Why?" Jai wished he didn't always feel as if he lagged ten steps behind everyone else.

"She will be empress." Robert shifted his weight. "It is necessary to, uh, avoid the implication—that is, you might say . . ."

Jai regarded him wearily. "Yes?"

"Your Most Gracious Highness, I would never imply—"

"I know, Robert." Jai rubbed his eyes. "Just tell me."

Robert cleared his throat. "It is necessary to avoid the appearance of coercion by the Qox Dynasty to make the bureaus pay monies above those specified in the hearing."

"Of course I'm not trying to make them give my future wife more money." Like Tarquine needed it. In preparation for joining the Qox and Iquar Lines, one of his aides had shown him her financial records. She was even wealthier than he would have guessed in his most generous estimates.

"No, certainly, of course not, Your Glorious Highness." Robert's face had gone red. "This can be made clear in your meeting with the bureau chiefs."

Jai considered him. He had chosen Robert as his personal aide over several others with more experience, in part because Robert's mind exerted no mental pressure, but also because the aide knew all sorts of useful palace scuttlebutt. He had been at the palace for ten years and had served Jai's grandfather, Ur Qox, until Ur's death three years ago.

"Robert," he said. "Prepare a statement for me to give in tomorrow's meeting."

"Certainly, sir." Robert entered commands into his comp. "What would you like to say?"

"You write a first draft. Have it for me to read in the morning."

Again surprise came from Robert's mind; Ur Qox would never have allowed him such a responsibility. From what Jai had seen in the records, Ur Qox had wasted his aide's talents.

Robert sat up straighter. "I will have it ready for you at breakfast."

"Good." Jai leaned back, too tired to stay upright. "Anything else I need to know tonight?"

Robert checked his comp. "The delegation from the Diamond Coalition canceled their request for an audience."

Jai inwardly swore. Corbal had worked for years on that project, a new banking system in Sapphire Sector that he was establishing with the Diamond Coalition. With the right ties between the palace and the Coalition, they could all profit from the partnership. But the Diamonds had been skittish lately. "Why did they cancel their request to meet with me?"

Robert scanned his screen. "They sent a lengthy and extremely complimentary document to you."

Jai grimaced. "Can you summarize?"

"They want more time to work on their plans."

Jai didn't believe it. "What do you think really happened?"

Robert looked up at him. "The Blue-Point Diamond Line changed their minds about wanting to work with the palace on this project."

A memory jumped into Jai's mind: the dinner at Kaliga's home. *Damn.* One of the guests had been an elder Blue-Point lord. Jai didn't doubt his own behavior that night had put off the lord. And Corbal, who set up the deal with the Diamond Coalition, was in ESComm custody. Corbal probably could have dealt with the situation, but Jai had no idea what to do.

Propping his elbow on the arm of his chair, Jai rested his head on his hand. "Leave the report for me. If you have recommendations, leave those, too."

"Certainly, sir."

"Anything else?" He hoped not; he desperately needed sleep.

"I have an answer to your inquiry about Jafe Maccar."

Jai lifted his head. Ever since Kelric had asked him to pardon Maccar, the Skolian merchant captain, Jai had wondered why. ESComm wouldn't tell him anything. Although the military was supposed to be under his command, they were impressively adept at bypassing him. He had to fight for every scrap of information he wrested from them.

"What did you find out?" Jai asked.

Robert read from his screen. "Jafe Maccar commanded a Skolian merchant ship, the *Corona*. In the chaos after the Radiance War, trade restrictions between Eube and Skolia eased for a while. Maccar arranged a lucrative deal with Lady Zarine Raziquon, who owns the habitat *Chrysalis Station*. She offered him a large payment for a shipment of Targali silks, jewelry, spices, china, silver, and antique boxes."

"Let me guess," Jai said dryly. "Lady Zarine tried to cheat him, he protested, and ESComm threw him in jail."

"I'm not sure." Robert's forehead furrowed. "She paid for the shipment. As he was returning to his ship, she sent him an escort of vessels."

"An escort? Why?"

"To guarantee him safe passage out of Eubian space."

"Then why did ESComm imprison him?"

Robert continued reading. "For some reason, Maccar's flotilla attacked hers. The ships did battle, and most of the Skolian vessels escaped. But ESComm caught Maccar's ship. They deported the crew back to Skolia and sentenced Maccar to ten years in prison."

Jai stared at him. "Why the blazes would Maccar attack his escort?"

Robert scrolled through more files. "The attack appears unprovoked."

"Appears?"

Robert regarded him uneasily. "Maccar was under the protection of a Highton noblewoman. She would have done everything in her power to ensure his safe return home."

Sure. It was also possible that Lady Zarine had tried to steal Maccar's ships, forcing the crews to defend themselves. But he needed to know Maccar hadn't committed a crime before he could act on Kelric's request. "Look into the matter, Robert. I need more details."

"Right away." Robert made another entry on his comp. "Anything else?"

His aide hesitated. "Your Most Gracious Highness—"

Ah, no. He became a "Gracious Highness" whenever his staff feared they were about to say something he wouldn't like. "Go ahead."

"It is the matter of your betrothal."

"My betrothal." He was afraid to ask.

Robert crinkled the screen of his comp, then realized what he was doing and smoothed it out. "It must be announced."

Jai tried to focus his weary mind. "I did that at the hearing."

"Well, yes, you did." Robert quickly added, "And a wise decision you made." He did his best not to look doubtful. "However, it would be most glorious, Your Esteemed Highness, if you were to announce it to the public."

Jai winced. "Oh. Yes, of course." An insurance hearing was hardly the venue for the announcement of an imperial betrothal. "Can you put the Protocol Office on it?"

"Certainly." Robert looked relieved. "You and Minister Tarquine will be expected to appear on the broadcast."

"Have Protocol let us know what they want."

"I will do that."

"Anything else?" *Please say no.*

"No, sir." Robert averted his gaze and carefully rolled up his screen. He slipped the rod into the sheath inside his sleeve.

Jai could tell Robert was troubled. He eased his mental barriers—and discovered his aide was in pain.

"Are you all right?" Jai asked.

"Yes, Your Highness." Robert wouldn't meet his gaze.

"Can I help with anything?"

Robert hesitated, then ran his finger under the metallic ring that circled his neck. It resembled bronze, but was more flexible than metal. "Your Most Gracious Highness, please know I would never presume—but I—"

Baffled, Jai said, "But you . . . ?"

"It no longer fits."

"The collar?"

Robert paled. "Yes. Please forgive my deplorable presumption."

Jai stared at him blankly. "What deplorable presumption?"

"To refit the collar will require removing it."

"And?" As far as Jai was concerned, Robert could throw the blasted thing away.

"You must authorize the removal."

"All right." Jai rubbed his eyes. "I authorize whatever you need. Let whoever fixes those things know."

"Your Highness." Robert cleared his throat.

"Yes?"

"I cannot request this work." He was stumbling over his words. "You must do it."

Like the shift of an optical illusion, Jai's perception changed. He kept thinking of his staff as people hired at the palace, but they weren't employees. He *owned* them. He had let himself believe, subconsciously, that they could take off their slave restraints when they went home. Of course they couldn't. Judged from Robert's behavior, even suggesting temporary removal of a collar could be a punishable offense. Jai *had* to think about it, whether he liked it or not; he was responsible for their lives and health.

Jai realized he was clenching his fist on his knee, his fingernails gouging his palm. He opened his hand and stretched his fingers. "Be assured I will have the matter taken care of so you no longer experience discomfort."

"You are most kind, Your Gracious Highness."

Jai didn't feel kind. He felt like a monster. "Please make

it known among my staff that if anyone else has such a problem, they can tell me."

"I will take care of it, sir."

"Good."

After Robert left, Jai walked to the bed and collapsed across it, fully dressed. He lay there longing for home, for the people he loved, for a sane universe. Just a few months ago he had been spending his free time at the arcade with his friends, playing hologames. He had never had to worry about military intrigues, insurance bureaus, coalitions, imperial protocol, deadly brides, or kidnapped providers. He hadn't been responsible for thousands of people who couldn't even go to a metalworker without his permission. Hell, it wasn't just his staff; he owned entire *worlds*. In hologames, ruling an empire had been fun.

In reality, it terrified him.

17

Beginnings

The meeting will take place on Earth," the Minister of Protocol said. She was speaking to one of her aides, so she could be direct, but her words were meant for Jai. She stood next to him on a holostage. A gaunt Highton woman from the Haquail Line, she had a mind that grated like sandpaper. Jai was too tense to speak at all, let alone cope with the labyrinth of Highton speech. Mercifully, the aides with them had too little Aristo heritage to exacerbate his headache.

The holostage took up one end of the media studio. A screen curved around half of the elliptical stage, and consoles filled the room, as operators prepared to transmit Jai's words. Media techs were setting up a white chair in one focal point of the stage. Protocol aides bustled around Jai, dusting off his clothes, making sure he presented an impeccable appearance. His rich garb was solid black and severely cut, both the trousers and high-necked shirt.

A tech came over and knelt with his head bowed. Embarrassed, Jai motioned for him to stand. When the tech had risen, Jai said, "You have a message?" He tried to ignore the protocol people combing his hair.

The tech motioned at the chair on the stage. "Just to warn you; it may look odd during the transmission. We'll be overlaying it with an image from the Hall of Circles."

An image? "Of what?"

"The Carnelian Throne, Your Highness."

Jai nodded, disrupting the efforts of an aide to blot non-existent sweat from his forehead. No matter how imperial they made him look, it wouldn't give him more confidence in his ability to pull this off. Today was too important to muddle, but he felt painfully unprepared.

Protocol spoke to the tech. "Any word on whether the transmission will be in real time?"

He bowed to her. "None yet, ma'am."

She frowned. "I don't see how the Allieds expect us to believe they can do this transmission. Neither they nor we have access to a Kyle web."

The tech spoke carefully. "They have Ruby psions in custody on Earth. Perhaps they can create a temporary bubble of Kyle space."

Jai wondered at that. The Kyle web, what Skolians called the psiberweb, was a network of comp nodes in Kyle space, outside of spacetime, making instant communication possible among the stars. But the web had collapsed during the war. He had his doubts that the Ruby psions in custody on Earth could re-create even a temporary webnode without a Lock.

Protocol didn't look convinced either. She glanced at Jai. "Your Highness?"

Jai lifted his hand in the gesture that allowed the tech to leave. He wanted to rake his fingers through his hair, but he held back, knowing it would horrify the aides working so diligently on his appearance. It was hard to stay still; Protocol's mind made him want to twitch.

A console operator came over to them and knelt to Jai, her long hair curtaining her face.

"Please rise," Jai said.

As she stood, she spoke with deference. "We're ready to start, Your Highness. We've received a signal from Earth."

Jai tensed. "You mean a real-time signal?"

"Yes, sir. No delays."

Protocol exhaled. "So. They did it." She didn't sound

pleased that the Allieds had managed to create a Kyle node.

Jai understood her reaction, though he didn't share it. If the Allieds could make one node, they might soon make more. Could they create a Kyle web from Earth? Personally, he hoped so; it would help keep a balance of power among Skolia, Eube, and the Allieds. Hightons didn't want a balance; they wanted ascendancy over the rest of humanity.

The aides finally quit fussing over him. With Protocol at his side, Jai crossed the holostage and sat in the white chair. A tech put a comm button in his ear, and Robert's voice came over it. "We're ready, Your Highness."

Jai wished his hands weren't so clammy. He took a deep breath. "Begin."

Everyone withdrew from the stage, leaving him alone. A console operator started the sequence to receive the signal from Earth. No one spoke. Jai realized he was holding his breath.

Suddenly a woman's voice came out of the console, speaking an unfamiliar language. Another voice translated it into Highton: "His Royal Highness, Eldrinson Althor Valdoria, Web Key to the Triad and the King of Skyfall."

Astonishment sparked in Jai; that first voice, the woman he hadn't understood, had come from Earth, many light-years away.

He was about to speak to his grandfather.

Jai wondered at the title, "King of Skyfall." His mother had described her father as a judge, with the title "Dalvador Bard." His people had no king, though some of his duties were similar to those of kings from cultures on Earth. Jai supposed the Allieds thought "King" sounded more imposing than "Bard."

The operator at the console near Jai spoke, her words going to Earth: "His Esteemed Highness, Jaibriol the Third, descended from the Line of Qox, son of Jaibriol the Second, grandson of Ur, great-grandson of Jaibriol the First, and great-great-grandson of Eube, Sublime Founder of the Concord."

Listening to a man with a deep voice translate the words, Jai found himself wishing they didn't have to recite his predecessors every time they introduced him. He felt sorry for his descendants; in a few generations, the lineage would become truly unwieldy.

A blurry image formed on the holostage about five paces away from Jai. It sharpened into a man who was sitting in an elegant chair encrusted with gold and rubies—and Jai's pulse jumped. The man had violet eyes, and wine-red hair streaked with silver brushed his shoulders.

His grandfather.

Do you recognize me? Jai thought. His grandfather knew about Jai's parents; it was Eldrinson who had arranged for the two lovers to go into exile. Jai saw the resemblance between Eldrinson and his son, Eldrin, the uncle Jai had traded himself for on Delos. It had amused Jai's mother that her parents had given the name Eldrin to her brother, who was the *son* of Eldrinson. Jai suspected they thought Eldrinsonson was overdoing it. No doubt existed about who was the father, though; the man facing him now looked much older. He watched Jai from across the stage, and across the immensity of interstellar space.

The silence grew strained as everyone waited to see who would speak. They had decided in advance to use English, a neutral language. Skolian and Eubian protocols both derived from the ancient Ruby Empire. They required the person who had requested the communication to speak first. In cases such as this, where both sides had orchestrated the meeting, the lesser power spoke first. If powers were matched or disputed, the newest leader went first. If the experience was matched, the youngest spoke.

Of course neither side would acknowledge being a lesser power. That meant Jai should go first, in deference to Eldrinson's age and experience. But such would imply that Eldrinson—a man the Hightons considered a provider—had higher status than the emperor of Eube. It violated the very basis of Aristo beliefs.

As far as Jai was concerned, no question existed that Eldrinson had higher status. But Jai had bungled too many of his dealings with the Aristos; he didn't dare misplay this. Aristos tolerated the peace negotiations because the Radiance War had exhausted Eube. No one wanted more conflict. But if Jai stumbled here, his uneasy support would collapse.

So he and Eldrinson sat in silence.

Do you see my mother in me? Jai wished he could talk to his grandfather about his parents. He could say nothing, but they couldn't sit here forever, either. Someone had to break the deadlock.

An idea came to Jai. He spoke—in Highton instead of English. "The Line of Qox acknowledges the Ruby Dynasty."

An audible sigh came from the aides, techs, and operators. Relief washed out from Protocol, who was standing near the stage. By using Highton instead of English, Jai asserted the Aristo claim of authority, but he recognized Eldrinson's greater experience by speaking first.

In a voice resonant with power, Eldrinson answered in Highton. "The Imperial Dynasty acknowledges the ascension of Jaibriol the Third to the Carnelian Throne."

A chill ran through Jai. His own grandfather had just accepted him as the leader of a despotic interstellar empire.

So he and Eldrinson began their discussions.

This meeting was a symbol: their diplomats and staffs would set up the actual peace talks. Now they discussed who would attend. The Skolians representatives would come from their Assembly, the Ruby Dynasty, and Imperial Space command; the Eubian participants drew from the Qox Dynasty, Jai's ministers, and ESComm. Everyone would be present as VR simulacra only; the risk of putting so many interstellar leaders in one place was too great. They chose Earth for the virtual conference site. Not only was it neutral territory, it was also the birthplace of humanity, a potent symbol.

Then Eldrinson dropped his bombshell.

"The Imperator," he said, "will represent Imperial Space Command."

Jai barely stopped his sharp inhale. "We had not known a successor to the late Imperator had assumed the title." The words hurt: the "late Imperator" had been his mother.

"The Triad is complete." Eldrinson looked beyond the range of the holocams and motioned. Then he waited.

A man appeared.

Towering and massive, with gold hair, skin, and eyes, the man walked into view, his image sharpening as he entered the center of the holocam's focus. He moved with assurance, and his limp did nothing to detract from his imposing presence. Heavy gauntlets covered his arms from hand to elbow, embedded with conduits and controls. He stopped behind Eldrinson's chair and stood facing Jai like a fortress, his face impassive, his gaze unwavering. And he challenged the Aristos with the most shocking defiance they could imagine— he wore a provider's collar.

Someone whispered, "Skolia be damned." Protocol stared at the man, her face a livid red. Murmurs broke the silence, rapidly growing in pitch.

Robert's excited voice came over the comm in Jai's ear. "Your Highness, I'm getting an ID on that man. He's the provider that escaped from Minister Iquar!"

Fierce gratification swept through Jai. Let Eube choke on that. He could guess why Kelric still wore the collar: it would have extended neural threads into his nervous system. To remove it, his doctors would have to map the entire system and surgically remove each thread. They couldn't rush the job, lest they cause neural damage. But Jai suspected Kelric had another reason for letting the collar show. It sent a bold message to the Hightons: *I am your worst nightmare.* Nothing could be a greater outrage—except a provider on the Carnelian Throne.

My greetings, Uncle, Jai thought.

"Saints almighty." Robert spoke over the comm again. "We have more. Your Highness, that man is Kelricson Garlin

Valdoria, the youngest son of the Foreign Affairs Councilor, Roca Skolia, and Web Key Eldrinson." When Jai didn't answer, Robert added, "Sir—you must decide whether or not to acknowledge him as Imperator."

Jai glanced at Protocol. She looked furious, but she didn't intercede. That no one tried advising him gave Jai a good idea how nonplussed they all were.

His uncle's triumph had come at a price. In the Lock, Kelric's limp had been far less pronounced than it was now. And his eyes tracked Jai now. It was a subtle effect, one Jai noticed only because a friend of his on Earth had lost his sight in an accident. After the doctors implanted an optical system that let him see, his eyes had tracked in the same way. Jai could only wonder what Kelric had endured, struggling to reach Earth while his body failed him. It seemed impossible he could have done it alone. If anyone had helped him, they had a great deal of courage, risking the wrath of Eube.

Jai spoke quietly. "The Line of Qox acknowledges the ascension of Kelricson Garlin Valdoria to the Imperial Triad."

Kelric nodded, restrained, but with recognition. Jai felt a bittersweet joy; he could never return to his family, but his uncle had, and in doing so, he might help pave a road to peace.

Eldrinson and Jai resumed their discussions, and Kelric listened, standing behind Eldrinson. When the appropriate time came, Jai said, "As proof of our good intent in this endeavor, I have pardoned Jafe Maccar, the Skolian merchant arrested and imprisoned by ESComm."

Protocol's mouth fell open. The aides and techs around the studio stared as if Jai had gone insane. Anger sparked from someone, he wasn't sure whom. He knew his decision would engender hostility, but Maccar deserved the pardon. Now that Jai had the details of the incident, it was obvious the Highton noblewoman had sent out her pirate fleet to steal Maccar's ships and crews after she paid for his goods.

Robert had dug up several other telling facts: Kelric had been the weapons officer on Maccar's ship. And the Highton who had captured Maccar's ship was none other than Admiral Azar Taratus, who had sold Kelric to Tarquine. According to the Halstaad Code of War, POWs couldn't be auctioned as slaves. But Taratus had listed Maccar's weapons officer as lost and presumed dead. The admiral truly did astonish Jai in his brazen disregard for the law.

Jai doubted ESComm would make trouble over the pardon, at least not openly. They wouldn't want Taratus's misdeeds to become public. That he was the brother of a Joint Commander would make the scandal even worse.

Eldrinson looked puzzled. "A magnanimous gesture, Your Highness."

Jai inclined his head. Then he glanced at Kelric. Although his uncle's face remained impassive, Kelric nodded slightly, with understanding in his gaze.

So it was done. Eube and Skolia would meet at the peace table. What they would achieve, if anything, Jai didn't know.

But they would try.

Jai had never seen the Hall of Circles without an audience of Hightons. Now media techs filled it, along with the infernal protocol aides from this morning, when he had spoken to Eldrinson. They were at it again, fixing invisible flaws in his appearance. He wished they would go away.

The great doors of the Hall swung open, admitting a large retinue. Tarquine Iquar strode in its center, listening while her staff briefed her. Her retinue included the four Razers Jai's people had sent her as bodyguards. It was the first time Jai had seen her since five days ago, when he had announced his decision to make her empress.

When she looked up, Jai inclined his head. She paused and bowed, then resumed her walk to the dais where he stood. He couldn't pull his gaze away; she mesmerized him even more now than before. He didn't understand how she worked this madness. Part of him responded to her as a *High-*

ton. She was the ultimate product of their caste, which was supremely ironic given that both she and Jai lacked the main attribute that defined Hightons, an ability to transcend.

Her retinue slowed as they climbed the dais. When they reached Jai, her aides knelt to him and the Razers bowed. Tarquine also bowed, but then she stood appraising him like a hawk watching a pup in the fields. She spoke huskily. "My honor at your presence, Your Highness."

Jai flushed. "It pleases us to see you, Minister Iquar."

"Good," she murmured.

Remembering himself, Jai moved his hand, palm down, permitting her aides to stand.

Protocol joined them and bowed to Tarquine. "An auspicious day, Minister Iquar. Soon all will know its splendid favor."

Jai supposed that was Hightonese for, "We're ready to start." His aides went to work on Tarquine, straightening her black tunic and trousers, and fixing her hair, which she wore in an elegant roll on her head.

The Protocol Minister surveyed the Finance Minister. Then Protocol spoke to one of her aides. "Minister Iquar needs garb more befitting an empress, eh? Bring me a formal dress, black diamond cloth."

Tarquine turned an icy gaze on the aide. "On the other hand, perhaps you value your well-being."

The aide flushed. "Ma'am?"

"If you do value it," Tarquine continued, "I suggest you desist with the dress."

Protocol scowled. When Tarquine raised an eyebrow at her, Protocol started to speak, then apparently thought better of it. To her alarmed aide, she said, "Perhaps Minister Iquar's garb will be fine after all."

Jai blinked. He wished he knew how Tarquine did that. He had ended up wearing exactly what Protocol wanted, conservative trousers and high-necked shirt, all black, even their fastenings. But as cool as Tarquine was on the outside, he picked up unexpected emotions from her mind. She had never expected the title of empress; now, faced with its reality, she alternated among misgiving, satisfaction, ire, and incredulity.

Aides clustered around them, conferring and checking their palm-meshes. Amid the bustle, Jai watched Tarquine and she watched him back, inscrutable. He couldn't absorb that this woman would be his wife. It brought home the extent of his influence, that he could simply announce his intent to marry one of the most powerful human beings alive, and have it come to pass.

Right, he thought dryly. Had Tarquine wanted to refuse him, this betrothal wouldn't be taking place. Incredible as it seemed, she was willing to take him. Or, more realistically, she would take the title he offered.

His mood darkened. He wasn't the one she had given up fourteen million credits for. What would she think when she learned her escaped provider was now the Imperator of Skolia? Would she crave Kelric even more?

It doesn't matter, Jai told himself, trying to believe it. He had her now.

The aides finally withdrew, leaving Jai and Tarquine side-by-side, facing the holocams. He knew how they looked: the same height, black hair shimmering, eyes ruby red, their faces snow-marble smooth, their clothes severe and black. A brace of perfect Hightons.

The Eubian anthem played, its haunting strains filling the Hall with a beauty so heartbreaking, it hurt to hear. Jai wished he could see that beauty among the Hightons, instead of the cold formality that defined them. He felt as if he were facing a lifetime of starvation, but of the soul rather than the body.

The lights of holocams blinked, but he knew that right now the broadcast was showing views of the palace. After an eternity, Protocol's voice came over the comm in his ear. "We're ready for your part, Your Highness. Three, two, one—go."

Jai took a deep breath. "People of Eube, I bring you joyous news."

So Jai announced the betrothal, his speech peppered with the requisite lavish praise for the Line of Iquar, including the previous empress, his grandmother, Tarquine's niece. If anyone objected to his kinship with Tarquine, they had the sense to keep their mouth shut. Given that Jaibriol I had married his sister because he considered no one else elevated enough for his bloodline, Jai doubted his relation to Tarquine would cause much shock. That she was his Finance Minister and so much older was far more likely to stir controversy.

After Jai finished his speech, High Judge Calope Muze officiated at the betrothal, sanctifying it for their wedding, which would take place in three months.

Then it was done. Qox and Iquar were once again united. Standing with Tarquine, Jai thought darkly of a phrase he had learned on Earth.

Until death do us part.

18

Ascending Sun

Lord Raziquon hit the wall with his fist, causing a nearby table to shake. The vase on the table toppled off and shattered on the floor.

A wry voice spoke behind him. "Destroying pottery rarely accomplishes anything."

Raziquon swung around. Xirad Kaliga, Joint Commander of ESComm, stood in the arch of Raziquon's office, leaning against its side, his arms crossed.

Raziquon gave him the minimalist greeting favored in their circle. "Admiral."

Then Raziquon saw who else had entered his office, and sweat beaded on his forehead. Both Joint Commanders had come to visit. General Kryx Taratus was half-sitting on the desk across the room, facing him. A large man in both height and physique, Taratus had thick eyebrows and a blocky chin. He had also brought his younger brother, Azar Taratus, a taller, thinner man with sharply handsome features. Azar stood by a window, staring out at the gardens of Raziquon's estate.

Kaliga smiled slightly. "It must be gratifying to have so many antiques that you need to be rid of them."

Raziquon scowled. "What I need to be rid of is the dawn." It enraged him that his interrogation of Sunrise had so far come to naught; he had risked his good name when he arranged her abduction.

General Taratus was watching him. "The Line of Xir continues to inquire into confidential ESComm cases."

That was no surprise; Raziquon had no doubt Corbal's kin were "inquiring" with great vehemence about Sunrise. At least he had succeeded in having Corbal blamed for her disappearance. "Perhaps the Line of Xir forgets it is, itself, one of those confidential cases."

"One cannot hold a Highton indefinitely," Kaliga said. "Proof makes the difference."

"Holorecords offer proof," Raziquon said. Although the holos that showed Sunrise stealing files didn't directly implicate Xir, she couldn't have acted without his permission.

"Records can be doctored," General Taratus said. His posture indicated sarcasm. "Or so Security tells me."

Raziquon didn't like the sound of it. If Xir's people could prove the records implicating Sunrise were false, the case against Corbal would fall apart.

"Security could be wrong," Raziquon said.

"Perhaps." Kaliga's stance indicated skepticism. "But I suspect it will please Corbal Xir to attend his cousin's nuptials."

Raziquon's rage deepened. If Xir's people demonstrated that the records had been doctored, their lord could indeed be free before the wedding. Then suspicion could ricochet back to the other guests who had dined that night with the emperor, may the gods scorch his Esteemed Imperial Self. And Sunrise had revealed nothing they could use against Xir. No provider should have such strong mental protections. It wasn't legal. It wasn't *decent*.

Kaliga spoke in his calculating voice. "The Line of Xir gathers strength. It pleases me to see it so blessed in favor with the palace." He was holding his thumb and forefinger together at his side, implying he intended the opposite sentiment to what his words expressed.

Azar Taratus had been staring out the window, but now

he turned. His usually sardonic mien had darkened. "The Line of Iquar is likewise blessed."

General Taratus glanced dourly at his younger brother. "With help from the Line of Taratus, eh?" When Azar scowled, the general raised an eyebrow. Raziquon supposed that the general meant Jaibriol III might not have betrothed himself so precipitously to Tarquine Iquar if not for the court case that had brought them together.

Admiral Kaliga spoke to Raziquon. "It is fortunate you have an omega clearance, my esteemed friend."

Raziquon blinked. What did his security clearance have to do with this? He let his posture indicate wariness. "It is an honor to have the trust of ESComm."

"So it is," General Taratus rumbled.

"Trusted enough," Kaliga continued, "to know that Minister Iquar gained a certain provider cheap."

Raziquon didn't see what they were about. "You are wealthy indeed, to consider fourteen million cheap."

"Cheap," Kaliga repeated. "Just ask Imperator Skolia."

"Imperator Skolia is dead." Raziquon had watched the holo of her shuttle exploding many times. Kaliga's tone suggested a revealed confidence, but Raziquon saw no secrets.

"Those who die often leave heirs." The younger Taratus spoke in a deceptively soft voice. "It seems our new Imperator enjoys remarkably good health, especially considering his supposedly dreadful state when Tarquine Iquar's doctors examined him."

It took a moment for his meaning to register on Raziquon. No. *Impossible*. Had Tarquine Iquar owned a member of the Ruby Dynasty—and let him *escape*? Gods, what a debacle. "Then may our dear Finance Minister rest in peace."

"But a well-paid peace, eh?" General Taratus said.

Raziquon narrowed his gaze. Well-paid? "Your wishes for the Finance Minister are benign." Bizarre, too, given Tarquine Iquar's aggravating existence.

"Benign, hell." Taratus crossed his beefy arms, left over right. "Imperial decrees, now, they go beyond benign." His posture, in the context of his words, implied he meant the decrees made by Jaibriol III at the insurance hearing.

"Indeed." Raziquon still didn't see their point.

"Hell of a thing, these imperial decrees," Taratus continued. "Just think; if an independent evaluation of the escaped provider sets his worth higher than that determined by the bureaus, they must pay double the difference between their most recent assessment and the independent appraisal."

Raziquon stared at him. "Skolia be damned."

"Damned indeed," Kaliga said. "What is an Imperator worth, eh? More than fourteen million, I'd wager."

Hell and damnation. Raziquon wanted to punch the wall again. Tarquine Iquar was about to receive an obscene insurance settlement, and she would soon combine her odiously vast power base with the Qox Dynasty. If that wasn't enough, Corbal Xir would go free, and suspicion would taint Kaliga's guests from that miserable dinner. It all added up to the wrong people gaining power and the right people suffering for it, namely himself, Jaibriol Raziquon.

Something had to be done.

Sunrise ran.

The forest around Raziquon's estate seemed endless. She recognized nothing. She didn't think she was even still on Glory; the air smelled wrong and her body felt too heavy. The sky had no moons. Her silk pajamas offered little warmth from the night, and twigs and rocks jabbed her feet, but she didn't care. After what she had endured from Raziquon, a few scrapes were nothing. Terror spurred her as she ran among the trees, stumbling in the unfamiliar gravity.

Days had passed since the kidnapping, she didn't know how many. Her life had narrowed to Raziquon and the interrogation room. During every reprieve she had rationed her sanity, praying he would grow bored with his futile attempts to make her talk, and every day he had crushed her hope.

But everyone erred sooner or later. Today he had slipped, a small mistake, one that didn't matter according to his view of reality. He hadn't put on her ankle restraints, though he had left her locked in her suite. She was a provider; she could no more think her way out of a locked room than could an animal. Or so he thought.

Sunrise had let the Hightons misread her intelligence. Their arrogance made them careless. By closely watching her jailers, she had figured out the passwords that locked her suite, and tonight she used those codes to escape. Then she had stolen a palmtop. Such a small thing, a palmtop, but she had been forbidden to use the technology Aristos took for granted. Supposedly she was incapable of understanding it. Perhaps that was true for some providers; she didn't know. But she had made the palmtop do what she wanted, disguising the signature emitted by her collar so she could flee the estate.

She had to leave this place fast, before her disguise failed. A provider couldn't travel alone; if she tried, the authorities would contact her owner. That would be good, but only if their records listed Corbal. The starport was her best hope, if she could find her way without alerting Raziquon.

So she ran, desperate, fleeing from one unknown to another.

After preparing Tarquine Iquar's financial report, the Iquar Accounting Office sent the report to the Committee on Ethics and Morals for the Ministry of Finance, which went over it in detail, making changes, and then sent it to the Protocol Office at the Qox palace, which went over it in detail, making changes, then released it to the palace Ethics and Morals Committee, which made changes and released it to the Accounting Office, which had numerous questions for the Ethics and Morals Committee, which contacted the Protocol Office, which contacted the Ethics and Morals Committee at the Finance Ministry, which contacted the Iquar accountants.

Eventually, after the palace accountants investigated, reinstated, recovered, and otherwise put back what everyone else had deleted, added, and changed, they sent the report to the emperor. When Jai opened the huge file at the console in his office, he had a complete record of where it had been and who had done what to it before the file reached him.

"Good gods," he muttered to Robert. "This is crazy."

"They have your best interests in mind." Robert assured him. He was sitting next to Jai with his comp screen unrolled in his lap. "Your staff wishes to ensure you receive a full accounting of your betrothed's assets, and that no awkward questions arise when you and Minister Iquar combine assets."

"That they feel the need to do so many checks doesn't exactly ease my mind." Jai motioned at the document on his screen. "Tarquine's accountants hid her investments in the Sapphire Sector platinum mines. Ethics and Morals at the Finance Ministry put it back in, Protocol here took it out, and our Ethics and Morals people put it back in." He scowled at Robert. "Why the blazes would anyone care if my future wife invests in platinum?"

"Perhaps because of the shortage?"

Jai just barely restrained his groan. Apparently he was about to learn yet another fact he should have already known. "What shortage?"

When Robert hesitated, Jai understood: Aristos took exception to having a taskmaker lecture them. But they weren't stupid; they knew they needed the expertise of their staffs. Taskmakers walked a precarious line between being invaluable and becoming a threat by knowing too much.

"Go ahead," Jai said.

"Most platinum comes from asteroids in the Platinum Sectors," Robert said. "The mining operations were hit hard during the war. Now we have a shortage."

"I take it Sapphire Sector doesn't have a shortage."

"You are perceptive."

Jai answered dryly. "And you're a diplomat." It didn't surprise him to find Tarquine in the middle of this. Platinum had great economic value; many technologies used the metal. A shortage could provide a windfall for a financially savvy person—including one who shouldn't be exploiting her knowledge to her own financial gain.

"Let me guess," Jai said. "Tarquine used her connections as Finance Minister to buy up huge quantities of Sapphire Sector platinum at a price that undercut the market. Her accountants don't want us to know, the ethics committees do want us to know, and my protocol people don't want it to appear I'm involved in this questionable 'little' business."

Robert gave a strained smile. "That about sums it up."

Jai swore under his breath. "This could backfire on us."

"The Protocol Office can offer guidance for dealing with political shrapnel."

"I'd rather not be hit." Disheartened, Jai scrolled through the immensely annotated report. If the rest of his betrothed's finances were as bad as the bit with platinum, he was in deep, deep trouble.

He turned to Robert, and a difference registered on him. "You've a new collar."

"Yes. Thank you."

"Does this one fit better?"

"Much better, Your Highness."

"Good." It wasn't good, it was appalling, but at least Robert would be more comfortable. "Let me know if you have any more trouble."

"I will, sir." Although outwardly Robert showed little emotion, surprise came from his mind. Jai's grandfather, the last emperor Robert had known, would have never bothered to ask such a question. Jai gritted his teeth. He wondered how his purportedly esteemed predecessor would have felt if he had had to wear one of the wretched things.

A light blinked on his console. Jai tapped it with his finger. "Yes?"

"Your Highness, this is Vitar Bartholson in Security."

Jai froze. *Vitar.* It was his younger brother's name. Memories flooded him: Vitar laughing, running after him, or entreating his big brother for a ride. It was several moments before he could answer. "Is there a problem?"

"Not exactly," Bartholson said. "The Domestic Affairs Office contacted us. They intercepted a message sent to the Xir estate on Glory."

Jai sighed. Gods forbid someone should say, *Your Highness, we received a message through proper channels without spying on anyone.* "What did it say?"

Excitement leaked into Bartholson's voice. "The authorities on Halizon Two have Xir's provider. Sunrise."

Jai sat up straighter. "Are they certain?"

"They say so."

Although Jail would need more verification, it sounded far more promising than their other leads. "How is she?"

A pause. "She will be all right."

"That isn't what I asked."

Vitar audibly exhaled. "She has had a difficult time, Your Highness. But she will recover."

"I hope so." Jai turned to Robert. "What do we know about Halizon Two?"

Robert had already brought up the information. He studied his screen. "It's the second planet in the Halizon system of Emerald Sector. Lord Jaibriol Raziquon owns it."

Pah. Jai hadn't liked Raziquon when they had met in Kaliga's home, and he liked him even less now. On the comm, he said, "Major Bartholson, have Sunrise brought to the palace." Grimly he added, "And arrest Jaibriol Raziquon." It would enrage the Hightons, especially Raziquon's kin, given the lack of evidence, but Jai couldn't delay. The longer Raziquon had to prepare himself, the less chance they had of bringing him to justice.

Jai had no intention of letting him escape.

19

Ceremony

The palace media people spent most of the three months after Jai became emperor building up his wedding. By the time the day came, estimates placed the number of news services that would carry the broadcast in the billions. Jai tried not to think about it. He was in a daze, moving by rote, going where his aides sent him, wearing what his valets put on his body, and saying what protocol wrote.

They outfitted him in startling clothes. The black cloth felt soft but glittered like gems, an effect enhanced by holographic fibers. Elegantly cut trousers accented the length of his legs. A tunic set off the breadth of his shoulders and tapered to his hips, tailored to display his physique. They said the cloth alone cost thousands. Jai would have taken it all off right then if his valets hadn't stopped him. They added a black belt inset with carnelian stones. Red gems encrusted his shirt cuffs, and a clasp of carnelians set in a gold claw closed the high neck of his tunic. Black shoes and gloves completed the picture. When Jai looked in the mirror, a stranger in immaculate formal attire gazed back, his eyes like rubies. Vertigo swept him; he had lost Jai and found Jaibriol III.

The suite where his valets dressed him was furnished in ivory, with gold accents. In his dark clothes, he felt like a shadow on the decor. At least he wasn't the only one; his bodyguards also wore black. Omnipresent and unavoidable, they had become so much a part of his life that he felt odd when they left the room, as if he had misplaced something he had no wish to find.

His refusal to let his bodyguards approach him too closely had added to his reputation for eccentricity. He was slowly replacing them with Razers who had too little Aristo heritage to exert pressure on his mind. He couldn't do it all at once, lest he draw attention to himself, but each replacement helped.

Now he stood restlessly while his valets straightened his tunic. He wished they would stop fussing. Surely the Eubian Concord would survive if a hair on its emperor's head was out of place. He sometimes thought his ministers just wanted him to stand around looking hologenic, to benefit their propaganda machine, while they ran his empire.

The door across the room opened, and a tall man strode into the room. The valets stopped their ministrations so they could bow to the newcomer. Jai didn't feel up to facing Corbal now, but here was his cousin, resplendent in elegant clothes, dark blue with gold holoribbing on the cuffs and high neck.

Too agitated for any more preparations, Jai dismissed his valets, standing his ground when they resisted. Finally they departed, leaving him to Corbal's nuanced arrogance.

It was hard to believe nearly three months had passed since Corbal's release. About the same time that Sunrise had escaped, Corbal's security people had proved the records of her supposed crime were false. The case against Corbal had already been weak; the new evidence left ESComm no choice but to release him. He hadn't exactly been the worse for wear, given the luxury of the mansion where he had lived, the many taskmakers who had waited on his every whim, and the providers ESComm had lavished on him in the hopes of spying on his mind. He returned looking as if he had been to a resort. Only Jai had felt the anger underlying his facade of nonchalance; the high lord of the Xir Line would not soon forget what had happened.

Corbal gave him an appraising look. "Your bride will be pleased."

Pleased indeed. More likely, she would feed him to venom-eels. Jai had seen nothing of Tarquine since their betrothal. She had gone off-planet soon after, to attend to her various estates in preparation for her upcoming change in status. Today, when he stood in the Hall of Octagons to wed his bride, he would speak vows with a stranger.

"If she recognizes me," Jai said.

Corbal spoke dryly. "She recognizes your title."

Jai wished Corbal would quit harping about Tarquine wanting his power rather than him. Knowing it was true didn't make it any easier to hear.

"ESComm seems busy these days," Jai said.

"So does the Ministry of Finance."

Damn. Corbal wouldn't let it go even now. Well, tough. He could express his disapproval from today until forever. Jai had no intention of changing his mind. He knew why Corbal hated the idea of his marriage; it would increase the influence held by the Line of Iquar, rivaling the Line of Xir. That was just fine with Jai; Tarquine and Corbal could wear themselves out sparring with each other for power and leave him alone.

A knock came at a door behind Jai. Relieved to escape Corbal's scrutiny, Jai turned to one of his Razers. The guard bowed, acknowledging the unspoken command. He opened the door to reveal Robert.

The aide hurried inside, beaming, dressed in his elegant best, dark blue trousers and tunic with the Qox insignia on the chest. When he knelt to Jai, his body seemed to vibrate with energy.

"Please rise," Jai said.

Robert almost jumped to his feet. He grinned. "You will dazzle your bride, Your Highness."

Jai couldn't help but smile. At least Robert, who loved

pomp and circumstance, was enjoying this wedding, more even than he had taken pleasure in the recent celebrations for Jai's eighteenth birthday. It hadn't really been Jai's birthday, but Corbal had insisted on that date and Jai hadn't argued. For Jai's story about his Highton mother to be convincing, he needed a birth date from *before* his father disappeared rather than after.

Jai rubbed the back of his neck, trying to ease the kinks. He wished he could relax, but nothing helped. For all he knew, Tarquine wouldn't even show up. "Has Minister Iquar arrived yet?" he asked, for the fifth time.

"Ah, yes, Your Highness." Robert gave him a reassuring look. "She and her retinue are secluded in the Obsidian Wing of the palace."

"I hope she survives her valets better than I have mine."

Corbal was watching him with amusement. "Don't women call their helpers something other than valets?"

It startled Jai now when Corbal used a more direct style of speech with him. Although Hightons spoke more openly among their nearest kin, Corbal didn't really qualify as a close relative. But it was the best Jai would ever do, given that he could barely endure the presence of his other Highton kin.

"I don't have much experience with what words women use," Jai admitted.

Corbal's lips quirked up. "One's level of experience often increases."

Jai reddened, picking up what he meant by "experience." There were times when he could have done without telepathy. The speculations of his kin and staff about his upcoming wedding night were more than he wanted to deal with right now.

Apparently oblivious, Robert pulled his palmtop off his belt, all efficiency. Jai could tell, from Robert's mind, that the aide knew exactly what Corbal had implied, but he took mercy on the frazzled groom and pretended otherwise.

Robert waved his finger through a blinking holo above his

palmtop. Then he looked at Jai, composed, but with underlying excitement. "They are ready, Your Highness."

Jai was glad at least one of them was enjoying this. "Very well." He fortified his resolve. "Lead on."

So they headed for the wedding chamber. They followed a secluded route through the palace that few people knew and even fewer had clearance to use. The floors were laid with hexagonal tiles in snow-marble and black diamond. Tessellated mosaics tiled the walls and sparkled in the groined ceilings far overhead.

Jai heard the pounding of booted feet just before a formation of Razers burst out of a side corridor. No one spoke, but he could tell the newcomers were communicating with his guards using wireless implants in their brains, a sort of crude, technology-induced telepathy. Jai's guards responded fast; two took his arms, one on either side, and two more grasped Corbal. They set off running, pulling Jai and Corbal with them.

"What's going on?" Jai asked, forced into a run. His Razers suddenly felt more like kidnappers than bodyguards.

The captain on his left answered. "Palace security has been violated, Your Highness. We are taking you and Lord Xir to safety."

Ah, hell. "Safety where?"

Corbal raked his gaze over the new guards running with them. "You're part of the Special Operations Cordite Team."

One of the new Razers said, "That is correct, Lord Xir."

Jai didn't know which irked him more, that Corbal had interrupted him or that Jai had no idea what "Cordite Team" meant. They all raced down the hall: Jai, Corbal, both teams of Razers, and Robert, who was guarded by two Cordites.

A boom thundered deeper within the palace. The floor shook and Jai stumbled, lurching into the captain of his Razers.

"My apologies." The captain steadied Jai as they ran, helping him regain his balance. Corbal and his guards were ahead now. Despite his age, Corbal was barely out of breath, his body obviously bio-enhanced for speed and strength.

As Jai pulled up alongside the Xir lord, Corbal glanced at him. "That blast came from the Hall of Octagons."

Jai felt ill. His wedding was supposed to be in the Hall of Octagons. He spoke to the captain, spacing his words between breaths. "Any contact—with Minister Iquar?"

"The last we knew," the captain said, "her retinue was headed for the Hall. We can no longer contact them."

"Why the hell not?" Corbal was starting to sound winded. "This place is packed with security."

"Whoever infiltrated the palace has sophisticated enough jammers to block our systems," the captain said.

Jai felt the blood drain from his face. Security here was the best ESComm had to offer. Either someone had developed better, which meant his safety was severely compromised, or else this attack came from within ESComm, which would be even worse. Speaking sharply to the captain, he repeated his earlier question. "Where are you taking us?"

"To a safe room, Your Highness." He sounded more like a machine than a man, with no trouble breathing despite their grueling pace. Jai didn't think he wanted to know how much augmentation the captain had in his body. He preferred to believe his bodyguards were human.

The floor suddenly bucked under Jai's feet, throwing him forward. As he hit the ground, Razers dropped all around him, covering him with their armored bodies, bracing themselves on their arms so they didn't crush him. For interminable seconds, the ground heaved and debris showered over them.

Then they were scrambling to their feet, with dust and powder swirling in the air. As the two Razers grabbed Jai's arms again, a medic ran a scanner over his body. "Bruises, scrapes, and a broken rib. He can run."

Jai didn't even feel the injured rib. His adrenaline drove him forward as they scrambled over debris that seconds ago had been a corridor. Corbal had been farther from the blast and wasn't hurt, but Jai didn't see Robert. Looking around, he caught sight of his aide following them, bracketed by two Razers. So he took off, running hard with his guards.

Within moments they cleared the worst of the wreckage. The Razers pulled them into a corridor that sloped downward. Jai was gasping now, choked by all the dust. He could hear Corbal's breath rattling as well.

They rounded a corner—into a dead end. Jai swore and started to turn back, but his guards stopped him. Several Razers were crouching on the floor, pushing tiles in quick succession, like bankers entering a code into a vault. The pressure of their minds combined with the swirling dust made Jai feel suffocated. He struggled to breathe, holding one hand over his ribs, which had begun to ache.

One of the Razers looked around, his forehead furrowed. The captain grunted, then shook his head as if to clear it. Dismayed, Jai realized he wasn't damping his empathic responses enough. His discomfort was causing the Razers to transcend, probably at too low a level for them to realize it, but enough to distract them.

Jai's alarm surged, and this time it had nothing to do with explosions or dead ends. His fear of discovery outweighed it all. He intensified his mental barriers, buttressing his mind until he felt walled into a mental vault. The world became muffled, distant, not fully perceived. His mind was sluggish. Heavy.

"That's it!" As the Razer spoke, a circular section of the floor began to descend.

Jai's guards pulled him forward, fast and efficient. The circular plug was big enough for nearly everyone to fit onto it, though they had to leave two Razers behind. As they all crowded together, the plug sank into a chute of diamond-steel composite. Watching the walls slide past, Jai battled his shortness of breath. Razers hulked around him, shielding his body. Even through his deadened thoughts, their minds pressed on him, relentless.

The light faded. With growing apprehension, Jai looked up and saw a cover closing over the chute. Claustrophobia hit him like a jolt. When the chute became completely dark, he wanted to scream and pound the walls. He could almost feel the palace exploding above them, collapsing this chute, burying them in tons of rubble.

He didn't scream. It took every shred of his control, but he kept his voice calm. "How far down does this go?"

"It isn't far, Your Highness." That came from a Razer, the captain maybe, though Jai couldn't see in the dark.

So they descended.

The chute suddenly ended, and the plug continued to descend, lowering into a cavern lit in the center by harsh lights. Machines hulked in the shadows beyond, rank upon rank of robots, from small cleaning droids to military strikers that stood at twice the height of a man on their segmented legs.

Rails had risen around the circumference of the plug while it descended, protecting them from falling off as it came down to the cavern floor. When it reached the ground, Jai closed his eyes in gratitude. He opened them immediately, as Razers guided him off the plug. When he tried to pull away, they wouldn't let go. He looked around for Robert; his aide was behind him, between two Razers.

Jai didn't know what Robert saw in his face, but as soon as their gazes met, the aide strode forward. With deft confidence, he insinuated himself between Jai and the Razers and maneuvered Jai away from his guards. Robert even evaded Corbal, who had been closing in on Jai from the left.

As they drew ahead of the others, the pressure on Jai's mind became more manageable. He spoke in a low voice. "Thank you."

"It is my honor."

They were crossing a floor made from a steel-diamond composite. Robert stopped at a platform piled with crates and pulled out a chair with nervoplex padding. Jai hated nervoplex; it responded to his every move as if it were alive. He shook his head and sat on the edge of the platform instead, planting his well-shod feet on the floor. Resting his elbows on his knees, he lowered his head and drew in a shaky breath.

"Are you all right?" Robert asked.

Jai looked up. Robert had sat down on the platform, but not too close. Several hundred meters away, Corbal was speaking with the captain. The other Razers had dispersed throughout the cavern, some guarding Jai, others at consoles. One was running checks on a suit of power-armor, what ES-Comm commandos sometimes wore, becoming the walking fortresses known as waroids.

The group of Razers closest to Jai, including the medic, were speaking among themselves and checking meshes, but Jai knew they were also keeping watch on him. The medic would want to treat his injuries. Had Jai been in any more serious trouble, he doubted they would have waited for his permission to approach.

"Your Highness?" Robert sounded worried.

Jai glanced at him. "I am fine."

"Shall I bring the medic?"

"Not yet. Catch your breath."

Resting his elbows on his knees, Robert clasped his hands. "It is my honor to serve Your Highness."

"You always say that." Jai spoke tiredly. "Everyone does. It loses its meaning."

"I regret if it sounds false." Robert seemed genuinely troubled. "Please be assured of my sincerity."

Guilt tugged at Jai. When he eased his barriers, he could read Robert's moods like holos in an open book. He knew his aide had never been anything but loyal.

Jai spoke quietly. "I greatly value your fidelity."

Robert's troubled expression calmed, but his worry for Jai didn't fade. He glanced at the medic and beyond to where Corbal was conferring with the captain. Jai knew he should be over there, taking charge. But even if he could have endured so many Aristos up close, he wasn't as well qualified as Corbal to deal with the situation. If he survived long enough, he would gain experience with Aristo culture, but he didn't see how he would ever adapt to their cutthroat politics. He had begun to question whether he could truly function as emperor. He had no wish to adopt Highton mores or motivations. No doubt the Aristos would consider him hopelessly unsophisticated, but he had liked himself better before he became one of them in name, if not in his heart.

Jai inhaled deeply, trying to calm his agitation, then winced as pain shot through his torso.

"Your Highness." Robert watched him with concern. "May I allow the medic to approach?"

"All right." He couldn't put it off forever. "Send the captain over too. I would like a report on the situation."

"Yes, sir." With obvious relief, Robert jumped up and bowed, then strode over to the medic. They conferred, and the medic headed toward Jai while Robert went on to where Corbal stood with the captain.

Jai steeled himself as the medic approached. After the requisite kneeling, the doctor stood and unhooked a holotape from his belt. "May I do a scan, Your Highness?"

"Yes. Certainly." Jai wondered if it seemed as surreal to the medic as it did to him that they needed his permission to heal him. That was only true up to a point, though; if his life were in danger, they would save him first and apologize for touching his imperial personage later.

The medic sat on the platform and unrolled the tape. But when he tried to lay it against Jai's neck, Jai jerked back, his reflexes kicking in before he could control them.

The doctor took his emperor's peculiar behavior in stride. Instead of setting the tape against Jai's neck, he pushed up the sleeve of Jai's tunic and laid the tape on his forearm. Holos formed above it, views of Jai's upper body: bones, organs, circulation, and more. The broken rib showed in his skeleton. Strange, that. He felt relatively little pain. Perhaps he had too much adrenaline pumping through his body to register how much he hurt.

The medic took an air-syringe off his belt and dialed in some drug Jai hoped would make him numb, not for the rib but because of how the Aristos and Razers affected his mind.

As the medic treated him, Jai stared out at the cavern.

Seeing him, Corbal lifted his hand. Then the Xir lord approached, with the Razer captain at his side. Jai didn't know much about the captain except that he was the son of a Red-Point Diamond Aristo and one of her providers. Razers rarely if ever used names; it had taken Jai weeks to find out that some people called this one Redson.

The captain bowed to him. "I am gratified to see you looking so well, Your Highness."

Jai was tempted to say, *I look like hell.* Instead, he spoke in his carefully cultured Highton voice. "Thank you. Do you have information for me on this disruption?"

The captain glanced at Corbal, who inclined his head. Jai gritted his teeth. His Razers ought to ask his permission to speak to Corbal, not the reverse.

Redson did address Jai with deference, though. "It appears a traitor within the palace has given Qox security codes to another Highton Line. We are tracking the leak."

Jai relaxed his barriers enough to absorb a sense of Redson's mind. The captain had no idea what had happened, but he dreaded telling Jai, whose grandfather had thrown people in prison for having the wrong answers. Jai wanted to heave his purportedly revered ancestors into the ocean for making it near to impossible to do this job. How did they expect their staff to operate when everyone was afraid of being drawn and quartered for failing to achieve the impossible?

"Let me know as soon as you find out more." Jai feared the answer to his next question. "Has anyone been hurt?" *Like Tarquine.*

"We have reports that four taskmakers were killed in the explosions," the captain said. "Sixteen injured."

Heaviness settled over Jai. "We must take care of the families of those who were lost."

Redson blinked. "Yes, sir." He seemed surprised to have the emperor concern himself with the loss.

The captain still hadn't told him what he wanted to know. Jai gave up trying to be oblique. "And Minister Iquar?"

"We believe she is safe," Redson assured him. *We haven't*

a damned clue, he thought, with so much apprehension that Jai picked up the actual words.

Jai didn't think he could live with himself if his attempt to marry Tarquine had caused her death. "Has anyone been apprehended? Any more explosions?"

"No more explosions," Redson said.

Jai noticed what he didn't say. "Do you have any idea who set the blasts?"

Sweat sheened the captain's forehead. "We have many promising leads."

In other words, they had no clue. Jai suspected that no matter what he asked, the guards wouldn't admit their uncertainty. Their apprehension was too ingrained. "Very well. Let me know how the leads turn out."

Redson bowed. "Most assuredly, Your Glorious Highness."

Jai lifted his hand, dismissing the captain. Corbal was standing back, watching, but he didn't interfere. As Redson returned to confer with his team, Jai raised his mental barriers again, with relief. Whatever painkiller the medic had given him, it wasn't enough to mute the headache caused by his exposure to Aristo minds.

Jai couldn't fathom how Aristos could bear to live this way, stiff and formal, with assassination just around the corner. They seemed to have no real friendships, the kind where you just enjoyed each other's company, laughed about nothing, and trusted each other. He felt sorry for the Highton children growing up in this chill, deadly atmosphere. No wonder they turned out so strange as adults.

And yet . . .

Jai knew his father had treasured his memories of Ur Qox, Jai's grandfather. Ur Qox had secluded his son in childhood, determined to protect his heir. Incredible as it seemed, he had loved his Ruby telepath son.

Jai laid his palm against his ribs. He felt no pain at all. His head hurt more from the presence of the half-Aristo medic. He inclined his head to the doctor. "You have done a fine job. You may go now."

"But I should—" He stopped when Jai scowled at him. "Of course, Your Highness." The doctor withdrew, leaving Jai with Corbal, which Jai doubted was likely to help his blood pressure. At least his bodyguards were standing far enough back to respect his reputed idiosyncratic need to surround himself with empty space.

Corbal frowned. "Good health benefits a sovereign."

"I was tired of being poked." Jai spoke bluntly, even for kin-speech. "They have no idea who tried to blow me up, do they?"

Corbal sighed. "Do you know, Cousin, you might be more successful if you learned to master the intricacies of proper speech."

"The hell with proper speech. I want to know who tried to kill us."

"Antagonizing people isn't the way to find out."

"Who do you think did it?"

Corbal finally relented. "Probably Raziquon's kin."

"I should think they would be relieved he is away." He had ordered Raziquon put into a real prison, with no luxuries, servants, providers, or any other privileges such as Corbal had enjoyed during his ESComm custody, the pleasures an Aristo took for granted. "Now they don't have to put up with him."

"Jaibriol."

"Jaibriol, what? The man is insane."

"He is perfectly sane." Corbal's manner cooled. "Questions of sanity are far more likely to arise over your behavior."

"He deserves to be in prison."

"You didn't have enough evidence."

"I had Sunrise's testimony."

"She is a *provider*."

"So?"

Corbal made an incredulous noise. "You are hopeless."

Jai crossed his arms. "If his kin killed Tarquine, I will execute Raziquon."

"Don't be a fool."

"Damn it, Corbal, she is my *wife*."

"Not yet."

Jai clenched his fists. "For all I know, you set this up to stop the marriage."

Corbal raised an eyebrow. "Setting up my own death would be rather ill considered on my part."

"You don't look dead to me."

"We were lucky."

"Maybe." Jaibriol stood up, wincing as pain stabbed his torso. "But this assassination is more Xirad Kaliga's style. He framed you in his own home."

"You have no proof of that, either."

"He did it, Corbal. You know it. The only reason he isn't in prison, too, is because you interfered when I tried to put him there."

His cousin shook his head. "Don't be foolish. Kaliga controls ESComm. Push him, and you're pushing the entire military. Take on your Joint Commanders and you won't survive a day."

Before Jai could respond, a rumble vibrated through the floor. Jai froze, his pulse surging as he imagined the cavern collapsing. Then he realized the rumble came from the plug that had brought them here. Slowly and smoothly, it rose from the floor, ascending until it disappeared into the chute in the ceiling.

"Why did it do that?" Jai asked. His bodyguards were moving into formation around him and Corbal.

Corbal pressed the cuff of his tunic and the gold designs on it flickered into an active comm mesh. "Captain, what's going on?"

Redson's voice came out of the comm. "A precaution, Lord Xir. We're closing the chute."

Jai stiffened, his claustrophobia returning. He could almost feel the weight of the palace above them. "How do they know this place won't cave in?"

"The walls are held by a quasis grid." Corbal motioned toward a line of shadowed machines against the curving wall of the cavern. "Those are the generators."

Jai took time to absorb that. ESComm kept a tight rein on its quasis generators, yet he counted five here. A quasis field fixed the quantum wavefunction of anything it touched. The affected system didn't freeze; its atoms continued to move as they had when they went into quasis. But their behavior couldn't change, not even one particle. On a macroscopic scale, everything in the field became rigid. In theory, even explosions couldn't deform it, though if you hit it enough times, the quasis would fail. He suspected that the fields here formed a grid that reinforced the cavern, rather than a solid surface, so communications and the plug could pass through.

The floor shuddered.

Jai froze. Had he been wrong about the strength of the quasis fields—but no, the vibration wasn't from an explosion or structural collapse. The elevator reappeared, coming down from the ceiling. People crammed it: Razers, aides, soldiers, even waroids.

A tall figure stood in their midst.

The woman wore a dark red dress, ankle-length and gleaming like carnelians. Her hair fell in a shimmering black waterfall over her shoulders. She stood tall and proud, a fiery goddess in the midst of dark warriors.

His bride had arrived.

20

Merger

As the lift settled onto the floor, Jai's mouth went dry. Tarquine stood regally, devastating in her red dress, which clung to her long curves from neck to ankle.

"It would seem she survived," Corbal said dryly.

Jai knew Corbal was studying him. Ignoring his cousin's scrutiny, he headed for his bride. Corbal came with him.

"You can wait for me back at the platform," Jai said.

"So I could." Corbal continued on at his side.

He didn't want to argue with Corbal when Tarquine could see. She was stepping off the lift, watching their approach. Jai was having trouble breathing. He might as well have heart failure now and get it over with, because he wasn't going to survive the wedding night if she kept looking at him like that. She let her gaze travel upward, moving up his legs like a caress, taking in his hips, gliding over his torso and chest. By the time she reached his face, his cheeks were so hot, he wondered that he didn't incinerate.

He made himself walk slowly. As he reached Tarquine, she murmured, "My greetings, Your Highness."

At least I'll die happy, Jai thought. "You look lovely, Minister Iquar."

She inclined her head.

Jai indicated the cavern. "I had intended to offer you a

better wedding hall, but I'm afraid this will have to do." In his side vision, he saw Corbal stiffen, a familiar scowl on his face. Even the Razers looked flustered this time. No one expected the imperial marriage to happen here in a bunker, or safe room, or whatever they called this place. Jai didn't care. He had no intention of letting whoever had tried to assassinate him win. He would marry Tarquine now.

Robert performed the ceremony.

Jai asked him to officiate because Robert had so savored the preparations. It only seemed right that at least one person should enjoy the wedding. Jai was too agitated. He and Tarquine stood side by side, surrounded by guards, many armed with laser carbines now in addition to the miniature arsenals they carried on their hips, boots, and belts. Waroids in full armor patrolled the perimeter of the area.

Robert read the vows, and Jai and Tarquine gave their agreement. Tarquine's personal aide had brought the Iquar documents and Robert had the Qox documents. So Jai and Tarquine signed the contracts, and gave their retinal scans and voice imprints, fulfilling the legal requirements.

Then it was done. Eube once again had an empress. It remained only to name a moon after her.

Jai turned to Tarquine, running through phrases in his mind, searching for the right words to greet his new wife. She regarded him with her dark gaze, her lips parted. Before Jai could decide what to say to her, Robert motioned to him. The aide and Captain Redson were talking urgently, in low voices.

Jai held back his sigh. Perhaps, in another century, he might actually hold a conversation with Tarquine.

"Is there a problem?" he asked Robert.

"We have news of the Skolians," Robert said. "The Ruby Pharaoh."

Sweat beaded Jai's temples. The Pharaoh was his aunt. "What news?"

Captain Redson spoke, agitation marking his usually implacable demeanor. "ESComm intercepted a broadcast from Earth. Ships are carrying it throughout Allied, Skolian, and Eubian space."

"It's that important?" Jai asked. Without the Kyle web, it was hard to spread news in a timely fashion to the star-flung settlements of humanity. It would travel fast only if its importance justified the effort of so many ships carrying it quickly among the various worlds and habitats.

Jai caught a thought from Redson's mind: the captain would have rather been anywhere but here right now, giving this news to the emperor. But he spoke with laudable composure. "The Skolians sent a commando team to Earth. It rescued the members of the Ruby Dynasty imprisoned there."

Jai blinked. "The Ruby Pharaoh was on Earth?" *That* fit none of the rumors he had heard.

"No, Your Highness." Redson was almost stuttering. "She has taken command of the military."

"She can't," Jai said. "Her title is titular."

Robert was reading from his palmtop. "It isn't clear—reports are conflicting—but it looks like she instigated a coup over the Skolian government, backed by the most powerful branch of ISC, the Imperial Fleet."

Jai stared at him. What the blazes were the Skolians doing? ISC meant Imperial Space Command, the combined military forces of the Skolian Imperialate. The name "Imperialate" was historical, given that an Assembly of elected councilors governed the Skolians. The reign of the Ruby Dynasty had ended long ago. But if the military had supported his aunt in a coup, it meant the Ruby Pharaoh once again ruled. Such a political upheaval could shatter the fragile balance among Skolia, Eube, and the Allieds.

Another thought hit Jai: his uncle Kelric had been on Earth. If ISC had freed the Ruby Dynasty, that included Kelric. He truly was Imperator now.

Jai was painfully aware of Tarquine at his side. Better than anyone else here, she could predict what Kelric would do now. But even if Jai had been in private with her, where he could have asked a direct question without insult, he didn't think he could bear to hear her speak of Kelric, the man she truly wanted, the one who was far more her match than Jai would ever be.

Somehow he kept his face composed as he turned to his wife. "The Ministry of Finance must have interests that will be affected by changes in the status of the Ruby Dynasty." There: indirect and understated. Much more appropriate than *What do you think about your former pleasure slave becoming Imperator?*

Her face was unreadable. "Many observers might assume it makes no difference to the Finance Ministry where peace talks between our people and the Skolians take place. But our offices have a great deal invested in the outcome."

The talks. With a start, Jai realized everything had changed. The Skolians had agreed to talks when they were prisoners on Earth. They had more options now. And the Ruby Pharaoh hadn't agreed to anything. With the might of ISC behind her, she would be a formidable foe if she chose war over peace.

Jai knew he needed to deal with these new developments, but he couldn't do much, trapped here while his people tried to figure out who wanted to kill him. He turned to Redson. "How long until we can return to the palace?"

The captain scanned a small screen on his gauntlet. "Security is doing a final check. Then we can go back up."

"Good." It would be a relief to escape this cavern and its oppressive sense of burial. Soon he would be free.

Until the next assassination attempt.

Kelricson Valdoria, Imperator of Skolia, stood on the dais. Light bathed him, slanting through windows in the cathedral-like Hall of Chambers on Parthonia, the capital world of Skolia. Media teams surrounded the dais. Soon they would broadcast the speech of Dyhianna Selei, the Ruby Pharaoh, the woman he knew as Dehya, his aunt, his mother's older sister. Dehya had re-created a fledgling psiberweb. Telops would use the newly birthed web to send her words throughout space faster than any ship could carry them.

Only a few days had passed since ISC had freed the Ruby Dynasty from Earth. But in the months prior to that, Kelric had been healing. He would never have made it to Earth if not for Jeejon. She had lived on an asteroid near the border of Skolian and Eubian territory, an outpost that the Allieds had liberated from Eube during the war. It was the only place his ship had enough fuel to reach after he escaped the Sphinx Sector Rim Base. By that time he had no more than days to live. Jeejon thought him crazy when he told her he was the Imperator, but she helped him anyway. She was his age, fifty-seven, a Eubian taskmaker. *Former* taskmaker. Now she was the consort of the Imperator. He had married her on Earth.

Kelric stood waiting on the dais with Dehya, his aunt, a slender woman with her dark hair swept up on her head. The streaks of gray in it hinted at her age, but she otherwise appeared young. Only the timeless quality of her gaze revealed the truth: she was over one and a half centuries old. Although she was the Pharaoh and he the Imperator, they both dressed simply, Dehya in a blue jumpsuit and Kelric in gold trousers and tunic. Neither of them wore medals or ornamentation. Their Jagernaut bodyguards paced the hall, cyberwarriors in black. Less visible, but just as deadly, Evolving Intelligence defense computers monitored the great hall.

Trillions of people would receive this broadcast through the psiberweb, and in months to come ships would carry it to places the newborn web didn't yet reach. When the media tech gave the signal, Dehya began. She had a strong voice, melodic and clear. "My people, I greet you. I come before you today with great hope."

Dehya's advisers had written the speech. They had wanted Kelric to speak as well, but he refused. Taciturn even in personal conversation, he dreaded public speaking. He preferred to stand in silence, a bulwark to protect Dehya, Eldrinson, and himself—Pharaoh, Assembly Key, and Imperator. The Mind, the Heart, and the Fist of Skolia. The Triad.

"It has been five thousand years since the height of the Ruby Empire," Dehya continued. "Almost six thousand since the Ruby Dynasty first rose to power. Throughout our history, Skolia has been our heart. Now today we honor that heart with the advent of a new and greater era."

Kelric waited for her next words: *With a smooth transition to the new government, the Ruby Dynasty again assumes full sovereignty of the Skolian Imperialate.* That one phrase had caused relentless debate among her speechwriters. It was the closest they wanted Dehya to come in acknowledging the price of the coup that had made her a true Pharaoh—she would have to order the execution of the First Councilor, the head of the government she had deposed, a distinguished leader who had been her friend and colleague for decades.

Dehya spoke stiffly. "With a smooth transition to the new government—" Then she stopped.

Kelric tensed, as did many of the people watching them record this broadcast. His older brother, Eldrin, was leaning against a column, his arms crossed. It gratified Kelric to see his brother free from the Traders; he would wonder for the rest of his life why Jaibriol Qox had shown Eldrin mercy, trading himself so Eldrin could go free.

Dehya was watching Eldrin, too, her husband of over fifty years, a marriage between kin, one forced by the Assembly to produce more Ruby psions. The match, however unwillingly made, had become a union of love. But the Assembly had again and again shattered the Ruby Dynasty in its desperation to control them, an irony, given that destabilizing the Rubies destabilized Skolia. So Dehya had overthrown the government. But that coup could destroy the fragile bubble of peace that protected humanity in the aftermath of the Radiance War. Executing the First Councilor, the elected leader of Skolia, would create havoc.

Dehya suddenly finished her sentence in a clear voice.

"We will meld an alliance unlike any Skolia has known before."

Kelric blinked. *That* wasn't part of the script.

"Several tendays ago," Dehya said, "the government of Skolia shifted from the Assembly to the Ruby Dynasty. I stand before you now as full sovereign. During the Ruby Empire, the rule of the Dynasty was absolute."

The media techs were scrambling to make sure they caught every detail of this unexpected change from the planned speech. Some spoke hurriedly into comms, their attention split between Dehya and whatever protests they were hearing.

"Skolia has identified itself for six millennia through the Ruby Empire," Dehya said. "Yet in this modern age, we chose a representative government instead." She paused. "And so it should be."

The techs froze. Kelric wondered what the blazes Dehya was doing. She had just gone to great lengths to overthrow that representative government. Her mind was guarded; he couldn't feel her thoughts, only her tension.

Dehya spoke slowly, as if even she wasn't sure what she would say next. "The uneasy meld of modern politics with tradition has often rent our civilization. We think of ourselves as an ancient race from Raylicon, yet compared to humanity on Earth we are incredibly young. We have no history prior to six thousand years ago, only distant memories of our birth world. We are new. Raw. At this crucial time in our growth, we dare not destabilize Skolia. We need *both* the Ruby Dynasty and Assembly."

Kelric began to see her intent. She spoke the essence of their dilemma: six thousand years ago, some unknown race had moved humans from Earth to the planet Raylicon and then vanished, stranding the displaced humans with no explanation. Since that time, their people had evolved independent of Earth. They thought of themselves as Skolians, children of the Ruby Empire, which had arisen five thousand years ago, and then fallen a few centuries later, followed by millennia of dark ages. They weren't ready to cut those ties, but modern civilization had outgrown that method of governance.

"For that reason," Dehya continued, "our government will join old and new. The Ruby Dynasty and Assembly will share the governance of Skolia. So begins our future." She turned to another holocam, as the techs had previously instructed. But instead of finishing with the planned tribute to the Ruby Dynasty, she said, "I accept the offer of Jaibriol the Third, Emperor of Eube, to meet at the peace table. Let us work together—Skolian, Trader, and Allied—to heal the rifts that have divided our common humanity."

The Hall became a tumult, as people shouted questions. Kelric and Dehya stood together, surrounded by their bodyguards. Kelric wondered at this decision Dehya had so precipitously announced. He could see its promise; a joined government would return to the Skolian people the heritage that defined them, but retain the stability of the Assembly. Nor would they have to execute the First Councilor; he would be a part of this melded government.

Dehya's idea was a good one.

It was also going to be one holy hell of a mess.

21

The Stone Table

Jai's canopied bed waited, gold and ivory. He stood next to it, considering the lacquered table in front of him. It hadn't been there this morning. A decanter of gold liquid and two crystal tumblers sat on it. Jai picked up the decanter and took a deep swallow. He had no idea what he was drinking, but it went down like summer heat and kicked like a blizzard.

He had triple-checked the room earlier to make sure no monitors spied on him tonight. Scanners would warn the staff if he had a heart attack or other crisis, but no one could see him swigging alcohol like a drunk on the stardocks.

At least his rib didn't bother him. He had expected it to ache, but he felt nothing. On Prism, injuries had been a great danger. They had no hospitals there, only a medical comp and a few medicines. It told him a lot about the care available to an emperor, that just a few hours ago his rib had broken and now it was nearly healed.

The only light came from an antique stained-glass lamp at the other end of the suite. The breakfast nook curved out on Jai's left, shadowed, its curtains drawn. He glanced across the bed to the archway that led to the bathing chamber, with its tiled pool, sauna, whirlpool, and underwater VR center.

Right now he could think only of its most prosaic function, as a changing room.

Restless, Jai went down into the breakfast nook. He sat on a wing chair with ivory and gold pinstripes, then rose and paced to a wardrobe against one curving wall. A black velvet robe hung inside. He removed his clothes and slipped on the robe. It fit perfectly, covering him from shoulder to knees, but it was open halfway down his chest. He fought the urge to pull it closed. He had to stop acting like a boy who had never touched a woman. Well, all right, he pretty much never had, except Silver. But he had to handle this.

His bride had little in common with Silver.

Jai pushed his hand through his hair. Unable to hold still, he went back to the dais and sat on the bed. A tickling in his throat made it hard to swallow. *Get a grip.* Surely the emperor of the most powerful empire in human history could show more cool than this. He wished the EI hadn't turned the lights so low. It seemed . . . blatant. He could have it brighten them, but that would be tantamount to confessing his embarrassment.

The door to the bathing room opened.

Jai froze. Tarquine entered the bedroom, a tall shadow with lithe grace. Jai suddenly didn't give a damn what the EI thought; he wanted to see her. "Lumos up," he said in a low voice.

The light increased enough to show Tarquine clearly. She wore a robe similar to his, but red. The velvet rippled along her angular curves as she moved, and her hair shimmered around her shoulders. Her face was perfect, unmarred by any flaw, making her seem more like a statue than a human being.

The empress met his gaze. She stopped at the other side of the bed and stood, her eyes dark in the muted light. Her throaty voice evoked thoughts of whiskey. "Good evening, Your Highness."

Warmth rushed to his face. "Good evening, Wife." If she kept looking at him like that, he was going to drag her over here right now. Flustered, he lifted the decanter. "Would you care for a drink?"

She sat on her side of the bed. "You may give me one."

He smiled. "Thank you for the permission."

Her lips slowly curved upward. He didn't know how she could be so icily aloof and yet look so seductive, as if she would incinerate him with her sensuality.

Distracted, he filled two glasses. On Earth he had never seen anyone drink liqueur from tumblers, but then, few other Highton customs were familiar to him, either. Sliding into the middle of the bed, he sat against the headboard. In the smoky moment, with a slow burn of alcohol warming him, he let his mental barriers ease.

An image of what Tarquine saw jumped from her mind to his: he was sitting sprawled against the headboard, his long legs stretched across the covers, pillows tumbled around him. The robe accented the breadth of his shoulders and his narrow waist and hips. On the outside, she was ice; on the inside, he excited her more than she would ever admit.

The eroticism of knowing she found him that desirable was more inebriating than any liqueur. Jai offered her a drink. Her gaze became heated, as if he had propositioned her. He caught another image from her mind: himself, extending the glass, his hair tousled, his gaze half lidded, nothing at all like a properly remote emperor. It aroused her in a way Highton reserve could never have done.

She moved closer and took the glass. As she sipped her drink, he gulped his, then realized what he was doing and stopped. At this rate, he would get himself drunk before she felt anything.

"An interesting day," she murmured. Her ruby eyes, large and slanted upward, were half veiled by the black fringe of her lashes.

Jai wondered if she had any idea what she was doing to him. He tried to think of a suave response, but all he came up with was, "I didn't expect our wedding to cause so much commotion."

She laughed, as cool as the snowmelt of a river. "Indeed, Your Highness."

"Jai."

She tilted her head. "Jai?"

"That's my name."

"Jai." Her voice caressed the word.

He finished his drink in one gulp. Then he took her tumbler, prying it out of her hand, and reached across the bed to set both their glasses on the table. He felt her surge of desire as she watched him stretch out, his robe shifting to reveal more of his legs.

Sitting up, Jai grasped her arm and spoke in a dusky voice. "Come here."

Tarquine gave him an appraising stare, as if she knew exactly how flustered he felt. Nudging him back against the headboard, she leaned forward and brushed her lips over his. So controlled. If Jai hadn't been an empath, he would have never known how much she wanted him. He pulled her across his body as she kissed him, her tongue teasing apart his lips. He tried to match her control, but what he really wanted was to throw her down on the bed.

When she tugged his robe off his shoulder and began to stroke his chest, he gave up. The hell with control: he rolled her over and stretched out on top of her, pulling open her robe. Like him, she wore nothing under it. Gods, she was so *long.* Her legs went on forever. As he moved his hands on her body, hungry for her, a thought in the back of his mind warned against losing himself this way. He pushed it away, too ravenous to listen.

"So eager," Tarquine murmured, her voice like molasses.

Then she flipped him over.

Jai barely had time to grunt before she had pinned him on his back. Straddling his hips, she bent over him, holding down his wrists, one on either side of his head. Then she gave him a long, slow smile.

Jai tried to yank his hands away, but he couldn't. He struggled harder, but he still couldn't free himself. She had to

have enhanced skeletal and muscular systems; even a weight
lifter couldn't have held him down this way without the help
of bio-augmentation.

Jai scowled. "Let me up."

"Now, why would I do that?" She kissed him again.

He meant to resist, to pull away, but the warmth of her
lips made it hard to remember that. He kissed her back, still
straining to free his wrists.

She raised her head. "So sweet."

Ai! Not "sweet" again. He tried to sound rugged. "Let go
of my arms."

She gave him a drowsy look, her hair falling around her
face. "Why would I want to, Your Delectable Highness?"

"I'm not your dessert." Jai finally succeeded in freeing his
wrists. Grasping her around the waist, he rolled her over and
pressed her into the bed, his pulse surging as his desire for
her built.

So they tangled together, wrestling, touching, burning
within, Tarquine's ice transformed into a devouring flame.
She introduced him into her darkling universe of sensuality,
and he lost himself in her fire until it consumed him.

A long time later, Jai stirred. Tarquine was dozing next to
him, but when he moved, her lashes lifted. Her smile formed
like the embers of a conflagration, barely perceptible now,
but ready to ignite. She trailed her long, elegant finger down
his cheek. "Now you are mine."

"You can't own me." He had meant to sound firm, but the
words came out dusky and provocative instead.

She just smiled and closed her eyes.

That night, as Tarquine slept, Jai watched her—and wondered what force of nature he had unleashed by making her
the empress.

Mist curled around a circular table made from stone. It stood
alone, incongruously, on a shelf of rock high in the mountains. On one side of the shelf, a cliff sheered down in a
vertical wall; on the other three sides, cliffs rose up into the

fog. Admiral Xirad Kaliga waited by the cliff behind the table. His bodyguards had faded into the mist, but he knew they remained nearby.

An engine rumbled. A flier was coming down, veiled by fog, landing on a field Kaliga's personal security people had carved out of the mountains nearby. Laser-based defense systems protected these pockets and shrouded them from monitors. Even ESComm had no record of this place.

Three figures coalesced out of the mist: two bodyguards and the hefty form of General Kryx Taratus, the other Joint Commander of ESComm.

Kaliga nodded to his counterpart. "Taratus."

"Hell of a time to meet," the general grumbled. "Damnable fog."

"Veils have their uses," Kaliga said.

Taratus waved his hand. "Everything has its use. If not, then I say dispose of it."

Kaliga suppressed his frown. Taratus often balanced on the edge of insult by direct speech. But Kaliga was used to it. He sat at the table, facing the general across the stone disk. "Even if something has a use, one may want to dispense with it." Like their tiresome emperor.

Taratus lowered himself onto the curved bench. "The plans for peace talks with Skolia continue to progress."

"A shame." This time Kaliga did frown. "One could imagine instead the great heights Eube could achieve if we chose to seize the initiative over the Skolians."

Taratus snorted. "It takes a great leader to seize such initiative."

"So it does." Kaliga paused. "I understand that an assassination attempt was made against the emperor on his wedding day. I am aghast." It truly had appalled him; he would have thought Taratus's people could have done a better job. "May the emperor live a long and glorious life."

"Glorious, indeed," Taratus muttered. "It is fortunate the Line of Qox has support from the Line of Xir." He drummed his fingers on the table, revealing his sarcasm. "Failures come in many forms, including uncooperative dawns."

Thinking of Sunrise, Kaliga scowled. "The dawn seems to shed its light on the Line of Raziquon." It disgusted him. The emperor had treated Raziquon worse than Kaliga would have expected even if the palace had found evidence against him—which they hadn't. Convicting Raziquon on the testimony of a provider was an unspeakable outrage. Jaibriol's decision to throw Raziquon in prison was made even worse by the contrast with how well ESComm had treated Corbal Xir while he was in custody.

"Appeals can chill the dawn." Although Taratus sounded detached, the rhythm of his words indicated his anger.

Kaliga nodded. Of course Raziquon's kin had appealed the prison sentence. The incarceration of their lord was the true crime. Questions of legality in Sunrise's abduction were unimportant; if ESComm needed such an action, it became acceptable.

The girl's resilience had surprised him, but her silence also revealed Corbal's secrets. Too many defenses protected her mind. True, an Aristo could train or adapt his providers to resist interrogation, but the law allowed only limited protection, precisely for this reason, in case ESComm needed to question the provider.

Sunrise obviously had protections beyond the legal limit. That Kaliga's agents had found no evidence of an ESComm operative working for Corbal Xir suggested Xir had trained her himself, which made it even worse. He was a Highton. For him to teach his provider how to resist other Hightons was treason.

Kaliga understood what motivated Xir; he had been tempted to give Silver similar safeguards. But he resisted the weakness that drove him to betray his Highton lineage by giving his favored provider illicit protections. Corbal Xir should have done the same.

After Kaliga had pondered in silence for several moments, Taratus grunted, a most un-Highton sound. "I've heard it said silence is worth more than platinum. Apparently we only have a shortage of the metal."

Kaliga raised his eyebrow. For Taratus, that was an unexpectedly clever joke, with Sunrise as the "silence," and Kaliga, too. The double meaning surprised him; Taratus generally had a much cruder wit.

"One wonders how High Judge Muze will hear the Raziquon appeal," Kaliga said. Her ruling could go either way. Common sense and Highton decency said she should pardon Raziquon, but her kinship with the emperor could motivate her to support Jaibriol. "The political landscape changes."

"For the worse," Taratus grumbled.

"Evolution is an ongoing process."

"Perhaps we ought to evolve it more to our liking."

Kaliga leaned forward. "You have a suggestion?"

"Consider the Skolians."

Kaliga moved his hand in dismissal. "If ever I wondered about the mental stability of the Ruby Dynasty, I no longer doubt their insanity. The only intelligent thing they have done in the past five hundred years is to overthrow that Assembly of theirs. Only a government run by providers would come up with the idiotic notion of giving the Assembly *back* half its power. What the hell kind of coup is that?"

Taratus laughed. "One could compliment the Ruby Pharaoh on her originality."

"Your tact is laudable." Kaliga would have liked to do many things with the Ruby Pharaoh, but complimenting her originality wasn't one of them.

"Eubian tact always is. We aren't Skolians."

"Were Eube ever to engage in activities similar to those of the Skolians, we would follow a more elevated course." If ESComm overthrew the Qox Dynasty, Kaliga damn well wouldn't hesitate to execute Jaibriol III and install his own emperor.

Taratus drummed his fingers on the table. "Fortunately, our government is more stable than that of the Skolians."

There was that, unfortunately. The people of Eube practically worshipped their emperor. Even most Aristos maintained a certain awe, though that was more because the Qox Dynasty had extended its political and economic hooks into the affairs of every Aristo Line, manipulating fates and finances. And the populace favored Jaibriol III, the handsome, charismatic youth who had appeared at Eube's greatest hour of need. It would be virtually impossible to garner support in ESComm for an overthrow of the Qox Dynasty.

"You are right, of course," Kaliga said. "We are fortunate to have a superior government." He gave Taratus a thoughtful look. "The only way I can imagine such an upheaval would be in the unlikely event that our emperor turned out to be a fake. We are lucky such could never happen."

Taratus looked as if he had eaten a sour fruit. "I am so pleased we all accepted his imperial DNA."

Indeed. They had all seen the proof of Jaibriol III's claim to the throne. His genetics had been verified and reverified. They had little hope of convincing anyone the emperor was a fraud. Jaibriol II had sired Jaibriol III, just as Jaibriol III would probably soon produce his own heir.

Kaliga's mouth quirked upward. "Maybe the imperial hormones will do the trick. Distract him from his job."

Taratus smirked. "Of course we all wish the emperor well in his marriage."

"A truly matchless pairing." Kaliga couldn't believe Jaibriol had the effrontery to marry one of his ministers. The job of an empress was to look aesthetic, not hold the most influential financial position in the empire. Hell, Jaibriol would do better with the aesthetic duties than his hard-edged wife. Kaliga didn't know which gave him worse heartburn, the idea of Corbal Xir as the power behind the Carnelian Throne or Tarquine Iquar practically in the throne.

Maybe Jaibriol could be discredited. His reign so far had been anything but glorious. With all his mistakes and bizarre decisions, he confused people as much as he annoyed them. Isolating him from Corbal had been a stroke of genius; without the Xir Lord's advice, Jaibriol had alienated an impressive number of people. In fact, it wasn't the emperor they had to discredit; given the chance, he would do it himself. Corbal and Tarquine were the ones to focus on. Without them, Jaibriol would be easy prey.

"Silence and platinum," Kaliga mused. "It appears our empress has experienced a shortage of neither."

Taratus's posture indicated interest. "Not that the Line of Qox would use its power to destabilize the economy by allowing the empress to corner the market on platinum."

"Of course not," Kaliga said. "Any rumors to the contrary must be false." He rested his elbow on the table and his chin in his hand. "So, too, must be rumors suggesting Corbal Xir has violated both imperial law and Highton decency by training his provider to protect her mind."

Taratus grinned. "Terrible, isn't it, the way rumors start?"

"Terrible indeed."

"It is fortunate for us that Raziquon has no platinum mines."

Kaliga blinked. How had Raziquon come into this? Not knowing what Taratus was about, he gave a generic reply. "Many possibilities exist."

"Consider a scenario, purely hypothetical of course."

"Of course."

Taratus leaned forward. "Suppose a Highton with no link to ESComm has reason to interrogate the provider of another powerful Highton. Trained as a spy, she 'listens' to his mind even as he questions her. Suspecting as much, he puts false information in his thoughts. Just in case she escapes."

That intrigued Kaliga. It would be like Raziquon to let Sunrise "overhear" a false story. He would have had to take care, though, lest she also pick up his intent to lie. It would be a difficult undertaking, but Raziquon could probably pull it off. It was why Kaliga paid him so well; irritating though he was, he was also thorough.

"He could plant disinformation in the camp of his adversary," Kaliga said.

Taratus laughed. "He might even make her think he owns illegal platinum mines."

Kaliga frowned. "So what?"

Taratus could have taken offense at the blunt question, but he chose to overlook it. "False accusations, Admiral. Such a shame for the accuser—*if* he's caught."

Kaliga mulled it over. False accusations were the blight of an Aristo. They could be valuable currency, but if the accusers were caught, they suffered severe repercussions: shunning, civil suits, even criminal charges. If Corbal accused Raziquon of owning illegal mines and was proved wrong, it would weaken his standing among Hightons and could cause him legal problems. For one thing, Raziquon could sue him for defamation of character. In a culture where appearance and reputation were everything, no Aristo would tolerate such an offense. Of course Corbal wouldn't risk an open statement—unless he had reason to believe it posed him no risk.

Kaliga weighed the possibilities. Minister Iquar *did* have questionable investments in platinum. With her marriage, she and Corbal became kin. If Corbal falsely accused Raziquon, and then his own kin were proven guilty of the same misdeeds, it would stain the Qox name as well as the Line of Xir.

Another idea came to Kaliga, a way to deal with the emperor's disgraceful pardon of Jafe Maccar, the captain of the Skolian merchant vessel. ESComm couldn't openly censure the pardon; the emperor could retaliate by revealing how Taratus's fool brother had ignored the Halstaad Code of War and auctioned Kelric Valdoria, the weapons officer on that vessel. Nor did they want to draw attention to the fact that Valdoria—now the Imperator—had walked off right under their noses.

But suppose the emperor's kin committed an even worse violation of the Code than that perpetrated by Azar Taratus? It would give ESComm ammunition against the palace.

Kaliga rubbed his chin. "I am gratified to know that no

ships owned by our illustrious emperor prey on Skolian vessels." In truth, he had no doubt the Line of Qox owned numerous pirate ships that raided the Skolians, though the emperor was probably too naive to realize it.

Taratus waved away the comment. "You'll never trace any pirates to the emperor. His predecessors were too careful."

Kaliga stiffened at the direct response. "Your depth of perception astounds me."

Taratus guffawed. "No, it doesn't."

"Rumors, General. Rumors."

"Rumors are often misleading."

"A shame they can't be prevented."

Taratus laughed and slapped the table. "A shame indeed."

Kaliga smiled. If properly played, rumors might topple a dynasty.

22

Power Base

Kelric walked through the stone mansion. It had been built high up on the slope of the valley where his family lived on the space habitat known as the Orbiter. Almost two decades had passed since he had seen this secluded valley, even longer since he had entered this house.

He came alone, seeking solitude. This was the home of the Imperator. His half-brother Kurj had lived here for decades. When his sister Soz had become Imperator, she had chosen another home. Kelric thought he knew why; it would have been like living with Kurj's ghost. It wrenched him to come here after having been gone so long and changed so much.

The main entrance to the house was big enough for three men to walk through abreast. It needed no door; in a space habitat, they could have perfect weather every day, if they chose. So Kurj had left the house open to the air. Airy and spacious, the building was all stone. Its dimensions were huge, as if designed for a giant.

Kelric walked down the steps into the sunken living room. When he entered, the dormant walls showed just the barest line of gold at waist-level. As his presence awoke the mansion, the line of gold brightened into the silhouette of a desert, sand below the horizon, amber sky above.

The room had scant furniture. Its large size and simplicity appealed to Kelric. Like Kurj, he was taller and more heavily muscled than a normal man. On a world with standard gravity, humans wouldn't evolve such a heavy build. His ancestors had altered themselves, their size adapted to a lower gravity world where it was an advantage rather than a liability. Kelric had never lived in a place with such gravity; for his entire life, he had needed to adapt to the how other humans lived. But the pseudo-gravity in this region of the rotating Orbiter was only 70 percent human standard, and his brother Kurj had tailored this mansion for his unusual size.

Kelric made his decision.

He went to a console by one wall. When he touched the comm panel, his aide answered. "Lieutenant Qahot here."

"Lieutenant, this is Imperator Skolia."

"Sir! Yes, sir." She almost stuttered.

"Have the Imperator's house prepared for me to move in."

"Yes, sir. Right away. Can we do anything else?"

"I'm going to the War Room." Kelric had doubts about how well he would understand its operation. He hadn't seen an ISC command center for decades. "Have its ranking officer meet me there in an hour."

"I'll notify her immediately."

"Thank you, Lieutenant." He paused. "Also—please send my wife down here."

"Right away, sir."

After signing off with the lieutenant, Kelric walked through more of the spare rooms in his stone house, with desert silhouettes bordering the square doorways and windows. At his age, near sixty now, he moved more slowly. The nanomeds that delayed his aging hadn't operated well for two decades; although he had the physique of a young man, his age showed in the lines around his eyes, the gray in his hair, and the severity of his limp. His quest to join the Triad and deactivate the Lock had nearly destroyed him; by the time he had reached Earth, he had been blind, deaf, and almost dead.

The doctors in Sweden had rebuilt him. Parts of his skeleton and internal organs were synthetic now. He had state-of-the-art nanomeds, those molecule-size laboratories that monitored health and repaired cell damage. Synthetic optics allowed him to see, and implants in his ears let him hear. He would never have the strapping health he had enjoyed in his youth, but he was as healed as modern medicine could make him.

So Kelric limped through his home. Eventually he found a long gallery. Breezes gusted through its many windows and ruffled his hair. Outside, a green hill rolled to the bottom of the valley.

A voice came from far down the gallery. "My greetings."

Kelric turned. Jeejon, his wife, was standing in the entrance. It seemed only days had passed since he had met her, but it had been much longer. He marked his recent life in the events that had so dramatically shaped it: his escape from Tarquine three months ago; his infiltration of the Lock a few days later; his escape from the Lock; his arrival four days after at the asteroid where Jeejon had lived; their desperate flight to Earth; and his recovery these past months.

Jeejon's presence warmed him. Logically, he knew that the compatibility he felt with her, what seemed like "warmth," came about because the fields produced by her brain cells had an unusually good resonance with his. He didn't care about the science. He just liked being with her.

She had strong features, with a softening around the edges. Although she had kept herself in excellent shape, as required of a taskmaker, she had never had aging treatments. Her white hair curled around her lined cheeks. Years ago she had suffered a broken nose, and the Aristo that had owned her then had never bothered to have it fixed.

Kelric found her beautiful.

He grinned. "Greetings."

Jeejon smiled, coming toward him, and they met in the center of the gallery. Taking her into his arms, he laid his cheek on her head. "Your hair smells good."

Her answer sounded like, "Hmmph."

Kelric laughed. "What, I can't compliment my wife?"

Lifting her head, she frowned, though its effect was diluted by the mischief in her gaze. "What am I supposed to think, when you go and turn into king of the universe?"

"I just command the military. I'm not king of anything."

"Pah. I was already intimidated enough when I thought you were just a provider."

He smiled. "You call this being intimidated?"

"Hmmph." She put her arms around his waist and let him pull her close. With her head against his chest, she spoke in a quieter voice. "Do you think the Hightons will deal with you as Imperator?"

"They have no choice." It would be gratifying to see them forced to treat him as an equal. He had only one hesitation: Tarquine Iquar. His responses to her had always been conflicted.

He doubted he would ever truly know whether he craved or hated her.

Tarquine stood before a door tiled in gold and black mosaics. Obsidian columns flanked the entrance, rising to a height of three meters. At their top, an arch curved in a graceful onion shape filled with stained glass. When she touched a gold tile, the door swung inward, revealing an octagonal room with black walls. Gold mosaics bordered the ceiling and framed the arched windows. Within the gold floor, points of lights glowed in star patterns. A glossy holoscreen covered the desk, and a VR system stood to one side. All in all, an impressive room.

With a satisfied nod, Tarquine entered her new office.

As she settled behind the desk, her Razers took up posts around the walls. She wasn't used to them yet. Although in the past she had traveled with guards from her security force, she hadn't felt the need for them in her own home. Now four went everywhere with her. It had to be a boring occupation; they spent hours just standing around. They apparently had extensive computer augmentation to their bodies, and at times she thought they were running calculations. The captain of this foursome had cybernetic arms that glittered with lights.

Tarquine went to work.

During first hour, just after dawn, she organized the transfer of files from her ministry office to the palace. She had spent the last few months preparing, so the transfer didn't take long. Shifting her actual duties would require more time. No precedent existed for an emperor marrying one of his ministers, so she had to start from scratch in deciding how to blend her dual offices.

To say the other ministries weren't happy with her new status was an imperial understatement. Intelligence and Trade had been the most powerful ministries, followed by Finance, Science and Technology, Foreign Affairs, Domestic Affairs, and Protocol. That had changed now. She smiled. Finance had leapt over the others.

It would be a rough ride as the other ministers adjusted to—and schemed against—the new order. She had no doubt about her ability to thrive in such an environment, but her husband was another story. He was too damned innocent. Given the chance, his enemies would pulverize him. Except now, they had to go through her. Smart boy, to make her empress. He had given her the best possible reason to see that he thrived—her own vested interest.

During second and third hour, Tarquine interviewed her new staff. The late empress, Viquara Iquar, had put together a reasonably good team, but they seemed more competent at throwing parties than doing useful work. Viquara always had liked the social aspects of her position. Tarquine had little interest in gaudy celebrations of Aristo extravagance, aside from their value as a place for making political connections. Truth be told, she had been relieved to have her wedding in an underground bunker. Whoever had tried to assassinate them had done her and Jaibriol an unintentional favor, rescuing them from the pageantry.

After lunch, Tarquine opened Viquara's personal files and investigated what her niece had been up to as empress. Viquara had access to an impressive range of files relating to the work of her husband, Ur Qox, grandfather of the present emperor. After Ur's death, when Jaibriol II had become emperor, Viquara had gained even greater access. In fact, close examination suggested Viquara had known far more about the emperor's work than had her son, the emperor.

Tarquine smiled slightly. *Naughty niece. She has grown up.* Viquara had ruled Eube after the death of Ur Qox.

Viquara's second husband, Kryx Quaelen, the previous Trade Minister, had apparently also held great power. Tarquine had never figured out why her niece married him. Although his high status befitted the widow of an emperor, he came from a questionable Line. His great-grandfather had married a Silicate Aristo rather than a woman of the Highton Aristo caste. The scandal had reverberated for decades. Although the Quaelen Line had since maintained an impeccable bloodline, many considered it tainted. Tarquine didn't care; Quaelen had been brilliant, far more accomplished than the current Trade Minister. But she would never have married him.

As the matriarch of the Iquar Line, Tarquine had been the one who supervised the investigation into Viquara's second marriage. She had found nothing untoward beyond the obvious offense of a Quaelen marrying an Iquar. But this new information bore a closer look.

Tarquine brought up her spy programs. She had been trying for decades to crack the emperor's far-flung networks. His security had always been a step ahead of hers. She could see now that the palace web wizards were even craftier than she had known. They had an amazing system here. She was thoroughly impressed. Of course, she had a better one.

As empress, she finally had access to enough of the palace networks to utilize the full extent of her spy systems. The palace defenses were soon falling to her EI crackers. So she took stock of her husband's influence.

And so her astonishment grew.

Tarquine had known the emperor had great power, but even she hadn't appreciated his reach. His influence had become so vast, it could operate of its own volition regardless of who sat on the throne. It extended into every aspect of Eubian life. He had bureaus she had never even heard of, with links to every Aristo Line that existed. Even expecting to find his Line intertwined with hers, she was stunned by the depth of his infiltration into Iquar affairs.

Nor did his influence extend only to Eube; his merchant empire, anonymous investments, pirate fleets, and private contacts spread among the Skolians and Allieds. No other Aristo empire was so vast or strong.

"Gods," Tarquine muttered. All that glorious power concentrated in the hands of an inexperienced boy. She doubted Jaibriol even came close to comprehending what he had inherited.

No matter. She did.

Late that afternoon, Tarquine sat sprawled in her chair, her long legs stretched out. She was glaring at a holomap, which rotated serenely above her desk. According to her research, this map of the palace was missing entire rooms and corridors. She would bet anything someone had altered it to hide secret chambers and corridors.

"I'll admit, it isn't the most aesthetic floor plan," a deep voice said. "But it can't be that bad."

Tarquine looked up. Her husband stood in the doorway, leaning his aesthetically pleasing self against one column of the horseshoe arch.

"Greetings, Husband." It felt odd to say. She hadn't wanted a husband. She still didn't. Given that this one came with more power than anyone else in the history of the human race, though, she could live with it.

Besides, Jaibriol had his own charm. For all that he acted the emperor in the presence of other Hightons, his behavior was too perfect. Alone with her, he let his *newness* show. Warmth was not a word one associated with Hightons, yet he seemed to have it, even if he did pretend an arctic front in public.

Jaibriol crossed her office, dismissing her guards with an imperial wave of his hand. Tarquine almost laughed. She wondered if she was the only one who realized he was faking his mannerisms. Clearly his mother hadn't steeped him in Highton protocol. Tarquine didn't blame her. Protocol ranked about as high on her list of desirable activities as eating hospital food.

The last Razer closed the door behind him as he left. Smart guard. Tarquine languidly rose to her feet. She didn't know how she appeared, but Jaibriol's face turned that charming shade of red it often did when they were in private.

He came around her desk and, with no preamble, pulled her into his arms. "Come here." His voice was husky.

"I've work to do." Remembering herself, she added, "Your Highness."

"Why do you keep calling me that?" He stroked her hair back from her face. "It's too formal."

She sighed. "You must learn your role better."

His look of welcome vanished. "What the hell does that mean?"

So touchy. Sometimes he acted more like a provider than a Highton. Technically her job as empress consisted of catering to his whims and making him feel good. Well, helping him survive ought to make him feel better.

"If I call you Jai," she said, "it will hurt your esteem among your staff."

A wicked gleam came into his eyes. "Then I might have to call you Tarquiette."

"Good gods, I should hope not."

He kissed her neck. "It's late. We should go sleep."

"Saints above. It's only seventh hour." She pushed on his shoulders. "I won't sleep until tomorrow night."

His smile turned drowsy. "Then I must make you tired."

"Ah, Jaibriol." She wished he would stop looking so appealing. She couldn't drop her work. Besides, sleeping with one's husband in the middle of the day was anomalous, and Hightons never indulged in anomalous behavior.

Of course, most Hightons didn't care for their spouses either. Marriages were hereditary, political, and financial contracts. If you wanted warmth, you went to your providers. Like Kelric. Except she wouldn't think about Kelric, damn it. He had escaped and had the bad manners to make himself Imperator.

Jaibriol confused her. He acted like an Aristo in public and a provider in private. He was the perfect fantasy, a Highton of impeccable pedigree, the most elevated of all, yet when they were alone, his passion blazed. No Highton man with normal socialization would show such ardor. Aristos made an art out of the oxymoron "aloof intimacy." Going with him now would be irregular—but pleasant, she had to admit. Odd, to think of one's husband as pleasant.

As Tarquine put her arms around him, she reminded herself that they had married to strengthen their power bases. Their motives were pragmatic. Concepts like "affection" had no place in this.

None.

She would not fall in love with her husband.

23

Discrepancies

Jai strode along a shaded path with Robert. His Razers accompanied them even in these secluded woods that separated the private wing of his palace from his offices. Today he had a meeting with his advisers to discuss protests lodged by Azar Taratus about the insurance rulings against him. It amazed him that the admiral could have committed such obvious fraud, yet remain so unrepentantly convinced he should suffer no consequences. Even more fantastic, most Hightons agreed with him. Jai wished he could throw them all in reform school.

Right now, though, it was Robert who had him worried. "Platinum Sector?" Jai asked. "I don't understand. I never made any decree about their asteroid mines."

Robert looked as if he were about to jump off a cliff. "You did make a—a sort of decree, Most Glorious Highness?" He turned his statements into questions when he was nervous. "Actually, it was organized by your Office of Protocol? After someone leaked Minister Iquar's financial statement to the media?"

"Do you mean the press conference I gave?"

"Yes, Your Highness."

"But I didn't make any decrees." Jaibriol regarded him uneasily. "I just explained Tarquine's platinum investment."

He hadn't actually explained it all; he had "neglected" to mention that she used her position as Finance Minister to manipulate the cost of platinum, letting her buy up large amounts at an artificially low price. Although Jaibriol resented having to cover up her misdeeds, his advisers said he had no choice. Their growing alarm didn't surprise him; his charming wife was turning out to be even more crooked than Azar Taratus. She was just better at not getting caught.

"You gave a superb speech, Most Gracious Highness."

Jai really, really didn't like it when they called him "gracious." It always meant he was in trouble. "But?"

"Superb," Robert repeated. "Including—uh—your statement, 'The Palace Committee on Ethics and Morals will seek out and remedy irregularities.' "

"What's wrong with that?"

"It is rather vague."

"Most Highton statements are."

"Yes, certainly, you are right." Robert cleared his throat. "But, uh, it seems the Diamond Coalition has less understanding of such nuances than yourself."

Jai squinted at him. "What 'less understanding'?"

"It seems they have misinterpreted your statement to mean you will prosecute anyone found tampering with the price of platinum."

"Ah, hell." Jai drew him to a stop. His Razers also halted, far enough away to maintain the distance he insisted they keep. "Let me guess. They want an investigation into my wife's platinum deals."

Robert looked apologetic. "I'm afraid so."

"Damn."

"An apt evaluation, sir."

"Now what do I do?"

His question had been rhetorical, but Robert answered. "Her Most Beauteous Highness, the empress, might have thoughts on the matter."

Jai nearly choked. " 'Her Most Beauteous Highness'? Robert, have you ever said that to her face?" He could just imagine her reaction. It would be on par with calling her "pretty" or "dainty."

"No, sir," Robert admitted. "Never."

"I would suggest you don't. She might take it wrong."

"I would greatly regret if anyone mistook my admiration." He blanched. "Especially the empress."

Jai thoroughly understood his reaction. "Especially her."

"She is quite a woman."

"That's one way to put it." Jai headed back to the private wing of the palace they had just left. His meeting would have to wait. "Come on."

Robert hurried after him. "Where are we going?"

Jai dryly said, "To see my beauteous wife."

High Judge Calope Muze paced in her private chamber, her robes rustling as she walked back and forth. Azile Xir, the Minister of Intelligence, sat sprawled in a smartchair, watching her.

"The High Court cannot indefinitely avoid an appeal," Calope said. She would have to let Raziquon's kin have a hearing. She couldn't put them off any longer.

Azile crossed his arms. "Some appeals deserve nothing."

Exasperation threatened to make Calope direct. Azile was as fond of Sunrise as his father, and it compromised his judgment. He was also angry that ESComm had kept his father in custody. But he knew perfectly well the situation with his father was different from what Jaibriol had done with Raziquon. Putting the Highton lord in an actual prison was tantamount to treating him like a taskmaker. A slave. They needed proof of Raziquon's involvement in Sunrise's abduction and they didn't have it. Period. Even if they had uncovered evidence, it would be folly to incarcerate a Highton. Jaibriol seemed bent on making enemies.

Calope knew she had to pardon Raziquon. But then what? If Jaibriol rescinded the pardon, it would further antagonize his enemies. If this kept up, ESComm might take drastic action, seeking to put their own emperor on the throne. Such an upheaval now, after the war, would be a disaster.

She stopped pacing. "The perfection of the Hightons is in their union of mind and purpose." The problem with Jaibriol III wasn't really his inexperience. He wasn't inept, he was *unpredictable.*

Azile unfolded himself from his chair and walked over to her. "It depends on whose mind and purpose."

"ESComm has the power to assert both, if it feels threatened."

Although Azile frowned, he didn't refute the statement. "As High Judge, you serve the emperor."

She didn't miss how he phrased it: *serve the emperor,* not *serve Eube* or *serve justice.* But what Jaibriol wanted would only hurt him. If he had any sense, he wouldn't undermine her efforts to avert a crisis between the palace and ESComm.

Unfortunately, she feared he had a very different view of the matter.

Sunrise served Corbal dinner in a dining room of the Xir mansion. While he reclined on plush rugs among scattered pillows, she placed a small table in front of him, black with gold edges, and set it with pastries filled with nuts and covered by sweet sauces.

Corbal watched her pour the wine. Tonight, she matched her name. The chains on her ankles were dark blue, like the sky before dawn. Their bells chimed. Her skirt, which fit low on her hips, was a translucent blue, as when dawn washed out the night. Under it, her G-string shimmered gold. The chains of her halter were the deep pink of dawn, and she had braided topazes into her gold hair. Her blue eyes matched her skirt and her eyelashes sparkled with glitter. The overall effect took his breath away.

Even now, months after her return, he couldn't make peace with the sheer intensity of his relief. When she had vanished, the bottom had dropped out of his life. He didn't understand the ferocity of the emotions that gripped him. Hightons didn't experience such passions. Having her here now, with him, soothed the unnatural fury that had gripped him since Raziquon had kidnapped her and framed him for treason. Jaibriol had chosen well when he threw Raziquon in prison. Corbal hoped the lord rotted there.

When he smiled, Sunrise blushed and averted her gaze. Corbal sighed. Why after almost three years, did that simple gesture still have the power to make him want her so much?

"Shall I dance for you?" she asked.

"Yes." His voice was low. "Do that."

She rose gracefully and walked to a console, where she chose one of his favorites, a mesmerizing work of music, its beat steady under a haunting melody played by pipes. She seemed to know he wanted to hear it. Perhaps she took it from his mind in that mysterious way of empaths.

She swayed with the beat, undulating. Her skirt fluttered around her thighs. Watching, Corbal wanted her with a depth that disturbed him. It went beyond desire. She affected him on some level he didn't understand.

He spoke hoarsely. "Come here."

She padded across the carpets and knelt next to him. Pulling her down on the rug, he kissed her hard. He wasn't a gentle man; a century of transcending had seared away any capacity he had for tenderness. But he tried not to hurt her as he stretched her out in the pillows. Even knowing she produced synthetic pheromones, he wasn't immune to those chemical cocktails. It had to be chemicals. That was the only way he could explain her effect on him.

He wanted to take her the way he had taken providers all his life. But he could never hurt her. He gritted his teeth. He hated feeling guilty. He had a life of privilege. He liked it. He deserved it. He was, after all, a Highton, overlord of the Xir Line and kin to the Line of Qox. He didn't aspire to be an upstanding member of his community. He had no interest in building his character or developing integrity. He liked being a hedonist, with his relationships no more demanding than this pleasure girl who catered to his every whim. Guilt had no place in his life.

But damn it all, he felt it.

Reluctant, he eased his hold on Sunrise. He wondered if he even knew how to be gentle. Not really. But for her sake, he would try in their lovemaking. At least, he thought "love" was the correct term. He had never experienced it before, certainly not with his wife, may her glacial heart rest in peace and never freeze him again. Perhaps he was wrong in thinking he felt it with Sunrise. Maybe he just had indigestion.

He lifted his head. "Do you know my thoughts right now?"

"A little." She traced her finger across his lips. "You're thinking of making love, yes?" Then she drew him into another kiss.

Corbal put aside his thoughts and submerged himself in the heady ocean of pleasure she created for him. Later, as they lay in the pillows, he tried to sleep. But he couldn't forget how Raziquon had hurt Sunrise. Corbal scowled. He should maintain the proper separation of his emotions from his pleasure.

Separation, hell. He wanted to shove Raziquon inside the thrusters of a starship and fire up the engines. Someone in the prison ought to make the universe a better place and assassinate him. Corbal doubted it would happen, though; Raziquon would soon go free, now that his appeal had reached the High Judge.

He had thought Sunrise was asleep, curled against him, but now she spoke sleepily. "His mind opened."

He slid his hand across her stomach. "He?"

"Lord Raziquon."

Corbal tensed, knowing how much pain the memories caused her. "You need never worry about him again."

She sighed, half asleep. "I felt his mind."

"I know." After she had come home, he had discovered he couldn't ask if she had spied on Raziquon's mind, not when it meant she would have to relive that experience. And yet, on her own, she had spoken. He had held her close, offering comfort when she cried. It was a strange experience.

He wasn't used to comforting anyone. She hadn't told him anything he didn't already know, but it didn't matter. That she tried for him of her own choice, despite what it cost her, meant more than he knew how to say.

Sunrise yawned against his chest. "His platinum mine."

He blinked, realizing she had meant *his mine opened.* Her mind must have relaxed as she drowsed, letting her remember more. "Raziquon has a mine?"

"Hmmm . . . platinum."

"I didn't know he had mining interests."

"Cheat emperor . . ." She burrowed into the pillows. "Never reported income . . ."

Raziquon owned illegal mines? He kissed her temple. "Sunrise, you are a gem."

Asleep now, she didn't respond.

Her news might mean nothing. If Raziquon had failed to include the revenues from just one mine in his financial reports to the government, it would cause little trouble. But then, he had never known Raziquon to do anything small.

Corbal grinned. This could prove useful.

The War Room was located in the hull of the Orbiter. Its amphitheatre contained many consoles, VR rigs, and holomaps, as well as robot arms that carried telops throughout the area. High above the amphitheatre, a massive arm suspended a command chair in a dome lit with holographic stars. Conduits from all over the War Room fed into the blocky chair—and into the brain of whoever sat in that great mechanical throne.

Kelric entered the War Room on the walkway that circled the holodome and summoned the chair. The amphitheatre below hummed with activity: officers monitoring ISC forces, telops in the newly birthed psiberweb, aides running errands, cranes moving through the air. When the chair swung over to Kelric, many people looked up. He felt their surprise. It was as if a ghost had entered the War Room. No one had sat in this chair since the death of the last Imperator, his sister, Soz, and before her, his half-brother, Kurj.

Kelric knew he looked like Kurj. A living ghost.

Kelric settled into the throne. As it returned to the center of the dome, its exoskeleton clicked prongs into his ankles, wrists, spine, and neck, linking to the biomech web inside his body. Impersonal puzzlement came from the chair as it registered its new user. The hood lowered and extended a spiderweb of threads into his scalp. Data poured into Bolt, the oldest node in Kelric's spine, and Bolt organized and shunted it to the cluster of new nodes, leaving Kelric free to think. As his mind became sensitized to the chair, and through it, to the webs networking the War Room, he could trace lines of thought in the amphitheatre.

This felt right. He belonged here.

The chair resembled the one in the Lock. He would never forget. He had met an emperor there who claimed to want peace talks. Kelric found it hard to believe Qox genuinely wished to negotiate peace. The emperor had to have other motivations.

"Bolt?" he said.

A voice came out of a comm mesh on the arm of his chair. "My greetings, Kelric."

"How do you like the chair?"

"It is exhilarating."

Kelric smiled. Although Bolt was part of his brain, it had arranged to use the chair's comm when Kelric linked the throne to the biomech web in his body. Bolt hadn't always been able to perform such feats; over the decades it had reconfigured itself for new tasks and even emotions, though how it managed that, Kelric didn't know.

His biomech web also linked to the gauntlets he had found in the Lock and wore all the time now. He had little idea how the gauntlets worked, but he suspected they involved some type of machine intelligence in Kyle space. He couldn't be sure; his interactions with it came only as undefined impressions. But this much he knew: the gauntlets were at least five thousand years old.

"What can I do for you?" Bolt asked.

"I was wondering how the peace talks were shaping up."

"Our people are verifying with the Allieds that the talks will go forward even though the Ruby Dynasty is no longer on Earth."

That didn't surprise Kelric. Now that his family was loose again, the Allieds were more determined than ever to have Skolia and Eube talk peace. "Have you found any more information on Jaibriol Qox?"

"A bit. Apparently he is eighteen, not seventeen."

"Why did the news services say he was seventeen?"

"The error was introduced on Earth, after the war. His high school listed him as five months younger than the age he gives now."

"Five months?" Kelric raised an eyebrow. "That would be quite a feat. It would mean he wasn't born until eleven months after his father disappeared."

"Which is impossible."

"Not if his mother conceived artificially."

"Such a procedure would be contrary to Highton mores."

"They store their genetic material, so it can't be unheard of." The empress would have been desperate if her husband disappeared without an heir. It could explain the secrecy surrounding Jaibriol III's childhood. Hell, maybe the Hightons had been playing with genes, trying to make a telepath. Kelric couldn't shake his feeling that the youth he had met in the Lock had been a psion. He couldn't imagine the Hightons accepting a provider as their emperor, though.

"It is improbable but not impossible that she conceived artificially," Bolt acknowledged. "In any event, his official age is eighteen."

Kelric rubbed his chin. "Let me see if I have this straight. Nineteen years ago Ur Qox was emperor of Eube. His son and heir, Jaibriol the Second, secretly married and sired a son, Jaibriol the Third. Before the boy's birth, Jaibriol the

Second was supposedly killed trying to escape our military. Fifteen years later, Ur Qox dies. Not long after that, Jaibriol the Second miraculously reappears. About two years later Jaibriol the Second dies in the war. A few months later, his son, Jaibriol the Third, shows up to claim the throne."

"That about sums it up," Bolt said.

"It's a bizarre story."

"But valid, apparently."

"You know, if the Traders weren't such fanatics about verifying their bloodlines, I wouldn't believe all these Jaibriols were the real thing." He pushed his hand through his hair. "We know too little about Jaibriol the Third. If we misjudge his motivations, the talks could fail." They would probably fail anyway, but he wanted at least to try.

"I had the impression he was sincere when you met him in the Lock," Bolt said. "Why would he let you escape, otherwise?"

"I don't know." Kelric thought back to his meeting with the youth. "He didn't talk to me the way Hightons talk with one another. He was too direct."

"He would consider you a provider. Not an equal."

"That's why it was so strange. He treated me like an equal." Kelric thought of the other Hightons he knew. "He's hard to fathom. Highton brains work differently than ours. Their thought processes are like fractals."

"He might not think like other Hightons," Bolt pointed out. "He grew up in isolation."

"That assumes their thought patterns are cultural rather than genetic. My guess is that it's both." Kelric tapped his finger on the comm. "Bolt, widen your search. Check every web you can reach no matter how small. Do a running comparison of him with our files on other Aristos. Look for patterns I can use to predict his behavior and motivations."

"I will need to access interstellar webs, trillions of them, many still off the psiberweb. It will take time."

"You have until the peace talks. About a month."

"I can work with that."

"Good."

Bolt's mention of the psiberweb gave Kelric pause. Only two people now powered the former Triad that created the web: himself and Dehya. Although it had been many tendays since the death of his father, and though they had all known the span of his life was coming to an end, Kelric still found it hard to accept that he was gone. Eldrinson Althor Valdoria had passed away quietly, from old age, surrounded by the people who loved him, his wife and children. It meant more to Kelric than he knew how to express that he had been able to see his father before Eldrinson died. Now Kelric would carry on for him, protecting the family, their people, and the Skolian Imperialate.

So Kelric went to work, integrating his mind with the War Room. If Skolia and Eube found their way to peace, he might never need this room in its full capability. Yet as much as he hoped they could establish a treaty, he doubted it would happen. If they had to go to war again, he would mourn the lost peace—but he would be ready.

24

Secrets

Lake Mirellazile stretched like a silver sheet in a forested valley of the Jaizire Mountains. The sun burned in the stonewashed blue of the sky. Centuries ago, this rocky planet had supported no life, but Eube Qox had seen its promise. Biosculpting had produced a fresh, crisp world well suited to humans.

A beach of glittering black sand curved along the lake. Jai sat on a metallic blanket there, watching breakers roll into the shore. On a world like Eube's Glory, with its fourteen moons, even the lakes had wild tides.

The body of water took its name from Mirella, the largest moon as seen from Glory. Right now Mirella hung near the horizon, bloodred. Eube Qox had named the moon for his wife, the first empress, and surfaced the satellite with synthetic carnelian. It wasn't actually the largest moon; that distinction went to Zara, named for the second empress, the wife of Jaibriol I. In her honor, he had surfaced it in gold. Although Zara was four times farther away than Mirella, it appeared half the size in the sky. Right now it hung above Mirella, almost full. They made a startling pair, gold and red against the blue sky.

Viquara, the third largest moon, wasn't visible. Named for the third empress, it had a diamond surface. The fourth largest moon, G4, was reserved for the wife of Jaibriol II. With his father's death, it fell to Jai to name it for the Highton mother who had supposedly birthed him. Although he could never acknowledge his true mother, he would find a name that honored her.

Jai couldn't see the fifth largest moon, G5, but he had no doubt about its new name: Tarquine. How to resurface it was another question. Zara was already diamond, but many other hard, brilliant materials existed. Maybe he would use a steel-diamond composite. Perhaps he should ask Tarquine. Traditionally an emperor made the decision and then told his wife, but Jai valued his survival over Qox tradition.

He wondered what his descendants would do when they ran out of moons, or how the last few empresses would feel about having the small ones. It might behoove future emperors to create some bigger moons. The sky of Glory could end up as crowded as a starport concourse.

Leaning back on his hands, he gazed down the beach. A woman was coming toward him, accompanied by four Razers. A breeze ruffled her hair. The sensual quality of her walk came naturally, so much so that she had no sense of its effect. It wasn't that no one had ever told her, but rather that she simply didn't care. His wife was the antithesis of an ingénue, going so far in the other direction that she came full circle. Her complete disinterest in her own sensuality aroused him far more than any deliberate seduction.

When Tarquine reached him, she bowed.

"Join me," Jai invited.

Tarquine sat near him while her Razers faded into the scenery. She said nothing, just gazed at the lake. It stretched for several kilometers, with fern trees swaying on its shores. Vines hung in loops from their branches, blooming with delicate gold and red balls. On every side, blue-gray mountains cut sharply against the sky.

"A beautiful day," Jai said.

She slanted him a glance. "A good day for me to further

the glory of your empire, Husband, by doing my job. As opposed to sitting around sunbathing."

Jai imagined her sleek and dripping with water, lolling in the sun. "Everyone needs rest."

To his surprise, Tarquine smiled. "The way you look at me sometimes, I wonder if you realize I'm not food."

"I would never dare call you a sweet. You might pulverize me." He was only half joking.

She actually laughed. "Ah, well. It is true, few would put Eube's Finance Minister and sugar in the same thought."

"Too much sweetness can be cloying."

Tarquine considered him as if he were an impudent young man she had just met. "You prefer tart?"

He moved closer. "I do indeed."

"You have a one-track mind, Husband."

"I can't help it, with you as my wife."

She sighed. "Jaibriol, you are impossible. I should think you would have more reason to send an imperial summons for me than for us to begin the night early."

Jai was tempted to tell her he could think of no better reason, but he held back. He could only push her so far before her annoyance at having her work interrupted would overcome whatever contributed to her good nature at the moment. And right now he needed that good nature.

"It would seem," he said, "that one other matter would have to be attended first, before we enjoy the night."

"One other matter?"

"A financial matter."

"I deal with many financial matters."

"A platinum matter."

Tarquine frowned. "Perhaps you should be holding this discussion with the merchants from Platinum Sector. They are the ones who can't mine enough metal from their asteroids."

"Actually, I was thinking of Sapphires."

Her good humor had vanished. "Cheap rocks."

"Cheap platinum."

"Perhaps the merchants in Sapphire Sector should learn how to bargain better."

Jaibriol scowled at her. "No merchants, Sapphire or otherwise, could hold their own against a ministry that uses its financial influence to drive down the price and then buys up the available product."

Tarquine didn't look the least bit remorseful. "Such a ministry would be formidable indeed. If it existed."

"Such a ministry could cause me a lot of grief."

"Or bring you great wealth."

"I already have great wealth." Jai wished he could make her understand. "What I don't have, Tarquine, is Aristo support. Now the Diamond Aristos in Sapphire Sector want me to investigate the financial activities of a certain ministry."

Her look turned incredulous. "They dare suggest you investigate your own wife? Perhaps they would like to dine with our dear friend Raziquon."

"For saints' sake, Tarquine. I can't keep throwing Aristos in prison."

"Why not? A lot of them belong there."

How could he get through to her? "Many would say the same about a minister who used—or should I say abused—her power to cheat an entire sector."

"The Diamond Coalition wants something from you, Jai." She rubbed the back of her neck. "You have to figure out what it is and give the bankers enough to make them think they worked a good bargain."

That caught Jai by surprise. Corbal had told few people he was forming a partnership with the Diamonds, and Tarquine certainly wasn't one of them. "You know about the Coalition?"

"Of course. Corbal is making a bank with them."

Jai couldn't hold back his frustration. "He's worked on this for years. I've managed to ruin it in a few months."

"You haven't ruined it." She watched him under half-closed lids. "He is repairing the breach even as we speak."

"He is?" Corbal had given him no hint.

She tapped her long finger on his cheek. "The Coalition is testing you. Seeing how far they can push."

"It's gone beyond that. They want an investigation."

"You give in too easily."

He wanted to groan. "You don't have the least bit of regret for what you did, do you?"

"I've done nothing, dear husband."

"Yes, well, the nothing you've done is going to blow up in our faces."

"That depends on how you deal with it."

"And now you're going to say I should refuse their demands, right? I can't. It will only antagonize them more."

"I would never suggest such a thing."

Jai blinked. "You wouldn't?"

"Of course not." She smiled, resembling a cat that had caught a bird. "You must, of course, have an investigation."

Jai shifted uneasily. "Why must I, of course, do that?"

"When your investigation turns up no wrongdoing by your beloved and loyal wife, the Diamond Coalition will have made an inexcusable mistake."

"And what, pray tell, is that?"

"They would have wrongly accused me."

"So?"

She laughed softly. "You are so green."

"Fine." Jai glared at her. "See if you can dye me a different color. Enlighten me."

"Reputation is everything. Appearance means more than fact. A false accusation is a severe offense. A Line making such an accusation against the empress would suffer enormous shame."

For all its bizarre logic, it actually made sense with what he had seen of Aristo society. "That's all fine, Tarquine, but you missed one small point."

"And what might that be?"

"The accusation isn't false."

"Oh, that." She waved her hand. "It only needs to look false."

Jai couldn't believe this conversation. "The bigger the cover-up, the harder we will fall when it is discovered."

"You are Qox. I am Iquar. We do not fall."

Jai didn't know whether to be appalled or awed by her attitude. "Gods help me, the day I married you."

She smiled blithely. "They did indeed."

The conference center in the countryside outside Paris startled Kelric. He had never associated beautiful architecture with the home world of humanity. He had thought Earth's people too pragmatic for such art, but apparently he had been wrong. The building soared on its hillside, an ethereal framework of gold with so many windows that it was more glass than metal. It sparkled in the streaming sunlight from Sol. The sky arched above, a heartrending shade of blue that he recognized at an instinctual level, though neither he nor his ancestors had lived on Earth for six thousand years.

He was visiting the center as a virtual simulacrum; his body remained in his chair in the War Room, linked through the psiberweb to a command center on Earth, which relayed the signal to the Allied United Centre in Paris where the peace talks would take place.

The air in front of Kelric shimmered. The light formed into his aunt Dehya, the Ruby Pharaoh. She walked to him, her hair swinging around her body. "My greeting, Kelric."

He answered in English. "Hello."

She smiled. "I didn't know you spoke Earth languages."

"Only a few words," he admitted, switching into Iotic. He motioned around them. "What do you think?"

Dehya spoke wistfully. "It's so incredibly beautiful." She indicated the building. "It is hard to imagine we will meet with Hightons here."

"I suppose the symbolism is good. I doubt the location really matters, though."

"You don't believe they're coming to talk peace." She didn't make it a question.

"I don't know what to think." He began walking up the

hill with her. "The more I learn about Jaibriol the Third, the less sense he makes to me."

"Why?"

"He doesn't act like a Highton."

She considered him. "You are the only one of us who can make that judgment with any reasonable accuracy."

"That isn't saying much."

Dehya fell silent. When she finally spoke, her words jolted. "She is empress now. Will that matter to you?"

"No." Tarquine Iquar was the last person he wanted to discuss.

"You're sure?"

No, he wasn't sure. He had no intention of admitting it. Instead he said, "In the past, the Traders have been false with us. They want to woo Earth as an ally, so they pretend to negotiate peace, then blame our bellicose nature when the talks fail."

She spoke dryly. "Hightons thrive on misdirection."

"Something about this emperor just doesn't seem right." Kelric smiled wryly. "Actually it *does* seem right. That's the problem. He comes across as honest."

She gave a soft laugh. "You're right, that doesn't sound Highton." Her hair swirled in the breeze as they walked. Had they been on a real hill, they would have already reached the top, but Kelric had set the simulation to let him wander, so it kept extending the hill.

"He lived on Earth for over two years," Dehya said. "He probably learned their customs."

"I suppose." Her guarded responses puzzled him. Then again, it was no wonder if she had conflicted feelings, knowing that Eldrin, her consort, was free only because the Traders exchanged him for Jaibriol III.

"How is Eldrin?" he asked.

She stared off in the distance. "He is fine."

Kelric wondered if he could ever fully express his joy at having his brother safe. "I am glad he is home."

"Yes." She let a wealth of emotion show in that one word:

gratitude, relief, love, and an underlying wish for vengeance against the Traders who had hurt the man she loved. Her manner was exactly what he would have expected. And yet it seemed off somehow. Her simulacrum could show whatever she wanted; she could easily hide her true mood.

Dehya glanced at him. "You stare at me most intently."

"You know more than you say."

She made an exasperated noise. "People always say this. 'You know more.' You would think my life was full of secrets. I'm afraid the reality is far more boring."

Kelric had no doubt that his aunt, whom many called the "Shadow Pharaoh," had more than her share of secrets. "I need to know. It could make a difference in how I deal with Qox."

"I don't know anything." She drew him to a stop. "But I've wondered if a provider raised Jaibriol the Third rather than a Highton. It would explain his behavior."

Although similar thoughts had occurred to Kelric, he found it hard to credit. "So where was the empress?"

"Dead, maybe."

He frowned. "That boy has an odd history."

Too odd. It made Kelric uneasy.

She ran through the night. Tree ferns blocked her way, and she plunged through them, scraping her skin. Her breath came in gasps. Still she ran. Raziquon was so close—

Sunrise sat up with a gasp, straining to scream, but she couldn't make a sound. Gradually her pulse calmed. She was home. *Home.* Corbal lay next to her, sleeping. It was only a nightmare.

As she lay down, Corbal stirred. "What is it?"

"Nothing."

He pulled her close. "I will make him pay for what he did to you."

"Cori—"

"Shhh." He laid his finger on her lips. "I have a plan. Don't worry."

Sunrise tried to sleep, but long after Corbal's breathing had deepened into a steady rhythm, she remained awake. For some reason, she felt convinced Corbal's plan for vengeance would end up hurting him far more than Raziquon. *Why? Why?* She had to delve into her memories of Raziquon, hated as they were, and understand what disturbed her.

She couldn't let Raziquon win.

25

Nanomeds

Four pirate frigates ambushed the Skolian yacht when the ship dropped out of inversion into normal space. Everyone knew the Eubian military denied such pirates existed, but the weapons on the frigates clearly came straight from ESComm.

Willex Seabreak owned the yacht. Born to a prosperous Skolian family, he had accrued even more wealth by designing virtual reality vacations for bored socialites. He had a good life—until the raiders showed up. They surrounded his yacht, matching speed as the ships hurtled through space. The yacht's defenses were nothing compared to the firepower on the frigates. Seabreak took stock of his situation and made the only possible decision. He surrendered.

As Seabreak decelerated his ship, he told his passengers what was happening and asked them to gather in the lounge of the yacht. He tried to sound assured, but fear made him terse. He had more people onboard than usual: his girlfriend Saria, three other couples, and several entertainers, as well as his crew.

The computer system on one of the frigates infiltrated the yacht's system and took over navigation, leaving Seabreak unable to pilot his craft. His presence on the bridge didn't really matter then; he was needed more to provide moral support for his passengers. He joined them in the lounge, and everyone waited, their faces pale, all with the same question: Would the raiders take any of them to sell?

Standing next to Saria, Seabreak held her hand. The pirates had slowed the yacht's rotation so they could dock with it, but they had left enough motion to create a light pseudo-gravity. Sweat beaded Seabreak's forehead and dripped down his sides, under his shirt. The Traders didn't need task-makers: they had plenty. They wanted providers. The combination of mutated genes that produced empaths and telepaths was both rare and difficult to replicate in a lab. So the Traders abducted Skolian psions.

Saria watched him with a terrified gaze, and Seabreak swallowed against the lump in his throat. Her tawny hair, large green eyes, and angel's face turned heads even in this age when anyone with a good income could fine-tune themselves to whatever ideal they admired. But he loved her because she responded with such sensitivity to other people. It wouldn't surprise him if she was an empath. She might be exactly what the Traders sought.

After the ships docked, Seabreak left the lounge and went to meet his unwanted guests at the airlock. A large group boarded: three men with shimmering black hair and rust-red eyes, and ten mercenaries, hardened men and women in body armor.

The tallest of the red-eyed trio appeared to be in charge. With a mocking smile, he spoke to Seabreak in Skolian Flag. "My greetings, Captain."

"You're in Skolian territory." Seabreak doubted they cared about the legality of their actions, but he had to try. "You're violating the Halstaad Code and Skolian law."

"But we aren't at war, my friend. As for your laws—" The man shrugged. "I'm sure we're in Eubian territory. By our laws, that makes you all escaped slaves."

Seabreak stiffened. "We're nowhere near your territory."

The pirate waved his hand. "Would you care to tell my frigates? I'm sure their crews would be happy to debate with you." Malice lurked in his smile. "Your choice of weapons."

Seabreak knew his yacht couldn't survive a battle with the frigates. "We've no wish for violence."

"Well, then." The Trader lifted his hand as if inviting him to dinner. "Shall we meet your passengers?"

Clenching his jaw, Seabreak led them to the passenger areas, aware of the raiders assessing him. They could have his ship and all the wealth onboard. Hell, they could have the codes to his accounts. He just prayed they didn't take Saria or anyone else.

The pirates strode into the lounge as if they owned the ship, which for all practical purposes they did. They were well trained and didn't seem at all bothered by the low gravity. They lined everyone along the bulkheads, men on one side, women on the other. When several passengers balked, the mercenaries drew their spikers, guns that could set a person's nerves on fire with pain. No one protested further.

The raider captain walked along the line of women. When he stopped at Saria, Seabreak's pulse surged. He stepped forward, and one of the mercenaries raised his spiker. Seabreak looked at the gun, then at Saria. If they tried to take her, he would do whatever it took to stop them, spikers or no spikers.

The captain appraised Saria as if she were a rare vase he was considering for purchase. She met his gaze, her face red. Putting his finger under her chin, he turned her head from side to side, then stepped back and looked her over—a woman in a silver jumpsuit that did nothing to hide her spectacular figure. In the past, Seabreak had loved that outfit, but no more. He wanted to kill the captain for the way he was surveying her.

"Pretty," the captain said.

Seabreak tensed, preparing to lunge. But the captain continued down the line, looking over the other women. Then he moved on to the men against the other bulkhead. When he stopped in front of Tandy Marzin, Seabreak began to worry again. Tandy was an athlete, obviously strong enough for hard labor, possibly a lucrative find for the Traders.

But the captain went on. He paused at Seabreak, and Seabreak met his gaze, defiant. He barely hid his exhale of relief when the raider continued down the line. The captain also stopped in front of Jacques Ardoise, who stared back, unable to disguise his fear. Lithe and blond, with blue eyes, Jacques was a musician. Although women found him attractive, Seabreak couldn't fathom it. The young fellow looked fragile. At least that benefited him here; the raiders probably couldn't auction him for much.

The captain apparently had the same thought. He turned away and went back to the other raiders. They conferred quietly, and one of the men indicated Saria. The captain shook his head. Seabreak wasn't sure what he said, but it sounded like, "I've seen better."

Seabreak had never been so glad to have someone find his girlfriend less desirable than he did. They could think whatever they wanted as long as they left her alone.

Finally the captain turned to them all. "We will take the yacht. You may have the lifeboats. Go where you want."

Seabreak's relief was so intense it threatened to make him dizzy. He caught Saria's gaze across the cabin and she managed a shaky smile, her eyes luminous with tears.

Then the raider said, "Except for one of you."

Seabreak froze. No. *Gods, no.*

The captain motioned at Jacques. "You come with us."

"*What?*" The color drained from Jacques's face. "No!"

Seabreak blinked. Jacques? Belatedly, he saw the flaw in his reasoning. Why would the Traders need slaves for hard labor? Robots were cheaper and stronger. His own interest in beautiful women had made him overlook the obvious; the raiders could get just as much for a beautiful man, especially if he was an empath.

The artistic gifts that made Jacques such a dramatic performer might well arise from empathic ability. The traits would have to come from both parents, given the recessive nature of the genes. Jacques had listed them in his employment application: his father was a stardocker on the Skolian world Jalliope, and his mother had been a musician and Earth citizen in a place called France before she married his father and became a Skolian. The few times Seabreak had met them, he had noticed their sensitivity to each other. It wouldn't surprise him if they and their son were empaths.

When the mercenaries closed on Jacques, Seabreak and the others attacked. It was stupid and desperate, but he had no intention of standing by while Traders kidnapped one of his employees. A female mercenary easily held the struggling musician while the raiders spiked the prisoners. Seabreak screamed as the serum attacked his nerves. Dimly, as he convulsed on the deck, he saw the raiders drag Jacques out of the lounge. Then someone shot him a second time and the excruciating pain became his entire universe.

Gradually he became aware again, the agony ebbing enough for him to think. Mercenaries were carrying him into a lifeboat. They loaded him into the pilot's chair and strapped his passengers into seats behind him, including Saria. As the other raiders set the autopilot, the captain swiveled Seabreak around to face him. "Leave now, and we'll let you live. Fight us, and we will kill you. Understand?"

The spiker had induced a partial paralysis, but Seabreak managed to croak, "Yes."

"Good." The captain jabbed the controls and the engine roared. But before he went out the airlock, he turned back to Seabreak. "You can tell the boy's family he was taken by the Line of Xir." Enmity glittered in his eyes. "You remember. Corbal Xir."

Tarquine almost missed the bombshell.

She found it in a report on Jaibriol's health. Cracking open his secured medical files had taken a good deal of work, but when she finally had them, they revealed nothing she didn't already know. She could have told the doctors her husband was a strong, healthy young man. But she copied them anyway.

Something bothered her about the file on his nanomeds,

though she couldn't say what was wrong. Everything seemed in order. He had the best meds available. Their chemistry looked odd, but nothing too unusual. All Hightons had customized meds designed to optimize their own personal health. Of course an emperor would have many unique species, the best available. He had probably inherited some of them from his mother while he was in the womb.

But the differences seemed familiar.

Tarquine frowned, trying to remember where she had seen similar meds. She was sure it had been within the last year. She had the computer compare his file with the records of every Highton that she had encountered or investigated in the past two years, but no match came up. So she checked every Aristo, including Diamonds and Silicates. Still no match. She widened the search to Razers and high-level taskmakers.

Still nothing.

She rubbed her chin. Could it have been a lower status taskmaker? It seemed unlikely, given the elite quality of the meds. Providers had top-of-the-line species, especially to delay aging, but theirs were also designed to suppress aggression, heighten their desire to please, make their minds more susceptible to Aristos, and act as aphrodisiacs. Of course Jaibriol's had none of those modifications.

Well, so. She might as well look. She had the computer check every taskmaker and provider she owned whose file she had looked at in the past two years.

Still nothing.

Tarquine shrugged. She must have been mistaken. She spoke to her EI. "I guess that's it."

"You haven't looked at one file."

"Why didn't you bring it up?"

"You asked about slaves you owned or sold."

"That covers every—" Tarquine stopped. Ah, yes. One of her providers fit neither category. He had had the unmitigated audacity to escape. "You mean Kelric Valdoria?"

"That is correct. Shall I make the comparison?"

"No, don't bother." Tarquine started to stand up. Then she paused. "Oh, why not. Go ahead."

After a moment, the EI said, "Comparison complete."

She looked over the results. The general meds Jaibriol and Kelric carried had nothing in common. Of course.

Except—

"Gods almighty," Tarquine whispered.

Of the nanomeds that Kelric and Jaibriol had inherited from their mothers, most were an exact match.

PART THREE

Penumbra

26

Hall of Ancestors

"They will excoriate us," Jai said.

With Robert at his side, Jai paced through an ancient wing of the palace, one that had survived both the war and the assassination attempt on his wedding day, mainly because it housed nothing useful enough to destroy, unless one counted the dour holoportraits of Jai's ancestors. His dead relatives stared down at him with icy faces. The hall seemed to brood, from the bronze and black tiles on the floor to the black marble pillars. It fit his mood.

"Excoriate," Jai repeated. "I can't cover up what Tarquine did to Sapphire Sector."

"I don't see that you have much choice," Robert said. "You must never admit it."

Jai wanted to kick himself. He had married Tarquine fully aware of her financial shenanigans. The platinum business was the worst offense, but she had plenty of other transgressions. He had wanted her anyway, and now he had to deal with the consequences.

He stopped under a portrait of his great-grandfather and scowled at the long-dead founder of the Eubian Concord. *What possessed you to create Eube?* He would never know the full story, anymore than he would ever fully know why his Skolian grandfather, Eldrinson, had helped Jai's parents go into exile. Eldrinson had taken that secret to his grave. Even having never met his grandfather in person, Jai mourned his death.

Robert was waiting. "Your Highness?"

Jai turned to him. "Xirad Kaliga isn't helping either. I can't get straight answers from him about anything."

"I can requisition additional ESComm reports."

"I doubt it will help." Jai grimaced. "And I have to respond to Azar Taratus. Do you remember the credits he had to repay my wife for Kelric Valdoria? Well, now he wants his money back. He says Valdoria was worth even more, as a Ruby prince, than what Tarquine paid."

"Taratus fully intended to cheat her," Robert said. "That the provider turned out to be worth more than anyone knew doesn't change the fact that the admiral committed fraud."

Jai rubbed his eyes. "Do you remember what I said the insurance bureaus had to do if an independent assessment determined Kelric was worth more than the low value they set?"

Robert paused. "I believe, Your Highness, you required them to pay the empress double the difference."

"Yes, well, Tarquine made them do it. It came to almost thirty million." Jai started walking again. "And she has the settlement from Taratus. I can't let her keep both, Robert. Everyone is furious. I have to do something."

His aide blanched. "She may not appreciate your telling her to return one."

"She'll *pulverize* me." It would make no difference that she would still be better off even if she gave back one of the settlements. She would never willingly part with her wealth. He stared up at his allegedly estimable ancestors on the walls and wondered what they would do. Whatever it was, it would probably appall him.

Nor was Tarquine his only problem. "High Judge Muze says we must let Raziquon out of prison."

"You can refuse," Robert said.

"He belongs in prison."

"Of course."

"Ah, hell." Jai hit his fist on his thigh. "I've made too many enemies. If I refuse the High Judge, someone will try to assassinate me again."

His aide looked alarmed. "Being alive is definitely more desirable."

"Sometimes I wonder," Jai muttered.

Robert pulled him to a halt, forgetting no one could touch the emperor without his permission. "You mustn't say that! All Eube would mourn if anything happened to you."

"Sure they would. They have to. I own most of them."

"It is *more* than that. Much more." Robert spoke earnestly. "You are a just man. Good. Decent." He paused, and Jai could almost feel him searching for the right words. "These unique traits make you a Highton among Hightons."

That was tactful. Robert could have just come out and said the Hightons were greedy, self-centered sadists. They would make anyone look good and decent. Maybe that was why Aristos talked in such convoluted forms. It made the truth less stark.

"Eube needs you," Robert added.

"Thank you." Jai doubted his advisers shared that opinion, but he appreciated his aide's loyalty. He regarded Robert curiously. "I was wondering."

"Yes, sir?"

"Your name. It sounds Allied."

"It is my father's name. He came from Earth."

"Pirates attacked his ship?"

"Yes." His expression closed. "My mother bought him. She is a taskmaker, but her father was a Highton lord. She runs a factory that makes robots." A muscle twitched under his eye. "My father was her provider."

Jai spoke quietly. "I'm sorry."

He expected Robert to give the canonical platitude about his mother honoring his father. Instead, the aide's face worked as if he were fighting to hide his anger. His memories of his father came through despite Jai's barriers, images of a man who had grieved for his lost freedom but loved his son. "At least my father is no longer her favorite. He has a quiet life now."

"Would you like him to come here? To the palace?"

Joyful surprise leapt in Robert's mood, but he guarded his response. "If it would please Your Highness."

"I had the impression you missed him."

Robert stared at him. Then, remembering himself, he said, "I appreciate your generosity. I've hardly seen my father in years. And I think he would like to come. But I don't know if my mother would let him go."

Jai thought of Silver, Kaliga's provider, the girl who had introduced him to love. He knew now he would never see her again. But Robert had said his father was no longer his mother's favorite. "I can make an offer. What do you think would work?"

Hope came from Robert's mind. "My mother likes jewels. Real ones, not synthetic gems."

"I have plenty of those." Jai grimaced. "More than I'll ever need."

Robert hesitated. "I don't know what my father could do for you. He has no training for your staff."

"What did he do on Earth?"

"Art. He still paints. Mother gave him a studio."

Jai beamed at him. "Well, there you have it. He can have a studio in the palace. You make arrangements."

Robert's cautious expression gave way to a smile. "Yes, certainly, I will take care of it. Thank you, Your Highness." His gratitude overflowed his thoughts. "You are most kind. Thank you."

Jai wanted to say, *How can you thank me when you wear that collar around your neck?* "I wish I could—"

The scream of a siren drowned out his words. Jai clapped his hands over his ears, but that only made the agonizing noise echo inside his head.

"Aaai!" He stumbled forward, aware of his Razers bursting out of shadows around the marble columns. Robert was speaking urgently, but Jai couldn't hear. Others grasped Jai, trying to pull his hands off his ears.

"Get away!" Jai shouted. He lurched away from them and pushed the heels of his hands against his ears, but the unbearable sound kept going on and on, inside of him.

Backing up, Jai thudded into a pillar. He slid down to the ground, and bent over, folding his hands over his head. Someone was kneeling next to him and someone else was yelling orders. His head felt as if it would burst. The painful sound came at several frequencies, some so low he felt rather than heard them. Dark spots danced before his eyes and nausea surged in him.

"Help me." Jai looked up into Robert's terrified eyes. One Razer had a medtape on Jai's arm and another was scanning him with some device, he didn't know what. Had they betrayed him? It had to be someone who could get close enough to trigger whatever was shattering his head now.

Jai groaned and doubled over. Clenching his fists, he hit them against his head.

A rumble penetrated the unbearable noise, boots thudding on stone. Then more people were kneeling around him, doctors, officers, soldiers. Jai rocked back and forth, ready to add his own scream to the one killing him.

"Gods, make it stop," he cried. Yet no one else showed any sign of discomfort, or even that they heard the noise. "It must be the medical alarm in my body. It's gone crazy."

Someone said, "Can you verify that?" and someone else said, "Yes, we've confirmed it."

A medic shot Jai with an air-syringe. He felt as if a blanket fell over him, taking his sight, his speech, and then—mercifully—his hearing.

Gradually Jai became aware of the hall. His retinue had moved him to a black marble bench behind the columns. He closed his eyes and sat slumped, never so glad for silence. He wiped his palm against his cheek, smearing tears.

"Your Highness?" a woman asked.

He opened his eyes. A doctor was sitting with him on the bench. She wore the uniform of a lieutenant colonel in the ESComm medical corps, and the name patch on her shoulder read Lyra Qoxdaughter. She was one of his relatives, perhaps even a daughter of his grandfather. Jai's Razers towered around the bench. He regarded everyone in stony silence, wondering just what, if any, connection they had to what had just happened.

"How do you feel?" the doctor asked.

"Fine." He couldn't bear the minds of his bodyguards. Raising his head, he saw Robert standing nearby. He motioned tiredly, hoping his aide understood.

Somehow Robert managed, with efficiency and discretion, to nudge, coax, urge, and otherwise persuade the Razers to move back. Although they didn't withdraw far enough to eliminate the pressure on Jai's mind, the improvement made him breathe out in relief.

The doctor continued to watch him. "Why do your bodyguards bother you?"

"I like privacy." The shorter his answers, the better.

"They can do their job better if they don't have to stay so far away."

"They're still with me." Jai knew if he didn't give her a plausible explanation, she would keep probing. "I'm not used to people. I lived alone for most of my life." He rubbed his head. "Do you know what happened to the alarm in my body?" His voice turned cold. "I want the names of everyone who has worked on it."

Her face paled. "I programmed it, Your Highness. Please be assured I would never do anything to harm your person. I never set it up to hurt you."

Jai could tell, from her mind, that she told the truth. "Then what happened?"

"Someone altered it to affect your nervous system and brain as if you were actually experiencing the sounds you heard. It was triggered from a distance. Had it continued long enough, it would have killed you."

Another assassination attempt. He wasn't going to let them win, damn it. "Who could have done it?"

She pushed back tendrils of yellow and gray hair that had escaped the roll on her head. "I can't say for certain."

"Then guess."

"I've seen this technique before. Diamond Aristos in Sapphire Sector use it to control their taskmakers." The doctor hesitated. "I suppose that doesn't make much sense."

"Unfortunately it does." Tarquine was siphoning millions out of Sapphire Sector. Jai rose to his feet, then grabbed the doctor's shoulder as dizziness swept over him. After his head steadied, he took a long breath and let go of her shoulder. Qoxdaughter stared at him in undisguised shock. Even through his fortified barriers, he caught her thought; she wouldn't have expected him even to touch a taskmaker, let alone lean on her for support.

Jai inclined his head to her. Then, motioning to Robert, he set off down the hall. Robert hurried after with him. "Your Highness, you mustn't push yourself so hard after such an attack."

Jai scowled. "I have business to take care of."

Robert continued to protest, but Jai refused to slow down. His bodyguards and Dr. Qoxdaughter caught up and kept pace with them, but no one attempted to stop him, which was a good thing, because in the mood he was in right now, Jai thought he might have punched anyone who tried.

Jai would have slammed open the new door to Tarquine's office if it had been slammable, rather than a molecular airlock that remained solid until he approached, at which time it shimmered and vanished. Actually, it underwent a change in molecular configuration that made it transparent and permeable to humans. It was impressively effective in ensuring no unwanted gases seeped into the office, but a dud when it came to door-banging.

Inside, Tarquine was standing behind her desk, studying a

holomap. As Jai strode in, she looked at him over the map. "Did we have an appointment?"

"What?" Jai demanded. "I need an appointment to see my wife? I don't think so." He stalked to her desk and smacked a panel on its surface, making the map vanish. "Someone just tried to assassinate me. It might be the Diamond Aristos in Sapphire Sector. Surely you remember them."

Tarquine looked around the office, at the many Razers, the medic, and a very agitated Robert. "Is that why you've acquired all these alarmed looking people?"

"I'm not the only one who has acquired them." Jai swung around to the Razer captain. "See that my wife is protected."

The Razer nodded. "We are on alert status four right now, Your Highness. The palace is secured. No one can enter or leave, and we've stepped up protection for both you and Empress Tarquine."

"Do it for Lord Xir, too," Jai said. Corbal was staying at the palace, supposedly to get to know Jai better, though Jai knew perfectly well his cousin was keeping an eye on Tarquine.

As the captain spoke into his gauntlet comm, Jai turned back to Tarquine. "For some reason the Aristos in Sapphire Sector aren't happy. I can't imagine why."

Her gaze turned icy. "I'm not that easy to kill."

"Neither am I. That hasn't stopped people from trying." He wanted to shake her. "Gods, Tarquine, we can't keep turning the palace into an armed camp."

She regarded him with a scrutiny that would have bored a hole through him if it had been a laser. "We?"

"Yes, we."

"I've no idea what you mean."

Jai threw his hands up into the air. "Of course not! What was I thinking? You're just in here planning balls and galas like a nice empress."

Unexpectedly, she smiled. "No, I suppose not."

"We have to do something about Sapphire Sector."

"I agree."

That was a surprise. "Any ideas?"

Her voice hardened. "I rather liked your solution with Raziquon."

Jai stared at her, a lock of his hair falling over his forehead. "You want me to throw the entire Diamond Coalition in prison? On what the hell grounds?"

"They tried to kill you. I should think that is grounds enough."

"And I convict them on what evidence?"

"A lack of evidence didn't stop you with Raziquon."

"I *had* evidence there. Sunrise's testimony. I don't have *any* now."

Her calm demeanor didn't show the slightest crack. "I'm sure you can find some."

"You're out of your mind."

"You have a better idea?"

"Yes. Give Sapphire Sector back its platinum."

Her laugh held no hint of humor. "You've a sharp wit."

He braced his fists on her desk, resting his weight on them as he leaned toward her. "How many more of your deals are going to blow up in our faces?"

"You would let these cowardly attackers send you running?" She crossed her arms. "You shame your ancestors."

"Bullshit." Jai met her gaze. "If it wasn't for my esteemed ancestors and their wonko ideas about how to run things, we wouldn't have to live this way, always afraid of assassins, crooks, and torturers."

"Bullshit? Wonko?" She put one hand on her hip. "What do these words mean?"

"It's retro-slang from—oh, never mind." Reminding her that only a few months ago he had been in high school was hardly going to increase his influence now. He pushed away from the desk and paced across the office. The Razers were checking the room, and Robert stood by the door, waiting. Dr. Qoxdaughter kept a discreet distance, but Jai could tell she was monitoring both him and Tarquine.

Jai stopped in front of the Razer captain. "Any news on my cousin, Lord Xir?"

The captain somehow straightened even more, though that seemed impossible given his already rigid posture. "Your Most Glorious Highness—" Then he cleared his throat.

Ah, hell. "What's wrong?"

"Lord Xir left the palace just before you were attacked."

"Well, well," Tarquine murmured.

Ignoring her, Jai pushed the lock of hair off his forehead. "Where is he?"

"We're searching for him." The captain's mind leaked fatalism; he fully expected Jai to punish him for delivering such unpleasant news. "Lord Xir received a transmission through the Kyle web before he left."

Jai stiffened. Although the web was slowly coming back up, it was still rare for Eubians to receive messages through it. They had access to the webs only on the sufferance of the Skolians. No Aristo would put up with the humiliation of requesting Skolian help unless the message was important and worth that humbling price. "Do you have a record of it?"

The captain shook his head. "The message was too well secured. However, Security did trace the transmission. It originated in Sapphire Sector."

"How inconvenient for Corbal," Tarquine said.

Jai swung around and scowled at her. "Stop it."

"Your loyalty is charming, Husband. Fatal, too."

He went over to her desk. "Corbal wouldn't be this obvious."

To his surprise, she nodded in the Highton style that indicated she agreed with him. "He may be many things, most of them aggravating, but 'obvious' isn't one of them."

Jai blinked at her. Then he glanced at the captain. "Find Lord Xir."

"Right away, Your Highness."

"I doubt he's still on the planet," Tarquine said.

"Do you now?" Jai considered her. "How interesting."

She raised an eyebrow. "Interesting?"

"That the Diamonds attacked me instead of you."

"Perhaps my security is better than yours."

"We have the same security." He had no doubt she commanded resources neither he nor his staff knew about, but that didn't matter. He had picked up what he needed from her mind: she hadn't tried to murder him. If he hadn't been a psion, he knew nothing could have appeased his doubts.

The Razer captain spoke. "Would you like us to take the empress into custody, Your Highness?"

Tarquine gave the captain a forbidding stare. "You overstep yourself."

Jai didn't want her in custody; he needed her savvy if he intended to continue breathing. Of course his enemies wanted him to mistrust her. The Diamond Coalition had probably set her up, if they actually were the assassins and hadn't been framed by someone else. Given all the schemes Aristos inflicted on one another, gods only knew who had done what.

To the captain he said only, "No, don't take her into custody." He gave Tarquine a measuring gaze. "You may be many things, my love, but 'obvious' isn't one of them."

A smile curved her lips. "You have wisdom."

"Your Highness." The captain sounded urgent.

Jai turned around. "Yes?"

"Security has located Lord Xir."

The muscles in Jai's back spasmed. They had become so tight, he wondered if they would ever relax again. "Go on."

The captain kept his face neutral, as if he were dealing with explosives. "He went to the starport."

"So." Tarquine said more with that one word than an entire speech on betrayal.

Jai refused to believe Corbal was trying to escape. "Why did he go there?"

"We are checking," the captain said.

"Yes, you do that," Tarquine murmured, watching the Razer as if she were a hawk and he a rodent. "Take him into custody, Captain, just like you wanted to do with me."

Jai gritted his teeth. He wanted to tell her to stop, but he couldn't risk making her feel as if she had lost face in front of his staff. In the suffocating atmosphere, the minds of the Razers pressed on him. Resting his palms on Tarquine's desk, he leaned his weight forward and dropped his head. "Go," he said through clenched teeth. "All of you. Find Corbal and detain him."

Robert cleared everyone away. Only half the guards left the room, but the rest doubled their distance from Jai. No one was imprudent enough to ask Tarquine to move. Jai could see her hand resting on the desk near his. He didn't raise his head, though he knew she was seeing him fight an internal battle she could never understand. He told himself he didn't care what she thought. His head throbbed and nausea rolled over him.

She spoke quietly. "Jaibriol?"

Lifting his head, he looked into her eyes. He expected to see scorn but found concern instead. It disconcerted him. He sensed how much she wanted to ask, *What is it?* But she held back, giving him the same face-saving respect he had given her. Gods willing, none of them would ever guess he couldn't bear the Highton minds of his Razers. Tarquine was the only one he let stay with him, and she had more Highton lineage than any of his guards.

As Jai straightened up, the medic stepped toward him. He shook his head, stopping her advance. Nothing she could do would help. He felt trapped, with no escape.

None.

27

Accusations

Corbal waited in the arrivals lounge. In the distance, the spires of ships in dock gleamed against the sky. A magrail car was crossing the port. Most such cars followed a set route, picking up arrivals and delivering passengers, but Corbal had arranged for this one privately, to honor his guests.

As the car pulled up to the platform outside, Corbal went to the window with his bodyguards. Normally he would have sent an aide to the port to meet his business associates, but given the difficulties in this deal, he had come in person. The message from the Diamond Coalition had subtly indicated they would appreciate the implied honor.

A woman stepped out of the magcar, a taskmaker rather than the expected Diamond Aristo. Puzzled, Corbal went to the entrance. The wall there shimmered and vanished.

The taskmaker approached him and bowed deeply. "My honor at your presence, Lord Xir."

"My Line gives you welcome." Corbal considered her. "You represent the Diamond Coalition?"

"Yes, sir. My lords and ladies of the Coalition invite you to their yacht as an honored guest. They wish to express their appreciation for your diplomacy and expertise in restoring their confidence." She indicated the car. "Please allow me to offer you transportation to their ship."

Corbal hesitated. The invitation was well made, and he would enjoy a night hosted by Diamond Aristos in the fashionable hospitality of their yacht. It also boded well for the reestablishment of relations with the Coalition. But he didn't like it. He couldn't say why, but he didn't trust the invitation.

"Your hosts are gracious," he said. "Please extend my appreciation to them. It is with regret that I must decline; I have duties to the emperor I cannot miss." He actually had nothing scheduled, but he needed only stop by Jai's office to make his excuse real.

The woman flushed. Obviously she hadn't expected a refusal. "Yes, of course, sir."

After a few more exchanges, the aide boarded the magcar and departed. Deep in thought, Corbal crossed the lounge, flanked by his Razers. He couldn't isolate why the invitation troubled him. It was something about the aide's attitude, perhaps unintentional clues she gave with her tense posture. But clues to what?

Kelric felt the mind of the Ruby Pharaoh. Standing at a window of his home, contemplating the hills outside, he knew when she entered the gallery. He turned to see her walk out of the shadows. Wind gusted through the open windows, carrying the fresh smell of the hills and stirring her hair, which hung dark against her pale jumpsuit. She seemed ethereal, intangible. Decades before she ascended to the throne, she had been a renowned mathematician. Then she had focused her luminous intellect on the Kyle web. She might share authority with the Assembly now, but it was she who ruled the webs.

She joined him at the window. "My greetings, Kelric." Her voice had a lyrically resonant quality.

"My greetings, Dehya."

They stood together, gazing at the hills that rolled from the mansion down into the valley. Kelric felt at ease with the silence. When she was ready, she would speak.

"The Traders have moved against us," she finally said.

He glanced at her. "How?"

"Their pirates boarded a Skolian yacht." She turned to him. "They stole the ship, terrorized the passengers, and kidnapped a Skolian man named Jacques Ardoise."

Kelric swore under his breath. With the peace talks set to begin in a few tendays, they and the Traders had kept an unspoken truce, neither side upsetting the precarious ceasefire that allowed the talks to proceed. This could collapse that fragile accord.

"Is Ardoise a psion?" Kelric asked.

Anger sparked in Dehya's mind. "Yes."

Damn. They would sell him as a provider, making this even worse. "Did the other passengers survive?"

"Yes, but they all suffered spiker injuries."

He clenched his fist at his side. "We can't allow this to pass."

She pushed back tendrils of hair that had blown across her face. "The passengers said the pirates claimed to work for the Line of Xir. Corbal Xir."

"The same Corbal Xir who would have become emperor if Jaibriol the Third hadn't shown up?"

"Yes." She sounded tired. "That Xir."

Kelric leaned his arm against the top of the window and rested his forehead on his forearm, gazing at the pastoral valley outside, though its beauty no longer calmed him. They couldn't talk peace with the Traders while Trader pirates terrorized Skolian citizens.

Security fliers apprehended Corbal when his hovercar was five kilometers from the port. Corbal sat, stiff and uneasy, while the captain of his bodyguards spoke with a Razer in one of the oncoming fliers. Corbal had never been so glad to have proof, in the log of his hovercar, that he was returning to the palace.

The fliers escorted them back. At the palace, aircraft and soldiers were on patrol everywhere. Laser systems blinked on the roof, and Corbal had no doubt many other defenses were activated. Vitar Bartholson, the head of palace Security, met them at the landing field. He treated Corbal with respect—and made him a prisoner. Corbal was heartily tired of being taken into custody.

Security officers surrounded them as they walked through the palace. At least they headed for the suite where he and Sunrise were staying; if he had to be a prisoner, he preferred the familiarity of his own rooms and provider. He covertly studied Bartholson. According to the files compiled by Xir security, this Qox security chief was the half-Aristo son of Barthol Iquar, brother of the current empress and father of the previous empress.

Although Corbal didn't want to speak first, his need to know what had happened outweighed his reticence. He could just ask Bartholson why the palace was under a lockdown, but the commander had enough status to merit a less direct approach, particularly given his control over the present situation.

"I would regret," Corbal said, "to see any misfortune befall His Imperial Highness."

"It would be unfortunate," Bartholson said, meticulously neutral.

"Is His Highness well?"

Bartholson glanced at him. "Yes, sir. The assassination attempt failed."

Hell and damnation. Corbal knew then that his decision to decline a visit to the Diamond yacht may have saved his life. If he had been discovered leaving the planet during an assassination attempt, the implication could have been deadly—for him.

With careful prodding, he convinced Bartholson to give him the details. They puzzled Corbal. Although it looked like the Diamonds had set him up, he didn't believe it. The explanation was too convenient. How he was going to convince anyone else of that, and his innocence, remained to be seen.

———

Jai strode into Corbal's suite, again wishing he could slam a door. Across the living room, Corbal was studying a wall-size holomap of the local starport.

"What the *flaming hell* were you thinking?" Jai demanded. "Why don't you just shoot me, Corbal, and get it over with?"

His cousin turned, his body silhouetted against the holomap. "I would never bring harm to your person." He even sounded sincere.

"I'm not talking about the fucking assassination attempt."

Corbal's mouth tightened. "One might suggest, Your Highness, that observing proper court protocol will yield more productive results than profanity."

Jai stalked over to him. "Did you really need a Skolian yacht? Your billions of slaves and trillions of credits aren't enough? Never mind that this may have trashed our talks with the Skolians. What does interstellar peace matter compared to your attaining a little more wealth?"

"Are you done?"

Jai struggled with his anger. "*Why?* Why did you do it?"

"Do what?"

"Oh, excuse me, I forgot that proper Highton discourse includes denying culpability for everything and anything."

A muscle twitched under Corbal's eye. "I went to the starport to meet representatives of the Diamond Coalition. I didn't trust their invitation, so I came back here."

"I'm not talking about that."

Corbal blinked. "Then what?"

"Your pirates."

His cousin's gaze unfocused slightly, the way it always did when he lied. "I know of no pirates."

"Right. You forget those frigates that work for you?"

Corbal crossed his muscular arms. "When making accusations, it behooves the accuser to have proof."

"That's all you have to say?" Jai wanted to burst. "Damn it all, Corbal, couldn't you at least have called them off until after the peace talks?"

His cousin lowered his arms, his forehead furrowing. "It is difficult to call off what isn't on."

"A thousand denials won't undo the truth."

"A 'truth' may be false."

Jai paused. As he had come to know Corbal better, he had grown attuned to his cousin's mind and tended to ease his defenses in Corbal's presence, at least as much as he could bear with his Razers around. Confusion came from the older man now, not deception. Jai picked up other details, too; if he had ever doubted Corbal financed a fleet of pirates, he no longer did. But Corbal hadn't sent them out recently; if anything, he had shown unusual restraint.

"Ah, hell," Jai said.

"I would hear this accusation against me."

"The Skolian Assembly sent a protest to our Foreign Affairs Ministry." Jai spoke tiredly. "Pirates boarded a Skolian yacht, spiked the passengers, stole the yacht, and kidnapped a Skolian citizen."

Corbal stared at him. "I had nothing to do with it."

Jai had no doubt Corbal could look him straight in the eye and deny any link to the pirates. Had Jai not been a psion, he would never have believed him. The trail led straight to his cousin, and palace security had found no evidence of anyone else involved. If Jai had accused Corbal in public, he could never have retracted it, even if he later found proof that someone set up the Xir lord. Taking back the accusation would have meant admitting the emperor himself had leveled a false accusation of major proportions, a crisis that would undermine his reign.

But Jai was a psion. He knew Corbal was telling the truth. He felt as if he had just dodged another attack, this one on his character rather than his life. He spoke in a subdued voice. "I have heard that those without wisdom sometimes foolishly accept accusations when the truth is anything but obvious."

Until Corbal's shoulders relaxed, Jai hadn't realized how

much the older man had tensed. "Your Highness shows insight." It was probably the closest Corbal could come to saying, *apology accepted.*

Jai walked to the couch and sank down onto it. His Razers remained at their posts, discreet as always, but he felt their disapproval. They thought him foolish, to back down so easily.

Corbal spoke with care. "The Line of Xir supports the peace talks."

Jai rubbed his eyes. "The evidence says otherwise."

"Such evidence can be convenient to those who wish to discredit someone."

Jai rested his elbows on his knees, clasping his hands between them. "That leaves the question of who created the evidence." Bitterly he added, "Perhaps those people sparkle, just like my would-be assassins."

"It would be stupid for the Diamond Coalition to set me up or attempt an assassination."

"Then who?"

"I don't know."

It didn't surprise him that Corbal said no more. Jai was acutely aware of the Razers listening. Neither he nor Corbal dared make accusations. He had an odd sense, as if Corbal were *trying* to create pressure against his mind. Jai took a deep breath. Then he did what he had dreaded since coming to Eube; he completely lowered his barriers.

Jai silently gasped at the onslaught from the Razers. He felt as if an avalanche was burying him in suffocating darkness. Struggling against the sensation, he focused on Corbal. His cousin's thought came through like a faint voice in a roar of noise: *Check ESComm.*

Jai could take no more. Pressing the heels of his hands against his temples, he rebuilt his barriers. He hated that the Razers were transcending at a low level because of his discomfort. They weren't conscious of it; they just knew they felt better when they were around their emperor. Jai didn't miss the irony, that the distress they caused him also increased their loyalty to him.

He lowered his hands. "I should check on Tarquine."

Corbal's voice cooled. "One might wonder why the Diamond Coalition spared your wife."

Jai stiffened. "Do not presume too far on our kinship."

"My apologies, Your Highness."

He recognized Corbal's challenge from his cousin's stiff posture rather than his apparently conciliatory words. Corbal wanted to know how Jai could be so sure in his belief that the empress hadn't tried to kill him.

Quietly Jai said, "The same way I am sure about you."

The Xir lord stared at him, startled into silence, his response so strong it penetrated even Jai's rebuilt barriers: Corbal understood exactly what he meant. Jai had an answer then to a question that had troubled him since he first met his cousin.

Corbal knew he was a telepath.

28

Psions

The false leads went nowhere. The Intelligence Ministry conducted an investigation, thorough and detailed, aided by palace Security. Jai and Robert also searched every database they could find. No Diamond yacht had been in orbit the day Corbal went to the port. The Coalition denied sending him a message, yet he had a verified record of their conversation. Despite the circumstantial evidence against the Coalition, no proof surfaced to justify an accusation of assassination, just as none had ever been found against the Line of Raziquon in the first attempt.

Innuendo swirled everywhere. Rumors about Jai's eccentricities proliferated. Speculation about Corbal ranged from insulting but harmless suggestions of abnormal behavior with his providers to deadly whispers of treason. Hightons shunned the Diamond Coalition. The economy of Sapphire Sector sagged and antagonism deepened against the Line of Iquar, though the recession had little to do with the platinum trade. Lies spread that Jai had pardoned Jafe Maccar because Maccar was smuggling platinum for the Line of Xir, taking it to the Skolians, who paid inflated prices. Protests against Raziquon's imprisonment grew louder.

Within the rank and file of ESComm, cracks appeared in the bedrock of support for the emperor.

Jai turned over in bed, groggy, unsure what had awoken him. His mind formed one thought: *assassin.* He knew he should wake up, but he was too tired.

A rustle came from across the bedroom. He decided that living was better than getting enough sleep and opened his eyes. His new optical enhancements let him see infrared light; the hotter an object, the brighter it glowed. A red blaze with human shape was approaching.

Ah yes, definitely a shapely human.

Jai smiled drowsily. "When did you get up?"

"A few hours ago." Tarquine sounded tired.

As Jai sat up, rubbing his eyes, Tarquine climbed the dais. She sat on the bed and started to pull off her boots.

Jai slid over and put his arms around her waist, his front to her back. "Why did you get up?"

She leaned against him. "I am glad, my husband, that we have privacy from monitors in here."

Jai wondered what she was up to. "What happened to the monitors?"

She pulled off her other boot and dropped it on the floor. "I redirected them."

"How?" He wasn't sure he had ever managed that feat, though he had tried.

She turned in his arms, facing him. "With discretion. The same way I traced the Diamond Coalition transmission that Corbal received from Sapphire Sector."

Jai went very still. "We've all traced it."

"Not well enough." Her voice hardened. "I can't prove it, but I know what I found. Xirad Kaliga framed the Diamonds."

"Admiral Kaliga? The Joint Commander of ESComm?"

"Yes." Her voice sounded muted in the large suite. "You can bet General Taratus is in it, too."

"We have no evidence of their involvement." Jai didn't want to believe his Joint Commanders were plotting against him. "None."

"They hide well."

"You must be mistaken."

"And why is that?"

He swallowed. "Because I can't take on ESComm."

"You need only take on Taratus and Kaliga."

"They're too strong."

She shook her head. "No one is invincible."

"Can you prove your accusations?"

"No."

"I *need* evidence."

Tarquine spoke in her shadowed voice. "Do you?"

"Why should I trust your word?" He couldn't read her expression in the dim light, and she had guarded her thoughts well. "Maybe you have motives for accusing them."

"You know my motives." She had become deadly quiet. "You know them without doubt."

"Doubt always exists." Easing his barriers, he tried to probe her thoughts more deeply.

"No," she said. "You *know*."

Jai felt her surety: she believed with certainty that he could tell if she lied. It chilled him—because she was right: as a telepath, he would know. But she couldn't know he was a psion. She *couldn't*.

"Tell me something," she asked. "Have you tried, lately, to find an image of yourself on the webs?"

"What?" Jai released her, disoriented by her change of subject. Even now, with his barriers relaxed, he had trouble picking up more than a sense of her mood: tension, sexual desire, anticipation. It disquieted him that she shielded her mind so well.

She motioned at the console by the wall. "See what you can find."

Puzzled, Jai pulled on his black sleep trousers and went to the console. After accessing the planetary web, he began a search.

An hour later he gave up. He had checked every database on Glory; he had tried every offworld network he could reach; and he had even managed to access some of the Skolian and Allied webs. He knew public images of him existed, but he had found absolutely none from before he became emperor, and despite his more recent appearances on news broadcasts, very few of him existed even from the past few months.

He looked up at Tarquine, who was standing next to his chair. "What happened to them?"

"I think Corbal deleted most. I disposed of some he missed."

"But why?"

She pulled over a chair and sat by him. Then she spoke into the comm on the console. "Tomjolt, access my private directories and bring up the file labeled 'Jaibriol One.' "

"Verification required," the EI answered.

Tarquine gave her passwords and submitted to retinal and voice scans. A moment later, a holo appeared above a flat screen on the console, a laughing youth in a blue sweater and jeans, with blond highlights streaking his dark hair. He was standing in a meadow, under a blue sky with a yellow sun.

Jai blinked. "That's me." The holo had been taken on Earth a few months ago, just after his seventeenth birthday, his real birthday, not the false one he used now.

Tarquine studied the image. "Did you know, Jaibriol, that my provider, Kelric, had metallic hair?"

Jai felt as if the air suddenly left the room. "He isn't your provider. He is the Imperator of Skolia."

"So he is." She spoke to Tomjolt again. "Comp, give me the eighth Jaibriol file."

Jai shifted in his chair. "What are you doing?"

"Watch."

The image of him vanished, then reappeared, larger, with only his head and shoulders. A holo of Kelric formed next to it, an older man with metallic hair graying at the temples.

Jai tried not to grit his teeth. "What makes you think I want to see this?"

"Look." She touched a panel and the image of Jai changed, the bright streaks in his hair spreading until all of the locks turned yellow. No, not yellow.

Gold.

Sweat beaded Jai's forehead. He had never realized the streaks had such a metallic quality. "Tarquine, this is sick, comparing me to your provider."

She spoke pensively. "Do you know, for decades I had fantasized about owning Kelric Valdoria." She turned to Jai. "But then he died, all those years ago."

The blood drained from his face. "You knew," he whispered. "You knew his identity the whole time."

"Well, I can't admit that, now can I?" Her gaze hardened. "But I can tell you other things."

He didn't want to ask. He didn't want to hear. But he had to know. "What things?"

"Nanomeds."

Sweat beaded on his temples. She couldn't be going where he thought. She couldn't know. His mother and Kelric Valdoria had been sister and brother. They would have received the same nanomeds from their mother, in the womb. Jai had inherited those same meds from his mother. Some of the species had undoubtedly been altered, but not all of them. And of all the people alive, only Tarquine was in a position to compare his meds to those Kelric carried.

She spoke to the EI. "Tomjolt, age the holo of Jaibriol Qox twenty years and make his hair dark again."

Jai clenched his hands on his knees, watching his holo age. He obviously resembled his father, Jaibriol II, the previous emperor, but he began to see more similarity to someone else as well.

His mother.

Jai couldn't breathe. It took a conscious effort to make himself stay in his chair. Laying his hand over the holoscreen, he made the image fade to nothing. "Stop this. It's sick."

"Is it?" She nudged away his hand, bringing back the holos of Jai and Kelric. "Tomjolt, compare the two holos. Tell me if those two men might be related."

"Tarquine, stop," Jai whispered.

"Comparison complete," the EI said. "I calculate a six to eleven percent probability that the subjects are brothers, nine to twenty-seven percent that they are father and son, and five to forty-two percent that they have a kinship relation one level removed from immediate family."

Relief surged over Jai, so intense it felt visceral. Complete strangers could come up with those statistics. He frowned at Tarquine. "Shall I compare you to the Ruby Pharaoh? You both have black hair, after all." He waved his hand. "I have better things to do than play this game."

"Indulge me just a bit longer." She tapped a panel. "Computer, compare the image of Jaibriol Qox and the holo in file 87T5. Just consider close kinship."

Jai tensed. "What is file 87T5?"

"Watch."

"Comparison complete," Tomjolt said. "I calculate a fifty-three to eighty-eight percent probability that the subjects are brother and sister, and eighty-four to ninety-two percent that they are mother and son."

Only through a great effort of will did Jai speak without revealing his agitation. "Whose image is in file 87T5?"

Tomjolt answered. "The late Skolian Imperator, Sauscony Valdoria."

Adrenaline surged through Jai. "I don't know what you're trying to prove, Tarquine, but you've gone beyond insult. You walk the edge of treason."

No doubt showed in her expression. "If I could find the resemblance, so can others. Corbal suspects, I'm certain. You must change your face, subtle alterations, but enough to destroy the resemblance."

"This is absurd." He could never acknowledge the truth. Never. Blackmail, government coups, betrayal—gods only knew what she would try. "It means nothing that I have similar features to a Skolian. We all come from the same stock, and our ancestors had a small gene pool."

"You can't take chances."

"You go too far."

"Jaibriol, listen to me." Her quiet tone did nothing to disguise her urgency. "Aristos bodysculpt themselves all the time. It would surprise no one if you fine-tuned your features to resemble your ancestors more, better to establish yourself as emperor in a time of crisis." She traced her fingertip over his nose, cheek, and lips. "You are so very, very beautiful. I would hope for only minor changes. But it must be enough to ensure you no longer resemble a dynasty of providers."

Jai caught her hand. He took a moment, letting his pulse calm. "I will give it some thought."

Tarquine turned to the console. "Tomjolt, destroy all the files in the current directory. Clean your memory of any fragments. Then erase all evidence of the deletions."

"Tomjolt has protocols to prevent such erasures," Jai said. "Even I can't override them."

"Erasures complete," Tomjolt said.

"Gods almighty," Jai muttered.

Tarquine glanced at him. "One should take care not to underestimate one's wife."

He took a deep breath. "What is it you want?"

"For my husband to stay alive."

"Why?"

Her eyes glinted. "Because then I remain empress."

It made sense. And yet . . . she was lying, or more accurately, she wasn't telling the full truth. More than a desire for power motivated her, he just wasn't sure what.

She rose to her feet. "Come, let us return to bed."

Jai stood up slowly. "You compare me to a provider, then ask me to bed? Such insults hardly inspire affection."

"Affection?" She took his hands. Her smile had an edge. "Are you fond of me, sweet Jaibriol?"

He pulled away his hands. "Don't patronize me."

"You evade my question."

Jai clenched her upper arms. "You madden, exasperate,

and irritate the hell out of me. And yes, you arouse me." That had to be the understatement of the century. "But that is all I feel, Tarquine. Nothing more."

"I don't think so," she murmured. "Such might be true for me, but not you. Admit it, Jaibriol."

"Admit it yourself." He jerked her closer. "I can tell you're lying about what you claim you don't feel for me."

"You think so?" Her look turned speculative. "And can you judge so well when your Joint Commanders are lying?"

Jai stiffened. If she meant what he thought, she was right; he could spy on their minds. It was more evidence that she believed him a telepath. As he had done with Corbal, and even Tarquine herself, he might discover in their thoughts what they knew about the assassination attempts. But it would work only if he lowered his barriers in their presence. Jai didn't think he could endure making himself that vulnerable.

Regardless, he had no intention of admitting anything to Tarquine. "I wish I had some way to uncover their secrets. But of course I don't."

"Of course." She put her arms around his neck, holding her thumb and forefinger together against his skin. "But you could invite them here to, oh let's say, repair deteriorating relations between the palace and ESComm."

Jai slid his arms around her waist. "Even if their visit led me to believe, for some reason, that they were involved in the assassination attempts, my basis for those conclusions would be circumstantial."

"In a court of law, yes."

Jai laid his finger over her lips. "I want only to improve relations with ESComm."

"Of course. As do I." She lied so smoothly.

Jai knew he had to consider her idea no matter how much he dreaded it. If she was right, that his Joint Commanders were trying to kill him, he had to know.

Jacques Ardoise huddled in the corner, ignoring the plush divans and luxurious bed of his room. The ivory walls, the tapestries, and parquet floors—nothing in this mansion reassured him. He pulled his legs closer to his chest, wrapped his arms around them, and put his head on his knees.

Tears ran down his face. He had always questioned whether his ability to empathize so well was a gift or a curse, but he had never realized he was a true empath. The Traders had tested him; he was even a marginal telepath, able to discern the rare thought from a more generalized mood, if it came strongly enough. It delighted his captors. They expected to make a lot of wealth from him. But they hadn't yet held the auction; they had wanted to transcend themselves first.

So they had.

Jacques sat shivering against the wall, wondering how soldiers learned to resist interrogation. He would have told his tormentors anything to make them stop. But they weren't interested in information, only transcendence. The female mercenaries also "liked" him. They took him to bed regardless of how much he fought, and they did what they pleased.

He had no idea where he was. The pirates had brought him to this mansion after they landed on some planet. It wasn't Earth; the air was too thin and the low gravity disoriented him. The raiders had cuffed and collared him, and given him expensive new clothes, shirts and trousers, but no shoes or socks. The garments covered his body, but fit snugly, obviously designed to display his build.

A chime sounded. As Jacques lifted his head, the wall across the room faded into an open archway. A man of average height and build stood there, a stranger with brown eyes and black hair, *dull* black. Jacques choked with relief. No glittering Aristo hair, no red Aristo eyes. Nor did this visitor create the mental pressure Jacques dreaded. Whenever the pirates with rust-red eyes had approached, their minds threatened to crush him. They were like mental voids swallowing his mind. They used his empathic abilities to fill a hollow where their capacity for compassion should have existed.

As the stranger approached, Jacques stiffened. Four of the mercenaries came behind him, two women and two men, all in body armor, with carbines. Four unfamiliar Razers followed, their minds reaching toward Jacques, bringing horror. He pressed against the wall, prepared to fight, knowing it was useless.

The man with brown eyes knelt in front of him. "Jacques Ardoise?"

"What do you want?" His voice rasped. He spoke in French, his native language. He also knew Allope, his father's tongue, but he doubted anyone here had heard of it. He thought some of the mercenaries had language modules in their brains, and every now and then they spoke ragged French to him. He had learned a few Highton words, but his captors didn't really seem to care if he understood them.

The man spoke in heavily accented French. "I am Robert. I take you to palace."

"Robert?" Jacques wasn't sure he had heard correctly. "Are you from Earth?"

"Not me. My father." He hesitated. "Like you."

Jacques went cold. *Like you.* Would he have children born into slavery? Images of his family flooded his mind: his wife, the two girls, the baby. It had angered him when Willex Seabreak decided at the last minute that Jacques couldn't bring them on the yacht. Jacques had wanted to cancel his job with Seabreak, but his family needed his income. As much as he wished now that he had broken the contract to play the synthesizer and sing for Seabreak's friends during the cruise, he was more grateful than he could ever say that his wife and children had stayed on Earth.

Based on what he had learned from the Traders about his mind, he suspected his wife was also an empath, which meant their children probably were as well. The Traders would have taken his family. A tear ran down his cheek, this time from relief that the people he loved were safe from this nightmare.

Robert spoke quietly. "I am sorry." He stood up. "Come, please."

Please. It was the first time he had heard the word since his capture. But he didn't rise. Instead, he laid his head on his knees and closed his eyes. What did it matter? He had lost too much: his life, home, family, everything, ripped away. Damn Corbal Xir, whoever he was.

Someone touched his arm. Jacques lifted his head to see one of the mercenaries bending over him. She smiled, her metal teeth glinting. Then she hauled him to his feet. "Come on, pretty boy." She pulled him closer, speaking in splintered French. "We miss you, eh?"

Jacques jerked back from her. "Go to hell."

"Let him be," Robert said.

She immediately dropped Jacques's arm, which surprised him, given the lack of respect she showed most people. She spoke to Robert in Highton. "Yes, sir." Jacques understood those words; it was the first phrase his captors had taught him.

So they left the room, Jacques following Robert, accompanied by the mercenaries and Razers.

And the world exploded.

29

Ardoise

The blast threw Jacques to the floor. The mercenary dropped over him, protecting him with her armored body, holding herself up on her hands so she didn't crush him. As the walls collapsed over them, she let loose with a river of unintelligible but vehement words that Jacques suspected were oaths.

After what felt like eons, the world grew quiet. The mercenary shifted, making debris clatter. Then she stood up, her booted feet planted on either side of his hips. The hall was in shambles. Razers and mercenaries picked themselves off the floor, brushing away dust, but no one seemed hurt. From the pattern of the collapse and the powdery debris, Jacques suspected the building had been designed simply to crumble if it were bombed, to minimize damage and injury. That precaution told him more than he wanted to know about the lifestyle of his captors.

Leaning down, the mercenary grabbed his bicep and pulled him to his feet. "You okay?"

Jacques wondered what language file gave her "okay." He moved stiffly, shaking powder off his clothes. "I'm all right." His voice was even more hoarse than before, his raw throat irritated by the dust.

"Good." The mercenary grinned. "Come here." She was taller and heavier than him, and the boots of her armor added six inches. Jacques tried to pull away, but she locked her gauntleted hand around his arm. It didn't hurt, at least not compared to what they had already done to him, but bile rose in his throat anyway. When she pulled him against her side, he thought she had gone nuts, pawing him after a bomb had blown up the place. Then he realized she was keeping him close in case she had to protect him again.

While the mercenaries and Razers checked the area, the man called Robert spoke into his palmtop. The collapse had trapped them in the hall, but Jacques could hear robots or people digging, presumably to rescue them. As much as he hoped no more blasts went off, a part of him wondered if it wouldn't be better to die now than to suffer anymore.

Why someone would want to blow them up, he had no idea.

Robert stood in Jai's sitting room, his face drawn, his usually impeccable clothes rumpled. He continued his report, his voice weary. "If any evidence existed in the mansion of who hired the mercenaries, the blast destroyed the records. We found nothing."

Jai motioned him to another wing chair at the octagonal table where he sat. As Robert sat down, Jai said, "The frigates that attacked the Skolian yacht must have records."

Robert pushed back his tousled hair. "We haven't been able to track down the ships."

"What happened to their crews?" Supposedly, they had worked for Corbal, though the Xir lord claimed otherwise. The irony was that Jai thought Corbal was telling the truth. Of course no one believed it; Hightons always denied knowledge of the pirates that worked for them.

"They disappeared after the blast," Robert said. "The mercenaries can't tell us who hired them. They test out with lie detectors."

Damn. After Azile Xir's intelligence people had put so much effort into tracking down the pirates, it was frustrating to have them escape. "Who set the blast?"

"Supposedly an enemy of Lord Xir."

"Does that mansion really belong to Corbal?"

"Apparently so." Robert checked his palmtop. "One of his taskmaker descendants lives there for part of the year. She claims it was supposed to be empty right now."

A sense of defeat rolled over Jai. He had held out too much hope that they could confiscate records of the attack on Seabreak's ship, snatching them from the mercenaries who had helped in the raid. If any other records existed, he had no idea where to find them.

"What about the man they kidnapped?" Jai asked. "What was his name? Ardoise?"

"Yes. Jacques Ardoise. He is shaken, but safe. We brought him to Glory."

Jai thought of the Intelligence reports he had skimmed. "Is he a Skolian or Allied citizen?" It could make a difference in how they dealt with the situation.

Robert flicked several holicons floating above his mesh, then read from the screen. "He lives on Earth, but he is a Skolian citizen. His wife is an Allied citizen, a physicist at a place called CERN. She and their children have dual citizenship."

Jai nodded, appreciating how Robert judged so well what he needed to know and had the information ready. "Good work."

Robert had an odd look. "Thank you, Your Highness."

Puzzled by Robert's expression, Jai eased his barriers. He picked up an image from his aide of Ur Qox and Viquara Iquar, Jai's grandparents. Robert had served both. Jai didn't catch details, but he could fill them in with what he already knew; had Robert brought such disappointing news to Jai's predecessors, they would have put him in isolation, deprived him of sleep, inflicted pain, or demoted him. Supposedly the fear of such punishment drove aides to make sure they didn't fail. Jai thought it was a stupid philosophy. It just led to cover-ups worse than the original problem, as demoralized aides scrambled to save their own backsides at the expense of anyone else they could blame.

Robert's mesh chimed. He flicked the comm holicon. "Yes?"

A voice came out of the comm. "The provider is here, sir."

Robert glanced at Jai. When Jai nodded, Robert said, "Bring him in."

An archway across the room shimmered open. Two Razers escorted in a young man with blond hair and vivid blue eyes. He wore a white shirt and blue pants made from gilter-velvet. A sapphire collar circled his neck, and sapphire cuffs flashed on his wrists and below the hem of his pants. Jai had never been a good judge of what women found attractive, but even he could tell Jacques Ardoise was unusually good-looking. The musician also looked terrified.

The Razers bowed to Jai, and Ardoise went down on one knee, lowering his head. He may have lived on Earth, where people no longer knelt to leaders, but he had learned Highton customs well, probably as a survival mechanism.

"Please rise." Although Jai was becoming more used to the kneeling, it still bothered him.

Ardoise stood slowly. He kept his expression guarded, but nothing could hide the hatred in his mind. After being so long among Eubians with no empathic ability, Jai was startled by how strongly Ardoise's emotions hit him.

Jai indicated a chair across the table. One of the Razers pulled out the chair for Ardoise, and the musician sat down. Although Ardoise tried to act calm, his agitation beat against Jai's mind.

Jai waited, as Hightons usually did when meeting a stranger. He didn't do it for long, though; the intent, as far as he could tell, was to make the other person uncomfortable, which wasn't his goal. After a few moments, he spoke in the French he had studied on Earth. "Are you recovered well from the explosion?"

Ardoise jerked, then sat up straighter. He answered in French. "Yes, Your Highness."

"We regret you were caught in that problem."

"Thank you." The loathing in Ardoise's mind belied his courteous words.

Jai was at a loss. He didn't know what to do with Ardoise. The musician had no political connections Jai could use to justify sending him home. Had he been an Allied citizen, it might have worked, but freeing a Skolian was a touchier proposition. Jai would have done it anyway if he could have managed it without further eroding his support among the Hightons. But he could take no risks that might scuttle the peace talks. Unfortunately, if he didn't release Ardoise, that could also wreck the talks. Eube had violated the unspoken truce; now Jai had to appease the Skolians. No matter what choice he made, it would anger someone.

He glanced at the captain of his Razers. "You and your men may leave. I will talk to our guest in private." It was, in fact, the truth, though Jai knew no one believed it. The Razers were disappointed; they wanted to stay and transcend while Jai interrogated his new provider. It made Jai sick. Ardoise looked as if he wanted to die—or else kill Eube's emperor.

Jai glanced at Robert. "You may return to your office. Please tell my wife I would like her to attend me."

"Yes, Your Highness."

Robert wouldn't look at him. At first Jai thought his aide had made the same assumption as the Razers. When Jai concentrated, though, he realized Robert didn't believe he would torture a provider, which by Highton standards made Jai aberrant. Yet despite his many years among Aristos, Robert approved of Jai's behavior. His loyalty went beyond the expected fealty; he genuinely believed Jai had the makings of a great leader.

Even after everyone had gone, leaving Jai alone with Ardoise, Jai wasn't certain they were safe from monitors. His people had scanned this room, but he wasn't ready to trust the results. So he settled in his wing chair and motioned to Ardoise. "Please. Be comfortable." He hated knowing what Ardoise thought about him.

The musician inched back in his chair, but stayed stiff with tension, his fist clenched on his knees.

"So." Jai didn't know what to say. "You live in France?"

Ardoise answered in a low voice. "Yes."

After another silence, Jai tried again. "Are you thirsty?" He indicated the decanter and goblets on the table. "Would you care for some wine?"

"Wine . . . ? Y-yes." Then, remembering himself, Ardoise said, "Thank you, Your Highness."

"It is my pleasure." Jai poured two glasses of wine and gave him one.

Ardoise hesitated. "Do you want me to drink first?" His face had paled.

Remembering Corbal's "lesson" with the bird, Jai said, "No. It has been tested." He tried his drink. The bioguards in his body verified it was an excellent vintage—free of poison—and let him swallow the wine.

Ardoise sipped his drink, paused, then closed his eyes and downed the rest in one swallow. Opening his eyes, he regarded Jai with a despair he had quit trying to hide. As much as Jai wanted to offer reassurances, he could say nothing until he was certain of privacy. He set his goblet on the table, having lost his taste for the wine.

A chime broke the silence, and the entrance to the room shimmered open. Tarquine stood within the archway like a sleek, svelte weapon. Jai sat up as straight as Ardoise.

"Greetings, Husband." She walked into the room, long and sensuous, and the entrance solidified behind her, leaving the Razers outside.

Jai rose to his feet, and Ardoise jumped up as well so he wouldn't be sitting while the emperor stood. Tarquine stopped at the table and looked over the musician, her gaze appraising.

Jai spoke in Highton. "This is Jacques Ardoise."

"He is a beauty, Husband. But an unusual gift."

Jai scowled. "He isn't for you."

"For you, then? I didn't know you liked—"

"No!" Jai reddened. "I don't."

She gave Jai a sultry smile. "Pity. It might be fun, the three of us."

"Tarquine, cut it out." His face flamed.

Ardoise was watching them with a horrified fascination. Jai could tell he understood none of their Highton words.

Tarquine turned back to Ardoise and spoke in Skolian Flag. "You would treat your empress with such disrespect?"

Ardoise froze. At first Jai wondered at his lack of response. Easing his mental barriers, he found the answer; Ardoise didn't speak Flag. Living on Earth with his wife, he had needed French more. Now, faced with Tarquine, what little Flag he knew had deserted him.

"My, my," Tarquine murmured. "Are we a statue today?"

Jai glared at her. Then he spoke to Ardoise in French. "My wife bids you welcome."

The Skolian obviously knew Tarquine wasn't giving him welcome, at least not the warm and fuzzy variety. Averting his gaze, he knelt to her with his head bowed.

"Our manners are improving," Tarquine said in Skolian, looking down at him.

"Not 'ours,'" Jai muttered in Highton. "Only his." In French, he said, "My wife thanks you for your gracious gesture and bids you please to rise."

As Ardoise stood, watching them both, Tarquine frowned at Jai. "So you bought yourself a provider. I didn't think you even knew what to do with one."

Jai wanted to retort, but not in front of Ardoise. He never won arguments with Tarquine anyway. Instead he spoke quietly, in Highton. "It would be preferable if we had more time." It was a code they used to mean "more privacy." If anyone could outwit the monitors, it was Tarquine.

Her face remained inscrutable, but he could tell his behavior baffled her. She didn't believe for one moment he wanted to transcend. Corbal, Robert, and Tarquine had all noticed his behavior as unusual in that regard, which meant others probably would as well, if they hadn't already. He had to learn to play his role better if he wanted to survive.

She went to a console against one wall. "It would be my pleasure to free up more time."

As Tarquine worked, Jai sat back down and gestured for Ardoise to do the same. The Skolian sat on the edge of his chair. Sweat sheened his forehead.

Jai spoke in French. "Are you all right?"

Ardoise answered in a low voice. "Your Highness, please. No more."

Jai wanted to crawl under the table. How could Hightons live with themselves, reducing people to this state, thinking it was their exalted right?

Jai glanced at the console. "Tarquine?"

She held up her hand, intent on whatever she was doing. After entering more commands, she flicked her finger through a holicon. "That should do it." Standing up, she turned to him. "We had plenty of time already, but I've arranged for extra, to be certain."

Jai exhaled. "Good."

She came over and dropped into a wing chair at the table. In Highton, she said, "One might wonder what we plan to do with all this time of ours."

He smiled at her. "I have to keep you guessing. Otherwise you would become bored."

"Boredom is never a word I've associated with your reign." Dryly she added, "Things keep blowing up."

Jai winced. "That they do." Switching into French, he turned to Ardoise. "The empress has secured the room."

Ardoise remained silent, watching them.

Jai finally said what he had wanted to tell Ardoise since they met. "No one will harm you. You have my word."

A muscle in Ardoise's cheek twitched.

"Whatever you told him, I don't think he believes you,"

Tarquine said in Highton. "Maybe he doesn't understand. What language is that?"

Jai glanced at her. "French. From Earth."

"You speak Earth languages?"

"I learned it in high school."

She raised an eyebrow. "*This* well?"

"I pick up languages fast." His parents had brought him up speaking Highton, Iotic, Skolian Flag, and Eubic. Shifting from one to another had been second nature to him since he began to talk. He also had an empath's natural advantage; knowing a person's mood helped him understand their words. As a result, languages had always come easily to him. He had studied many, including a few from Earth.

"Impressive," she said. "Can you translate for me?"

"Certainly."

"Good." She contemplated Ardoise. The musician watched her like a deer caught in the lamps of a hovercar.

Jai switched into French. "Monsieur Ardoise, it is not our desire to keep you here against your will."

Ardoise's forehead furrowed. He started to answer, then hesitated.

"Please speak," Jai said.

Ardoise took an unsteady breath. "You paid a lot for me. Why would you let me go?"

Jai wanted to say, *Because buying people is appalling.* But he couldn't go that far. "My people and yours are trying to set up peace talks. Your abduction stalled the process." He nodded toward Tarquine. "I'm going to translate our discussion so my wife can understand." After Ardoise nodded, Jai repeated his words in Highton for Tarquine.

"You want the talks to proceed?" Ardoise asked Jai.

"Yes. I do." Jai spoke carefully, first in French, then in Highton. "The situation is difficult. If I send you home, I lose influence among the Hightons. I need their support for the talks to succeed. But if I don't send you back, your government may cut off negotiations. They consider the raid where you were taken a hostile action, potentially a prelude to war."

Ardoise's forehead furrowed. "Why would you want peace?"

For my parents, Jai thought. "The war debilitated our people. It is time to heal."

"A noble goal." Ardoise obviously didn't believe him.

"We hope to achieve it."

"How, if you can't send me back?"

As Jai translated for Tarquine, she tilted her head toward Ardoise with an expression Jai recognized. She wanted to question the Skolian. When Jai nodded, she spoke to Ardoise, and Jai repeated her words in French.

"We need evidence of who planned the raid where you were captured," Tarquine said.

Ardoise answered without doubt. "Corbal Xir."

Jai scowled. "That's a lie."

Ardoise chose silence over disagreeing with the emperor.

"Can you describe what happened in the raid?" Tarquine asked. "Any detail, no matter how small, might help."

Ardoise stiffened, becoming so tense the tendons in his neck stood out. "I answered everything the mercenaries asked. *Everything.* It's in their records."

Jai gentled his voice. "We aren't going to interrogate you. We need your help to bring the perpetrators of this crime to justice. We have no access to records made by the raiders."

Ardoise pushed back his hair. His arm was shaking. "What do you want to know?"

Jai nodded to Tarquine, whom he suspected could see implications he might miss. She questioned Ardoise skillfully, with Jai translating. At times Jai could barely listen to Ardoise's account of his captivity. More than ever, Jai despised what Aristos stood for and hated that all humanity considered him one of them.

Tarquine surprised him.

Jai had thought Corbal was the only Aristo who felt remorse for the behavior of his caste, but now he felt the anger that smoldered in Tarquine's mind as she listened to Ardoise. It seemed his wife had a conscience after all. She might be as crooked as the path of a particle in Brownian motion, but transcendence sickened her.

After they finished talking with Ardoise, Jai stood up. Tarquine and Ardoise immediately rose to their feet, though Tarquine did it with that quirk of her eyebrows that so flustered him. He didn't know how she managed it, observing all the toadying behavior expected toward the emperor, yet making him seem subservient to her.

When Jai called his Razers into the room, he felt Ardoise's apprehension. Jai spoke in Highton to the Razer captain, taking the time to translate his words into French. "Please escort Monsieur Ardoise to the Emerald Suite. Have my staff provide him with anything he needs for his comfort. He is our honored guest." Until he figured out what to do with the Skolian, he would treat him as a dignitary. Having his staff take care of Ardoise instead of the guards would also free the musician from the mental pressure exerted by the Razers.

After the proper formalities, the Razers escorted Ardoise from the room. When Jai was alone with Tarquine, he settled back into his chair. "What do you think?"

She lounged in her chair, her legs stretched out under the table. "That raid doesn't fit Corbal's style."

Jai scowled. "I didn't know abduction had a style."

"Corbal's pirates test their prisoners for psi traits before they kidnap them. Not after."

"You can't determine a rating from one test."

"But you can get an idea." She shrugged. "They have to be careful. Why steal something with no worth?"

"It's called kidnapping, Tarquine. They aren't fencing stolen goods, they're selling *people*. It's reprehensible."

She went very still, regarding him with a scrutiny that made the hairs on his neck lift. Too late, he realized he had gone too far, condemning the very basis of their economy to one of the highest placed members of his government. He could qualify his statement, try putting it in a better light, but it wouldn't fool her.

Tarquine spoke quietly. "Take care, Husband."

Jai gripped the armrests of his chair. He remembered how she had looked at Ardoise in that instant when she thought Jai was giving her the Skolian. *Hungry.* Tarquine had stopped transcending, but the impulse lived within her, locked and suppressed. He glimpsed its edges every night and skirted it every second in his life with her, never certain how much she knew about him and what she would do with the knowledge, unable to confront her and afraid to delve too deeply into her thoughts, yet just as afraid of what would happen if he left it unspoken.

Jai shook his head. What could he say? *I can't keep on this way.* He had no choice; he couldn't give up and go home.

Tarquine exhaled, her face drawn. "We have a problem."

"Only one?" He managed a weary smile. "The last time I checked, we had too many to count."

"Jaibriol—give up this idea of peace talks."

"I can't."

"These 'problems' aren't going to stop." She shook her head. "The assassination attempts, the propaganda wars, the lies and deceptions, the undermining of your authority—it will only become worse if you continue to push the talks."

"I have to try." He fought to keep his face impassive, but he was losing the battle. So he tried to make a joke. "It isn't as if I have anything to live for besides you." It didn't sound funny. His voice caught on the words.

She started to reach across the space separating them, then held herself back. "No Highton emperor should ever make such an admission."

Her intensity stunned him. She tried to shield her thoughts, but they were too strong to hide; his life, well-being, and happiness mattered to her in a way no Highton empress should ever admit.

Jai took her hands and pressed his lips against her knuckles. She let him for a moment, then pulled away. If he hadn't been an empath, the rejection would have hurt. She responded to him in the only way she knew how, resisting her affection for him because she believed it would weaken them both. Yet the reason she wanted him to be strong, to survive, was because she cared what happened to him.

Tarquine sat back, retreating into her reserve. "We must discover who is behind this war of rumors against you."

Jai let the moment go. "Raziquon, probably. Or the Diamond Coalition."

"Or ESComm."

"We need proof."

She met his gaze. "I doubt we will find it. Whoever is doing this is too adept at hiding."

"I can't give up the peace talks."

"Then bring Kaliga and Taratus here."

He clenched his fist on his knee. "I can hardly stand to be in the same room with them."

"You must try."

"It won't do any good." If he used telepathy to find the evidence he sought, he couldn't reveal how he knew. In theory, he had the authority to replace Kaliga and Taratus without giving a reason, but it could backfire spectacularly. Although his support in ESComm was eroding, he still had the military behind him. If he challenged his powerful Joint Commanders, his support could disintegrate.

Jai leaned his head against the back of his chair and closed his eyes. He had nowhere to turn. He couldn't even convince his own people to trust him, let alone the Skolians.

Tarquine spoke softly. "Just find out what you can from them."

Jai didn't want to do it, but he knew she was right. "Very well." He lifted his head to look at her. "The Qox Dynasty will extend an invitation to the Joint Commanders of ESComm to visit the Qoxire palace."

Her eyes glittered. "Good."

30
Valley

The Ruby Pharaoh played the Kyle web like music.

Kelric stood among the girders that crisscrossed the Triad Chair Chamber. Far above him, supported on massive robot arms, the Chair hung under a dome. Dehya was sitting in the Chair, surrounded by cables and conduits, sheathed in a mesh that linked to her internal biomech web. She looked small and otherworldly, lost in the immensity of the throne and its systems, but it didn't fool Kelric. Mental strength ran through her like a diamond-alloy rod, brilliant and unfathomable.

The Chair slowly lowered from its dome. When it reached the floor, the techs went to work, unfastening Dehya from its tenacious grip. Only a few Triad Chairs survived from the Ruby Empire, including this one and the one in the Lock where Kelric had become Imperator. In this modern age, no one understood how the ancient thrones worked. This much Kelric did know; Triad Chairs were sentient, a form of intelligence so alien, it had little intersection with human thought. He had no idea why the Chairs allowed Triad members to use them to power and develop the Kyle webs.

As the techs worked on Dehya, she opened her eyes and looked straight at Kelric. He had an eerie sense, as if she wasn't completely solid, that part of her remained in the ghostly webs spanning Kyle space, where her mind had been for the last two days. Intravenous feeds had provided nutrients and kept her hydrated. A medic spoke to her, and she shook her head. Kelric knew she was refusing to go to the cool-down facility, a small hospital with the sole purpose of aiding Triad members who had been in the web.

The doctor finally gave in, probably because Dehya was standing on her own, glowering as she adamantly refused help. Four Jagernaut bodyguards accompanied her across the chamber to Kelric. Surrounded by the towering cyberwarriors, she looked like a waif in a white jumpsuit.

"My greetings," Kelric said as she came up to him.

"And mine to you." Her voice sounded like leaves blowing over a distant plane. "It is so raw."

"The web?"

"Yes. So new."

"Did you find anything?"

She nodded, preoccupied as they walked together through the struts and girders, accompanied by their bodyguards. It wasn't until they left the chamber that she spoke. "I'm not sure what I found, though. Glimmers throughout Eube, but nothing definite."

Glimmers of light: it was how she perceived the minds of other telops in the web. Kelric rarely had impressions that distinct; for him, the web was more of a sparkling fog.

"One light was radiant," Dehya said. "It could have been an unusually strong psion, but I'm not sure."

Kelric considered the thought. The psions who lived among the Eubians were providers, their minds traumatized and constrained. It dimmed their light. If Jaibriol III was a psion, his mind could be hurt now, too, like the providers, clenched into itself as a defense against the Aristos.

"Radiance suggests a healthy mind," he said. "I don't see how that could be."

"I know." Fatigue saturated her mood. "It hurts even to think of."

Softly he said, "Yes."

"I found nothing concrete on Jacques Ardoise."

Kelric had discovered nothing about Ardoise, either, but he didn't have Dehya's finesse. Although she lacked his sheer mental power, he had hoped she could find details he had missed. Then again, she had said *nothing concrete*. With Dehya, that word choice could be significant. "Anything less definite?"

"Perhaps." They were walking down a bronze corridor now with their bodyguards. "ESComm might be involved in the raid where Ardoise was kidnapped."

Kelric snorted. "No surprise there."

She smiled slightly. "I checked for connections between the Line of Xir and ESComm. Some appear on the surface, but when I delve deeper, the threads disintegrate."

Interesting. That suggested Xir's links to the pirates might be illusory. Had the Eubian military set him up? "ESComm has a vested interest in stopping the peace talks."

"But does Xir?"

"I wish I knew."

She exhaled. "I also."

Had Kelric never met Jaibriol, he wouldn't have believed the emperor genuinely wished to negotiate. Now he was less certain. The peace process had to be making Jaibriol enemies among the Hightons. If he lost his throne, Corbal Xir would probably become emperor. But Xir was no fool; he knew that whoever sat on the Carnelian Throne became a target. He might prefer wielding power from the shadows, as he undoubtedly did now. If ESComm sought to weaken Xir's power, they might frame him for acts that would anger the emperor.

Then again, maybe Xir didn't give a damn and just wanted providers to auction. It wouldn't surprise Kelric after what he had seen of Azar Taratus, the Highton who had auctioned him and seemed to care for nothing but his own gain.

Lost in thought, Kelric continued on with Dehya, headed to a private magrail station. The Jagernauts kept pace, two in front, two in back. They rode the magrail out to the valley where the Ruby Dynasty lived on the Orbiter. The bodyguards came no farther than the station just outside the valley; within the secluded vale, the Ruby Dynasty homes were protected with the best defenses known to the Imperialate.

Dehya's gracefully terraced house was built against a hill and shaded by trees, dappled in light and shadow. On the next hill over, far up the slope, the Imperator's home stood, bare stone, striking in its simplicity. Kelric thought of his wife up there, Jeejon, and smiled.

As they neared Dehya's house, she asked, "Would you like to come in?"

"Yes, thank you." Kelric enjoyed visiting his kin.

The door within the scrolled entrance arch shimmered and vanished as they approached. It looked lovely, but Kelric knew many deadly systems had monitored their approach before letting that door open. Inside, sunlight slanted through the windows, gilding the empty living room. A glorious singing greeted them, coming from some other room. Kelric recognized the voice; it was his brother, Eldrin, Dehya's consort, the man the Traders had given up for Jaibriol Qox. Eldrin's spectacular baritone filled the house.

Dehya stopped and sighed. "He hasn't sung much since he came back from the Traders." Her small fist clenched at her side. "He could barely talk at first, his voice was so hoarse."

Anger surged in Kelric. "I'm sorry."

She made a visible effort to relax. "It is over now. That is what matters."

Kelric knew her anger wouldn't release any more easily than his. Yet incredibly, she was right: it *was* over. Against all the odds, Eldrin had come home.

The singing eased into silence. Dehya headed toward an archway across the room that opened into a hallway. She had only gone a few steps when Eldrin stepped into the hall. It didn't surprise Kelric; his brother had probably picked up their mental signatures when they entered the house, just as Kelric picked up his now. Kelric didn't think his brother really understood the positive effect he had on people. Eldrin's mind was like the swells of a sunlit ocean with waves that rocked in deep, soothing motion. If Kelric was strength and Dehya finesse, Eldrin was warmth.

Eldrin met Dehya in the archway, and he took her hands. "My greetings."

"And to you," she murmured.

It gratified Kelric to see how much better his brother looked now compared to when he had first come home. Thinking of Eldrin's captivity and his own experiences as a provider, he found it hard to imagine talking peace with the Traders. And yet—Corbal Xir had freed Eldrin. Kelric couldn't reconcile that with the Highton who had so cavalierly crippled the peace process by abducting a Skolian. The Allieds could claim from now until forever that they had arranged the trade of Eldrin for Jaibriol III, but that wouldn't change the truth; when Dehya had tracked Eldrin to Delos and come for him, the Allieds hadn't even known his identity. Jaibriol Qox had orchestrated that trade himself.

Did Qox truly want peace? It seemed impossible to believe.

The house EI said, "Councilor Roca is here." In that instant, the door chimed.

Dehya started, turning around. "Let her in."

The front door shimmered open, revealing a woman. Her eyes were gold and her hair fell over her arms in gold and bronze waves. Seeing her in the entrance, Kelric relived the moment on Earth when she had thrown open the doors at Allied United Centre and run to him, the son she had believed dead for eighteen years. He had been blind then, but she had created such a vivid impression that he had seen her in the minds of everyone else in the lobby. He remembered his tears. Joyful tears.

Eldrin walked into the living room with Dehya. "Greetings, Mother."

Roca joined them. "Gorgeous day outside." Her disgruntled tone contrasted with her cheery words.

"Is everything all right?" Dehya asked.

Roca scowled at Kelric. "Light of my life, my youngest,

sweetest child, it pleases me more than I can say to see you today."

Kelric blinked. He was about as sweet as iron shavings. "What's wrong?"

She glared at him. "Far be it from me to suggest that my impressive Imperator son is ignoring his wife."

What? Jeejon was always in his mind. "Is she all right?"

"So you remember you have a consort." Roca crossed her arms. "Good. It's a start."

Exasperated, he touched a panel on his gauntlet, keying in the code for Jeejon's palmtop. After waiting, he glanced at his mother. "She's not answering."

"She doesn't want to disturb your work."

"I'm not working."

"Did you tell her that?"

"Surely she knows she can talk to me." His face relaxed into a smile. "I like to talk to her."

Roca relented a fraction. "Kelric, all she knew before she met you was life as a low-level taskmaker. She was a slave, and now she is married to one of the most powerful men alive. Of course she's having trouble with it. She didn't even know, at first, that when you disappeared for days at a time, you were working in the web."

Gods. What kind of empath was he, if he hadn't picked up on his wife's distress? He understood why his mother noticed, though; since the death of his father, she had mourned deeply, her grief sensitizing her even more to the loneliness of others. He strode toward the door.

"Kelric, wait," his mother said.

He turned back. "Yes?"

Roca sighed. "You are a brilliant man, my son, when it comes to military strategy or mathematics, but with women you could use a bit more subtlety."

"What do you suggest?"

"Help her adjust." She spoke quietly. "So far you've protected her from publicity. But you can't much longer. It will soon become known that you married a Eubian taskmaker."

Kelric frowned. If anyone had a problem with his wife's common birth, they could go to the devil. "I stand by her."

Her voice softened. "I know. *She* is the one having trouble dealing with it. For her entire life, since before her birth, she was molded, trained, and designed to think of Aristos as godlike and of herself as nothing. Now she has to face them as your consort, possibly soon, if the talks go forward."

"Why didn't she say anything to me?"

"You know Jeejon. She never complains. She thinks it would be ungrateful of her to disturb you."

"Ungrateful?" He gave her an incredulous look. "Gods, she saved my life. I would never have made it back to Earth without her help. I was *dying*. I'm the one who owes her."

"For saints' sake," his mother said. "I hope you didn't tell her you married her because you were grateful."

"Of course not." He thought back to his proposal, when he was lying in a hospital bed on Earth. "I told her we had a good neural resonance."

Dehya, who had been standing with them, laughed. "Now *that* was romantic."

Kelric scowled. Jeejon, if he recalled, had made a similar comment, and in about that same tone of voice. "What's wrong with that?"

"Kelric." Eldrin took his arm and led him away from the women. When Roca started to follow, Dehya intercepted and herded her over to a recessed window across the room. Kelric had no doubt Dehya was distracting her with talk of politics. Perhaps they would solve the Eube-Skolia conflict while he and Eldrin grappled with the more difficult question of wives.

Despite Kelric's several past marriages, he had a remarkable lack of experience in certain ways. Most of his marriages had been against his will or arranged, where he hardly knew his wife on his wedding day. Even when he had been offered a choice, the woman had been the one to court him. He had been pursued, seduced, coveted, kidnapped, bought, and sold, but only once in his life had *he* sought the relationship—with Jeejon. And that hadn't involved courtship. He had no experience with wooing a woman, either before or after they said their vows.

Eldrin spoke without preamble. "Do something to show Jeejon that you think she is special."

"I do that all the time."

"How?"

Kelric squinted at him. "I think about her a lot."

The corners of Eldrin's mouth quirked up, though he tried to hide his smile. "Oh, well, that ought to do it."

"It's true."

"You know that saying women have, 'I can't read your mind'? Well, my wife *can* read my mind, and it doesn't make a whit of difference. You have to show them."

Eldrin was too tactful to add, *you've never had to work at this,* but Kelric caught the thought from Eldrin's mind. "What do you suggest?" Kelric asked.

"What does she like?"

"Me."

Eldrin looked like he was trying not to laugh. "If you want to make your wife feel desired, I suggest you could come up with something more than, 'Here I am. Aren't you lucky?' "

Kelric winced. "I didn't mean that." He scratched his chin. "I could give her flowers."

"Too generic. What can the two of you do together?"

"She likes to play those VR games."

Eldrin grinned. "So take her to an arcade."

Kelric regarded him dubiously. "As Imperator, it would be anomalous for me to go to an arcade."

"You could have one installed at the house."

Kelric considered the thought. "Yes, I do think she would like that."

"Well, there, you have an answer."

It seemed an odd answer to Kelric, to build his wife a VR arcade, but perhaps she would like it. "Very well." He glanced at Roca and Dehya, who were standing by a window, bathed in light. They looked serene, but he doubted their argument was anywhere near as peaceful. Their tension emanated through the room.

Eldrin followed his gaze. "Perhaps we should find out what they're talking about before they do something drastic, like declaring war on someone."

Kelric smiled. "Only I can do that."

Eldrin gave him a dour look. "Don't be so sure." Then he headed across the room.

As Kelric and Eldrin drew nearer, Roca turned to them and motioned irately at Dehya. "Perhaps you can talk sense into her."

"About what?" Eldrin asked.

"I think we should go ahead with the peace talks," Dehya said.

Kelric spoke. "No."

"We must," Dehya said.

"Not while they hold Ardoise prisoner."

Dehya frowned at him. "That is exactly what ESComm wants, for us to pull out."

"Jaibriol Qox controls ESComm," Kelric said.

Eldrin spoke dryly. "He is eighteen. He's probably lucky if he can control himself, let alone ESComm."

"His advisers will be the ones with power," Roca said. Grimly, she added, "And Corbal Xir."

Dehya looked around at them. "I can't give you proof Jaibriol Qox is sincere. It's more my sense of what I found in the web. But I think he wants peace. If we let ESComm destroy the talks, we play right into their hands."

"That may be," Kelric said. "But if we go to those talks now, we're telling them they can brutalize our citizens and we'll still negotiate. We can't undermine our position that way, especially not with Aristos."

Dehya turned away and stared at the window. "We need those talks."

Kelric wanted them, too. But he knew the Hightons. "We can't give in on this."

"Has Qox responded to our protest over the Ardoise incident?" Eldrin asked.

Roca answered. "Nothing." She glanced at Dehya, who was still staring out the window. "Not a word."

"What should he do?" Dehya said, more to herself than to them. "If he sends Ardoise back, ESComm will shred him."

"If he can't handle ESComm," Kelric said, "then any agreements he makes with us mean nothing."

"I know." Dehya turned to them. "I had just hoped this time might be different."

Kelric understood. For centuries, their people had hoped that someday, somehow, it might be different with the Traders. But it had never happened in the past, and it looked like it wouldn't happen now either.

The silence in the house seemed to echo, though logically Kelric knew that made no sense. He walked through the spacious rooms searching for Jeejon. When he found only empty space and polished stone, he grew concerned. Surely she wouldn't leave. Not Jeejon.

Sensing what he wanted, his gauntlet activated its comm and paged his aide. A voice came out of the mesh. "Lieutenant Qahot here, sir."

"Qahot—" Kelric paused, self-conscious. He pushed the words out all at once, before he could back out. "I need you to find out what it would require to install a VR arcade in my house."

"Yes, sir. Certainly." Qahot sounded amused.

"Thank you, Lieutenant. Out."

"Out, sir."

Kelric winced. Saints only knew what his officers would think if the rumor spread that he wanted an arcade. Well, never mind. An Imperator and his wife had a right to relax once in a while.

He touched another panel on his gauntlet, and the house EI said, "Attending."

"Comp, can you locate my wife?"

"She is outside, behind the house."

Kelric went out the back of the house and crossed a slope covered by green grass. As he came over a swell of the land, he saw Jeejon seated on the hill, facing away from him, staring out over the ravine and the silver ribbon of a stream that wound along it far below. A breeze stirred her hair, fluffing the silvery curls.

As he reached her, she turned with a start. "Kelric."

He smiled, warmed by her presence. Maybe no one else approved of his telling her that they had a good neural resonance, but it was true. Her mind affected his, making him feel good whenever he came near her.

Sitting next to her, he took her hand in his. The hill was steep enough that they didn't need to lean back much to have its support. The slope rolled away more gently at their feet, almost flat, then plunged down to the river.

Kelric thought of his brother's advice to express his emotions. "You look beautiful today."

She snorted. "Have you been drinking?"

Laughing, he said, "No."

Jeejon made a *hmmmph* noise, but she settled against him, her mood pleased even if she pretended otherwise. She said no more, in keeping with the terse dialect used by taskmakers where she had lived, a minimalist speech style that rationed words. It was one reason he liked her; she could be as taciturn as him.

Kelric put his arm around her shoulder and they sat enjoying the view. It took a while to decide how to phrase his question. Finally he said, "The peace talks may fall through."

Jeejon sighed. "I am sorry. I know you had hopes."

"Yes." When she said nothing more, he tried again. "But we haven't lost hope."

"Good."

"If they do proceed, we will meet on Earth. As VR simulacra, not in person."

"Smart idea."

"Jeejon?"

"Eh?"

"The talks won't just be discussions. There will also be diplomatic-type events."

" 'Diplomatic-type'?" She laughed. "What does that mean?"

"You know. Dinners. Receptions."

"People need to eat in VR?"

Kelric smiled. "No. But the social aspect is part of the process."

"It seems a waste of time."

"I suppose." He paused. "As my consort, you will be expected to attend."

She went very still. "With you?"

"Yes. With me."

"Wouldn't know what to do."

"Who wouldn't? You or me?"

"Ha. Funny." She didn't sound amused.

"We have people who can help you adapt."

"I feel like I would need a new brain."

He brushed his lips over her hair. "The one you have is perfect."

"Heh." She started to speak, then stopped.

"Yes?" Kelric asked.

"What Aristos would come to the talks?"

"Emperor Qox. One of ESComm's Joint Commanders. Qox's advisers."

"Ministers?"

"Some of them."

"Like Finance."

Kelric tensed. "Yes, Finance."

She pulled her hand out of his. "The emperor needs financial advice to make peace?"

He took her hand again. "Jeejon, she is the empress. She has to be there."

His wife didn't answer.

"It makes no difference to me," he said.

"You still love her?"

He let out an explosive breath. "Gods above, where did you get the idea I loved that barracuda?"

"You think about her all the time."

"Yes, I do. Every day I thank the saints I'm free."

She said nothing, but he felt her disbelief.

"How do I make you believe me?" he asked.

"With the truth."

Kelric knew she would see through any platitudes he tried. So he said, "Yes, I slept with her. I didn't have much choice in the matter. They gave me drugs."

"Drugs, pah."

"I didn't love her, Jeejon. I hated her."

"You liked the sex." She didn't make it a question.

"It meant nothing."

She turned in his arms, facing him, her face flushed with uncharacteristic anger. "She's a *Highton*. I can't compete with that."

Kelric took hold of her shoulders. "She's no one. And you don't have to compete with her."

She put her palms against his shoulders. "I'm afraid."

"Don't be." He pulled her close. "I need you."

"I don't know how to help you."

"Just be yourself." He searched for the words to explain. "You settle me."

She rested her head against his shoulder. "Maybe."

"Jeejon—"

No answer.

Kelric laid his head on hers, knowing she would say no more. But he had felt a slight shift in her mood, less uncertainty and more optimism. He would continue this way, each day, until she believed him.

So they sat, two players in the twilight of a truce between Skolia and Eube that was dimming despite the best efforts of many people to make it work.

31

The Blue Room

A gonizing.

It was the only way Jai could describe the visit of his Joint Commanders to the palace. Being in the same room with Admiral Kaliga and General Taratus was agonizing, but he could show no sign of it, lest they perceive weakness in him.

The Grand Ballroom—ceiling, floor, walls, and columns— was made from sparkling white stone veined with black. Jai stood with Tarquine while Highton after Highton filed into the reception. Everything glittered: their black clothes, their black hair, and their diamond finger cymbals, one on the thumb and one on the index finger. The only color in the room came from their red eyes.

Each Highton walked along a line of Razers to the emperor and empress. The Razers never moved. Jai wasn't even sure they were breathing. Were they more machine than human? They never gave their names. He didn't even know if they went home at night or just turned themselves off. They could stand this way for hours, always vigilant.

When the Hightons reached the end of the Razers, they bowed to Jai, then to Tarquine. They tapped their cymbals twice, sending chimes through the hall. Then they walked along another line of Razers away from the emperor and empress. No one spoke. The process made Jai's head hurt. This reception was meant to be a party, but as far as he could see, no one was having fun. The Hightons didn't dance; they didn't eat; they didn't drink. After they went through the line, they stood in groups and watched Jai greet other Hightons.

Finally the procession ended, and the Razers dispersed throughout the ballroom. Scanning the room, Jai saw Corbal standing by a column. When the Xir lord nodded, Jai raised his arm and, for the first time that night, tapped his finger cymbals. A melodic note vibrated in the air.

Providers filed into the hall, carrying trays with crystal goblets and decanters of a clear liquid. Jai froze. Although he knew his staff had arranged refreshment, he hadn't realized providers would serve it. They flustered him. They wore no colors. In fact, they wore almost nothing at all, neither the women nor the men. Their G-strings were chains of diamonds, and diamonds studded their slave restraints. The women had diamond chains slung low on their hips and diamond rings in their nipples. All of them had the same pale platinum hair. The only color came from their eyes, a vivid blue.

He didn't know which appalled him more, the display of providers or that he enjoyed watching the women so much. He tore his gaze away from one girl, praying Tarquine hadn't noticed him looking. As the providers circulated, Jai and Tarquine split up and moved among their guests. The Hightons finally began to converse, though their discussions were more like duels than small talk. Jai took refuge in silence. It worked surprisingly well; Aristos used silence as a form of manipulation, so his lack of response made him seem in control rather than at a loss for words.

Corbal maneuvered people around the room like chess pieces, gradually bringing together Jai, Admiral Kaliga, and General Taratus. A pleasure girl served them drinks. As Kaliga stared at her, she flushed, her mood a hazy blend of fear and unwilling desire. Her gaze had a glossy sheen. With a start, Jai realized she was drugged with aphrodisiacs. Looking around the hall, he realized the other providers had the same look. Well, surprise. Apparently the emperor's hospitality extended beyond food and drink, regardless of whether or not the emperor knew.

As Kaliga took a goblet from the tray, he brushed his thumb across the girl's nipple. She averted her gaze, her face turning red.

Kaliga nodded to Jai. "You are a most gracious host, Your Highness."

Jai gritted his teeth. He knew why Corbal had sent over the prettiest pleasure girl; it was an apology, supposedly from Jai, for having taken Kaliga's favored provider that night in Kaliga's home. Although Jai understood better now how he had offended the admiral, he couldn't regret his actions, not when he knew what Kaliga would have done to Silver that night.

Taratus surveyed the hall, less circumspect than Kaliga about leering at the servers. He raised his goblet, his florid face ruddy from the liqueur. "The Line of Qox entertains well."

Jai inclined his head. It both mortified and aroused him to realize why the ballroom had so many alcoves hidden behind those stately columns; tonight, the providers would also be dessert. If Jai really intended to win back the support of ESComm, he had made a good start, judging from Taratus's and Kaliga's moods, but plying his Joint Commanders with expensive liqueur and beautiful pleasure slaves had hardly been his intent. As much as he knew he had to concentrate on their minds and discover their secrets, he couldn't make himself do it. Even with his defenses fortified, he could barely keep from leaving the hall.

"A serene gathering," Kaliga commented.

Jai blinked. *Serene?* Hardly. He tried to focus on Kaliga, easing his mental defenses, but his headache and anxiety increased immediately. As soon as he picked up what Kaliga meant by "serene"—the peace talks—he snapped on his barriers. If any Hightons felt the effects of his discomfort, Jai hoped they would attribute it to the presence of so many providers.

"Serenity has its time and place," Corbal said, neutral.

"And its limitations," Taratus muttered.

"So it does," Jai said. He hadn't intended any hidden meaning with the remark, but he sensed wary approval from Kaliga. Damn. The admiral thought Jai was exploring the idea of limiting the peace talks. If he wasn't careful, he might end up promising to give up the negotiations.

Unfortunately, Jai couldn't discern much else from Kaliga. To find the answers he sought, he would have to lower his defenses again, even more than before, and for longer. He couldn't do it here; he would go catatonic from the pressure of so many Highton minds.

Corbal sipped his drink. "Limitations can become opportunities."

"Opportunities are always appreciated," Kaliga said.

Jai could have throttled Corbal. His cousin was encouraging them to think Jai might cancel the talks. That Corbal put out the idea without consulting Jai didn't bode well for the rest of the night. Jai drained his goblet and set it back on the tray. His hand shook slightly, but he managed to cover the motion. His urge to escape increased.

Corbal lifted his goblet. "A long and successful evening, Your Highness."

Jai dreaded finding out what his "success" had been. Emotions swirled around him; Taratus and Kaliga remained guarded, but the visit was easing their enmity. Taratus in particular enjoyed Jai's "hospitality."

"Long indeed," General Taratus said. He thunked his empty goblet on the tray. If it hadn't been for his Highton appearance, Jai thought he would have looked more at home in a holo-bar on Earth, swigging beer. The general considered the provider with undisguised hunger. "It will be good to rest."

Corbal gave him a cool Highton smile. "I have heard it said the wicked never rest."

Jai almost choked on his wine. What was Corbal doing, insulting Taratus? But rather than taking offense, the general guffawed. "Then surely we deserve a long rest, eh?"

"Surely," Kaliga murmured, with a ghost of a smile.

Corbal motioned toward an arch behind several columns. "Perhaps you would enjoy a tour of the palace?"

"A tour, eh." Taratus took a full goblet off the tray. Then he tugged on the ring in the provider's nipple. "Bring our nectar, doll."

Kaliga slid his arm around the girl's waist. "Such a fine vintage." As Kaliga pulled the girl along, her fear diffused through the drugged haze of her mind.

Jai wanted to sock both Kaliga and Taratus. He barely held back the urge as he walked stiffly with their group toward the archway. If they didn't stop pawing the girl, he might be tempted to do it anyway, Joint Commanders or no.

When they reached the arch, another group joined them, four Razers escorting a Highton.

Tarquine.

Ah, hell. Jai was excruciatingly aware of the almost naked girl in their midst. Tarquine inclined her head to him, but her manner was chillier than ice, and sweat broke out on his forehead. Neither Kaliga nor Taratus seemed surprised to see her. Corbal hid his annoyance, but Jai felt it in his mind.

They all left the hall together.

Kaliga relaxed among the many cushions, lying on his side, his weight supported on his elbow. This circular chamber had no furniture, nothing except the pillows and a blue carpet so thick it felt like a cloud. The walls and ceiling were tiled in shades of blue, making Jai feel as if he were inside a jewel box.

They made a rough circle, with Taratus reclining next to Kaliga, and Jai sitting by Taratus. Corbal had left, Jai wasn't sure why, but the others didn't seem to mind. Tarquine was sitting cross-legged between Kaliga and Jai. She glanced at Jai, her face neutral, but he understood her unspoken question: Had he found out anything? Even if he could have answered, he had nothing to say. He couldn't relax his barriers enough to spy on either Kaliga or Taratus.

The provider was kneeling between Kaliga and Tarquine, her hair spilling over her lovely body. As she offered the admiral a drink, she averted her gaze. Jai didn't blame her. He didn't want to look at those icy red eyes, either. The girl also wouldn't look at him, though, an unwelcome reminder that his eyes were just as disturbing. At least she didn't seem to have picked up his differences. She wasn't a strong telepath, and with aphrodisiacs muddling her mind, she would have trouble distinguishing individual minds. She probably couldn't tell he and Tarquine didn't affect her in the same way as other Hightons.

Intent on the girl, Kaliga took her tray and set it on the rug behind him. She continued to kneel, staring at the floor.

"Platinum," Kaliga said in a low voice. "Such a pretty metal." He twirled a strand of her hair around his fingers.

"Pretty," Taratus mumbled. He finished off his fourth drink, then tossed the goblet behind them. When it hit the wall and shattered, he didn't even look. Jai had to bite the inside of his mouth to keep from swearing. That one goblet was worth more than what some people in the Appalachians, where he had lived on Earth, earned in a month.

As Taratus put his arm around the girl and kissed her, he played with her breast. Kaliga closed his eyes and stretched out his legs so he and Taratus were penning the girl inside the circle of Hightons. Taratus kept at her, pulling on her nipple rings. Every time the girl twitched, Kaliga breathed out as if he were the one caressing her.

Jai clenched the carpet, almost pulling out the pile. He knew he was a prude by Highton standards, but gods, all five of them *together*? This was too much. He tried not to stare as Taratus fondled the girl.

When Tarquine sighed, Jai almost jumped. She was lying on her side now, watching him from half-closed eyes, her red irises dramatic through the black fringe of her lashes. But behind her sensuous look, Jai recognized the warning in her gaze. She might be pretending to the languorous, hazy mood, but her mind remained as sharp as a trap.

Taratus lifted his head and looked down at the provider. "Pretty," he mumbled. Then he splayed his palm against her chest and pushed. She fell backward, landing on her back, the top of her head brushing Tarquine's stomach, her silky hair flying across Jai's lap.

Tarquine laughed softly. "How kind of you, General." With her head propped up on one hand, she stroked the girl's hair. General Taratus grunted at Tarquine, kneeling over the pleasure girl now, his weight braced on his palms. Kaliga continued to lie on his side, his eyes closed.

Jai wanted to leave. No matter how hard he tried to act blasé, their casual approach to intimacy shocked him. For all his dismay, though, he couldn't help but notice the provider. Here she was, naked and nubile, ready for them. Filling his hands with her silky hair, he lifted it to his face and inhaled. It smelled like perfume. From the way his desire surged, he suspected it was also producing an aphrodisiac. He was beginning not to care. Straitlaced or not, he was growing dazed with pleasure.

Taratus ran his finger along the chain of diamonds around the girl's waist. She sighed, moving under him, pressing her hips against his pelvis. When Tarquine began to fondle the girl's breasts, Jai flushed, unable to believe this was happening. His wife and the provider? He couldn't do that. Really. All the time he kept telling himself he couldn't make love to a pleasure girl and his wife at the same time, he kept caressing the girl's hair. She was murmuring now, her eyes closed, her body undulating from their attentions. Then Tarquine gave Jai the full force of her sultry stare, and he thought he was going to perish right then and there.

"Tarquine—" His voice came out in a husky whisper.

As the empress leaned in and kissed him, his hand slid across the pleasure girl's breast and he groaned. Vaguely, in his side vision, Jai saw Kaliga take something sharp from his belt, a syringe of some kind. The admiral reached for the provider. Jai wanted Kaliga and Taratus to go away, leaving the girl and Tarquine here for him—

Then the provider screamed—and her agony blasted through Jai.

32

Siren Call

Jai wasn't sure how he left the blue-tiled room. He found himself in a nearby bathing chamber, kneeling over a gold-tiled pool, vomiting his guts out. He knew his bodyguards were hovering over him, that one of them started to talk into a comm, and that someone else stopped the Razer from making a report. Jai didn't care. His mind had been blasted open, wide open, leaving him in agony.

Raising his head, he spoke hoarsely to the captain. "Flood the blue room with gas. Knock out everyone in it." His mind was raw to his bodyguards, undefended. If he hadn't replaced some of his Razers with non-Aristos, the pressure they exerted on him would have been unbearable. Desperate, he shored up his demolished barriers.

Tarquine knelt next to him. "It is your illness." Her voice was low with warning. "Shall we go to your rooms?"

Jai clenched the rim of the pool. "What, this is just the emperor being bizarre again? Blame his behavior on his 'eccentricities,' is that it?" Standing up, he pulled away from her. "Not this time." He swung around to the captain. "Gas the goddamn room."

The captain's usually impassive face was set in tense lines—and Jai finally discovered how far his authority went with his bodyguards. The captain made no move to carry out his order.

"Do it," Jai ground out. "Or you're dead."

The Razer stared at him, obviously trying to decide if Jai was bluffing. Then he raised his wrist and spoke into his comm, giving the order. Jai watched, aware of them all staring at him.

Jai knew when the gas took effect. The screams of the provider faded in his mind. He inhaled, suddenly free of her pain. Taratus and Kaliga had been so deep in their brutal transcendence, they had barely realized he had left. But nothing would ever erase her agony from his mind. Even though she had known how their ménage might end, the shock of pain had caught her hard; multiplied by her undefended telepath's mind, it had shattered Jai's barriers as well, ripping his mind wide open.

He wanted to die. Before Kaliga and Taratus had gone to work on her, he had been with them, wanting her for himself. He felt so ill he thought he would vomit again.

Without another word, Jai left the chamber. As the Razers fell into formation, Tarquine caught up with him.

"Jaibriol," she said.

"Go to hell."

She stiffened but didn't answer. She and the Razers kept pace as he strode down an arched hallway tiled in blue and gold. The walls curved at the floor and ceiling, and no cross-hall came in at right angles. Nothing met anything else square on. Oblique and convoluted: Aristo built as they thought.

Tough.

In his side vision, he saw Tarquine turn to the captain. He felt her intent; she wanted the Razers to stop him before he trapped himself in a situation he couldn't escape. Jai had no intention of changing his plans, regardless of what she told his bodyguards.

He stopped abruptly. "Captain, where is Corbal Xir?"

The Razer lifted his arm to speak into the comm embedded

in his gauntlet. Then Jai realized he wasn't wearing a gauntlet; his entire arm was cybernetic.

Tarquine spoke in a low voice. "Be careful, Husband."

"Of what?" He turned a hard gaze on her. "Or should I say of *who*? Taratus? Kaliga? Corbal? You?"

A flush tinged her cheeks, marring the snow-marble skin. His ice empress was losing her cool. "Do you have any idea the magnitude of what you have done?"

He met her gaze. "I gassed my Joint Commanders."

She had the look of someone who had just seen a wild person jump off a cliff. "It's called suicide."

The captain looked up. "Lord Xir is in his office, Your Highness."

"Good." Jai set off again.

Jai didn't like Corbal's silver and steel office any more today than the first time he had seen it. That day, the octagonal shape and domed ceiling had startled him; today, they were more symbols of Highton duplicity.

As Jai strode into the room, Corbal stood up behind his desk, his white hair glittering in the harsh light. Jai stopped at the desk and rested his clenched fists on its surface. "I've made my decision."

Corbal met his bluntness with his own. "I have no doubt it is the wrong one."

"I'm sending Jacques Ardoise home to Earth."

A muscle jerked in Corbal's cheek. "While you're at it, why don't you sign the death warrant you took out for yourself when you gassed your Joint Commanders?"

Tarquine came to the desk and spoke in a measured voice. "Perhaps, as kin, the three of us might hold this discussion in a more appropriate setting."

Just say you want to get rid of the damn guards. Jai was sick to death of Highton speech. He was wound so tight, he felt like he would snap. He spoke to the captain. "You and your team may wait outside."

The Razers bowed and left, their footsteps muted on the

carpet, like stealth robots. Jai turned to Tarquine and Corbal, but they still couldn't talk, not without verifying security. Corbal met his gaze, then sat at his desk and went to work. Holicons appeared above the glossy surface, symbols for security systems in the palace. Jai didn't even recognize some of them.

Tarquine leaned over the desk and tapped several glyphs on the screen. When Corbal frowned at her, she shrugged. With a scowl, he redoubled his efforts, and the glyphs soon disappeared. He and Tarquine repeated the procedure several times before Jai realized she was revealing security flaws Corbal hadn't known about. At one point, Jai was certain she showed Corbal a system he had never before seen. Jai paced the room, too angry to stay still.

Finally Corbal pushed back his chair and stood up. "Perhaps we should have some wine."

Jai gave a harsh laugh. "Is that your solution to everything? Have a frigging glass of wine?"

Corbal's mouth tightened. "Better than destroying all hope of working with ESComm." He walked around the desk and came over to Jai. Then he lifted his hand, holding his thumb and forefinger close together. "We were this close to reestablishing good relations with ESComm. Now you've destroyed it. What the blazes possessed you to attack them?"

Incredulity cracked in Jai's voice. "Gods forbid I should 'attack' while they tortured that helpless girl."

A long silence descended as Corbal and Tarquine stared at him. Finally Corbal turned to Tarquine. "Your Highness, I believe my cousin and I need to discuss—"

"I'm not leaving," Tarquine said.

"My, aren't we direct," Jai said. "You aren't related to Corbal. Then again, given how everybody here marries their relatives, you probably are."

"Stop it," Corbal said.

"You both transcended." Jai wanted to fold up and die. "For *decades*."

"Jaibriol, don't do this," Tarquine said.

Jai was losing his battle to stay calm. "I could make myself 'forget' because I never had to witness it, not from either of you." He couldn't bear to tell Tarquine the truth, that she had become the only thing that made his life worth anything. She and Corbal were all he had, which meant he had nothing. *Nothing.*

Tarquine and Corbal looked at each other, and Jai felt their shock as they each realized the truth, that neither of them transcended. He also knew the moment when each realized the other suspected Jai was a psion. He felt as if a band were constricting across his chest, making it impossible to breathe.

Jai stepped behind Corbal's desk. When he stabbed his finger at its screen, an array of holicons appeared, floating above the surface.

Corbal came to the front of the desk. "Deactivate." His voice had deepened into command mode.

"Deactivated," it answered. The holicons disappeared.

Jai clenched his fists. "Ardoise goes home. The peace talks go forward. And Raziquon stays in prison."

Corbal started to answer, then turned to Tarquine. "I must speak to His Highness alone."

She glanced at Jai. "Do you want me to stay?"

"Yes," Jai said.

"No," Corbal said.

Jai could tell Corbal genuinely felt it would endanger him if Tarquine stayed. Tiredly, he spoke to his wife. "We can talk later."

She gave him one of those enigmatic looks he dreaded. Then she bowed and took her leave.

The moment they were alone, Corbal said, "We may be able to convince Kaliga and Taratus they were caught in another assassination attempt against you."

Jai gave a bitter laugh. "How believable is that? They helped Raziquon's kin with the first and masterminded the second."

"How do you know?"

"Don't ask." A shudder wracked his body. That moment

when his barriers had shattered, when he had been wide open to Kaliga and Taratus—he had learned everything from them.

Corbal was worried Taratus and Kaliga would have their poor Highton feelings hurt by the gassing. If they had picked up the truth about Jai when his mind opened, he had a lot worse to worry about than their feelings.

Corbal faced him across the desk. "These peace talks aren't your only alternative."

Jai hit the desk with his palm. "What else is there? Warring with each other until we destroy civilization?"

"You can ensure its survival by bringing all of settled space under your sole command."

Jai scowled. "That isn't survival. It's tyranny. And in case you've forgotten, Eube has tried for centuries to conquer Skolia and never succeeded."

Corbal met his gaze. "That was before we had a Kyle web."

"We still don't have one."

"But we have a Lock."

"It doesn't work."

"It needs its Key."

"We don't have one."

Corbal's voice went deceptively quiet. "Just think—if we had a Key, he could use the Lock to join the Triad. He could build a Kyle web. And he could ensure that no one who mattered to him came to harm when Eube absorbed all settled space into its empire."

Jai braced his palms on the desk, leaning forward. "And if some Highton had the mistaken belief that he could control such a Key, and through him, the empire, then that ill-advised Highton would have to think again."

"It needn't be a matter of control," Corbal said reasonably. "People with similar goals can work together."

"Only if they trust each other enough."

Corbal spread his hands out from his body. "You found answers about ESComm. Find them about me."

Jai crossed his arms, feeling the black-diamond cloth of his tunic against his skin. He didn't want to do what Corbal suggested. Now that he had brought his mental defenses back up, he didn't ever want to lower them again. But he had to know his cousin's true mind. Unwilling but driven by fear, Jai lowered his defenses for the second time that night. With only himself and Corbal, it didn't shatter him this time, but he still felt shaken, raw, and vulnerable.

Corbal had natural mental barriers, as did most humans, and he had made an effort to fortify them. Now he was trying to lower his defenses. Just as he didn't fully know how to build them, so he had trouble bringing them down. But Jai caught enough. Corbal wanted power, yes, but he would rather wield it from behind the throne; he liked his life now too much to change how he lived. Corbal saw him as naive, unpredictable, intelligent, and . . . worthy of loyalty.

Jai blinked. Loyalty. He hadn't expected that.

Unable to take the exposure for long, Jai raised his defenses again. They had become so ingrained that lowering them took more effort than bringing them back up. It was a relief to retreat into his mental fortress.

Corbal stood watching him, waiting. Jai wondered what it was like for his cousin never to feel the emotions of others, to be locked forever in his own mind. Less painful, certainly. Jai wanted to sit down and rest his throbbing head, but he could show no weakness, especially not with so much balanced on the edge of his indecision. And yes, it was indecision, for he knew all too well now what Corbal wanted. If Jai built a Kyle web, he could claim Jacques Ardoise was the Key, that the initial tests to determine the musician's psi ability had underestimated it. What Highton would recognize the lie? None were psions. As long as Jai never released Ardoise, no one would know that the emperor rather than his provider was the true Key.

Corbal believed they might salvage the mess with ES-Comm if Jai canceled the peace talks and released Raziquon. And with the instant communications a Kyle web provided,

ESComm might finally conquer Skolia and the Allied Worlds.

Like a man responding to a siren call, Jai looked at what he had so long avoided. No human being, no matter how noble, could remain unmoved by the lure of such power.

He could rule humanity.

All of it.

The children of Earth had never seen such an empire. No reign would match his, not among the Allieds, not among the Skolians. He had within his grasp an empire unparalleled in the history of the human race. But in return, he had to allow an abomination, the ascension of the Highton Aristos to dominance over the sum total of humanity.

Jai sat slowly behind the desk, staring across the office but seeing nothing. *I could protect my Ruby kin.* As emperor, he could ensure none of the Ruby Dynasty suffered. No Highton would ever touch them. He would make certain. He had a lot to learn, but he had Corbal and Tarquine. And he learned fast. Very fast.

But . . .

He would condemn humanity to slavery, controlled by a few thousand Aristos. Nor could he guarantee that his successors would share his beliefs.

But . . .

Many taskmakers had a higher standard of living than their Skolian counterparts. Their material lives were better than those of the Skolian or Allied peoples.

An image of Robert came to him, his aide's face pale as he asked for permission to refit his collar; of Robert having no choice but to live at the palace, never seeing his father; of Robert's father condemned to a life of loss and pain, never able to see his son until Jai paid an exorbitant price to bring him here. Then Jai thought of Jacques Ardoise, who would have never seen his family again because the Hightons felt they had a right to own and torture anyone they pleased.

No.

Jai closed his eyes. Corbal offered a temptation both horrifying and seductive. All Jai had to do was give up his dream of peace. What use was it to hope? Kaliga and Taratus would never accept peace with the Skolians. The harder Jai pushed, the harder they would try to kill him. They would relent only if he became a conqueror.

But a conqueror needn't be cruel.

His could be a benevolent reign.

Power corrupts.

No. That was a stupid cliché. Reality was far more complex, an interplay of truth and deception. He had grown up with that knowledge, listening to his parents, learning why they had gone into exile, seeing them make interstellar history during the Radiance War. They had given their lives because their power hadn't twisted them. He could use his to protect his people. It wouldn't corrupt him, either.

The way it hadn't corrupted the Aristos?

Every Eubian and Skolian knew the truth, regardless of whether they acknowledged it: they had originally been one people, all descended from the Ruby Empire. As emperor, Jai had access to records no one outside Eube had seen, indeed, hardly any Eubians either. When Eube Qox established his empire, he hadn't envisioned slavery and brutality. In his writings, he had spoken much the way Jai thought now, envisioning a concord of peoples and culture, their great civilization guided by a benevolent race of Hightons.

Eube Qox had never transcended. Historians claimed it was discretion that kept him from indicating any familiarity with the experience Aristos now considered a gods-given right. In public, Aristos would no more talk about transcendence than they would about intimacy. But Jai could see what the historians refused to acknowledge: Eube Qox had come from the same people that birthed Skolia, a culture where the brutality practiced by Hightons was a crime, immoral, cruel. Those beliefs had been part of him.

Jai looked at his cousin. Corbal wasn't a gentle man, but neither was he the monster Jai had expected. Nor was Tarquine. Jai had surrounded himself with the few Hightons he could endure. Tonight Kaliga and Taratus had forced him to face the truths he had tried to deny. Whatever nobility the first Qox emperor had possessed, and whatever decency might be buried within some Aristos, their empire had warped beyond repair. Jai could no more control what happened after his reign than Eube had been able to prevent the cruelty that had twisted his empire after he died.

Standing up, Jai spoke tiredly, knowing he might be sealing his coffin. "The peace talks go forward."

Corbal closed his eyes. Then he opened them again. "Don't do this."

Jai touched a panel on the desk. "Robert."

His aide's voice came out of the comm. "Here, sir."

"Prepare a statement for me." Jai continued to look at Corbal. "We are returning Jacques Ardoise to Earth."

To Robert's credit, he only paused a moment. "What would you like the statement to say, sir?"

"I'm not sure." Watching Corbal, who was shaking his head, Jai said, "Research the procedures and write a draft."

"Right away, Your Highness."

"Good. And Robert?"

"Yes, sir?"

"Has Lord Raziquon left the prison yet?"

"We sent the pardon back to High Judge Muze with your signature. He should be free in a few days, as soon as the documents are processed."

Jai took a weary breath. "Notify High Judge Muze that I am rescinding my agreement. Raziquon stays in prison."

Robert spoke slowly. "Yes, sir."

Corbal waited until Jai signed off. Then he said, "You will live to regret these decisions."

Jai swallowed. "If I live."

33

The Price of Loyalty

Tarquine stood in an alcove high in the east tower. With one knee on a cushioned bench that bordered the enclosure, she gazed out at the city of Qoxire. It spread below the palace, a jumble of white buildings spilling down the hills, gilded in the evening sun. Only an hour had passed since Jaibriol had destroyed his relations with ESComm, but she imagined the city already knew somehow, and had become wild. Beyond it, the ocean crashed against glittering black beaches. The moon Viquara and several others shone in the sky, testament to the forces that drove the violent tides.

The door of the outer chamber whispered open behind Tarquine. She had no spy monitor running, but she knew who entered. He was the only other person her security systems allowed access to this tower.

She continued to watch the ocean batter the shore. The tread of feet sounded behind her. Then Jaibriol joined her at the window.

Tarquine glanced at him. "My greetings, Husband."

He didn't answer, only watched the ocean. Sun rays slanted over him, giving his face that antiqued look only late-afternoon sunlight could create.

Tarquine turned back to the city. She could smell the soap Jaibriol had used to wash, and a masculine scent that was his alone. It made her think of the nights he came to her in the brooding darkness, burning with his need. She found him often in her thoughts now. She didn't want him there. She tried to push him out, but he returned, undeniable.

In the mornings, she always woke while he still slept. He required the greater rest of youth, ten hours, almost twice what she needed. Sometimes she found herself breaking her rule of immediately rising, a habit that had been inviolate for most of her life. Instead she lay next to him, enjoying his slumbering warmth.

Jaibriol spoke. "You will attend me on Earth."

Earth. That could mean only one unwelcome, foolhardy thing. "You intend to go ahead with the talks."

"Yes."

So. She was empress. Of course she would be expected to attend the talks, even if they ended up killing her husband. She let her tone convey her displeasure. "Very well."

Jaibriol wouldn't look at her. "He will be there."

"He?"

The emperor finally turned to her. "Kelric Valdoria."

A familiar anger surged in Tarquine. Kelric's escape violated her sense of rightness at a deep level.

And yet . . .

The edge of that memory had dulled. It would always rankle that he had outwitted her. Only Kelric could have made that escape; no one else had the skills, talents, and mental ability. But oddly enough, he no longer experienced the fierce yet indefinable pain that had plagued her after he vanished. She sorted through her emotions, including those she had shut away so their intensity wouldn't interfere with her life. The pain had gone. She no longer felt a driving need to have Kelric back.

He had never touched her emotions like Jaibriol.

Outside, tempestuous waves tipped with blue-green froth shot up against rocks along the shore. Her husband was like that, wild and turbulent. He turned her life inside out. She had tried to lock thoughts of him in the hidden place of her mind that protected her from stark emotions, but it couldn't contain this response. If she had a sore tooth, she could have it fixed with hardly a thought. If she became sick, the na-nomeds in her body would make her better. If signs of age showed, she had the doctors make her perfect again. But nothing could cure her of Jaibriol.

She couldn't let him know how he weakened her. So she misdirected his attention. "Kelric Valdoria owes me a great deal of money."

Jaibriol blinked. "What?"

"He stole a fourteen-million-credit property of mine."

"He can't steal himself."

"He's the one who took my property."

He spoke dryly. "Both Azar Taratus and the insurance bureaus paid you for your 'loss.' "

She snorted.

"Tarquine—"

"Yes?"

"About the bureaus and Taratus."

She crossed her arms. "What about them?"

"You have to give one of them the money back."

"I most certainly do not."

"Yes, you do."

"You forget, esteemed Husband. Those payments were mandated by your decree."

"You *can't* have it both ways." He glared at her. "Either Taratus cheated you or he didn't. If the bureaus had to pay you that exorbitant amount, then Taratus didn't cheat you. If Taratus didn't cheat you, then he shouldn't have had to give you back your credits. So you must repay him."

She put her hands on her hips. "Taratus meant to cheat me. He owes me punitive damages."

"I want you to return the credits."

She considered him for a long moment. "Giving money to the little brother of General Taratus won't appease ES-Comm."

He stiffened. "This isn't about ESComm."

"No? It never occurred to you that making Azar Taratus happy might dissuade his boorish older brother, otherwise known as one of your Joint Commanders, from plotting against your appealing but woefully unsophisticated self?"

Jaibriol scowled. "You will give back the money. It isn't open to discussion."

"Very well," she lied. "I will give it back."

He shot her a look of alarm.

"What?" Tarquine asked. Honestly, he was moodier than a malfunctioning AI.

"You never give in that easily."

"It isn't worth arguing about." Time to deflect him. "Your Joint Commanders concern me more."

Like a restless beast unable to stay still, he paced out of the alcove into the tower chamber, his black garb stark against the pale marble walls. "It seems they have trouble holding their secrets."

Did he mean he knew their minds? "You have succeeded?"

He was standing with his back to her. "If you can call it success."

She spoke quietly. "Success would be discovering whether or not they have decided their 'duties' to the emperor include his assassination."

He took an audible breath. "Then yes, I have succeeded."

Tarquine waited.

Jaibriol turned to face her. "Taratus helped Raziquon's kin on the first attempt, with Kaliga's blessing." He sounded much too quiet, as if he were holding in a turmoil of emotions. "Both of them masterminded the second attempt. They intended to implicate you and Corbal. The Diamond Coalition had nothing to do with it."

Tarquine spoke with a deadly calm. "I see."

"I have no proof."

"This is enough for me."

"No one will consider you an impartial judge."

She met his gaze. "I'm not."

"Tarquine—" He lifted his hand as if to reach toward her, then dropped it. "The peace talks start in a tenday, if they go forward." Bitterly he added, "If I live that long."

She came forward and put her hands on his shoulders. "Give up this idea of talks."

He laid his hands over hers. "I cannot."

"If you die, you will achieve nothing."

"I can't give up."

She wanted to shake him, hold him back, lock him up, whatever it took to protect him from himself. Damn his integrity, his honesty, his gods-forsaken purity. "No one is worth these sacrifices." She clenched her hands on his shoulders. "Not even your parents."

He stared at her, his face pale. But he didn't deny her implication. "I won't let them have died in vain."

"You cannot take the problems of all humanity onto your shoulders." Her voice caught. "You will break."

He took her hands and brought them together in front of him. "We all do what we must."

Tarquine had no answer, for she was certain Eube would never accept his desperate peace.

The empress found the man she sought in a studio with many windows. Sunshine streamed into the high-ceilinged room. Actually, she found two people. The older man sat on a stool in front of an easel, working with holographic paints. The younger had settled in an armchair and was reading a holobook. It was a tranquil scene, domestic and cozy, or at least it was until she arrived with her bodyguards.

Robert jumped to his feet, tossing his holobook on a table. His father looked up from his easel like a diver surfacing in a lake. Then he saw Tarquine and dropped his paintbrush.

For an instant father and son remained frozen. In the same moment that Robert's father jumped off his stool, Robert stepped forward as if to protect him. Then they both knelt, averting their gazes.

Tarquine considered their bowed heads. "You may rise."

As they stood, she got a better look at the older man. Good gods. No wonder the pirates had taken him. Even with his auburn hair graying at the temples and lines showing around his eyes, the fellow was breathtaking. His maturity made him even more appealing, at least to Tarquine. Yet for all his striking looks, he left her unmoved in a way that would never have happened before her marriage. Her mind was muddled with thoughts of her husband, a most unacceptable situation, but one that seemed unlikely to go away.

The father, however, wasn't the one she had come for. Although she recalled seeing the younger man attending Jaibriol, she had never paid much attention to him. He resembled the older man in his auburn hair and brown eyes, and he was reasonably pleasing to look upon, as expected for a member of the palace staff. But his appearance was more subdued than his father's; he was professional rather than sensual, proficient rather than devastating. In short, he looked like a palace aide with unusually high rank.

Tarquine nodded to Robert. "You will come with me."

To her surprise, he didn't move.

She spoke coldly. "I assume it is unnecessary for me to repeat myself."

Robert's face had turned ashen. "Please accept my worthless apologies, Your Most Glorious Highness, but I am only allowed to serve the emperor."

Skolia be damned. The fellow had refused her. She would have ordered him flayed and hung out a tower window by his toes, except Aristos didn't do that to their taskmakers anymore, besides which, as the emperor's private aide, he *was* only allowed to serve Jaibriol, on penalty of death in fact, though she knew perfectly well Jaibriol would never hurt him. In any case, she needed Robert predisposed toward her wishes, which he would hardly be if she had him hoisted out the window by his feet.

"Robert." She put her hands on her hips. "It would please me to have your company in my sitting room to share a glass of Taimarsian wine."

He spoke carefully. "You honor me, Your Highness."

"Well, yes, I do." Remembering that she was softening him up, she added, "The pleasure is mine."

He was no fool. "It would be a great privilege to accept your generous invitation, Most Esteemed Highness."

"Very well." She nodded to him. "You may arrive at the Ivory Sitting Room at sixth hour this evening."

Both father and son bowed to her. Then Tarquine took her leave, striding out of the studio with her Razers. They headed for a staircase that swept down to more populated levels of the palace. Lost in thought, she didn't notice the captain until he cleared his throat.

Tarquine frowned at him. "Eh?"

"Would you like me to have some Taimarsian wine sent to the sitting room, Your Highness?"

"You mean we actually have some in the palace?"

"I believe so, ma'am."

"Oh. Well, good. Yes, send it down."

Then she took off for the palace hospital.

Xirad Kaliga awoke to the knowledge that enemies surrounded him. He remained motionless while the biomech web in his body analyzed his situation and sent him data. He was lying in a room, in a bed. Traces of gas remained in his bloodstream, a sedative that left his mind groggy and his throat raw. Three medbots moved in the room, tending medical equipment. A woman sat nearby. The rate of her breathing suggested she was awake but relaxed.

Kaliga opened his eyes. None other than the empress herself sat at his bedside. He spoke in a rasp. "My greetings, Your Highness."

She inclined her head. "Admiral."

"Please accept my apologies. I'm afraid my condition prevents me from greeting you properly." She wouldn't miss his implication: he shouldn't be here in this condition.

Tarquine stood regally. "It is most gratifying to see you

awake, Admiral. We deeply regret that you were caught in the assassination attempt."

"Indeed." Assassination? Kaliga waited.

Tarquine waited.

Kaliga closed his eyes. He had no energy for this.

Several moments passed. His internal sensors indicated Tarquine had settled into her chair again. Kaliga resisted his fatigue, but he hadn't yet recovered from the gas. Putting his biomech web on alert, to awake him if necessary, he allowed the healing sleep to take him . . .

Robert didn't recognize the woman who ushered him into the Ivory Sitting Room; she was one of the aides Tarquine Iquar had brought with her when she moved into the palace. The empress was standing by a window, her Highton profile limned with light from the setting sun. In her black-diamond trousers and tunic, she looked like a dark gem. The ceiling shed a warmer light than the sun, giving her an unreal look, as if she were a portrait rather than a person.

Turning, she spoke in the husky voice that had unsettled generations of Eubian men. "Come in, Robert." She indicated a table near the window. A black tray with two goblets and a decanter of wine sat there. "Please be seated."

"You are most kind, Your Highness." Robert went to the chair, then hesitated. He couldn't sit while she stood, but she had bid him to sit and he could hardly refuse.

Tarquine sighed, taking a last look out of the window. Then she came to the table. After she seated herself, he settled into his chair, relieved but alert, taking no liberties, not even sitting back. She had couched her summons as an invitation involving no formal work, so it didn't violate his responsibilities to the emperor, but Robert was neither naive nor arrogant enough to believe the empress had any wish to entertain him socially.

After Tarquine dismissed her bodyguards and aide, she poured the wine and gave a glass to Robert. Then she sat back. "It pleases me to chat with you. I haven't had sufficient time to meet my husband's staff."

Robert felt as if he were prey being stalked by a sleek, deadly gemcat. "Your dedication to your work blesses the empire."

"Well, yes, it does, doesn't it?" She scrutinized him. "As does yours."

"You are most generous."

"I am indeed." She took another swallow of wine. "Your father has talent."

"It is kind of you to say so."

She paused. "Perhaps a public exhibit could be arranged for him in the gallery."

Even knowing she was softening him up for whatever she wanted, Robert couldn't help his surge of excitement. A public exhibit at the Qox imperial palace—the number of artists offered that honor was astronomically small. Even if his father had realized a successful career on Earth, he could never have hoped for such an achievement. Word of his brilliance would spread everywhere, even among the Skolians and Allieds.

With a mental wrench, Robert halted his wild imaginings. If he angered the emperor by letting the empress talk him into some ill-advised scheme, it would backfire on his father, who was here only on the good graces of Jaibriol III.

Good graces. It was true. Jaibriol III had a grace of heart. Years ago Robert had begun his job at the palace determined to avoid mistakes and advance himself, and he had never lost sight of that purpose, but since the ascension of Jaibriol III to the throne, Robert's dedication had grown. He gave his fealty to Jaibriol for more reason than because it was expected. The young emperor had a goodness Robert had never associated with Hightons, for all that he acknowledged their power.

"You are indeed generous." This time, Robert put only enough warmth into his tone to express gratitude without appearing eager.

"Perhaps I speak too soon." Tarquine held up her goblet to the sun, making the wine sparkle. "If the emperor dies, my interest in art will likely vanish."

Gods. Where had that come from? "His Exalted Highness will live a long and glorious life."

"Yes, well, we all hope so." She lowered her glass. "If my exalted husband isn't careful, he won't survive the year."

Robert felt as if he were walking through a minefield. "Your Most Glorious Highness, please be assured that the well-being of your husband is my highest concern. I will do my utmost to make certain it continues."

She spoke dryly. "I wish the same could be said of him."

Robert had to admit she had a point. Jaibriol III, in the uncommon decency that motivated his life, rarely operated in his own best interest. "His Highness sets a high standard for himself."

"His Highness is woefully idealistic." Tarquine put her goblet on the table. "Have you sent the order he gave you yesterday evening, refusing the pardon for Lord Raziquon?"

"It is in process." Robert set down the wine he hadn't touched. He knew now what the empress wanted. He even knew it would be better for Jaibriol. But he couldn't "forget" to send the order rescinding Raziquon's pardon. It would be a betrayal of the emperor.

Tarquine rested her elbow on the arm of her chair, her posture a study in regal carriage. "We both want what is best for His Highness."

"More than anything else."

"Reason exists to believe the Line of Raziquon was involved with the first assassination attempt."

"I hadn't realized new evidence had come to light."

Tarquine waved her hand, dismissing his words.

Robert didn't doubt she had good sources or that they gave her reason to believe Raziquon's kin had plotted to kill Jaibriol. But if her evidence could have held up in court, an accusation would have been made. He hated the position she was putting him in. If the emperor rescinded Raziquon's pardon, he would further incite the Line of Raziquon and aggravate the crumbling relations between ESComm and the palace. Jaibriol had already released Jafe Maccar, the Skolian captain, and now he intended to return Jacques Ardoise to Earth. Refusing to free Lord Raziquon would be the final outrage.

Robert knew if he "mislaid" the order rescinding the pardon, allowing Raziquon to go free, it would be nearly impossible for Jaibriol to put the Highton lord back in prison. The emperor would lose face if he declared he had made a mistake by freeing Raziquon. It would be a debacle. But if Robert did what the empress wanted, he would incur the wrath of the person he most respected. Jaibriol wasn't likely to put him to death, and if Tarquine intervened Robert might not even suffer consequences. But Jaibriol would never trust him again. Robert valued that trust, deeply, even more than he had realized until now, when he contemplated its loss.

He spoke wearily. "The decision of what is best for those that we love is not ours to make."

"Sometimes we make it ours," Tarquine said.

Robert knew what he had to do. He hated it, but he knew. "It is odd," he said, his voice low. "I thought I had new orders regarding the pardon of Raziquon, but apparently not."

She said simply, "Thank you."

Don't thank me. He would have to live knowing he had betrayed the one emperor who actually deserved his loyalty.

34

The Balcony

___

Corbal found Sunrise curled in a fetal position, buried in the cushions on the floor of her favorite room. Seeing her shoulders shaking, he crouched next to her. "Suni? Why do you cry?"

She raised her face, her cheeks wet. "I am sorry. I don't mean to sadden you."

He took her hand. "You must forget Raziquon."

She clung to his fingers. "I had to remember."

He tried to read her face. It was *too* lovely, sculpted to his specifications, forever set in beauty, which made it hard to discern her true expressions. "What do you mean?"

"What Raziquon 'thought,' about his platinum mines—I— it was all there, I just—" Her voice caught. "I didn't want to remember."

He settled next to her, rubbing his hand along her arm. "Then don't."

"I already did."

Then she told him what she had learned—and destroyed his carefully planned revenge.

The second time Kaliga awoke, he was less disoriented. Stronger now, he sat up slowly, looking around. This was a room for an honored guest, blue and white, with gilt trim.

Again, Tarquine Iquar was seated beside his bed, with a holobook in her lap.

The empress set down her book. "My greetings, Admiral."

"You honor me, Your Highness." His voice was less hoarse now. "It isn't often an empress sits vigil on a patient."

She inclined her head. "The Line of Qox deeply regrets your injury in the assassination attempt."

Assassination again. She could be implying a great deal with that word. He personally knew of no attempts planned for the night of the emperor's celebration. Perhaps the Intelligence Ministry had uncovered clues of his involvement in previous attempts. No matter what they suspected, they would never find proof. He looked her in the eye. "It is always the honor of ESComm to protect and venerate the emperor." He even said it with a straight face.

Tarquine gave him a perfect Highton smile. "The Line of Kaliga has always provided exemplary military commanders."

True. It would continue to do so, in spite of Jaibriol III. "You honor my Line." He had to admit, she made an impressive empress. Deadly and extraordinary. She was wasted on Jaibriol.

"Indeed," she murmured. "The emperor also wishes to esteem the Line of Kaliga."

Kaliga held back his snort. "It is fortunate His Highness happened to leave the room prior to the attack." For all he knew, the odious emperor had gassed them himself.

Tarquine's gaze darkened. "Fortune can be capricious." She touched a button on the nightstand by his bed. Kaliga said nothing, guarding his responses as always.

Across the room, an entrance flickered open. Kaliga glimpsed several Razers outside, and then a woman entered, a lieutenant colonel in the medical corps. She wore her hair in a roll, the blond streaked with gray. With grace, she knelt to the empress.

"You may rise." Tarquine sounded bored. As the medic stood, Tarquine turned to Kaliga. "Dr. Qoxdaughter can answer any questions you have about what happened."

Qoxdaughter bowed to him, her manner polished with impeccable courtesy. She was probably the daughter of Ur Qox, grandfather of the current emperor; Ur had always given his taskmaker children the best educations and positions that decorum would allow.

"It would be my privilege to answer any questions," she told him.

Kaliga scrutinized her. "I understand you treated me after I was caught in an attempt on the life of the emperor."

"Yes, I did." She looked exceedingly contrite. "We are terribly sorry. Security released the gas. They had to act fast, before either you or General Taratus suffered worse injury."

Kaliga raised his eyebrow. "Palace security knocked out the general and myself?"

The doctor reddened. "Yes, sir. I truly am sorry. The poison in your bodies was set to activate when your pulse and breathing rate went above a certain level. It had nearly reached that point."

"What poison?"

"In your drink."

Tarquine spoke. "It would appear we were all poisoned that night." Although she addressed the doctor, she obviously meant her comment for Kaliga.

Following her lead, Kaliga also addressed the doctor. "Poisoned how?" It allowed him to be more direct without insulting the empress.

"We are investigating," Qoxdaughter said. "We found the poison in the wine."

Kaliga didn't believe it. He recalled how his provider, Silver, had forgotten to test the emperor's drink at that long ago dinner. Was this some sort of strange payback? Jaibriol would have to be even more unstable than he had thought, to risk his deteriorating relations with ESComm for such a petty revenge, especially given how he had taken Silver that night, asserting his rights as emperor and Kaliga's guest. It was foolish enough to make Kaliga wonder if the assassination story actually had some truth to it. He wouldn't be surprised if other parties wanted Jaibriol dead. He would have to investigate.

To the doctor, he said only, "I have protections against poisons."

She nodded. "Molecular sheaths hid this one. The chemicals passed even the emperor's safeguards."

It sounded unlikely. "I would like to see the design."

Qoxdaughter didn't blink. "Of course, sir."

"Who planned the assassination?" he asked.

"We aren't sure yet. Security is investigating."

It was a stock answer. Kaliga didn't bother to respond.

Tarquine spoke in her cultured voice. "To express his apology, the emperor has speeded up the release of Lord Raziquon. The pardon became effective today."

That fit more with Jaibriol's behavior prior to the gassing. Perhaps the boy might develop some sense yet, though whether it would be in time to save his reign, Kaliga had his doubts. "It pleases the Line of Kaliga to know the Hightons are once again coming into balance." Putting an Aristo in prison had been an abomination. "The Line of Kaliga and the Line of Raziquon have many kin in common."

Tarquine's lips curved in an icy smile. "We will see that Lord Raziquon receives a proper escort home."

Kaliga had no doubt she intended to question Raziquon, discreetly of course. The faster he removed Raziquon from Glory, the better. He had a great deal to discuss with the lord, and he preferred to do away from the emperor's intelligence systems, which networked the entire planet.

"The arrangements made at the Qoxire starport for my private yacht were impeccable," he said.

"It pleases me to hear." Tarquine was regal in her aloof demeanor.

"The Lines of Kaliga and Raziquon have long traveled together." Actually, that wasn't true; their Lines had battled more often than cooperated. But the statement would serve his purposes now. He had no doubt that Tarquine understood he was offering to escort Raziquon home. She wouldn't like it, but she had no good reason to refuse.

The barest hint of displeasure escaped the empress. Had Kaliga been any less adept at reading nuances of posture, he would have missed it. But her response was above reproach. "It would be fortuitous indeed if Kaliga could provide Raziquon the worthy escort its lord deserves."

He gave her his predator's smile. "Fortuitous indeed."

Releasing Raziquon was a start, but it wasn't enough, especially after this gassing incident. Jaibriol had to cancel the talks with the Skolians.

If the emperor persisted with this treason, Kaliga knew exactly how he could stop it.

In the night sky, six moons cast light across the palace gardens, all of them different shades of violet, amber, and blue. Corbal stood within a gazebo, hidden in shadow. Night-blooming ice blossoms twined around its lattice walls and up the posts to the roof.

"My greetings, Lord Xir," a throaty voice said.

Corbal turned, startled, though he had expected company. Tarquine was standing on the other side of the gazebo.

He inclined his head. "My greetings, Your Highness."

"A lovely night."

"So it is."

Her voice hardened. "A good night for freedom."

"I imagine Lord Raziquon thinks so." He couldn't keep the edge out of his voice. For all that it would have been political suicide to keep Raziquon in prison, Corbal would have gladly let him rot there.

"So he must," Tarquine said. "As does Admiral Kaliga."

"Kaliga?"

Her stiff, straight posture indicated anger. "He generously offered to take Raziquon home on his yacht."

Damnation. The last thing they needed was a stronger alliance between Kaliga and Raziquon. "May they both live in all the glory and esteem they deserve." Corbal gritted his teeth.

Tarquine joined him and gazed out at the distant palace. To the north, on a plateau, the needled spires of the emperor's starport rose into the sky. Her voice sounded shadowed. "Raziquon knows a great deal."

Too much. "He seems to have ties to ESComm."

"And to platinum mines. Illegal mines."

His hand tightened on the rail of the gazebo.

"Ghost mines," he said.

She turned to him. "Ghost?"

"False. He planted false information in Sunrise's mind. Had he remained in prison, he couldn't have defended himself against the claim that he owns those mines. But now—" He made himself release the rail. "Were some misguided Hightons to make such an accusation against Raziquon, it would cause them far more trouble than him." It astonished him that Sunrise had gone so deeply into her mind, enduring the pain of her memories, doing it for him, Corbal Xir, to stop him from making that false accusation. It made him want vengeance more now than ever.

"Mines can take new owners," Tarquine said. Dryly she added, "I have plenty to spare."

Corbal restrained the urge to remind her that those wretched mines of hers had helped cause this problem. Although they could forge documents making Raziquon the owner, it was too easy to disprove such evidence.

"Neural scans are almost impossible to forge," he said. "The falsely accused can use them to prove they are telling the truth when they claim their innocence." In prison, Raziquon wouldn't have had recourse to such tests, but he had plenty now.

Tarquine blew out a gust of air. "So."

As she and Corbal watched the starport, a ship lifted off in a dazzling display of fire and exhaust that seemed to mock them with its fiery show.

So Admiral Kaliga left Glory, taking Raziquon with him.

In the early morning light, Tarquine stood at her window above the moss-draped forest east of the palace. Beyond it, the Jaizire Mountains rose against the sky. On a distant balcony in an adjacent wing, she could see Jaibriol. Sunlight slanted across his face and wind ruffled his hair. She was too far away to make out details, but she knew his expression. She had seen his pensive gaze more and more lately, as he sought solitude on that isolated balcony.

The bodysculptors had done a superb job on his face. The differences were almost invisible; even someone who knew him well would have difficulty noting any change, except that he had a more regal aspect now. Far more important were the subtle changes he would never acknowledge: with a few well-chosen alterations, he had lessened his resemblance to the late Skolian Imperator, Sauscony Valdoria.

His guards stood back against the walls of the palace, far enough away to accommodate his need for space. Tarquine knew now that he couldn't bear their half-Aristo minds. She also knew another truth. He was mourning. She felt it every time he looked at her, every time he held her at night. It was more than his conviction that his Joint Commanders would soon succeed in killing him. He mourned the failure he feared for the peace talks.

He mourned his parents.

Watching Jaibriol, she knew he condemned himself with his own purity of soul. He had too much goodness to do what was necessary to ensure his survival.

He was too decent.

But she wasn't.

35

Summit

Robert gave him the news.

Jaibriol and his aide stood together on the shore of Lake Mirellazile, its surface a mirror of the sky.

"They agreed?" Jai had to hear it again. He couldn't yet believe this incredible news. "You're certain?"

Robert nodded with no hint of joy. "Yes, sir. The Ruby Dynasty has agreed to go forward with the talks."

Jai closed his eyes, giving himself over to gratitude. Whatever happened to him, however little time he had left, he at least had a chance to try. It was better, so much better, than nothing at all.

Opening his eyes, he smiled at Robert. "They agreed."

"Your decision to free Ardoise apparently made the difference."

"This is good."

"Yes, Your Highness."

Jai wished his aide didn't look as if he were going to a funeral.

The console curved around the control chair where Jai would sit. He stood next to the chair while his staff fussed over it. Several other Hightons also waited in the chamber: the Protocol Minister; Azile Xir, the Intelligence Minister; High

Judge Calope Muze; Corbal; and, of course, Tarquine.

Jai's head ached. He longed to submerge himself in the virtual reality console, which would put physical as well as psychological distance between him and the others. Their consoles were well separated from his, by his deliberate choice.

A tech approached and went down on one knee.

"Please stand," Jai said automatically.

She rose to her feet. "We're ready, Your Highness."

Jai nodded, aware of everyone listening. So this was it. Several techs fastened him into his console chair. The VR mesh folded around his body and inserted prongs into the sockets in his wrists, ankles, and spine, connecting to the newly implanted biomech web in his body so the console could communicate with his brain.

"Are you comfortable?" the tech asked.

"Yes, very good," he said. She had no idea how much she and the other techs were helping him. Their non-Aristo minds made a bulwark between him and the others in the room, easing the pressure.

She tapped the console. "This will connect you into the Kyle web, what Skolians call the psiberweb."

"They have a node available for our use?" Jai asked, yet again. He knew the Skolians had assured his staff they would create Kyle webnodes for the talks, but even after having used such a node before, he found it hard to believe his transmission would take only a few seconds to travel the light-years from Glory to Earth. Until it actually happened, it wouldn't seem real.

The tech smiled. "Yes, sir," she said, as patient now as the first time he had asked. "It is all set up." She checked the readouts on his visor. "Ready?"

His pulse jumped. "Yes. Go ahead."

She lowered the visor, enclosing him in darkness. A voice said, "Initiate," and another said, "Activating VR."

The voices faded. Jai waited, his hands clenched on the arms of his chair. The world brightened, until a white mist surrounded him. When it faded, he found himself standing in a white room. A *square* room. The strange angles disoriented him.

After a pause, he said, "I've arrived." In fact, he had gone nowhere; he was still in his chair at the palace.

A rectangular door opened and a woman entered, an officer in a blue skirt and blouse with gray hair cut stylishly around her face. She bowed deeply and spoke in Highton. "Welcome to Earth, Your Highness."

"Hello," Jai said in English.

The woman smiled. "Hello, sir." She spoke English as perfectly as Highton.

"Are you an EI?" he asked.

"That I am. Would you like anything before we continue?"

Jai looked at himself. As always, he wore elegant black garb. He sighed. "I wish my clothes had color."

The Evolving Intelligence paused, needing enough time to process his comment that it registered in real time. "You wish to change the protocols worked out by our staff and yours?"

"No. No, don't do that." Jai pushed his hand through his hair. It felt real. "I'm fine."

The EI smiled. "Shall we proceed?"

"Yes, let us go."

She ushered him into a corridor delineated marble columns. The airy spaces gave Jai a sense of freedom. A group of people waited down the hall, men and women in uniforms. As Jai and his host approached the group, Jai recognized the woman in its center—Hanna Loughten, president of the Allied Worlds of Earth. Two honor guards waited with her, one of Allied dignitaries and the other Eubian Razers. The comps had created the honor guards; Jai and Loughten were the only "real" people here, and even they were actually in consoles far away.

Loughten bowed to him. Disquieted, he realized he was becoming accustomed to Highton expectations; it felt strange to have her bow rather than kneel. Instead of the formal nod he would have given to another Eubian, he returned the bow, one leader to another.

"Emperor Jaibriol." She spoke with the minimalist form of address Hightons used to indicate respect.

He inclined his head. "President Loughten."

"Welcome to Earth, Your Highness."

He answered in a modern form of Gaelic that derived from the tongue of her mother's ancestors. "I thank you."

She blinked. Then she smiled. He didn't need empathy to see it pleased her that he had gone to such an effort to learn a greeting in her language.

The EI and honor guards escorted Jai and Loughten down the hall, which ended in a lobby bordered by an arcade. Above the balconies, sunlight poured through arched windows. The lack of right angles in the arches relieved Jai. It disquieted him to think how much he might eventually change, if after less than a year among the Hightons he had trouble adjusting to the geometry of Allied architecture.

They stopped before two great doors engraved with the Allied insignia, which consisted of concentric circles overlaid by a silhouette of the continents on the Earth.

Jai turned to Loughten. "Is everyone else inside?"

"Not quite," she said. "Everyone but the Ruby Pharaoh, Empress Tarquine, First Councilor Tikal, and yourself."

Puzzled, he looked around. "My wife isn't here yet?"

President Loughten glanced at the gray-haired EI. "Has the empress arrived?"

"Yes, ma'am." The EI indicated the hall behind them. Jai turned to see Tarquine approaching with her own honor guard. She wore trousers and a tunic similar to his, elegant and conservative, though with a more feminine cut. They made a matched pair, he and his empress, at least on the outside.

When she reached him, she bowed.

"My greetings." Dryly, Jai added, "I am glad you decided to join us."

She offered no explanations. "Shall we enter?"

Jai didn't want to know why she had tarried. He didn't want to hear that she had taken special efforts to prepare for this meeting that included Kelric.

The EI spoke. "First Councilor Tikal and the Ruby Pharaoh are ready to enter."

"Very well." Jai made a conscious effort not to look at Tarquine. He told himself he didn't care about her former provider. He knew he was lying to himself, but too much was at stake to let Kelric Valdoria rattle him.

Their guards grasped the grand handles on the doors and heaved. The portals swung open, slowly, their height and weight making them impressive. Everyone walked forward, but most of them stopped just short of the door. Only Jai and Tarquine went on, until they were framed in the entrance.

The hall beyond dazzled Jai. Chandeliers filled it with light, tier upon tier of bright spheres. A round table took up the center, its white marble embedded with silver flecks. Many Hightons already sat there: Corbal Xir, High Judge Muze, Azile Xir, the Highton Foreign Affairs Minister, and several high-ranking ESComm officers.

Jai recognized the Skolians from holos he had seen: Roca Skolia, the Foreign Affairs Councilor—and his grandmother; General Naaj Majda, Matriarch of the House of Majda, the Skolian counterpart of Xirad Kaliga, and by reputation just as unyielding and conservative as he; Admiral Ragnar Bloodmark, roughly the Skolian counterpart of General Taratus, though ISC didn't have joint military commanders. It had only one commander. The Imperator.

Kelric Valdoria.

He dominated the room. When Jai had met him in the Lock, his hair and eyes had been brown. Now he made no attempt to hide his metallic coloring. Gray streaked his hair and lines showed around his eyes. At two meters tall, over six feet six inches, he had broad shoulders, a massive chest, and long, muscular legs. This was no untried youth; his maturity added to his aura of power.

And he was looking at Tarquine.

Jai knew then that he could never compete with Kelric. He had no chance. Kelric could have enhanced his VR image or made himself look younger. Although all the parties had agreed to present their natural forms, anyone could have cheated if the enhancements were subtle enough. But Jai had met Kelric before. He knew the truth: his uncle had come as himself. That was more than enough.

Somehow Jai stopped himself from turning to see how Tarquine had reacted. He might be aching inside, but he refused to let it show.

Across the room, beyond the table, another set of double doors had opened at the same time as those where Jai stood with Tarquine. Jai finally absorbed who stood there: the Ruby Pharaoh and the Skolian First Councilor, respectively the hereditary and elected leaders of Skolia.

Jai recognized Barcala Tikal, the First Councilor, from the dossier he had studied. Tall and lanky, with dark hair, the Councilor projected confidence. But it wasn't Tikal who riveted his attention. Jai thanked the saints he was in VR; he could never have hidden his gasp in real life, but the programs monitoring his simulation easily deleted it. So he stood, silent, staring at Dyhianna Selei, the Ruby Pharaoh, while he fought the hotness in his eyes.

She was a slim woman, petite, with a gaze that seemed to miss nothing. Although her dossier had included holos, the images hadn't captured her essence, not for Jai. One aspect hit him above all else.

She looked like his mother.

The Pharaoh didn't have his mother's height or strength, but the curve of her face, her green eyes, the sweep of her hair—it was all painfully familiar. He had thought he knew what to expect, but nothing could have prepared him for this. Her appearance shook him like an electric shock.

The EI spoke over a comm in Jai's ear, using a private channel open only to Jai and Tarquine. "The two of you will walk to the table at the same time as the Ruby Pharaoh and First Councilor. Are you ready?"

"No." Pressing his thumb and index finger together, Jai activated the privacy shield on his VR console, so neither his words nor his frown showed in the simulation. "Where the hell is Admiral Kaliga?"

"I don't know, Your Highness," the EI said.

Tarquine spoke on the private link. "Do you want to wait until we find out why he hasn't shown up?"

Damn. Given the precarious nature of the talks, which very nearly hadn't taken place, Jai feared to delay now, lest it scuttle the session altogether. By not showing up, Kaliga undermined the process. It also meant one of his Joint Commanders had openly defied him, an offense that verged on a declaration of hostility by ESComm against the throne.

Jai made himself stop gritting his teeth. "No, I don't want to wait. The meeting goes on."

"Without either Joint Commander?" Tarquine asked. "The officers here don't have authority to speak for ESComm."

"I speak for ESComm." Jai knew if his decisions went against Kaliga's plans, it would be close to impossible to implement them and would further weaken his support among the military. Kaliga knew it, too, the bastard. Jai hoped he rotted in whatever palace or pleasure dome he had gone to instead of showing up here.

The EI interrupted his thoughts. "The Ruby Pharaoh and First Councilor wish to know why we are waiting."

Jai took a breath. "You may begin the count."

"Very well. On three, you will all walk to the table. One, two, three."

Jai and Tarquine entered the hall; at the same moment, the First Councilor and Ruby Pharaoh came forward. All four of them reached the table at the same time. Jai inclined his head, grateful they couldn't see the sweat on his forehead.

Tarquine spoke on his private channel. "This is an outrage."

Jai answered on the same channel. "Why?" He waited behind his chair while their honor guards joined them at the table.

"Tikal is a taskmaker," his wife said. "That would be bad enough. But that woman is a *provider*."

"You already knew that."

"They ought to kneel to us."

"Tarquine, for gods' sake."

"Well, they should."

"Like Kelric kneeled to you?" It came out before he could stop it.

She didn't answer. Whatever she felt in seeing Kelric, she hid it well. She was too far away in actual space for him to pick up her emotions.

The Razers pulled out chairs for them. Across the table, Skolian officers were doing the same for the Pharaoh and First Councilor. All four leaders sat down together. Technically, according to Eubian protocol, Tarquine should have waited until Jai sat. Neither the Pharaoh nor the First Councilor would wait, however, and they needed to maintain a balance in the proceedings. Nor was Jai insane enough to tell his empress she had to remain standing while a "taskmaker" and a "provider" took their seats.

They all watched one another, wary and guarded. No one let his or her simulacra give away anything.

At the head of the table, President Loughten spoke in a resonant voice. "We of the Allied Worlds welcome you to the birthplace of humanity."

So began the peace talks between the Eubian Concord and the Skolian Imperialate.

"Nothing." Jai was sprawled in a smartchair in his bedroom, brooding. "We achieved absolutely nothing."

"It's only the first day," Tarquine said mildly, looking up from her palmtop. "If you expected more than formalities, you are far more optimistic than the rest of us."

"Where the blazes is Kaliga?" Jai couldn't believe the admiral had so blatantly challenged him. It verged on treason.

Tarquine checked her palmtop. "Neither he nor General Taratus have responded to the summons you sent them."

"It could take days for the message to reach them by ship."

Tarquine glanced at him. "Only Kaliga has the go-ahead to use a Kyle webnode from his home. Even if we reach Taratus, he has no node that will let him attend the talks."

Jai crossed his arms. "We need better web access."

"So we do." She studied him. "If we had a Key, he could create our own web, and we would be done with our dependence on the Skolians."

Jai didn't miss the pronoun she used: "he." He swallowed, but said nothing.

To her credit, she didn't push, at least not now. He doubted she would ever let it go.

"You should rest," she said. "Tomorrow will be more grueling than today."

Jai lowered his lashes halfway. "Yes. Let us rest."

"Us?"

He stood up, extending his hand. "Us."

She motioned with her palmtop. "I'm not done working."

"Yes, you are." Jai took the palmtop and set it on a table. He felt as if Kelric's specter were in the room. "Come, Wife."

She stood slowly, and Jai felt as if he were on a knife edge, barely able to balance. He couldn't let her see how much he needed her, but he couldn't let Kelric's unspoken presence take her from him either.

Tarquine had a strange expression, as if he had stabbed her, but she was hiding her pain. Jai didn't understand. He saw no way he could have hurt her. Maybe she no longer wanted him after seeing Skolia's mighty Imperator. He tried to pick up her thoughts, but she was learning to guard her mind. Although he caught impressions, Kelric was in none of them. Only himself. He made her hurt inside, but why, he didn't know.

She took his hand, and they walked to the bed.

That night she made love to him with an intensity that

burned. She seemed darker in spirit, harsh, as if she wanted to drive him away, but an incongruous tenderness underlay her ferocity, giving her passion a bittersweet quality that threatened to break his heart.

Afterward, as they lay together, Jai knew he would never understand his wife, nor feel secure with her. But this much he did know: he never wanted to live without her.

In the darkness of the living room, the only light came from the faint glow made by the gold desert silhouettes on the wall. Kelric sat alone, unable to sleep. He had thought seeing Tarquine would leave him cold.

He had been wrong.

Kelric knew why Jaibriol had chosen her as his empress. It wouldn't have taken the boy long to discover she differed from other Aristos in the only way that mattered to a psion. If the emperor truly was a telepath, Tarquine might be the only Highton woman he could marry.

Kelric tried to untangle his responses. He had never been one to dwell on his emotions. As an empath, he often understood the moods of other people better than his own. He didn't know what he felt now, but it was keeping him awake.

He didn't want seeing Tarquine to affect him, but he couldn't deny he had found her compelling from the first day he met her. She was darkness, the opposite of Jeejon, his wife. Although Kelric would never feel the passion for Jeejon that had gripped him in other relationships when he was younger, he loved her in a quiet way. Whatever he felt for Tarquine, it bore no resemblance to love.

Kelric shook his head, trying to clear Tarquine from his mind. He had more pressing concerns about the peace talks. He didn't trust the Hightons, especially not this Intelligence Minister, Azile Xir, the son of Corbal Xir, who had owned Eldrin, and who had allowed his pirates to terrorize Skolian citizens. The absence of Admiral Kaliga was even worse. The explanation given by the emperor's office about a "change of plans" convinced no one. It looked like Kaliga simply hadn't shown up, and it sent an inescapable message: Jaibriol III lacked the authority to command his own military. Without their backing, the talks meant nothing.

Kelric had little hope now for the peace process. The Aristos would promise whatever they believed necessary to achieve their goals, but they considered nothing binding in their dealings with Skolians. Other motives drove them here, though what, he didn't know. Jaibriol III seemed sincere, especially after he had released Jafe Maccar and Jacques Ardoise, but he lacked support in his own government.

Whatever was going on among the Hightons, Kelric wanted no part of it. As long as Dehya maintained psiberweb links with Glory, they were giving the Traders a chance to hack the Kyle web and create interstellar havoc. Better to end the talks now and cut their links to Glory than become a pawn in some Highton intrigue.

His gauntlet comm buzzed. Lifting his wrist, he said, "Imperator Skolia."

"Lieutenant Qahot here, sir." Her voice crackled. "A priority alpha communication has come in for you."

Kelric sat up straighter. "What's the problem?"

"It regards the peace talks." She took an audible breath. "Empress Tarquine wishes to speak to you in private."

36

The Starlight Chamber

White radiance surrounded Kelric.

The light solidified into a room with luminex walls, ceiling, and floor. The EI he had met the last time appeared again, an athletic man in an Allied naval uniform.

"My greetings, Imperator Skolia," the EI said in perfect Iotic, the language of the Skolian nobility.

Kelric nodded to him. "Has the empress arrived?"

"I believe she is in process. Shall we proceed?"

"All right." Kelric had no idea what to expect.

They entered a luminex corridor. It was like walking in a tunnel of white light that ended at an arched doorway.

"Do you wish me to accompany you inside?" the EI asked.

"No, that won't be necessary. Thank you for your escort." Kelric felt odd thanking a computer, but in the years he had been gone, EIs had become more intelligent. He never felt sure anymore what they expected or wanted, if a computer could "want" anything.

The EI bowed and faded into the light.

When Kelric touched the door, it sparkled into a million pinpricks of light and vanished. He walked into an odd, asymmetrical chamber, apparently on a starship. It was shaped like a narrow pyramid, longer on one side than the other, so it seemed to lean. The opposite wall was a narrow triangle of dichromesh glass about twice his height.

Tarquine stood in front of the glass.

She was facing away from him, gazing out at space, her body silhouetted against the stars. Then she turned—and he felt as if a blast of wind had hit him. Her face had that alabaster perfection he remembered so well, her body its long, lean sensuality. The simplicity of her black jumpsuit underscored her elegance. She emanated power.

He walked to her, and they faced each other in front of the window. She was a tall woman, and her boots added more height, bringing her gaze nearly level to his own.

He said, "Tarquine."

She inclined her head. "Kelric."

"You wished to see me."

"I need to answer a question."

"Yes?"

She paused, showing hesitation for the first time since he had known her, a response even more startling in that she could have had her simulacrum hide it if she wished.

"It isn't a question I know how to ask," she said.

He spoke quietly. "You need to give me a better reason for this meeting. I am the Imperator of Skolia. You are the Empress of Eube. We have been lovers. Some might construe a private conference between the two of us a prelude to treason on an interstellar scale."

Her gaze didn't waver. "This is no treason."

"Good."

"You choose interesting words." In the deceptively soft voice, she added, "Such as, say, 'lovers.' "

Kelric exhaled, grateful the simulation allowed him to hide his disquiet. She was as potent across many light-years as she was in person. "It was a figure of speech."

"Perhaps."

He knew her direct speech carried a message. They weren't related; nor were their words meant to establish a hierarchy of dominance. That left only two possibilities, one being that she wished to indicate respect for the Skolian style of communication, which he doubted. The other implied an intimate link between them.

"Whatever we were," he said, "it ended the day I walked off your space habitat."

She put her hands on her hips and frowned at him. "You made many problems for me that day."

"You seem to be thriving." He had never seen her looking so well, in fact. Being empress obviously agreed with her.

She lowered her arms. "I do have a question I can put into words."

"Yes?"

"I would know your intentions in these talks. Do you honor my husband's desire for peace?"

"Of course." Kelric wondered what she really wanted. Had they truly been in the same place, he might have detected her mind, but she was light-years away on Glory. "The question of intent would seem more appropriate applied to a people other than mine. Such as, say, certain groups among the Eubian military."

Her lips curved. "Now you sound like a Highton."

"These talks seem to be missing a Highton."

"I hadn't noticed."

"Admiral Kaliga is hard to miss."

Tarquine clasped her hands behind her back and looked at the stars. "The Line of Kaliga is of no matter."

"'No matter'?" He let his incredulity show. "How genuine can your emperor's intent be if his Joint Commander doesn't even show up to the talks?"

"Emperor Jaibriol commands the Eubian military."

"In name."

She turned to him. "Any agreement made by the emperor is binding on ESComm."

"And if Xirad Kaliga decides otherwise?"

"It makes no difference."

"I find that hard to believe," he said. She had to know Kaliga's absence was a disaster.

"The Line of Kaliga serves the Line of Qox," she said.

"Neither of us is that naive."

Her gaze didn't waver. "Yes, Kaliga has a great deal of influence and my husband is young. But don't underestimate the emperor, Kelric."

Hearing his name on her lips startled him. He suddenly remembered a time he had fallen asleep with his head in her lap. And then later . . . no, he must let those memories go.

Kelric knew he wouldn't forget living in her universe. And yet somewhere, sometime, his craving for her had faded. For all that he had insisted he no longer desired Tarquine, until this moment he hadn't realized he spoke the truth.

Her motives eluded him, yet in talking to her now, he had the impression she truly wanted the talks to take place. He doubted Jaibriol could succeed without ESComm behind him, but Tarquine's support might make the difference. Kelric had seen and lived with the power she commanded; if she backed her husband, the peace process might have a chance.

"Very well," Kelric said. "I will accept what you say about your husband's intent in these talks."

Tarquine turned her haughtiest Aristo look on him, an impressive one he had to admit, fit for an empress. "And I will accept the same, for the Ruby Dynasty."

"So."

She exhaled. "So."

He knew he should end the conversation, but instead he asked, "Did you get the answer to your other question, the one you can't put into words?"

Sadness shaded her response. "Yes. I did." In a husky voice, she added, "Farewell, Kelric. May you have happiness in your life."

Softly he said, "And you also. Good-bye, Tarquine."

Seven people sat at the table in the War Room on the Orbiter: Dehya Selei, the Ruby Pharaoh; Barcala Tikal, First Councilor of Skolia; Kelric, the Imperator; General Naaj Majda, highest in the military after Kelric; Admiral Ragnar Bloodmark, next after Majda; Eldrin, the Pharaoh's Consort; and Roca Skolia, the Foreign Affairs Councilor and mother to both Kelric and Eldrin.

Roca spoke flatly. "I don't see the point in continuing the talks."

Kelric recognized her tone; she wasn't going to relent. For all that she looked like the proverbial "sweet angel" described in news broadcasts, she was one of the toughest politicians he knew.

Naaj Majda nodded, her iron-gray hair pulled back, accenting her austere, patrician features. "I agree with Councilor Roca. Without ESComm, these talks mean nothing."

Ragnar Bloodmark sat sprawled in his chair, his lanky frame stretched out. "ESComm has sent no explanation. All we get are excuses from the emperor's staff."

"We need to hear from the Joint Commander," Tikal said.

Ragnar's gaze darkened. "Xirad Kaliga can go to hell."

Eldrin spoke dryly. "Your military insight leaves me in awe, Ragnar." He made no attempt to hide his dislike of the admiral. Ragnar cocked an eyebrow at him.

Roca glanced at Kelric. "You've been quiet. What do you say?"

"That we continue the talks."

First Councilor Tikal scowled at him. "They're using us, Imperator Skolia, playing some political game among themselves."

"Possibly," Kelric said. "But I'm convinced they at least want to try this time."

Ragnar gave him a sardonic look. "Of course your sudden interest in these talks has no link to your clandestine meeting last night with the empress."

Damn. Kelric narrowed his gaze at the admiral. How had Ragnar found out?

"What the hell?" Tikal said.

Naaj turned a cold gaze on Ragnar. "You had better have proof to back up that accusation."

Eldrin smirked. "Or else you just bought yourself one load of trouble, Ragnar my friend."

Even Roca looked troubled. "Ragnar, you go too far."

Kelric spoke quietly. "Yes, my meeting last night with Empress Tarquine affected my opinion."

Everyone went silent.

Until now, Dehya had been listening only, as she often did, no doubt evaluating their comments with her ever-evolving brain. Now she spoke to Kelric. "You didn't talk to the empress for long."

For flaming sakes. Dehya also knew? In truth, though, Kelric wasn't all that surprised she had discovered his talk with Tarquine; Dehya was probably too interconnected with the webs to miss a link from the Orbiter to Glory. But he had secured the transmission himself and had expected it to hold against anyone else. Ragnar had better intelligence operations than Kelric had realized.

Naaj frowned. "Just how many people know about this 'clandestine' meeting?"

"Not enough, apparently," Tikal said dryly. "I've only just heard of it."

Tarquine was the last person Kelric wanted to talk about with anyone, let alone his top advisers. But this wasn't something he could pull back from, no matter how he felt. "We spoke last night, through the web."

Roca regarded him uneasily. "About what?"

"The Eubians doubt our motives in the talks."

"*Our* motives?" Naaj snorted. "Is that a joke?"

"Apparently not," Kelric said.

"Do you trust the empress?" Eldrin asked.

Kelric gave a wry smile. "No."

"You shouldn't have spoken with her." Tikal scowled at him. "It violates every protocol."

Malice glinted in Ragnar's eyes. "Maybe speaking wasn't what they had in mind."

Eldrin stiffened. "You're out of line, Ragnar."

The admiral slanted a dark glance at him. "Are you speaking for your *brother*?" His emphasis left no doubt what he thought about Eldrin's objectivity, or lack thereof.

In his youth, Kelric had never understood why Eldrin resented Ragnar. Their animosity had grown during the past two decades, but now Kelric had the maturity to recognize its origins. Ragnar coveted Dehya, the Ruby Pharaoh, Eldrin's wife. Kelric wished his brother could distance himself from the admiral; Eldrin had to know Dehya would never betray him. He played into Ragnar's hands when he let his rival bait him.

Kelric spoke quickly, before his brother could blow up at Ragnar. "The empress and I discussed only the talks." That wasn't completely true; a great deal had gone unspoken between them. But any record of their conversation would support his claim.

Roca's voice hardened. "Tarquine Iquar overstepped herself. She has no rights to you."

Kelric could feel his mother's formidable ire stirring. Even now, when her children were interstellar potentates, Roca viewed them as her brood. Poets and historians lauded her beauty, but Kelric had always thought she was at her most striking like this, intense and daunting, without the polish of the media techs, a queen ardent in protecting her own, whether it was her children or her empire.

"Tarquine doesn't claim any rights," he said. "She just wanted my assurance about our intentions."

"That's absurd," Naaj said. "What, shall I go to Intelligence Minister Azile Xir and demand to know what Corbal Xir intends with his pirate fleets?"

Tikal crossed his arms. "A reason exists for our rules of order, Imperator Skolia. Breaking those protocols undermines the entire process."

"Does Emperor Jaibriol know you met with his wife?" Dehya asked.

"I didn't ask," Kelric said. "But no, I don't think so."

Tikal shook his head. "One wonders what is going on with the Hightons, that the emperor's military leaders refuse his commands and his empress is off having private audiences with the Skolian Imperator."

Naaj rested her elbows on the table and steepled her fingers. "Qox seems to have relatively little authority. I suppose it isn't surprising, given his youth and protected childhood. But I don't see much point in continuing these talks."

"I disagree," Kelric said.

"You aren't an objective judge," Tikal said.

Kelric stiffened. Then he finally said aloud what they were all avoiding. "I was her provider. That is hardly likely to predispose me to trust her."

Naaj met his gaze. "You were her lover."

"Not of my own free will."

An awkward silence fell over the group.

Dehya spoke softly. "Enough." She was watching Eldrin, who was staring at the table. Although Eldrin had barricaded his mind, Kelric knew his brother was remembering his time as a Trader prisoner.

Tikal spoke quietly. "I vote we end the talks."

"I agree," Naaj said.

Roca nodded. "I also."

Eldrin gave Kelric a look of apology. "I also agree."

Ragnar spoke wryly. "It appears Prince Eldrin and I are actually in agreement on something."

Tikal exhaled. "That is five in favor of withdrawing from the talks. We have a majority."

Dehya spoke coolly. "This isn't a democracy, Councilor Tikal. I say we continue."

"Well, well," Ragnar murmured. "The Ruby Pharaoh and the Imperator say yes, and the First Councilor says no." He looked inordinately entertained. "How awkward."

Kelric held back his retort. His dislike of what Ragnar had to say didn't change its truth. The blended government, with the Pharaoh and First Councilor sharing power, was just barely established. They had no precedent for this situation, where the two of them were opposed in a major decision.

Tikal and Dehya appraised each other. Then Tikal said,

"It isn't in our best interests to continue the talks."

Dehya raised an eyebrow. "Peace isn't in our best interest?"

"If the Traders wanted peace," Tikal countered, "Admiral Kaliga would be at the talks."

"That a power struggle may exist between the Qox palace and ESComm doesn't mean they don't want peace."

"Damn it, Dehya, they're using us."

She leaned forward. "If we withdraw, we weaken whatever support the emperor has for his position."

"And if the emperor falls in a coup?" A muscle twitched under Tikal's eye. Only a few months had passed since Dehya had overthrown his own government, backed by the military. The Ruby Dynasty suddenly ruled again, after centuries of having their lives constrained, manipulated, torn apart, even lost due to Assembly decrees. Kelric understood the desperation that had driven the Assembly to use the Ruby Dynasty no matter what the cost—the Kyle web protected Skolia against Eube, and without Ruby psions the web couldn't exist—but that didn't change what his family had suffered.

Kelric doubted the First Councilor would easily forget or forgive how close the coup had brought him to death. Had Dehya kept absolute sovereignty, the ancient laws of the Ruby Empire would have required she execute Tikal. She had split the government instead because losing him and the Assembly would have weakened Skolia. The Eubians had a less benign view. If Jaibriol III fell in a coup, he would be very dead, very fast.

"If he falls, we deal with it," Dehya said. "We can't stop talking peace just because he *might* be overthrown."

Tikal leaned forward. "Every moment our links stay open to Glory, we give ESComm an opportunity to crack the web."

"We need real-time discussions."

"It isn't worth the risk."

"Without risks, we'll never attain peace."

Tikal snorted. "They don't want peace."

"And if their emperor is sincere?"

"Why would he be?"

Dehya let out a breath. "I can't say why I think so. It's intuition."

"Your 'intuition' is legendary," Tikal said. "With all those extra neural structures of yours, gods know you see more than most people. But you're not always right."

"I can't make promises. But I believe this."

Tikal glanced at Kelric. "You agree with the Pharaoh?"

"Yes."

"On the basis of your talk with the empress."

"That's right."

Tikal looked frustrated. "It's too little to go on."

"Barcala," Dehya said. "Don't give up on this now."

Tikal narrowed his gaze at her. It was a long moment before he spoke.

Then he said, "Bloody hell. All right. Let's continue."

37

River of Ciphers

Jai found these restricted sessions of the peace talks the most grueling. Today he and Tarquine met with Pharaoh Dyhianna and Kelric, only the four of them. The Ruby Pharaoh regarded him across the table, her voice startling in its rich timbre. "Eubian pirates continue to attack Skolian ships. It is unacceptable."

In his side vision, Jai saw Tarquine stiffen. Given how accomplished the Pharaoh had turned out to be at interpreting Highton speech, he had no doubt her direct language now was deliberate; she was testing them, probing their reactions. Her authority probably offended Tarquine more than her speech; providers weren't supposed to understand the complexities of Highton speech but they were expected to defer to Aristos. Dyhianna violated both expectations with a vengeance.

He also understood what Dyhianna left unsaid; his own cousin, Corbal, rated among the worst offenders when it came to raids in Skolian territory. He couldn't reveal that Corbal had been set up; it would only make his power base look weak.

"Any raiders that prey on your people are breaking our laws," Jai said. "They will be punished."

It was Kelric who answered, his voice a rumble. "An assurance easily made." He left the rest of the sentence hanging: *and easily broken.*

Tarquine focused on Kelric with an intensity Jai knew would have made his own face flame. Yet Kelric remained unruffled even when she spoke in that devastating voice of hers. "An assurance," she said, "backed by strength." Jai recognized the nuanced Highton message in her posture; she referred to military strength. ESComm.

The Pharaoh shrugged. "That requires a willingness to back the assurance."

"A requirement easily met," Jai said. He wanted to throttle Kaliga for weakening his position this way.

Tarquine's voice came over his private channel. "Don't let her push you. Setting 'requirements' gives them advantage."

Damn. Every time he thought he was making progress, he stumbled. Everyone at this table was many decades older than him, and they all had experience commensurate with their years. He knew he wasn't the first sovereign to assume his throne at too young an age, but he didn't see how other such rulers had managed. Then again, maybe they hadn't; very few hereditary governments existed now. Even the Ruby Pharaoh had foregone sole power.

Dyhianna bemused Jai. For all that she resembled his mother, she had a finesse his mother had lacked. Hale and hearty, Soz Valdoria had been the epitome of a cybernetic warrior, but no one would have ever called her subtle. Dyhianna had so much subtlety that on the rare occasions when she chose bluntness, it came as a shock, one she used to deliberate effect. Nor could he imagine anyone calling his mother "delicate," whereas Dyhianna seemed breakable. But the differences were superficial; he recognized the same strength of will and intellect in his aunt that he had known in his mother.

He wasn't certain what Tarquine thought of the Pharaoh. Dyhianna defied everything Tarquine considered right and proper, on top of which, Dyhianna had the audacity to be short, when Hightons valued height. But Tarquine was no fool. She had to recognize the Pharaoh's strength, the authority that Dyhianna wielded with confidence. Dyhianna and Tarquine were like two lionesses circling each other, each evaluating her foe and protecting her pride.

Now Tarquine spoke. "It is important to punish lawbreakers for their crimes."

Jai stiffened. After telling him not to let the Skolians control the discussion, Tarquine had just played into their hands, implying they had reason to censure Eube. Personally Jai agreed, but he and Tarquine had to represent the Aristos or he would lose what remained of his support.

The Pharaoh didn't seem to agree with his assessment. Her voice turned icy. "Unless the 'law' is itself a crime."

Jai suddenly understood Tarquine's intent. Slavery was anathema among Skolians; when Eubians escaped to Skolia, they became free and were granted asylum. According to Eubian law, the Skolians were committing a major crime by harboring escaped taskmakers or providers. He hadn't thought Tarquine was serious when she said Kelric owed her fourteen million, but now he wondered. What if she demanded reparations? Surely even she wouldn't be that outrageous.

"It should be possible," Jai said, "to find compromises for differences in legal systems."

"Some laws are too opposed," Dyhianna said coldly.

"Opposition can be resolved," Jai offered.

"Opposition, yes." Kelric showed no sign of relenting. "Morality, no."

Tarquine narrowed her gaze at him. "Whose morality?"

Dyhianna answered. "Some principles should be universal." Her voice could have chilled ice.

Tarquine raised an eyebrow. "Indeed."

Jai knew they were debating the slave trade. Skolians would never accept it and Eube would never relinquish it. Quietly, he said, "Must billions die for this opposition?"

Kelric met his gaze. "If it is important enough."

"And if those deaths aren't necessary?" Tarquine asked.

Anger edged Dyhianna's voice. "How can you stop them, when laws we consider an abomination are forced on unwilling populations?"

Jai took a deep breath—and plunged ahead. "Suppose such force became illegal?"

Kelric went very still. "It already is illegal."

"Illegal on both sides," Jai said.

Silence descended on the table. Jai was glad none of them could see him sweating. He had just offered to outlaw the pirate fleets. Although neither ESComm nor any Aristos admitted owning such fleets, no Eubian law forbade the raids. Only the Halstaad Code of War even addressed the issue; it prohibited selling Skolian POWs. Given that most Aristos had no wish to own hostile Skolian soldiers, it wasn't hard to enforce the Code. But that was for taskmakers, who weren't psions. If Kelric's experience was any indication of what happened with a psion, it could be a nightmare trying to forbid *all* raids. But Jai was willing to try, if the Skolians would offer a compromise he could take to the Hightons.

Tarquine spoke on his private channel. "ESComm will never allow you to outlaw the raids."

"I have to try." He answered Tarquine privately, but then he spoke to the Pharaoh on the channel everyone could hear. "Skolian citizens should have the right to remain Skolian— just as Eubian citizens should remain Eubian." In other words, if he stopped Eubians from taking Skolians, then her people should send escaped slaves back to Eube.

She regarded him for a moment. "I see."

No one else spoke. Jai knew the compromise was abhorrent to both sides. The Aristos would revile any law forbidding the raids; the Skolians would revile any law requiring them to return escaped taskmakers and providers to Eube. But gods, it was better than world-slagging wars that would never end until they destroyed human life.

Kelric leaned forward. "No Skolian would force people he cares for to return to a life of slavery."

Jai wondered if the rumors were true, that the Imperator

had married a former taskmaker. If so, Kelric would never agree to such a compromise. In this VR simulation Kelric could edit his responses however he wished, but even given that, Jai thought he detected an unusual degree of tension in the stoic Imperator.

Jai spoke slowly, thinking it through. "Perhaps a statute of limitations could apply to the return. After a certain amount of time, if the Eubian is still in Skolian territory, she may remain." He used "she" deliberately, thinking of Kelric's wife.

"How long?" Dyhianna asked.

"Ten years," Tarquine said.

Kelric didn't bother to edit out his look of disgust. "No."

"Ten days," Dyhianna said.

Tarquine raised an eyebrow. "I didn't know absurdity was an imperial trait, Pharaoh Dyhianna."

From what Jai had heard, Kelric had married a woman who had helped him reach Earth. That would have been over three months ago.

"Three months," Jai said. "If the Eubian is still in Skolian territory after that time, she can apply for asylum."

Tarquine's voice came over his private channel. "That is no way to bargain, Jaibriol. Hold out for longer."

"They won't agree to longer," he said.

"You have to push it harder."

They all sat, considering one another. As the silence stretched to the breaking point, Jai feared they had reached a deadlock.

Then Dyhianna spoke, her voice heavy. "A flawed treaty is better than none at all, when the alternative could very well be mutual annihilation."

"Good gods!" Tarquine's voice came on Jai's private channel. "Is that what it sounds like, that she might negotiate? If we can find a way to talk about this, we might actually make progress." She sounded so stunned, Jai wondered if she had ever believed the talks could accomplish anything.

"I hope so," Jai told her. He kept his simulacrum silent,

aware of Kelric studying him. He didn't know what to think of the Imperator: enemy, uncle, rival? In another life, he might have sought out Kelric as a father figure after his own father died, but this was the only life he had, and Corbal was the closest he would ever come to a mentor.

Just as Jai started to answer the Pharaoh, the voice of an EI came over his private channel. "Your Highness, you have a priority transmission from Glory."

Jai paused. Everyone was waiting for him to respond to Dyhianna. "Who is it from?" he asked the EI privately.

"Robert Muzeson. He says it is an emergency."

"Tell him we're in the middle of an important session."

"Muzeson didn't think it could wait, Your Highness."

Jai knew Robert wouldn't interrupt him without good reason, but the timing couldn't have been worse.

Tarquine spoke over the private channel. "Jaibriol, you must answer the Pharaoh. She just offered the opening we've hoped for."

"I'm getting a page from Robert." To the EI, Jai said, "Relay the message to myself and Empress Tarquine."

Robert's voice came in his ear. "Your Highness, you are needed immediately on Glory."

"That's it?" Jai asked.

"That is all," the EI said.

Kelric was scrutinizing him even harder now. "Emperor Jaibriol?"

Jai knew he had to make a decision. "I'm receiving a transmission from Glory. I regret that I must invoke a temporary close to these proceedings."

Tarquine swore on his private channel. "Don't do this! Robert can wait. We may not get an opening like this again."

"This is rather sudden," Dyhianna said.

"Please accept my apologies," Jai said. Before Tarquine could curse at him for apologizing to a provider, he spoke to his wife on the private channel. "Robert wouldn't interrupt if it wasn't important."

Kelric said, "We can have our Protocol Office set up a new session with your Protocol people."

Jai nodded. "That would be good."

"Ah, hell," Tarquine muttered privately. "Once Protocol gets involved, it will take forever."

Dyhianna was studying Jai. "I hope all is well."

So do I, Jai thought.

After the requisite formalities, Jai and Tarquine took their leave. They split up outside the conference room, and he returned to the white chamber where he always "arrived" in Paris. As its walls faded, he became aware of voices, techs talking in the console room on Glory.

Light flared as a tech removed the visor over his eyes. He could see the console room now. As the techs unfastened him from the chair, Jai stood up. Tarquine was standing in the center of her console a few meters away, being checked by medics. As soon as Jai's medics finished with him, he strode toward the exit of the room. Tarquine joined him, accompanied by their ubiquitous Razers.

After they left the VR room, Jai spoke into his wrist comm. "Robert?"

"I'm in your office, Your Highness."

"Why did you interrupt the session?"

"Perhaps we should speak here," Robert said.

Jai put his hand over the comm and glanced at Tarquine. "Do you have any idea what this is about?"

She shook her head. "None."

Bile rose in his throat, but he fought it down. Had someone tried to kill him while he was in the VR sim? Or maybe ESComm had followed the example of their Skolian counterparts and overthrown his government. Right now he might be a prisoner of the military he was supposed to command. He doubted he would fare as well as the Skolian First Councilor.

"I wonder if I'm still emperor," Jai muttered.

Tarquine drew him to a stop. "I have taken precautions in case we ever need to leave the palace quickly."

He swallowed, aware of the Razers forming a bulwark around them, one that had never seemed benign and now felt like a prison. "Yes. Make your precautions ready."

They set off again, with Tarquine talking into her comm. It sounded as if she was just checking her net mail, but Jai didn't question her. Either she had created a cover to disguise her commands or else she had lied. He chose to believe the former, mainly because he didn't have much choice.

At Jai's office, he and Tarquine left the Razers outside and went in alone, closing the entrance behind them. Jai was surprised to see Corbal standing behind the desk. The desk itself glimmered with a river of hieroglyphics flowing across its surface.

Corbal looked up, his face drawn. Robert was standing behind the Xir lord, a palmtop clenched in his hand, watching Jai with quiet horror.

Jai's pulse ratcheted up. "What is it?"

Corbal moved back. "You had better see for yourself."

Jai went around the desk, focusing on the glyphs streaming across its black top. "This looks like some sort of offworld transmission."

"It's from a ship that just entered the system," Corbal said at his side. "If it had dropped out of inversion any closer to Glory, it would have violated the regulations against using star drives too close to a settled planet."

Tarquine came to the front of the desk and peered at the glyphs. "I can't read them upside down. They're going too fast."

"The ship started broadcasting the moment it arrived." Corbal's voice had a strange quality, as if he were struggling to contain a reaction. "The message is on a secured ESComm channel."

Jai went cold. "This is from an ESComm ship?"

Corbal nodded. "Yes."

Jai studied the message, which was encoded in all three dimensions of the glyphs. With the node implanted in his spine analyzing the message, it didn't take him long to absorb its meaning.

He read the message four more times to make sure.

Jai slowly sat down in the chair. "Gods." He swallowed. "Gods almighty."

It wasn't until he looked up and saw Robert's dismay that Jai realized he had spoken in Iotic, the language of the Skolian nobility. Robert had served as a translator; he would recognize not only the language, but how well Jai spoke it. In his childhood Jai had tended to think in Iotic rather than Highton. Apparently under stress he still did. And he spoke it perfectly, with no accent. Yes, any Highton could study Iotic. Every Qox emperor had spoken it. Jai might even learn it well. But no true Highton would revert to perfect Iotic when he was in shock.

Robert shot a panicked look at Corbal and Tarquine, knowing they had heard. But they simply continued to watch Jai with neutral expressions. Neither said a word.

Jai rose to his feet, his hand resting on his desk, the glyphs flowing around his fingers.

Tarquine spoke quietly. "What does it say?"

He answered with a numbness he knew wouldn't last long. "Admiral Xirad Kaliga and General Kryx Taratus, the Joint Commanders of ESComm, are dead."

She didn't even blink. "How?"

When Jai saw her lack of surprise, a chill went through him. "Taratus assassinated Kaliga." The news felt like dust in his mouth. "Lord Raziquon was on Kaliga's yacht when it exploded." He glanced at Robert, his voice hardening. "Apparently my order rescinding Raziquon's pardon never reached the High Judge."

Robert blanched. "I will look into it, Your Highness."

"You do that," Jai said coldly.

"How did Taratus die?" Tarquine asked.

Jai turned to her, feeling as if he were in a surreal painting. "The Raziquon and Kaliga Lines discovered what they considered irrefutable evidence that the Taratus Line had assassinated their lords. So they retaliated. They shot Taratus."

"Gods." Even she seemed stunned. "They moved fast."

"Didn't they now." Jai remembered her delayed arrival at the peace talks. And Kaliga had never showed up. Jai's heart was beating so hard, he felt it in his whole body. "This will cripple ESComm. It could throw Eube into chaos."

"You must appoint new commanders as fast as possible," Corbal said.

"Astonishing, that." Jai continued to stare at Tarquine. He didn't know how he kept his voice calm. "Now I must choose two new Joint Commanders."

"So you must." Fierce satisfaction sparked on her face.

"You must call an investigation," Robert said.

Jai glanced at him. He still couldn't believe Robert had betrayed him. He couldn't absorb any of this. Yet.

Corbal motioned at the glyphs scrolling across Jai's desk. "According to that, an investigation has already been done and evidence produced."

"Evidence can be faked," Jai said.

"For an accusation of this magnitude?" Corbal gave him an incredulous look. "It would be impossible. Kaliga and Taratus were too powerful."

"Almost impossible." Jai turned to Tarquine. *"Almost."*

"I believe the operative word is 'impossible,' " she murmured.

"Is that right?" It wasn't until Jai's hand began to ache that he realized he was clenching the desktop, his fingers stiffened into a claw.

"Apparently so." No chink showed in her cool demeanor. "No one would dare make such an accusation without proof." She stepped forward and rested her hands on his desk, submerging them in the river of glyphs. "You must act quickly to avoid a disaster. Select new commanders."

He had to make a conscious effort not to clench his teeth. "And I've no doubt you can offer me advice on that."

"Of course."

It astonished Jai that he wasn't shaking with anger as he

turned to Corbal. "No doubt you have advice, too."

His cousin inclined his head. "If it pleases Your Highness, I can offer my humble thoughts on the matter."

Humble, hell. Jai felt as if the world had gone silent, muffled by his shock. With icy formality, he nodded to Corbal and Tarquine. "I will speak to you both later."

Although neither looked pleased to be dismissed, they didn't seem surprised. Jai had his Razers escort them from the office. But just before she left, Tarquine turned back to him. "Husband."

"Yes?"

"Your speech is exalted," she said softly. "Never forget."

Jai swallowed. Never forget. *Never again speak your mother's tongue.* Hotness filled his eyes, but damned if he would let his grief show—and he would turn to ashes in hell before he mourned Taratus or Kaliga.

None of the Razers even blinked at her comment. Why should they? Given the megalomaniacal way Hightons spoke about themselves, her "compliment" was mild. Only he, Corbal, and Robert understood its true meaning.

When everyone had left but Robert, Jai lowered himself into his chair and rested his elbows on the desk. Putting his forehead in his hands, he closed his eyes. He wished he could float away, out the window, free.

Robert spoke. "Your Highness, may I help you?"

Weary, Jai lifted his head. "It is so odd, Robert, that Lord Raziquon happened to be aboard Admiral Kaliga's yacht when it exploded. I wonder how he received his pardon after I refused to grant it."

"I will do my utmost to discover how such a terrible mistake occurred."

"Yes, do your utmost." Jai swiveled his chair around to him. "So, Robert my trusty aide, do you also find my speech exalted?"

His aide met his gaze squarely. "Yes."

"Just 'Yes'?" Jai raised an eyebrow. "No, 'Yes, Your Most

Supremo Emperor'? What happened to that glib tongue of yours?"

Sweat sheened Robert's forehead. He went down on one knee and bowed his head. "I revere you now and always, and will attend you with the greatest loyalty."

Jai clenched the arms of his chair. "Don't kneel to me."

Robert rose to his feet. "I wish only to serve you."

"Then serve me. Not my wife."

He averted his gaze. "Yes, sir."

Jai knew, from Robert's mind, that his aide had acted in what he believed was Jai's best interest. What stunned Jai more, though, was that Robert never intended to question his lapse into Iotic. He would serve his emperor even if he had reason to believe that emperor might be other than what he claimed.

"We have a great deal of work ahead of us," Jai said.

"Shall I see to the investigation into the deaths of Admiral Kaliga and General Taratus?"

"Yes." Jai stood up, rising to his full height, half a head taller than Robert. "But first, I would like to know where my wife went."

Robert checked his palmtop. "She is in the arbor of the North Garden." He started to say more, then seemed to think better of it.

"What is it?" Jai asked.

His aide took a shaky breath. "I am immensely grateful, Your Highness, that the empress is not our enemy."

Softly Jai said, "So am I."

38

The Garden

---

*J*ai stood with his siblings in the pew of the church. For the first two Christmases they had spent on Earth, they had come here with Seth to celebrate the holiday. It had become special to them because it meant so much to him.

But this third year was different. This year, on newscasts that played over and over, they had watched their parents die. Time after time, Jai saw the shuttle bearing his mother and father explode; time after time, he saw debris hurtle through space, the detonation recorded by hundreds of other ships during battle. His parents, who had dreamed of peace, had died for their hope. The scene replayed endlessly, everywhere, in a horrible parody of the peace that this season was supposed to bring.

His grief was too big. He had never been able to weep.

Now he stood with his sister, Rocalisa, and his brothers, Vitar and Del-Kelric. Lisi was almost fifteen now, her pretty face much like their grandmother's, Roca Skolia. At ten, Vitar was growing like a sprout, his black hair streaked with gold, his eyes red. Four-year-old Del-Kelric resembled a cherub, but with ruby sparkles in his gold eyes.

They were listening to the priest say Mass when the double doors of the church creaked. Jai glanced back, uneasy. The church held hundreds of pews, and he was near the front, far from the doors, so he couldn't see clearly. It looked like a man was in the foyer, but the darkness beyond the doors made it hard to make out anyone who hadn't entered the main church.

Then the man came all the way inside—and Jai's pulse leapt. Outfitted in the full battle armor of a cybernetic warrior, the man carried a laser carbine.

When the priest went silent, staring at the back of the church, the members of the congregation looked as well. The church was packed for the holiday service, which meant hundreds of people were turning to the soldier.

He wasn't alone.

More warriors filed in, boots clanking, guns glinting. The priest walked to the rail that separated the area where he said Mass from the main church, but when he tried to step out, a soldier moved quickly to him and put out his hand to stop the older man.

Sweat beaded on Jai's forehead. A soldier was coming up the central aisle, carrying a laser carbine. Jai recognized his armor: the man was a Skolian Jagernaut. He kept coming, nearer and nearer, his tread relentless.

Jai felt as if he were dying inside. He had no doubt why these soldiers had come. He stepped to the end of the pew, putting himself in front of Lisi, Vitar, and Del-Kelric. He was aware of Seth moving to the other end of their line, so he and Jai bracketed the younger children.

The Jagernaut stopped at their pew and stared at Jai, making no attempt to hide his shock.

Seth spoke in a firm voice. "These children have political asylum. You cannot touch them."

Jai wondered what good political asylum would do against so many armed warriors.

"Gods almighty," the soldier whispered, more to himself, it seemed, than to Jai or Seth. Then he spoke into the comm on his gauntleted wrist. "All four of them are here."

A sinking sensation spread in Jai, deepened by a sorrow greater than he knew how to handle. The soldier turned toward the back of the church. The doors were open, both those to the foyer and the doors that led outside. It was night. Light from the outdoor lamps slanted through the dark foyer, silhouetting two figures entering the church.

Then the two entered the light, and Jai's sense of time slowed down. They seemed to walk in slow motion, a woman in a dusty black commando uniform with a carbine slung over her shoulder, and a man in Highton clothes that had once been elegant and now were ripped and rumpled. Two people—

Two achingly familiar people.

Jai heard Del-Kelric cry out, but in his shock he didn't move fast enough. The small boy squeezed by even as Jai grabbed for him. Then Del-Kelric was running down the aisle, oblivious to the armed intruders, his face radiant.

As warriors all over the church whipped up their guns, the soldier at Jai's pew yelled, "Don't shoot!" In that same instant, the woman in the commando uniform shouted into her wrist comm, "*Hold your fire.*"

Del-Kelric ran on, oblivious to the firestorm of laser shots he had nearly started, his pudgy arms extended, his face wreathed in smiles. Then Vitar and Lisi pushed past Jai and raced down the aisle as well, Vitar's long legs devouring the distance, Lisi's hair streaming behind her. Jai couldn't move. He couldn't break the icy shock that had frozen him.

The man in the ripped Highton clothes went down on one knee—Jaibriol II, the Emperor of Eube, was kneeling, reaching to a little boy. Del-Kelric barreled into him, throwing his arms around the emperor's neck, his father, at the same time reaching for the woman in the commando uniform, his mother, Soz Valdoria, the Imperator of Skolia. Then Lisi and Vitar reached them, and the two rulers gathered their children close, everyone crying as they embraced, uncaring that hundreds of strangers and armed soldiers were watching their reunion.

Jai finally walked down the aisle. Two steps away from his family, he stopped, unable to continue. They all gazed at him, his father holding Del-Kelric in one arm and his other arm around Vitar's shoulders. Lisi stood next to their mother, tears on her face.

Jai couldn't speak. For the past two years he had seen his parents vilified on the news as brutal tyrants who had broken two empires. Were these the parents who had given their children such a deep, abiding love?

Yes.

Seeing them now, Jai knew that whatever the rest of humanity chose to believe, he would always have the truth. They were the two finest people he had ever known. He stepped forward and they took him into their arms.

So he held his family, his mother, father, brothers, sister, his tears streaming as they rejoiced . . .

Jai opened his eyes into darkness, his face wet. Grief wrenched through him. The dream wasn't real. Yes, he and his siblings had gone with Seth to church that last Christmas, but no miracle had occurred. His parents hadn't come home.

Finally, after so long, he cried. He couldn't stop. The tears tore out of him, his mourning as raw as a new wound. He was alone. Tarquine had already risen, as she often did. Sometimes she woke him, her touch sensual in the dark hours, but this time she had been wise enough to leave him alone. He didn't want to touch his dangerous wife, not tonight.

So Jai wept. The tears released, giving way to the sorrow he had locked within himself for so long.

Kelric waited on the balcony of the apartment that Dehya and Eldrin kept in the city on the Orbiter. The great lamp that served as a "sun" had completed its arc across the sky and now night filled the spherical habitat, lit by star lamps that sparkled in the hemisphere above them.

Standing at the rail, he gazed at the graceful bridges and buildings below. As he took a swallow of his drink, a rustle came from behind him. Then Dehya joined him.

"I've always loved this view," she said.

"It is beautiful."

For a while they stood appreciating the city. Strains of music came from within the apartment, as Eldrin worked on his latest composition.

"Do you believe he did it?" Dehya asked.

Kelric didn't need to ask whom she meant. "No, I don't think so." He doubted they would ever know the truth, but he didn't believe Jaibriol Qox had killed his Joint Commanders.

"I'm not sure I believe they assassinated each other," Dehya said.

"Why not?" Gods knew, Hightons spent an inordinate amount of time plotting against one another.

"It's hard to explain." Her face was pensive in the silvery light. "Intuition, maybe, or the calculations I've been running on my neural nodes." She tilted her head, listening. Eldrin's voice graced the night, soaring into high notes, then dropping into deep, rumbling tones. Softly she said, "I should so like to make the stars safe for the people I love."

Kelric thought of Jeejon, captivated by the VR arcade he had built for her. "I also."

"Perhaps hope exists for the talks after all."

He felt less optimism. "Even if the emperor forbids the raids, I doubt he can enforce such a law."

Dehya sighed. "Nor can I imagine any Skolian sending escaped slaves back to Eube."

Kelric thought of Jeejon. "Nor I."

"I hate the suggested compromise."

"Yet still we negotiate."

She spoke with pain. "Perhaps it is because we hope this treaty will lay the first stones in a path that leads to compromises we can better accept."

Seeing her face luminous in the starlight, he thought that here, in the forgiving night of home, she was willing to hope. He didn't yet dare give in to that gossamer dream.

"Perhaps someday," he said.

Dehya sipped her drink. "It may take decades. Half a century. But perhaps someday."

"Why half a century?"

"The models I've been running predict something then. Lightning?".

"A storm?"

"I don't know. But changes will come."

Kelric looked out over the city sparkling in the night. "He is unusual, this new emperor of Eube."

"A miracle," Dehya murmured.

"Maybe." It was as far as he could go in speaking his wish for peace. He had seen too much of the ugliness humanity produced to believe the Traders could ever change.

But deep within his heart, hope stirred.

Jai knew he had to face Tarquine. He could put it off no longer. In the day that had passed since the deaths of Kaliga and Taratus, he had barely had time to breathe, let alone talk to his wife. But he couldn't avoid this forever. When Robert told him she had gone to one of the palace gardens, Jai went in search of her.

Fog wreathed the grounds. He couldn't see the sky, where the moons G4 and G5 shone. He knew now how he would surface G5, Tarquine's moon. As a geode: steel-diamond on the exterior, brilliant crystals underneath, knife-edged but startling in their beauty. He had also chosen a name for his mother's moon. Prism. It was what his family had called the world where they had lived in exile for fifteen years, the place where he had been happy and loved. If asked, he would say it was what his father called the sanctuary where Jai and his mother had lived in seclusion.

He followed an overgrown path that wound through a lush woods, with hoary trees on either side, and trellises covered by vines heavy with silver, blue, and rose flowers. Walkways crisscrossed the garden. Deeper in the woods, ancient trees leaned over a latticework tower, their branches dripping long fronds of moss. The tower was three stories tall.

Tarquine stood framed within an opening at the top.

Jai wondered how such beauty could exist amid such violence, both in Eube and in his wife. He entered the base of the tower, a circular area ten paces across, its lattice walls threaded by vines with curling tendrils. He stopped at the stairs that spiraled up around the inner wall and turned to the captain of his bodyguards. "You may wait here."

The captain bowed. "As you wish, Your Highness."

Jai started up the stairs, his hand on the rail. But after a few steps, he paused, looking down. "Captain."

"Yes, Your Highness?"

"It would please me to know your name."

"I haven't one."

"Nothing at all?"

"I have a serial number. Would you like that?"

Sadness filled Jai. To grieve for a living being designed to be more machine than man hurt at a level too deep for him to define. He spoke his younger brother's name. "Vitar."

The captain's forehead furrowed. "Your Highness?"

"You have a name now," Jai said. "Vitar." The Razer resembled Jai's younger brother. "If I had ever had a brother, I would have liked him to have that name."

The captain's gaze widened, giving lie to the serial number that labeled him as a machine. "I am honored."

Jai tried to smile, but he couldn't. He inclined his head, then resumed climbing. His Razers stayed below, monitoring his progress on their cybernetic arms.

The staircase ended at the third level. Tarquine was a few paces away, her back to him, her black-garbed figure silhouetted against the overcast sky. Mist curled around her legs.

Jai went to stand with his wife.

Tarquine turned to him. "You look well today."

He wondered if he would ever be well again. "So do you." That much was true. She was devastating. Such cold, deadly beauty.

"Have you heard news from the Skolians?" she asked.

"Yes." In the muffled day, Jai felt unnaturally quiet. "They have agreed to resume the talks." He thought of General Barthol Iquar, Tarquine's nephew, and of Admiral Erix Muze, the grandson of High Judge Calope Muze. "Both of ESComm's new Joint Commanders have sworn to support the talks. General Barthol will attend."

"Good." Dark satisfaction showed in Tarquine's gaze.

Jai wondered if he even knew how to define *good* anymore. "My security people found evidence of a message that Admiral Kaliga sent from his hospital room in the palace. It was well hidden. It took them a long time to uncover it."

"A message?" Her face was inscrutable.

"To Raziquon's kin. It includes reference to Kaliga's involvement in the attempts against my life."

"So," Tarquine murmured. "Kaliga implicated himself."

Jai didn't believe for a moment Kaliga had sent the message. Someone else had been in the admiral's room during that crucial time. Whoever it had been would never speak, and no neural scan of the admiral's brain could prove his innocence now.

He wanted to ask Tarquine the questions that burned within him. Why had she gone to such drastic lengths to further peace talks she had never seemed to want in the first place? Had she done it for Kelric? But he didn't know if he could bear to hear her answers.

He said only, "Without opposition from Kaliga, Taratus, or Raziquon, we may establish a treaty with the Skolians."

"The newscasts are already calling it the Paris Accord."

His voice caught. "So I've heard."

She searched his face. "Are you happy, Jaibriol? It is what you wanted, yes?"

"Yes." He had dreamed of it. He should rejoice. And he did feel a bittersweet joy. But he had never expected it to come at the price of murder. That Tarquine had told him nothing of her plans made no difference; unknowing or not, he was responsible.

She spoke pensively. "A thought has come to me."

"What do you mean?"

She turned back to the gardens, her hands clasped behind her back. "That it may be desirable, sometimes, to act in benefit of Eube rather than of oneself."

Jai didn't know whether to weep at her words or disbelieve them. Her calmness contrasted with her usual tension. She seemed to have made peace with something, but what, he had no idea.

"Is that why you support the talks?" he asked.

"I wouldn't have chosen to have them."

"Then what is it you think may benefit Eube?"

Facing him, she spoke quietly. "To have an emperor with decency rather than avarice, one who desires what is best for his people over what will satisfy his greed."

Jai's perception suddenly shifted. She hadn't done this for herself; she had done it for him. He had agonized for so long, fearing her avarice and ambition, and her hunger for Kelric. Even knowing her mind, he hadn't seen the truth until now. It wasn't Kelric she wanted.

It was him.

He didn't know where to put that knowledge. Tarquine was a force of nature he had unleashed. She would never share his beliefs in right and wrong, yet she would support him to the death. Literally. Was it worth the devastating price she exacted from his conscience? He would pay that price, if it meant Eube and Skolia could someday find their way to peace, but the stain on his soul would never leave.

He spoke in a low voice. "I'm not sure I will ever understand you."

She spoke quietly. "I have discovered I understand myself far less than I thought."

"You have questions?"

"One." She gazed at the ancient trees. "I found the answer without ever asking it aloud."

"What did you find?"

She hesitated. "I could be wrong about it."

"About what?"

"I don't know if I am truly capable of this."

"Of what?"

Another silence.

Then she said, "Of loving another human being."

Tarquine faced him then, really faced him. "You are goodness and I am not. Nor will I ever be. I cannot change that much." She took his hand. "But whatever hells our marriage was made within, I am glad of its making."

Jai spoke softly. "I, too." It was true, gods help him.

Standing together, the emperor and empress looked out at the new universe they were creating, one shrouded in mist, but with the hint of sun lightening the overcast.

Author's Note: The Moons of Glory

The Science in Science Fiction

The moons of the planet Glory are a dramatic presence in its sky, with brilliant colors and marked size variations. I based their behavior on the moons of Saturn. The two systems aren't identical; Saturn has at least eighteen moons (probably more), whereas Glory has only fourteen. But many similarities exist.

I've called the moons G1, G2, G3, and so on; the smaller the number, the closer the moon's orbit to Glory, the capital world of Eube. Some of the moons are very close in, but the smallest orbit is still outside the Roche limit that determines how close a moon can orbit before gravitational forces pull it apart.

Glory is a large planet with a light core, a radius three times Earth's, and an average density a bit less than one third that of Earth, which gives it a surface gravity of 92 percent of ours. The sun of Glory subtends an angle of 0.45° in the sky, which means it appears slightly smaller than the sun in our sky.

The two innermost moons of Glory, G1 and G2, are small, about 30–40 kilometers in diameter, less than 1 percent the diameter of Earth's Moon. Their distance from Glory is roughly eleven percent the distance of our Moon from Earth, with G1 closer than G2. As seen from Glory, each satellite subtends an angle of 0.04°–0.05° in the sky. For comparison, Earth's Moon subtends about 0.5° in our sky, making it more than ten times the width that G1 or G2 appear as seen from Glory.

The next two moons, G3 and G4, have orbits close together, separated by only 50 kilometers. Their behavior follows that of two Saturn moons—Janus and Epimetheus.

Specifically, they periodically switch orbits. The swap occurs because they approach each other closely enough to trade momentum. Suppose G3 is initially closer to Glory; it then travels a bit faster than G4 due to its smaller orbit. As G3 approaches G4, the gravity of G4 pulls G3 into a larger orbit, which slows G3 down. Similarly, G3 pulls G4 into a smaller orbit, speeding G4 up. So G3 becomes the outer moon and G4 drops into the inner orbit. In other words, as the two moons near each other, they swap orbits. The inner moon then speeds off from the outer, and the process repeats when the moon comes back around.

Seen from Glory, the two moons would gradually appear to approach each other but then "bounce" away again without touching or passing. If you were on the satellite that lags behind, you would see your moon approach the leading moon. As the two neared, yours would slow down while the other sped up, seeming to "run away" every time you almost caught up.

Eube Qox, the first emperor, originally named G3 and G4 in honor of his sisters, Tarquine and Ilina. However, those designations are falling out of use. The satellites of Glory are named for empresses, with the moon that appears largest from the surface of Glory named for the first empress, the second largest named for the second empress, and so on. Although G4 and G3 appear the same size, they are, respectively, the sixth and seventh largest, and will be renamed for the sixth and seventh empresses. Each subtends an angle of 0.13° in the sky, about one quarter the width of our Moon as seen from Earth. They have an elongated shape, particularly G3.

The next satellite is G5, which appears in the sky as the fourth largest moon; as such, it should be named for the fourth empress, the wife of Jaibriol II and mother of Jaibriol (Jai) III. Jai cannot give it his mother's name—Sauscony Valdoria—so he chose one that honors her without revealing her identity as the military leader of Eube's enemies. Her moon subtends an angle of 0.28° in the sky, more than half the width of our Moon in Earth's sky.

The next moon, G6, is the third largest in actual size and also as seen from Glory. The third emperor, Ur Qox, named it Viquara in honor of his wife and surfaced it with synthetic diamond, making it the brightest object in Glory's sky. It subtends an angle of 0.39°, about three-quarters the size of our Moon.

G7 is the fifth largest moon as seen from Glory. Jaibriol III (Jai) named it Tarquine in honor of his wife (which is another reason G3 lost its name). He had the moon resurfaced to resemble a geode, with a steel-diamond composite on the outside, brilliant and hard. Just under the surface, it has a crystalline structure in incredible colors.

Three moons share the eighth orbit: G8a, G8b, and G8c. The largest, G8b, is called Mirella after the first empress. She married Eube Qox, who founded the Eubian Concord. In her honor, he surfaced the moon with a ruby composite, turning it a vivid red. As seen from Glory, Mirella is the largest moon, but in actual size, it is the second largest, with a diameter only about 40 percent that of G11. However, G11 is over four times farther away from Glory, so in the sky it appears smaller than Mirella. The diameter of Mirella is about half that of Earth's Moon, but its distance from Glory is only about one quarter the Earth-Moon distance; Mirella thus subtends an angle of 0.98° in the sky of Glory, twice the width of the Moon in our sky.

Two tiny moons share Mirella's orbit. G8a is 60° ahead in and G8c is 60° behind, each of them at a *Lagrange point,* which is an unusually stable point in an orbit. They have blocky shapes and each subtends an angle of 0.02° in the sky, which is about 1/25 the width of Earth's Moon in our sky. Together, the three G8 moons form the same type of system as the Trojan moons of Saturn—Tethys and its tiny companions Calypso and Telesto.

G9 and G10 are tiny moons that appear the same size as G8a and G8c. They are actually a bit larger than Mirella's companions, but they orbit farther out from Glory. G9 is about three times as far from Glory as G1, the innermost moon, and subtends an angle of 0.03° in the sky of Glory; G10 is four times as far out as G1 and subtends an angle of 0.02°.

G11 is the largest moon. As seen from Glory, however, it appears as the second largest because it is so far out from the planet. It is called Zara for the wife of Jaibriol I, the second emperor. Zara subtends an angle of 0.59° in the sky, making it about 60 percent the size of Mirella as seen from Glory and about 120 percent the width of our Moon in the sky. Jaibriol I had its surface turned into gold to honor his empress.

Zara raises substantial tides on the Glory, exerting a force about one and a half times that of the Moon on Earth. Mirella has an even greater effect, exerting a tidal force over six times that of our Moon. Several other Glory satellites also have a significant effect: Viquara, at 47 percent the effect of the Moon on Earth; G4 (Soz's moon) at 20 percent; Tarquine (G5), at 5 percent; G4 at 4 percent; and G1 and G3, both roughly 1 percent. The other moons exert smaller forces. The combined effect of the moons and the sun of Glory creates huge, complicated tides and distorts the planet.

The last moon, G12, is tiny. Its unusually large orbit puts it approximately one hundred times farther out than G1, the innermost satellite, and ten times as far out as Zara, its closest companion.

Shadows

During an eclipse of a sun by a moon, the moon moves between the planet and the sun so that its shadow falls across the planet. From the surface of the planet, the sun appears covered by a dark disk. In a total eclipse, all of the sun is covered and a period of darkness results; in a partial eclipse only part of the sun is covered.

An eclipse is total when a planet passes through the inner portion of the moon's shadow—the *umbra*—the central cone of shadow created by the overlap of shadows from all edges of the moon. Surrounding the umbra is an outer, lighter cone of shadow—the *penumbra*. In a total eclipse, the planet passes through the penumbra, into the umbra, out of the umbra, and finally out of the penumbra again. In a partial eclipse, the planet passes through the penumbra.

The three parts of *The Moon's Shadow*—Penumbra, Umbra, and Penumbra—represent the stages in Jaibriol's attempts to establish himself as emperor. They also symbolize his efforts to keep his vow that his parents won't have died in vain, that he will bring Eube and Skolia to the peace table.

The Moon's Shadow contrasts to *Ascendant Sun,* which chronicles Kelric's rise to power as Imperator of Skolia. The sun is Kelric, whereas the shadow refers to Jaibriol's experiences. In some senses, Jaibriol can be thought of as the moon to Kelric's sun; Jaibriol leads the darker of the two empires and Kelric the lighter.

The moons of Glory symbolize the reign of the Eubian emperors, represented by their empresses. Each casts a shadow over Jaibriol's life. In that sense, the title refers to Tarquine. She symbolizes the conflict in Jaibriol's ascension; to achieve his goal of peace talks, he relinquishes a part of his inner light. In other words, to bring light to the peoples of Skolia and Eube, he must let darkness into his life. The reverse is true of Tarquine; by the end of the book, she emerges from certain shadows of her own heritage. Neither she nor Jaibriol change their fundamental nature, but each is deeply affected by the other.

The cyclic nature of the moons and their eclipses represent the cyclic nature of Jaibriol's quest to bring peace to Eube and Skolia. He will never escape the shadows of the previous reigns nor the civilizations they created, but each time he enters the shadow, hope exists that he can emerge.

Other interpretations exist for the moons, their shadows, and their symbolism. Readers interested in talking more about the allegories or other aspects of the Ruby Dynasty universe can join an online listserv on yahoo groups started by Skolia fans. To subscribe, email asaro-subscribe@ yahoogroups.com.

Family Tree: RUBY DYNASTY

Boldface names refer to members of the Rhon. The Selei name denotes the direct line of the Ruby Pha
All children of Roca and Eldrinson take Valdoria as their third name. All members of the Rhon within the
Dynasty have the right to use Skolia as their last name. "Del" in front of a name means "in honor of."

= marriage   + children by

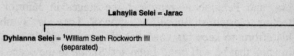

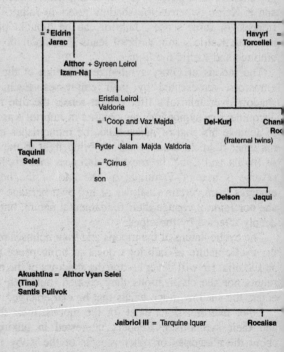

Lahaylia Selei = **Jarac**

Dyhianna Selei = [1]**William Seth Rockworth III**
(separated)

= [2] **Eldrin**
Jarac

Havyrl =
Torcellei =

Althor + Syreen Leirol
Izam-Na

Eristia Leirol
Valdoria
= [1]**Coop and Vaz Majda**

Del-Kurj   **Chani**
Roc
(fraternal twins)

Ryder Jalam Majda Valdoria

= [2]**Cirrus**
son

Taquinil
Selei

Delson   **Jaqui**

Akushtina = **Althor Vyan Selei**
(Tina)
Santis Pulivok

Jaibriol III = **Tarquine Iquar**   **Rocalisa**

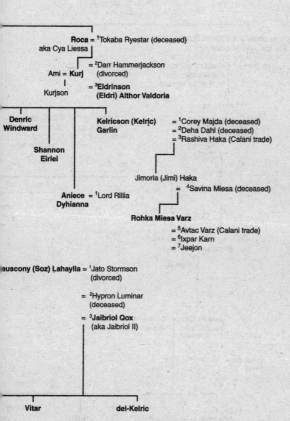

Roca = [1]Tokaba Ryestar (deceased)
aka Cya Liessa

     = [2]Darr Hammerjackson
Ami = **Kurj**   (divorced)
  |
 Kurjson = [3]**Eldrinson**
      (Eldri) Althor Valdoria

Denric
Windward   **Kelricson (Kelric)** = [1]Corey Majda (deceased)
      Garlin   = [2]Deha Dahl (deceased)
           = [3]Rashiva Haka (Calani trade)

Shannon
Eirlei
        Jimorla (Jimi) Haka

         = [4]Savina Miesa (deceased)
  Aniece = [1]Lord Rillia
  Dyhianna
      Rohka Miesa Varz

        = [5]Avtac Varz (Calani trade)
        = [6]Ixpar Karn
        = [7]Jeejon

auscony (Soz) Lahaylia = [1]Jato Stormson
        (divorced)

      = [2]Hypron Luminar
      (deceased)

      = [3]**Jaibriol Qox**
      (aka Jaibriol II)

Vitar   **del-Kelric**

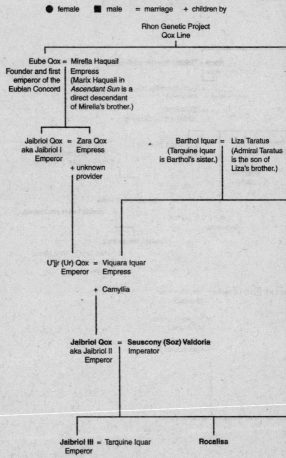

Family Tree: QOX DYNASTY

Boldface names refer to members of the Rhon.

● female   ■ male   = marriage   + children by

Rhon Genetic Project
Qox Line

Eube Qox = Mirella Haquail

Founder and first
emperor of the
Eubian Concord

Empress
(Marix Haquail in
Ascendant Sun is a
direct descendant
of Mirella's brother.)

Jaibriol Qox = Zara Qox
aka Jaibriol I
Emperor

Empress

+ unknown
provider

Barthol Iquar = Liza Taratus
(Tarquine Iquar
is Barthol's sister.)

(Admiral Taratus
is the son of
Liza's brother.)

U'jjr (Ur) Qox = Viquara Iquar
Emperor

Empress

+ Camyllia

Jaibriol Qox = **Sauscony (Soz) Valdoria**
aka Jaibriol II
Emperor

Imperator

Jaibriol III = Tarquine Iquar
Emperor

Rocalisa

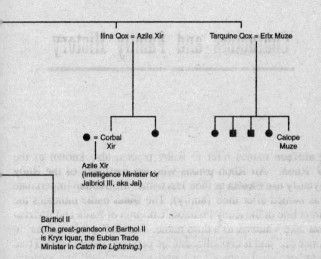

Ilina Qox = Azile Xir

Tarquine Qox = Erix Muze

= Corbal Xir

Azile Xir
(Intelligence Minister for
Jaibriol III, aka Jai)

Barthol II
(The great-grandson of Barthol II
is Kryx Iquar, the Eubian Trade
Minister in *Catch the Lightning*.)

Calope Muze

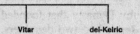

Vitar

del-Kelric

Characters and Family History

Boldface names refer to Ruby psions, also known as the "Rhon." All Rhon psions who are members of the Ruby Dynasty use **Skolia** as their last name (the Skolian Imperialate was named after their family). The **Selei** name indicates the direct line of the Ruby Pharaoh. Children of **Roca** and **Eldrinson** take Valdoria as a third name. The "del" prefix means "in honor of," and is capitalized if the person honored was a Triad member. Most names are based on world-building systems drawn from Mayan, North African, and Indian cultures.

= marriage

Lahaylia Selei (Ruby Pharaoh: deceased) = **Jarac** (Imperator: deceased)

Lahaylia and **Jarac** founded the modern-day Ruby Dynasty. **Lahaylia** was created in the Rhon genetic project. Her lineage traced back to the ancient Ruby Dynasty that founded the Ruby Empire. **Lahaylia** and **Jarac** had two daughters, **Dyhianna Selei** and **Roca**.

Dyhianna (Dehya) Selei = (1) William Seth Rockworth III (separated)
                      = (2) **Eldrin Jarac Valdoria**

Dehya is the Ruby Pharaoh. She married William Seth Rockworth III as part of the Iceland Treaty between the Skolian Imperialate and Allied Worlds of Earth. They had no children and later separated. The dissolution of their marriage would have negated the treaty, so neither the Allieds nor the Imperialate recognized Seth's divorce. Both Seth and Dehya eventually remarried anyway. *Spherical Harmonic* tells the story of what happened to **Dehya** after the Radiance War. She and **Eldrin** have two children, **Taquinil Selei** and **Althor Vyan Selei**.

Althor Vyan Selei = 'Akushtina (Tina) Santis Pulivok

The story of **Althor** and **Tina** appears in *Catch the Lightning*. **Althor Vyan Selei** was named after his uncle/cousin, **Althor Izam-Na Valdoria**. Tina also appears in the story "Ave de Paso" in the anthology *Redshift* and *The Year's Best Fantasy*, 2001.

Roca = (1) Tokaba Ryestar (deceased)
      = (2) Darr Hammerjackson (divorced)
      = (3) **Eldrinson Althor Valdoria**

Roca and Tokaba had one child, **Kurj** (Imperator and former Jagernaut), who married Ami when he was about a century old. Kurj and Ami had a son named Kurjson.

Although no records exist of **Eldrinson**'s lineage, it is believed he descends from the ancient Ruby Dynasty. He and **Roca** have ten children:

Eldrin (Dryni) Jarac (bard, consort to Ruby Pharaoh, warrior)
Althor Izam-Na (engineer, Jagernaut, Imperial Heir)
Del-Kurj (Del) (singer, warrior, twin to **Chaniece**)
Chaniece Roca (runs Valdoria family household, twin to **Del-Kurj**)

Havyrl (Vyrl) Torcellei (farmer, doctorate in agriculture)
Sauscony (Soz) Lahaylia (military scientist, Jagernaut, Imperator)
Denric Windward (teacher, doctorate in literature)
Shannon Eirlei (Blue Dale archer)
Aniece Dyhianna (accountant, Rillian queen)
Kelricson (Kelric) Garlin (mathematician, Jagernaut, Imperator)

Eldrin appears in *The Radiant Seas* and *Spherical Harmonic*

Althor Izam-Na = (1) Coop and Vaz
                    = (2) Cirrus

Althor has a daughter, Eristia Leirol Valdoria, with Syreen Leirol, an actress turned linguist. Coop and Vaz have a son, Ryder Jalam Majda Valdoria, with **Althor** as co-father. **Althor** and Coop appear in *The Radiant Seas*. The novelette, "Soul of Light" (Circlet Press, anthology *Sextopia*), tells the story of how **Althor** and Vaz met Coop. Vaz and Coop also appear in *Spherical Harmonic*. **Althor** and Cirrus also have a son.

Havyrl (Vyrl) Torcellei = Lilliara (Lilly) (deceased)
                            = Kamoj Quanta Argali

The story of **Havyrl** and Kamoj appears in *The Quantum Rose,* which won the 2001 Nebula Award. An early version of the first half was serialized in *Analog,* May 1999–July/August 1999. The story of **Havyrl** and Lilly appears in "Stained Glass Heart," a novella in the anthology *Irresistible Forces*, February 2004.

Sauscony (Soz) Lahaylia = (1) Jato Stormson (divorced)
                            = (2) Hypron Luminar (deceased)
                            = (3) **Jaibriol Qox** (aka **Jaibriol II**)

The story of how **Soz** and Jato met appears in the novella, "Aurora in Four Voices" (*Analog,* December 1998). **Soz** and **Jaibriol**'s stories appear in *Primary Inversion* and *The Radiant Seas.* They have four children, all of whom use Qox-Skolia as their last name: **Jaibriol III, Rocalisa, Vitar,** and **del-Kelric.** The story of how **Jaibriol III** became the emperor of Eube appears in *The Moon's Shadow.* **Jaibriol III** married Tarquine Iquar, the Finance Minister of Eube.

Aniece = Lord Rillia

Lord Rillia rules Rillia, which consists of the extensive Rillian Vales, the Dalvador Plains, the Backbone Mountains, and the Stained Glass Forest.

Kelricson (Kelric) Garlin = (1) Corey Majda (deceased)
= (2) Deha Dahl (deceased)
= (3) Rashiva Haka (Calani trade)
= (4) Savina Miesa (deceased)
= (5) Avtac Varz (Calani trade)
= (6) Ixpar Karn (closure)
= (7) Jeejon

Kelric's stories are told in *The Last Hawk, Ascendant Sun, The Moon's Shadow,* the novella "A Roll of the Dice" (*Analog,* July/August 2000), and the novelette "Light and Shadow" (*Analog,* April 1994). **Kelric** and Rashiva have one son, Jimorla (Jimi) Haka, who becomes a renowned Calani. **Kelric** and Savina have one daughter, **Rohka Miesa Varz,** who becomes the Ministry Successor in line to rule the Twelve Estates on Coba.

The Novella "Walk in Silence" (Analog, April 2002) is set in the Skolian universe, but doesn't invole members of the Ruby Dynasty.

Time Line

circa 4000 BC	Group of humans moved from Earth to Raylicon
circa 3600 BC	Ruby Dynasty begins
circa 3100 BC	Raylicans launch first interstellar flights; rise of Ruby Empire
circa 2900 BC	Ruby Empire declines
circa 2800 BC	Last interstellar flights; Ruby Empire collapses . . .
circa AD1300	Raylicans begin to regain lost knowledge
1843	Raylicans regain interstellar flight
1866	Rhon genetic project begins
1871	Aristos found Eubian Concord (aka Trader Empire)
1881	Lahaylia Selei born
1904	Lahaylia Selei founds Skolian Imperialate
2005	Jarac born
2111	Lahaylia Selei marries Jarac
2119	Dyhianna Selei born
2122	Earth achieves interstellar flight
2132	Allied Worlds of Earth formed
2144	Roca born
2169	Kurj born
2203	Roca marries Eldrinson Althor Valdoria

2204	Eldrin Jarac Valdoria born; Jarac dies; Kurj becomes Imperator
2206	Althor Izam-Na Valdoria born
2209	Havyrl (Vyrl) Torcellei Valdoria born
2210	Sauscony (Soz) Lahaylia Valdoria born
2219	Kelricson (Kelric) Garlin Valdoria born
2223	Vyrl marries Lilly ("Stained Glass Heart")
2237	Jaibriol II born
2240	Soz meets Jato Stormson ("Aurora in Four Voices")
2241	Kelric marries Admiral Corey Majda
2243	Corey assassinated ("Light and Shadow")
2258	Kelric crashes on Coba (*The Last Hawk*)
early 2259	Soz meets Jaibriol (*Primary Inversion*)
late 2259	Soz and Jaibriol go into exile (*The Radiant Seas*)
2260	Jaibriol III born (aka Jaibriol Qox Skolia)
2263	Rocalisa Qox Skolia born; Althor Izam-Na Valdoria meets Coop ("Soul of Light")
2268	Vitar Qox Skolia born
2273	del-Kelric Qox Skolia born
2274	Radiance War begins (also called Domino War)
2276	Traders capture Eldrin. Radiance War ends
2277–8	Kelric returns home (*Ascendant Sun*); Dehya coalesces (*Spherical Harmonic*); Kamoj and Vyrl meet (*The Quantum Rose*); Jaibriol III becomes emperor of Eube (*The Moon's Shadow*)
2279	Althor Vyan Selei born
2287	Jeremiah Coltman trapped on Coba ("A Roll of the Dice")
2328	Althor Vyan Selei meets Tina Santis Pulivok (*Catch the Lightning*)

ABOUT THE AUTHORS

SHARON SALA

Sharon Sala is a longtime member of RWA, as well as a member of OKRWA. She has seventy-seven-plus books in print, written as Sharon Sala and Dinah McCall. First published in 1991, she's a five-time RITA® Award finalist, winner of the Janet Dailey Award, four-time Career Achievement winner from *Romantic Times BOOKreviews,* and in addition, has won the National Reader's Choice Award and Colorado Romance Writer's Award of Excellence five times each! Her books are *New York Times, USA TODAY, Publishers Weekly* and Waldenbooks mass market bestsellers. She believes writing has changed her life, her world and her fate.

ISABEL SHARPE

Isabel Sharpe started reading romance in high school, back when she claims it should have been called "Men who plunder honeyed depths and the women who let them." After she quit work to be with her firstborn son and nearly went out of her mind with boredom, she started writing. She admits she was the clichéd bored housewife writing romance, but it was either that cliché or seduce the mailman, and her mailman was unattractive. Twenty-plus sales later—romance novel sales to Harlequin Books and women's fiction sales to Avon/HarperCollins—the mailman is still not tempting, and Isabel can safely say she made the better choice.

LINDA CARDILLO

Before she became a novelist, Linda Cardillo wrote nonfiction, from articles in the *New York Times* to business texts on marketing and corporate policy. Between earning her Harvard MBA and publishing her first novel, she's been an editor, teacher and fund-raiser. She plays the piano every night and does the *New York Times* Sunday crossword puzzle in ink, as her mother did. When she isn't writing, puzzling or making music, she cooks. Her first novel, the Maggie Award-winning *Dancing on Sunday Afternoons,* was published by Harlequin Everlasting Love; her novella "The Hand That Gives the Rose" appeared in the Harlequin Superromance anthology *The Valentine Gift;* and her next novel, *Across The Table,* will be released in October 2009.

New York Times Bestselling Author

SHARON SALA
ISABEL SHARPE
LINDA CARDILLO

A

Mother's

Heart

HARLEQUIN®

TORONTO • NEW YORK • LONDON
AMSTERDAM • PARIS • SYDNEY • HAMBURG
STOCKHOLM • ATHENS • TOKYO • MILAN • MADRID
PRAGUE • WARSAW • BUDAPEST • AUCKLAND

ISBN-13: 978-0-373-83731-1
ISBN-10: 0-373-83731-3

A MOTHER'S HEART

Copyright © 2009 by Harlequin Books S.A.

The publisher acknowledges the copyright holders
of the individual works as follows:

THE PROMISE
Copyright © 2009 by Sharon Sala

YOU BELONG TO ME
Copyright © 2009 by Muna Shehadi Sill

A DAUGHTER'S JOURNEY
Copyright © 2009 by Linda Cardillo Platzer

www.eHarlequin.com

Printed in U.S.A.

CONTENTS

THE PROMISE

Sharon Sala

Mother's Day is always on Sunday. When I was a little girl, everyone—women and men—wore a rose on their clothing in honor or in memory of their mothers. A red rose meant your mother was still living; a white rose signified she had passed away.

I remember sitting in the church house, leaning against my grandmother's ample bosom and smelling the sweetness of the white rose pinned to her dress. My grandfather had one just like it pinned to his shirt.

Mother's rose was red, as was mine and my sister's. We would bend our heads forward until we could bury our noses in the roses pinned to our dresses, then look at each other and giggle. We didn't "get" how special it was to be able to wear that red rose, or how empty lives became as our loved ones aged and passed away.

These years, as so many other things from past generations, the tradition is slowly dying. It's rare to see people wearing flowers on Mother's Day, and if they do, it's often a big showy corsage made of orchids.

When I do see roses pinned to people's Sunday finest, I can't help but remember the sweetness of times gone by, and the safety of being held beneath my grandmother's arm with the soft scent of roses swirling around my head.

I am one of the lucky ones. At this writing, my mother is still with me—living with me—and still sharing memories.

I am dedicating this book to my mother, Iris Shero Smith, and to my daughter, Kathy, my daughter-in-law, Kristie Ann, and to my niece, Crissy, for being great mothers to their own children, and for giving me seven of the best grandchildren a woman could have.

CHAPTER ONE

THE MORNING SUN WAS just coming up when Liberty Farraday walked into her son Sammy's room to wake him up. Not only was today a school day, it was also Sammy's birthday. He was eight years old. She could hardly believe it. Eight long years of raising Sam Holt's son—without Sam. Of course, when she thought about it, which was more often than she wanted, she had to admit it was her fault she was on her own, because Sam didn't know Sammy existed. But it was Sam who'd walked out on her and hadn't come back. The way she figured, if he didn't want her, he wouldn't want Sammy, either.

Most of the time, her reasoning worked, but every now and then, like this morning, watching her son as he slept, and knowing that with each passing day he was growing into the image of the man who'd broken her heart, she doubted her judgment.

Libby frowned, then shook off her sadness. Today was a day for rejoicing. Sammy's eighth birthday and all it entailed. She glanced at the *Star Wars* clock hanging over his bed, and leaned down with a smile.

"Good morning, little man," Libby whispered, then tickled the back of Sammy's ear as he began to rouse. "Happy birthday, Sammy. Better hurry up and get dressed. I'm making pancakes this morning and you don't want to be late for school."

With the skill only a child can manage, Sammy came awake within seconds, talking before his eyes were even open.

"Mama, are you bringing cupcakes to school this afternoon for my birthday?"

Liberty Farraday stifled a sigh. One more thing to squeeze into an already hectic work day. But a guy only turned eight one time, and celebrating the day with your school friends was a must in Azalea, Tennessee.

"Absolutely, little man," Libby said.

"Are they gonna be chocolate?" he asked.

Libby grinned. "Is there any other kind?"

"Mama, you're funny," Sammy said, and rolled out of bed and headed for the bathroom.

"Don't forget to wash your face and brush your teeth," Libby said as she laid out the clothes for him to wear to school.

"Okay, Mama," Sammy said, and so their day began.

Not only did Libby have pancakes waiting at Sammy's plate when he came to the table, but his birthday present was there, as well.

"Yea! Can I open it now?" Sammy asked.

"Of course you can," Libby said, then sat back with a delighted smile on her face. She tried not to think of how much her little boy looked like his daddy.

"*Star Wars* stuff! Way to go, Mama!" Sammy said, and gave her a high-five as he tore into the box. "Cool! There's Lando Calrissian, Han Solo, Yoda...oh, oh, look Mama, an Ewok. They're funny."

Libby nodded in all the right places but had no clue as to who the characters were. Although they owned every one of the Star Wars DVDs, she had yet to sit all the way through even one of them. Then she glanced at the clock.

"Oops, better get at those pancakes. You can play with your *Star Wars* stuff this evening when you come home from school."

"All right, Mama. Boy. I can't wait to tell Pete what I got."

Pete Wyatt was Sammy's best friend, and his grandmother, Kate Wyatt, was probably Libby's best friend, although their ages were separated by more than forty years.

A short while later Libby pulled up in front of Robert E. Lee Elementary and handed Sammy his book bag.

"Have a great day, my love," Libby said. "I'll see you later… cupcakes and all."

"'Bye, Mama. Make pretty bouquets," he said, referring to her job at Faye's Floral Fantasies, then waved as he headed toward the main entrance to the school.

Libby gave Sammy a last wave, then paused, watching his funny swagger and thought again, the older he got, the more he looked like Sam. Then she bit her lip and looked away. No need to think of that man. He'd walked out of her life even before she'd known Sammy was on the way. And the breach between them had been so devastating that the idea of calling him later to inform him she was pregnant was impossible.

It hadn't been easy being a single mother, and there were times when she felt the guilt of Sammy growing up without a man in his life. But on the rare occasions when he asked what happened to his father and why he wasn't in their lives, Libby always said his daddy just got lost. So far it had worked, but the older Sammy got, the less he would be satisfied with the answer. However, life wasn't perfect; Sam Holt had taught her that.

Someone honked and her focus shifted. She looked up just in time to see Kate Wyatt waving at her as she dropped off her grandsons, Pete and Charlie. Libby waved back, then as soon as the street was clear, she pulled away from the curb and headed to work.

Libby was a skilled floral designer, which prompted her boss, Faye, to willingly work around Libby's schedule so she could be home when Sammy got out of school. It was the best job in Azalea for a woman in Libby's situation. She didn't make enough money for day care, but thanks to Faye's generosity, she made enough for them to get by. As she paused for a red light, she mentally ticked off the time it would take to get home after work, pick up the cupcakes and then get back to school at the appointed time. When the light turned green, she accelerated slowly and was in the middle of the intersection when she heard brakes screeching. She was vaguely aware of something coming at her from the driver's side of the car. Then everything went black.

THE AMBULANCE pulled up to the emergency entrance of Jackson Memorial Hospital with lights and sirens blaring. The staff had already been alerted to their arrival and met the EMTs at the door. The woman on the gurney was covered in blood, and there was a brace on her neck and an IV in her arm. The paramedics were running as they pushed her into the E.R. One of them was calling out her vitals as the other one pumped the bag on her oxygen mask.

"She got T-boned by a semi at the intersection of Elm and Main. Her BP is 80 over 60. Her pulse is erratic and thready. We lost her twice on the way here. She's bleeding into her abdomen, got broken ribs and God knows what else."

"Put her in Two," a doctor said, while a team of nurses followed behind.

They transferred the woman onto the bed, and then the team took over.

"What's her name?" the doctor asked as they began to assess.

"Farraday. It's Libby Farraday."

There was a collective gasp. This woman was unrecognizable as the pretty little thing they all knew who made deliveries from Faye's flower shop. They quickly began trying to assess her immediate needs and stabilize her long enough to get her to surgery.

SAMMY KNEW something was wrong when he was called out of his classroom just after second hour had begun. When he was told to bring his book bag, he knew he would be leaving, which didn't make sense. He didn't think he was in trouble, but with grown-ups and rules, it was always hard to know.

He entered the principal's office, expecting to see his mother, but saw Pete's Grandma Kate, instead. She'd been crying. That was when he started to get scared.

"Come here, honey," Kate said, then wrapped her arms around Sammy and hugged him so tight he couldn't breathe.

"What's wrong?" Sammy asked. "Where's Mama and why are you crying?"

"Honey, your mama had a wreck on her way to work this morning. I'm going to take you to the hospital."

"But today is my birthday," he whispered, as if nothing this awful could possibly happen on his special day.

Everyone in the office had already been in tears, but hearing the fear and the shock in that little boy's voice was more than they could take. The secretary excused herself and left the room while the principal blew his nose and then patted Sammy on the back.

"You're excused to leave, son. I'm sure your mother is going to be okay. When you see her, tell her we said to get well soon."

He didn't answer. He couldn't.

Kate Wyatt had already been told how serious Libby's injuries were. She prayed all the way to the hospital that Sammy's mother would still be alive when they got there. She couldn't imagine what would happen to this precious little boy if Libby didn't pull through; they only had each other.

SAMMY WAS TOO SHOCKED to cry. Mama didn't look like Mama anymore. Her turned-up nose was swollen to twice its size, and her lips and face had lots of tiny cuts. They'd told him it was because of all the broken glass from the wreck, but he didn't want to think about it. He kept watching all the machines hooked up to her and frowning at the needles in her arms.

"That's not Mama…is it?" he asked.

"Yes, honey, it's Mama. She's just swollen from the accident. That will go away as she heals."

His stomach hurt and the words burned the back of his throat so bad he didn't think he could say them. But he had to ask.

"Is she gonna die?"

Kate wouldn't lie. "They're doing everything they can to make her well," she said, then stroked the top of his head.

"Can I touch her?"

"You sure can, honey. And you can talk to her, too. Just because she looks like she's asleep doesn't mean she can't hear you, okay?"

Sammy walked to the side of the bed, carefully sliding three fingers across the sheet, then worked them beneath her hand. He kept wishing Mama would wake up and squeeze his fingers back, but she didn't. All he could hear were the machines—beeping, beeping, beeping.

"It's me, Mama," he whispered. "It's okay you couldn't bring the cupcakes. I don't wanna have a party without you."

Finally, tears welled and spilled, running down his face in two steady streams. "Mama. Please wake up. You have to get well, okay?" Then he put his head down on the side of the bed and sobbed.

He was still sobbing uncontrollably when Kate picked him up and carried him out of the intensive care unit. Once she got him outside into the hallway, she got down on her knees and made him look her in the eyes.

"Sammy! Sammy! Listen to me, darling. You're not alone. Pete and Charlie and I are here for you. And until Mama gets well, you're going to come stay with us. You like spending the night with Pete. It will be like a long sleepover, okay?"

He was afraid to answer. Decisions were out of his control. He just laid his head on her shoulder and held on for dear life.

PETE WYATT was the opposite of his best friend, Sammy. Where Sammy was tall and on the thin side for his age, Pete was short and stocky, with red hair and green eyes. Sammy's hair was straight and black, and his eyes were brown.

Pete had seen Sammy cry before, but he'd usually been bleeding. He didn't know what to do about sadness. He'd never seen anyone cry from being sad before, except once when Melissa Stewart had torn her new pants on the playground and he was pretty sure she'd been sad about that when she'd cried all through recess.

Grandma Kate told him and Charlie that Sammy was sad because his heart was hurt. Pete wanted to fix

Sammy's heart, but he didn't know how. Instead, he pulled a half-dozen tissues from the box, and crawled up onto the bed beside Sammy and patted his shoulder.

"I'm sorry your mama got hurt," he said as he handed him the tissues.

Charlie came in and sat down on the bed, too. "Yeah, I'm real sorry about your mama, too."

Now Pete was scared. Charlie usually picked on them. Instead of talking, he just rolled over and buried his face in his arms.

Pete patted Sammy on the back and then went to find his grandma.

Kate was in the kitchen with the phone to her ear as she worked. Everyone in Azalea knew she and Libby were friends, and the phone hadn't stopped ringing since the news had spread. Her back was to the doorway, so she didn't see her grandson's arrival. If she had, she might have chosen to voice her fears to the pastor at a later date. But she didn't know Pete was nearby, and she let her worries overflow.

"No, Pastor, they don't have any other family that I know of. Hmm? Oh. Yes, of course, I guess he has a father somewhere. Libby never talks about him, but if he was dead, I think she would have said so."

There was a pause. Pete knew he should speak up, or at least let Grandma know he was there, but he wanted to know what was happening and knew she'd stop talking if she saw him, so he stepped back into the hallway and continued to listen. Charlie walked up behind him, started to thump him on the back of the head, when he realized what was happening. Instead of picking on Pete like he usually did, he stood beside him, a cohort in eavesdropping.

"If she dies? Lord, Lord, please don't say that. I know, the possibility exists. But the accident just happened today. What would happen to Sammy if she did? I suppose the state would step in. I would offer to foster him, but I'm already treading on thin ice with my own grandsons. You know how small this house is, and with my health issues they'd never give me custody of another child."

"What's wrong with Grandma?" Pete whispered.

Charlie sighed, then patted his little brother on the head. "She just has arthritis. That's all." He didn't see any need to let the twerp know that Grandma also took pills for her heart. He knew because he'd recognized the name of the medicine on her pill bottle as the same one being advertised on a late-night television commercial.

"What's gonna happen to Sammy if his mother dies?" Pete asked.

Charlie frowned and shushed him as they continued to listen to Kate's conversation with the preacher.

"It would break my heart if he wound up a ward of the state. All those news stories about how awful foster care is, and orphanages…well, don't get me started."

Pete backed up, swiped the tears off his cheeks, and then turned to his big brother.

"We have to do something, Charlie."

"Like what?" Charlie muttered.

"I don't know," Pete said. "But you're the oldest. Figure something out."

Then he walked away, leaving Charlie alone in the hall with yet another burden on his shoulders besides the ones he already had.

One week later

SAMMY HADN'T MISSED a day going to see his mother, although Libby Farraday was still in a coma. The hospital had bent the rules so that he could stop and see her every day after school, rather than wait for proper ICU visiting hours. He was quiet as a mouse and usually sat in a chair beside her bed without moving. Once in a while, the nurses could hear him talking to her, although they didn't hear what he was saying. But for Sammy, his message was always the same.

"Mama, it's me, Sammy. School was okay today. Our teacher took us outside for science class. I found a praying mantis on the side of a tree and saw some ladybugs in the grass. The teacher said I had sharp eyes."

As usual, Libby maintained her silence, but Sammy wasn't finished.

"I ate my vegetables at lunch, even though they weren't as good as the ones you make. The ones in the cafeteria never have any salt on them, and they are always too squishy. You cook the best ones, Mama."

He waited the usual ten-second count for a response that didn't come, then moved on to the next topic.

"Mama, if you'll wake up, I'll tell you a secret."

His gaze was fixed on her face, looking past the green and purple bruises and scabs on the cuts to her eyes, praying for the lashes to flutter—praying that her lips would move.

When she didn't answer, he just sighed and patted her hand.

"It's okay, Mama. I'll tell you anyway. Pete heard his grandma talking to the preacher. If you don't wake up, they're gonna make me go live with strangers…some people named Foster, and I don't wanna leave you. So, you know how you always told me that Daddy got lost from us? Well, Charlie has a plan to fix that. It's gonna be the best Mother's Day present ever. You just have to wake up."

A nurse walked up and touched his shoulder. "Sorry, Sammy, but it's time for you to go."

He nodded, then leaned over and whispered, "Remember what I said, Mama. The best Mother's Day present ever. I promise. You just have to wake up to get it."

SOMETHING SHIFTED in Libby's darkness. There was a flash of cognizance, reminding her of life, and then it was gone and she fell back into the shadows, unaware that her little boy had come and gone.

IT WAS SATURDAY. Kate was up to her neck with laundry and worn out from the extra work of taking care of Sammy, along with his visits to the hospital every day. So when Charlie offered to take the boys to the park for the day, she was all for it.

"I'll watch them good, Grandma, I promise," Charlie said, and held up his duffel bag. "I'm taking Frisbees and the soccer ball and I've got us some snacks."

Kate sighed, thinking there was hope for her fourteen-year-old grandson yet.

"I appreciate this, Charlie."

"I know, Grandma."

She pointed at the clock. "Watch the time. You boys come on home by three. It'll be too hot by then for you to still be out in the sun."

"Yes, ma'am," Charlie said, and then yelled, "Come on, you two, or I'm going without you."

Kate winced from the blast in her ear, but refrained from mentioning Charlie's faux pas. She heard the boys coming and sighed again. A little peace and quiet would be welcome.

"You boys mind Charlie," she said, when Pete and

Sammy came running through the laundry room on their way out the back door.

"Yes, ma'am," they both echoed, and out they went.

The quiet they left behind was so startling that it took Kate a few minutes to acclimate herself, but she soon fell back into the rhythm of folding and sorting as the washer sloshed and the dryer hummed.

THREE BLOCKS OVER, Charlie's friend, Howard, was waiting. When he saw the three boys coming up the driveway, he ran out to meet them. Then he led them into his house the back way and down to the basement where his father kept his video equipment.

"You sure this is okay with your folks?" Charlie asked.

Howard shrugged. "As long as they don't know, it is." He grinned.

Sammy's eyes widened nervously. He wasn't in the habit of breaking rules and defying adults, but he viewed this as an emergency.

"Did you bring the picture?" Howard asked.

Charlie pulled a frame out of his duffel bag and handed it to Sammy.

"Here, kid. You're gonna hold this in front of you like we planned. Remember?"

Sammy nodded and took the photo, then looked at Pete, who gave him a thumbs-up.

"You know what you're doing with this stuff, right?" Charlie asked as Howard pulled a tripod out into the middle of the floor and then mounted a video camera on it.

"Yeah. I help Dad do this all the time. We took a bunch of film at his bowling tournament last month. I even uploaded the two gutter balls Mr. Waychoff bowled onto YouTube for him."

"You ready for this, Sammy?" Charlie asked, giving

Sammy a nervous glance. Charlie knew the dangers of posting images of children on the Internet. His grandma had talked long and hard to him about porn sites and perverts before she'd let him use her computer. He didn't think what they were doing was going to put Sammy in any danger, but he wasn't sure. Still, he felt sorry for the kid and, like Pete, didn't want to see the little guy placed in some awful foster care place.

"You ready for this, Sammy?"

Sammy nodded as he clutched the eight-by-ten photo of him and his mother. "Where do I sit?" he asked.

Howard pointed to a straight-back chair he'd pulled from the dining set. "Sit there, kid and when I say go, you start talking."

"His name is Sammy," Pete announced.

"Whatever," Howard muttered.

Charlie frowned and shook his head at Pete. They needed Howard's help, so antagonizing Howard wasn't a good idea.

Pete stuck his tongue out at his brother, then gave Sammy another thumbs-up.

"Do you remember what you're going to say?" Charlie prompted.

Sammy nodded. "I've been practicing it in my head for two whole days."

A phone rang somewhere in the rooms above. Howard glanced up at the ceiling. When no one yelled his name, he breathed a sigh of relief.

"We gotta do this fast," he said, then pointed at Sammy. "Ready?"

Sammy nodded again.

Howard punched a button, checked the camera for clarity, upped the volume, then pointed at Sammy and mouthed the word *go*.

Sammy clutched the picture against his chest and started talking.

"My name is Sammy Farraday and I'm eight years old. My mama's name is Liberty Farraday but everyone calls her Libby. This is a picture of us taken on Valentine's Day this year, only Mama's hair is longer now. A truck crashed into my mama's car on my birthday and hurt her really bad and she won't wake up. My best friend, Pete, heard grown-ups talking about making me live in Foster's care. I don't know any people named Foster and I don't wanna go live with strangers. I don't know who my daddy is, but Mama always told me that he got lost from us and doesn't know where we are anymore."

When Sammy's chin started trembling, Howard's own eyes welled. The kid was getting to him. Hopefully the rest of the nation would pay attention, too.

"So the reason I'm doing this is because I promised my mama the best Mother's Day present ever if she would wake up. Pete's big brother, Charlie, told me the Internet goes all over the world, and if I was lucky, maybe my daddy would see this."

Howard pointed at Sammy. "Say it now, kid."

Sammy took another deep breath. "Daddy, I know you don't know me, but I'm a good boy. If you see this, would you please come find us? I don't want them to take me away from Mama and give me to the Fosters. If you came, it would be the best Mother's Day present ever. We live in Azalea. It's in Tennessee. If you look on the map, it's not too far from Nashville." His little voice was trembling as he ended. "I guess that's all. Amen."

Howard stopped the recording. There was a long moment of silence. No one moved. No one spoke. Then Sammy asked, "Was that okay, Charlie?"

Charlie cleared his throat before he could answer. "Yeah, kid. That was great."

Sammy beamed, then looked at Howard. "When are you gonna put my movie on the Internet?"

"Right now," Howard said, and grabbed the camera off the tripod and hustled over to the computer in the west corner of the basement.

The trio watched, unaware that, within days, Sammy Farraday's plea was going to explode beyond the World Wide Web to media coverage all over the world.

KATE WYATT was putting the last pan of cookies into the oven when her phone rang. She glanced at the clock, making a mental note that the cookies would be done in plenty of time before she had to go pick up the boys from school. Then she wiped her hands before answering the call.

"Hello?"

"Kate. It's me, Myra. Turn on the television! Hurry!"

"What on earth?" Kate muttered, as she reached for the remote to turn on the little set she kept in the kitchen. "What channel?"

"Ten. Channel Ten."

Kate hit the number then gasped as Sammy Farraday's face and voice filled the screen. She heard all the way from "Daddy I'm a good boy," to "I guess that's all. Amen." Then she groaned. "I didn't hear the first. Where did this come from?"

Myra was a busybody and loved knowing stuff first. There was a hint of satisfaction in her voice as she filled Kate in.

"The newsman said it was one of those videos that people put on that Internet site, YouTube. He said it had become the most watched video ever and was getting thousands of hits a day."

"Who did this?" Kate asked.

"Obviously, Sammy and most likely your two, as well. He could hardly do this by himself now, could he?"

Kate bit her lip to keep from saying something she might regret later and just hung up in Myra's ear. She set the timer on the cookies and then paced until it went off. Within seconds, she had the cookies onto the cooling rack along with the others, then headed for school. She knew three boys who were going to get out of school a little early today, but she didn't think they were going to like the reason why.

CHAPTER TWO

STORYTIME was the last class on Thursdays and Sammy's favorite. Mrs. Lowrey had just begun the third chapter of *The Boxcar Children* when the school secretary's voice came over the school intercom.

"Peter Wyatt and Sammy Farraday, bring your things and come to the principal's office."

Sammy's heart sank. The last time he'd been called to the office, Grandma Kate had come to tell him about Mama's wreck. The only thing that went through his mind was that Mama had died. He couldn't move. He couldn't bring himself to speak. He just sat, staring at a stain on the hardwood floor, pretending he hadn't heard. Then Mrs. Lowrey walked over to him to hurry him along.

"Sammy. Get your things and go with Peter."

Sammy and Pete gathered their backpacks and walked down the hall to the principal's office.

As soon as they entered, they saw Charlie. He was sitting beside Grandma Kate. Neither of them was looking all that happy. Sammy felt sick to his stomach, and his voice was shaking.

"Did my mama die?"

Kate groaned as she jumped up from her chair. Of course this would be what he thought. "No, no, darling, nothing like that. I'm sorry you were scared, okay?" she said, and then hugged him to punctuate her words.

Sammy was so relieved he couldn't speak. He just nodded and followed her out the door. It wasn't until they got in the car that she started to talk.

"Boys, what on earth prompted you three to make a video of Sammy and then put it on the Internet? Don't you know how dangerous that could be? All kinds of perverts and crazy people could come claiming to be Sammy's father."

The three boys were stunned. They'd never looked at it from that point of view. All they'd known was that Sammy needed to find his dad.

Sammy came to the rescue and took the blame for what they'd done. "Don't be mad at Pete and Charlie, Grandma Kate. They heard you talking to the preacher about me going to live with the Fosters. I told them I didn't want to live with strangers and asked them to help me figure out a way to stay with Mama."

"Lord, Lord," Kate muttered, pulled the car over to the curb, wiped her eyes, blew her nose and took them to the Dairy Queen for ice cream.

Broken Bow, Oklahoma

GRACIE HOLT was finishing off the last few stitches on an afghan she'd been crocheting for a baby shower when the evening news came on. She set the afghan aside, grabbed the remote and upped the volume, then reached for her glass of iced tea as the anchorman began to speak.

"Normally, this news station is not in the business of catering to the frivolity of the Internet videos. But there was a video uploaded onto YouTube a few days ago that has pierced even the hardest of hearts throughout the nation. We did some research and found out that the scenario, which seems like something straight out of

Hollywood, is all too true. There is a woman named Libby Farraday in Azalea, Tennessee, who survived a devastating car wreck, but is into her third week of a coma. She does have an eight-year-old boy named Sammy who is, as he states in his video, looking for his biological father so that if she dies, he won't be put into foster care. And I'm going to admit at the outset, even though I've seen this video several times now, it still brings me to tears.

"So for all you fathers out there who are shirking your duties, listen up. If you ever knew a woman named Liberty Farraday, and you have an ounce of decency left in you, do the right thing."

Gracie was in shock. Everything around her seemed to stop. Could this possibly be the same Liberty Farraday who'd come home with her son Sam the Christmas before he'd left for Saudi Arabia? Then a little boy's face filled the screen. She saw the picture he was holding against his chest and moaned.

"Dear God, dear God, it's her."

Gracie's gaze moved from the picture to the child's face, and she felt as if she was going to faint. It was like looking at her Sam all over again, right down to the black hair and brown eyes—and in an eight-year-old body too tall and too thin for his age.

The video started. By the time it was over, she was in hysterics. That was her grandson in the video. She knew it. She just couldn't prove it. There was only one person who could make this right.

"Oh Sam, Sam…what in God's name have you done?" she cried, then reached for the phone.

SAM HOLT had been in Amman, Jordan, for eight months. Before that, on offshore rigs in California and Louisiana.

Before that Saudi Arabia. Wherever a troubleshooter was needed, he was there. The last eight-plus years of his life had been a blur of work, work and more work. He wanted to be so tired when he went to bed that he passed out. No dreams. No endless replay of the fight with Libby Farraday that had ended his world.

When he let himself think about it, which wasn't often, he still couldn't believe what had happened—how two people who'd been so perfect for each other had gotten so messed up. By the time he'd come to his senses, two weeks had come and gone. Then he'd called her and gotten a disconnect message. The panic that set in afterward still haunted him. He'd gone back to Tulsa, Oklahoma, to find out she'd left her job without giving notice. She hadn't left a forwarding address with the post office, and the few friends she'd had were as in the dark as he was. All they knew was what Libby had told them—Sam Holt didn't love her anymore. For the next eight years, that had been a private hell of his own making.

Also, with the passing years, he was bigger and stronger at thirty-two than he had been at twenty-four. His skin was darker from countless days on offshore oil rigs and in the oil fields. The laugh that had been ready on his lips rarely made it to the surface. He hid his emotions behind a stoic countenance and an empty heart. His days seemed to run one into the other, and had for years. Until last night. He'd been in bed less than an hour when his cell phone began to ring. He'd started to let it go to voice mail, then thought of how difficult it usually was to get a clear signal to return calls and grabbed it as he turned on the light.

When he saw the name on caller ID, his heart skipped a beat. Mom? He tried not to panic. She never called him unless someone died. He was mentally running through the family names, wondering who's time had ended while he was half a world away and trying to figure out what kind of an excuse he could give her for not coming home for the funeral.

"Hello?"

The minute he heard her voice, he knew it was bad.

"Sam! Sam!… You have….going to….should have…. can't believe…"

"Mom! Mom! Your call is cutting out! I can't hear you!" he shouted, as if raising his voice would somehow take care of the bad connection.

"I said…all over the news…you…..don't wait any longer…."

"Mom! Are you all right? Is it Aunt Susie? What's happening?"

"Just come home, Sammy!….you….home. *Now!*"

The line went dead.

He shuddered. She'd called him Sammy. He hadn't heard that name since his eighteenth birthday when he'd announced he was now a man and would she please just call him Sam. Something was terribly wrong and it was going to take him a few days to get home to her.

"God help me," he muttered, then headed for the office. He had calls to make and a suitcase to pack.

SAM MADE IT to Broken Bow, Oklahoma, in just under two days, with less than six hours of sleep. He'd tried calling his mother off and on since he'd reached the States, but the calls kept going to voice mail. When he pulled up into the driveway in his rental car, he was almost afraid to get out. Then the front door swung inward and Gracie Holt was coming from the porch with her arms open wide and tears on her face. He knew whatever it was was bad. Gracie Holt was a woman who never bothered to cry until the urgency of the moment had passed.

"Sam! Sam! Thank God you're here!"

Sam caught her on the run and just held her. Her body was trembling so hard he thought she would faint. But then she pushed out of his arms, grabbed him by the hand and almost dragged him into the house.

"Hurry," she said. "There's something you have to see."

When she turned on the TV and then began scanning her digital video recorder, he frowned. "Mom! Your phone call scared me half to death. Please do not tell me you had me come halfway around the world to watch television."

Gracie spun, pointing a finger in Sam's face.

"Do not mess with me, Samuel Wade Holt. The past few days have been hell for me, but nothing compared to what this child is going through."

She hit Play, then upped the volume on the television.

"What the hell, Mom? Child? What child? I want to know why you called me. I want to know why it was so urgent that I come home."

"That's why," she said, pointing to the screen. "Now shut your mouth, watch and listen. The rest of your life depends on what you do afterward."

He glanced at the screen, saw the little boy, but didn't catch his name. Then he saw the photo the kid was holding and his heart stopped.

"Libby."

It was the look on his face that told Gracie she'd been right.

Then Sam focused on the boy, and even as he was listening to the child say his mother wouldn't wake up, and he was in fear of being sent to foster care, all Sam could think was that little boy looked just like him. His mind was racing.

The boy said he was eight. That part fit. He said his mother told him that his daddy was lost. That part fit. Sam had been lost since the day he'd last heard her voice.

But when Sammy stated in his little-boy voice that he was a good boy, Gracie went from teary to an audible wail.

"I can't bear it," Gracie said. "That's my grandson, isn't? Why doesn't he know you? Why doesn't he know about me? Sam, Sam, I thought better of you. How could you do that to a child?"

Sam was in shock. "I didn't know," he mumbled. "I swear to God, Mom, I didn't know." Then he jumped to his feet and began to pace. "Libby and I had a fight. It was stupid, but it was a bad one. I thought she was cheating on me. She swore she wasn't and I didn't believe her."

"Why?" Gracie asked.

Sam groaned, and swiped his hands across his face, as if trying to wipe out the bad memories. But they were buried so deep they'd become scars on his soul.

"One of the men at work swore he saw her with another man. She said it wasn't her and I didn't believe her. I still don't know why. She never lied. But I opened my mouth and turned into someone else. Someone I didn't like, but couldn't call back. I broke her heart and ruined my relationship with the only woman I ever loved."

Gracie sighed, then got up and hugged him. "You have to make this right," she said. "You go to Azalea, Tennessee, and you find your Libby and your son, and you make things right. Do you hear me, Samuel Wade?"

"Yes, Mom, I hear you. But what if I'm too late? What if Libby dies? Lord, Lord…what if she's already dead? What have I done?"

"Then you get your son. I can't bear another night of thinking of that little boy alone and afraid. You get him now, and figure out how to be a father later. Here's a map of Tennessee. Go do what's right. Oh…and you might need this, as well."

Sam looked down at the small picture she'd put in his hand.

"It's your second grade school picture and I want it back," she stated.

Sam shuddered. The picture looked identical to the kid on the video. He slipped the picture in his wallet, pocketed the map and grabbed his suitcase on the way out the door.

SAM HOLT was a changed man. It had happened somewhere between his mother's house and the hospital parking lot in Azalea, Tennessee. Before, he'd lived without purpose other than work; now it was the furthest thing from his mind. All he could think about was Libby dying before he could tell her he was sorry. Before he could tell her he still loved her, that he'd always loved her. Before he could let her know that, if she would still have him, he'd take care of her and their son for the rest of his life.

He'd driven all night without stopping for anything but food and fuel. It was just after sunup when he arrived in Azalea. The town was small. According to the sign at the city limits, the population was under three thousand, which meant everyone knew everyone else's business. Like Broken Bow. Small town people with great big hearts. He could picture Libby coming here, alone and pregnant and trying to start her life over.

He was overwhelmed by the thought of the countless milestones he'd missed in his son's life. A baby's first laugh, first word, first hurt. The first time he cried because he was afraid. His first Christmas. The first birthday cake.

Sam became sad all over again.

And Libby. If she lived, would she forgive him? He didn't know how serious her injuries were, but what if she didn't even know him? His thoughts were as crazy as he felt.

After stopping to ask directions, he found the hospital, parked and headed inside, trying not to run. A quick stop at the front desk and he had the floor Libby was on. It was the ICU. The receptionist gave him a curious stare that he ignored and headed for the elevator. A couple of minutes later, he stepped out onto the third floor and headed for the nurses' desk. A short, blonde with a long ponytail and too much eye shadow was sitting behind the desk. Her blue scrubs were a couple of sizes too small, but that didn't seem to affect her competency. When he paused at the desk, she finished making her notes before she bothered to look up.

"May I help you?" she asked.

"I want to see Libby Farraday."

She frowned. "Sorry. No one but family is allowed in ICU."

Sam felt off center, as if he'd been on something going too fast and had just stepped onto firm ground. He was family. In a way.

"But I am family," he said. "I'm Sammy's father."

She gasped, then stood abruptly. "Oh. Oh my," she whispered, her eyes filling with tears. "Um, I have to… I mean…you need to…" She took a deep breath and then pointed to a pair of chairs against the wall. "Have a seat. I need to contact her doctor. He'll have to okay it."

Frustrated, Sam backed away, but he didn't sit. He couldn't. Somewhere behind one of these doors was the only woman he'd ever loved. And somewhere in this town was the son he didn't even know he'd had.

Everything felt surreal. He paced the floor, only vaguely aware that he'd become the object of much curiosity. As word of his arrival spread, patients got out of their beds to come look at the wayward father. Nurses sailed past him with judgment on their faces. Even the janitor had an opinion about Sam's absence in Libby's life when he ran the floor polisher right up to his feet without excusing himself.

Sam understood. It was no less than he felt about himself. Then suddenly, a doctor appeared, followed by a man in uniform. Sam sighed. Damn. They'd even called the cops. He guessed he couldn't blame them. At least they were looking out for Libby and Sammy's welfare.

The doctor introduced himself first. "I'm Doctor Livingston, Libby's doctor. This is Marcus Fite, our chief of police. I understand you're claiming to be Sammy Farraday's father."

Sam nodded. "Sam Holt," he said, offering his hand. The police chief hesitated, then shook it.

"I don't suppose you have any proof of your claim?" Fite asked.

"I didn't even know Sammy existed until two, no, three days ago…when I got a call from my mother telling me about the video."

"How could you not know about the video? It's been on the national news for almost a week now," Fite countered.

"I'm a troubleshooter for an oil company. I work all over the world. For the last eight months, I've been in Amman, Jordan." Then he pulled out the picture his mother had given him. "Here, maybe this will help," he said, and handed the police chief the photo.

"If you didn't know about Sammy, then where did you get a picture of him?" Fite asked.

"That's not Sammy Farraday. It's me," Sam said.

"Lord have mercy," Fite said, handing the photo to the doctor. "Talk about cloning yourself."

"I agree there's quite a resemblance," Doctor Livingston said. "But you understand our concerns."

"Take any tests you need to take. Make any calls you need to make. Here's a list of phone numbers…my employer, my banker, even my preacher from back home. They'll all vouch for me. Just please let me see Libby. I've been looking for her for over eight years."

A nurse standing nearby burst into tears. "Just like in the movies," she wailed, and then hurried away.

"I guess a visit would be all right," the doctor said.

"I'll go in with him," Fite offered.

Sam glared. "If you tell me not to, I won't even touch her. I promise. Just let me see her. I need to tell her that I'm sorry. I need to tell her I'll take care of her and of Sammy. I just need her to know I'm here!"

Now they were surrounded by onlookers, waiting to see what would happen next.

Livingston nodded. "Yes, of course, but not for long. She is in ICU and the visiting is strictly limited for reasons I am sure you can understand."

Sam sighed. "For whatever time you'll allow me, I thank you."

Moments later, he was walking through a pair of double doors and into a ward. The constant beep of machines monitoring vitals was unnerving.

"Where is she?" he asked, scanning the ward for a sign of the woman he'd known.

"That's her over there," Dr. Livingston said, pointing to the bed against the wall.

Sam started walking, but the closer he got, the faster his heart began to beat. By the time he reached the side of her bed, it was hammering.

"Most of the swelling is gone," the doctor said. "The bruising is fading, too. There were a couple of places on her face that had to be stitched, but as you can see, the stitches have already been removed and are healing nicely. In time, you won't be able to see them. She had broken ribs, but they're healing, as well."

"Why hasn't she woken up?" Sam asked.

"Her worst injuries were head injuries. Her brain was swollen, although that's subsided, too. To be honest, we're not sure why she hasn't woken up. All signs point to the possibility of that happening at any time. But you also need to understand that, when she does, we have no way of knowing what she'll remember or if she'll remember anything. Amnesia is a big possibility."

"Lord have mercy," Sam whispered as he stared at Libby's face. She looked the same, and yet she was different. Eight years had come and gone, changing the young girl of twenty to a woman of twenty-eight. Then he looked at the doctor. "Can I touch her?"

The doctor nodded. "Sammy pats her hand when he visits. And he talks to her nonstop the nurses say."

That image was more than Sam could bear. "Could I have a couple of minutes alone?"

Dr. Livingston nodded. "Make it brief. We're already breaking rules to let you in."

Sam nodded and, as the doctor walked away, leaned down and kissed the side of Libby's cheek. Time had not dimmed the memory of how soft her skin was, or how she tasted.

"Libby…sweetheart…it's me, Sam. I've been looking for you forever. I just want you to know that I'm here, and that I'll take care of Sammy until you can get well. And Libby…God, Libby…I didn't know about Sammy. I looked and looked for you afterward but you were gone.

It was almost as if you'd never existed, except for the big hole in my heart. I wouldn't have abandoned you. Somewhere down deep in your heart, you have to know that. Libby, please get well. I don't ever want to lose you again." Then he kissed her again, this time on the lips. The kiss was fleeting, but it was enough to begin Sam's healing.

All too soon, the doctor was back. "I'm sorry, but you need to leave now."

Sam gave Libby one last look, as if imprinting her face in his memory until he could see her again, then followed the doctor back out into the hall. The police chief was still there. Sam went straight for him.

"I want to see my son."

Chief Fite nodded. "I figured that would be your next request. I've already called Kate Wyatt."

"Who's she?" Sam asked.

"She's the grandmother of Sammy Farraday's best friend, Pete. She's been raising her own grandsons for six years now. Their father was Kate's only son. He died in a truck accident a few years back and their mother abandoned them years ago."

Sam nodded. "When can we go?"

The police chief glanced at his watch. "I suppose now is as good a time as any. Kate already picked the boys up from school, so they're at the house with her right now. You can follow me in your car."

"I'll be right behind you," Sam said, then turned to the doctor. "I'll be back at regular visiting hours."

The doctor nodded, then watched the men walk away. He had to admit he'd never thought this day would happen, but hoped it worked out for all concerned.

LIBBY CAME OUT of a darkness, unaware of where she was, of what had happened. All she knew was that something

was wrong. She couldn't move. She couldn't hear
Sammy's voice. And she couldn't find the strength to open
her eyes. Slowly she began to realize something was
beeping nearby. She inhaled slowly and smelled antisep-
tic. Then a voice came over an intercom, paging a doctor
to the E.R. and she thought, *I'm in a hospital? But how?
Why?*

In the back of her mind, she thought she'd been
dreaming about Sam Holt, although when he invaded her
sleep, she usually referred to them as nightmares. Reliving
the joy of loving him and then the pain of losing him was
just too much. If it hadn't been for Sammy, she often
thought she would have gone mad. Before she could get
any answers, she began to fade, falling under the curtain
that seemed to hang between her and the rest of the world.

SAM PULLED UP behind the police cruiser and parked.
They'd stopped at a small, white frame house with a
wraparound porch and yellow trim—obviously the resi-
dence of Kate Wyatt. There was a porch swing on one end
of the porch and a set of white wicker furniture on the
other. Two big wing chairs, a small circular table with a
giant fern spilling over the lips of a red-glazed pot and
what amounted to a small wicker love seat completed the
ensemble. He could see three bicycles parked under a
shade tree in the back. One large. Two small. Sam sighed.
Talk about small town perfection. Places like this didn't
exist anywhere else. As he got out of the car and followed
the police chief to the front door, he realized that the next
five minutes were going to be the most important minutes
of his life.

Most men meet their children for the first time in a
hospital nursery. They have time to get to know each
other the old-fashioned way. Sam sighed. He'd never

done anything the easy way. It figured he would have screwed this up, too.

Then the door opened inward and a short woman with reddish gray hair was in the doorway. The look on her face was somewhere between disbelief and shock.

"Kate, this here fellow is Sam Holt," Chief Fite said. "Claims he's Sammy's daddy. We've done some preliminary checking and he seems to be on the up and up."

"Where the hell have you been for the past eight years?" Kate asked.

Sam flinched. "Lost."

"Well…I'd say so," she muttered. "Libby showed up here about six months before Sammy was born, as alone in the world as a woman could be. She's never talked about her past and we didn't ask, but it seems to be a body would have checked up on her once in a while, especially since there was a baby involved."

Sam lifted his chin. His face was expressionless. "Libby and I had a fight. People have fights. All the time. Ours was a bad one, I'll grant. But most people don't disappear off the face of the earth. She left. No forwarding address. Nothing. I looked for her for a year, then left the country. I guess in my way, I ran away, too. I had no idea she was pregnant when she left, and I was in Amman, Jordan, when my mother called to tell me about the video. Now that's the last time I'm going to explain myself until I meet my son." At this point, his voice cracked. "I've lost eight years of his life I can't get back."

Kate exhaled on a sigh. "Well, he's in the kitchen with the boys. We were just about to sit down to supper. I suppose you could join us."

"He's okay, Kate," Chief Fite said. "He's clean. Not even a speeding ticket on his record, and like he said, he's spent most of the last six years out of the country. Now, if you're okay, I'll just get on back to the station. If you need anything, you can always call."

Then he gave Sam a quick look. "You're not planning on leaving town with Sammy or anything like that, are you?"

"Hell no," Sam said shortly. "I'm not going anywhere."

"Well, come on in, then. Supper is getting cold. And don't go and scare Sammy any, you hear? He's been through the wringer these past three weeks," Kate said.

"Thank you, ma'am. I'd be grateful," Sam said. "As for Sammy, the last thing I want to do is scare him. But he sent out his own brand of SOS and I want him to know that the minute I heard it, I came. That'll be the first step we both take to building some trust between us."

"Yes, of course," Kate said. "It's this way," she said.

Sam closed the front door and followed her through the house and into the kitchen. The table was set. The food had already been dished up. Three boys were already at their places, waiting for her return. Sam saw the tallest boy eye him curiously. Then he saw a little red-headed boy sneaking a chicken leg off the platter onto his plate. But it was the dark-haired boy with the big brown eyes staring back at him that nearly stopped his heart.

He walked past Kate without waiting for an invitation, circled the table and then stopped at Sammy's chair.

"You're Sammy Farraday, aren't you?" Sam asked.

"Who are you?" he asked.

"I saw your video, Sammy. It was a really smart thing to do because I've been looking for your mother for a long, long time. My name is Sam Holt. I'm your father, and I'm really happy to meet you."

Sam held out his hand, hoping the boy would at least shake it, but was unprepared for Sammy's reaction.

"Daddy? You're my daddy?"

Sam's vision blurred. He didn't know whether Sammy was just upset or uncertain. Then he remembered the photo his mom had sent and quickly pulled it out of his pocket.

"Look," Sam said. "This is a picture of me when I was seven. Almost the same age as you are now."

Sammy stared at the photo for what seemed like an eternity. Then he looked up at Sam.

"I'm eight," he muttered, then added, "That looks like me."

Sam nodded. "Fathers and sons are supposed to look like each other," Sam said softly.

"My mama is in the hospital."

Sam heard Sammy's voice tremble. He couldn't stand it any longer. He reached down and picked him up, then cradled Sammy's head against his shoulder. To his surprise, Sammy let him.

"I know, Sammy, I know."

Sammy leaned back long enough to eye Sam one more time.

"Did you know about the people wanting to give me to the Fosters?"

Sam swallowed past the knot in his throat, and managed a nod.

"You're not gonna let 'em…are you?"

"Hell, no," Sam said. "You and Mama aren't alone any longer. You two have me now. And you have a grandmother, too. Her name is Gracie. She's the one who told me about your video."

"My mama won't wake up," Sammy said, and then put his face against the curve of Sam's neck and started to cry. "What are we gonna do if she won't wake up?"

Sam could hardly say the words. "I don't know, Sammy. I don't know. But whatever it is, we'll do it together. Okay?"

Every muscle in the little boy's body seemed to relax at once. It was as if the weight of the world had been lifted off his shoulders.

Kate was in tears, too, but she couldn't let herself break down. Not when there were boys to feed and a man she didn't know well enough to trust.

"Well, then," she said, blowing her nose twice before stuffing the tissue into her pocket and pointing at Charlie and Pete. "Fill your plates, boys, before everything gets cold…if it's not already. Maybe I should warm up the—"

Sam put a hand on her shoulder. "No, ma'am. We're all fine with it as is, aren't we, guys?"

"Sit here," Kate said, pointing to the place where she usually sat. "I'll get another place setting and join you."

Sam sat, still holding Sammy. "Everything sure smells good," Sam said softly. "I'll bet you're hungry, too."

Sammy nodded, then crawled out of Sam's lap and back into his chair. But he didn't seem to be able to focus on food, even though Kate helped him fill his plate. He kept staring at Sam over and over until finally Kate intervened.

"Eat, Sammy. He's not going to disappear." Then she eyed Sam closely, as if daring him to make a liar out of her.

"She's right," Sam said. "I'm going to get a room in a motel and I'm not leaving this town. I've been looking for a very long time. Why would I leave? You also have a grandmother who's anxious to meet you."

"She is?" Sammy asked, and then turned to Pete with the first hint of excitement in his voice. "I have a grandma, too, Pete. How about that?"

They finally finished the meal, but not without Sam answering a thousand questions in between bites. Sam couldn't quit looking at Sammy. He saw himself in the boy, but he also saw Libby in the easy way he laughed and the way he tilted his head to the side when he was listening. He knew he was going to have to leave him soon. The boys had school tomorrow and he needed to find a motel. But not until he went back to the hospital to see Libby. He and the boys were helping clear the table when he brought up the subject of a motel again.

"Mrs. Wyatt, do you—"

Kate sighed. "You might as well call me Kate, since it appears you're going to be part of the family." Sam smiled, and for the first time, Kate saw what a handsome man Sam Holt really was. "You should do that more often," she added.

"Do what?" he asked.

"Smile."

Sam's smile slipped. "Up until today, I haven't had a whole lot to smile about. So, down to business. Could you recommend a motel?"

Sammy bolted toward Sam from across the room and grabbed him by the hand.

"You can stay at our house," he cried, looking to Kate for backup. "Mama would want him to stay at our house."

"I don't know," Kate said.

"No, Sammy. I don't think that would be right," Sam said.

"You have to!" Sammy wailed. "I have to stay here until Mama is better, but you should stay at our house. You can sleep in Mama's bed. Sometimes I sleep with her if it thunders." He frowned, then ducked his head, as if he'd admitted to something babyish. "I don't like thunderstorms," he muttered.

"Shoot, Sammy. It's nothing but a little noise," Sam said. "You know what my grandpa used to say about thunder?"

Sammy's eyes widened as he considered, for the first time in his life, what it meant to have an extended family.

"No, what did he say?" Sammy asked.

"I used to be scared of thunder, too, then Granddaddy told me it was just God poking holes in the clouds so the rain would fall. After that, I wasn't scared anymore."

"Really?" Sammy asked.

"Really."

No wonder Libby Farraday had fallen for this man, Kate thought.

"I don't suppose there's any harm in staying at Libby's house," she said. "But you keep it clean, now. Libby doesn't like mess in her house, you hear?"

Sam nodded. "I know all about that," he said. "I caught her mopping the floor at midnight one night when I came in late from work. She lit into me for tracking on her clean floor. After that, I pulled my boots off at the door."

Sammy giggled.

Everyone stared. Sam didn't know it was the first time in three weeks that Sammy Farraday had laughed, but he could tell by the look on Kate's face that whatever had happened was a good thing.

"So, does anyone have a key to the house?"

"I do," Kate said, opened a cabinet door and then took a small gold key off a hook inside. "Don't make me regret this," she muttered.

Sam took the key, and then laid his hand on Kate's shoulder. "I know I'm a stranger to you, but I hope that will soon pass. It's obvious you're a very important person in Libby and Sammy's lives. They are very blessed that they have you."

"Well, then," Kate muttered, took off her apron and hung it on a door knob. "Boys…load up in the car. Mister…. I mean, Sam can follow us over to Libby's house. Sammy can show him where everything is, and then we'll come back and let him get some rest."

"I appreciate it," he said, and within minutes, he was back in the car.

He waited until Kate backed out of the driveway, then followed her up the street. He couldn't help but notice that Sammy had climbed out of his seat belt and was on his knees, staring out the back window. Obviously afraid to lose sight of him for fear he'd disappear from his life as quickly as he'd come in.

"Don't you worry," Sam said, more to himself than to the boy in the car ahead of him. "You couldn't get rid of me if you tried." He then waved to reassure Sammy.

When Sammy grinned and waved back, Sam knew his life would never be the same. One bridge had been crossed successfully. He'd met his son, who was obviously willing to forge a relationship. Now all he had to do was get Libby well and convince her he was no longer the sorry jerk he'd once been.

CHAPTER THREE

KATE AND THE BOYS stayed at Libby's house long enough for Sammy to give Sam a personal tour.

"Wanna see my room?" Sammy asked. He didn't wait for an answer as he bolted past Sam and led him down a small hall. "I like *Star Wars,*" he said, as he opened a door and turned on the lights.

Sam grinned at the assortment of Starfighters hanging from the ceiling with fishing line, giving them the appearance of "hovering" in outer space. There were posters of Han Solo and Yoda on the walls and a small stash of toy light sabers in a waste basket that was being used as a storage bin.

"Look!" Sammy said, as he grabbed one of the light sabers from the basket and punched a button. It immediately lit a bright, pulsing green, and when Sammy swung it, the accompanying sound effects came with it. "Mama got me this stuff for my birthday," he added.

"That's pretty awesome," Sam said.

"And look at my Darth Vader cape and mask! Mama made the cape but we bought the mask with my can money."

"Your can money? What's that?" Sam asked.

"I pick up aluminum cans from everywhere and when I get a garbage sack full, Mama takes me to the recycle place where I sell 'em. I make good money that way."

Sam's conscience tugged. Good money, indeed. Libby

was teaching their son to work for his money. Good for her. But it didn't make him feel so good, knowing that it was his lack of faith and distrust in her that had caused this eight-year split.

"This is Mama's room," Sammy said, as he bolted across the hall. "You can sleep here."

Sam only glanced at the room. He needed to be alone to face that. This would be the closest to any kind of intimacy with her since their fight, and he wasn't taking it lightly.

"That's great. I will take good care of everything," Sam said.

Sammy nodded, then felt obligated to remind him. "Remember, Mama doesn't like messes."

"I'll remember."

Kate appeared in the hallway. "Sammy, we need to leave now. You boys have school tomorrow."

"If it's okay with Mrs. Wyatt, I would like to take you to visit your mama tomorrow."

Sammy turned to Kate. "Can I, Grandma Kate? Can he take me to the hospital tomorrow?"

"We'll see," Kate said.

They knew better than to argue and Sam didn't push the issue. Instead, he took Kate's hand in both of his and squeezed it gently. "It was a pleasure to meet you…you and your boys. Thank you for everything, including looking after Sammy's welfare."

Kate nodded. "He's like one of my own," Kate said. "I wouldn't have had it any other way." Then she gathered up the trio. "Boys…load up," she said. However, Sammy lingered behind after the others were heading for the car.

"Um…uh…am I supposed to call you Dad or something?" Sammy asked.

Sam sighed. So much confusion for such a little guy.

He got down on one knee so that they were eye to eye. "What do you want to call me?" Sam asked.

"Daddy. I want to call you Daddy."

It was impossible not to catch the anticipation in Sammy's voice. "I'd like that," Sam said. "And would it be okay if I sometimes call you Sammy and sometimes call you son?" Sam countered.

Sammy beamed and nodded.

"Guess we'd better shake on it," Sam said and offered his hand, but his son had other ideas. He threw his arms around Sam's neck.

"Thank you for coming to find us, Daddy," he said softly.

Ignoring the shaft of pain in his heart, Sam nodded, then added a quick kiss on the side of the little boy's cheek. His voice was thick with emotion as he added, "Sleep well, Son, and I promise, I won't get lost from you and your mama again."

"Okay. 'Night, Daddy," Sammy said, and bounded off the porch toward Kate's car with a spring in his step.

Sam waved from the front door, then went inside.

Now he was alone.

In Libby's house.

The whole situation was surreal. He pulled out his cell phone and dialed his mother's number, knowing she would have been anxious to hear how the meeting had gone. She answered on the second ring.

"Hello?"

"Mom, it's me. I made it here just fine. I've already seen Libby. She's in ICU, still in a coma. Doctors aren't giving out much details, but I think it's because they don't know what else to do for her. As for Sammy...I don't know what to say."

Gracie frowned. "What's wrong? Didn't you two hit it off?"

"No, no, it's nothing like that. I'm just overwhelmed by what seeing him made me feel." Then he sighed. "How long did it take you to bond with me when I was born?"

"True love at first sight," Gracie said.

"Yeah…me, too," Sam said softly. "Sammy isn't quite as sure, but he's willing to give me a chance."

Gracie sighed. "Thank God."

"Yeah, and thank you, too, Mom."

"For what?"

"Oh…the phone call, and everything."

"You're welcome, Sam. Have a nice night."

"You, too. I'll call you when I know something new."

The silence afterward was comfortable, just like Libby's home. He made a second sweep through the rooms, this time taking note of the small things she'd done to make the house a home, such as the baby pictures of Sammy scattered throughout and his school papers tacked in different places. One of his art projects had been taped to the front of the refrigerator. His raincoat was hanging on a peg by the back door with matching rain boots beneath. A small metal car she'd probably picked up from the floor was sitting incongruously beside a clear glass vase filled with delicate seashells. And there was a grocery list she'd left posted on the refrigerator. It was the single notation at the bottom of the list that startled Sam into a fresh realization of how little he knew about the child who was his son.

Sammy's birthday tonight. Going to the bowling alley.

He didn't even know his own son's birthday. What a screwup he'd made of their lives.

He picked his suitcase up from the hall where he'd put it earlier and carried it into Libby's bedroom. He stared at the pale blue coverlet and the white, fluffy pillows for a few painful moments, then put his bag on a nearby chair, and quickly unpacked only the necessary things. He had an hour left before visiting hours were over for the evening and he wasn't going to sleep until he'd looked at Libby Farraday one more time, just to make sure the last few hours were not a dream.

THIS TIME when Sam showed back up at the hospital, he was treated with a little more respect. He was allowed in ICU for fifteen minutes, cautioned to keep conversations quiet, then left on his own. He pulled a chair up beside Libby's bed, noticing that the other two beds next to hers were now empty, which gave him a bit more privacy. Not that it mattered. Libby had yet to participate in a conversation. He couldn't help but notice her breathing seemed steady and her color was good. There was a pink cast to her skin, rather than a wan, sickly pallor. The fading bruises left hints of how horrific her initial injuries had been, and he couldn't quit thinking of how Sammy must have felt, seeing his mother in such a terrible state. Then he sighed. That was the past. This was now. And he needed for Libby to be well so that she would be a part of their future. He leaned forward and cupped her hand with his own.

"Libby, it's Sam, again. I came back like I said I would." Then his voice shook as he began to talk about Sammy. "I met our son today. He is a great kid, and you're obviously a phenomenal mother."

Libby's eyelids fluttered, but Sam didn't notice. "I don't know how many times I'll have to say I'm sorry before you'll believe me, but if it takes the rest of my life to make things right between us, I'm there." Then he took a deep breath before he began his confession. "So, there's something you need to know. Eight years ago I came back for you…to say I'm sorry and to beg your forgiveness. I didn't run out. You ran away, and I've been living half a life ever since. Thanks to Sammy, I've found you again." His voice began to shake. "Please, baby, you have to wake up and get well. Don't make us live the rest of our lives without you."

THE NEXT MORNING, Pete and Sammy were fighting over the toothpaste when Kate came running into the bathroom. Her expression was somewhere between shocked and excited, but the boys figured they were in trouble for making a mess.

"I asked for the tube first, Grandma," Pete said.

"But I was already squeezing toothpaste on my brush," Sammy countered.

"Sammy! The hospital called. Your mother is waking up!" Then she clasped her hands together. "Praise the Lord for answered prayers! Sammy, finish getting dressed. Your father is on his way over here to get you. You're both going to see her together."

"Yea!" Sammy screamed, flung his toothbrush into the sink and headed for the bedroom.

"Grandma, Sammy didn't brush his teeth," Pete argued.

"This is one morning when I think he can be excused," Kate said. "Now hurry up. Charlie is already eating breakfast and I made French toast."

That was all the urging Pete needed, while Sammy's impetus was something else altogether. All Sammy could think about as he was putting on his clothes was that Mama was waking up. That meant she would be well and they would all go home and everything would be like it was before.

Then he stopped. No. That wasn't exactly right. Because of what he and Pete and Charlie had done,

Daddy was now in the picture. He thought Mama would be happy, but now he wasn't so sure.

He was combing his hair when he heard the front doorbell ring. He flew out of the bedroom and down the hall before Kate could get to the door. He flung it open, saw the tall, long-legged man from yesterday standing on the doorstep and the nervous worry in the pit of his stomach disappeared. Daddy had come back, just like he'd promised.

"Daddy! Mama's waking up. I wore my blue *Star Wars* T-shirt and my newest jeans because Mama likes me in blue. I tied my own shoes but I think one's gonna come undone pretty soon. I didn't have time to brush my teeth and I didn't eat breakfast yet. Do you think Mama will say my name?"

Sam's heart had been thumping overtime ever since he'd gotten the phone call from Kate Wyatt that Libby was waking up. When she'd offered to let him take Sammy, he'd been beyond grateful. Now, facing this tiny whirlwind of testosterone upped the joy in his heart. He wouldn't think about what condition she'd be in when she woke up. The fact that she was alive was enough for now.

"Does Kate know I'm here?" Sam asked.

"I do now," Kate said, as she appeared from the hallway. "Good luck at the hospital. When you're done, get him something to eat and drop him off at school. He'll show you the way."

"Yes, ma'am," Sam said.

Kate started to turn away, then stopped and fixed him with steely intent.

"You *are* going straight to the hospital, right?"

Sam knew what she was thinking. "Hey, Sammy, go ahead and get in the car and don't forget to buckle up," he said.

Sammy bounced past him and headed for the car as Sam stepped across the threshold.

"Mrs. Wyatt…"

"Kate. I told you to call me, Kate."

"So…Kate. I swear, on my mother's life, the last thing I would do is harm Sammy or Libby. I am not going to run away with him. I am not leaving Azalea. We are going to go see Libby and I'm going to ask you to pray that she wakes up the same woman she was before the wreck. I could handle it…I think…if Libby had amnesia, but not Sammy. I don't want him hurt any more than he's already been, okay?"

Kate sighed, then relaxed. "Okay."

Sam nodded, then pivoted quickly and headed for the car. Within minutes they were out of sight.

LIBBY WAS in a pit. She didn't know how she'd gotten there, or how long she'd been trapped, but every time she tried to climb out, she could only get so high and then she'd fall back. It was deep and dark, and the sides were too steep and slick to get a good grip. She'd been screaming for help for what seemed like ages, but no one seemed to be able to hear her.

Once she'd seen someone looking down at her from the opening above. When she'd finally realized it was her mother, she'd started weeping.

"Mother. Mother. Thank goodness you found me. I fell in, but I can't get out. I'm tired and cold and I'm afraid. Help me out. Please, help me get out."

But her mother had only shaken her head. "I'm sorry, my love, but you can't come with me. You have to find a way out and go back on your own. Sammy needs you."

Then she'd disappeared and Libby had fallen to the ground in a huddle, weeping helplessly. It had taken her some time to remember that her mother was dead, that she had died when Libby was seventeen and if she didn't get out, Sammy would wind up an orphan, just like her.

Later, she'd heard someone else and looked up, but couldn't even see daylight above her. She thought it was Sam's voice that she heard, but she had to be wrong. Sam was gone. He'd left her just like Mother had. She wondered what it was about her that made the people she loved keep leaving her behind?

Sammy. Sammy. Sammy.

Sammy hadn't left her. She'd just gotten herself lost. She had to get out and find Sammy. He was too little to be left on his own.

So she'd started digging footholds up the side of the pit. It had taken what seemed like forever. But she couldn't give up. Every time she felt too tired to continue, she would think of Sammy laughing at Saturday morning cartoons. Sammy at the watermelon-eating contest in the park on the Fourth of July with the pink juice running down his chin and onto his shirt. He hadn't won, but his picture was the one that had wound up on the front page of the paper the next week. Sammy saying his prayers at night. Sammy crying. Crying? Why was Sammy crying? Oh God…she had to wake up and find Sammy. Please God, help me get out!

DOCTOR LIVINGSTON was standing at Libby's bedside when Sam and Sammy entered ICU, escorted by a nurse.

"They're here, Doctor," the nurse said unnecessarily, as Sam sailed past her, clutching his son's hand.

Livingston held his fingers to his lips, making sure Sammy still understood he had to be quiet.

"All of her vital signs indicate she's coming to," he said.

"How long has she been like this?" Sam asked.

"A nurse noticed the changes sometime after midnight, but nothing drastic until about an hour ago. She's restless, and I suspect hurting and confused, so don't expect her to recognize people or talk normally. Okay, Sammy?"

Sammy nodded. His daddy had already warned him his mother might be mixed up because she'd been asleep so long.

"Could Sammy talk to her?" Sam asked. "Maybe if she heard his voice…?"

"Might be a good idea," Livingston said, then motioned Sammy closer. "Just talk to her as you have been, Sammy. Tell her what day it is. What you've been doing. Talk about your daddy's arrival. Whatever you want."

Sam held his breath. So much was riding on the next few minutes. He said another silent prayer, then patted Sammy's back.

"It's okay, son. Whatever you want to say is okay."

Sammy put his hand on Libby's arm and started to pat it, just as he had every day since she'd been admitted.

"Mama, it's me, Sammy. Today is Friday, but I got to be excused from school this morning so I could come see you wake up. You remember when I told you if you would wake up, that I would have the best Mother's Day present ever for you? Remember, Mama? Well, your present is here! I know Mother's Day isn't until Sunday, but if you wake up, I could give it to you early."

Sam was shocked. Was he the present Sammy had promised his mother? He looked down at his son's earnest expression and realized what a special little boy Sammy Farraday really was. He put his hand on Sammy's shoulder in a gesture of support and added his own brief greeting.

"Libby…sweetheart…it's me, Sam. I'm here with Sammy. He's been waiting for a very long time for you to wake up."

Nothing happened. Sammy looked up at Sam nervously, then at the doctor.

"Why isn't she talking?" the boy asked.

"It doesn't work like that," the doctor said. "She is waking up. You just can't tell it yet."

"How about we just sit down in a chair beside her bed," Sam suggested.

Sammy shrugged. This wasn't how he'd expected the visit to go, but when his daddy pulled up a chair and then patted his leg, Sammy crawled up in his lap, and then sat, stiff-backed and nervous, unwilling to loosen his grip on Libby's arm.

"Talk to her, Sammy," Sam said. "It's okay. She'll hear the sound of your voice."

"Mama. It's me, Sammy. Wake up, Mama. I need you to wake up."

LIBBY GROANED. Sammy. She could hear his voice. Was he crying? No. But he sounded scared. Sammy? Sammy? Where are you?

She kept digging and climbing. She had to get out.

Mama.

There! She heard it again. He was calling for her.

I'm coming, Sammy. Mama's coming.

Then suddenly her fingers felt the edge of the pit. She began to climb with every last ounce of strength she had left, pulling herself up with nothing but the muscles in her hands and arms. Then her toe found firm footing again and again until she was halfway out. She could feel the grass against her cheek and the sun on the side of her face. With her last ounce of strength, she crawled the rest of the way out, then rolled over onto her back, breathless from the exertion.

MAMA!!!

It was panic in his voice that made her open her eyes. Then she saw him…her precious little boy. He was here beside her after all.

"Sammy," she whispered, as she felt his hand on her arm. She tried to lick her lips, but her tongue wouldn't work right.

"Mama!" Sammy cried, then he turned to Sam, his eyes wide with excitement. "Daddy! Daddy! Look! Mama woke up!"

Libby's heart skipped a beat. Daddy? She wasn't awake after all. She was still dreaming. What she was seeing was never going to happen in real life. Her fingers curled, then clenched. Would this nightmare never end?

When Sam saw her make a fist, he couldn't stand it any longer. He grabbed her hand.

"Libby! It's me—Sam. I'm here, too."

The monitors hooked up to measure Libby's blood pressure and pulse rate began to beep erratically as she began grabbing at the tubes and needles connecting her to the machines.

Sam scooted Sammy off his lap and jumped up from the chair. He grabbed Libby's hands to keep her from pulling out the needles as the doctor and a nurse came running.

"Libby, you're okay, you're okay. You had a wreck. You're in a hospital but Sammy is safe. He wasn't with you. He's here with me. Sammy is okay. Just wake up and see for yourself. Sammy is okay!"

Libby inhaled sharply. Her eyes flew open; there was a brief moment of recognition, then disbelief as she stared up into the face of the man above her.

"Sam?"

He sighed. *Thank God.* "Yes, it's me."

"Where…"

He let go of her arm and pulled Sammy out from behind a chair to stand between them.

"Sammy found me."

"Happy Mother's Day, Mama," Sammy said.

Libby blinked. She kept looking at Sammy, then at Sam, and back again. "Wha…" she mumbled.

Sammy beamed as he took Sam's hand and laid it on Libby's arm. "Here's your present, Mama. It's Daddy. I found Daddy for you."

Libby blinked once, then closed her eyes, but it didn't stop the tears from seeping out from under her eyelids.

"She's crying," Sammy said, frowning.

"Sometimes people cry because they're happy," Doctor Livingston said. "Now I think you two have been here long enough. Tell her goodbye for now. We'll have her moved into a regular room by this afternoon. You can talk more then."

Sammy patted Libby's arm. "Bye-bye, Mama. I'm sure glad you woke up."

Libby grabbed his hand, then pulled it to her lips. "Love you," she mumbled.

Sammy grinned. "I love you, too, Mama. See you later."

Sam leaned down and kissed the side of Libby's face. The salt of her tears were on his lips as he whispered against her ear. "Rest well. We'll be back."

Libby heard the words, but didn't know what to think. Sam? Sam Holt? Where had he come from? And why? The last words out of his mouth had been something to the effect that he never wanted to see her again. But that had been a lifetime ago. She exhaled on a sob. She couldn't think about it anymore, only this time when she felt herself drifting, she knew it wouldn't be back into the pit. She was out of that for good. When she woke up again, maybe this crazy business would have been nothing more than another dream.

Or maybe not. She'd dreamed of Sam many, many times since he'd walked out of her life, but she'd never had one this vivid before. And she'd never felt his kiss this distinctly, or heard his voice as clearly as she had this time. What was it Sammy said about a Mother's Day gift?

Sammy, Sammy, what on earth have you done?

SAMMY WAS ELATED. He talked all the way through breakfast at a local diner, then all the way to school. When they arrived, Sam parked and started to get out.

"You don't have to go in with me, Daddy. I'm a big boy. I can take myself in," Sammy said.

"I know that," Sam said. "But since you're going to be tardy, won't the office need me to sign something so you won't be in trouble?"

"Oh yeah," Sammy said, then frowned. "Darn. I forgot my book bag at Grandma Kate's."

"Maybe she brought it for you," he said, and gave Kate a quick call, during which she confirmed Sam's suspicions.

"I sent it with Pete," she said. "How was Libby?"

"Great," Sam said. "She woke up, recognized Sammy…and me."

"I'll bet that was a jolt," she muttered.

"She was crying when we left," Sam said, then noticed Sammy's expression and added. "But they were happy tears."

Kate sighed. "I hope you're as good at smooth talking as you are good-looking, young man."

Sam was a little taken aback, then grinned. "I've had my moments."

Kate chuckled. "Yes, I'll just bet you have. Anyway, reassure Sammy that his stuff is already awaiting him inside."

"Yes, ma'am, and thank you again."

"You're welcome. Come for supper tonight. Six o'clock."

Sam was still smiling as he hung up the phone.

LIBBY WOKE UP off and on the rest of the morning. Each time she was awake, she continued to ask whoever was in the room with her at the time if Sam Holt had really come to see her. To her disbelief, the stories she got from different nurses continued to remain the same.

Yes, Sam Holt was in Azalea. Wasn't she proud of her little boy? Was he really Sammy's father? What happened that split you two up? Why didn't Sam know about his son?

The questions were often phrased in gentle terms, but they were basically the same. She opted out of answers by pretending to go back to sleep, but it was becoming evident that she didn't have any really good answers. Of course she was proud of Sammy. She'd always been proud of her son. She just didn't get the connection between her pride in Sammy and Sam Holt's arrival in Azalea.

She kept going over the last time they'd been together before he'd disappeared. Their fight had been horrible. The fact that he thought she'd cheated on him and was lying about it afterward had been shocking. And no matter how many times she'd denied it, he hadn't believed her. It had nearly destroyed her. Later, when he'd walked out of their apartment, she'd still expected him to return after he'd calmed down. Only he hadn't. She'd waited almost two weeks before finally coming to the realization that he was never coming back. And so she'd left.

She didn't know where he'd been, but it was obvious he no longer hated her. What she didn't understand was how he found them. And even more, she didn't know how she felt about him anymore. The man she'd loved had broken her heart. She didn't want a repeat of that again.

CHAPTER FOUR

By THE TIME they transferred Libby from ICU to a private room on a lower floor, she was worn out from all the commotion. But after that, it hadn't taken long for flowers to start arriving as word of her awakening began to spread through Azalea. On a normal day, she would have been the one taking orders at the flower shop and creating the bouquets, but now she was the one receiving them.

As two o'clock rolled around, Sam Holt walked into her room. When Libby saw his face, her heart skipped a beat. Dear Lord. He *was* real. When she saw what he was carrying, her vision blurred. Lilacs. He remembered. Then she steeled herself for what was obviously coming as he neared her bed.

"Where's Sammy?" she asked.

"School's not out yet. Kate said she'd bring him by when she picked them up."

Kate? So he was already on a first-name basis with her friends.

"Where did you come from?" she asked.

"Amman, Jordan."

It was the last thing she expected him to say.

Sam put the vase of lilacs on the table nearest her bed, started to take her hand and then stopped. He'd done it before, but she'd been asleep. Now, he felt he needed permission and she didn't appear to be offering it. He couldn't blame her.

"You are a hard woman to find," he said softly, then brushed the tip of his finger against her cheek.

Libby's chin lifted. She didn't want to care what his answer would be, but she did. It prompted the question. "I didn't know you were looking."

"For eight years."

Libby's heart skittered. This couldn't be right. "I waited for you, but you didn't come back."

Sam sighed. "I did, but you were already gone. I tried to call you, but when I got a disconnect message, I headed for Tulsa. Panic set in when I found out you'd quit your job and hadn't left a forwarding address. None of your friends knew where you'd gone."

"That's because I didn't tell them," she mumbled, while thinking of what might have happened if she hadn't run.

"Why, sweetheart? I'm the one who'd hurt you, not them."

Eight years of pent-up anger and disappointment spilled out. Her voice rose as her eyes filled with tears. "Because by then, I knew I was pregnant with Sammy. I didn't want to look at their faces every day. They knew you were gone. They knew you thought I'd been cheating. Some of them believed you. Some believed me. I didn't want to have to sort through the crap you'd made of my life by wondering who the baby's daddy really was."

Sam felt sick for the hurt in her voice and the tears on her face. "You hate me and I don't blame you, but you will never hate me more than I've hated myself. Losing you destroyed me. I haven't had one happy day since, and that's the truth. I work. I eat. I sleep. And more often than not, my dreams are of you." He exhaled wearily. "Unfortunately, the dreams were always of the fight." He shoved a hand through his hair, then shrugged. "I can't change the past, but if you would let me back into your lives…in any capacity…I would be forever grateful."

"Did you come back because you found out about Sammy?"

"Not exactly…Sammy found me."

"What?"

"It's true. Do you know how Sammy found me?"

"I didn't know he'd been looking," she said.

She was shocked, he could tell, and hurt.

"Not in the way you're thinking," Sam said. "It was after the wreck. And it all started with a video he put on the Internet."

Libby gasped. "What?"

"He put a video on YouTube. Can you believe it? According to Kate, Pete overheard her talking to your pastor, who was inquiring about extended family. Kate said you didn't have any. At that point, she said Pete heard something to the effect that if you didn't wake up, Sammy would wind up in foster care. He panicked and spilled the beans to Charlie and Sammy. I'm not sure how Charlie filmed it or uploaded it on the Internet, but it happened."

"Oh dear Lord," Libby whispered. Tears spilled and ran down her cheeks as she swiped at them with shaky hands. "My poor little man. He must have been so scared."

Sam grabbed a handful of tissues from a small box on the table. When she reached for them, he grasped her hand and lifted it to his lips. Just the touch of his lips was enough to make her crazy. Sam blotted her face with the tissues, then handed them to her.

"Yeah, he was scared. In the video he was holding your picture as he related what was happening to you. He said something to the effect that his mama had always told him the reason he didn't have a daddy like everyone else was because he got lost from them." At this point, Sam's voice was shaking. "And he was right, sweetheart. I've been lost…so lost. It was my own damn fault for losing the only woman I ever loved, and I have spent the last eight years in my own personal kind of hell for it."

Libby's heart was racing. This couldn't be happening. She wanted to believe him, but he'd sworn he loved her before and had broken her heart.

"Then how—"

"Sammy's video was one of the most viewed videos on YouTube and it went national."

Libby gasped. "As in television?"

"All over the country. My mom saw the video, remembered you and called me in Jordan. You will be happy to know that I got the worst chewing out of my life because of how I screwed up with you. She was bawling her head off when I left and told me not to come back until I'd straightened out my mess."

Libby's head was reeling. She wanted to believe in him again, but it was hard.

"Did you come because she made you?"

Sam groaned, then sat down on the side of the bed and gently took her hands.

"No, baby…never. I came because of you. Knowing I have a son is just an added bonus. I still don't know what made me act the way I did. All I can say is that I was a stupid, immature jerk. I'll spend the rest of my life on my knees for you if you'll just give me a chance to make things right."

Libby inhaled on a sob.

"I have a small confession to make, too."

"What is it?" Sam asked.

"Right before the wreck, I saw movement from the corner of my eye. I turned just as the truck ran a red light and slammed into the side of my car. The last two things I thought of were regrets. I thought…I'm going to die…and Sam doesn't know about Sammy. I'm sorry, too. Even though I knew you hated me, I should have told you I was pregnant."

"Oh, sweetheart…no, no, you have it all wrong. I didn't hate you. I hated myself. I loved you. I know I've got a lot of ground to recover with you. A lot of faith to be built back up, but would you give me a chance to try?"

"For now, just hold me, Sam. We'll worry about the future tomorrow," she said, then lifted her arms.

"Libby…baby," Sam whispered, as he slipped his arms beneath her shoulders and lifted her to a sitting position. When he felt her arms slide around his neck, he laid his cheek against the crown of her head and wept. "I am so sorry, so sorry that I let you down. It won't ever happen again. I swear."

Libby couldn't stop crying. It wasn't all Sam's fault. So much had been lost because they'd both made the wrong decisions. But before she could say so, a nurse came running into Libby's room.

"Mr. Holt! Mr. Holt! You'd better get down to the lobby. It looks like every television station and newspaper in the country found out about your appearance. They have Mrs. Wyatt and the boys trapped down in the lobby and won't let them get to the elevator. The hospital administrator called the police, but they're out of town working a wreck and can't get here in time to help."

It was as if Sam Holt had gone from zero to eighty within the space of a heartbeat as he shifted into trouble-shooter mode. He eased Libby back down onto the pillows, then cupped the side of her cheek. "Don't worry," he said shortly. "I'll take care of this."

Libby's heart was racing. Her son was in trouble and she couldn't get to him. Then she saw the set of Sam's jaw and the glint in his eye and told herself he could do this. When he strode past the nurse with his fists doubled and his shoulders back, she relaxed.

"SAMMY! SAMMY! This way! This way! Talk to the camera, Sammy. Tell us, Sammy, how does it feel to have a daddy? Where has he been? Are you mad at him for abandoning you and your mother? Sammy! Sammy. What did your mother say when she woke up? Is she glad you found your father?"

Sam was furious. He could barely see the top of Kate's head and could only assume Sammy and the boys were somewhere behind her. He knew why the reporters were here. His little boy's plea for a father was newsworthy, but by God, they'd crossed a great big line and he was about to put them back behind it where they belonged.

He began pushing people aside as he moved through the crowd, and yelling even louder than they were to "get the hell away" from his son.

It was the word *son* that caught the crowd's attention. All of a sudden, they realized who he was and all the cameras turned toward him. When he finally got to Kate, he could tell she was rattled. He touched her shoulder once, caught Sammy's eye and then turned to face the crowd.

They were shouting louder now. Sam raised his hand but maintained his silence until he could be heard.

"Are you Sammy's father? Why haven't you—"

"I need all of you to shut the hell up," Sam said shortly.

There was a moment of shock, then another reporter cried out, "The country has a right to know wh—"

Sam pointed at the man and then took two steps forward. Surprisingly, the crowd moved two steps back as he repeated, "I said… Shut. The. Hell. Up."

Silence.

"Were you people raised by wolves?" Sam asked. "Look at what you've done. You've pinned a grandmother and three kids against a wall, shoved a bunch of microphones and cameras in their faces and proceeded to scream at them. What did you hope to achieve? Is a news story that important?"

"But we—"

Sam's gaze caught the errant reporter who dared to argue. Then Sam looked away, as if the man didn't exist.

"This is a hospital. There are people in here who are sick and there are people in here who are dying. They are all at some of the worst places they'll ever be in their lives and you're down here raising hell and scaring old women and kids…sorry, Kate. No offense for the remark."

Kate sighed. "None taken," she said, as she gathered Pete and Sammy in her arms while Charlie stood beside her.

"So, you're here. Turn on your cameras and recorders…do whatever it is you people do and pay attention, because I'm only going to say this once. My name is Sam Holt. I am Sammy Farraday's father. I have been in love with his mother, Liberty Farraday, since the day I met her, which was almost nine and a half years ago. A little over eight years ago, we had a fight. It was stupid. It was my fault. I am a man, therefore I am an occasional jackass. I think it's embedded into our DNA but I can't prove it."

There was a ripple of laughter, but he now had their attention. He could hear recorders running while cameras were aimed at his face. This was the last thing he would have chosen to do, but after Sammy's video, it was inevitable. And because of what he'd done to Libby and Sammy, they deserved it.

"Libby thought I didn't love her anymore and she moved. I thought she was still in Tulsa and as soon as I got off the job site, went back to make up with her. It's sort of like Sammy said in the video…we got lost from each other. And in a horrible twist of fate, if Libby hadn't nearly been killed, none of this might have happened. There has never been another woman in my life but Libby. To find out that we had a child was a shock, but a phenomenal one. I couldn't be happier. My only regret is that I've missed seven years of Sammy's life."

"Eight, Daddy! I'm eight now!" Sammy cried.

Sam sighed and then shrugged. "See what I mean. Libby's wreck was on Sammy's eighth birthday, right, son?"

Sammy nodded, and then slipped out of Kate's arms and took his father's hand.

Sam gave his son's fingers a gentle squeeze as he continued. "Sammy and I have a lot of catching up to do, but I am proud to call this little boy my son. As far as I'm concerned, he is a hero. He promised his mother if she woke up, he would get her the best Mother's Day present ever. I was the present, flawed and at fault as I am, but never lacking in love. He did what he had to do to put his world back together again, and in doing so, he put mine and Libby's world back together, too. Libby is out of the coma and talking, and tomorrow is Mother's Day and I am here. Call it a miracle or whatever you want. No, you may not interview her…ever. I know Libby. She has nothing to say to any of you except to maybe give all of you grief for terrorizing her son. And you have had your last interview with Sammy and me. Now I would seri-

ously suggest you get the hell out of this hospital and go
back to wherever you came from because the hospital administrator has already called the police. Every last one
of you can be arrested for, at the least, disturbing the
peace. And if Kate wants, I'd venture she could add four
counts of assault for you all pinning her, her boys and my
son into a corner and not letting them go."

Then he picked Sammy up in his arms and turned to
Kate. "What do you say we all go see Libby now?"

"But Mr. Holt, surely—"

Sam spun. "What's your name?"

The reporter glared, but he got the message. Then, to
punctuate Sam's warning, they began hearing the sound
of approaching sirens.

"Too late," Sam said. "Don't say I didn't warn you."

The crowd parted as Sam, Kate and the boys walked
toward the elevators, then began to disperse. But it was,
as Sam said, too late. The hospital administrator met the
police at the front door and began pointing. Sam looked
at Kate and winked.

"Now they're the ones backed against the wall."

"They should have left sooner," Kate muttered.

"That's why I kept talking," Sam said. "I figured Chief
Fite would show up soon enough. No way was I going
to let them get away with scaring my son or bullying you
and the boys."

Sammy grinned when Sam said "my son." When they
got to the elevator, Sam put him down. "I know you're
too big to carry," he said. "I just didn't want anyone
messing with you again, okay?"

"I didn't mind," Sammy said softly. "I never had a
daddy carry me before. You're way taller than Mama. I
can see a lot more up this high."

Sam's heart twisted at the poignancy of the remark,

then he laid a hand on Sammy's head and grinned. "Glad I could be of help."

"Is Mama still okay?" Sammy asked, as Sam pushed the button for the second floor.

"She's more than all right," Sam said. "She's awake and talking a lot. They even moved her to a room all her own. We can't be loud, but we can talk to her for a bit and then I know she'll have to take another nap, okay?"

"Yeah. I have to take naps when I'm sick, too. You get well faster. Did you know that?"

Sam nodded. "Today, I'm learning all kinds of things, including just how smart you really are."

Sammy beamed, then looked at Pete and giggled.

Kate knew the boys well enough to know that when they giggled in such a conspiratorial fashion, she needed to know why.

"What's so funny?" Kate asked.

"Sammy's dad said hell a whole bunch of times. Hell is a bad word. We're not allowed to say bad words," Pete said.

Sam rolled his eyes, then looked at Kate. "Sorry."

"You'll learn," she muttered. "When they're not eating you out of house and home, they turn into parrots."

Sam laughed out loud. Suddenly, he couldn't wait to begin this new job. Being Sammy's father was going to take practice—a whole lot of practice—but he would prevail. His biggest challenge was going to be Libby. He'd hurt her so bad and in so many ways he didn't even want to count. He'd broken more than her heart. He'd broken faith and trust and everything it takes to make a relationship work. But he was going to fix that, too, if she'd let him.

A few moments later, they got off the elevator and headed for Libby's room. Sammy started talking as soon as they entered.

"Mama! Mama! You're awake. I'm so glad to see you. Are you still sleepy? Can you stay awake long enough to talk back to me today?"

Libby was sitting up, waiting for Sam to arrive with Kate and the boys. Relieved that they were all in one piece, she grinned and then patted the side of her bed. "Sit here for a minute, honey. Mama needs a big hug."

Sam lifted him up. "Hug easy," he said.

Sammy nodded. "I love you, Mama," he whispered.

"I love you, too, little man."

Sammy patted her shoulder, then when Libby leaned back against the pillows, he began telling her about what happened.

"Mama, there was a whole bunch of people downstairs shouting at us and taking pictures and it was crazy, and someone grabbed my arm and pulled me out from behind Grandma Kate and she couldn't make them get back, and Charlie was holding on to me and Pete so we would be safe and then Daddy came. He made them shut the hell up and—"

Sam rolled his eyes and mouthed the word *sorry* to Libby. It was all she could do not to laugh.

"...then he told them he was a jackass and—"

Libby looked at Sam, then laughed out loud. Sammy kept talking without missing a beat.

"...and said he loved you forever and that if it hadn't been for me, you and Daddy would still be lost. And he called me a hero. He did, Mama. He said I was a hero for finding him. Do you think I'm a hero, Mama?"

Libby didn't know whether to laugh or cry. "I know you're a hero," she said. "You've always been my hero." She patted his knee, which seemed to be the signal for Sammy's story to continue.

"Then he told them to leave or get rested and they didn't

run fast enough and Chief Fite got 'em first. Right, Daddy?"

"Pretty much," Sam said.

"I've got something to add," Kate said. "Libby, you don't know how grateful I am that you're awake. I love you like a daughter and have been half out of my mind with worry."

She hugged Libby quickly, then looked at Sam before continuing.

"I might have had reservations before, and I don't know where you two are with fixing what's between you, but after today, I say go for it. When I saw him pushing his way through that crowd to get to us, I knew it was going to be all right. And while I'm sure you'll be seeing what he said on the evening news for at least a week, I'll tell you right now he said all the right things." Then she patted Sam's arm and gathered up her grandsons. "I'm going to leave you three to visit on your own. Charlie…Pete…tell Libby goodbye. We'll visit longer when she's feeling better."

"'Bye, Libby," they echoed, and hurried out the door.

"Better take the back exit," Sam said. "Just in case there are some stragglers."

"Oh Lord…you're right," Kate said, and hustled out the door to catch up with the boys.

Sam slid an arm across Sammy's back, then took Libby's hand with his other so that they were all connected.

"I have something to say to both of you, and it needs to be said now before another moment passes. I'm so sorry for not being a part of your lives and I hope you'll give me a chance to belong. Sammy, I love your mother very much, and I've already said you are my hero. But you don't really know me, and that's my fault."

"Yeah," Sammy said. "But I'm learning."

Sam sighed. "I'm learning, too. Like I won't be saying bad words around you anymore because they're not okay."

Sammy shrugged. "I already knew that. If you'd asked, I could have told you myself."

Libby arched an eyebrow, then smiled as she leaned against the pillow and closed her eyes.

"Looks like your Mama is pretty tired," Sam said. "Maybe we'd better go."

"Are you gonna eat supper with us again?" Sammy asked.

"Yes, Kate invited me. Maybe I could bring dessert."

"She loves the pineapple cheesecake from Bryan's Bakery," Libby offered.

"I'll show you where it is," Sammy offered.

"Sounds like a deal," Sam said, then leaned over and kissed Libby, this time on the lips. It was brief and gentle, but Libby heard the catch in his breath just the same.

"One day when you're both ready, my mom would like to meet her grandson."

Sammy grinned. It was obvious that he liked the idea of having a grandmother, too.

"It's going to be a while before I can take a trip, but she can come anytime she wants," Libby said.

"I'll get us both a room at the motel," Sam said. "You don't know it, but I've been staying in your house. Sammy graciously offered it the day I arrived."

Shock rolled through Libby like thunder. Knowing Sam had been sleeping in her bed shifted everything to a level she wasn't ready to consider.

"Don't worry," Sam said. "When you get to come home, I'll be in the motel. I wouldn't assume anything else."

Libby nodded.

"You're not mad, are you, Mama?" Sammy asked. "He isn't making any messes. I checked."

Libby sighed. For a child, life was so simple. It was all about messes, the kind that can be swept up with a broom.

"No, I'm not mad. It was a kind thing to do. Thank you for thinking of it."

Sammy beamed.

Sam must have guessed she was rattled because he said, "It's okay, Libby. I understand. I just didn't have the heart to turn him down."

She looked at Sammy, then ruffled his hair in a loving gesture. "I know. He's like his daddy…quite a charmer."

Sammy beamed. "Mama! You never said that to me before!"

"I know, Sammy. I'll try to do better, too."

"So, son…let's go find that bakery before all the pineapple cheesecakes are sold."

Sam winked at Libby, then took Sammy by the hand and out the door they went.

A fresh wave of guilt washed over Libby again as she watched her little boy trying to emulate his father's stride. She and Sam had made so many mistakes. Hopefully, they had the rest of their lives to correct them. Then she closed her eyes, letting the weariness envelop her.

CHAPTER FIVE

One week later

LIBBY STOOD on the porch, waving goodbye to Sammy as Kate and the boys headed to school, then winced slightly as she turned too quickly. Her ribs were healing. The doctor had even given his permission for her to resume light duties around the house. Except for the occasional headache, and a myriad of fading bruises and healing cuts, she felt blessed to be alive. And, to her growing surprise, Sam had been a rock. He'd come every day the house after Sammy left for school and had helped her with everything—from washing her hair, doing her laundry and even changing the sheets on their beds. This morning, he was coming to get her grocery list to do their shopping. She wanted to believe this run of good will would last, but the hurt he'd caused her before had cut deep and left scars. She heard the sincerity in his voice, and acknowledged his efforts on her behalf, but trust, once broken, grew slowly again.

As she closed the door behind her, she paused in the living room, looking at all the things she'd gathered around her over the past eight years, remembering how drab and empty this little house had been when she'd first moved in, and how, month by month, she'd turned the house into a home. Her roots ran deep in Azalea. She wasn't sure how Sam's reappearance in their lives was going to impact the future, but she wasn't making any rash decisions.

With a sigh, she combed her fingers through her hair, then headed for the kitchen to finish the grocery list. She refilled her coffee, and as she did, thought how wonderful it was just to be able to pour herself another cup. After what she'd survived, it was nothing short of a miracle. She would never take the simple things in life for granted again.

A few minutes later, she was still working on the list when she heard a knock at the front door. Before she could get up, she heard Sam's voice.

"It's me. Okay if I come in?"

The sound of his voice was enough to set her pulse racing, which made her somewhat irked at herself. Slow and steady, Libby. Remember.

"I'm in the kitchen," she shouted, then looked toward the doorway, anticipating his appearance. She could hear his footsteps, quick and sure, and remembered how that used to quicken her heart. He was smiling as he walked in wearing blue jeans, a white T-shirt and a pair of old cowboy boots that were mud-brown and slightly run-down at the heels. He looked good enough to eat.

"Good morning, honey," he said. "You're looking great. How do you feel? Did you sleep good last night? Are you and Sammy managing okay on your own at night?"

Libby smiled. "Hi. Thanks. Good. Yes and yes."

Sam chuckled. "Okay...so that was probably one question too many. Got the list ready?"

"Just about," Libby said. "Would you please check and see how much toilet paper is left in the bathroom cabinet? I can't remember and your legs are longer than mine."

"You bet," Sam said, and turned on a dime. He was back in moments. "Only two rolls. Better add it to the list."

Libby sighed, unaware that the worry of her financial situation was showing on her face.

"What's wrong?" Sam said, as he slid into a chair beside her.

"Hmm? Oh. Nothing," Libby said.

He ran his finger along the frown line between her eyebrows. "That frown isn't nothing."

She shrugged. "I don't know how long it's going to be before I can go back to work. And I don't know why I'm even thinking about it yet because I don't have a car to drive to get there. So much to take care of and I'm so not up to it."

Sam laid his hand over hers, then gave it a squeeze.

"Look at me," he said softly.

Libby sighed, then met his gaze, fearing that his dark brown eyes, so very like her son's, saw too much.

"What?"

"I didn't just show up here in Azalea for the hell of it, Libby. I know how much you love Sammy. I know that you would do anything for him and gladly. But you no longer bear the burden of being a single parent. Now I'm here, too, and I'm not going anywhere."

"But your job—"

"Is all over the place and ready any time I want to go back to it. I don't do a nine-to-five at the same office every day, remember?"

She nodded.

"And just so you know, I checked with Chief Fite a couple of days ago regarding the trucker who hit you. He walked away without a scratch. Did you know that?"

Libby shook her head. Truthfully, she'd been so busy trying to readjust to everything else, that she hadn't allowed herself to dwell on the accident.

"Well, he did. He was ticketed for running a red light.

His company is liable for what he did to you. Chief Fite had already started checking into this for you…but I picked up where he left off. The company is paying for all your medical bills. You're also getting a new car out of the deal and…they're more than willing to talk cash settlement with you."

Libby's lips parted in shock. "Are you serious?"

"Yes. But…and this is just a suggestion because it's totally your call. If it were me, I'd hire a lawyer. You need a go-between to make sure what they offer is fair. It's going to be a long time before you're physically able to work at a job all day. And they have to compensate you for lost wages and pain and suffering. God knows you've had it. Thanks to Sammy, the whole world knew what happened to you, so it's not like the company can deny their culpability."

Libby leaned back in the chair, taken aback by the news. "I was worried about running out of money to pay rent and buy groceries."

Sam sighed. "Libby. You aren't hearing me. You will never have to worry about money again. I'm here. Whether you want me back in your life or not is your call. But you will always be in mine…you and Sammy…and I take care of what's mine."

Libby's vision blurred. She took a slow breath, trying to calm her thoughts, and choked on a sob, instead.

"Oh, Sam," she said softly, then covered her face with her hands.

"Libby…baby," Sam whispered, pulling her to her feet and into his arms. "You've been strong for Sammy a long, long time. Let me be strong for you. Lean on me, baby. Let me help both of you."

Libby shuddered. "I don't know if…I'm trying to believe—"

Sam put his fingers across her lips, silencing her before she could finish. "I know I have to earn your trust again. All I ask is for the chance. I'm not asking you for more than you're willing to give, okay? What I'm offering is no more than you and Sammy deserve. I'm not trying to buy my way back in your life."

"Thanks. You've been amazing, and I'm so grateful. You didn't know Sammy before, but you have no idea what an impact you've made in his life. He even carries himself differently. You've made him feel important in a way I never could, no matter how hard I've tried. All his life he's been a child without a father. I knew it bothered him, but I had no idea how deeply much until this happened," Libby said.

Sam rubbed his chin against the side of her face. "And I will be paying for being a jerk to you for the rest of my life because of what I've missed in Sammy's life. He is such a super kid."

"Thanks," Libby said, reaching for the tissues on the shelf behind her. She wiped her eyes and blew her nose, then took a deep breath and looked him square in the face. "Then…since you're offering, I'm adding ice cream to the grocery list. Sammy loves it and I only buy it for special occasions."

He leaned forward and kissed her. Just once and softly, then he backed off.

"I was wondering…would you like to go with me to the supermarket?"

Still rattled by his kiss, it took her a few moments to focus. "Um…yes, actually I would," she said.

"I thought maybe you would like to get out of the house for a bit."

"That would be great," Libby said. "Just give me a couple of minutes."

"You already look good to me," Sam said, eyeing the black slacks and pink knit top she had on.

Libby stuck out a foot. It was bare.

"Oh. Right. Shoes. I'll wait here."

A few minutes later they were on their way to the supermarket.

As they headed downtown, Sam had no idea he was following the same path that Libby had the day she'd had the wreck, or that they were coming up to the intersection where the wreck had occurred and where she'd nearly died.

Libby's heart started pounding when Sam stopped at the red light, just as she had. She heard Sam talking, but she couldn't focus on the words for staring at the light. When it turned green, she automatically leaned back, as if bracing herself for impact.

Sam sensed something was wrong when she hadn't answer his last three questions. As soon as he braked, he'd turned and looked at her. Curiosity turned to shock when he saw the expression on her face.

"Libby! What's wrong?"

"Drive, just drive," Libby said. It wasn't until they'd driven through the intersection that she began to relax again. "Oh my God," she whispered, and then leaned back and closed her eyes.

Sam quickly pulled over to the curb and parked. "Honey…what's wrong? Are you sick? Do you want to go home?"

"No. No. I'm okay. It's just…" She shuddered, then made herself look up. "I had no idea that would happen. That's the intersection where I had the wreck."

Sam's eyes widened, then he looked back over his shoulder, imagining her trapped in the car, as he knew she'd been, with the fear of fire and explosion increasing with every minute the EMTs worked, trying to free her from the mass of twisted metal. He sighed, then slid his hand beneath her hair.

"I'm so sorry. I had no idea."

Libby shook off her panic. "You don't need to apologize," she said. "I mean...I live here in Azalea. It's not like I could bypass this intersection for the rest of my life. I'm fine."

"You're not fine. But with time, you will be," he promised.

"Right. So...let's get those groceries, okay?"

A few minutes later, they reached the parking lot of the local supermarket. Sam parked, then circled the car to help Libby out. They were halfway across the parking lot when someone called Libby's name.

"Libby! Libby!"

Libby turned around just as Guy Porter jumped out of his pickup truck and came running toward her. Before she knew what was happening, he'd thrown his arms around her shoulders and hugged her, then exuberantly kissed both her cheeks.

"Lord, have mercy, girl. The last time I came through Azalea, you were still in a coma in intensive care. I just got back into town yesterday. I was going to give you a call later to see if I could come over."

Libby felt herself getting nervous all over again, wondering how Sam was going to react to meeting the only man she'd ever dated in Azalea.

"It's good to see you, Guy," she said, then turned to introduce him to Sam. "Sam, this is Guy Porter. He owns Porter Trucking on the south edge of Azalea. His mother, Mildred Porter, was Sammy's first grade teacher." To her surprise, Sam's reaction was easygoing and friendly.

"Great to meet you," he said. "And, my thanks to your mother for helping educate Sammy."

Guy grinned. "Yep. Mom has been teaching so long, some of the kids coming through her class are third generation."

"Wow," Sam said. "Talk about dedication."

Guy laughed. "Yeah…that and the fact that some girls marry young around here." Then he winked at Libby. "Unfortunately, none of us single guys could ever talk Libby into taking that step. Now I see why."

Sam glanced at Libby and caught a look on her face that he read as fear. For a few moments he couldn't understand why, and then it hit him. Even though Sam had lost all claims to her affections, she must be remembering the jealous fit he'd had during their relationship, and was afraid of how he'd react when being confronted by someone who was obviously an old boyfriend.

"No one ever accused Libby of being stupid," Sam said. "After the way I behaved, she probably didn't have the guts to trust another man." He glanced at Libby again. "Maybe one of these days I will have earned her trust again."

Libby couldn't believe it! Not only had Sam's reaction been unexpected, his genuine friendliness toward Guy was the last thing she would have predicted. Then Guy decided to leave and Sam was the first one to say goodbye.

"It was great to meet you," Sam said.

"Yeah. You, too," Guy said. "Sammy is a great kid. The best of luck to the both of you." Then he nodded at Sam, winked at Libby, got back in his truck and drove away.

Sam squeezed Libby's hand. "You still okay to walk around for a bit?"

"Yes."

Sam smiled, cupped her elbow, and together, they entered the store. The brief reunion between Libby and Guy was relived over and over throughout the store as Sam and Libby continued to shop. Everyone was elated to see her out and about, and curious about the famous "absent" father. While the news clip of his confrontation with the reporters had been shown almost as many times as Sammy's video had been viewed on YouTube, everyone still wanted a personal introduction. By the time they'd finished shopping, Libby was exhausted.

"I'm sorry," Libby said, as they finally left the parking lot and headed home. "I had no idea that would be so...so..."

"Trying?"

She nodded.

"No big deal," he said. "I've already had my share of incidents here. This was just the first time I'd had them with you."

Libby's eyes widened. "For real? Have people been rude to you?"

He grinned. "No. They just made sure I knew they were on your side."

"Oh. I had no idea."

"You have a lot of good friends in this town. I'm really proud of you, Libby. You have made a good life here for you and Sammy. I hope you'll let me share it...in any way you choose."

"You already are," she said, but didn't elaborate.

Sam sighed, then reminded himself to be patient. She'd already given him more access than he deserved. He kept reminding himself—slow and steady, slow and steady.

SAM HAD STAYED around the house with Libby all day, putting away groceries, fixing their lunch, taking a walk around the block with her in the afternoon. It was almost time for school to be out, which meant that Kate would come by soon dropping Sammy off.

Sam felt as anxious as a new father in the delivery room. He loved spending time with Sammy, listening to his wise, little-boy view of the world and the daily drama of an eight-year-old boy. After promising Libby he would be here when Sammy got home, she'd reluctantly gone to her room to take a nap.

Sam had gone to her bedroom several times to check on her, and each time, it became harder and harder to walk away. Standing beside her bed, watching her sleep, was his miracle. He'd given up hope years ago of ever seeing her again, and now, with the growing chance of renewing their relationship, he found it hard to stay away. He glanced at the clock. Sammy would be here any minute. With a regretful sigh, he leaned down and very gently kissed the side of her cheek before walking away.

He was on his way back into the living room when his cell phone began to ring. He answered it quickly, not wanting the sound to wake Libby.

"Hello?"

"Sam, it's me."

Sam started to smile. "Hey, Mom. How's it going?"

"I'm not the one with the interesting life," she snapped. "How's it going down there?"

He grinned. Typical of his mother. No messing around. "It's all good. I'm at Libby's right now, but she's taking a nap and Sammy's due to come home from school any time."

"I want to meet my grandson."

Sam sighed. He'd been expecting this and, truthfully, there was no reason now that she couldn't.

"So come meet him."

"Really? Is it all right now? Is Libby up for company?"

"Sure. And Sammy is really excited to know he has a grandmother, just like his best friend Pete."

"Oh my," Gracie said, and then started to cry.

"Mom, don't cry," Sam said.

"I'm not sad. I'm just overwhelmed," Gracie said.

"We all are. Now tell me when you're coming and I'll get you a room at the same motel I'm staying at."

"Um…well…I'm already packed."

"It's too late in the day for you to start out now, don't you think?"

"No. I can get halfway there tonight. I already have a room booked in a motel. I can be there by noon tomorrow. And since tomorrow is Saturday, I thought…"

"You're right. It's a perfect day for meeting a grandson."

"I'm bringing presents," she warned.

Sam grinned. "For me?"

She snorted.

He laughed.

"I'm bringing birthday presents and Christmas presents…for Libby and for Sammy…one for each year and each holiday that I've missed. That way, when Christmas comes around this year, I'll be caught up."

Emotion caught Sam unawares. "That's great, Mom. Drive safe, and call me tonight so I'll know you reached your motel safely."

"Okay. See you tomorrow. I love you, Sam."

"Love you, too, Mom."

Then the connection between them was gone. Sam dropped his cell phone back into his pocket, but before he could dwell on the call, the front door opened.

"Hi, Daddy! I'm home!"

Breath caught at the back of Sam's throat. Those were four of the most amazing words he'd ever heard.

"Hi, Sammy. Did you have a good day?" Sam asked.

Sammy nodded. "Yep. Pete got a bloody nose at recess. His Grandma Kate had to bring him a clean shirt and everything."

"Oh, man, that's too bad. Did he hurt himself?"

"Naw…he just picked his nose too much, I think."

Sam stifled a grin. Too much information…but he'd asked.

"Where's Mama?" Sammy asked.

"She's taking a nap," Sam said. "Are you hungry?"

Sammy's eyes widened. "Yeah! How did you know?"

"I was always hungry when I came home from school, too."

"You were? Wow! That's so cool, Daddy! We really are a lot alike, aren't we?"

"Yes, it looks like we are," Sam said, as his son's face suddenly blurred before his eyes. Sam glanced away so his son wouldn't know he was crying.

"Do you have homework?" Sam asked.

"A little bit," Sammy said.

"So, go wash your hands, then bring your homework into the kitchen. We can eat our snack and do homework at the same time while your mother finishes her nap, okay?"

"Yeah!" Sammy cried, and stormed down the hall, oblivious to the fact that he needed to be quiet for his sleeping mother.

Sam swiped at the tears in his eyes, then headed for the kitchen.

A few minutes later, Sammy burst into the room, saw the bowls of ice cream on the table and slapped his hands together in a gesture of delight.

"Oh boy! Ice cream! I love ice cream!"

"That's what your mom told me," Sam said, as Sammy scooted into his chair and grabbed his spoon.

"And it's chocolate! My favorite!" Sammy said, as he shoved the first bite into his mouth. "Umm, good. We don't have ice cream except at special occasions," Sammy said.

"That was in the past," Sam said. "From now on, you and your mama can have ice cream any time you want it. I promise."

Sammy's eyes widened in disbelief. "For real?"

"For real," Sam said, and then took a bite of his ice cream as well. "Umm, you're right. It is good."

"Yeah. I know my ice cream," Sammy said, and took another bite.

At that, Sam laughed out loud.

"So…Daddy…can I ask you something?"

"Sure," Sam said, as he, too, dug into the chocolate ice cream.

"How good are you at fractions?"

"As it happens, I'm real good at all kinds of math," Sam said.

Sammy nodded, as if something had just been confirmed for him. "You know what?" he asked.

"What?" Sam said.

"It's gonna be real handy having a daddy."

Sam couldn't help it. He laughed out loud again.

It was at that point that Libby walked into the kitchen.

"Hey, guys. What am I missing? I could hear you two laughing all the way down the hall."

"Mama! Guess what?"

"What?" Libby said, as she slid into the chair beside her little boy and gave him a kiss on the top of his head.

"Daddy said we can have ice cream anytime we want it, and he's good at math. I think we hit the jackpot!"

Sam and Libby looked at each other at the same moment, then at the same time, burst into laughter.

"I think I'm the one who hit the jackpot," Sam added,

and pushed his bowl of ice cream toward Libby. "Take mine, honey. I'm suddenly full to overflowing."

Libby felt warm all over. She knew what he meant had nothing to do with food. Sam Holt was slowly but surely worming his way back into her heart.

"Oh. There's one more thing you two should probably know," Sam said.

Libby paused with the bite of ice cream part way to her mouth.

"Like what?" she asked.

"My mom is on her way here to meet Sammy, and to see you again, Libby. She should be here around noon tomorrow. Hope you're okay with that."

Sammy's eyes widened as he glanced up at Libby. "Mama! Is it okay? I sure do wanna meet my grandma. Then Pete and I would be just alike."

Libby sighed. Once more, another absence in Sammy's life was being filled.

"Of course!" Libby said. "It's absolutely okay."

"Great," Sam said. "In fact, I just remembered I promised to get her a motel reservation. Excuse me while I make that call."

Sam got up from the table with a wink at Sammy and touched Libby's head as he passed. Then he was gone.

Libby shuddered. It felt as if all the air had gone out of the room. Then she focused her attention on Sammy.

"So…did you have a good day at school?"

Sammy nodded. "Yep. I was telling Daddy…Pete got a bloody nose and…"

Libby listened to her little boy rattle on about the day in his life, but she was also wondering what it would be like to see Gracie Holt again. The one time they'd met, she'd felt a connection. She hoped it would still be there.

CHAPTER SIX

SAMMY HAD BEEN STANDING at the window for almost an hour, watching for Gracie Holt's arrival. "Is that her car?" he yelled, as an unfamiliar sedan turned the corner and started down the street.

It wasn't the first time he'd asked the question, but Sam came to look again, just as he had the last four times Sammy had asked. He walked up behind him, slid a hand on his shoulder and gave it a squeeze.

"Nope. That's not it, either," Sam said. He'd driven his mother's car here and knew she'd been driving her sister's extra car, a red Toyota, ever since.

"Aww, man," Sammy muttered.

"Remember, I said her car was red. That will be an easy one to spot."

"Oh, yeah. Red."

"She'll be here soon, son. She called less than an hour ago, remember?"

Sammy nodded, and turned back to the window. All of a sudden, a red car turned the corner.

"Daddy! Daddy! That one's red! Do you think it's her? Do you think it's my grandma?"

Sam looked out the window, then sighed. Thank goodness. "Yep. That's her," he said.

Sammy bounced, then started yelling. "Mama! Mama! Grandma's here!"

Libby came hurrying out of the kitchen, wiping her hands on a towel. Sam sighed. She looked as anxious as Sammy, but with a tinge of panic.

"It's all good," Sam reminded her.

Libby managed a smile. "I know. It's just been a long time."

"Trust me," Sam said. "You are so going to become the princess in her life."

Libby sighed. "Considering I've never been anyone's princess before, I might be liking that."

"You can be mine," Sam said. "All you have to do is say the word."

Libby smiled, but didn't answer and Sam had to be satisfied with that.

He couldn't change the past, but he intended to spend the rest of his life making sure Libby never wanted for anything again—including love. But right now, it was his son who was demanding their attention.

"She's here!" Sammy shrieked. "Come on, guys. We need to go out to meet her, right?"

"He's right. We need to go out and meet her," Sam said, and held out his hand. Libby hesitated briefly, then took it.

Together, the three of them went outside. Sam never let go of Libby. He wanted her to know she no longer had to face anything alone.

At that point, Gracie Holt got out of her car, waving and crying all at the same time.

"Hello, everyone! I didn't think I'd ever get here!"

Suddenly Sammy got shy. Libby saw the look on his face and put her hand on his head and then whispered in his ear.

"She's just as nervous as you are, honey. We'll have to help her feel welcome, okay?"

Sammy's eyes widened, and then he nodded.

"Come on, Sammy. We're gonna have to help her carry stuff in," Sam said.

"Her suitcases?"

"No. She's not staying here, remember. But knowing your grandma, I'm betting she brought presents."

A huge grin spread across Sammy's face as Gracie approached. Sam went to meet her, then walked with her to the porch.

"Mom, you remember Libby."

"Absolutely," Gracie said. "Are you well enough to hug?"

Libby grinned. "Yes, ma'am."

"No ma'ams between us," Gracie said. "Either Gracie or Mom. Whichever feels best," she said and then enveloped her in a hug only a mother could give, holding her close and kissing her cheek before letting go.

Libby was reeling from the overwhelming feeling of acceptance when Gracie turned to Sammy. She could see Gracie Holt's nervousness, but gave her credit for maintaining a calm in the face of such an emotional moment.

"Hi, Sammy. My name is Gracie Holt. Your daddy was my little boy, so that makes you my grandson and me your grandmother, right?"

Sammy nodded.

"Do you think I might give you a hug?" she asked.

Sammy grinned. "Yes, ma'am."

As Gracie hugged him, she said, "I've been wanting a grandson for the longest time and didn't know I already had one. So, do you think you might like to call me Grandma?"

"Yeah!" Sammy said, and began to unload everything he'd been thinking. "Now I have a grandma just like Pete. You'll like, Pete, Grandma. He and his brother Charlie live with their grandma. They call her Grandma, but I call her Grandma Kate, 'cause she's a grandma, only she's not mine. And it's not polite to call your elmers by their first name. I think you two would be friends because you both have gray hair and like little boys."

"Elders," Libby said, while trying not to laugh. "It's not elmers, it's elders."

"Oh, yeah. Right," Sammy said.

"I can't wait to meet Pete and Charlie…and Grandma Kate," Gracie said.

"I knew that's what you'd say," Sammy said.

"I hope you're hungry," Libby said. "With Sam's help, dinner is ready."

"I'm hungry and happy and feel like I'm walking on air," Gracie said. "And…I have a car full of presents. One for every birthday and Christmas I've missed in both your lives." Then she handed the car keys to Sam. "Maybe you and Sammy could carry them in while I go wash up. They're in the trunk."

"Yes, ma'am," Sam said.

Sammy frowned. "Wait, Daddy. You're not supposed to call her ma'am, remember?"

Sam laughed as he ruffled Sammy's hair. "Come on. Let's go carry in those presents while I explain the reasons for when you say ma'am, and when you don't."

"Okay," Sammy said. He was still talking when Gracie and Libby went inside.

Immediately, Gracie hugged Libby again, then cupped her face. "Honey, I have to tell you this while we have a few moments alone. I won't delve into whatever was between you and Sam that made you deal with all this on your own, but I'm sorry you didn't feel comfortable enough with me, either, to have let me help."

Once more, Libby felt sideswiped by the love. "I know I made mistakes," Libby said. "And truthfully, most of it

had to do with always having been on my own. I didn't
know how to share my feelings, whether they were
troubled or painful. Having Sammy has changed a lot of
that. Growing up did the rest."

Gracie sighed, and then nodded. "Enough said. So,
point me to the bathroom. I'm thinking we're going to eat
the fastest meal on record, or open presents first. It's your
call."

Libby grinned. "The food will keep. I doubt if we
could say the same for Sammy if I asked him to wait until
after dinner. Bathroom is down the hall on the left. We
will wait for you to get back."

THE LIVING ROOM FLOOR was littered with bits of
wrapping paper, ribbon and presents. The laughter
coming from the kitchen was evidence of the joy within
Libby Farraday's small house. A little boy's promise
made to his mother in hopes of keeping her alive had
changed three people's worlds forever.

That night when Libby put Sammy to bed, he slept
with the present his grandma had given him for his first
birthday—a black-and-white stuffed panda. The rest of
his gifts were scattered around the room, including what
had been deemed a "cool" Lava Lamp that continually
"burped" red and black blobs and a Star Wars poster.

After reading Sammy his good-night story, Sam and
Gracie left to get her settled in at the motel. Libby walked
through the house, picking up bits of wrapping paper and
making sure everything was locked up, but her thoughts
were not on the neatness of the rooms. Today had been a
turning point—in more ways than one. Sammy hadn't just
gained a grandmother. He and Libby had become members
of a family—a really big family. Now Sammy not only had
a father, he had a grandparent, aunts, uncles and, as Gracie

said, a whole slew of cousins. It boggled the mind. Knowing this filled Libby's heart to overflowing and gave her a sense of peace she'd never had. If anything ever happened to her again, Sammy would never be alone.

She passed a mirror on the way to the kitchen to turn off the lights, then backed up and stopped, staring intently at her reflection. Her scars were fading. Her face looked the same, but she would never be the same again. Sam was back in her life, and if she trusted his words, he was here to stay. But could she trust him enough to chance heartbreak again? And if she didn't, how would she deal with the guilt of walking away from him a second time?

She blinked slowly, then closed her eyes, thinking back over the past week. When she opened them again, she could see that the face was still the same, but she wasn't. A decision had been made.

GRACIE LEFT on Monday, but not before meeting Kate, Pete and Charlie, and forming a bond with Kate Wyatt that surprised them both. And she'd elicited a promise from Sam and Libby that, despite whatever they decided about their own relationship, they would all spend Christmas with her at her home in Broken Bow, Oklahoma. It was going to be their chance to meet the "rest of the family."

Sam had watched his mother drive away, then left to take Sammy to school, promising Libby that he'd be right back. Libby knew he wanted to talk. And she did, too. There were things needing to be said that had been festering for eight years.

SAM KNEW something had changed with Libby and he was scared. He'd seen the look on her face as he and Sammy were driving away. She said she'd be waiting for his return. He didn't know what that meant, but he was prepared to face the consequences, whether he liked them or not. He drove back to the house with a sick feeling in the pit of his stomach. The rest of his life hinged on what happened afterward. He parked in the driveway, then headed for the porch. But when he got inside, he couldn't find her.

"Libby! Where are you?" Sam called, as he shut the front door behind him.

"In here," she said. "In the bedroom. Could you come here a minute?"

"Sure," he said, striding toward her bedroom with an easy stride. The door was ajar. He pushed it inward, then froze. Libby was standing at the foot of the bed, wearing a towel. If there was anything on beneath it, he couldn't tell. "Uh…sorry, I—" Then he took a deep breath and started over. "What was it you needed, honey?"

"You."

Sam's heart stopped, then kicked in so hard he momentarily lost his breath.

"Oh…baby…"

"I love you, Sam Holt. I always have. I'm saying this now because after today we're never going to discuss the past again."

Sam nodded, then sat down.

Libby waved a finger at him. "Start pulling stuff off. What I have to say won't take long."

He didn't have to be told twice. "I'm listening," he said, pulling off his boots.

"We both made mistakes eight years ago, but having Sammy wasn't one of them. You shouldn't have said what you said to me. You should have trusted me."

"I know, and—".

She held up her finger. "I'm not through and you still have on too many clothes."

He popped the snap on his jeans and began pulling them off one leg at a time as Libby continued.

"I should have let you know I was pregnant. Even if you'd doubted Sammy's paternity, you would have known the truth once you saw him. He's practically a clone of you. You deserved to know and I took that away from you, so we're both at fault. We were young and stupid. We are no longer young and stupid. We're parents. Our first obligation, for the rest of Sammy's childhood, is to him. Understood?"

He nodded as he tossed his jeans on top of his shirt. He had his thumb in the waistband of his briefs when he paused.

"Is it my turn now?"

She eyed the briefs and the arousal beneath, then, unable to answer, met his gaze and just nodded.

He took off the briefs and put on a condom, then walked toward her. Just before he touched her, she dropped the towel.

Sam picked her up and laid her on the bed. "Libby, sweetheart, I promise, I will love and trust you forever."

Libby put her arms around his neck. "That's a promise I expect you to keep," she said softly.

Sam groaned, then leaned down and captured her lips with his. She was as sweet as he'd remembered, but better. He stroked her body over and over, mapping the contours and valleys that he'd once known so well, until their love-making became wild and their bodies were bathed in sweat.

Libby grasped his face between the palms of her hands, deepening a kiss until they were both gasping for breath. When Sam cupped her breast, she encircled his arousal with her hand, bringing them both to a quick and burgeoning need.

"Now, Sam. Take me now," she finally begged, and he did.

The moment he filled her, Libby cried, "So long…so long," and then she arched her back and, together, they began to move. The climax built quickly, coming to a boiling point so fast it was scary. All of a sudden Libby lost control.

Sam felt her give way, bathing him in heat. It was all it took to push him over. With one final thrust, he shattered. When he found the strength to move, he cradled her in his arms and rolled onto his side, still holding her close.

Libby's heart was pounding as she came down from the sexual high, but she knew in her heart she'd done the right thing. For better or worse, she loved Sam Holt.

"So, what do you have to say?" she finally asked.

"Will you marry me?"

Libby closed her eyes as a satisfied sigh slid through her lips.

"I thought you'd never ask."

LIBBY'S WORLD was in a tizzy. Thanks to Sam's intervention on her behalf, she had a new car and a lawyer who was working on a monetary settlement that was most likely going to be enough to put Sammy through college someday.

She'd finally been released to go back to work at Faye's Floral Fantasies, and when she had, Sam had taken the opportunity to take Gracie's car back to Broken Bow. Then he flew back to his place in Dallas to pick up his SUV, close up the condo, and have his things shipped to Azalea.

During the three days he was gone, Libby had felt aimless, unable to focus, constantly watching the driveway, hoping to see him drive up. For the past eight years, she'd focused every ounce of energy she had on being the best mother she could be, and had taken pride and satisfaction in a job well done. And then Sam Holt had walked back into her life and reminded her she was also a woman.

She was at the flower shop, making a bouquet for a twenty-fifth anniversary party when the phone rang. She wiped her hands on her work apron, then hurried to answer.

"Faye's Floral Fantasies."

"Hey, honey, I'm home."

Libby's heart leaped. Sam was back!

"Yea! Did you have a good trip?"

"Yep. Are you okay? Not working too hard are you?"

Libby's smile widened. "I'm fine. I'll be through here in about half an hour. As soon as I pick Sammy up at school, we'll be home."

"Can't wait," Sam said.

"Oh. Just so you know, today was the last day of school so Kate is having a sleepover for the boys. They're having a barbeque in the backyard and then supposedly sleeping outside in the tent she set up. Sammy is so excited."

"Have they ever slept outside before?"

"Nope."

Sam laughed. "I'll bet the first time some dog howls in the neighborhood, they'll be inside."

Libby giggled. "Probably, but Kate's a glutton for punishment. She seems to think that's going to be fun."

"So…we're on our own tonight, then?"

"Mmm hmm."

"Fantastic. So…how about I take you out for supper?"

"That would be great!" Libby said.

"The diner or the roadhouse?" Sam asked.

"Oooh, the roadhouse. I haven't had steak in ages."

"The roadhouse it is," Sam said. "See you in a few."

Libby was still smiling when she turned around to find her boss, Faye, grinning at her.

"I bet I can guess who that was," Faye said.

"Sam's home," Libby said.

"As soon as you finish that bouquet, call it a day."

"Thanks," Libby said.

A couple of hours later, Libby was on her way to Kate's to drop Sammy off for the sleepover. She pulled into the driveway, then leaned toward her son.

"I need my good-night kiss early," she said.

Sammy threw his arms around her neck and kissed her soundly, then grabbed his bag just as Kate walked out onto her porch.

"There's Kate," Libby said. "Be good and remember your manners."

"Yes, ma'am," Sammy said, and then beamed. "Be sure and tell Daddy I said ma'am like I'm 'posed to."

"I will," Libby said. "Love you."

"Love you, too, Mama," Sammy said, and then he was gone.

Libby turned the car around and headed home—home to Sam.

SAM AND LIBBY were on their way to supper when he took the wrong turn.

"Sam. Honey…you missed the turn."

"Oh. Shoot. I'll just circle the block and get back on track."

Libby smiled, then leaned back in the seat. But when it came time to turn right, Sam kept on driving.

"You missed it again," Libby said, with a laugh.

"I know. There's something I want to show you."

"Oh. Okay."

A couple of blocks farther, Libby suddenly pointed.

"Oh, look, Sam! The old Turner place sold. I love that house. See how the white verandah wraps all the way around the first story, and then mimics it again with a tiny balcony across the second story?"

"Yeah, it's great," Sam said, and gently tapped on the brakes.

Libby kept talking, unaware they'd started slowing down. "There's something so solid and traditional about red brick and white trim. Even the shutters are pretty. All that cutwork makes them look like lace. Kate told me it was one of the first houses built in Azalea. Some banker built it for his wife. It's never been out of the family before, but the last couple never had children, and so it's been for sale ever since they died."

"Ever been inside?" Sam asked.

"Only to the foyer once to deliver flowers," Libby said, and then realized Sam was slowing down and pulling into the driveway. "Oh…you don't need to slow down. I've seen it countless times. I wonder who bought it."

"I did," Sam said softly.

Libby gasped, and then stared at him in disbelief. "What? Why?"

"For you. Kate said it was your favorite house in the whole town. And since you've already agreed to marry me, I figured it was the perfect wedding present."

Libby was in shock. "You bought it? Are you serious?"

"As a heart attack," Sam said. "Want to see it?"

"Can we?"

He handed her the key.

Libby grinned, then grabbed the door. "Oh my gosh. I am so excited."

They got out, then walked up the steps hand in hand.

But when Libby tried to put the key in the lock, her hands were shaking too much.

"You do it," she said, and handed the key back to him.

He unlocked it, then let the door swing wide as he picked her up and carried her across the threshold.

"Aren't people supposed to be married before they do this?" Libby asked.

"People are supposed to do lots of things," Sam said. "But we're not ordinary people, are we, sweetheart? We fell in love, then lost each other. We made a son together, but we're still not married. Why go against the grain and start following rules at this late date?"

Libby giggled, then threw her arms around Sam's neck and kissed him—and didn't turn loose until she heard him groan.

"I love you, Sam. So much."

"Love you more," he whispered, as he nuzzled the side of her neck. Then he put her down. "Would you like to see the rest of your house?"

Libby sighed, then gazed around at the spacious rooms and the antique furniture, unable to believe this was all hers.

"Are all the rooms furnished like this one?" she asked.

"Yes, but you can do anything you want to change the—"

"Is there a bed in the master bedroom?" she asked.

He started to smile. "A four-poster that's so high you have to use steps to get in it."

"Don't you think we should maybe try it out?" Libby asked.

Sam grinned. "Like I said before, we aren't exactly the traditional type. I see no reason why we can't start the honeymoon right now. We can worry about dinner and the wedding later."

"I love you, Sam Holt. Please make love to me before I die from want."

Sam eyed the grand staircase spiraling upward. "Are you gonna make me carry you up that thing?"

"Not if I can have seconds."

A grin started spreading across Sam's face. "We're not talking about food here, are we?"

"No, Sam. We're talking about my present. My Mother's Day present. I think it's time I began putting it to good use."

Sam took Libby by the hand, and together they walked up the stairs and into the rest of their lives.

YOU BELONG TO ME

Isabel Sharpe

To Laura Iding, who excels at writing,
friendship and keeping me sane

CHAPTER ONE

DEAR CLARISSA (my name for you),

If you are reading this, I assume you have contacted the adoption agency to find me. Giving you up was a hard and brave decision, one I have regretted about half the time and been glad of the rest. By now you are nearly twenty years old, and odds are you aren't named Clarissa.

I hope you can understand that twenty years ago I could not have been any kind of decent mother or given you any kind of decent life. Your father was not in the picture, which is the kindest way I can put it. I'm still not sure about the mothering, but I would love to meet you, make up for lost time and find out who you have become. Last I saw you, you were seven pounds, seven ounces and screaming your head off. I trust you've grown and adjusted to being out in the world.

I won't give you my phone number. I don't enjoy talking to strangers on the phone—I can barely tolerate my friends butting into my day that way. I don't have e-mail, though I'm told it's only a matter of time before I give in. Please just come. I'm not likely to move and if I do, I'll send another card to the registry for your file. Any time, I'll be here, the

door will always be open to you. And if you choose
not to come, then know that I respect your decision
and will carry you in my heart forever.
Sincerely,
Clara Schultz
Your birth mom

MAGGIE CHESTERTON gripped the steering wheel of her
rented Vibe much more tightly than she needed to. She
still wasn't sure coming home to Princeton was a good
idea. In fact, from the time she received the shock of her
life—in an envelope from the New Jersey Adoption
Registry—until now, sitting parked on Mount Lucas
across the street from Clara Schultz's house, she wasn't
sure she knew anything anymore.

She loosened her death hold and started tap-tap-
tapping the wheel instead. So many memories while
driving back into town. She'd been back only once, for
her Princeton Day School fifth reunion; work had kept
her from the tenth. Since her adoptive parents, Jane and
Michael Chesterton had moved to London right after she
graduated high school, there hadn't been much to come
back for. Her few close friends had left town. The only
other person she'd really liked to have seen—her first
boyfriend, Grant Conroy—hadn't come to the fifth
reunion. She'd been disappointed, but not surprised.
Grant had been one of the few kids bussed to PDS from
Trenton, and he made damn sure everyone knew he
wasn't a Princetonian. Given the rate at which he got into
trouble, she doubted his high school experience in the ex-
clusive private school had been something he was
anxious to relive.

She'd passed a few places coming in to town that held
some pretty crazy memories of him, as well as tender

ones. Like the Princeton Shopping Center, where he'd dared her to run naked with him in the little adjoining park after dark. Grant had always brought out the wild girl in her. He'd been angry and exciting, creative and destructive, and very, very bright. Who knew where he was now?

A pink blossom drifted down from the crab apple tree in the yard next to her car and landed on her windshield. She'd forgotten how beautiful Princeton was in May. Magnolias, forsythia, crab apples like this one in full pink bloom, dogwoods lending a touch of pure white, azaleas in many shades, pink to peach to purple. Practically every yard burst with color.

Her birth mother's house across the street, which she'd been staring at nervously for about fifteen minutes, was tiny, nestled among three or four huge oaks and maples which made it look like a fairy-tale house in the woods. A steep discolored slate roof, dormers here, bay windows there, the house seemed to have started in several directions and never made any of them work. Maggie had pictured a neat nondescript Colonial, like most of the other houses in the neighborhood. This one delighted her.

And terrified her. It had been hard enough deciding to find out if her birth mother had registered to find her. Emotionally explosive to find instead of an impersonal report from the registry, a personal card from Clara written nearly ten years earlier. Deciding to follow up and visit took every last ounce of Maggie's courage. She'd booked her reservation impulsively, taking an unheard-of week off from work—though she did bring her laptop since the office collapsed without her—then had agonies of regret mixed with excitement. What if Clara was a clingy mess of a person who'd intrude into Maggie's well-ordered and very full life and make her crazy?

But then…what if she was everything warm and loving and supportive that Jane and Michael Chesterton tried to be, but…well, couldn't quite get there.

Finally Maggie had concluded that if she didn't go, she'd drive herself crazy wondering what might have been. Stupid to have thought she could inquire at the Adoption Registry risk-free. Once Maggie set that boulder in motion, it wasn't going to come to a stop until it had rolled as far as it was going to roll.

She'd only told her ex-roommate Amy about the trip. Depending on what she found and how the relationship with her birth mother moved forward—or not—she'd decide when and what to tell her adoptive parents. The registry had confirmed that the Chestertons knew nothing of Clara and vice versa. Maggie couldn't help wondering if they'd ever passed each other on Princeton's streets, or met at a party without realizing.

It was possible. But while musing on these things was delightful, Maggie should probably remove herself from the vehicle, cross to 256 Mount Lucas and ring the doorbell, since meeting Clara Schultz was the entire reason she'd come to Princeton in the first place.

Ya think?

She got out of the car and made her way, step by step toward her birth mother's front door, set back under tree limbs so it was like going through a tunnel.

Standing inches away, she stared at the dimly glowing cracked doorbell. *Okay, Maggie. Go.*

Her finger made contact. The bell played a single tone, then made a bizarre agitated buzzing, as if it had choked on its own tune.

Silence. Breeze sighed through the leaves overhead. An ant crawled over a sill smudged with fine black dirt.

Then footsteps and the deep bark of what sounded

like an enormous dog. A metallic clank as a deadbolt shot back. The rattle of the handle. A muffled female voice inside. Maggie held her breath. The door swung open.

Yikes. Clara Schultz—if that's who had answered—was not the tall, stylish woman Maggie had expected, or maybe hoped for. All of probably five feet three inches—which made five-foot-seven Maggie feel like a giant even in her sensible-heeled pumps—wearing pink flowered pajama bottoms, a blue-striped pajama top and a large white apron covered with paint splotches, she was standing looking at Maggie with her graying head of medium-length, tangled brown hair tipped to one side as if she were listening intently to something in the apartment behind her.

Or to voices in her own head.

Help.

Strangest of all, she barely seemed to register Maggie's presence. The dog, a collie with matted fur, had no trouble registering Maggie's presence, however, which meant Maggie had to find some way to keep the dog's nose out of her privates without being rude. The woman didn't seem to notice the struggle. She was still lost in whatever world she appeared to inhabit.

It seemed completely impossible that this woman could belong to Maggie's gene pool, which made it suddenly easy to speak.

"Are you Clara Schultz?"

The woman lifted her head. Hers eyes were the exact shade of Maggie's, unusually bright blue, which often had people guessing she wore color-enhancing contacts. That shared physical characteristic was enough to take away Maggie's recent calm and bring back the initial shock.

"Yes. I'm Clara." She pulled the black-framed half-glasses off her head and jammed them onto her nose, peered at Maggie as if she were looking over produce in the supermarket. "Who are you?"

"I'm…" Maggie would never go into a meeting of any kind unprepared. But faced with this extraordinary, plump, mismatched character standing in the doorway of her fairy-tale house while her dog explored forbidden areas, Maggie's polished presentation fled in panic. "I got your note."

"Wobbles, back." Clara spoke softly, but the dog immediately retreated into the house, to Maggie's unutterable relief. "What did you say now, a note?"

"You sent it through—"

"Oh, yes. The one about the…" She frowned and shook her head. "No. That's been taken care of. What note?"

Dear God, was Clara Schultz all there?

"It was a card, really. From you. The agency sent it. I'm your…I'm Clarissa. Only I'm Maggie. Your…" She took a deep breath. Braced herself. "Daughter."

"Oh-h-h-h." Clara put a hand to her heart, then to her mouth, singing the syllable in a fluid mezzo. "Oh-h-h-h."

"I…your note said just to show up, so…" Maggie gestured stupidly. "Here I am."

"Yes. My goodness, so you are. Well." Clara moved back from the door, catching her breath a few times in bizarre hiccups. "Well. My goodness. Please come in. My goodness."

"Thank you." Maggie stepped into the house, registering increasing dismay. The place was a shabby mess. Piles of newspapers, catalogs, books and various papers covered every surface and chair. Bookcases overflowed with books stacked vertically, horizontally and on the floor. The smell of wet dog permeated the hallway, and, she guessed, the rest of the house.

It was about as far from her immaculately organized condo in Chicago as any place could get.

"My goodness, look at you." Clara pressed clasped hands to her mouth. "Just look at you. You're so beautiful."

"Oh. Well, thank you." She stood awkwardly under the scrutiny, understanding how necessary it must be. But instead of a wave of daughterly warmth, she felt slightly sick and claustrophobic. And guilty for feeling that way. This woman was her mother. Shouldn't some portion of her subconscious recognize that and be overcome? Overjoyed? All Maggie could manage was overcritical.

"Well I shouldn't stand here staring, come on in, let's find you somewhere to sit." Clara led the way into a small living room that would be cozy and welcoming if it were neat and beautifully arranged. The sofa—in fact, most of the furniture and the floor—was covered with large floral sheets, on top of which were stacked jars and tubes of paints, brushes, palettes, sketch pads.

"You're an artist." In front of a corner window an easel stood, turned to capture the natural light. Maggie headed toward it, wanting to see while dreading what she'd find. What were the chances her mother's paintings would be as odd and haphazard as she was?

"Yes. Well, yes, I am."

Maggie stepped over a tray on which lay the remains of a lunch she hoped had been prepared that same day and turned to look at the canvas.

"It's not finished. Almost. Not quite."

"Oh, how beautiful." The words came to Maggie's lips, but didn't do the painting justice. It was extraordinary. The recognizable figure of a woman, sitting on the ground holding an infant, looking up at a bright red cardinal in the branches of a tree. Lots of colors, very few lines, yet the look of pain and longing on the woman's face nearly brought Maggie to tears.

Her mother was indeed an artist.

"You like it?"

"I love it." Her voice cracked with emotion; she stayed hidden behind the easel until she could regain control. She'd wanted to be an artist, but her adoptive parents hadn't considered sculpting a suitable career. Undoubtedly they were right, though beautiful work like this could still give her a pang of regret along with the pleasure.

"Do you paint?" The hope in Clara's voice was unmistakable.

"I sculpt. Used to, that is."

"You stopped?" Her surprise bordered on outrage, as if she were wondering what kind of true artist would give up the very thing that fed her soul.

Maggie cringed. "I had to make money."

"Oh, dear. That is sad."

"Yes." She suddenly missed the feel of clay and stone under her fingers. "But it's okay. I make a good living, and I'm satisfied."

"Satisfaction is good. Joy is better. What do you do?"

Maggie stepped out from behind the easel, ready this time for the sight of her mother. "I'm an advertising executive."

"Well my goodness." Clara clasped her hands together and nodded, obviously trying to look thrilled at her daughter's choice. "That is impressive."

"I don't know about that. I sort of fell into it. Do you show your work around Princeton?" She desperately wanted the subject changed.

"Oh. No. I don't. No." Clara shook her head so vigor-ously her glasses loosened from where she'd put them back on top of her head and landed on the bridge of her nose. "I don't show anywhere."

"Why not? I should think a local gallery would love to have your paintings. Heck, you might be able to get a show in New York. Do you have an agent?"

"An agent. Goodness no." She frowned severely. "My art isn't about money."

"Oh, but your talent should be recognized. You can always—"

"Now sit down and I'll make a cup of tea. Or well, do you drink tea? What time is it?" She looked at her watch, held it to her ear, shook it and looked again. "That can't be right."

"It's close to six."

"Oh." She squinted at her watch again. "I guess it is. Well, then, six o'clock is cocktail hour in this house. Would you like wine? Or gin? I might have a beer some-where…" She looked around vaguely as if hoping a frosty mug would magically appear.

"I'd like to take you out to dinner. Is Lahiere's still around?" A sudden vision of her mother's half-and-half pajama outfit surrounded by the elegant dark wood and low-ceilinged coziness of one of Princeton's oldest and finest restaurants made Maggie almost want the invitation back. When she had planned to take her mom to dinner…well she'd had a different picture in mind.

"Oh, no, I've waited years to have you at my table. Please don't deprive me of that." Clara headed toward the kitchen, then turned back, nearly tripping over the fold of a sheet. "How long are you staying? I'll make up the guest—"

"Oh, no, don't bother. I'm at the Nassau Inn."

"Oh." Her face fell before she propped it up with a smile. "How long can you stay?"

"I go back Sunday." Right now it seemed an eternity.

"A week at the Nassau Inn? At those prices? Nonsense. You stay here."

"Thank you. That's so sweet. But I…have a thing for…" She glanced around at the mess, wondering if things besides Wobbles crawled through the house at night. "Privacy."

"Ah. Yes, okay." Clara rubbed her head, looking so disappointed Maggie nearly agreed to stay. Except…no.

"But I'd love to have dinner here. And see you every day."

"How nice. Thank you." She smiled, a radiant beam that made her look years younger. Not that she was old; in her mid-forties, probably. "I'll pour us a drink and…now what was I going to have for dinner? Maybe I have a bottle of champagne somewhere…"

Fifteen minutes later, the champagne turned out to be standing in the corner of a cupboard, covered with a thick layer of dust. Maggie was pretty sure champagne should be stored on its side to keep the cork moist. This trip was turning out to be…interesting. She had to continually remind herself to relax her jaw and shoulders. In spite of her efforts, both throbbed with tension. She wanted to be back home in her peaceful, ordered living space with all her emotions intact, and her birth mother a safe, distant fantasy.

"Well, this will be festive." Clara blew on the bottle, then coughed harshly as most of the dust flew into her face. "Now where are my glasses?"

Oh God. "Um. I think you're wearing them…"

"Oh!" She giggled until her face turned flatteringly pink. "No, no, my champagne glasses."

Another ten minutes and the glasses were found in their original box under a pile of canvases in the dining room. Maggie's stomach started growling; her legs were getting shaky. The bag of peanuts on the airplane hadn't done much to substitute for lunch, but she'd been too nervous to eat after landing.

The cork came out with a sad *thwip,* not even a small whoosh of air to reassure them of the presence of bubbles. "Oh dear. Well, I guess this is more like wine than champagne."

Five minutes passed while Clara washed the glasses and put ice into each, heresy for such good champagne. Though without bubbles…

"Here's to our reunion twenty-nine years after our first meeting. I hope it's the first of many." Clara toasted cheerfully, and clinked her glass with Maggie's

"Here's to…this meeting. Yes." Maggie couldn't think of anything else to say. Warm sentiment would sound shallow and false. She didn't think she'd been this un-comfortable in a long time. Even at bad moments at work, she was in her element, in charge, sure of her role in every encounter. She might be related to Clara, but she didn't belong here.

By eight-thirty, with the dining table still bare, Maggie's stomach had turned as sour as the tired wine in her glass. Clara had decided she absolutely must make an elaborate meal to welcome her daughter, and since she was imbibing healthily from the bottle, the details of recipes kept getting confused. She'd provided stale crackers when Maggie finally broke down and asked for something to protect her insides from acid and alcohol, but Maggie didn't want to betray her starvation by emptying the box, stale or not.

"And now, I need…" Clara suddenly threw up her hands. "I haven't got any eggs."

Okay. This was it. They were going to go out to dinner. Or Maggie was going to fake a heart attack and get the EMTs to take her to Burger King.

"I hate you to go to all this trouble, Clara. I'm sure we can still get a table at—"

"Never mind, I'll call my neighbor. Where did I put my phone?"

Maggie counted to ten. Then twenty. Then thirty. At fifty-five, the phone was located under last week's newspaper. By sixty, the number was actually dialed. Unfortunately, Maggie's last hope for cancelling the meal due to lack of eggs was dashed when someone obviously picked up.

"Hello, dear, it's Clara. Be a sweetheart and run four eggs over, would you? I'll pay you back when I go to the store. And I have a surprise for you." She winked at Maggie.

Oh no. An introduction to a neighbor. Small talk. Maybe offering him a drink. Further delay.

"See you in a sec." Clara hung up the phone and giggled. "He'll drop dead when he sees you."

"Really." Maggie clutched her glass of champagne, wondering if it would be rude to grab the eggs and crack them right into her mouth when this guy showed up, because she was the one more likely to drop dead. Forget low blood sugar. She was on her way to no blood sugar.

The doorbell rang while Clara was investigating a burning smell coming from the oven. "Oh dear, I—"

"I'll get it." Maggie put her glass down on a clear corner of the kitchen table and headed for the door, dodging the dog, trying not to roll her eyes. She'd imagined by this time she and her mother would be on the dessert course, pleasantly buzzed on excellent wine, finding they had tons in common, catching up eagerly on the last thirty years.

Not this.

She got to the door, pushing Wobbles away, yanked it open…

And nearly dropped dead, yes. But not from hunger. Standing in her birth mother's doorway, clutching two eggs in each hand was her first love, Grant Conroy.

CHAPTER TWO

GRANT STARED stupidly at the beautiful blonde who answered Clara's door. Several seconds went by before he could wrap his brain around the fact that he was staring at Maggie Chesterton.

"Grant."

"Hi." His voice cracked like a teenager's. The eggs clenched in his fingers were in danger of the same fate. Wobbles pressed blissfully against his legs and nearly knocked him over. A feather could have done it. "What …"

"*You're* Clara's neighbor?" She was obviously as stunned as he was.

"Yes. Who are you?"

Her face fell. "Maggie. Maggie—"

"No, no." He shook his head, nudged Wobbles away. "I meant who are you in relation to Clara?"

"Oh. Well she's my…" Her lungs seemed to run out of air.

She was so beautiful. Too thin and somewhat harder-looking, but—

"*Grant? That you?*"

"Yes." He grabbed on to Clara's familiar voice to ground himself. "I've got the goods."

"You are a lifesaver once again." Clara emerged from the kitchen in another crazy outfit, flour on her hands, a smudge of something red on her cheek. "I'm making a jelly roll, and you can't make those without eggs. Have you met my daughter?"

"Your—" He stared from Clara to Maggie, then tried to move his stare back to Clara but it was stuck on a pair of bright blue eyes with dark lashes that he hadn't expected to be staring into ever again.

"She's Clarissa."

"*You? Are Clarissa?*" He handed the eggs to Clara. "Here. Take these."

"Thank you. Let me pour you some champagne." She turned, then abruptly turned back, fumbling one of the eggs, which Grant managed to catch about six inches from the floor. "Where are my manners? Maggie Chesterton, my long-lost daughter, this is Grant Conroy. Grant Conroy, my wonderful neighbor, this is Maggie Chesterton."

"Grant and I knew each other in high school." Maggie fidgeted awkwardly. She'd changed her hair. It was longer, carefully blown dry and styled. He preferred it going wherever it wanted, but God, she was beautiful. Even too thin and anxious-looking.

Some men held certain girlfriends or lovers in a special category: The One That Got Away. Maggie was his. No matter how many other women he fell for or desired, he couldn't help comparing all of them to her.

"You knew each other?" Clara beamed. "Well, how amazing. My two favorite people."

A sudden hissing and splattering from the kitchen sent her running. Grant and Maggie winced together, waiting for the sound of eggs smashing or boiling liquid sloshing or pots crashing to the floor.

Nothing.

"Well." He turned to her, hands on his hips. Had she

gotten shorter? No, he'd grown—they were kids the last time they saw each other. "This is…a surprise."

"I had no idea you were still in Princeton. I thought you'd be…" She made a vague gesture. "Anywhere else."

He knew what she meant. "Princeton has changed, and so have I."

"Yes. You've really…"

"Grown up?" He hoped she was nervous because she was struggling with emotion and attraction as he was, and not because she'd turned into a stress junkie like her parents. He didn't like the tightness around her mouth and eyes, or the way her fingers tapped against her leg.

"I wasn't going to say that."

"But maybe you were thinking it."

She twisted her lips, the way she did when she was caught in a tough place. "Maybe."

"You'd be justified. I'm not that kid anymore."

"Here we are." Clara reemerged from the kitchen holding a glass of pale liquid on ice, suspiciously bubble-free. "Champagne to celebrate. Grant, you must stay to dinner."

"Dinner?" He took the glass. "It's after nine."

"No. It is?" She looked horrified. "Maggie, you must be famished."

"Oh. Well." Maggie shrugged. "I could eat, yes."

Grant chuckled under his breath. Maggie was probably ready to pass out. At her weight, she'd need food every couple of hours just to keep going.

He took a sip of the diluted, still wine, remembering the first time he saw her, his first day at Princeton Day School, a trial for any "new kid" but worse at a small private school in a small college town he didn't belong to. He'd compensated for his fear by striding up the front walkway looking as angry and tough as he knew how.

Maggie had been outside talking to Kristy Payne,

who'd taken one look at him, whispered something to Maggie and burst into giggles. Maggie had caught his eye, tipped her head quickly toward Kristy and rolled her eyes, including *him* in a joke on her friend. He'd experienced the immediate thrill of attraction, and, given her preppy porcelain perfection, of challenge.

"Come in, come in. I've cleared the table in the dining room. We can begin with soup. Grant, it's so late you're probably ready to eat again. I'll give you half portions."

"Thanks, Clara." He gestured Maggie ahead of him, and couldn't resist touching the small of her back as she passed through the door. Her jeans fit low on her hips and her pink top allowed a glimpse of the firm, smooth skin he'd known intimately.

He wanted to touch her a whole lot more. He always had. Back in high school, every embrace had felt stolen as well as given. Every kiss had been a crazy mixture of right and impossible. A golden girl like her didn't belong with a guy like him. He was a scholarship kid from "Joisey" and she was from Princeton, and everything about the lives they led pointed to the big fat difference.

Two months before graduation, she'd been accepted into Vassar. He'd been about to start a job pumping gas, and with less than no interest in or money for college, he was facing a possible brilliant future of becoming a drugged-out garage mechanic. What hope did he have of holding on to her? She'd be surrounded by guys she fit in with, guys who'd had her same upbringing and opportunities, who could give her the same life she'd always had. What could he give her?

He'd been frustrated, angry, horrible to his mother, worse to his friends. He wasn't going to wait around and get his heart broken. He'd taken her to Marquand Park, and during what she thought was going to be a romantic stroll, he'd dumped her, brutally, saying his feelings had changed. If anything they'd gotten stronger.

Now she was miraculously sitting across from him peering at her oddly colored soup, fingers restless on the table, glancing at Clara and back at her soup, wondering either if food in this house was safe to eat, or whether she could begin yet.

"Please, dig in before it gets cold. I'll get the jelly roll out of the oven," Clara said.

He smiled at the speed with which Maggie grabbed her spoon and brought the soup to her lips. Then looked at him, slightly startled.

He'd had this soup before. Asparagus and leek, boiled viciously until the vegetables were a sickly olive green, scorched and begging for mercy.

"Well." He shrugged and started in on his bowl. "She's an incredible artist…"

Maggie covered her mouth to smother laughter, which made him absurdly happy. She still got his humor.

"How's the soup?" Clara called from the kitchen.

"Just the right temperature." Maggie determinedly spooned more into her mouth. "And…perfectly salted."

"You're a dear. I just whipped it up. Asparagus with leek and a little sour cream. I've made it for Grant before."

"I remember." He grinned at Maggie who was gracious—and hungry—enough to be emptying the bowl. Or did she always attack food as if it would be taken away too soon?

"When did you get here?" He passed her the bread basket containing rolls from the Princeton Shopping Center's excellent bakery.

"About three hours ago." She grabbed a roll and told him the story of the adoption registry between eager bites.

He listened but had to make himself concentrate in order to hear. His mind wanted to wander down memory lane and his eyes wanted to wander all over Maggie. So many years later, she could still disrupt him like no one else. He felt as on edge as she acted, nerves stretched and alive.

Her story unfolded and he managed to pay enough attention to realize she'd formed her first impression of her birth mother in mismatched pajamas in a disaster of a house. Jane Chesterton, Maggie's adoptive mother was one of those women who could throw on a T-shirt and shorts and still look totally put-together, who could open the refrigerator, pull out three ingredients and make something a chef would envy. One of those women half the guys who went to Maggie's house developed a hopeless teenage crush on.

Grant only had eyes for Maggie, which meant to the Chestertons, he was worse than bad news. Jane and Michael must have celebrated for weeks when he broke their daughter's heart and was therefore finally out of her upper class life. Funny how the bitterness lingered.

"So you've only just met your…Clara." He couldn't quite say mother. Clara didn't seem capable of producing her own child. Which, she'd told him, was why she'd given "Clarissa" up. He tried to picture a Maggie raised by Clara and came up empty. Her Chesterton side was so much a part of her.

"Yes. Just now." She looked down into her soup, stirring it around a few aimless times. "So…what do you do now, Grant?"

He felt a pang of sadness on Clara's behalf at the abrupt change of subject, even while he savored the familiar way Maggie said his name, slightly broadening the vowel, which he'd mocked as an aristocratic affectation but secretly liked.

"Grant is director of multimedia design at Princeton."
Clara reentered the room bearing an enormous platter on
which rested a sadly shriveled chicken and a few wrinkled
carrots. "He is superb at what he does. The university types
are beside themselves. They're so lucky to have him."

Grant grinned, used to Clara's somewhat out-of-
control exaggeration, at the same time having to hold
back pride at what he'd accomplished, and nutty hope
that Maggie was impressed. The same impulse that had
him causing trouble in high school—to stand out from
the crowd, since he couldn't with grades or athletic
prowess or breeding. "It's a new job. I moved up and am
still getting used to it."

"You were always brilliant with paper and pen,"
Maggie said.

He ignored the flash of pleasure which other people's
compliments didn't give him to the same degree. "Nice
getting paid instead of getting into trouble."

"I can imagine." Her eyes danced and he knew she was
thinking of his infamous caricatures of faculty and classmates that he managed to post all over the school without
being caught, except for one notable time in the principal's office that nearly got him suspended. Happily, Principal McClellan had a sense of humor.

"How's that soup, Maggie dear?"

"It's great. Thank you." She smiled at her mother, but
Grant could see her reserve. The Maggie he knew would
have looked past Clara's cover to make her judgment—
she'd seen something in *him*, after all—but this new,
older Maggie…who knew what she thought of Clara's
flakiness and disorganization?

"How long can you stay, Maggie?" He desperately
hoped long enough that she could get to know her birth
mother better. What you saw wasn't even close to what

you got with Clara. And yeah, maybe she'd have a few hours left over to spend with him, too. Or a lot of hours.

"A week." Clara patted Maggie's hand, eyes misting over. "Can you believe I found my daughter? Or that she found me?"

"No." His gaze met Maggie's; he experienced a jolt of the familiar electricity. He used to get turned on sitting across the classroom if she happened to look up. "It's amazing."

Her eyes softened, just a flicker. What had changed her? She'd always been high-energy, but not as if the slightest change in the breeze would make her jump out of her skin. He wanted to get her alone and find out how her life had been, whether she was doing what she wanted, whether she was involved with anyone, whether the guy made her happy.

He became aware of Clara watching them speculatively. By now she'd have figured out that he and Maggie had been something more than just "classmates." Intensive matchmaking efforts would result, which sounded fine to him. There was a woman at work he'd been vaguely interested in, but after this short evening Ann already seemed to belong to another galaxy. Maggie did that to him. Some things never changed.

The sad bottle of champagne was quickly drained to give moisture back to mouths sucked dry by the chicken, then a pitcher of water passed and refilled. The jelly roll was sawed through and dutifully consumed, washed down with cups of sawdust-tasting chamomile tea. Grant offered to help with the dishes, but Clara shooed him and Maggie out of the kitchen, insisting that Maggie had to see the remarkable transformation he'd effected on his house, which would mean nothing to her since she hadn't seen it before.

But given the volcano of feelings she'd started in him again, he had absolutely zero objections to getting Maggie Chesterton alone.

CHAPTER THREE

THE LAST TIME—eleven years earlier—Maggie had been anywhere Grant lived, she'd been invited into the tiny apartment he shared with his single mother. Elena Conroy had been flattened by the recent desertion of Grant's father, who hadn't been the best provider and role model even when he'd bothered to be around. Maggie had walked into the cluttered dingy living room, prepared to be her most polite and charming self, to find Mrs. Conroy slumped on the couch in clothes Maggie's mom wouldn't wear to do yardwork.

Jane and Michael Chesterton wouldn't dream of receiving anyone without a perfect house and plenty of food and drink to offer, nor would they dream of letting Grant escape at least five minutes of welcoming conversation on each visit. The first time they met him, even though they hadn't been thrilled with her choice—to put it mildly—they'd made a special point of greeting him warmly, and the get-to-know-you conversation over tea and cookies had lasted a good hour.

Grant's mother had nodded brusquely to Maggie from where she lay watching TV and picked a fight with her son, who had sullenly argued back, using language Maggie couldn't imagine using in front of her parents, even now. She'd been shocked, repulsed and fascinated, aware suddenly of her life of privilege in a way she never had been when immersed in it.

Hadn't she pledged right then to reject everything Princeton stood for, and to dedicate herself to helping others? Hadn't she planned to be a social worker? Sure she had. And a world-famous sculptor. The big dreams of youth.

Grant had scoffed, saying dreams were the stuff of that same privilege she'd been forced to acknowledge so directly. He'd seemed proud not to have any. A place to live, a car and a little extra for beer and cigarettes, that was all he claimed to want from life. She'd never been sure if he was serious or sticking it to her. Or maybe protecting himself from fear of failure.

Look at him now. No sign of failure whatsoever. The house, a beige Colonial, had been lovingly updated. Hardwood was newly refinished, and walls knocked out to create larger spaces. Those remaining had been painted tasteful rich shades of blue, green, ochre and rust, so the flow seemed to evoke sky, sea and land.

"This is gorgeous." It was the type of place she'd love to live. Her own condo seemed soulless and lacking warmth in comparison. She wandered through the soft blue dining room, trailed her hand over the beautifully finished Shaker farm table. "You must love living here."

"The upstairs isn't finished yet. It's hard to find time."

"*You* did this?" Astonishment froze her.

He nodded, hands on his hips, watching her quietly but not able to conceal all his pride. He was so different, so polished, so…restrained. She couldn't quite get used to this new version of Grant.

"I'm even more impressed now. How did you learn?"

"After you left, I was—"

"You mean after you dumped me." The hurt still showed through the teasing remark.

"Yes, but you *left* for college."

"Okay, yes. I did. Go on."

"After our paths no longer crossed…" He made a face and she found herself laughing harder than the joke warranted. "The courts finally pinned Dad down, and Mom got enough money to buy a fixer-upper outside Trenton."

"And you did the fixer-upping?"

"We had a retired neighbor who'd been a cabinet-maker and a lifelong do-it-yourselfer. He taught me a lot. The rest I figured out on my own."

"Wow. I'm amazed. You've really…" She wasn't sure how to ask what inspired him to achieve so much. "You've put a lot into this. Into your life. I mean you've changed. A lot. Which is good. I mean not that you were…uh…"

He quirked an eyebrow. "Need rescuing?"

"Please." She exhaled her relief. "I have no idea how to put this."

"No problem." He walked into the kitchen. "Want some coffee? Tea? Brandy?"

Maggie followed, feeling queasy. It was so odd being with someone she once knew so well, and now…didn't. "I hope I didn't offend you."

"Not at all." He turned from the sink where he was filling the coffeepot and smiled. "I need something to help digest Clara's dinner. Maybe you do, too?"

"A very good idea, yes."

"Then we can sit and talk. If you'd like that."

"I would. A lot. Yes." She closed her mouth before she kept up the string of affirmations. Totally. Completely. For sure. Abso—

"Are you staying with Clara?"

"No, I'm at the Nassau Inn."

"What, the hourly rate motel was full?" He made a face to show he was kidding.

She laughed, glad he didn't seem to see the differences between them as so threatening anymore. Not that there really *were* any differences anymore. And why did that make her feel so oddly vulnerable? "I'll have decaf if you're making it."

"Decaf it is." He ground fresh beans and set the machine going. "Grapes? Cookies? Chocolate? Nothing overcooked, burned or otherwise massacred, I promise."

"No. Thank you, though." She hid her smile. Grant Conroy, the perfect host. It was very nice…and a little disconcerting. Where was her wild rebel? Could people change that much? She certainly hadn't.

"So you wanted to know how I became a functioning member of society." He gestured her to one of the blond wood chairs at his kitchen table.

"I wouldn't have phrased it quite that way."

"I was being flip. It's a natural question." He lowered himself across from her, and the atmosphere changed, she couldn't tell why. Maybe it was the intimate domesticity of sitting together at a kitchen table.

"I loved fixing up the house, and loved even more that I was good at something besides screwing up. But I was still pretty wild. Still drinking too much, smoking, partying harder than was healthy or smart. Or legal." He laughed humorlessly and shook his head. "Typical angry kid. Typical chip on a pretty typical shoulder. Meanwhile, of course, I was thinking I was something really unique in a cookie-cutter world."

"You were unique." The emotion in her voice startled her.

"Among the crowd at PDS? Yeah, probably."

No, that wasn't what she meant. But she didn't know how else to put it without betraying how much she had adored him and how much he hurt her.

"Then Mom had a car accident." He stared down at

the table. "She was in really bad shape. Touch and go for a while."

"Oh, Grant." She was helplessly drawn into tenderness for what he must have gone through. His relationship with his mom might not have been destined for a greeting card commercial, but they were all each other had. "I'm so sorry."

"It was horrible. But suddenly I was responsible for someone else's life instead of just for ruining my own." He shrugged. "So I grew up."

The coffee machine made a rude gurgling noise into the silence, which saved her from bursting into tears.

"Is your mom okay now?"

"Completely recovered, yes." He got up, and took down a pair of navy mugs from one of the beautiful maple cabinets. The masculine grace of his body was familiar, but so little else about him was. "Still take it black?"

"Still." She was pleased he remembered. "Where does she live?"

"In a development just north of town, in Kingston." He poured their coffee—he still took his black, too. "She works in a bank on Nassau Street. I see her at least once a week."

"Devoted son." She let her admiration show in her eyes.

"The accident changed our relationship for the better. You don't ever want to catch yourself being glad someone you love had to go through something like that, but…a lot of good came out of it." He put the steaming mugs on the table and sat, curling his long fingers around his. "So now your turn."

"For what?"

"Why have *you* changed so much?"

"Me?"

He pretended to scan the room. "Anyone else around? Nope. Must be you, then."

"I haven't changed at all."

"Yes." He leaned back in his chair, arms crossed over his chest. "You're different, too."

"How?"

"Well…" He narrowed his eyes, thoughtfully, tipped his head one way and the other as if she were a work of art he was trying to decipher.

She laughed, but the sound was nervous. "If it's so obvious, why can't you say it?"

"You're tougher. Wound up. On edge." His hand landed over her fingers, which she hadn't been aware were drumming the table next to her mug. "Unable to sit still."

"Oh. Well. I… It's been… I'm…" She made the mistake of looking into his eyes, and registering how warm his hand felt over hers. Her mouth closed. She had nothing to say in the first place, and this sudden connection took whatever remained of her brain activity and stilled it as effectively as he'd stilled her fingers.

"Maybe it's just the stress of meeting Clara." He moved his hand over hers in a light caress. "But I don't think so. You wear it like a habit."

She made a huge effort and jumpstarted her mind. "Nun's?"

"Never. Not you."

Even that much innuendo undid her. She took her hand away with the pretense of needing another sip of coffee. "I have a high-pressure job. It's creative, which I enjoy, but…there's a lot going on, and deadlines all the time, sometimes conflicting, and projects to juggle, and staff to manage, and—"

"Shhh." He put his finger across her lips and she realized she'd been speaking faster and faster and her voice had been rising. "You're making me tired just listening."

"Oh, come on." She backed away from his finger. "Your job has long hours, too, I'm sure. And responsibility. And pressure."

"Yes, it does." He got up and brought the coffee back to the table. "A little more?"

"Sure, thank you."

He topped off their mugs and put the pot back on the machine to keep warm. "Remember figuring out how much coffee we'd need to drink to offset all the shots we did on prom night?"

She giggled. "As if *that* would work."

"You're only young and stupid once." He sat down again, grinning. "If you're smart, you don't end up old and stupid, too. What do you do to relax?"

His question startled her. He had this odd way of backing off subjects, then zooming in again when she thought she was off the hook. "Oh. Well, I read for half an hour before bed, and I exercise every day for an hour before work, and once a week I—"

"This sounds like a schedule, not relaxing."

"Ah." She sent him a look. "Sorry it doesn't meet with your approval."

He put his mug down, leaned forward across the table. "Everything else about you does. That hasn't changed."

Maggie took in a long breath. *Then why did you break up with me?* But that was a road she didn't want to drive down tonight. The day had already been too complicated. "Thank you, Grant."

"You're welcome."

She stared into her mug, feeling awkward and out of place in the second house today, a feeling she wasn't used to. He'd spoken matter-of-factly, but her emotional response…maybe it had just been too long since a man complimented her. "So how did you meet Clara?"

"Ah." He straightened again and she felt easier breathing. "Typical Clara story. I was at McCarter Theater one night for a play. My date didn't show and I was about to give up and go in, when Clara comes rushing up, in a panic. She managed to make it on time but forgot her purse."

Maggie laughed. "Somehow I can picture that."

"I offered her my extra ticket and we sat together. At one point I mentioned I was looking to buy a house and she said the one next to her had just gone on sale for a good price."

"And the rest is history. How does she live? I mean if she doesn't sell her paintings?" Maggie asked.

"She inherited plenty from her parents. Let me show you upstairs. You can bring your coffee."

"I will." She pushed back from the table, both relieved and disappointed to be released from the conversation. "Lead on."

The second floor was a work in progress, the bathroom dingy with cracked hideously pink tile. Two empty bedrooms were just that—empty.

But the master bedroom...

The room had beautiful flooring he'd salvaged from homes slated for destruction. Each plank was a slightly different shade, some pinker, some tinged more yellow, others a soft tan. The effect was rich and pleasantly varied. A beautiful cherry bed stood opposite the window, with a matching nightstand, industrial-style lamp and deep brown leather chair with ottoman. The wall behind the bed had been textured and done in a muted deep blue. The adjoining walls he'd painted a warm orange-brown with a bold red stripe at eye level. The bed was made simply with a striped comforter in muted earth colors that picked up the shades in the paint and tied them together.

Good taste, appealing colors and definitely masculine. "Forget graphics, you should have been an interior designer."

"Clara helped. I would not have had the nerve to try out the colors on these walls."

The phone rang and he strode over to the cordless on his night table. She studied his broad shoulder and newly—to her—adult body until she realized that study was leading her to thoughts she didn't want to be having. Not now, anyway.

"Sure. Yes, I have them. They're downstairs, hang on." He walked toward the door.

"Clara needs more eggs?"

"I wish." He rolled his eyes. "Drawings for work. I said I'd bring them tomorrow, but one of my co-workers wants them now."

"Oooh. Tsk-tsk. Sounds like someone is *working too hard.*"

"I'll be right back." He grinned the wide grin that had always undone her.

Guess what? It still did.

Oh boy. To distract herself, Maggie wandered over to examine a print of several women, heavily painted in bright colors. His bookcase was dense with nonfiction and literary books, graphic design books and reference books. A work table sat in the light from a dormer window, papers scattered across its surface, books piled at its legs, the only space not ordered.

The room fit the man he had become. She was almost wistful for the boy she'd known, giving authority the finger, riding his own ride his own way as recklessly as possible. What good little girl wouldn't be drawn to such a joyous expression of unsuppressed living? Had he lost something along the way in his transition to respectability?

She was halfway back to the middle of the room when

she saw it, in the bookcase, used as a bookend. One of her sculptures, a clumsy bust she'd done of herself at his request.

Wow. She backed up, oddly not wanting to go near it, or think about why he might have kept it after rejecting her so cruelly. The edge of the bed hit the backs of her thighs and she sat abruptly, then let herself fall back, feeling an odd jumble of pleasure, despair, longing and frustration. The pain of that breakup had stunned her. Out of the blue, her first experience with terrible grief—she hadn't been convinced she could survive. And now, seeing him again...

A sound made her sit up as quickly as she'd flopped down. Her blood quickened and rose to her cheeks. Grant's no-longer-a-boy's body filled the doorway, one arm up on the jamb, watching her with undisguised heat in his narrowed eyes.

Ohhhh my. There he was. Exactly as he used to be. And she responded exactly as she always had. Her brain turned off and her body revved up, ready to go. She never gave in all the way, didn't lose her virginity until college, but...they'd certainly tried everything else. Given how horrible her first experience had been, and how desperately she'd adored Grant, she'd often wished he'd been the one.

"Maggie."

"Grant..." Her arms folded instinctively across her chest. "Whatever you're thinking—"

"You know what I'm thinking."

"—stop thinking it. I've had a really great day today, but it's been emotionally draining, first meeting Clara, then finding out you, of all people, are her neighbor, and—" *Shut up, Maggie.* "I think it's better not to go there."

"Ever?" He walked into the room, stood beside the bed, hands on his hips, still watching her intently. "Or just now?"

"Is that what you brought me up here for?"

"No." He shook his head, almost regretfully. "But once I saw you lying on my bed…a lot of memories came back."

"Of a lot of years ago."

"True." He rubbed the back of his neck; the look went out of his eyes. He became the civilized man she'd met again that evening. She was grateful and…desperately disappointed.

"We both have changed. Me for the infinitely better and you…whew." Grant shook his head. "I don't know *what* happened to you."

"Ha!" Maggie jumped off the bed. "I'm leaving."

"You need a ride?"

"Not from you. I rented a car. I even know the way still."

He grinned and gestured to the door. "I'll walk you out."

"The perfect gentleman?"

"The sooner you're out of here, the better."

Ouch. Her face fell, she couldn't help it.

"Because…" He stepped closer; her nerve endings were still waiting for his touch. "If you're in my bedroom much longer, Maggie Chesterton…"

"No more gentleman. I get it." She left the room as best she could on seriously weakened knees. Her face was no longer fallen.

He followed her downstairs; she was aware of his body behind her in a totally primal way. Two serious boyfriends after him, a few shorter liaisons, and no one had ever affected her physically like this. What would it be like to make love to him all the way?

She needed to think about something—anything—else. Too much to process today. She needed space and calm to figure out the smart thing to do about Grant.

Outside, the chilly air was still and faintly scented with lilacs. They stopped by her car opposite Clara's house; the atmosphere grew tense with her desire to avoid an awkward good-night, and who knew what emotions on his end.

"Thanks for the coffee, Grant. It's so nice to see you again." She tried to keep her voice light and held out her hand, a stupid mistake. The last thing either of them wanted to do was shake hands, which became obvious when he took gentle hold of her shoulders.

"I want to see a lot of you while you're here, Maggie." He leaned closer. She knew what was coming, didn't make a move to object, but still, the touch of his mouth shocked her. Brief, gentle, so familiar and so strange, too. It sent electricity ricocheting through her body. "Would that be okay?"

"Mmm-hmm." She could barely speak. "That'd be nice."

Oh my goodness. Somehow she managed to get into her car, start the engine and drive away with a casual wave. Totally dazed from one quick kiss—if he did anything more serious, she'd probably go up in flames.

Down, girl. Think about this in logical and practical terms. Yes, it would be nice to see more of Grant while she was in town. He could help her figure out her confusing and eccentric mother. He could give her a good excuse to get away when being a new daughter became too much.

Mount Lucas turned into Witherspoon; she was heading toward Hulfish, then Palmer Square in downtown Princeton, where her lovely room at the Nassau Inn waited.

And he could also turn her carefully controlled life completely upside down.

CHAPTER FOUR

MAGGIE OPENED one eye, then bolted upright. She'd over-slept. She'd be late for work. She was…

…in Princeton. At the Nassau Inn. In a room on the third floor, done in soothing pale colors.

Okay. She put her hand to her still-panicked heart and slid back down onto the beautifully poufed pillows. Yesterday had ended up being one of the most exhausting days of her life. Starting with travel, meeting Clara, rediscovering Grant, and then being assailed with a work crisis the second she arrived at the hotel and checked her messages. Seven of them, all problems, all requiring her intervention, decision, action.

That's what she got for thinking she could be out of touch for a few hours. By 2:00 a.m. she'd gotten everything straightened out, smoothed feathers, typed up about a dozen e-mails, left a few voice mails, took a shower, finally fell into bed…

And couldn't sleep.

Too many emotions whirled, and no matter how often she went through progressive exercises to relax her body, her thoughts refused to calm down.

Around four, she got up and went to the hotel's fitness center, trying to exhaust herself to the point where she could sleep. Another shower, another hour lying in bed trying to think of anything but Grant and Clara, Clara and Grant, and Grant and Grant…

Yeah, good luck. When she finally dozed off she'd even dreamed of him. He'd been chasing her across a field with that familiar heat in his eyes. Maggie had been running away, not in fear but in taunting challenge. Then she'd tired of the game and let him catch her; he'd scooped her up and kissed her with such passion that she'd become wildly aroused, woken up…then had to go through more relaxation exercises to fall back asleep again.

She pushed her hair out of her face. What was her plan? Already 10:00 a.m., she should call Clara and see what time to come over. Today would be easier since Maggie was going to the little house knowing what to expect.

And Grant…

Maggie turned over, rested her cheek on the cool soft sheet, remembering his lips on hers last night, his arms around her, in reality and in the dream. She needed to stay in control, not to allow tender memories to take over her common sense. Meeting Clara had already made her emotionally vulnerable; she was ripe for thinking she was falling for Grant just because she needed support for this complicated reconnection with her birth mother.

The room phone's peal made her jump. She dragged herself out of bed and picked up the receiver, opening the room's curtain to the sunshine. Beautiful day.

"Hi there." Grant's deep voice sent shivers of pleasure through her that she did not want to be having. "How did you sleep?"

"Terribly, you?"

"The same. I couldn't stop thinking about you."

"Oh." Uh-oh. If she admitted she'd been thinking

about him, too, this would get very intense in exactly the way she most wanted to avoid. Grant might have changed, but this was his old go-with-the-feeling behavior and she needed to be on her guard. He'd broken her heart once already; she wasn't going there again. "I had a work crisis. Kept me up for hours."

"You *worked* last night?"

"I had to."

"I thought you were on vacation."

"Yes, but they needed—"

"They needed to remember you're on vacation."

She rolled her eyes. "Are you completely unavailable when you go away?"

"Completely. I wrap my cell phone in foil, bury it in the backyard, then disappear."

"I don't believe you."

"Have lunch with me today?"

Maggie sank into the grey-green upholstered chair next to the phone, sideswiped by the abrupt invitation. She wanted to go. Definitely. But if she saw him every day while she was here, if he kissed her again…then what? She had no desire to re-open old wounds. "I should spend time with Clara today. She'll want me to—"

"She wants you to have lunch with me. I spoke to her this morning to make sure I wouldn't be interrupting any plans. She said she wanted to paint this afternoon, and that we should catch up."

"I see." Maggie wrinkled her nose. She did not like being boxed into situations. Even ones she wanted to be in. Grant had always been a pro at getting her to do what he wanted. Once he decided back in high school that she was going to belong to him, she practically had no say in the matter. "Well…"

"You can't tell me you weren't planning to eat. And I

thought you might appreciate being rescued from one of Clara's meals."

She laughed and felt herself giving in. Lunch wouldn't hurt. She could talk to him then, tell him that while it was great to find him again, she was really here this week to see Clara. "Lunch would be nice, thank you."

"I'll pick you up at Clara's at twelve-thirty."

"Yes. Okay." She replaced the receiver, guiltily giddy. This man had carved Maggie and Grant Forever on a tree by her house and had broken that promise when it no longer suited...

So shoot her, it was just lunch.

Since she was at the phone anyway, she dialed the number Clara had given her the night before, fantasizing that her mother had magically transformed overnight into a fashionista neatnik foodie with an ambitious life plan.

"Hello, good morning, dear. I knew it was you by the way it rang."

Maggie was about to comment on the joys of caller-ID, when she remembered Clara had an old-fashioned land line. "Uh, really?"

"No, I just guessed. I don't get many calls. When are you coming over? I can't wait to see you. Even Wobbles says he's anxious for you to get here."

She laughed nervously. "He said that?"

"Of course not, he's a dog."

"I slept late. I'll dress and be on my way." And make sure she grabbed breakfast from anywhere that wasn't Clara's house.

"Lovely, dear. Can't wait to see you."

Maggie hung up, feeling slightly sick—headachey from lack of sleep, yes, but also...she so wanted to be eager to spend time with her mother, but the thought of entering that cluttered dog-smelling house still didn't do it. Maybe Clara would want to take Wobbles for a brisk walk.

A quick shower and session with the blow dryer to tame her hair, then a trip to Nassau Bagel Company for bagels, orange juice and the largest espresso she could find, and she was again parked across the street from her birth mother's house, noticing today how desperately the lawn needed seeding in some spots, mowing in others. Maybe while she was here, she could help her mother get organized.

The idea cheered her enough to propel her out of the car and to Clara's front door with quick firm steps. She liked goals, tasks, ways to keep busy and productive. This would benefit both of them. And maybe by working in and around her mother's house, Maggie could break through the weirdness of her initial impression of Clara and find common ground between them.

The door opened as Maggie raised her hand to knock. Her birth mother appeared, today dressed in hot pink and black checked knit pants and a yellow turtleneck with glittering silver streaks of lightning and green paint smudges on one shoulder. On her feet were fuzzy yellow and brown cartoon character slippers.

This time Maggie was ready. Stomach and jaw tense, but ready. And actually, she liked this outfit better than the pajamas.

"Good morning, good morning." Clara ushered Maggie in while Wobbles attempted his usual thorough investigation. "Looks like a beautiful day."

"You haven't been out yet?"

"I was reading the paper. What a state the world is in. Makes me want to move to another planet sometimes."

"Very true. I brought you some bagels." She held out the sack, not wanting to hear anymore about her mother's possible access to other planets. "With cream cheese."

"Oh, aren't you nice." Clara took the bag and gazed at it reverently. "We love bagels, don't we, Wobbles?"

Wobbles gave a muted woof, apparently appreciating the sound of his name.

"Come in, sit down and let's have a chat."

"Okay." She walked toward the living room, hoping against hope that her mother had been embarrassed by the state it was in and had cleaned.

Um, no.

"Here." Clara cleared an armful of magazines from the paint-splattered, sheet-covered sofa. "Have a seat. How was your night?"

"Oh. The Nassau Inn is so nice. Beds are very comfortable."

Clara put the magazines down on an already-laden wing chair and turned, concern evident in her eyes. "You didn't sleep."

Maggie's brows lifted in surprise. "How did you know?"

"You look tired, for one." She started counting on her fingers. "Two, you said you'd slept late. Three, you had a hugely emotional day yesterday and were most likely keyed up for hours after you left Grant's. Would you like some tea?"

"No, I just had coffee, I'm fine, thank you."

"Well, sit. We'll have a talk."

"Okay." She sat gingerly on the sofa, aware almost immediately of dust, which must have wafted up when disturbed by her weight.

"So." Clara smiled calmly.

"So." Maggie smiled nervously and had to stop her clasped hands from tapping up and down against her thighs.

"I imagine you want to know about your father and why I gave you up."

Maggie nearly jumped. Nothing like a gradual lead-in. "Uh, yes. Yes, I would."

"He was a wonderful man. And a complete sh—" Her gaze snapped to Maggie. "Um, well, you know."

"Yes."

"Grant reminds me of him a lot." She stared off dreamily. "They have the same animal magnetism, the same underlying bad boy aura. Only Grant has grown up, and I don't think Jake ever would have. He offered to marry me when he found out I was pregnant, but I knew he didn't have the least desire to be my husband, which made me less than enthusiastic to be his wife."

"I can imagine."

"I've lost track of him. Maybe you'd like to find him, too?"

"I…not right now. Not…soon." She could not deal with that much upheaval in this short a time.

"Of course not yet. Well, his name was Jake Crawford. I met him at school and was head over heels in about two minutes. Jake lived for getting in trouble, and for some reason he made me want to get into trouble, too. Which I certainly did." She shook her head, but more with amusement than regret. "Funny how opposites attract like that. I'm still not sure what he saw in me. Probably stability and respectability and a maternal figure, all the things he wanted so badly and at the same time wanted to destroy."

Maggie sat rigid. Clara could be telling Maggie and Grant's story. Had history repeated itself through the generations?

Wobbles dragged himself up to her and thrust his head under her hand, pawing at the sofa and stirring up a new cloud of dust. A sudden burst of claustrophobia made her jump to her feet.

"Can't sit still? Your father was like that."

"Oh. Well, no, but I—"

"Shall we go for a walk?"

"Let's." She had to keep from sounding too relieved.

"Excellent. Wobbles would like that, too."

And he would, but first Clara had to find his leash, which was eventually retrieved from under the bed in the guest room. Then it was necessary to find Clara's hat, which she finally did, squashed flat under a couch pillow and covered with dog hair. Then a tissue was necessary, to tuck in her sleeve, and finally, dark glasses, which were miraculously where they were supposed to be, on top of the refrigerator.

"Now. Off we go."

Maggie followed her outside. "I was thinking that this afternoon, after lunch with Grant, I could help you tidy up."

"Tidy what, dear? Oh what a day, smell that air." She took a long rapturous sniff. "Spring is such a gift every year, isn't it?"

"Yes, it is. I meant your house. I could help you clean."

"Why on earth would you want to do that?"

"I thought…"

Clara patted her on the shoulder. "You're on vacation. I've done my own cleaning for years, no need for you to pitch in."

She began to stroll, so leisurely Maggie itched to sprint ahead and keep circling back. To her a walk meant a chance to get out and stride, arms pumping, heart rate rising, calories burning.

Obviously to Clara this was less of a walk and more of an amble. Maggie had to concentrate on slowing her steps, which made her feel nearly as claustrophobic as she had sitting inside.

"I just thought since there's so much to do that you'd like some help."

Clara didn't answer for a while and Maggie finally glanced at her. Her mother was frowning at the sidewalk. "Is your place in Chicago neat? Spotless?"

"Sort of." She had a bad feeling about this. She'd wanted to help and was terrified she'd offended instead.

"The way I live must be...startling, then. Unpleasantly. Is that why you didn't want to stay with me?"

"No, no." Her heart sank guiltily. "Of course not."

Clara stopped, which forced Maggie to stop and face her. "The truth, Maggie."

"It had...something to do with my decision. But not all."

"Oh dear." She looked so crestfallen Maggie wanted to kick herself; why hadn't she kept her mouth shut? "I feel terrible. If you want me to clean, I can certainly do it. There always seem to be more fun and rewarding things to do with a day, though."

"No, no, please." Maggie put her hand on her mother's soft arm. "Forget I said anything. If you wanted help, I would have been happy to, but it's fine to leave everything the way it is."

"If you're sure it doesn't bother you."

"Yes. I am. Truly." She stared her birth mother down until Clara seemed satisfied Maggie was telling the truth and resumed walking...make that ambling...down the sidewalk.

"I hear you're spending the afternoon with Grant."

"We're having lunch..."

"Oh, yes, that's what I meant. Just lunch. Yes."

Maggie eyed her sharply. She sounded more vague than usual. "He's picking me up at your house."

"Mmm-hmm. Look at that star magnolia. Isn't it beautiful?"

"Gorgeous." She barely glanced, then caught herself and made herself pay attention. Yes, it was truly—

"You were in love with Grant."

Maggie nearly tripped over something that wasn't there. "Way back. Years ago, when I was a kid. In high school."

"I know." Clara stopped opposite a particularly full forsythia bush. "So pretty. I'd love to grow these, but I don't get enough sun. I can't bear to cut down my trees, though."

"No, they protect the house."

"They do, don't they. He's still in love with you now."

She actually gasped, the shock and thrill were that heady. "That's crazy. We haven't seen each other in—"

"Oh, but true love never dies. Didn't you know that?"

"I…well, I mean…" True love? Did people really think that existed anywhere except in fairy tales and people's fevered imaginations? "I don't think… He broke up with me. Poof, his feelings changed."

"Look, a robin. They're so cheering, aren't they?"

Used to Clara careening around subjects by now, Maggie watched it hop across a lawn, cock its head and dart to snag a worm. Life must be so blessedly uncomplicated when your brain was the size of a grape. "Did…Grant talk about me with you?"

Clara picked up a stick and threw it for Wobbles, who dashed off in ecstasy and brought it back, dropping it hopefully at her feet. "No, of course not."

"Ah." Maggie murmured a short prayer of relief. Clara was just painting an overly romantic picture of her own.

"But I have eyes. And he only has them for you."

"Well, we haven't seen each other in…it's natural that he…we have some history that…"

Clara chuckled and put her hand on Maggie's arm. "Don't fight it so hard. Just let it be what it is."

"Let what be what *what* is?"

"He's still in love with you. Accept it."

"How can you—"

"And no one's forcing you."

She was becoming truly exasperated. "To what?"

"Admit you still love him, too."

Maggie's mouth opened and she sputtered several times before she could get any words out. "Clara, I saw him for a total of what, two hours? After ten years?"

"If you insist. Oh look." Clara pointed off down the street.

Maggie didn't even look. She was really very close to done with this woman. Whatever connection she thought they'd established over their similar weaknesses years and years ago for a certain type of man had been thoroughly ruptured over this latest silliness. Grant in love with her? She in love with him? They didn't even know each other anymore. How could Clara possibly—

"It *is* Grant." Clara's happy voice broke into Maggie's internal rant. "I thought I recognized his car, didn't you?"

"Not really." Since she'd never seen it before.

Grant's arm waved out of the window of his green Prius, and his handsome head and shoulders leaned out as he slowed to a stop next to them. Maggie's heart went for a world-record tap dance, and a blush burned up her cheeks.

Great. Clara would notice with her sharp artist's eye and have a field day. And yes, in fact, she'd just glanced at Maggie and was now smiling smugly. Even Wobbles had on a told-you-so smirk.

Honestly.

"Hello there." Grant's eyes were only on Maggie's, and hers didn't seem to want to move away, either. "I left work early and thought I'd swing by, see if you were ready to go now."

"I—"

"She's ready. We were just finishing a nice walk."

Maggie sighed. Apparently she was not going to be allowed to answer the question herself.

"I'll turn the car around. Clara, do you want to join us?"

"Oh, no, no. Wobbles and I have some painting to do, don't we, Wobbles?"

Wobbles barked his agreement.

"Have fun!" Clara turned back toward the house, but not before she sent Grant a conspiratorial wink that had Maggie instantly suspicious. What were the two of them plotting?

"Ready?" Grant leaned over and shoved open the passenger side door, a gesture so familiar she got a lump in her throat. In high school he'd gotten out to open the door of his beaten-up, adored 1974 Dodge Dart until she'd told him she was perfectly capable of opening it herself. They'd compromised this way.

Did he get out and open the door for other women now? The idea hit her strangely, and she scoffed at herself. She'd moved on to other relationships; of course it was natural he would, too.

"I'm ready." She got in and buckled her seat belt. It felt strangely intimate to be in a car with him again. How often had they driven around Princeton, mostly at night after parties or dates? It seemed hard to imagine now that there had been any part of PDS that hadn't involved him, though he hadn't come until junior year. Everyone had wanted to know him, one of the few new kids in a school whose student body was small and mostly static year after year. She'd been so thrilled when he singled her out.

"How are you getting along with Clara?"

"Oh, fine. Fine. She's great." In spite of her effort to put enthusiasm in the words, she caught his glance. "Apparently we were both once attracted to wild men. I guess my father was like you as a teenager."

"Hmm." He looked over at her again; she kept her eyes on the road. "How about after me? What type did you date?"

"No one like you."

"Learned your lesson?"

"Guess so." She didn't add that she'd been attracted to pretty much every guy who reminded her of Grant, but few of them stayed around long enough to count as "dating" and none of them had his brains nor his hidden sweetness. "How about you? A string of 'good girls?'"

"Not a string. A few. Apparently I have a taste for them. You set the bar." He stopped at a light and took her hand, squeezing her fingers. She wanted to pull away, at the same time couldn't bear to lose the contact. And then she made the mistake of turning to look at him, and her cooled-off blush went hot enough to cook eggs on her face. His eyes were so damn intense; she hadn't forgotten, but she'd underestimated how vulnerable she'd still be. "Since we're early for lunch I thought I'd drive you around and see some favorite haunts. Sound good?"

"I'd love it."

He took her first to her old house on Cleveland Lane, and they sat parked across the street while she marveled she'd ever lived in anything so enormous. Until you became a citizen of a larger world, you knew only the world around you. Hers had been a six-bedroom, thousands-of-square-feet house with a pool and tennis court.

"Hey, Maggie." His warm voice made her dangerously fuzzy. "Remember when you snuck out at midnight and we went skinny dipping?"

"How could I forget?" She unbuckled her belt to face the house more fully.

They'd been having an erotically charged swim, tangled together kissing, when a huge—well it seemed huge at the time—frog had taken a leap toward the water and landed on Maggie's shoulder. She'd been so startled she'd screamed. Her parents had heard and charged out for the big rescue. "I thought my father was going to shoot you."

"Not as much as I did." He leaned close behind her to see out her window. "I think I broke laws of physics getting out of that pool."

Maggie giggled madly. "I've never seen anyone move that fast. It took me hours to convince them I wasn't screaming because of anything you did."

"They hated me anyway."

"No." She turned to him, minding and not minding that he was so close. "They didn't."

"Come on, Maggie…" He gave her a be-serious look.

"They liked you, Grant. They just…" She gestured toward the house. "They wanted someone for me who was exactly like them. It's their world, it's all they know. They didn't understand. I don't blame them, not really. They never forbid me to see you. And when you broke my heart, they were actually—"

"Relieved."

She smacked his shoulder playfully. "Not relieved."

"Come on, Maggie." The be-serious look got a comic repeat.

"Okay, okay, maybe on some level. But they were careful not to let me see it. They were very sweet to me. I remember Mom bringing me hot milk one night when I couldn't sleep. She sat with me, stroking my hair, got me tissues and told me men weren't worth it. It was actually one of my best memories of growing up with her."

"Well, see? You have me to thank."

She laughed, then sobered, staring back at the house, white and stately, guarded by ancient oaks, one of which still bore the inscription Maggie and Grant

Forever, and softened by bushes glowing green in the morning sun.

"I wonder how life would have been different if I'd grown up on Mount Lucas with Clara."

"Hard to say."

"If I grew up the way I am now, we would have driven each other crazy."

"Maybe. Or maybe you would have complemented each other." He grinned and touched her cheek, let his fingers rest there. "Like we did. You kept me relatively sane and out of jail and I tried to shake you out of your perfect tidy world and into some messy fun."

She whistled silently, trying for comic effect and to deny the effect his touch was having on her. "You certainly did that."

"It was great, Maggie." His hand cupped the back of her neck. He leaned closer, pulling her toward him. "It was the best."

If she didn't do something *right now*, then he was going to kiss her again, and if he kissed her again, she was going to want him to convince her to take off her clothes right here in his car, the way he used to be able to in high school. Only it was even more of a bad idea now, because thinking over the good times, being back here at her house where they'd spent so much time together, had her feeling even more vulnerable to him than she had before. And then what? They had a hot and heavy week, then she said hey, bye, went back to her life and had to get over him again?

The problem was that none of that seemed to matter when he was so close and his mouth was in the process of matching hers in that perfect, perfect way it always had.

"Please. Grant." Somehow she got the strength to pull away. "Let's keep things platonic this week."

"That means you'll kiss me next week?"

"I don't want to start anything. There's nowhere it could go."

His eyebrows went up. "I've got a couple of ideas."

"No." She'd had to look away before she could make herself sound as if she meant it. "No. It's not a good idea to get involved."

"Okay." He started the engine and pulled slowly away. "If that's what you want."

"It is." She buckled her seat belt, glancing back at the house she grew up in one more time, terribly afraid that she was lying through her teeth.

CHAPTER FIVE

"DESSERT?" Grant glanced at the unfinished hamburger on Maggie's plate, the barely picked-at salad. She'd ordered with such enthusiasm, oh, she was starving, oh, she hadn't had a burger in so long. Then she barely ate enough to keep a squirrel going. No, she didn't want a beer midday, even though Triumph Brewing Company brewed its excellent beer on-site. Beer made her sleepy.

So what if she got sleepy? What did she have to do?

Oh, she wanted to go back and help Clara clean. *Clean? That's* what she wanted to do?

He was worried about her.

"No dessert, thank you." Maggie patted her stomach. "I don't think I could fit anything more in."

"Really." He resisted rolling his eyes. "Well, I could."

He flagged their waiter, wanting to give Maggie a figurative shake. Where was the daring spontaneous girl he'd been so crazy about? He hated to think her parents' conditioning had taken over so completely. Had he been the only one who knew her shadow side and could bring it out? Since then, it seemed she'd gone over completely to the light side.

"Yes sir." The attentive server came right to their booth.

"Dessert?" He was not going to sit here and watch her starve herself, either of food or of life.

"Certainly." The waiter recited the list while Grant watched Maggie's face. When Chocolate Mousse Indulgence Cake was mentioned, her lips parted and her eyes went glassy, a distant relation to how she looked when she was aroused, which he better stop thinking about or he'd have to adjust his pants.

"That cake. Is it a large piece?"

"Enough for an army."

"Perfect. I'll have that. With vanilla ice cream. Two forks. And two coffee-and-cream stouts."

"Excellent. Coming right up."

"Um." Maggie narrowed her eyes. "Grant."

He grinned innocently. "Yes, Maggie?"

"Why are you ordering dessert and beer? For two?"

"Because we're going to toast our past, and doing that with water is depressing."

"Yes, but I said I didn't—"

"I know." He took out his cell and dialed his office, ignoring her annoyance because no serious protests accompanied it. "Hi, Susan. I won't be back to the office this afternoon. Anything important going on?"

His efficient assistant gave him exactly the answer he hoped for. Nothing they couldn't handle.

"See you tomorrow." He put the phone back into his pocket, thinking he hadn't played hooky in far too long.

"What are you doing?"

"Kidnapping you."

"Ah." Her eyebrows rose cynically. "Really."

"Really." He leaned forward, wishing there wasn't a table between them. "First I'm going to get you high on sugar and buzzed on beer."

Her eyes skittered to one side then back to his. "I see."

"Then, Maggie..." He focused on the smooth pale skin of her throat. Then the rose shade of her mouth.

Finally the bright, bright blue of her eyes. "I'm going to take you somewhere I bet you haven't been in far too long."

"Hmm." She tried to look cool but a flush was creeping up her cheeks and she started playing with her watch. He was getting to her. Which was a good thing because she was getting to him. As if no time had passed since they'd been together as almost-lovers, so alike under their obvious differences. "Where is that?"

"Bowling."

Startled laughter. "Bowling."

"Yup." Energy rose, a pure clean shot of adrenaline that had nothing to do with overload or stress. "And we'll rent kayaks and paddle the mighty Delaware and Raritan Canal."

"Ah-ha." She pinched her lips together.

"And…" He tried to gauge her mood, hoping she wouldn't put up a real fight, hoping the Maggie he knew wasn't that far gone. "We'll have dinner at Ajihei if you like Japanese. Then back to my place to talk until we fall asleep. In the morning I'll take you to Pj's Pancake House for—"

"Excuse me."

"Yes?" He faked surprise at the interruption. "You had a question?"

"Do I get a say in any of this?"

"Since when do kidnap victims get a say?"

"Chocolate mousse cake. Two forks." The waiter put a slab of cake down in the center of the table that could feed four people. "And two coffee-and-cream stouts."

"Thank you." Grant nodded to him, still mainlining adrenaline. He hadn't been bowling in a long time, either. Or kayaking, for that matter. He hadn't done much besides work out, go to the office and attend the same social events with the same circle. Who was he to criticize her life? He held up the black, foamy beer. "Here's to our afternoon."

Maggie looked down at the mountain of chocolate cake. "I was going to talk to you about us spending less time together, not more. I'm here this week to see Clara."

"Clara wants nothing more than to see us married and living next door."

"She—" Her horror broke the cake's hold on her gaze. He winked at her, then couldn't look away. Desire rose, sharp and hot.

He put down his beer and loaded a fork with mousse cake and as much ice cream as he could fit without toppling the whole thing over. "Open your mouth."

She glanced at the cake, then at him. Her mouth opened, she leaned forward; he could see the shadow between her breasts. Feeding her cake became less about making her lose control and more about fear he would. To hell with talking; he wanted this night to end tangled and sweaty in his bed, the way he'd fantasized about too many times in the years since he'd booted her from his life.

The cake went in; her lips closed around the fork. He came *this close* to saying forget bowling, forget the kayaks, he was going to drag her back to his place.

"Good?" His voice barely emerged.

"Mmm." She closed her eyes and chewed slowly.

Torture. Profound torture. He reached toward the cake, afraid he was more under her spell than she was under his. "More?"

"No." She picked up her own fork and loaded on a bite as impressively large as the one he'd just fed her. "Your turn."

The cake was moist and rich, the mousse creamy and bittersweet, the ice cream pure vanilla heaven. He savored it slowly, enjoying the way she watched him, color high, a tiny smudge of chocolate on her lower lip.

"Cheers." He held up his beer; their glasses clinked together; they took simultaneous sips. The sweet coffee and roasted malt flavor spread over his tongue.

"Cheers, Grant." She smiled, took another sip, forked up more cake and ice cream for herself this time.

What had changed? He didn't dare question. But some resistance had given way, and he felt like a goofy kid in puppy love. If anyone had asked him yesterday how his life was going, he would have said he had it all. Now it seemed the definition of *all* had changed. And he didn't want to follow that thought any further because it scared the hell out of him.

Between them they finished the entire cake, downed the glasses of stout and emerged into the still-early sunshine of the day, pleasantly buzzed, laughing over a story they'd dug up about the time they'd come home late from a party and had to get Maggie to bed without waking her parents. Somehow he'd gotten a ladder out and up to her window silently enough for success.

He didn't tell her, and he'd forgotten until she brought up the memory, that standing on the ground, watching her gorgeous rear and fabulous legs disappearing inside, then her beautiful head reappearing, waving and whispering good-night between breathless giggles, he'd been swept away by teenage passion and had wanted to ask her to elope with him out that same window, down that same ladder, right then.

Crazy idea; he'd recognized that right away. She was home in one of the six bedrooms in her house, and he'd be offering her half of the pullout couch in his mom's living room. No college plans for him back then, no plans at all besides get through each day, smoke, drink and feel good. That night he'd still struggled against the truth, but looking back he could see the seed had been planted then, the knowledge that he had to let her go. Maggie and Grant would not be forever.

"So what is it, Mr. Kidnapper? Kayaking or bowling first?"

"Kayaking." He took her arm and kept her close to him. "Cooperate and no harm will come to you."

They rented boats at Princeton Canoe and Kayak and paddled leisurely up the tree-lined Delaware and Raritan Canal, which flowed lazily through rural Princeton, then slid into Lake Carnegie.

The weather was perfect, sunny, warm, the trees proudly waving newly leafing branches, showing off their return to green. But the best part of the trip from Grant's perspective was watching Maggie's original purposeful pace relax as the scenery and their conversation distracted her. In the middle of the small lake, she was even content to drift.

Score one for Grant.

By the time they turned the kayaks over to the rental agent, Maggie was sexy and windblown, cheeks pink from sun, eyes heavy-lidded with fatigue. To his surprise and vague discomfort, more than wanting to make love to her, he wanted to curl up with her for a nap. Fine if she brought out the animal in him, but he wasn't anxious to set his heart up for any more pain where Maggie was concerned.

"Hey." He put his arm around her, intending a brief hug as they walked toward his car. When she didn't resist, his arm decided to stay. "Sleepy?"

"Oh, maybe a little. All this fresh air…"

"They don't have fresh air in Chicago?"

She giggled softly. "I don't get out in it as much as I should. Cities, you know how it is."

"Doesn't sound too healthy to me."

"I suppose not."

He was pleased she didn't put up a fight. Either she

was getting closer to seeing his point about slowing down—or she was just too tired to take him on. She was definitely too tired to watch where she was going. "My car's here."

"D'oh!" She got in and buckled herself, yawning. "Bowling now?"

"Soon." He started the engine.

"Somewhere else first?"

"You'll see."

She smiled and settled back into the seat, lids lowering and raising slowly, as if she was dying to give in to sleep. He took Alexander to Mercer down to Lover's Lane, then turned in to Marquand Park. The last time they'd been here, he'd said goodbye.

"Oh, the memories." Her voice sharpened.

"Time to make new ones." He got out and retrieved the blanket he kept in the trunk for unexpectedly chilly evenings, impromptu picnics, extra cover on camping trips and, ahem, yes, in case he was "entertaining."

Sad to say the blanket had been cleaned and returned to the trunk a long time ago.

"Ah, the infamous Conroy bedding."

He ignored the smirk in her voice. "You benefitted many times."

"Yes." She didn't seem to be able to look at him. "I did."

"New memories." He took her hand, led her toward his favorite tree, which had a huge branch grown nearly horizontal, on which they'd sat, legs dangling, many times and talked and talked—he'd never met anyone before Maggie who'd made him feel so worth listening to.

"Nap time." He spread the blanket nearby, under a large spruce.

"Just a nap?" Her suspicious tone raised a big red flag.

"If I wanted to seduce you, Maggie, I'd wait until

tonight when we're at my place with a real bed available and all the privacy we never used to have."

She still didn't look at him. "Is that the goal of this afternoon?"

"No." He was able to speak sincerely, but not for the reasons she might think. "This afternoon is a chance to get to know each other again and have fun in the process."

"Okay." She dared a glance up at him and for a crazy second he thought she looked disappointed. "Okay."

"So…" He sat on the familiar soft plaid wool and patted a spot respectably far away. "You look as tired as I feel."

She nodded and yawned as she sat next to him, closer than the spot he'd indicated, which put his noble intentions in a fair amount of jeopardy.

"This is nice." She lay down and stared up into the gently waving branches of the evergreen above them. "Thank you."

"Sure." He couldn't say much more. The sight of her, limp with fatigue, dark lashes drawn down to her cheek as if they had weights on them, made an impression on his heart as if it were burned on there. Maybe it always had been. He put his arm around her; she nestled her head into his shoulder and he held her as her breathing slowed and became regular, as the blood left his arm and pins and needles took its place. He'd lose a limb if that's what it took to be able to watch her sleeping, to feel her body so near again.

Finally he had to close his eyes himself or he was going to kiss her soft mouth and tell her he loved her, that he'd never stopped loving her and that odds were he never would stop loving her; he'd beg her to move to Princeton, share his bed, share his house, share his life.

He took a deep breath. *Slow down, Grant.* This was about memories of old, old feelings that had blossomed in his youth, when he and Maggie were different people heading for different lives than the ones they had now. He needed to send his overly romantic heart a strong dose of reality.

She made a small sound and snuggled closer, her head slipping off his shoulder so blood started flowing mercifully into his fingers again. He couldn't resist, curled his arm around her back, rested his chin against her hair, and let his body relax into the sweet smell of the pine and grass, the periodic caress of the breeze…

Who knew how much later, he opened his eyes to find her next to him. Waking up to Maggie. He had to shut down his next thought, which was about wanting to wake up to her tomorrow morning, too, and the next, and the next, as long as she was here. Maybe instead of indulging the excitement and lust they generated together, he should drop her back at Clara's after dinner. He hadn't counted on feeling vulnerable to this woman ever again. In fact, he'd sworn after high school that he never would.

"Hey." She moved to roll onto one elbow and winced, hunching her shoulder toward her ear.

"Let me help." He jumped on the excuse, masochist that he was, and pulled her close so he could massage the stiff muscles.

"Mmm, can you do that for the next forever? I won't mind, I promise."

"It's a deal." He worked across her upper back, up into her neck, savoring her soft skin, the tickle of her hair. Then the desire got too strong to touch her everywhere, and he knew he had to stop. Miraculously, his hands obeyed his brain's command to drop. "Ready to bowl?"

"Aww, now who's on a schedule?"

He chuckled. "You want to skip it?"

"What?" She jerked her head around as if he'd suggested she eat small children. "Skip *bowling!*?"

He laughed and pushed himself up, glad he'd escaped temptation relatively easily—and also not. "Okay, then. Let's go."

It wasn't until they were halfway into their first game that Grant remembered how erotic bowling with Maggie could be. She did this little shimmy with her perfect round rear when she prepared for her turn, and dove down the lane with power and grace. The pins couldn't withstand her; they tumbled for her as fast as he had his first day at PDS.

They reminisced and teased each other, drinking coffee to bolster their energy; she even sucked down a bag of chips as if she were eating forbidden fruit. After their second game, they left the bowling alley, still laughing, bumping into each other as if they were drunk, which they probably were, but not on alcohol.

"Want to go right to dinner?"

"I want to shower first. Can you drop me at the Inn?"

"Shower at my place."

"I'd like to change, too."

He probably sounded irrational, but instinct told him not to let her get away from him. "I can lend you clothes."

"Whoa. For what restaurant?"

"We can get takeout." He glanced at her when she didn't answer. She was sitting in his passenger seat with a worried look, fingers back to tapping on her leg. Damn it.

"Maggie." He covered them with his hand. "What is it?"

"I need to check in at work."

A jolt of frustration made him take his hand away and start the engine, putting the car in gear more roughly than he needed to. "You're on vacation."

"As you and Clara keep pointing out." She sighed exaggeratedly. "However, it is my vacation, my job and my life. So if I want to—"

"Point made." He merged onto Route One and headed toward Princeton. "I'll drop you at the Inn."

"Thanks."

He drove them into town and turned into Palmer Square, annoyed that their relaxed chatter had turned into occasional stilted comments.

"So." He pulled up to the Inn and got out to open her door, even though he knew it drove her crazy. Or maybe because he knew it did. "I'll be back in an hour and we'll go to Princeton's best spot for sushi, over on Chambers."

"Sounds good." She hopped out of the car and started briskly toward the Inn's front door, all business.

"One hour, Maggie."

She turned and rolled her eyes. "What, you don't think I can shower and change in an hour?"

"It's all the rest of the stuff you're going to do that takes longer."

Another exasperated look over her shoulder and she disappeared inside.

Grant drove home, the uneasy dark mood persisting. Back at his house, he ignored his blinking message light, showered and changed his jeans for neat khakis and a knit polo shirt, smiling grimly at what his younger self would say, "What happened to *you*, man? You sold out!"

Yeah, well life was more complicated than he, even with his complicated past, could have imagined.

His phone rang. He relaxed when he saw Clara's number. If Maggie blew him off now...

"Hi, Clara."

"I don't want to bother you and I don't want to pry,

but I saw your car come home and I was wondering how your afternoon went."

"But you don't want to pry."

"Of course I want to pry, but it's universally accepted that if you *say* you don't want to pry right before you do, it's somehow more polite."

Grant laughed. "I think you've got that right. The afternoon was nice. We went on a long, slow kayak trip. I even got her to take a nap."

"Well, that is something. Is she still with you?"

"She's back at the Inn changing for dinner."

"You'll have the most beautiful children. One of each, a boy and a—"

"You're sure you don't mind me hogging her for a whole day of your time together?" He didn't want to think about mini Maggies or a child version of himself. More to the point, he didn't want to feel the accompanying leap of excitement.

"Of course not." Clara made a dismissive sound. "You should be with her. She still loves you."

Oh, man. No way did he need or want to hear this. "You think so, huh?"

"I know so. The way she looks at you, reacts to you. Oh yes, I'm quite sure."

"Nice thought." He kept his voice neutral. If Maggie loved him, she'd be here right now, not back at the Inn with her head buried in her job.

"So, dinner now, and then…?" Her suggestive tone was unmistakable.

"Clara…"

"If you want breakfast here tomorrow, I'll be making muffins."

Grant shuddered. He remembered Clara's muffins. "You bought eggs?"

"Oh. Well, no, I forgot. But I finished my painting. And I was thinking…" She cleared her throat. "I'd like to paint my daughter."

Emotion welled up at the vulnerability in her voice. "I think she'd like that."

"I'm not sure."

"Ask her. Or I will, though she'd rather hear it from—"

"Would you?" Her relief was obvious. "I'd appreciate it. You can get an honest response. She'd feel she had to be polite to me. We still know so little about each other."

"I'd be happy to." His phone line beeped. "Clara, I have another call."

"Thank you, Grant. And have fun tonight."

"Thanks." He clicked to the next call, afraid it was—

"It's Maggie." Her voice was too loud and tight.

He leaned wearily against his kitchen counter. "What happened?"

"What makes you think something happened?"

"I know you. What is it?"

"It's work. This complete mess came up, the sales team misrepresented what we could do for a client, and now we're stuck with this project that's half-finished in entirely the wrong direction and I have to—"

"No, you don't."

"I do, Grant. It's my job. It's important. You and I had a great afternoon together. I hope we'll be able to have dinner while I'm here. But I can't tonight. This is going to take hours. They've already been frantic all day because they couldn't reach me."

He set his jaw, trying for perspective. He had crises at work where he had to stay late. He understood that. But while he was on vacation he could handle them with one quick e-mail or call. There were plenty of talented people on his staff who could make do when he wasn't there.

That was how companies ran. But if he tried any kind of power play right now, when Maggie was safely in her element and he was far away, she'd put her foot down and that would be that.

"Okay. Another time is fine." He kept the frustration from his voice. "Have fun."

Her silence told him she hadn't expected him to give in so easily. She'd better be disappointed.

"Grant…you know it's not personal."

"Of course not. Never occurred to me. Work is work."

"Oh. Well. Thank you."

Another silence. He hoped she was beside herself that he wasn't trying to talk her out of it. He wouldn't give her the satisfaction of that martyrdom. If she wanted to do the wrong thing for the wrong reasons, she could do that all on her own.

"So…um, maybe I'll see you tomorrow. After I go to Clara's in the morning."

"Sure."

"I'm really sorry about this. It's just—"

"You don't have to explain, Maggie. I'm a professional too, I completely understand." By some miracle he sounded calm and, more amazingly, sincere.

"Good. Good. Okay. Well…thanks." She sounded miserable. She deserved to.

He hung up the phone, imagining her alone in her room with the panic and responsibility that coworkers had thrown on her to get themselves off the hook. Did it make her feel needed? Powerful? In control? Why did she so desperately want those things? He didn't know. But in spite of what he'd just put her through, it wasn't in his nature to back down and wait.

He wanted answers to those questions as much as he wanted her to learn to value herself and her time more than other people's, something they'd argued about even back in high school. And he wanted to find out why she affected him so strongly even after all these years.

Grant grabbed his phone, dialed a familiar number and pocketed his car keys while he waited for an answer. One thing was sure, he couldn't accomplish any of those things sitting here without her.

CHAPTER SIX

MAGGIE STARED at her laptop. Something was very wrong here. She generally enjoyed a crisis, enjoyed that she was the one people ran to, the one who knew how to finesse a client and fly in with the save-the-day compromises everyone needed and could live with. Exhausting yes, stressful, no question, but ultimately satisfying.

Now that satisfaction had become the equivalent of feeling wonderful because you'd stopped beating your head against a wall. She knew what needed to be done. She could do it. But resentment was creeping…no, racing through her. The call had interrupted one of the most fabulous days she'd spent in a long time. How long since she went with the flow? How long since someone else organized her day and she got to sit back and enjoy it? How long since that person was the ex-love-of-her-life for whom Maggie was developing the beginnings of a dangerous relapse?

Who was Maggie, anyway? Big as the work crisis was, a bigger one brewed in her. She was either going nuts or becoming sane. Was there a Clara inside her dying to get out? Would she stop cleaning her apartment, take up sculpting again and get a smelly dog with a nose built for sexual harassment?

Would that end up being a good thing or not?

Her cell rang; she glanced at the number. George, her assistant. She closed her eyes, wanting the phone to self-destruct. Everyone at Anderson and Dargin must be convinced she was dead or lying in a hospital. When had she ever not answered? When had she ever not been available? Morning noon and night, vacation days, sick days...

"Hello?"

She listened wearily as he outlined staff problems, arguments, childish personality and ego issues.

"George, this is nothing new. Tell Stan the drawings stay the way the client wants them until we have a chance to explain his theory. Tell Darla to kiss up to their VP until I get back next week. And she should absolutely not let Stan speak with him. Clear?"

Yes, it was clear. He promised to handle it and hung up. Maggie's e-mail dinged. Two new messages. One from Stan, one from Darla. She got up and went to the window, heart like a cinder block in her chest. She could be with Grant right now. She could be feeling the way she'd felt all afternoon. Happy. Free. Relaxed.

Her e-mail dinged again. She crossed back through the lovely room which currently felt like a maximum security prison. From Loren this time, the VP at Barkson's Shoes. Maggie opened it and read his version of what an ass Stan was. Stan's e-mail, a version of what an ass Loren was. Darla's, predictably, announced that both Stan *and* Loren were asses.

Okay. This was her job. She had signed on to do it. Time to stop feeling sorry for herself and get busy.

Fifteen minutes and four e-mails later, the room phone rang and she reached absently, trying to figure out who she should—

"What room are you in?"

Grant. Her fingers stopped typing; her breath suddenly had trouble flowing smoothly. "Three-fourteen. Why?"

"Never mind." *Click.*

Maggie frowned at the receiver in her hand. What was that about? Was he going to have something sent up? Flowers? A smile tugged at her lips, first one since she'd been with him earlier today. Flowers would be so nice.

She sent her next e-mail, pulled up a new blank one and smiled goofily at it until she realized what she was doing. Work. Right. On with it.

A knock on the door made her jump. "Delivery for Ms. Chesterton."

Wow. She hurried for the door, all aflutter, and yes, it felt damn good to flutter again. How did he get a delivery guy here that fast?

She opened the door eagerly and gasped. "Grant."

"Ms. Chesterton?"

She couldn't stop grinning. Just the sight of him after she'd been so buried again in her work life was like Dorothy landing in Oz and opening the door of her black-and-white home to her first glimpse of Technicolor. "I'm Ms. Chesterton."

"One Conte's pizza with mushrooms, onions and olives and green peppers…"

"Oh, Grant." Their classic pizza battle—she wanted hers with veggies and he wanted his loaded with every possible kind of meat. "Conte's with vegetables! I'm in heaven."

"Your idea of heaven and mine are different. But only slightly." He produced a six-pack from behind his back. "New Jersey's own Rolling Rock beer. The mountain wouldn't come to Mohammed…"

"I know." She let him into the room, not even hesitating. Work could go to hell. She'd never been happier to see anyone in her life. "I'm sorry. I got swamped."

"Tell them you'll be back when you're back."

"These problems needed handling now."

"So tell them to handle them."

"They can't handle them, Grant. My position is—"

"Okay, wait." He put the pizza and beer down on the room's table, pulled out a bottle, opened it and held it out to her. "Go with me here. What would happen if you didn't help?"

She sat across from him and took the beer. "Stan would go screaming to the client VP, tell him he knows nothing about the market and that the changes he's requested are going to sink the whole campaign. Then the client will be furious, cancel the account, and I'll get fired."

"Really. This Stan guy is so stupid that he'll sabotage a project and jeopardize his own job in the process?"

"He's pretty hot-headed."

"Why hasn't he been fired?"

"He's also very talented."

"Did it ever occur to you that he only has fits because you're there to stop him?" He opened his own beer, took a swig.

"I don't…I mean he's—"

"Tell them you're not available until you're back. Stan isn't stupid enough to ruin the deal. Once you stop enabling the prima donna crap, the prima donna crap will stop itself."

Maggie took a swallow of beer to avoid answering. He'd always done this. Confused her by sounding so sensible when she was so sure she was right. Like when she'd volunteered to help decorate their senior prom and ended up doing ninety percent of the work. He'd told her to do her share and leave the rest. Who cared if the decorations weren't perfect? It wasn't fair that she was stuck with the whole job. If the rest of the committee wasn't willing to help, fine. The prom would go on, decorated or not.

Against her judgment, she'd taken his advice. For about twenty minutes during the prom she'd been mortified by how lame the gym looked. And then…he was right, it didn't matter. Everyone had a great time, including her. Okay, Grant had sneered the whole time because that was his thing, but she was pretty sure he'd had fun doing that, at least.

However, this situation was a lot more important than a decorated-or-not gym for a high school dance. This was her career. As manager, she was responsible for—

"Pizza?" He opened the box, picked up a fragrant steaming slice and handed it to her. She couldn't resist. The crust was thin and chewy, the sauce with just the right combination of zip and sweetness, and the toppings plentiful and fresh, scattered on the rich melted cheese. A person could forget him or herself eating Conte's pizza.

"Oh my God, it's still so, so good."

"*Much* better with various animal products, but okay." He took a healthy bite. "Remember that night we got to Conte's about a minute before they closed and begged for anything they could give us?"

"Yes, I was starving." She took another huge bite, not caring she'd have to talk with her mouth full. "Where had we been?"

"Martha Henderson's. Her parents were away and the party had been going on since noon. We got out just before the cops showed."

"I remember. Thank God. My parents would have killed me. They thought I was at Carol's house for a sleepover."

"We spent the night in the park, eating pizza."

"Double cheese and to hell with our arteries."

"Drank Diet Coke to help keep us awake all night."

Maggie concentrated on her pizza, down already to the crust. They had been awake all night, wrapped in the infamous blanket. That had been the night, the only night in the two years they'd dated, when Grant had asked her to go all the way. She'd finally said yes, and was astounded when he simply grinned and said he was fine waiting. He just wanted to know she was willing, that he was really the one. Maggie had cried, knowing deep in her heart that she and Grant were meant for each other, that they'd be together forever.

Her eyes filled up; she blinked them away. Grinned nervously when she found him watching her with a look on his face that told her he was remembering, too. "Good times, Grant."

"The best, Maggie."

Her phone rang. She sent it a look of pure hatred, which made him chuckle.

"Sorry." She reached for it on the table. "I've got to—"

He put his hand on her wrist. "Don't answer it."

"It may be important."

"Just try. This time. Let your voice mail get it while we're eating. Then if you want, I'll leave right after we're done and you can call them back. Twenty minutes, half an hour, tops."

She hovered half out of her seat, looked at the pizza, at Grant, then at her phone. And sat back down, feeling as if she were embarking on a stroll across a minefield.

"What are you afraid of? That they'll stop needing you?"

"I guess I'm a control freak."

"Relinquish that control, just for tonight." He polished off his beer and put the bottle back in the cardboard holder. "Who knows, you may end up liking it."

"Could be." She was thinking of how often during the

years they were together he'd pushed her to the edge of what she would ordinarily do, and then over. Was that part of what drew her to him so strongly? That he gave her permission to step outside herself?

"I definitely like this." She held up her second piece of pizza, downed it, then her third, thinking that an afternoon of bowling and kayaking had done good things for her appetite. She could barely remember feeling so deeply hungry.

"Clara sends love, by the way."

Maggie jumped on the chance to change the subject. "I'm worried about her. Does she ever leave the house? And has she ever tried to sell a painting?"

He shook his head, looking at her strangely.

"I want to help her, Grant. She seems so lost. I wonder if she's depressed."

When he didn't answer, she looked up from considering a fourth piece of pizza and found him eyeing her with amusement.

"What?"

"I was thinking all those same things about you, Maggie."

"I'm nothing like her. I have a great job, a great apartment in which I can locate anything and everything, and which is not only tidy but clean at all times. I have plenty of reasons to leave my house, lots of friends…"

He was looking skeptical. "Two sides of the same coin. She's too messy, you're too neat. She's always home, I bet you never are. She's not ambitious, you let work rule your life."

Maggie's minefield became very threatening. She didn't want to take another step, not a single one. An angry fear inside her told her rational mind Grant had hit too close to home.

He drew his chair close to hers, took her hands and looked into her eyes, which made her insides tango. "You don't look happy. You're like an overstretched rubber band."

"You just called me a depressed workaholic neat freak, so no, I don't feel so terrific right now."

"I mean in general." He smiled, a slow sensual wicked smile that she recognized all too well. "Cut loose, Maggie. Let it all go. Remember who you were with me? Be that person again. You came so close this afternoon."

She felt the temptation, leaning forward as if he were pulling her. *Cut loose.* "I don't—"

"Look at you." He smoothed a gentle finger over her forehead; she realized only then that she'd been holding it tight. "Worry lines, and you're not even thirty."

"I'm close."

His finger drew down the bridge of her nose to touch her lips, which started buzzing. "Relax here."

She did and realized she'd been bunching her mouth.

"And here." He touched her shoulders, which were up nearly to her ears. "You're a mess, Maggie."

"Thanks a whole lot."

"Come here." He drew her up and over toward the bed. Immediately she pulled back.

"What are you doing?"

"Don't panic."

"I'm not panicking. Who's panicking?" She could hear the panic in her voice.

"You are. Lie down."

"Why?" If he made love to her she'd be lost, swallowed up by…something. She had no idea what she was feeling, only that it was big and potentially beyond her control. "What are you going to—"

"You don't have to know. Cut loose."

Cut loose. She gritted her teeth and lay stiffly on the bed, staring at the ceiling, knowing she must look as messed up as she felt.

"Turn over."

"Why should—" She made a face at him. "Cut loose, I know. Fine. Turning over."

"Now relax."

"I'm relaxed."

"Not even close."

"I'm trying."

"Try this way." His hands began on her shoulders, then did strong sweeps over the muscles of her back.

"Mmm."

"Good?"

"More than."

A few more sweeps, then his fingers concentrated on individual spots, probing and—

"Ow."

"My God, your back is practically macrame." His fingers kept working. "I'm surprised your muscles haven't all snapped."

Maggie sighed. "I suppose you think this proves your theory."

"Beyond reasonable doubt." He pushed at a sore spot and held the pressure. "Now concentrate on relaxing. One body part at a time, head to toe. Clear your mind."

"Yes. Okay." She moved into a more comfortable position and set herself to try. She did pretty well on the relaxing, but her mind would not come close to clearing. Not while hands that had known every inch of her body were exploring that territory again.

Uh-oh. She should stop him now. Because she wanted

to go to that blissful place with this man she was still crazy about more than she wanted just about anything else, and that was not good. Because…

Because…

No, she could remember, she had to remember. It was about him being impulsive, going with whatever he felt. It was about the shock she remembered so clearly, Grant loving her, Grant adoring her, Grant clearly the one, and then in Marquand Park that day, oops, he'd changed his mind.

And yet…he wasn't that boy anymore, not entirely. He had committed to a job, a house, and maybe now he was capable of committing to her.

Was that what she wanted? She didn't know.

"You're tensing again. What are you thinking about?"

She started to make up something about work, or a plan to clean Clara's house, and then his voice came back to her. *Cut loose.*

"I'm thinking about how much I love having your hands on me again. And I'm not sure that's a good idea."

His hands stopped. For a count of five. Then he let out his breath as if he'd been holding it. "Why not?"

"Call it instinct."

"Call it fear. Cut loose, Maggie." His voice was low and mesmerizing. "Don't keep denying yourself what you want out of life or you'll end up not living."

She closed her eyes, totally disoriented. Was he right? Had she shut herself away in the same carefully controlled ivory tower her parents inhabited?

Help.

When Grant's hands started again, his touch changed. His pace slowed, his hands explored her back again, but under her top, the contact between his fingers and her skin deliberately sensual.

"I love having my hands on you again, too, Maggie. You have no idea."

Her body heated to full-blast arousal, like one of those induction stoves that turns red-hot in an instant.

The ring of her phone was torture. Nothing mattered but Grant and this ache for him.

"Want me to answer it?" His hands slid along the edges of her back, nearly brushing the sides of her breasts.

"No." She turned over and pulled off her top. "Turn it off."

In two strides he crossed to her phone, then returned to the bed, sat on its edge, splayed his fingers possessively over her rib cage. He started to speak, then stopped.

"What?" His warm gaze nearly undid her.

"Only this." He leaned down to kiss her; she wrapped her arms around his neck, and in an instant, he was no longer Grant the responsible salary-earning professional. He was her rebel, all muscle and powerful urgency, who unleashed a part of her no other man had ever reached.

"You've only gotten more beautiful, Maggie."

She managed to whisper her thanks, thinking that with Grant she'd always felt beautiful, always felt accepted and cherished, instead of criticized and judged. Until that day at Marquand Park that blew her teenage world apart. She couldn't let him in far enough that he'd be able to do that to her again. She'd never let anyone in that far since.

Cut loose. She turned her brain off, turned off the warning signals as she had so many times on so many adventures with this man. His body was intimately familiar even in its more mature and masculine shape and she dove in, to his scent, to the warmth of his skin and to the joy of being so desired by someone who used to know her so well, someone she didn't need to pretend with.

His hands were large and possessive over her breasts. She didn't want him to stop touching her ever. Ever. His back and shoulders were strong, muscled, sexual. She stroked down the length, over the firm curve of his buttocks, wanting to feel them working on top of her. She was ravenous for this man, and she proved it with her lips and mouth and tongue until he stopped her, put on a condom and pushed her back against the mattress with his body.

"Is this what you want?" He was holding himself off her, breathing fast, arms solid on either side of her head. "Are you sure?"

She met his dark eyes without hesitation, drew her legs apart, pressed down on his lower back to bring him closer. "I'm sure."

Then for the first time ever, slowly, reverently, Grant slid inside her, and a wave of emotion built from her center and crashed over her heart.

It was useless to pretend she had any chance of keeping herself safe. She loved him. She'd never stopped loving him. Even after he hurt her, even after he rejected her, even after she let other men into her life and into her body, it was always Grant.

She'd come to Princeton to find herself in the woman who gave her up, and she'd found herself instead in the man who'd done the same.

CHAPTER SEVEN

"HELLO?" Maggie stuck her head into Clara's front hallway. She'd spent the entire night alternately dozing and making love with Grant, and she was exhausted, exhilarated and a bit sore. He'd dropped her here on his way to work, and she'd discovered Clara's front door wide open and no sign of her.

Her dog, however, lost no time in claiming sniffing rights.

"Hi, Wobbles." Even Maggie's exasperation was good-natured. She felt like a total cliché, starting the evening cranky, repressed and knotted up, and waking after a night of sex humming, stretching and smiling ceaselessly.

Yup. That was her. Cliché come to life.

She'd checked her messages this morning before leaving the hotel—while Grant was showering—and after listening guiltily through several panicked voice mails, miracle of miracles, there came a message from Darla saying they'd come up with a solution and everyone was happy.

Maybe Grant was right. Maybe she could loosen her hold a little, push her coworkers out of the nest. The idea was a little scary, but the fact that she reacted with fear to the idea of freedom only gave more credence to Grant's theory of her martyrdom.

Cut loose.

"Clara?" She heard banging noises from the living room, and a loud thump. *"Clara?"*

"Here, dear!"

Maggie followed her voice and turned the corner. She was so happy today she didn't even mind that her mother was wearing lime-green overalls with a man's brown polo shirt. Then the rest of the room registered. "Wow."

The paint-splotched sheets had been taken off the furniture. The piles of newspaper and books had been cleared away. It even looked as if she'd vacuumed. What's more, the pieces of furniture turned out to be of good quality in colors that complemented the room and each other.

"This is amazing. It's gorgeous!"

"Thank you, dear." Clara ran a dustcloth across a bookcase, looking vulnerable and slightly perplexed. "It's funny. I didn't realize until you said… I mean I'd lived here so long, I got used to it."

"Oh, Clara." Maggie put a hand to her chest. "I'm so sorry, I never meant to make you feel—"

"No, no. It's good that you did. I never thought about how the place must look to other people, and how they must judge me. I suppose I seem like a kook."

"No. No. Not at all." Her voice came out too high and thin.

Silence. Wobbles sneezed. Clara gave her an oh-come-on look.

"Okay. Um. Maybe a little…eccentric."

"I'll take it." Clara smiled, to Maggie's intense relief. "It's good that you came, Maggie. Apparently I needed to be reflected back to myself."

"Strangely enough, I know exactly what you mean." She gestured toward the vacuum cleaner. "Can I help?"

"Of course not." Clara waved her off, bent to pick up a broom that had fallen behind a chair. "You're a guest, you shouldn't have to do my cleaning."

"I'm not a guest, Clara." Maggie was surprised by a wave of genuine affection. "I'm your daughter."

Clara blinked. Blinked again. "Well. Yes. So you are. I guess that's different, isn't it."

"A lot different."

"In that case…" She lifted the broom like a general leading a charge. "To the kitchen."

For hours they scrubbed and dusted and vacuumed, threw away and organized, recycled and repaired. Kitchen, front hall, bathroom, bedrooms. While they cleaned, they talked. About painting, about sculpture, about the creative process, about life in Princeton, life in Chicago, about food and exercise and being female in the twenty-first century. About love and motherhood and family.

Bit by bit Maggie lost her feeling that they'd come from different planets on different orbits in different galaxies. Under her spacey exterior, Clara was obviously tremendously intelligent. And Maggie shared more world and social views with her than she did with her adoptive parents.

"There." Clara brushed her hands together and looked around. "It does look nice, doesn't it?"

Maggie touched her mother's shoulder. "It looks wonderful."

"I feel like a new woman in a house this nice. Maybe I'll even go put on something decent." She shot Maggie a wry look. "Think that's a good idea?"

Maggie nodded, tired in body, giddy in spirit. "Go for it."

Clara reappeared ten minutes later in a long rose-colored sweater that fell to her still-trim hips over a pair of casual black pants. She looked lovely, elegant, and so normal Maggie almost missed the lime-green overalls. Almost. "You're beautiful."

"Nonsense, you're the beautiful one."

"I take after you, then."

Clara's eyes filled. She clasped Maggie to her impulsively. "Having you here, I feel as if I'm coming back to life."

Maggie squeezed her back, smelling lavender and vanilla and thinking she'd never inhaled anything so delicious or so dear. "I feel the same way."

"Grant has something to do with that, I'm guessing."

"Are you?" Maggie blinked innocently.

Clara laughed in delight. "You belong together, my dear, you'll see. But now I have a more important question. When was the last time you ate at Hoagie Haven?"

"Oh boy." Maggie rubbed her stomach eagerly. "Way too long ago."

"My treat. Let's go."

They drove to Hoagie Haven and each ordered a whole sub loaded with cold cuts and soaked in the oil and vinegar dressing that made them so memorable. They took their sandwiches to a bench on Palmer Square and sat in the sunshine, gorging themselves.

"Oh these are so good." Maggie swallowed a mouthful blissfully, wondering why everything in Princeton—that Clara hadn't cooked—tasted so much better than at home.

"Sometimes the best food experiences have nothing to do with being gourmet." Clara took a sip of her Diet Coke. "I'd like to paint you. Would that be okay?"

The question came so suddenly that Maggie needed a few seconds to process her mother's request and react. When she did, it was with a lump in her throat that thickened her words. "Wow. Clara. I'm touched. Thank you."

"I wanted Grant to ask you. I was afraid you'd say no, or be annoyed. But I realized that was a stupid thing to be afraid of and that if you said yes, I'd want it to be to my face, not his. So I called him last night on his way to you and told him not to say a word."

"He didn't." She lowered her sub. Hadn't she and Grant just been talking about not giving in to fear of what might happen? Hadn't he said she and Clara were more similar than she realized?

"So is that a yes?"

"Absolutely. Yes."

Her mother beamed, and for a second Maggie saw herself in her mother's features, which made her beam back.

"Lovely. I'll have Grant take a picture of you. He's a very good photographer among all the other things he's good at."

Maggie pictured herself on her hands and knees suppressing a scream of ecstasy and had to stuff her sandwich in her mouth to stifle a giggle. Yes, he was good at many, many things. "I'd offer to sculpt you but I'm—"

"Oh, Maggie. I'd love that. Or even better, I'd love one of Wobbles. He won't last forever, and it would be great to have him around after he's gone. Thank you."

Maggie opened her mouth to object. She'd been about to refuse. She wasn't up to the job. She didn't have time. Then the thought of the dog's soulful eyes, his noble muzzle—which she wished he'd keep more to himself—being translated into clay under her hands, and she was suddenly and fiercely crazy to try. *Cut loose.* "It might be a disaster…"

"It couldn't be. Moms love everything their kids make, didn't you know that?"

Maggie smiled at the extraordinary woman next to her. "I guess I did."

"So not to change the subject, and not to pry, but—"

"You're going to do both."

"Of course." Clara pulled a strip of lettuce hanging from her hoagie and popped it into her mouth. "What is happening between you and Grant?"

"Oh. Well." Maggie felt herself blushing. "Good things I guess. At least for—"

"Wonderful!" The joy in Clara's voice was a surprise. "I knew he hadn't gotten you out of his system and you hadn't gotten him out, either, had you?"

She took a deep breath. "Not by a long shot."

"Scary?"

"Terrifying."

"Wonderful?"

"More than I dreamed."

"You're in love."

"I guess I am." She put the rest of her sandwich back down on its paper, which was threatening to blow off the bench. A surge of emotion made eating impossible. For one thing, being in love made her prone to both giddiness and tears, sometimes within seconds of each other. She'd forgotten. And for another…she couldn't imagine having this conversation with Jane Chesterton, whom she'd known all her life. Which made her sad.

"Now you need to move back to Princeton."

"Ha!" She sipped her soda. "Not so fast."

"I was serious. Why not? Great hoagies, great men, what's Chicago got?"

Maggie laughed so she wouldn't have to answer.

"Maybe too soon?"

"Just a little."

"Think about it. I'd love it. I *know* Grant would love it. And of course Wobbles."

"Why did you name him Wobbles? Not to change the subject."

"Of course not." She winked a knowing eye. "Well, when he was a puppy he was all over the place. Once I'd laid a yardstick between stacks of books and he tried to cross it. Wobbled all over but he never fell."

Maggie nearly got soda up her nose from laughing. "Weebles wobble but they don't fall down!"

"That's it." Clara finished the last bite of her sandwich and crumpled the paper. "He's a good dog. I'll miss him terribly when he passes."

Maggie's heart sank. She couldn't bear to think of her mom—her *mom!*—alone and sad like that. Of course Clara would have Grant next door. Maggie would be the only one alone, and much sooner than the end of Wobbles's life. "I'm sure you will."

"Well, life and death, it's all part of the bargain. Now." She gave Maggie's knee a gentle smack. "What would you like to do? Take a walk? Run twenty miles? Sightsee? Shop?"

Maggie put her arm around her mother. "How about we just go home and talk?"

CHAPTER EIGHT

GRANT FOCUSED on his assistant, who was looking at him expectantly. Uh-oh. She'd probably asked him something. Come to think of it, she'd probably been talking for the last five minutes. He couldn't remember a thing after, "Hey, good morning."

"Susan, sorry. I was distracted by..." He glanced down at his bare desk. His computer was off. No help anywhere. "Other thoughts about...things."

Susan clearly wasn't pleased, but luckily, since he was her boss, she couldn't tell him where to go, which he probably deserved. All morning he'd been absent mentally, brain stuck in a virtual loop, experiencing again the night of carnal pleasure that had weakened his body and strengthened his heart and mind.

"...because if you don't, then I should—"

Uh-oh. What had she said this time? She was offering him some choice. Maybe about the brochures for—

"Knock knock." The cheerful voice of Ann Baskins, a member of the university's development office saved him. Before Maggie showed up he'd thought he and Ann would get involved eventually.

"Hi, Ann, come in." He sent an apologetic look to Susan who all but rolled her eyes as she left the room.

"Hey, soldier, how's the battle going?"

"Not bad." He indicated the chair in front of his desk.

"I can't sit. If I sit I'll stay. I have to rush off to a meeting, but your door was open so, I thought I'd pop in."

"Glad to see you." She was a very attractive woman. Intelligent, extremely good at her job. Grew up in Princeton, went to Princeton and knew everyone around with money in the bank and how to get them to cough it up. Last time they'd been together for a drink, he'd felt the distinct burn of sexual attraction. Thank God he had the sense to follow his instinct and not show it.

"Looks like Mr. Juno is going to come through with a sizable gift in memory of his wife. I've been after the old buzzard for years."

"Good hunting." Today it seemed completely impossible he'd ever considered getting involved with her. He'd accused Maggie of changing, but maybe he'd let adult responsibilities push him too far from who he was, too. He and Ann had been dancing around each other for months. One look at Maggie and Grant played hooky at the office for the first time ever, got out of his activity rut with kayaking and bowling, and hadn't waited more than two days to take their relationship to the next level. He'd had a few girlfriends in the last ten years and had no complaints in the bedroom. But with Maggie there was so much more.

"Grant?"

Uh-oh. He pulled himself back to the present. "Yeah. Hey."

She looked at him curiously. "Where'd you go?"

"I…nowhere."

"You had this look on your face…" She smiled. "Thinking about me, I hope."

Had he said *uh-oh* enough times yet or was there room for one more? "Oh, well, actually work is sort of consuming at the moment…"

A perfectly plucked eyebrow rose. "You must really love your work."

"Right." He was busted. Better to be honest. "An old girlfriend is back in town and we've had something of a...reunion."

"Gotcha." She grinned lopsidedly. "Lucky girl."

"I don't know about that. But thanks."

She looked as if she were going to say something else, then tapped the jamb of his door smartly and gave a wave before she left.

He hoped he hadn't hurt their friendship or their good working relationship. His life had turned around so quickly. History was repeating itself, but he had enough to offer Maggie this time and no reason to let her go again.

Grant got up from his desk and moved to his window overlooking old Nassau Hall. An odd excitement had gripped him, making it impossible to sit still. Maggie could move back here, to be closer both to him and to Clara. If he could get past her fear, it was the perfect solution. Not only for himself, but for Clara, who deserved a chance to know her daughter. Most especially for Maggie, who needed out of the big city and her pressured job, and into the smaller-town feel of Princeton. Who needed what Clara could give her. And who needed what he could bring to her life.

Yes, he was jumping the gun. All had been roses and light when she left this morning, but emotions changed, and Maggie was off her home turf this week and vulnerable. Once she went back to Chicago, he could see her getting sucked back into the whirlwind of her life and not giving him and Clara serious consideration. Not because she wouldn't want to, but because she'd be spending every second trying to keep up.

So... He watched undergraduates hurrying toward the Firestone Library, probably desperate to cram for upcoming exams.

How could he get Maggie to stay? He didn't know. But out of her one short week in Princeton, only four days remained, one of which was Sunday, the day she flew back.

He walked out to his assistant's desk. "Susan. I'm taking tomorrow off."

Susan's jaw dropped. "Really?"

"Personal day. Would you let HR know?"

"Uh, yeah. Sure." She was obviously trying to figure out where her suddenly irresponsible boss had gone so wrong.

He knew how. After his mom's accident, he'd done everything to prove he could change, that he was mature and responsible, someone she could depend on. He'd gone to college, first at Trenton State, then transferred to Rutgers. He'd gotten a job in a graphic design firm in New York, then burned out on the city and moved back to Princeton, continuing to care for and support his mother even now that she no longer needed him to. Somehow in all of this he'd lost track of himself.

Which meant now that he needed Maggie as much as she needed him.

MAGGIE LEANED HER HEAD back in Grant's car. Was it possible to swell up and burst from conflicted happiness? Because she felt as if she just might. The last two days had been perfect. More than perfect. Whatever ice had been broken between her and Clara had stayed broken. Clara had responded to her clean house by dressing with more care. Together they'd tackled the yard and even given poor Wobbles a bath. In the evenings before Grant showed up, they'd chatted in her backyard holding steaming mugs of tea. Clara was even considering contacting an agent to show some of her work, though she insisted any profit should be donated to charity.

Maggie and Grant had spent blissful days together. Yesterday he'd taken her to Terhune Orchards, where he'd kissed her the first time their junior year. Back then, they'd visited in late fall with friends, a group of them enjoying being kids together away from their parents, feeding the ducks and geese corn available from coin-operated dispensers. The other kids had gotten cold and had gone inside the store for hot cider. She and Grant had stayed outside to dole out one more handful amid greedy honks and quacks.

Maggie remembered so clearly how hot he'd looked in ripped jeans and layered T-shirts and shirts under a frayed jacket. She'd felt so dull and uptight in her neat pants and top and classic hooded parka. She remembered that fierce, almost sexual longing to be the kind of girl who'd capture this wild rebel's attention.

A particularly persistent goose had waddled towards her, and she'd backed away, giggling half in amusement, half in alarm. Grant had grabbed her by the arm with a melo-dramatic shout and dragged her away, running with her past the chicken coop, into the old barn and behind a tractor.

Maggie had been breathless from running and laughter, then suddenly found herself pressed against the wall. He'd stared at her, eyes full of such intensity she'd found out how much more breathless she could become.

"Maggie." His voice had been a hoarse whisper. "What am I supposed to do about you?"

She still remembered her surprise, her disbelief and the burning sensual thrill that had run around her young body when he'd cut off her answer with their first kiss. The memory still turned her on.

After the Terhunes re-visit, he'd taken her to Ajihei, a

little basement restaurant on Chambers Street for the excellent sushi they'd missed the night he brought Conte's pizza to her hotel room. After, they'd gone to the Princeton Shopping Center, and before she knew what was happening—okay, okay, she knew what was happening, but she still couldn't believe at her age that she'd done it—they'd gotten naked again in the little park next to the parking lot.

Sometimes reliving old memories could be really, *really* fun.

Tonight they'd been to Acacia, a wonderful restaurant in the next town, Lawrenceville. She'd been having a fabulous time as always, but running through her happiness was the awful truth. She was going back to Chicago the next day. Most of their evening she'd kept the thought at bay and lived as if there were no tomorrow, but now, with dinner over…

Another painful goodbye for Maggie and Grant.

He turned onto The Great Road, heading north toward their old high school. He seemed unusually keyed up, which fired her up, too. Whatever he was planning, she knew she was going to like it. They'd been to PDS once before, the previous Thursday to take a tour of the new additions and another stroll down memory lane. This time he passed the main entrance to the school and turned onto the road to the skating rink, where he parked, the lone car in the lot.

The facility was lit outside, dark within. Sports fields flanked the building, including the softball field, which was where, on a chilly damp night like this the spring of their junior year, he'd first told her he loved her.

They got out into the cool air, Maggie hardly daring to breathe in the reverent quiet. Her instincts were telling her this wasn't going to be a moment for giggling and arm-punching reminiscences. Mist showed around the rink lights in white cloudy halos. The thunk of their doors closing was loud in the silence. Grant took her hand and led her purposefully to the field behind the rink. Softball. Home plate.

"Familiar spot?"

"Yes." So much of her time with him she remembered in so much detail so many years later. He'd been wearing a black T-shirt bearing the picture of a wavy distorted skull, ripped black jeans and untied black high-top sneakers, his dark hair in its usual curly disarray. She'd driven to the rink in her parents' Mercedes and waited here. At the agreed-on time, he'd come out of the woods to meet her, as if he were a runaway who lived there. His eye had been swelling from a fight with some kid, and he'd been breathing hard, trying not to show his pain and upset.

He'd said her name with desperation that had made her want to wrap herself around him and carry him into her safe and sheltered world. And then he'd said the words, no preamble, no warning, *I love you.* And she, brimming with joy, but struck stupid coming from a family where those words were never spoken, had managed only painful awkward silence, then a mumbled *me, too.*

"Your eye looks better tonight."

"It should by now." He took her hands, facing her with the same runaway-sheltering woods behind him. "I wanted to bring you back here, but it didn't feel right before."

"Oh?" Her jolt of adrenaline rivaled the one she felt that night, but this time there was an element of panic. "What changed?"

"I realized something I probably should have known."

"What's…" Her voice jammed; she had to clear her throat and try again. "What's that?"

"I love you, Maggie. Again. Still. Doesn't matter which."

Air rushed into her open mouth and exited in a long, "Ohhh."

Then again that joy mixed with the awful awkward silence she knew she had to break but couldn't. She loved him. She'd never stopped. But something kept the words she'd never spoken clutched in her throat.

"I want you to think about us together moving forward."

"Yes. Yes, I will. I mean, yes, I want that."

His hands relaxed. She hadn't realized how hard he was gripping her fingers until blood started flowing again unimpeded. "I could move to Chicago."

"Wow." Her heart gave a leap of joy and more panic. Grant in Chicago!

"But there's another solution that is much better for everyone."

"What's that?" She didn't realize her fingers were pulling away from his until he tightened his grasp again.

"You move here. Back home. Be with Clara, your mother. Be with me. You can move into my house, there's plenty of room. Or get your own place if that's too much too fast."

Oh my. This was so wonderful…and so typical. Based on one week of perfect fantasy reunion, he wanted her to change her life completely. Move here, move in.

"Maggie, let's finally take the time to find out what's between us and how far we can take it. You must know it's the right thing to do."

Her heart chilled; she pulled her fingers away. "This is too much, too soon, Grant."

"No fear, Maggie. Cut loose."

"No." She backed up a step. "This isn't getting naked

in the park. You're asking me to make a major change after only a few days together."

"Right." He put his hands on his hips, dropped his head, an exact replica of his sullen younger self. "I just want this so much."

"It sounds…so great. Really. But this week has been a vacation, Grant. A fantasy. I mean it's been amazing, seeing you again and meeting Clara. And yes, I've learned a lesson about me and my life which I will take back with me, but I still need to figure out who I am, where I came from, where I want to go."

"Why can't you do that here?"

She looked around as if someone might be there to tell her how he could be so dense. "Because you're talking about a huge uprooting. I'd have to quit my job—"

"Which makes you miserable."

"Which I love and am good at. I'd have to give up my apartment—"

"Which is lonely and cold. And too neat."

"Which is an excellent investment."

"Investment!" He gave her the you-must-be-crazy look that had always surfaced along with their deep differences. "This is your life you're talking about. Your sanity. Your heart."

"I know. I don't mean to sound—"

"Like your parents."

She laughed bitterly, gestured and let her hands slap back onto her thighs. "Like my parents. But making important decisions on a whim like this…it's crazy."

"Do you love me?"

"I…yes. I mean, this week it feels like I do. But…"

"But." His head dropped again, he kicked at a tuft of grass. Maggie put her hand on his arm.

"What about when I get home? What if this was

just…a temporary revival of something we both found out long ago wasn't meant to be? I don't know. I'm not even me right now."

"You're more you than when you arrived a week ago."

"Point taken. But I can't live my life kayaking and bowling and taking naps in a park. Not even making love with you."

"Whoa. Why not?" He gave her a sidelong grin.

She laughed. "I know, I know. But life isn't like that."

He stepped forward, took her wrists and brought her flush against him, brushed his hand over her hair. "Life should be like that. Since you've been back, we've both changed, both come more alive. I want more of that. Why don't you?"

"Because it's not about acting on what you want at any given moment. It's about responsibility and commitment and following through on things you've—"

He cut her off with a kiss that made her brain melt down and her thoughts scatter. "You want to leave this?"

"No." She pressed her lips together, tried to retrieve her logic. "But as wonderful as this is, as you are, I can't give up everything for it. At least not yet."

He nodded, and nearly broke her heart letting her go. This was their basic difference coming up again. He leaped at life—whatever felt good, whatever made him happy, there he went. He might have found a job, a house, made those commitments at least, but look how he was ready to toss it all after seeing her again for a few days. Look how he expected her to toss it all for him. Look how he'd tossed *her* away after two years together in high school.

She'd been raised with a strong responsibility to others that made her an excellent team player, but, yes, sometimes also a martyr. On his side, circumstances forced him to develop a strong responsibility to himself, which made him fiercely independent, but also self-indulgent. She couldn't turn her back on who she was any more than he could.

"I'll think about it. I promise."

He nodded, and she knew they both knew she wasn't going to move here, and that while they might try to keep the relationship going long-distance for a while, eventually the Maggie and Grant story would end the way it had the last time: in bitterness and disappointment.

CHAPTER NINE

MAGGIE SAT on her balcony overlooking Lake Michigan, trying not to sweat in spite of the record heat. She couldn't bear to be indoors, even if it was beautifully cool there. Inside lurked her laptop and all the e-mails she should return, her bills and her mail from the last four days which she hadn't had time to open. Usually she kept on top of all that stuff. Recently…

At work, another long day of intrigue and the usual mix of successes, failures, progress and setbacks. In the weeks since she'd been back from Princeton, she'd felt unusually detached from the process. The empty, shaky feeling that used to bother her occasionally was now her constant companion. She'd been without Grant for eleven years, seen him for less than a week and had missed him horribly for the last month.

Of course they'd been in touch, but their conversations were haunted by their frustration at not being able to come to a solution satisfying to both, which allowed them to be together. Maggie couldn't see them continuing to beat themselves over the head with the same problem for much longer.

Could she move? Of course she could. But she wasn't yet convinced it was the sensible thing to do. Sometimes, given her recent restlessness and dissatisfaction, she'd ask herself what the hell was stopping her? Just fear? Same old stick-in-the-mud Maggie? Hadn't she learned to look past that?

And yet, there were so many obvious risks. What if her renewed feelings for Grant were just part of the romance of reuniting with an old boyfriend? Wouldn't their old problems ambush them again once the exciting newness wore off? Could she change her entire life just for the hope and the early thrills? Maybe. But wouldn't it be more sensible to try to bring the fun and spontenaiety Grant reintroduced her to back into her life here? Maybe that would be all she needed.

Yes, brilliant plan. So she'd decided. But her rut was extremely reluctant to let her out. Maggie had planned to start sculpting again and had gone so far as to dig out her old tools. Great start, but…she hadn't made it to the store to buy the clay. The picture of Wobbles remained tacked to her bulletin board in the room she called her office, which in a burst of optimism she'd considered renaming her "studio."

Right. Because of all the art she wasn't going to do there. She had an hour before bedtime tonight, and she was so exhausted she couldn't even think of doing anything but sitting here, staring at the water, feeling the heat baking around her—an oven at 9:30 p.m. Even the breeze was hot.

She'd talked to her adoptive mom that morning. She and Maggie's father were fine. She'd complained about a train delay that had fouled up their planned trip to Brighton. Was Maggie working hard? Good, good for her.

Her father had come on the phone. How was the job going? Had she helped land any new accounts lately? How was her bank account faring, did she need any money?

Maggie knew they loved her, of course she did. But… Had they ever just asked if she was happy? And more to the point, why couldn't she tell them she wasn't?

Her cell rang. She fumbled for it and glanced at the screen. If it was someone from work she'd hurl her phone off the balcony and too bad for anyone passing on the sidewalk below.

Whew. Not work. "Hello, Clara. How are you?"

"What's wrong, Maggie? You sound miserable."

"Oh, no, I'm just—" She gestured out into the black depths of Lake Michigan while a surprise rush of tears clogged her throat.

"Having a tough day?"

"Yeah, pretty bad."

"I'm so sorry." Clara made a tsk-tsk noise; Maggie could picture her shaking her head grimly. She was suddenly ludicrously homesick for the time she'd spent with this kooky, wonderful woman. "Things okay with Grant?"

"They're fine. Except that he's there and I'm here."

"Oh, yes." Clara sighed heavily. "Worst part of long-distance relationships is no hugs."

"No kidding." Among other things. She sniffed, feeling horrifically sorry for herself, which was not like her.

"I finished your painting."

Maggie sat up straighter, pleasure giving her a little more energy, even in the heat. "That was so fast."

"I don't have much else to do. I hope you'll like it. Grant promised to take a digital picture and send it to you."

"That would be wonderful. I can't wait."

"I'm going to hang it in my living room so I can see you every day."

Maggie's smile of pleasure sagged at the thought of her mother missing her after such a short visit. And at the thought of her having to make do with a painting after so many years apart. "Thank you."

"I could have done a better job if you'd been here, you know. And even though Grant can get you a photograph of it, you'd like the painting better if you could see it here in person…"

She nodded in the darkness, fighting tears. "I know."

"Maggie. I don't want to butt in, which as you know means I'm going to, but are you happy? I know you're not at the moment, but are you? Do you get up every morning and face the day with joy? Do you revel in your womanhood and in your creativity? Do you nurture your body and soul, or spend hours at a time depriving both? I'm asking you, but I think you also need to ask yourself. Concentrate on what you have, the ways you've chosen to live your life. Would you choose them again?"

The tears won the battle, sliding down Maggie's cheeks; she couldn't speak. What else would she have chosen? How else would she survive? Not by sculpting.

"I consider the years I spent without you as a waste. Not of my life, but of the chance to love someone besides myself. That's what life is about, Maggie. Now I've met you, I'm happier than I've ever been. Because you belong to me, and I love you."

Maggie's tears came harder. She tried to speak and couldn't. She needed to say something. Fill that horrible post I-love-you space her parents left her unable to cope with. A decade ago, had she given up on her own path, her own passion, her own chance at love because it was what she wanted or what they did? Was she living the life she wanted or the one they wanted for her?

"But it's not too late." She spoke forgetting Clara

hadn't been listening to the words in her head and would have no idea what she was talking about.

"Of course it's not. It's never too late."

She did understand. She was Maggie's mom. "I have to go, Clara."

"I'll be seeing you soon, won't I?"

"Yes." She nodded her head, tears now coming down from happiness. "Very soon. And Clara?"

"Yes, my sweet."

Maggie got up and went to the edge of the balcony, focussing east and slightly south, where she imagined New Jersey might be, where the two people dearest in the world to her were waiting. "I love you, too."

GRANT HUNG UP the phone and stalked back into the bathroom on his second floor, which he'd finally gotten around to renovating. His third call to Maggie in the last five hours, and no answer. This was crazy. What kind of relationship was this when he couldn't even reach her when he wanted to talk? He'd encouraged her to be less tied to and dependent on her cell, but not when *he* was calling. Ha-ha.

For the last month he'd been in an agony of frustration. What would it take to convince her to move? He was willing to move to Chicago, but for the problem of Clara being left without both of them. Even Maggie agreed her relocating to Princeton made more sense. Except…she couldn't bring herself to do it. He'd tried very hard to be patient and understanding. Lately, however, he'd been fantasizing about less noble options, like begging, pleading, manipulation and threats. Except he didn't want her to cave and do it for him, he wanted her to do it for herself.

What was the point in stubbornly resisting what she

knew was right? He thought he'd finally proved to her how good it was to jump in with both feet. Didn't she trust they could land safely together?

He was sure they could. And it felt pretty lousy being apparently alone in that conviction. Once in a while, he got the feeling she was seriously considering the move, but her natural caution won out every time.

Grant was coming closer to issuing an ultimatum: choose, or take a break from each other. Because the subject hung over all their phone calls, throwing its shadow even on innocuous conversations. "How was your day? Is it hot there? What are you having for dinner?" While playing in his mind, like a song he couldn't get out, "Move here, be with me. I love you but you're frustrating me to the point of insanity."

He squeezed a thin line of grout to bond the edge of the sink he'd just installed to the new beige tile wall, shaped the paste carefully so it would be even and smooth. Thank God he had work to do here or he'd go stark raving loony.

His doorbell rang downstairs. Grant rolled his eyes. Someone wanted him to donate something or sign something or buy something, or all three. He put the caulk gun down and strode across the hall and into the spare bedroom where he peeked out the window. Unless there was a truck or car outside, he wouldn't bother answering.

An unfamiliar car in his driveway. The doorbell rang again.

"Coming." He thudded downstairs, hoping it wasn't a social call. He wasn't in the mood to chat. Sundays were his work day and he didn't like interruptions.

At the front door, he peered through the peephole.

The door had never opened faster. He was surprised he didn't rip it clear off the hinges.

Maggie.

"Delivery for Mr. Conroy."

He wouldn't stop grinning for the next decade. "I'm Mr. Conroy."

"I've got a large Conte's pizza, sausage, bacon and pepperoni with extra cheese. And…" she pulled something from behind her back "…a six of Rolling Rock, New Jersey's finest."

"Hi, Maggie."

Her brilliant blue eyes softened. She hadn't styled her hair and it framed her face in glorious disarray. His Maggie. "Hi, Grant."

"Should I even bother saying 'this is a surprise' or is my jaw landing on the floor enough?"

"It's enough. Can I come in?"

"Oh yes." He took the pizza and beer and put them down right on the floor, because he couldn't wait to get her in his arms. Why she was here could wait.

Several kisses later, she broke away, laughing. "Aren't you going to ask me what I'm doing here?"

"Not yet." He kissed her again, hands traveling places inappropriate in public. Her breathing changed and she let out the small sound he loved so much, which betrayed her arousal.

"Ask me now."

He sighed, as if her request were a grave imposition, while trying not to show either nerves or too much hope. "Okay. What are you doing here, besides bringing me pizza?"

"I'm here to look for an apartment. And a job. And sculpting clay."

"Oh-h-h, Maggie." He was too scared to allow any happiness yet. "You're sure this is what you want?"

"If you promise not to dump me the minute your feelings change, then yes."

He could only stare, his brain trying to make sense of her words. Dump her the minute his feelings changed? Is that what she thought—

Oh God. That's what he'd told her. "Don't you know why I really broke up with you, Maggie?"

"Sure." She rolled her eyes for comic effect, but he could sense her pain. "You didn't want to go out with me anymore."

"No. God, no. I broke up with you because I would have held you back from the life you were raised to live. I had no prospects, no ambition. I knew in college you'd fall for some pre-law Ivy Leaguer and I'd get shafted anyway. So it was a preemptive strike." He had to look away to grapple with his emotions. *He* hadn't trusted they could land safely together. Not back then. "I might have broken your heart, but I swear, I ripped my own out in the process."

"Grant." She took this in, and he could see what it cost her. His fault all the pain, all their wasted years apart. Then, miraculously, on her beautiful face, the beginnings of a triumphant smile. "And you accused *me* of living too much in fear of what might happen?"

"Touché." Relief made him weak. They were going to be okay. The past was past, and they were about to start their future—delayed, but not destroyed. "See how much we're the same?"

"Except for the pizza thing, which will always drive us apart."

"Tragically." He chuckled because he couldn't stay silent with this much joy growing in him. Maggie was here. She'd come back. "What changed your mind about moving?"

"Believe it or not, Clara finishing the picture of me."

"Uh…you're going to have to walk me through that one."

"I realized it could be months before I saw it. And that once I finally made time to sculpt Wobbles it could be months before she saw it. So here she'd be with a fake piece of me and there I'd be with a fake piece of her, and that's not what either of us wanted."

"I'm glad, Maggie." He was, very glad, for her and for Clara. He also, selfishly, didn't want Clara to be the only reason Maggie decided to move.

"And the next reason…" she kissed him twice and stayed close "…is that I don't want to wait until I'm old to realize I should have taken this second chance to be with you, Grant, but was just too much of a coward. I don't want memories to be all I have of you anymore."

He nodded, too moved to speak right away. How many times had he dreamed of this? "But you came thinking I was an unstable mess who could back out of a relationship at a moment's notice. That's not cowardly."

"No, it's completely insane."

He laughed, resting his forearms on her shoulders, burying his hands in her glorious cloud of hair.

"One more thing, Grant." She wrapped her fingers comfortably around his wrists. "Something I haven't given you yet, that I should have a long time ago."

"Besides meat-loaded pizza?"

"Besides meat-loaded pizza. Three words."

Three words. Grant went still, expectant, feeling as if the rest of his life were about to start.

"I love you."

He knew she did. But given how hard the words were for her, those beautiful lips opening and saying them meant more to him than he could ever tell her. "I love you, too, Maggie. Always have."

"Always will?"

"That's a no-brainer."

"So…" She sidled up to him, all warm curves and promise. "Want to go wild?"

"You need to ask?"

"Let's go upstairs…" she spoke slowly, suggestively "…and have missionary sex in a bed with the lights out."

"Whoa." He pulled her close, surrounded her leg with both of his. "That's almost too wild for me."

"Rather do it on the eighteenth hole at Beden's Brook Country Club?"

"Too long a trip." He turned her toward his staircase. "Let's go crazy and risk the first option."

"I'll get the pizza, you get the beer." She picked up the box and climbed the stairs eagerly, Grant a step behind her. They put the beer and pizza down, already taking off their clothes while tumbling onto his bed.

A lo-o-ong thrilling time later, they sat contentedly side by side against his headboard, having lukewarm pizza and beer. Grant wasn't sure he'd internalized that they had all the time they wanted now. No limits, no end. She wasn't about to go to college or back to another life in Chicago. Her life would be here, with him. He'd wait until she was settled in Princeton, then he'd ask her to marry him, plan some spectacular way to do it that she wouldn't expect, put the ring in the finger hole of a bowling ball or plant it in a Thomas Sweet ice cream cone. Now he still had to pinch himself that this was really happening, but someday soon he no longer would.

"Mmm, I'm stuffed." She licked her fingers and drained her beer.

"Now *that* was a pizza." He patted his stomach with satisfaction. "See, Maggie? Vegetables don't belong on a pizza. They belong in a salad."

"If you say so."

"And you...you belong to Princeton. And to Clara." He kissed her, draped his arm around her shoulders so she was as close as possible to his side. "But most of all you belong to me."

A DAUGHTER'S JOURNEY

Linda Cardillo

For my mother

Acknowledgment

I'm deeply grateful to Aaron Lazare, M.D.,
Chancellor Emeritus of the University of
Massachusetts Medical School, for sharing
with me his family's experience of adopting three
Vietnamese children.

Part One

THE STACCATO TAPPING of the keys on Melanie Ames' portable Smith-Corona was echoed by the monsoon rains beating relentlessly on the tin roof of Mr. Bao's tea house across the alley from Mel's open window. Sweat dribbled down her neck below her cropped, dark brown hair as the ceiling fan cranked ineffectually above her, shoving the moist overheated air from one side of the cramped one-room flat to the other. Mel reached for another Marlboro from the pack in the breast pocket of her loose-fitting shirt. Close up, in the yellow pool of the light cast by the lamp on the table, one could see the slender wrists emerging from the sleeves of the shirt, the delicate bone structure of her face. But from a distance, as she moved in and out of the shadows in a disintegrating Saigon, the casual observer might not notice that she was a woman. It was one of the ways she protected herself. She defined it as making herself invisible, something she had learned as a young girl living abroad with her father on diplomatic missions. People tended not to notice or realize she was there because they didn't expect her to be. And thinking she was not there, they often said or did things she was not meant to hear or see.

She now used that talent in her profession as a journalist. People trusted her: bar girls in the noisy clubs that lined the teeming alleys of the city; shopkeepers; Navy lieutenants who ran river operations in the Delta; South Vietnamese army officers who talked to her over a beer and a cigarette.

Above the night voices of the rain and the ancient fan she heard the far-off reverberation of an explosion, then another. Despite the South Vietnamese government's insistence that it could defend Saigon, the word trickling through the city like the overrun sewers in the monsoon was that, as in Yeats' poem, the center would not hold.

Mel knew it was time to go. But after three years of writing about the country, Vietnam was under her skin. Her pulse beat to the singsong rhythm of its language. And she knew she still had one more story to write in the mounting panic and confusion of impending loss.

Her journalism professor at Columbia had described it as fire in the belly. If you didn't have it, the burning desire to get the story no matter what the cost, you'd never make it in the news business. And Mel knew she had it.

As she hit the return on the typewriter and rolled out the thin sheet of paper with her latest story, she heard tapping on her door.

"Missy! Telephone call for you."

It was late, and there were few people left in Saigon close enough to her to call her here. She followed Mrs. Bao down the narrow stairs to the phone in the teahouse.

"Melly, this is Anh. I call because I have no one else to turn to. Please, I need your help."

Anh was a bar girl Mel had first met when she arrived in Saigon three years before. Where Mel had camouflaged her femininity to work and survive in Saigon, Anh had flaunted hers to the same end. Both had paid a price, and in that had found some common ground to ease the loneliness of life in a war zone, cut off from family. But

Anh had dropped out of sight, and Mel hadn't seen her for over a year.

Her distress on the phone was palpable. She was insistent, a rising note of desperation in her voice that Mel had never heard before. Anh, the one with the veneer of bravado, the silken note of teasing promise, was voicing the despair whispered all over the city.

"I have to see you. Tonight. Can't talk on the phone."

Anh was working and Mel reluctantly agreed to meet her at the bar. She threw on a poncho and hurried the few blocks in the rain to meet her friend.

When she arrived she bought a drink for each of them to appease Anh's boss and Anh sat with her at a battered, sticky table. The place, once swarming with American servicemen and throbbing with Motown music, was nearly deserted.

Anh reached into her purse and pushed a photograph across the table to Mel. She looked at it, a smiling image of Anh in traditional Vietnamese dress (not the miniskirt and halter top that was her working outfit). In her arms was a baby.

"Who?" Mel asked.

"My daughter, Tien."

Mel knew that she and Anh had secrets, pieces of their lives they hadn't shared with one another. But this piece stunned her. Anh, at nineteen, was like a kid sister to twenty-three-year-old Mel. How could she not know Anh had a daughter?

"Where is she?"

"In the St. Agnes Orphanage on the outskirts of the city. I—I cannot care for her. Every month I send money. I thought, when I first left her there, it would be only until the end of the war. But now, I think there will be no end for me. That is why I am turning to you.

"I am thinking, if I can get her out of Vietnam to America, you can find her a family who would care for her. She is half-American. She will have no life here."

"Does her father know about her?"

Anh shook her head. "He died before she was born."

"I don't know what I can do, Anh."

"You are smart, Melly. You have power—your boss in America, your father. Help me. I beg you. There is nothing I am asking for myself. Only for Tien. Please!"

Anh clutched Mel's hand, and in her touch Mel felt a force that she knew would stop at nothing to save her daughter. Mel had already witnessed that force in her friend.

Anh had once saved Mel's life. The first year she was in Saigon, Mel had made mistakes, not knowing whom to trust, where it was safe for a woman to walk alone. She'd been grabbed, dragged into an alley. Anh had seen her attacker, followed them and put the knife she always carried against the attacker's throat, spewing a string of expletives and threats. The boy let go of Mel and ran.

It was after that experience that Mel cut her hair and took to wearing baggy clothes.

Mel knew she could not refuse to help.

"Take me tomorrow to St. Agnes. I'll see what I can do."

The next morning before she met Anh at the orphanage, Mel made some calls. She learned that some American agencies were indeed trying to arrange for adoptions of Vietnamese babies, especially those with American fathers. At least she could try to get Tien onto the list.

The morning rains had eased some when they arrived at St. Agnes. The woman at the door greeted Anh with a cold familiarity. It was clear to Mel that, while the children might be welcomed here, their mothers had earned only disapproval.

The stench of unchanged diapers assaulted Mel when the woman who had greeted them opened the door to Tien's ward. Two dozen cribs, most shared by two babies, filled the room. Mel saw a nun, harried but caring, moving from crib to crib changing diapers. It was quiet. No babbling or even crying followed them as they walked down the aisle to Tien's crib.

Anh reached for her daughter and murmured to her. The little girl, about six months old, was thin and pale, with dark eyes that moved solemnly from Anh to Mel and back again to her mother. She didn't smile in recognition, and Mel had no idea how often Anh had been able to visit.

They took the little girl to a small room where Anh bathed her and dressed her in fresh clothes she had brought with her. Then she fed her with some formula she'd asked Mel to buy.

"They do the best they can with so many children. But I know it's not enough. And can you imagine what they will face when the Americans are gone? You see why I have to get her out!"

Mel left Anh to spend a few more minutes alone with her daughter and wandered through the maze of rooms in the building that had once been one of the villas housing some expatriate merchant during the French occupation. Its former elegance was lost in the aging, dilapidated rooms now crowded with nearly four hundred children. Unlike the nursery, the rooms filled with older children echoed with the shouts and energy of kids cooped up after too many days of rain.

In one room she saw a small group clustered around a man chatting animatedly with them as he examined throats and listened to heart beats.

Mel was surprised to find a doctor. Behind her, the Mother Superior spoke, as if anticipating her question.

"He's Doctor Phillip Coughlin. One of your country-men. An ex-Marine who came back to help us care for the children. He's a gift from God." Then with a wry smile, she added, "And he knows it."

With a swish of her skirts, she walked away.

Mel was waiting for Anh in the vestibule when Dr. Coughlin emerged like the Pied Piper, trailed by several of the children.

He stuck out his hand. "Phil Coughlin. Are you here to help?"

He flashed a smile, his brilliant blue eyes meeting her hazel ones with a direct and intense gaze. Mel imagined that he was one of those people who could walk into a room, address a crowd of people and have each one believe he was speaking only to him or her. He was ar-resting. But rather than finding it attractive, Mel was un-comfortable with his attention focused on her. She felt far too visible. Too vulnerable.

"No. Rather, I'm here to help one of the children. I'm trying to arrange for her adoption."

"Who the hell are you?" Coughlin's welcoming charm had been abruptly short-circuited.

"Mel Ames. *Newsweek* correspondent."

Coughlin was silent for a moment.

"I know your work," he said thoughtfully. It wasn't clear *what* he thought of her work, however.

"You're younger than I imagined. And I didn't know you were a woman."

Mel was used to both perceptions, but they still made her bristle. She had trained herself not to take the bait and simply smiled.

"You could do something more with that pen of yours, you know. You've got the talent, and you've probably got more of an audience than you realize."

She didn't like people telling her how to do her job. She was used to the military, the politicians telling her what she should write, how she should slant an article. She never listened to them. And she had no intention of listening to Phil Coughlin.

"You say you're trying to help one baby. Why that one? Why only one?"

"I've made a commitment to a friend to help her get her daughter on an adoption list. It's a personal request from someone I care about."

"You could save this whole orphanage."

"What are you talking about? You're as naive as my friend. I don't even know if I can get *one* child out of here, let alone hundreds."

"You underestimate your own power. Or you are incredibly selfish, to see only the suffering of one you know and ignore the others."

"I've seen the others. I'm not blind to the need here."

"Then *do something* about it! Of all the people who have walked in here with their hearts on their sleeve bearing boxes of formula or clothing donated from their neighbors, you can do more with your words than a hundred of them!"

"What do you mean?"

"Tell the world about this place—and the tens of others in the city—caring for the children abandoned by their sons and shunned by their mothers' people. Tell the world."

And he walked away, dismissing her.

Despite her dislike of Phillip Coughlin and her resistance to being told what to do, Mel admitted to herself that rescuing one child was not enough. The already desperate conditions in the orphanage, coupled with the uncertain fate of the country, were overwhelming. She still doubted that her words alone could make a difference, but now that she had seen St. Agnes she didn't think she could forget it.

She spent the rest of the morning talking to the Reverend Mother, got a list of contacts and went to the *Newsweek* office in the Hotel Continental on Catinat Street to start making phone calls. She talked to adoption agencies, government officials, her editor in New York.

Within a few days she had accomplished her original mission—one of the agencies agreed to include Tien on its adoption list, provided Anh was willing to sign away her maternal rights. Mel found Anh at the bar that evening.

"Were you able to find a way to save Tien?" Anh's face was tight with hope.

Mel nodded and handed her friend the papers she would need to sign.

"Do you understand what this means? Relinquishing your rights to your daughter?"

"I have no choice, Melly. This is what I must do." She hesitated. "One more thing. I can still see her at St. Agnes, say goodbye?"

"I'm sure Reverend Mother wouldn't keep you away."

Anh's hand trembled as she put her signature on the pale yellow sheets Mel placed on the table. When she was done, she blew on the ink, quickly folded the papers and thrust them into Mel's hands.

"Take them away from me before I change my mind." She got up and strode away from Mel without looking back. At the bar she slid next to one of the few customers, whispered in his ear and then led him onto the dance floor. As Mel left, she saw a vacant, haunted look in Anh's eyes as she melted into the stranger's embrace.

That night in her flat Mel pounded out her story—the

desperate conditions in the orphanages, the excruciating choices and personal cost of the war to women like Anh, the thousands of children who were innocent victims and the individuals who were racing against the approaching North Vietnamese army to rescue them.

She had gotten permission from the Reverend Mother to bring a photographer to the orphanage and had managed to convince one of her *Newsweek* colleagues to take the photos. The next morning she sent the film and the story via courier to her editor in New York. She went back to her flat, thinking she was done.

But she was mistaken. In the short time that she had spent at St. Agnes, its children and the adults caring for them had affected her more than anyone else she had encountered in Vietnam. She found a reason every day to return to the orphanage—sometimes meeting Anh there as she spent her final days with her daughter and other times arriving with whatever she could scrounge from the dwindling number of expatriates in the city.

When her article appeared the following week, it set off an avalanche of concern for the orphans of Vietnam and launched an extraordinary concerted effort to rescue them. Mel was astounded. Her years in Vietnam had hardened the armor around her soul. What she had seen and reported on had accumulated and weighed upon her—young men with broken bodies and shattered minds; an unseen enemy hiding among the innocent; villages burned; trees stripped bare. She had not anticipated that this story of hers would have such impact.

Despite the hopeful activity that followed her story, Mel was suddenly plagued one night by nightmares. But rather than revisiting the horrors surrounding her in the city, her mind thrust her back to her childhood and the day her mother died giving birth to Mel's brain-damaged brother, David, when Mel was ten. Another dream placed her in her grandmother Dessie's house in Georgetown, abruptly pulled from her school in Bonn when her father, devastated by the loss of his wife, shut himself up in his work as a diplomat and took an assignment in the Congo.

The dreams woke Mel up in the middle of the night, the sweat seeping through her thin cotton T-shirt caused by more than the oppressive heat. She reached for a cigarette and went out on the narrow balcony that overlooked the street. In the distance, to the north, she could see flashes of light, a phosphorescence that spread out in the mist.

How many days? She shook off the fears of the child who hadn't understood why she'd been left by first one and then the other parent. There were far more real fears only miles away.

Unable to go back to sleep, she paced until dawn, then dressed and hurried to the orphanage. She told herself with the firefight so near she wanted to make sure that Tien wasn't forgotten in what might be a chaotic departure.

She rang the ancient bell and waited for the shuffling feet of the night porter. The old woman's face registered surprise at Mel's presence on the crumbling doorstep, but let her in.

"Reverend Mother at matins," she announced. "Too early to speak to you."

"I'm not here for Reverend Mother. I came…"

Mel didn't know how to explain the urgency of her trip across the city. It occurred to her that the old woman might very well understand that Mel had been summoned by a dream, but she felt suddenly foolish.

"I came to help with the morning feedings." She finally uttered a reasonable excuse for her unorthodox arrival.

"Okay. Okay. Sister be very happy to see you. You know the way to the babies?"

Mel nodded and made her way across the cracked terrazzo floor to the nursery. Diapers that had been scrubbed so many times they were nearly transparent hung from lines stretched across one end of the room. The smell of urine mingled with sour milk hovered in the room. A single infant was crying and Mel hurried to Tien's crib.

But Tien was still asleep, curled in her corner of the crib, thumb in mouth.

Mel looked around. The sister in charge of the ward must also be at matins. The crying continued, persistent and building to a crescendo that Mel feared would soon wake the other babies. Her eyes scanned the cribs for the needy child and found him clutching the bars of his bed and banging his head against them.

She moved quickly, striding down the narrow aisle between the crammed metal cribs until she reached the screaming little boy. His diaper was soaked and full, and Mel could see little brown rivulets dripping down his legs. She hesitated.

Come on! You've seen a lot worse than this out in the field.

She reached into the crib and picked up the boy, holding him away from the front of her shirt. He abruptly stopped his wailing. Mel remembered a stone sink near the end of the room where the diapers were strung and moved toward it quickly.

She sat the boy in the sink. She turned on the faucet and a trickle of water emerged, but it was enough. When he was clean, she lifted him again, holding him awkwardly with one arm while she grabbed a clean diaper from the line above her head. It had been a long time since she had held a baby. She remembered sitting very still when her grandmother had placed her infant brother in her waiting arms.

"You have to support his head, Melanie. He can't hold it up by himself yet."

She had held her breath, afraid to move the elbow where David's oddly shaped head had rested. He hadn't been a squirming infant, but lay very still, no sign of recognition in his eyes. He looked like her mother.

The child now in her arms was twisting and kicking, his wet skin slippery. The unfamiliarity of this weight and shape against her body was unnerving.

I have no idea what I am doing.

She managed to sort out how to pin the diaper around him and then returned him to his crib, where to her relief he put his head down. She retreated to the sink, found a battered plastic bucket and filled it with water to soak the soiled diaper.

Other children were beginning to stir, although Tien still slept. Mel thought about leaving the nursery, finding some pretext for taking out her notebook. But she stayed, and as babies woke up she repeated the bathing and diapering.

Mel was at the sink rinsing diapers when she saw Phil Coughlin in the doorway at the opposite end of the room, stethoscope around his neck and a small piece of paper in his hand. Mel was surprised that he'd be here at such an early hour. He looked as if he'd had as sleepless a night as she'd had, but she guessed it hadn't been nightmares that had kept him awake. His skin had the gray pallor of too many hours spent in smoke-filled bars and he hadn't shaved. She assumed he'd come directly from whatever nightclub was still serving the remnants of the American community still in Saigon.

She'd heard a few stories about Phil Coughlin since the day he directed her to write about the orphans. A couple of the Marines guarding the embassy had served with him a few years before.

"Phil Coughlin? Man, that guy was a wild man in town. Everybody knew if you were looking for a party, just put a tail on Coughlin and he'd lead you to it. But on duty, there was nobody else in the Corps I'd rather have putting me back together when I got hit. I've seen the guy under fire, hands steady as a robot, blood from a severed artery pumping all over him and he kept the grunt alive. Saved his leg, too."

"What's he doing back in Nam? I was at his farewell party last August. He was joking about some plush job in Boston he had lined up—he was going to be the doc to some big-shot politician's family."

"Why would anybody come back?"

No one Mel talked to had the answer to that question and it was unlikely Phil Coughlin would answer it himself. Her contact with him since the day she'd met him at St. Agnes had been limited to seeing him surrounded by children clamoring for his attention.

From her end of the room, Mel now watched Phil approach one of the cribs and examine a tiny girl with pale, almost blue skin and a bloated belly. She noted how deftly and gently he touched the child, in sharp contrast to Mel's own clumsy grasping of the squirming children she'd been bathing. He made some notations on the slip of paper as Sister Agatha, the nun in charge of the nursery, rushed in.

"I didn't expect you so early, Doctor Coughlin. Matins were delayed because we were waiting for Father Joseph to bring communion."

She was tying a gingham apron around her gray habit as she spoke and pulled a notepad from the pocket. She took a position at his side as they stopped at the beds of the sickest children.

Mel, sweaty and damp, her shirt stained from too many equally damp babies pressed against her, considered easing herself quietly out of the nursery. She suddenly felt like an intruder, an interloper in the domain of those with a far more important mission. She imagined Phil Coughlin would certainly perceive her that way (although Sister Agatha, she hoped, would appreciate the freshly diapered babies, however awkwardly it had been accomplished).

Mel was in no mood for another of Coughlin's condescending remarks. Despite her constant activity and the repetitive, mind-numbing nature of bathing and changing the children, she hadn't dispelled the unease that her nightmares had precipitated. If anything, the work of the last hour had only amplified her sense of the desperation in the orphanage—not only the physical limitations of the crumbling building and its insufficient supplies, but the emotional deprivation of the children. Sister Agatha, as efficient and compassionate as she had to be, was only one person. The babies barely cried because they had learned that no one responded to their cries. They withdrew into a realm of isolation, staring at the patterns of light and shadow made by their own hands.

Mel's brother David had done that. No cooing or smiling or returns of affection. Just a blankness and emptiness where she had hoped to find an emerging personality, a brother who would love her. But in addition to his damaged brain, David was also physically frail. When he was four, his congenitally weakened heart had simply stopped, and he was gone.

Mel shook off the brooding memory. She didn't dwell on losses; life threw too many at you. Soldiers who had shared a shot and a beer on a humid night returning the next day in a body bag; her father receding from her life as he spiraled deeper into his work, unable to recover from his own losses; the boyfriend at Columbia who had resented her winning the *Newsweek* assignment, accusing her of taking a spot that she didn't deserve.

"First of all, you'll never get the kind of stories a man would be able to write. There are places you can't go, people who won't talk to you because you're a woman. And second, even if you're able to get the experience, it'll be wasted on you. You'll come back after a couple of years, get married and decide to stay home with your kids."

Mel had no intention of having children. Her mother's death giving birth to David had sealed that decision. But she didn't tell her boyfriend that. She didn't want to waste her breath trying to justify why she was as deserving as a man to be writing for *Newsweek*. But it was after his resentment surfaced that she decided to use Mel for her byline, not Melanie.

Each of those losses had felt as if someone had punched her in the belly, knocking the breath out of her. She had wanted no more of caring so deeply about anyone that their loss could cause her pain.

She cautioned herself not to allow her concern for the plight of the children of St. Agnes to drag her back to the vulnerability and weakness she had put behind an impenetrable wall of detachment.

She was thinking too much—an observation her grandmother had often made about her growing up. So she thrust herself back into activity. If she kept moving and doing, she distracted herself from such thoughts. That was why she had left her flat so early this morning, driven from the unnamed fears in her bed. There was little in Saigon to occupy her now except the orphans.

She slipped out of the nursery before she had to speak to Coughlin.

On her way back to the front of the house she encountered a girl of about seven.

"Reverend Mother heard you are here. She's looking for you."

Mel followed the girl. She didn't particularly want to be pulled into the superior's circle. Whenever she had seen her, the nun peppered Mel with questions, demanding information she thought Mel had access to. Mel couldn't blame her. The woman, like everyone else in Saigon, was desperate for whatever fragments she could glean to protect her charges.

But this time it was Reverend Mother who had information for her.

Reverend Mother was just returning the phone's receiver to its cradle. Mel saw that her hand was trembling.

"Something has happened." Mel was certain.

The nun's face crumpled in anguish.

"The first planeload of children left Tan Son Nhut this morning. It crashed shortly after takeoff."

Mel felt the nun's words as if a grenade had torn through her chest. She gripped the desk and leaned toward the nun.

"Survivors?" She could barely speak the word.

"We don't know. I got the call from Madame Deng. The children were from her orphanage. They were supposed to be the lucky ones to get out first. She was watching from the terminal.

"I have experienced more than my share of horror in my life, Miss Ames. God has granted me the strength and the will to lift a child bloodied but unharmed from under the body of her mother, who threw herself over her child to protect her. And I've accepted babies from their mothers who cannot return to their families with a dark-skinned child.

"I thought we were doing the right thing—your story, the outpouring of concern, the airlift. How can it be that we are putting these babies in harm's way by trying to bring them to safety?"

She seized Mel's hand, her grip at once both powerful and needy.

"We cannot be deterred by this catastrophe, Miss Ames. We can grieve, we can pray for the souls of those on board. But we cannot stop. You must let the world know that."

At that moment Phil Coughlin burst into the room.

"I just heard. They'll need assistance at Tan Son Nhut if there are any survivors. Ames, if you're finished changing diapers, come with me."

Reverend Mother released her hand. "Do what you can," she said. Behind her wire-rimmed glasses, Mel saw tears welling up in the nun's eyes.

Coughlin grabbed his black bag and Mel followed, adrenaline kicking in after the horror of what she had just learned. She forced herself to ignore his deprecating remark about the diapers. She knew her usefulness in the nursery was limited. There was no need for him to rub it in.

But at the airport she'd be in her element. Amidst the chaos she knew would greet them, she'd find her way. Coughlin was simply a means to get there, and she put aside her anger that he had ordered her to come with him. Once a Marine, she thought, having been at the receiving end of far too many comments intended to intimidate her.

She wasn't expecting their mode of transportation to be a Vespa scooter. Somehow she thought the esteemed doctor would have had access to a Jeep. Reluctantly, she climbed on behind him. At first she gripped the seat, but his speed as he wove through the crowded streets forced her to clasp her arms around his waist.

She hadn't been this close to a man in a long time. She could smell the bite of his sweat, hear the shallow pant of his breathing, feel the accelerated beating of his heart. The intensity of his physical response to the news they had heard echoed hers. She tried to calm herself and prepare for what she knew awaited them at the airport. But she was too aware of Coughlin—his restlessness, his impatience as he raced toward the crash. She hated the sensations rippling through her and pushed them aside. She felt sucked in by him in ways she had never experienced before, and she didn't like it.

When they arrived at Tan Son Nhut, she leapt off the scooter, eager to distance herself from his intensity. But he grabbed her by the hand.

"You won't get through without me, so stick close. If anyone asks, you're a nurse, not a journalist."

She followed him reluctantly, acknowledging that he was right. An agitated mob, witnesses to the crash, pushed up against the chain link fence. Some women were wailing, clawing their way through the crowd, while others stood off on a small rise in a state of profound grief, stunned and motionless. In the distance, beyond the end of the runway, Mel could see billowing clouds of dense black smoke. Sirens wailed.

She plunged forward with Coughlin, his arm now tightly around her, as they made their way to the securely guarded entrance to the terminal. The soldiers were letting no one through except rescue personnel, their faces grim with the strain of holding back the distraught crowd, their weapons raised and ready.

Mel kept her mouth shut with difficulty as she listened to Coughlin, a civilian without authority over them, talk the soldiers into letting the two of them beyond the checkpoint. Even though the soldiers didn't know him, they knew *of* him. But it was more than his reputation—part of which she realized she was responsible for, thanks to including him in her article. The image of a frail child in the arms of the handsome, blue-eyed doctor had been beamed around the world. His vivid commentary had had as much impact as any of her descriptions of the severe plight of the orphans.

"Sergeant, I'm Doctor Phil Coughlin, retired Marine Corps, and the physician to the children who were on that flight. If any of them are still alive, I need to be at their side. I know you understand that. I also know you have orders and if I need to speak to your C.O. to give me permission to proceed, I'm more than happy to do that."

Phil flashed them a smile. Rather than intimidate them, he was professing to understand their position while expecting them to recognize his moral authority. Mel grudgingly admitted that his moral authority was authentic. He cared deeply about those children and believed himself responsible for their very lives.

Mel knew that, had she been alone, she would have been her scrappy, combative, persistent self. She hadn't gotten as far as she had in the few short years she'd been a journalist by making nice to all the people who told her, "No, you can't go there."

But Coughlin displayed a muted self-confidence, absolutely convinced that he had a right to be on the tarmac saving "his" children. Apparently, he convinced the guards as well.

"There's no need to contact the C.O., sir. I have the discretion to let someone as significant as you onto the compound."

"Thank you, Sergeant, in the name of the children."

And with that, Mel and Coughlin were waved through. Once inside the terminal they raced onto the airstrip and grabbed a ride with one of the emergency vehicles heading toward the site of the crash.

The stench of burning aircraft fuel and the thickening smoke engulfed them. Mel looked over at Coughlin and saw that the charming smile had disappeared. In its place was an emotional barrier as opaque as if he had tied on a surgical mask. His whole body leaned forward, poised as if ready to pounce on an attacker.

When the rescue truck came to a halt at the edge of a marsh, Coughlin jumped out, his eyes scanning the smoke-filled, boggy area for signs of activity. He shouted to Mel to stay close.

"I need your help here, Ames. I didn't bring you along so that you could score another journalistic coup. I've already handed you your Pulitzer Prize on a silver platter. Now it's time to get your hands dirty."

"I think I've already earned that stripe," Mel shouted back. She wasn't looking for a story now. She was looking for signs of life.

All around them was chaos—the choking smells, the sounds of screams, the swarm of rescuers trying to get close to the plane, the pulsing of foam cannons on the fire trucks smothering the flames.

Coughlin wove his way through a staggered line of soldiers aiming hoses at the wreckage to a clearing where Mel could see a pile of stretchers near a van emblazoned with a red cross. When they reached the stretchers she could see that they were empty.

The control and focus that seemed to be propelling Coughlin since they had left the orphanage slipped for a few seconds. Mel caught a glimpse of what she took to be despair behind the mask. She began to tremble, absorbing Coughlin's realization as if it were her own. Were there no survivors? She couldn't accept that. Something possessed her—an outrage that she couldn't quell; a surge of unfamiliar strength and invincibility.

She plunged farther into the smoke-filled bog toward what she thought were voices. She couldn't see more than a few feet ahead of her, but she kept moving toward shouts and the frail but definite sound of a child's cry.

She nearly wept when she stumbled into a soldier carrying a child—not the body of a child, but a breathing, screaming child. He thrust the baby into her arms.

"There are more. Parts of the plane are still intact. We're trying to get them out."

Beyond him she could see children being passed from one set of arms to another.

"We're trying to get them away from the plane in case the rest of it blows. Tell the medics in the clearing we've got survivors."

He turned back to the plane.

Mel ran with the baby. Coughlin had followed her and met her halfway to the clearing.

"Survivors coming!" she choked out the words. The despair she had seen in his eyes had disappeared. In its place was something else. Not just relief that some of his children might be alive, but a grudging respect that was directed at her. He took the baby from her and held her gaze long enough for her to absorb that it was meant for her.

She turned back toward the plane to retrieve another child, distracted by the effect Coughlin was having on her. It was as if he had swallowed her emotionally. Each shift in his mood was reverberating through her. She'd been close enough to exploding mines before to have felt the shock waves, and that was what she now compared to the sensations coursing through her. Dangerous. Overpowering.

She steadied herself both physically and emotionally and concentrated on the task ahead of her, forcing herself to act with purpose as the noise and confusion of the rescue mounted. The mud of the bog sucked at her feet and slowed the movements of everyone trying to evacuate the shattered fuselage. She joined a ragged line that was passing babies from the wreckage back to the hastily organized triage area where Coughlin was.

She had no doubt that he had established himself at the center of that operation as soon as she had handed him the first baby. Mel kept her thoughts on moving the children to safety and medical treatment and tried desperately not to react to what was being put in her arms—the bloodied, frail bodies, most of the children in shock. Out of some long forgotten memory, she began singing a lullaby she had learned from her grandmother to calm David when he'd been restless. Someone had dumped a pile of blankets at her feet and she wrapped each child handed to her, crooning to them as she carried the almost weightless bundles to the medics.

Ambulances were arriving and leaving in a steady stream, carrying the most severely injured away. Stretchers had been brought to the wreckage for the adults on the flight. Like the faces of the children, theirs were dazed, stressed, looks of profound disbelief and confusion staring out at their rescuers. Some of them held babies in their arms and Mel couldn't tell if they were alive or not.

She kept putting one foot in front of another, not stopping to process what she was observing, what she herself was experiencing. She had lost track of Coughlin and that was just as well. It was a relief not to be so aware of him. His presence earlier had been a hot breath on her neck, an unwelcome pressure on her heart.

When it was clear that there were no more survivors, Mel's attention shifted to the triage area. Children needed to be held as IVs were inserted; extra hands were called for to stem bleeding or grab supplies.

It was hours before the last ambulance left the marsh. Body bags were lined up, waiting to be picked up and delivered to a temporary morgue. The chaos and noise of the rescue had given way to a hollow emptiness as the enormity of what had occurred began to seep through the clearing. The adrenaline that had been sustaining everyone was rapidly diminishing, and with its loss came the exhaustion and pain that had been held at bay throughout the day.

Mel's head jolted up with the roar of a plane taking off again from Tan Son Nhut. She could hear shelling to the north and realized it must have been going on as always. Time had been frozen for her, and she had believed that all else had stopped around her. The understanding that the world had gone on while she had been in the middle of a nightmare filled her with loneliness. Who would understand what she had experienced today, what she had lived through in the last three years?

She felt a hand on her shoulder and was too numb to even flinch.

"You're going to need a ride home. I asked one of the MPs to bring my Vespa up here from the terminal."

He pointed to the muddy scooter leaning against the wheel of a truck.

She was going to refuse, not willing to put herself once again in close contact with him. But she was bone tired, and a quick glance around convinced her she'd have to search a while for transportation. Reluctantly, she followed him to the bike.

"You surprised me today, Ames. Usually the members of the fourth estate around here are merely observers—and not very accurate ones. You also held it together pretty well, for all that you saw. As far as I could tell, nobody had to hold your head while you lost your breakfast."

"I had no breakfast to lose," Mel answered. It no longer surprised her that, even in apparently complimenting her, he managed to dismiss her because of her profession. As far as she could tell, Phil Coughlin was willing to see some slight value in journalism only when it suited his own ends.

She'd saved lives today, damn it, not holding a pen in her hand but cradling barely breathing children and bearing them to safety. Why did Phil Coughlin's grudging acknowledgment of what she'd done chafe so much? She tried to attribute her vulnerability to fatigue and hunger. But she sensed that these feelings, however unwelcome, were not going to disappear with a meal and a night's rest.

"We both could use something to eat, not to mention a shot of scotch. There's a noodle shop a few doors from my flat. I'll buy you dinner."

He pushed down on the kick-starter and they took off into the dusk, Mel's "No thanks" muffled by the low rumble of the bike.

She had no idea where Coughlin lived, but hoped it was near enough to her own neighborhood to get home under her own power. She was more tired than she realized and found herself leaning against his back, damp with sweat and reeking of the fumes that had billowed from the wreckage. It should have been off-putting in many ways, but there was a familiarity and comfort that tugged at her and she didn't pull back. She caught a glimpse of herself in his side mirror. Her face was streaked with soot and her shirt, already christened from the diaper changing early that morning, now bore witness to the hell she had thrashed through in the marshes. She wanted a bath; she wanted a hot bowl of noodles; she wanted her bed, however haunted it had been the night before.

The night before. How long ago that was! The dreams that had disturbed her now seemed childish and embarrassing compared to the true nightmare the orphans today had suffered through. Her reverie came to an abrupt halt as the motorbike skidded to a stop in a narrow alley somewhere in District 1.

The stop threw her off balance, thrusting her closer to Coughlin. She stayed that way a few seconds longer than she meant to, aware of her breasts beneath the loose-fitting shirt pressed against his back. Realizing what she'd done, she released herself from her hold around him and quickly jumped off the bike, turning her head away so that he wouldn't see how red her face was. Not from embarrassment, but from anger with herself. How could she be throwing her body at him—a man who seemed to find her as annoying and useless as she found him insufferable. She needed to get a grip on herself, get some food into her belly and get home.

She ignored the soft smile on Coughlin's face as he pushed open the rickety screen door to the noodle bar. With dismay, Mel saw that it had no tables—not even a counter with stools. It was takeout only. She'd thought this was going to be simple—a bowl of noodles surrounded by other diners who also looked upon the meal as no more than necessary nourishment, not as a social engagement. But now she had to add to her already overwhelmed brain the question of where she and Coughlin were going to eat.

That worry was replaced for a few minutes by the

aromas drifting from the bubbling pots on the stove in the corner of the cramped and crowded shop. Coughlin steered her to the front, his touch on her arm as deft and gentle as the one she had observed in the nursery that morning at the orphanage. Nevertheless, her skin where his fingers rested prickled, as if Fourth of July sparklers were shedding their sparks. Dessie had always procured a small supply every summer when Mel had been a girl and her grandmother had lit them for her on the beach in front of their cottage on Martha's Vineyard. She had loved to hold one in each hand and wave them in wide arcs, watching the trail of white light float through the night air. Sometimes the sparks fell on her bare toes and she danced the tiny pricks of heat away.

She could not dance away from Phil Coughlin's heat tonight.

Instead, she nodded at the vegetable pot, refused the fish and watched without words but with a suddenly grumbling stomach as Mrs. Ling ladled her choices into battered tin pots with lids and handles. Phil let go of Mel to pay Mrs. Ling and take the pots. Mel followed him out of the shop and the question loomed again about where they would share this meal. If she had paid attention to the route Phil had taken from Tan Son Nhut instead of burying her head against him, she might recognize where she was, take her pot and walk or flag down a cycle taxi.

But the alley looked like dozens of others she'd wandered through.

"My place is just around the corner. If you take the noodles, I'll walk the bike. I've got a bottle of Glenlivet and even two clean glasses in the cupboard."

He handed her the steaming pots and she followed him as he guided the bike through the puddles in the alley to a small padlocked shed. He pulled a key from his pocket, unlocked the door and rolled the bike into the dirt-floored space. In the rear corner Mel could see neatly stacked boxes marked with red crosses.

Phil followed her glance.

"Medical supplies I've managed to scrounge. As I need them I deliver them to the orphanage but there's little left—just what you see there."

He closed up, took the pots and led her up an external flight of wooden stairs to a landing above the shed. He flicked on a light as he opened the door and Mel followed him inside.

The room they entered was starkly neat. A small counter held a hot plate and a line of canned goods. On shelves underneath were a small stack of plates and a couple of pots. A desk flanked the one window and on its surface Mel saw a well-thumbed copy of a *Physician's Desk Reference* and a few medical textbooks. Through a doorway hung with a bamboo curtain Mel saw a mosquito-netted bed.

"I've actually got a bathroom if you want to clean up before we eat."

He set the pots on a table in the middle of the room and pointed toward the bedroom.

"It's through here. I'll get you a towel and can offer you some clean clothes." His glance moved down from her face to her blood- and grime-spattered shirt. "You probably will want to burn that."

He led the way to the bath and handed her a towel, shirt and shorts. "There's a tub if you want to soak. I can reheat the noodles when you're ready. Do you want a drink now or later?"

She turned down the drink and looked with longing at the claw-footed tub in the middle of the bath. This wasn't what she'd intended, but her flat had only a tiny box of a shower. She turned on the tap and peeled off her clothes while she waited for the tub to fill. When she finally eased herself into the warm water she could not imagine wanting to be anywhere else.

After she had scrubbed the vestiges of the day from her weary body she leaned back and let herself drift for a few minutes…

The knock was insistent, rapid.

"Melanie? Melanie, are you okay?" She heard genuine concern in his voice. And he had called her Melanie. Not Ames, which was the only way he had ever addressed her; and not Mel, which was how she referred to herself since she'd become a journalist. Only Dessie and her father called her Melanie.

She roused herself with a splash and rose from the tub.

"I'm fine. Sorry to alarm you. I'll be out in a minute."

She toweled herself dry, turbaned her hair and slipped on the crisply starched khaki shirt he had given her. The shorts came to her knees and were loose around the waist, so she slipped her belt off her own mud-caked pants and cinched the shorts tightly to keep them up.

Her fingertips and toes were wrinkled, but every inch of her was clean and smelled of Ivory soap. She was aware of his appraisal as she emerged from the bathroom.

"Now, that's an improvement. The noodles are on the hot plate. I'm going to wash up myself—be back a little faster than you were," he said, then ducked into the bath.

In the outer room she found the table set with bowls and spoons. An empty glass etched with Marine Corps insignia stood at one place with the promised bottle of Glenlivet next to it. She had noticed that Phil had taken his own glass into the bath.

She poured herself a splash of scotch and swirled it around the glass, breathing in the aroma. Glenlivet had been her father's drink and Dessie had kept a crystal decanter on a silver tray on the sideboard in the dining room at Georgetown, ready and waiting for his sporadic returns from whatever hot spot he'd been assigned to solve its crises. Mel remembered him on those nights when he first came home—the quick, stiff hug in the front hall and then the step back from her to assess how much she'd grown or to note the presence, and later absence, of her braces; the kiss to the cheek Dessie offered him; and then the retreat to the dining room. Mel sat and watched her father, hungry for his presence, as he sank into his chair at the head of the table, loosened his tie and clasped the double rocks glass. He drank slowly, his eyes closed at first, each sip easing the creases of worry and fatigue that to Mel seemed deeper each time he returned.

Mel wondered now if her father's Glenlivet had helped to obliterate the horrors that had assaulted him on his missions. She'd seen enough hard drinking during her years in Saigon to understand how many men used it as an anesthetic. More than likely, from what she'd heard about Phil, it was his drug of choice.

She took a small sip, the gold liquid searing her throat and then warming her empty belly. She rubbed the bridge of her nose. Too much of this and she wouldn't be able to hold on to the motorbike, much less find her own way back to her flat.

She stifled a yawn as Phil parted the bamboo curtain and stepped back into the front room. He brought the pots to the table and ladled noodles and broth into her bowl.

"Eat, before you topple over."

They ate silently, hunger and weariness overtaking any attempt on either part to be sociable. Like the bath, the food met a need so basic that it quelled the earlier disquiet Mel had felt about being with Phil any longer than absolutely necessary. She swallowed the noodles and shredded cabbage voraciously, registering the warmth, the flecks of hot chili pepper, the intense flavors of garlic and onion and basil from the broth that must have been simmering for days.

"Thank you," she was finally able to murmur when her bowl was empty. "I hadn't realized how much I needed to eat."

She pushed her chair back from the table.

"I'll help you clean up and then I should get back to my place. If you'll sketch out for me where we are, I can walk or hail a cycle taxi."

"It's late and, if you haven't noticed, it's pouring out. It's not safe for you to head out by yourself. I'd take you on the bike, but after finally being clean and dry I suspect that both of us would regret the ride.

"Look, you can stay here. Take the bed. I'll camp out here on the couch. I need to be close to the phone anyway. The Seventh Adventist Hospital, where most of the survivors were taken, has my number. I spoke to them while you were in the tub. If they need me, I'll be on my way. It's another reason for me not to take you back to your flat—I don't want to miss their call."

"I can certainly travel on my own at night. I've been doing it for a long time."

"I imagine that you haven't been doing it when the city is streaming with desperate refugees from the north and today, especially, in the aftermath of the crash, when rumors are careening from one end of Saigon to the other. Stay put. It's not a suggestion. You'll be no good for your precious Tien if you're abducted or worse. There's mortar fire hitting the fringe of the city."

Phil's reversion to his "I'm in charge, don't mess with

me" mode of communicating with her caught Mel off guard. Had he really been kind and solicitous earlier, or had she simply been lulled into thinking so by her fatigue and hunger? Under normal circumstances, Mel would never have allowed herself to be in this situation—dependent on a man who thought he knew what was best for her. Under normal circumstances, she would pick herself up and go, rain and mortar fire and panic in the streets be damned.

But she knew herself well enough to acknowledge that she was close to physical collapse. Whatever had driven her through this horrific day was gone. She bit back words that she knew might only fuel Phil's sense of her weakness and vulnerability. And she reluctantly admitted to herself how right he was with the clinching words of his argument to keep her at his place for the night. She had a responsibility beyond herself to Tien, a duty to fulfill to Anh.

"Fine. I'll stay. But I'll be on my way with first light."

She picked up the dishes and carried them to the bath, where she had seen a dishpan, sponge and incongruous container of dishwashing liquid stowed under the sink. She washed and dried the dishes while Phil placed another call to the hospital.

When she was finished she found him making the bed.

"Clean sheets. You're all set for the night. Get some rest."

He left her, and she climbed into the bed. Like the rest of his flat, the bedroom was almost monastic in its simplicity and starkness. The bed was narrow, not something she had expected, given Phil's carousing reputation. But then, he may have carried on that part of his life in other beds, rather than bringing women home to what appeared to Mel to be a sanctuary.

Next to the bed Mel found a stack of books on the night table. As tired as she was, as depleted of nearly all her resources, the journalist in her couldn't resist investigating. She ran her fingers along the spines: Thoreau's *On Walden Pond;* Teilhard de Chardin's *The Phenomenon of Man* in the original French; and Faulkner's *The Sound and the Fury.* She had expected Ian Fleming or Ed McBain, but was beginning to understand that what she had previously expected of Phil Coughlin and what she was discovering about him were worlds apart.

She had read de Chardin at Columbia and began to leaf through the pages. Marginal notes in deep blue ink and a jagged, angular handwriting were scattered throughout the well-thumbed book. She was filled with a profoundly curious urge to read the notes, seeking some insight into why Phil Coughlin was so disturbingly compelling. It might give her some edge in dealing with him, provide her with some understanding of him with which to defend herself. Protect herself. But she hadn't read more than a few words, straining to decipher the script in the dim light of the single lamp by the bed, when her eyes and her brain simply refused to perform for even a few more minutes. Her head fell heavy into the pillow, the book sprawled open across her chest and she was asleep.

But it wasn't a restful sleep. Jumbled images of the smoke-filled bog, the broken fuselage, scattered limbs, her father's distant, sorrow-lined face, and Coughlin's intense blue eyes crowded her subconscious, accompanied by a cacophony of sirens and explosions and fragments of the lullaby she had sung as she carried the babies. She was lost in the smoke, the mud immobilizing her feet. She was hearing the cries of a child in the distance but couldn't reach her, despite struggling with every ounce of her strength. Panic rose in her and guilt, as the screams continued and she was helpless to stop them. She was frantic, clawing at her feet to dig out of the mud, but when she lifted her hands they were filled with blood.

Suddenly, cool hands grasped her own heated ones, and a voice she couldn't see because of the smoke spoke to her calmly.

"Melanie. Melanie, it's only a dream. You're safe."

She struggled for a moment and then the bog and the smoke vanished, replaced by yellow light and an unrecognizable room. Where was she? The voice whispered to her.

"It's okay, Melanie. You're with me, Phil."

She opened her eyes and stared into his startlingly blue ones. He was sitting on the edge of the bed, stroking her still trembling hands.

"You must have had a bad dream—no surprise, given what you witnessed today."

What she had witnessed flooded back and crushed her emotionally. She began to cry, keening as if she were one of her Irish aunts on her mother's side, mourning each of the shattered lives flung across the path of this war.

Phil took her face in his hands, wiping her tears with his thumbs, and then pulled her into an embrace, his arms wrapped around her as her body heaved with uncontrolled sobs. She emptied herself into him and he simply held her, absorbing her grief. When her tears subsided, he brushed her damp hair away from her face.

"Try to get some rest now. It's almost morning and you'll be needed at the orphanage. I'll stay here with you if you want me to."

She nodded, not willing to be separated from the steadying rhythm of his heart, the strength in his arms holding her up and keeping further nightmares at bay.

She settled down again onto the narrow bed and he slipped behind her, her back leaning into his chest. His arm reached around her and clasped her hand.

"Sleep," he said. "I'm here."

When she woke a few hours later she could see faint cracks of light through the blinds on the window. She groped for her clock, a small, leather-bound travel clock that her father had given her when she left for Vietnam. It was the last time she had seen him. But the clock wasn't there, and the room and the bed weren't hers. She sat up with a start, remembering where she was and vaguely aware of the disturbance during the night. She was alone in the bed. Perhaps Phil coming to her in the midst of her dream had been part of the dream, as well.

She wasn't sure which version of the night before upset her more—that her subconscious had been so consumed with him that he could be so present in her dreams, or that he had physically comforted her and she had welcomed him into her bed. But she had slept, wrapped in a cocoon of safety that he had somehow provided her.

She heard the water running in the bathroom and scrambled out of the bed. She didn't want to still be there in the midst of rumpled sheets if, indeed, he had held her and slept with her.

In the front room she found a pot of coffee on the hot plate and poured herself some into one of the thick ceramic Boston Red Sox mugs on the counter. Some caffeine and a cigarette would clear her fuzzy thinking. Whatever had happened the night before was an aberration, thrust upon her by the crash. She couldn't even remember the last time she had cried or needed comforting. She hadn't been herself, Mel Ames, seasoned war correspondent, that was all. She nearly dropped the mug when Phil entered the room behind her and spoke. He didn't have to touch her to evoke what convinced her now had definitely been a physical, not imagined experience. His voice held the same compassionate tone she remembered.

"You're up, and looking like your old self! I'm glad."

Mel realized with relief that he wasn't going to bring up the night spent entwined in his arms or even refer to her nightmare. For a fraction of a second, he held her gaze when she turned to answer him. Our secret, his mesmerizing eyes seemed to promise. No need to ever mention it again. She hoped she could trust him.

"If you want a ride to the orphanage, I'm headed to that part of town. It's on the way to the hospital."

"Have you heard any more news?"

"No. That's why I'm going to stop by and see for myself."

"You'll let me know if there's anything I can do? Write another Pulitzer Prize-winning article?" She flashed him a wan grin. I'm still a journalist, she was saying. Despite last night.

He nodded.

Twenty minutes later, he dropped her at the steps to the orphanage and waved goodbye.

When he was out of sight she turned in the opposite direction and headed toward the *Newsweek* office. She knew from the previous day the nursery at the orphanage would still be quiet. She had at least an hour before Tien and the other infants would be stirring.

She walked briskly. In alleys and under makeshift shelters, she could see the sleeping bodies of those who must have fled the north. Dogs wandered the streets sniffing at garbage. Somewhere in the distance, a siren wailed.

She let herself into the deserted office, pulled the cover

off a Teletype machine and sat down. Without benefit of notes, Mel began a firsthand account of the rescue. The senior byline writers in the bureau would be doing investigative pieces, confirming the rumors of sabotage that had floated above the smoke and despair in the marsh. But they hadn't been where she had been, mired in the mud, an eyewitness at the point of impact.

The words came quickly, images and vignettes pouring out of her brain as if exorcised by the act of telling. When she finished, she realized she was sweating. The story was on its way to New York when the first of her colleagues arrived.

"Where were you yesterday, Ames? All hell was breaking loose—at least, more than the usual chaos—and I didn't have anybody to get me the specs on that C-5A that went down. Did you start the coffee yet?"

Mel put the cover back on the Teletype. Despite earning her own byline at the magazine on the strength of her reporting over the last three years, the older reporters still treated her like one of their research assistants.

"Didn't have time, Joe. Gotta run. Doing some follow-up on the orphan story. The background on the C-5A is probably in the Lockheed file. The Ls are in the second drawer."

She picked up her knapsack and slipped past him, trying not to react to the chagrin registering on his face.

As she hurried back to the orphanage she could see the refugees stirring from their piles on the streets—gaunt women with babies strapped to their backs, old men being helped to their feet by children who looked no older than four or five. A boy ran up to her with outstretched hands.

She dug into her knapsack and retrieved an unopened sleeve of Ritz crackers, which she handed to the boy.

Dessie had religiously supplied her with care packages ever since she'd left home for university and hadn't stopped when she'd come to Vietnam. The familiar treats, plus necessities such as tampons and medications, had been a lifeline for her, even though she prided herself on her ability to adapt to Southeast Asian life.

The orphanage was astir with activity when she arrived. A group of unfamiliar women—aid workers, the porter said—were busy at a table in the former dining room of the villa with piles of documents. Mel went first to check on Tien. The little girl was awake in her crib, staring solemnly at a patch of light that had been prismed by an angled window.

Mel lifted her up and murmured a few words in Vietnamese. There was no recognition in Tien's eyes and her body was stiff in Mel's arms. The child lacked so much in caring and affection. Mel had hopes that a loving adoptive family would fill the emptiness.

"Can you help with the porridge this morning?" Sister Agatha was at her elbow. At least they were trying to fill the children's bellies here. Mel followed the nun with Tien still in her arms to the orphanage refectory, set her in a high chair and began spooning a soupy rice gruel into her eager mouth. Sister Agatha brought in more babies and they worked their way through the nursery, with Mel managing to get most of the food into the babies' mouths despite her fumbling. She was finishing up, wiping the remnants of the meal from the chin of the last baby, when two of the aid workers arrived in the refectory like women on a mission.

"There you are!" the older one blurted. She looked like a country club matron, with carefully coiffed blond hair and an outfit appropriate for shuffleboard on a cruise ship. The other one Mel sized up as ex-Army, all tightly buttoned up and rigid backbone compared to the flounce and pastel softness of the blonde. She had a clipboard in her hand and was wearing sensible shoes.

"Reverend Mother told us about you, and first of all, let me thank you for what you've done for the children. It's an honor to actually meet you!"

Mel wiped her sticky hands and put out her right one.

"Thank you. And you are…?"

"Oh, forgive me. I'm Pamela Boniface, and this is Trudy Parsons. We're volunteers from the Vietnamese Rescue League, here to organize the evacuation of the children. I just arrived in Saigon and Trudy's been on the ground for months. I'm the one who can pull the strings in Washington. Senator Smith and I go way back. His wife and I were college roommates and she's godmother to one of my sons. Anyway, it was the senator who got the president to authorize American military transport for us. After yesterday's tragedy, we need all the planes we can get, and we need to move quickly."

"Which is why we're coming to you," Trudy interrupted.

"I don't understand." Everyone seemed to think Mel had some direct line to power and the ability to work miracles.

"Now that we have the planes, we have to staff them, not just with a flight crew, but with adults who can accompany the children and care for them on the flights. We're putting the call out to any Americans within traveling range of Saigon. A contingent of Air Force nurses is coming from Hong Kong."

"And you want me to write a story about this?"

"Oh, no! We want you to fly with the children from St. Agnes."

Mel was stunned. It was the most ridiculous request that had ever been made of her.

"I'm not a nurse. Besides, my work is here in Saigon. I have no intention of leaving, especially not now."

Did these women not understand what was happening in the city? Did they think she wrote the news from a safe distance? She couldn't leave, not when one more story lurked amidst the chaos.

"I'm sorry. I'm not the person you need. I'm sure there are others here in Saigon who are desperately seeking to get out. The embassy must have a lengthy list."

"Oh, my. This is a disappointment. Reverend Mother thought… Well, if you change your mind, we've got a plane for St. Agnes that will leave in a week. We're trying to get the paperwork processed for all the children. It's more problematic than I expected. The South Vietnamese government is not being as cooperative as I hoped."

"Now *that* is something I can be more helpful with. I know my way around the Vietnamese bureaucracy. Tell me what you need."

The disappointment expressed by Pamela was temporarily replaced with relief at Mel's offer. Mel followed the two women to the dining room to gather the list of missing documents.

"I still hope you'll reconsider, Miss Ames. Surely your family is anxious to see you."

Mel didn't respond. It hadn't mattered to her father that she'd been gone for so long, since most of the time he'd been away, as well. But Mel knew how hard it was on Dessie. She'd been an incredible supporter, encouraging Mel to defy expectations throughout her upbringing, and had applauded Mel's accomplishments all along the way. But when Mel won this assignment to Saigon she had seen that Dessie had tried to hold her worry in check.

"You have to take risks in life if you are to truly understand what it means to live," she had preached to Mel whenever she had hesitated to do something she feared, or feared she might fail at. So Dessie had kept her mouth shut, hugged her hard at the departure gate the day she left and continued to send her care packages.

Mel took the list and headed off to the ministry. She was glad to be doing something familiar—extracting information from officials—instead of juggling the needs of children who couldn't express themselves. She also didn't want to be at the orphanage when Phil arrived to do his rounds.

The fear and unrest mounting in the city had breached the barricades of the ministry. Confusion, resistance and anger greeted her wherever she went. Department heads barked at her, fists were slammed on tables, more forms in triplicate were thrust into her hands.

Realizing that the direct approach was not winning her the cooperation she needed, she retreated to the *Newsweek* office and began making phone calls. If ever there was a time to call in favors, this was it. She spent the next few days shuttling between ministries and on the phone, tracking down those who had the authority, or access to the authority, to grant the children the permission to leave.

She didn't stop as offices closed, but offered to meet her contacts in person at the Hotel Continental. She needed signatures, official stamps. If it meant a few hours in a smoky bar buying contacts expensive drinks, it wouldn't be the first time.

She had just wrapped up one of those meetings, her own drink barely touched as she had coaxed and flattered the self-important bureaucrat opposite her. But she had gotten what she wanted, thanked him profusely and sank into the worn banquette as she watched him swagger out the door. She took a quick sip of her drink and began gathering up her things to leave. Her head was down, stuffing her knapsack, when she heard the familiar voice.

"You're relentless, aren't you?"

"Excuse me?" She was caught off guard by Phil's presence. She'd managed to miss him at the orphanage, something her intellect had told her was a good thing. She'd been able to focus on what she needed to do for the children of St. Agnes rather than agonize about her conflicted reaction to spending the night at his flat. But her emotional need catapulted to the forefront as he stood on the other side of the table.

"I watched you from across the room. You weren't going to let him go until you got what you wanted. I wonder if he realized how well you played him."

"I was playing for keeps."

"I know. Reverend Mother told me you've taken on the entire South Vietnamese government to get the children released."

Mel noted the admiration in his voice and acknowledged to herself that she cared about what he thought of her.

"Mind if I join you while you finish your drink?"

"Oh, I was going to leave it…get going…a long day." She started to stand.

"Stay. Just a little while. I promise not to get on my soapbox about journalists."

She hesitated. Every moment she spent with him widened the chink in her armor, exposed more of her vulnerability. No one had seen her cry like Phil Coughlin. No one had held her like Phil Coughlin.

She sat down. *I'm going to regret this, in one way or another.*

"Why have you stayed in Saigon?" He looked around the nearly empty bar. Mel was the only woman.

"I could ask you the same question. Or rather, why did you come back?"

"You first."

"Because there is still a story to tell."

"And you told it. So why not leave now? Reverend Mother told me you refused a seat on the airlift."

"Reverend Mother appears to be telling you a lot of things about me. Is she trying to get you to convince me to fly with the babies?"

"No. She didn't volunteer any information about you. I had to pull it out of her. You don't like having the tables turned, do you? It makes you uncomfortable to have someone else asking the questions." He smiled.

She was startled by his curiosity about her. He was right, she was agitated—not because she found his questions intrusive, but because she found herself wanting to answer him. The heat she had felt simmering between them the morning after the crash—and the feelings she had managed to temper by avoiding him since then—now filled this desolate room. She took a gulp of her drink, staring into the sweating glass to avoid the intensity of his gaze.

"My turn. Why did you come back? I heard you left a job that would have set you up for life."

"A life I didn't want. My father, who *did* want it, blamed my decision on the Jesuits. I spent eight years being educated by them—high school and then Boston College. Despite my best efforts to live up to my early reputation as a scruffy, troublemaking kid from the streets of South Boston, I seem to have absorbed the lessons of Ignatian spirituality that permeated everything we did at school."

"Ignatian spirituality?"

"The ideas developed by St. Ignatius Loyola, the founder of the Jesuits—basically, that we are on a continuous search for how best to live an authentic life. We were taught to ask where God will best be served and where people will best be helped."

"And the answer for you was not in Boston, but back here."

"Yes. When I recognized that, I had no choice but to come back. I was miserable and empty in Boston, just going through the motions."

"When I first met you, I thought that you were holding others to an impossibly high standard. Let me rephrase that. I thought that you were holding *me* to an impossibly high standard. But it's *yourself* that you demand so much of."

"You know, for someone who doesn't like me very much, you seem to have your finger on the pulse of who I am. There aren't many people who do."

Mel didn't deny that she disliked him. She'd never been able to camouflage what she truly thought of someone. But she was now recognizing that Phil's arrogance and party-boy reputation were barriers he had thrown up to mask a deeply felt compassion that an ex-Marine was not supposed to show. It was only when he was with the children—at St. Agnes and during the rescue—that he let down the mask. And the night he had comforted her in her nightmare.

"You're growing on me," she acknowledged. "Especially when you don't hide behind the perfect Phil Coughlin you present to the world."

"You're growing on me, too. I admit, I took you for a single-minded, hard-bitten journalist whose only interest in St. Agnes was to build your own reputation and pull some strings for the child of someone who had done you a favor. You've got your own mask protecting you. You're full of surprises, Melanie Ames. And I like what I'm discovering."

He lifted his glass to her.

"I guess that makes two of us," she said, touching her glass to his.

Beyond the windows of the bar Melanie could see dusk falling; the tension in the city was rising and she didn't want to be out on the street after dark.

"I can give you a lift home," Phil offered, when he followed her gaze.

Mel didn't trust herself to accept. The conversation had already dissolved her resistance beyond the conflicted feelings that had haunted her as relentlessly as her nightmares. If she went with him, she wouldn't want to leave him. It was insane to open herself up to the possibilities taunting her in this complex and compelling man who had reached out to her across the divide between them. Saigon was about to fall. She had no idea where she'd be when it did, and she knew that wherever it was, there was no room in her life for someone like Phil Coughlin. And she also knew that there was no room in Phil Coughlin's life for someone like her.

"I'd love to accept. But I need to make my own way home. Goodbye and thanks for…"

He stopped her, placing two fingers on her lips. "Not yet. Not goodbye. Not thank you."

As she left the room she watched him order another scotch, remaining alone at their table.

PHIL WAS RIGHT that it wasn't yet time for goodbye. They saw each other again at the orphanage, and Mel was relieved that, surrounded by the children and the heightened tempo of activity, the emotional charge between them was muffled. But she couldn't deny that she was acutely aware of the aura he spread throughout the villa even before she saw him. The children were more animated, dancing around him with gleeful smiles; the nuns, especially the younger ones, hovered near him, soaking up the energy field that seemed to surround him like the halo of a saint. Even Reverend Mother came under his spell, her austere demeanor somehow lightened, hopeful, by the reassurance he supplied, like the lollipop he pulled out of his pocket to hand to a child he'd just inoculated.

His presence was calming to Mel, as well. He possessed a sureness that what they were doing was right, and Mel began to understand what he meant by the spiritual force that had led him back to Saigon. She questioned whether she would ever know with such certainty that she was following the right path.

Phil sought her out after he finished what had brought him to the orphanage—delivering supplies that he had scrounged around the city for the flight, completing medical exams that were required before the children could leave, ministering to the gravely ill children who were still arriving at the doorstep. They were both exhausted, driven, acutely aware that they had little time left to save the children of St. Agnes. But they found a few moments to talk over a cigarette in the courtyard, Mel leaning back against the wall with her eyes closed and Phil crouched in the position he often took to bring himself down to the level of the children.

"What will you do when this is over?" Mel tried to tell herself that her reason for asking was simply the natural curiosity of a reporter.

"I'm not sure yet. I'll go wherever I'm needed. One doesn't have to look very far—perhaps just across the border in Cambodia. And you?"

"Wherever *Newsweek* sends me. The next war. There doesn't seem to be a shortage."

"Will you go home?"

Mel hadn't considered that question. She missed Dessie. But after three years in Saigon she felt completely detached from the life she had left behind in Georgetown.

"I don't know. I don't belong there anymore."

"I know what you mean. This place, this life, changes people irrevocably. One can't go back to who one was before." He put out his cigarette and rose. Both of them went back into the villa and the challenges confronting them within its walls.

The next day, the day before the flight was supposed to leave, Anh came to the orphanage for the last time to say goodbye to her daughter. Mel almost didn't recognize her in her *ao dai.* It was pale yellow, the silk dress skimming Anh's body over wide trousers. The traditional gown transformed her from tough, war-weary bar girl to elegant and stoically contained young woman. Her face was scrubbed of makeup and she had pulled her hair back into a chignon. Even the porter and the nuns noticed the difference.

Mel knew what it must have taken for Anh to make this last visit, reopening the wound caused by her decision to relinquish Tien to a future without her. She took her daughter from the nursery and sat alone with her on the verandah, rocking her silently for nearly an hour. No one disturbed them.

Elsewhere in the villa, Phil was busy organizing group photos of the children. He had arrived earlier with a camera, convincing Reverend Mother to gather the children to commemorate the final days of the orphanage. He offered to take a photo of Anh with Tien. She hesitated, then shyly agreed. Mel watched them—Anh solemnly staring at the camera, Tien curled into her mother's arms.

When Anh saw Mel, she waved her to her side.

"Take another one with us both, please," Anh said to Phil.

Up close, Mel could see the tears brimming in Anh's eyes. Mel put her arm around Anh and held her long after Phil had snapped the picture.

LATER THAT NIGHT, she wearily climbed the stairs to her flat, her mission almost completed. She'd succeeded in getting the papers for all but ten of the St. Agnes children and had promises that she'd have the remaining documents the next day.

Inside the flat she found a note on the floor, apparently shoved under the door. It was in Mrs. Bao's hand.

"Grandmother call. Father ill. Come home."

Mel glanced at her watch. It was late morning in Washington. She couldn't tell from the note when Dessie had called. Mel's grandmother might be frantic with worry, especially when news like the plane crash heightened the perception in the States of just how dangerous the situation in Saigon was. It wasn't like Dessie to exaggerate, to create a reason to call Mel home unnecessarily. Dessie always told the truth, unembellished.

Despite the hour, Mel retraced her steps and knocked on Mrs. Bao's door, the note still in her hand.

"Missy, I wonder where you are all day. Not want to worry Grandma. But you must call."

Mrs. Bao opened the door wider and ushered Mel inside to use the phone.

The connection took longer than usual. Mel found herself tapping her fingers on the table, impatient and anxious. Questions raced through her brain. She needed information to quell the unease that the news of her father's illness had set in motion. Despite his absence from her life, Mel had always considered him indestructible, a survivor of violent encounters, a man who confronted and triumphed over wrongdoing. Illness was something she had never considered.

When she finally heard Dessie's voice on the line Mel sought the reassurance and solidity that her grandmother had always provided her. But for the first time it wasn't there.

"Oh, Melanie, thank God! I thought you might be out of reach, off on some assignment, and it would be too late."

"Too late? What do you mean, Grandma? What has happened to Daddy? Where is he?"

"He's had a massive heart attack, honey. He's at Walter Reed Hospital, and needs surgery. They're going to operate today. It's time for you to come home, Melanie. For *your* sake. Can you get a flight out? We can probably call someone at the State Department if there's a problem."

Dessie sounded frail and exhausted, but unwavering in her conviction that Mel should come home. Mel knew there had been times in the past when her father had been in danger—death threats, consulates under siege—and Dessie had protected her from the knowledge, not burdening her with fear. But she wasn't protecting her now.

For the second time in a week, Mel began to cry, quiet tears slipping down her cheeks. She wiped them away and answered Dessie in as strong a voice as she could muster.

"I know of a flight that will take me tomorrow, Grandma. I'll be in San Diego by Sunday and grab a plane to D.C. from there. Don't worry. I'll make it home."

"Thank you, honey. I'll let your father know."

"Is he conscious?" she asked.

The phone crackled with static and the connection was broken. Mel replaced the receiver without learning the answer.

Mrs. Bao was waiting in the shadows, wringing her hands.

"Not good? You go now, not come back?"

Mel acknowledged that Mrs. Bao was right. Leaving on the flight to San Diego most certainly meant she would not be coming back.

Mrs. Bao, normally restrained and measured in her interactions, reached out and stroked Mel's tearstained cheek.

"You good girl, Missy. Good to Grandma, good to Saigon, good to Bao family. Take care of family. Take care of self."

Mel closed her hand over Mrs. Bao's.

"Thank you. Take care of yourself, too, Mrs. Bao."

THE NEXT MORNING, her duffel bag packed and slung over her back, Mel stopped at the *Newsweek* office to leave word of her departure. Joe was there, fumbling with the coffee pot.

"Good luck, kid. Sorry to hear about your dad. Hope everything turns out okay. See you in the next war."

At the orphanage, the tension was unmistakable. Several more unfamiliar people were in the villa, conferring with Reverend Mother, furiously leafing through documents, making phone calls.

Mel waded through a maze of boxes and people to find Pamela Boniface. Her flowered blouse was a little rumpled this morning, but she was still meticulously groomed, her bright red fingernails rifling through a sheaf of documents.

"Pamela, I've reconsidered. If there is still room, I'll fly with the babies."

Pamela looked up in surprise. "Oh, I knew we could count on you!"

Mel had no intention of telling this woman why she had changed her mind. She opened up her knapsack and pulled out a stuffed brown folder bound with a rubber band.

"Here are all the stamped release forms I was able to get. My contact is working on the forms for the older boys that the government is holding up."

She spent the morning with Reverend Mother, Pamela and Trudy reviewing the logistics: the buses that would carry the children to the airport; the boxes of supplies— diapers, formula, blankets—that had been gathered from around the city; the preparation of the final manifest.

Every hour some new piece of information was brought to their attention; plans were adjusted, expectations re-aligned. The pace of activity suited Mel. It didn't give her time to think about her father and what awaited her when she arrived back in the States. But it did not obscure the loss gnawing at the edges of her concentration. She had known for weeks that the time she had remaining in Saigon was limited and she had made her farewells to the few people who mattered to her. But with her unexpected departure now only hours away, she was acutely conscious of the one goodbye that remained unspoken.

"Do you expect Doctor Coughlin before we leave?" she asked Reverend Mother, trying to restrain the urgency she knew her voice must be conveying.

The nun looked at her, and realization spread across her lined face. "So his effect has reached you, as well. Oh, my dear girl, I should have guessed that two people so committed to saving our children would have found in one another a kindred soul."

Mel was about to deny such a profound connection, but acknowledged that the nun had spoken the truth. Her face crumpled in despair.

"Found, and lost in the same moment. Our lives are about to diverge. Who knows what lies ahead for either of us?"

The nun took her hands. "Life, especially in times

like these, is filled with uncertainty. Trust that if it's meant to be, you'll find each other again."

Mel wanted to believe her, but the turmoil of the last twelve hours in her own life, coupled with the desperation surrounding her in the city, had taken its toll. Nothing seemed permanent or secure. The image of her father in a hospital bed tethered to machines and the prophetic nightmares of the last two weeks had crushed her childlike belief that her father would always be somewhere in the world, that Dessie would always be her rock and her comfort, that she herself had the resilience and strength to make her way no matter what befell her.

The fear that she had been reading on the faces of the refugees inundating the city was now lapping at her ankles. She felt it rising in her, threatening to drown her. She had never known herself to be so adrift. The clamor and frantic pace of the preparations around her heightened her shattered sense of control. She managed to whisper a thank-you to the nun and retreated to the courtyard, hoping to compose herself.

It was there that Phil found her.

"I heard that you were leaving with the children. Is it true?"

He seemed as unprepared as Mel for her departure. The anguish in his question laid bare what was still unspoken between them, what they no longer had the time to reveal to one another.

She nodded.

"Why the change of heart? I thought you planned on writing the last story of this war?"

She hadn't meant to share with anyone the reason for her decision to leave, but in her vulnerable state the words came tumbling out, along with the self-doubt that she was neither as brave nor as strong as she had once imagined herself to be.

"I'm sorry about your father. But don't lose faith in yourself. We're all afraid, Melanie. But what I've seen in you since you first set foot in the villa convinces me that you'll prevail over your fears. Now, more than ever, the children need you to be strong. I know you won't fail them. You're an amazing woman. You have to know that you've saved the children of St. Agnes, not only with your talent, but also with your persistence."

He looked away from her and added, "And you've saved me."

"Saved you? From what?"

"From myself. One of the Jesuit tenets I never bothered to master was humility. I know I can be insufferably cocky and full of myself, buying into the humanitarian and healer labels the world has bestowed on me and convincing myself that because I was on a mission, anything I did to accomplish it was right. You stood up to my bullshit. You spoke the truth. Thank you."

"I'm the one who needs to say 'thank you.' You pushed me to see beyond myself."

"I wish we had more time. Just think of all the improvements we could effect in each other." He smiled, and she rewarded him with a smile of her own. It eased the intensity of their revelations and postponed for a few brief moments the reality that awaited them.

"Will you ride with us to Tan Son Nhut?"

"No. I'm leaving for Cambodia this evening. With the orphans being evacuated, my work here is done."

"Then this is where we say goodbye?" She couldn't hide the pain in her voice.

"Not goodbye. I told you that the other night at the Continental." He was gentle in his correction of her words.

"What do we say?"

"This," he said. And took her face in his hands, drew her toward him and kissed her. His breath, his pulse, his courage, his compassion filled the emptiness that had been carved out by her fear. They held each other in silence until the afternoon rain began its steady drumbeat and the buses pulled into the courtyard.

THE RIDE to Tan Son Nhut was wrenching. The familiar landmarks of the city rolled by the clouded windows of the bus. Many of the buildings were empty, abandoned by merchants who had been serving Americans for almost a decade but who had seen the handwriting on the wall. A Coca-Cola sign flapped in the steamy breeze hanging by one corner, a broken chain dangling from the other.

From the moment the buses entered the heavily guarded airport past a desperate throng pressed up against the chain link fence, Mel understood how challenging a journey lay ahead of her. Tien began to cry as soon as they boarded the plane and could not be consoled. Improvising, Mel wrapped her in a sling and carried her for hours—first as they settled the children in their seats and makeshift cradles and then as an emigration official compared the information on the tag pinned to each child with the documents Mel had secured, his face impenetrable as he scrutinized every detail. She felt out of character balancing a baby on her hip. It was at once both unfamiliar and reinforcing. It was something so simple, but so clearly right for Tien, who responded with her body. She realized how incongruous she might look to her *Newsweek* colleagues, standing up to power and authority with a baby in her arms. But in a strange way she felt infused with a power all her own because of Tien. She was the fiercely protective she-wolf guarding her pups from predators. No one was going to take any of these children off the plane.

As soon as the official reluctantly signed off on the manifest, they were cleared for takeoff. Mel glanced out the window. Night had fallen. "Farewell, Saigon," Mel whispered. "Farewell, Phil." They lifted off and the plane banked toward the China Sea and the unknown.

The next twenty hours were a blur, caring for the children, snatching a few hours of rest and all the while holding Tien close to her.

When they landed in San Diego, nurses and ambulances were waiting on the runway to whisk the children away to the base hospital for checkups and care.

Mel stood in the doorway of the plane, Tien asleep and still sprawled across her hip in the sling. She blinked in the brilliant California sunshine, her eyes adjusting from the dimness of the plane. Around her everyone was crisp and energetic and efficient. She descended the stairs and a pair of hands reached out to take Tien from her.

As the nurse slipped her out of the sling, Tien woke up, took one look at the strange face and began to scream. "It's okay, sweetie. It's okay." She held the unhappy, struggling baby with practiced ease. "I'm a pediatric nurse and I go through this all the time with kids and their moms. She'll calm down soon," she reassured Mel.

"She hasn't been separated from me since we left Saigon. I'm not so sure she's able to calm down."

"Don't worry. It's frightening for all children to have their routines disrupted. But the good news is, they're flexible and, at this age, their memories are short. We'll get her cleaned up and fed and before you know it, she'll be united with her adoptive family and settling into life as a little American girl."

"She doesn't have a family yet. The agency hasn't identified one. Where will she stay?"

"Here on base for a few days. Then the agency responsible for her will take custody."

All the while, Tien continued screaming and reaching out for Mel.

"You need some rest. We've got temp quarters set up for you aid workers in the gym. Hot showers, hot meal, a real bed. Go ahead, take care of yourself now."

She pointed to a bus waiting to transport the adults.

Mel felt the accumulated fatigue and emotional assault of the last few weeks; she also felt an emptiness where she had carried Tien against her body.

She reached out for the little girl and took her back into her arms.

"I'll stay with her until I know she's settled down," Mel said and went with Tien to the hospital.

MEL WAS GRATEFUL for the continued efficiency of everyone at the base, although the sunny can-do attitudes grated somewhat against her darker view of humanity. Tien was quickly examined and cleared. Rather than risk another bout of inconsolable crying, Mel bathed and dressed her herself.

Someone even provided a rocking chair along with a warm bottle and the two of them drifted into a state of contentment that Mel hadn't known before. When Tien was finally in a deep sleep, a nurse showed Mel to a crib where she could lay her down. Mel hovered over her for several minutes, expecting another outburst, but she was clearly sound asleep and Mel tiptoed out of the room.

As she passed the nurses' station, the nurse on duty stopped her.

"Are you Melanie Ames, the reporter who arrived on the babylift flight this afternoon?"

Mel groaned inwardly as she acknowledged who she

was. What, had *Newsweek* already tracked her down, chomping at the bit for a story about the flight?

"We have a phone message for you, asking you to call someone named Dessie."

Mel's heart, already pulled in so many directions in the last twenty-four hours, plunged. She found the phone the nurse pointed her towards and hoped as she dialed with trembling fingers that Dessie had called only to reassure herself that Mel had arrived safely in San Diego.

Mel almost didn't recognize Dessie's voice when she answered the phone, it was so frail and distant. She sounded to Mel like she was under water and later Mel understood that it had been the water of her tears that had so distorted her speech.

"Grandma, it's Melanie. I've arrived safely in San Diego."

"Oh, sweetheart, thank God! I couldn't bear it if I lost you, as well."

"Lost me, as well? What do you mean, Grandma?" But she knew exactly what Dessie meant.

"Melanie, your father passed away this morning after surgery. His heart…just not strong enough…too damaged…nothing they could do to save him."

She seemed to be repeating a litany, unable to truly grasp the reality of her son's death. She began to cry.

Mel held her own tears in check to comfort her grandmother.

"Oh, Grandma. I'm so sorry. I'll be home as soon as I can get a flight out of here. We'll be together. We'll be all right."

"Yes, hurry home, honey. I need to put my arms around you."

"I will, Grandma. I'll be there soon."

Mel hung up the phone, stunned. She had somehow

managed all during the flight to deny her reason for flying in the first place. She slid to the floor on her knees and leaned her head against the cool tile of the wall as her own tears finally began to flow.

It was the nurse who had given her the phone message from Dessie who found her. She handed her a box of tissues.

"I'm so sorry. When you're ready, I'll have someone come pick you up and get you over to the gym. You need some rest, probably some food. When was the last time you ate?"

The nurse helped Mel up and sat her in a chair by the nurses' station until she could catch her breath.

Another helpful soul ferried Mel across the base to the gym, where she stood under a hot shower for twenty minutes. There, mingled with her tears, the dust and memories of Saigon ran off her body and down the drain. She was crawling into a cot after picking at the roast beef dinner the base had provided, when a messenger came searching for her.

"Miss Ames? The hospital just called. The baby's been screaming for half an hour and nobody knows what to do for her. They're asking if you'll come back."

Mel swung her legs onto the floor and accompanied the messenger back to the hospital. She could hear Tien's wails from down the corridor, and her body responded as if she herself were in pain. She began to run down the hall, arriving breathless at the door to the nursery and throwing off whatever burdens of fatigue or need had plagued her earlier. In that moment, she understood that Tien had become a part of her. The aching loss that her father's death had precipitated had somehow been filled by the child who had clung to her since she left Saigon. The doubts that had swirled in her head during her last traumatic weeks in Vietnam were suddenly dispelled.

She knew now what she was meant to do. She was meant to be Tien's mother.

She went to the little girl and enveloped her with arms that seemed to Mel to have grown in strength since she'd left Saigon.

"I'm here, baby. Mama's here. And I won't leave you again."

Part Two

Present day

THE FERRY *Martha's Vineyard* eased out of its berth at Woods Hole on Cape Cod and turned toward the island after which it was named. Mel climbed the narrow metal stairs to the top deck and stood at the prow, the wind whipping her hair as gulls hovered overhead and a few early morning sailors tacked away from the shipping channel.

She could have flown from D.C. to the Vineyard—along with half the Massachusetts Congressional delegation—but in addition to not wanting to get stuck sitting next to a senator who would feel compelled to expound on the latest national crisis, she simply loved this early morning voyage across Nantucket Sound.

She had always driven her beat-up Subaru from Georgetown every summer when she came to stay with Dessie at the cottage on Cape Pogue that had been in the family since before Mel was born.

When Tien had been a child, all three of them had driven together—Mel at the wheel and Dessie in the back entertaining her great-granddaughter as they made their way up the congested I-95 corridor. When they arrived on the island they had opened the cottage for the summer, airing out rooms that had been sealed against winter storms, making beds, inspecting for weather damage or habitation by mice and squirrels. Mel enjoyed the industry of those first few days, rolling up her sleeves and attacking cobwebs and dust bunnies and mouse droppings. It was a far cry from the intellectual life she led as a reporter and columnist for *The Washington Post*.

Before Dessie had passed away last year at the age of ninety-six, she had asked Mel to promise her that she would go back to the cottage at least one more summer.

"Oh, Grandma! I wouldn't miss it. Cape Pogue is very special to me."

"I know, dear. That's why I don't want you to lose what I saw it giving you every summer. Not just a respite from work, but a replenishment of your soul. You've always been so hard on yourself, Melanie. Especially when you were young and felt you had so much to prove.

"I am certainly proud of all your accomplishments— not everyone at my women's club had a granddaughter who'd won not one, but *two* Pulitzer Prizes." Her eyes twinkled in amused recollection of her bragging rights even in the heady environment of Georgetown. "But more than anything, I want you to know that you are a wonderful mother."

WHEN MEL HAD EMBRACED Tien as her daughter she also made the decision to find work that would keep her close to home. She vowed not to abandon Tien for her job as her own father had her. Her reputation established by the work she'd done for *Newsweek*, it had been easier than she'd thought possible to secure a slot with the *Post*. She had expected the transition from war correspondent to a city beat at a metropolitan newspaper—even one in the nation's capital—to be confining. She had anticipated the dismissive attitudes of her male colleagues in Saigon, who were heading off to the next conflagration without her to make their coffee or do their research. But she hadn't known that the choices she made by Tien's crib in San Diego—to adopt Tien and stay home to raise her— would ultimately be so satisfying. Mel had no regrets.

Tien had developed into an extraordinary young woman, flourishing as a high school teacher in a challenging school in the Bronx after graduating from Mel's alma mater, Columbia. Most summers Mel stopped in New York to pick her daughter up on the way to Woods Hole, but this year Tien was making her way separately, flying in from Wisconsin, where she'd been working as a counselor at a camp for Vietnamese children who'd been adopted by American families. She'd gone there herself as a teenager, one of the attempts Mel had made to help Tien understand her own heritage.

The loudspeaker advising drivers to return to their vehicles broke Mel's reverie on the deck and she headed below to join the line of escaping vehicles as the ferry pulled into the harbor at Oak Bluffs. Even at eight in the morning the dockside was bustling, and Mel maneuvered through SUVs towing boat trailers and mounted with bicycle racks until she was on Barnes Road and headed for the airport.

Tien had caught a Cape Air flight out of Boston after traveling the day before from Milwaukee, so she was exhausted and more subdued than her usual chatty self. Mel knew that Tien loved coming to the Vineyard as much as she did and chalked up her daughter's withdrawn demeanor to fatigue. A nap in the hammock on the lawn overlooking the pond, a meal of freshly dug clams and a glass of wine on the porch as the sun set this evening would revive her.

It was the first time either of them had been to Cape

Pogue without Dessie. Jerry Soames, the handyman on the island who cared for the place in the off-season, had already removed the boards that protected the windows during winter storms and had made sure the propane tanks were full. The cottage had no electricity and every-thing—the stove, refrigerator, gas lamps and water heater—ran on propane. Jerry had even raised the flag on the pole outside the house. Glancing down the beach Mel could see flags snapping in the breeze in front of other cottages. It was a common practice among the few families who inhabited this isolated stretch of land on the northern tip of Chappaquiddick—their sign to neighbors that they were there.

Mel and Tien quickly dispatched the preliminaries of settling into the achingly familiar place and then Mel shooed Tien off to sleep. While Tien retreated to the cozy bedroom she'd always used, Mel took a deep breath and opened the door to Dessie's room.

It reflected Dessie's touches: a white iron bedstead, a quilted coverlet faded to pale blues and greens, a bundle of dried lavender hanging above the bed reawakening Mel's memory of her grandmother's scent. On a table next to the bed was a wooden box Mel had never seen before.

When Tien woke from her nap, Mel was still in the bedroom, the contents of the box strewn across the bed around her.

"What's all this?"

"Mementos Gigi had apparently saved of the times the family spent here."

"Gigi" had been Tien's name for Dessie, short for great-grandmother.

Tien joined her on the bed to look at the photos and notes. She picked up one of a smiling young woman in a sundress holding a little girl by the flagpole.

"Who are they?"

"That's me with my mother."

"Do you remember her?"

"Yes. I especially remember spending summers here with her and my grandparents while my father was away."

Tien stroked the photo thoughtfully. Mel watched a look of longing cross her daughter's face and was puzzled by Tien's reaction to the photo.

"You're lucky to remember her. There's so much family history here," Tien mused, as she glanced at the array of pictures spanning almost fifty years.

"Look, here's you and me in almost the same pose," Mel said. "Gigi must have remembered the older photo and had us recreate it."

Later in the day the two women walked along the beach, empty except for a couple of fly fisherman hoping to catch a few blues.

Their walk was a ritual for them every year when they came to the island, an opportunity to catch up with each other since they'd seen each other last.

Mel remembered the first time Tien had returned from the Wisconsin camp at the age of eight, armed with recipes and a vocabulary list. When Mel had first adopted her she gave her the American name of Christine, a common practice among the families adopting the babylift children. But in addition to the foods and language she'd been introduced to at camp, Tien had also learned the meaning of her Vietnamese name—fairy or spirit—and wanted to reclaim it.

"My name is Tien," she had corrected Mel and Dessie several times. "I want to be called Tien." So Tien she became.

As they walked, arms linked, along the water's edge, Mel sensed that once again her experience at the Vietnamese camp had triggered some transformation in Tien. She no longer assumed that it was merely jet lag and sleep deprivation that had silenced her daughter. Something was on her mind that she was finding difficult to share with her mother.

"You've been very thoughtful since you arrived. Anything you want to talk about?"

Mel felt Tien stiffen and turn to look out over the horizon. An osprey swooped overhead returning with food to its nestlings.

"I'm not sure where to begin. It's something that's been on my mind for a long time. I just haven't felt compelled to act until now. Being at the camp and then, this afternoon, sifting through all those photographs of your family, I realized it's always going to gnaw at me."

Mel did not miss that Tien had said *your* family, not *our* family.

Tien stopped walking and faced Mel, her hands at her side.

"I need to find Anh. I want to know my Vietnamese family."

Mel saw the longing in her daughter's eyes. She also saw her searching Mel's eyes for approval and acceptance. Mel put her arms around Tien.

"Oh, honey, of course you do!"

"It's okay with you?" Tien's voice was flooded with relief.

"Sweetheart, I know what it means to want to know who your mother is. There were so many times in my life when I wished and longed for mine."

"I don't even know where to begin."

"I can help you. I'm an investigative reporter, remember!"

For the next two weeks, while soaking up the peace

and serenity that Pogue always brought her, Mel began what she could of the search to reunite Tien with Anh. A trip to the library in Edgartown to use the computer gave her some of the information she needed; a phone call provided a few leads.

Mel was going through the motions, doing everything she could think of to support Tien—from that first embrace to reassure her on the beach to hunting down contacts who might still have knowledge of the orphanage.

But late at night alone in her bed, Mel feared that every step she was taking to help Tien was also placing one more step between them. Despite her intellectual grasp that bringing Tien closer to Anh was not a zero-sum game—her actions weren't taking Tien away from her—emotionally she felt at risk of losing her daughter.

The night before they left the island, they sat at the dining room table with Mel's notes. She had accumulated enough information and developed a list of contacts that it made sense for Tien to go to Vietnam and continue in person to seek Anh. Tien was excited, but also distressed.

"I don't think I can do this on my own. I'm a school-teacher who's used to lesson plans and curricula and established criteria. I like knowing what to expect. I'm not sure I can deal with the uncertainty and ambiguity. I don't want to do this alone."

Mel looked across the table. Instead of the competent grown woman she knew her daughter to be, she saw the frightened little girl who had clung to her on the flight from Saigon.

She knew she would pick her up and carry her this time, as well.

"Shall I come with you?" she asked quietly.

"Would you? Thank you, Mom!"

IN THE NEXT FEW WEEKS, they made preparations for the trip. Mel took a leave of absence from the newspaper with her editor's blessing—she suspected because he anticipated she might be persuaded to write a story about Tien's quest for her mother. Mel's writing was deeply personal and often tapped into her own experience, but she had always drawn the line when it came to Tien's life. Raising a daughter had been challenging enough without having to deal with her feeling that her mother had told her secrets to the world. Tien was no longer a teenager, but this journey was as emotionally draining as adolescence.

Mel also acknowledged to herself that returning to Vietnam awakened feelings she thought she had long put to rest. Although Phil Coughlin had disappeared into the killing fields of Cambodia after Saigon fell, he had not disappeared from her heart. What might life have held for them if they had been able to fulfill the promise of those last few days in Saigon? As she had been when she was in her twenties, Mel wasn't one to dwell on loss. But in anticipating this journey she found herself tinged with regret that they had let slip from their hands something she knew now had been precious and irredeemable. With her usual practicality, she brushed aside these flickers of distraction. She had work to do.

Before she knew it, she and Tien had their visas and tickets, letters of introduction to the ministries that might have records, and a short list of contacts to start their search.

The night before they were to leave, Tien took the Acela from Penn Station in New York City to D.C. Normally composed and self-contained, she spent the evening at Mel's pacing, repacking and questioning every aspect of their plans.

"Do you think the gifts I've gotten are appropriate? How do I know what she'll like?"

"Tien, let's find her first. And the best gift will be you—a beautiful, happy woman who cared enough about her to seek her."

"Am I being selfish? What if she doesn't want to be found?"

"Then we won't violate that wish. There are no guarantees here, Tien. Let's try to get some sleep. We have a long journey ahead of us."

As the plane descended into Tan Son Nhat International Airport, Mel found herself with her face pressed against the window, searching for the familiar. She didn't know what she was looking for—and after thirty years of postwar reconstruction, it was doubtful that she'd recognize it. But with a jolt she understood that this trip was as much a homecoming for her as for Tien. Even to be landing at Tan Son Nhat, the new name for what had once been Tan Son Nhut airbase, and the incongruity of it now being an international airport and major hub for Vietnamese flights, seemed unbelievable.

The terminal was a chaotic mess of tourists scrambling to check in and find their gates. They'd arrived smack in the middle of monsoon season, and delays flickered across the departures and arrivals board. Tien seemed almost paralyzed by the assault on her senses, staring at the waves of people pushing past her, trying to decipher the lettering on the signs with her limited command of the language, unable to focus on any one thing as they moved through the airport. Her only comment to Mel was a revelation.

"They look like me. All of them. I'm not different here."

Mel should have grasped a long time ago what it had meant to her daughter to look out at the world and not see herself reflected in the faces looking back at her. Even if this trip did not result in their finding Anh, Mel understood even in these first few moments that what they learned—about themselves, about each other—would be immense.

They emerged from the terminal into oppressive heat and a curtain of rain. Mel had forgotten how aware one always was of the weather in Vietnam; she wondered if she was experiencing her first hot flash as they waited for the bus that would take them into the center of Ho Chi Minh City. With sweat dribbling down her armpits, she and Tien maneuvered their suitcases onto the bus and settled into two of the open seats. Mel had chosen the bus to bring Tien as close as possible to the life Mel remembered being lived on the streets of Saigon. The cocoon of a taxi or limousine sealed one away from everything there was to absorb in a city. With a map open on her lap, Mel pointed out landmarks, but what she saw passing by the windows of the bus resembled nothing that she remembered from the last bus ride she had taken on these same streets.

This was no longer "her" Saigon. The tawdriness, the sense of impending disaster, the frisson of danger that electrified every encounter, the mud were all missing. In its place was a scrubbed and orderly city, new buildings, parks in which families strolled rather than sought refuge from the enemy to the north. Here and there she saw an older building, its facade still pockmarked. As the bus crossed Dong Khoi Street, she caught a glimpse of neon and saw that the bar district had not disappeared, only switched its clientele. She might find one or two of her familiar haunts and be able to say to Tien, "This is where Anh worked and where she asked me to help her get you out of the country."

They settled into their hotel and Mel asked at the desk for the closest noodle bar. The hotel staff tried to steer her toward Western-style restaurants, thinking they were a pair of neophyte American tourists. But Mel dragged up her rusty Vietnamese and convinced them she didn't need coddling, just good information.

They ate, returned to the hotel to sleep and began their search in earnest the next morning. As they trekked from one ministry to another and made contact with each name on Mel's list, they felt themselves weaving a web. Their expectations were high as possibilities started to open up for them—the location of Anh's village; the name of a cousin.

A setback occurred three days into their search when they discovered that the villa that had housed St. Agnes had been destroyed as a vestige of the colonial era. No one knew what had become of the nuns. The news distressed Mel more than she expected. She'd not always understood the women who had run St. Agnes with such discipline and efficiency in the face of devastating deprivations; but to have even the memory of their existence wiped away as thoroughly as the building was to her incomprehensible and chilling.

Other fragments of her own history were missing as well—the Baos' tea house and the whole cluster of alleys where her flat had been located seemed to have been replaced by a block of modern apartments. She was disoriented by the transformation of the city and missed its seediness and dark corners.

On the fourth night they ventured to the bar district. As Mel had noted on the bus ride, it was still in the same place, throbbing with Japanese techno music and black lights. They wandered up and down the main avenue as Mel got her bearings, but as they rounded a corner a doorway hung with beads jogged her memory.

"That's it! That's the club where Anh worked." She steered Tien across the street and parted the curtain of beads. Inside was thronged with tourists—Chinese from Hong Kong, Australians, even some Germans from the conversations Mel was overhearing as they pushed further inside. The dance floor where Anh had entertained American soldiers was pulsating with young people while a DJ moved through his repertoire. The air was thick with cigarette smoke, knockoff perfumes and rum. Mel, for the first time since arriving in the city, felt the prickle of familiarity. She saw herself at twenty in the bodies on the dance floor, the barely contained seductions, the excitement of the unknown unfolding itself in the rhythm of the music and the sweet taste of umbrellaed drinks.

Tien, on the other hand, drew back. Mel saw the discomfort in her daughter's eyes. Perhaps this was not how she had imagined Anh's life. Beneath the energy on the dance floor she was seeing the spilled drinks, the furtive groping.

"What do you expect to find here?" Tien shouted to Mel, trying to be heard above the pounding music, her face in the flashing lights pained. "No one will remember her. The bar girls are younger than I am."

But Mel wasn't thinking about asking the waitresses. Instead, she made her way to the bar where an older woman was mixing drinks. Tien followed reluctantly. Mel managed to eke out a few questions between record changes. The woman had only been working at the club for a few years; she'd come from Hanoi after the war. But she knew of one or two women who had worked here before; she took Mel's cell phone number and offered to pass it on to them.

Mel would have lingered, soaking up this one sliver of her history here, but Tien so clearly wanted to leave that she reluctantly led her back out to the street.

"I just want to go back to the hotel and shower," Tien

said, as if to cleanse herself of any connection to that place so irrevocably tied to her mother.

Tien's discomfort with Ho Chi Minh City—what it had been for Anh and Mel, what it was now—grew stronger over the next several days. The food was spicier than she liked and upset her stomach; she struggled to use her limited Vietnamese.

"Why didn't you insist that I learn Vietnamese when I was a child? All I can speak or understand are the baby phrases you used to say to me. How will I be able to communicate with my mother when we find her?"

Mel noticed that Tien was referring to Anh now not by name but as my *mother*.

The conversation with the woman in the club set off a series of connections as Mel's phone number apparently was being passed from one possible source to another. They went on a round of meetings with women who claimed to know Anh or know of her. Then a man called, a lawyer who had developed a specialty in helping the children of the babylift find their families. He offered his services for a retainer.

Mel cautioned against trusting him, but Tien insisted on meeting him.

"We've turned up nothing so far. If he's been doing this as long as he says, he may have connections and access to records that we don't know about. At least hear him out!"

Mel acquiesced and accompanied Tien to the lawyer's office in a nondescript building, but only to protect Tien from what she suspected was an unscrupulous predator. When he pressed them for an advance payment before he began helping them, Mel refused.

"I need to see some evidence of your ability to assist

us—some assurance that you can make the connections you claim," Mel said.

They jockeyed back and forth, neither speaking the other's language well, but understanding enough to get the message across. Mel did not budge, and ultimately the lawyer threw up his hands. "Then I cannot help you."

When they left the office, Tien was furious.

"You treated me like a child in there!"

"You told me yourself that you feel unsure speaking Vietnamese. I was only trying to make sure he understood."

"But why didn't you want to pay him? What if we've lost our only opportunity to find her?"

"I wanted him to see that he wasn't dealing with someone he could easily exploit. I don't trust him."

"You think I can't handle this on my own!"

"Tien, you asked me to help you. I'm trying to do that. I'm also trying to protect you against false hope."

"But you keep throwing obstacles in the way. You doubt *everyone*. I think you honestly don't want me to find my mother!"

"Tien, I promise you that I will persevere for you until we've exhausted every option, explored every possible lead. But you're hovering on the edge of obsession if you're willing to believe that some snake oil salesman can magically make Anh appear.

"I know these last two weeks have been frustrating, and so much less than you hoped. But don't let your need to find Anh turn into desperation. That will only make you easy prey for someone like him to take advantage of."

"Stop patronizing me! How can you possibly understand my need? You *know* who your family is. You *know* whose blood runs through your veins."

"*You* are my family, Tien," she whispered, crushed

that her daughter did not understand the bond that had been forged between them.

They had been arguing in front of the lawyer's office. Mel believed that if she stayed there any longer they would both descend into a spiral of accusations about mothering and daughtering from which they might not recover.

"I need to be alone for a while. I'll hail you a cab to take you back to the hotel and meet you there in a few hours," Mel said.

"I can do that myself."

"Fine." Mel turned toward the center of the city and began walking. Out of the corner of her eye she saw Tien go back into the lawyer's building, but she resisted the impulse to stop her and walked on.

She was angry—with Tien for not recognizing how vulnerable she was, with herself for her own ambivalence. Was Tien right, that she didn't truly want her to find Anh? She longed to offer Tien wisdom and reassurance. Instead, she fumbled as awkwardly as she had decades before when she had first held Tien in her arms.

She continued to walk, futilely seeking refuge in a city that was no longer hers. The closer she got to the center, the more chaotic and alien it seemed. Horns blared. Motorbikes wove recklessly through a sea of three-wheeled trucks, pedestrians and bicycles. Heat simmered above the payment.

She felt oppressed—by the weather, by Tien's criticism, by her own weaknesses. She had a fleeting longing for the cigarettes she had given up when she became a mother. She could use something right now to distract her as she strode through the city, putting distance between herself and her daughter, between the past and the present. She doubted that a cigarette would do the trick, but decided she'd settle for some air conditioning and a long, cool drink. The afternoon rain had begun. Her sandals were soaked and starting to chafe, and her bare legs were splashed with mud.

She'd led herself to a neighborhood that held pockets of familiarity and realized she wasn't far from the old *Newsweek* office in the Hotel Continental. As she rounded a corner, she saw it up ahead. The hotel had been renovated rather than demolished. With relief, she rotated through the revolving door, shook out her umbrella and cast about for the bar, where she was happy to sink into one of the padded booths.

She ordered a tonic and lime and scanned the room. The place definitely appealed to a western tourist clientele. Copies of the *Financial Times* and *Herald Tribune* were scattered about.

She was leafing through the *Herald* absentmindedly, refreshed by the drink and lulled by the monotony of falling rain, when her eye fell on a familiar face staring out from page three.

Phil Coughlin, even in a low-resolution black-and-white photo, bristled with energy and a penetrating brilliance. It stunned her, especially when he had been so recently in her thoughts. She read on, hoping that the article would divert her enough from the unsettling tension with Tien.

The MacArthur Foundation had just announced its latest round of Fellows and Coughlin was one of them. They referred to him as the "Mountain Doctor" for his work among the hill tribes of northern Thailand. It appeared that he had never left Southeast Asia. After he had crossed into Cambodia, ministering to the victims of Pol Pot, he'd made his way north, building clinics in the remote territory above Chiang Mai in Thailand. The facts of his achievements as a humanitarian were spare—a list of dates and deeds that was long but lifeless. He had apparently impressed the award committee, but Mel had no sense of who Phil Coughlin was now beyond the label that had been attached to him.

She folded up the paper and was about to leave when her phone rang. She assumed it was Tien and flipped it open, but the number was a Washington area code.

"Mel, this is Sam."

The feature editor at the *Post*. It was 2:00 a.m. in Washington.

"I'm sorry to bother you on your vacation, but Susan told me where you are, and, well, I need you to take an assignment."

"Sam, I'm on leave taking care of family business."
And messing it up.

"I know. But hear me out first, please. The MacArthur Foundation just named a new set of Fellows and they are a quirky bunch, so we want to do an in-depth piece on them. It seems that one of them is in Thailand. You're closer than anyone I've got in the newsroom, and I understand that this guy rarely comes back to the States. He's something of a one-man Doctors Without Borders, a cowboy, from what little I could find about him. But he's willing to do an interview—maybe only because MacArthur told him he had to. I can fly you up there and back to Vietnam—thirty-six hours tops. Will you do it?"

Mel had enough stature at the paper to refuse, but she didn't immediately turn Sam down. She felt a duty to Tien to see this quest through to one answer or another, but the frustrations and hostility of the morning had left her questioning whether she was helping or hindering her daughter. She also was pulled in two directions by the subject of Sam's assignment. The flatness of the MacArthur press release had left her curious about what had shaped and driven Phil to a life so different from hers. But at the same time, she was wary of opening herself up— to her own regrets, to his judgment of the path she had chosen, even to why he had disappeared so thoroughly, never once trying to reconnect.

She drummed her fingers on the glass-topped table.

"Sam, let me think about it. I'll call you in a few hours."

She hailed a cab back to her own hotel, surprised by the discomfort Sam's request had triggered. She was a professional. A simple assignment like this—a profile of an accomplished man—was hardly challenging.

Sam was right; she could knock this off in a day or two. And the fear she had of getting drawn back into the vortex of emotion that Phil Coughlin had elicited in her so long ago seemed ridiculous. She had been young and inexperienced then, and more vulnerable than she had admitted to herself, caught up in the raw and desperate situation in Saigon.

She'd lived through a lot since those tumultuous days—raised a child; excelled in her profession; even been in and out of love a few times, although never married. She wasn't one to fall under anyone's charismatic spell now, no matter how piercing his blue eyes or engaging his smile or noble his mission.

Mel let herself into her hotel room. Through the open French doors she saw Tien sitting on the balcony and went out to join her. Although the rain had subsided, the air was still heavy and the balcony offered no relief from the sweltering heat.

Tien's face was taut and clouded with anger as she turned to Mel.

"Where have you been? I was worried."

Mel didn't answer her question. "Why didn't you call? I had my phone on."

"You seemed to want to be alone when you left me at the lawyer's office." Tien's voice was icy, accusatory.

"I thought we both needed time away from each other. How did you spend the rest of the day?"

"I met with someone. Mr. Nguyen made the arrangement. She was the right age, came from the same region. But she couldn't answer the questions you gave me."

Mel had prepared a short list of questions that only Anh would be able to answer.

Mel read the disappointment and frustration in her daughter's eyes. She refrained from asking Tien how much she had paid for this hastily arranged and failed assignation. She knew Tien didn't need to hear an "I told you so." But she was also wary of the barely camouflaged anger just below the surface of Tien's remarks. It was clear to Mel that Tien was gathering up all the false leads and dashed hopes into a bundle that she was laying at Mel's feet. She could hear the unspoken litany—if only Mel had made an attempt to maintain contact with Anh after she and Tien left Vietnam; if only Mel had recognized that Tien would want—*need*—to know her mother and had begun the search when Tien was younger and leads were still fresh. Mel saw it dawning on Tien that she had begun too late, that she might not find Anh, and that it was all Mel's fault.

Mel, weary and unwilling to engage Tien in another verbal battle, decided to retreat into work. She told Tien about the call from Sam.

"So I'm going to fly up to Chiang Mai and do the interview. You're welcome to come with me if you want to, or you can stay here and continue the search—maybe you should go to Anh's old village."

"I'll stay. If word is starting to circulate among people who might have known her, I want to stick around—not be on some inaccessible mountain. Who knows if you'll even have cell reception?"

"Do you want me to arrange for an interpreter while I'm gone?"

"Mr. Nguyen has already taken care of that."

"I hope this avenue works for you, honey." And with that Mel got up, went into the bedroom and called Sam to let him know she'd take the assignment.

By the next morning she had a round-trip ticket to Chiang Mai and a reservation for a four-wheel drive vehicle to get her up into the mountains to Phil Coughlin's compound. She felt both relief to be away from Tien's bitterness and an apprehension that she was heading into emotional territory that might be just as entangled.

As the plane landed in Thailand, she reminded herself that this upcoming interview was about Phil Coughlin and what compelled him to do extraordinary things, not what he thought about Mel Ames. Nevertheless, she steeled herself for an unsettling reunion.

Armed with the information Sam had e-mailed her and a map from the car rental agency, Mel navigated out of Chiang Mai and followed the highway toward the mountains. Sam had offered to get her a driver, but she'd always preferred being on her own. She wanted time to think, not have to banter in pleasantries with an eager-to-please chauffeur. She wasn't a tourist in need of pampering.

Although it was monsoon season here in northern Thailand, as well, the rain only lasted for an hour or so during the day and then brilliant sunshine burst onto the refreshed countryside. As the road became narrower and more serpentine, Mel discovered a breathtakingly beautiful landscape around each bend. But as she passed through tiny villages scattered up the mountain she also saw heartbreaking poverty.

It was mid-afternoon when she reached the intricately carved gate to the clinic compound. Her arrival was noticed first by a group of boys, who were scattered around a dusty pitch playing soccer as she rolled to a stop just inside the walls and parked next to a rusting Toyota pickup.

The boys clustered around her as she emerged from the car, chattering in a dialect that she assumed must be Lahu, the hill tribe in this region. She spoke Phil's name and one of the younger boys ran off to a large thatched bamboo building resting on stilts. As she listened to the boys, she glanced around, taking in her surroundings and cataloguing them for later inclusion in her article. Several stilted buildings rimmed the courtyard, simple but well maintained. She remembered how orderly Phil's flat had been in Saigon and saw that same precision reflected on a much larger scale here. The entire compound bustled with activity—women shepherding small children, awaiting their turn at what appeared to be the main clinic; men unloading supplies from a flatbed truck; an older woman tending a vegetable garden.

A tall, thin man, his face lined from years witnessing the pain and suffering human beings inflicted upon one another, descended the stairs of one of the houses and crossed the courtyard toward her. As he approached she realized with barely contained surprise that it was Phil. He stretched out his hand and greeted her, but with wariness and discomfort.

"Po told me a round-eyed woman with hair like a boy had spoken my name. I assumed it was either a desperately lost tourist or the reporter from *The Washington Post* the foundation had warned me to expect. They didn't tell me it would be Melanie Ames."

At least he recognized her, but beyond remembering

her name, he seemed both distrustful and unwilling to acknowledge their shared history. She wondered what had so damaged him in the intervening years.

"They said they had pulled you away from your vacation. I apologize for the disruption. If I'd had any say in this, you'd still be sitting on a beach drinking mai tais and I'd be left alone to do my good works, of which the foundation seems so enamored. However, it appears that neither one of us had the option of refusing, so here you are. Welcome."

She wanted him to know that she could have refused but had chosen instead to come. But he seemed to think that she was like any other journalist sent to irritate him. In the face of that indifference, her own apprehensiveness about falling once again within his sphere seemed foolish and self-absorbed.

"Thanks for agreeing to meet with me," she answered, determined to tamp down the churning in her gut and silence the voice that was asking plaintively, "How can you not care that it is *me* who has come to do this story?"

She followed Phil around the compound, notebook in hand, observing, questioning, showing suitable appreciation for the ingenuity of the Lahu tribesmen who'd been able to create a medical village with the most meager of resources.

Phil was comfortable expounding on the services he and his small staff of rotating medical workers were able to provide to one of the most impoverished of the hill tribes. He was willing to talk about the mobile clinic he brought to the more remote tribes at higher altitudes. He even described a plan he had for trying to prevent the younger generation from developing the opium addiction that was widespread among the elders of the tribe.

But he remained opaque and resistant whenever Mel

tried to steer the conversation to Phil himself—what had been the journey that ultimately brought him to these lush mountains? What about the hill tribes had so captured him that he would devote his life to them? He offered nothing that she could not see herself, presenting only the facade of the hero doctor, a self-aware and hardened version of the cocky bravado she remembered from decades before.

After little more than an hour, he was ready to dismiss her.

"I have the evening clinic to prepare for. Many of the Lahu men offer themselves out as labor in other villages and return late in the day. That's when I treat them. I can ask the cook to prepare you some tea before you go. Feel free to enjoy it on my verandah." He pointed up to the porch above them, jutting out on stilts. "The view is spectacular."

Mel, frustrated by her inability to elicit anything of the man's spirit and irritated by his abrupt dismissal and unwillingness to even sip a cup of tea with her, decided to leave without accepting his offer. Her phone rang.

"Excuse me, but it's my daughter. I must answer this." She turned and took a few steps away from him.

"Mom, oh, thank God you've got reception up there!" Tien sounded tightly wound, as if she wanted to leap out of the phone, grab Mel and pull her back.

"Tien! What is it?" The distance she had felt between them in the last few days evaporated. She was once again a mother responding to a cry of need from her child.

"I think I've found her! This isn't some scam artist passed off on me by that lawyer. Someone in the Ministry of Child Welfare called this afternoon. They gave me an address and assured me that this was the Anh Tran who had relinquished the infant Tien Tran in 1975."

"Have you tried to contact her?"

"I only have an address, and I can't find a phone number in the directory. I'm going to have to go myself…but that's why I called." She was silent for a moment. The bitterness and frustration were gone from her voice.

"Mom, I'm sorry I was so angry with you the other day. I said things I shouldn't have. And you were right about Nguyen. He was only trying to take advantage of my need."

"I understand, sweetheart. All is forgiven."

"Mom, I don't want to go to her alone. Will you come back and be with me?"

"Of course I will. I've got a flight out of Chiang Mai in the morning. There is nothing to keep me here any longer."

Mel clicked the phone off and absorbed what she had heard from Tien. Although there were no certainties, this latest information about Anh was probably as good as they could get, given its source. Mel was excited for Tien. She had heard the anticipation in her voice—the hope—and she shared that with her. But at the same time, she was hit with the old fear that she was about to lose something very precious.

"Is something wrong?" Phil's voice broke her train of thought. "You look like you've been given devastating news."

Mel was exhausted and drained. She'd already regretted making the grueling trip, a waste of time for both of them given the paltry, sterile information she'd managed to obtain. She was angry with him—for his arrogance, for his lack of understanding of what she could have done for him with her story, for his unwillingness to acknowledge that something—however tenuous—had once existed between them.

She should have just shrugged off his question, refused the tea and climbed into her car.

But she didn't.

Something seized her, perhaps ignited by the tentative reconciliation she'd just experienced with Tien on the phone and her own recognition that, as much as Phil had erected a wall between them, she'd allowed it to remain and had not even attempted to establish a connection with him. She'd played the objective, disinterested journalist instead of the woman whose life he had touched in an irrevocable way. Damn it, she was Mel Ames! Where was the fervor, the willingness to leap into unknown territory?

"I'll take that cup of tea you offered, but only if you'll join me and allow me to tell you what that phone call was all about."

She was about to make that leap and see if Phil Coughlin would follow her.

He shrugged and looked at his watch.

"I imagine I can spare a half hour."

He led the way up to the verandah and made the tea himself.

The view was indeed extraordinary, extending across the mountains to the west. Mel settled into a cushioned wicker chair and cradled the cup in her hands. With a jolt of recognition she saw it was one of the Red Sox mugs he'd had in Saigon.

"You still have these mugs!"

"I still have many things from Saigon. So you have a daughter. When did you marry?"

"I didn't. I adopted Tien."

"Tien?"

"The baby from St. Agnes I originally came to help before you persuaded me to rescue all of them."

"I had no idea." Phil seemed truly stunned, as if he had

not imagined her ever considering such an action. "I didn't realize you intended to adopt her yourself."

"I didn't—intend to, that is. But by the time we arrived in San Diego, she had made it very clear what she intended—she wanted no one else but me."

"So she's a grown woman now. But clearly close to you, and upset about something that has upset you, as well."

"Was it that obvious?"

"When you ended the conversation, some realization affected you. I could see the change in your face. When you were talking with her, your tone and your expression were totally empathic. You were a mother with a hurting child. But after you got off the phone, it was *you* who was hurting."

It was Mel's turn to be stunned. For someone who had barricaded himself from her an hour before, he had nevertheless been tuned in to what she was experiencing. She swallowed another sip of tea and realized this was the opportunity she had been hoping for—the breach in the wall. She plunged in, willing to open herself up to him in the hope that he would reciprocate.

"Tien is in Ho Chi Minh City, where we've been for three weeks. Not on a beach." She looked up at him. I'm not some dilettante tourist soaking up local color, she wanted to say to him.

"We've been searching for Anh, the bar girl who was my friend and Tien's mother."

"Any progress?"

"Not until today. But the frustration of the search and my own ambivalence about finding Anh had pushed us to the edge a few days ago. The mother-daughter dance is a complicated one. The rhythm keeps changing and the steps get more intricate as you move through life."

He smiled. "I know. I have three sisters. They each put

my mother through hell at one time or another. So now that there's a real possibility she may find her mother, you're thinking, who am I? Am I about to lose her?"

Mel nodded. "So much of how I define myself, so many of the choices I've made in my life, are tied to my being Tien's mother. I am in a totally different place than I imagined for myself thirty years ago. When I was working in Saigon I thought I wanted nothing else than to be a war correspondent, someone who could translate the reality, the horror, the underbelly of war."

"Any regrets that that's not who you are now?"

"None. I didn't understand then how deeply satisfying this life would be. So, no regrets. But costs—there have been costs."

"Like not being a war correspondent."

She nodded.

"Any others?"

She looked him in the eye, then reached into a deep part of herself.

"I didn't marry."

"Because of Tien?"

"I wanted a father for her as well as a husband for me. The man had to be both, and I didn't find him. What about you? What have the costs been for you?"

She waited, hoping that his willingness to listen to her and his perceptiveness about how vulnerable she felt would translate into a willingness to let down the mask.

"After I arrived in Cambodia I lost touch with everything and everyone who had meant something in my life. Including you."

"Why?" With this revelation of his, she was no longer the objective reporter.

"I was captured and imprisoned. By the time I was released four years later, I'd lost faith in humanity, and in the God whose will I thought I was following. I descended into a dark and hopeless time in my life. I disappeared more thoroughly from those who loved me than when I had been in prison."

One of the aides from the clinic stood at the bottom of the verandah stairs.

"Doc, the men are starting to arrive for the clinic hours. Will you be down soon?"

He seemed relieved to stop the revelations. It occurred to Mel that he had buried this part of his life and never spoken about it to anyone else.

"Look, it's getting late to start down the mountain. Why don't you spend the night here at the compound? We have plenty of room. We can have dinner when the clinic hours are over and continue our conversation. In fact, do you want to shadow me at the clinic?"

Mel smiled, accepted the invitation and followed him across the courtyard and up into the clinic.

The next two hours reminded her of the scenes she'd seen so many times at the orphanage. Phil bantered in Lahu as the men brought him their aches and pains, their faces lighting up as Phil bent to listen to their hearts or deftly probed a tender muscle. At times he turned to Mel to translate or explain—one man expressing worry about his son, who wanted to leave the village; another joking with Phil about his singing. Patients presented him with barter as payment—a scrawny white chicken, a net bag filled with cabbages, an embroidered cap, which Phil put on immediately.

What Mel witnessed was affection on both sides.

Dinner was communal, the entire staff at a long table in a large room in their quarters. Like Phil's house, it was on stilts with an open porch overlooking the mountain. Mel enjoyed the give-and-take of conversation and was surprised by Phil's rapport with them all. She had only known him as a loner, forgetting that he had once been a Marine. She had assumed he preferred to work on his own, not willing to engage in the compromise and balancing of everyone's needs that being part of a team required. But he seemed quite at home with the five people around the table.

After dinner, people dispersed to their own pursuits and Phil invited her back to the verandah for a continuation of their conversation. He didn't seem ready to pick up where they had left off, so she asked a more comfortable question.

"What will you do with the MacArthur money?"

A wide grin stretched across his face, and she saw flickers of the energy and drive she remembered in the young Phil Coughlin.

"Oh, my God! Let me tell you what I'm going to do— operating rooms, more mobile clinics, fellowships to bring specialists here for short-term assignments."

He grabbed a sheet of paper and sketched out the new building he had planned. His excitement was undisguised. The grant had unleashed the restraint he had practiced for years trying to make do with the most limited resources. He could accomplish so much that he had only dreamed of doing in the past.

As the evening deepened so did their conversation, meandering from one topic to another and eventually returning to how he had pulled himself out of the darkness. He talked about how he had stumbled upon the need among the hill tribes and why he ultimately decided to stay; the evolution of what he was trying to accomplish; his realization that he was on a mission to which he was passionately committed.

In all of what he described to Mel there was one thing glaringly missing. Like her, he had never married.

"My mother, the devoutly Catholic Margaret Mary Daly Coughlin held out hope for a while that I might enter the priesthood. In retrospect, what I've chosen to do with my life has been a kind of priesthood. I don't think one can do this without the kind of single-minded devotion you find in those who take vows."

"That single-mindedness is a two-edged sword," Mel interjected. "It's a strength, keeping us focused on the goal, but in the extreme, it also keeps us from letting anything or any*one* else share our attention."

They continued to talk. Late in the night, the sky overhead brilliant with stars, they reached the moment Mel referred to as the "crossing-over" point. The moment of true intimacy when the layers of disguise have been peeled away and one reveals one's deepest self. It was exhilarating and excruciating at the same time. For just as they bared their souls to one another and acknowledged what had occurred, they also realized that it was coming to an end. Morning was nearly upon them. Tien was waiting in Ho Chi Minh City; Sam was waiting for her article; the first of the patients were making their way up the mountain to the compound.

Phil wrapped her in an embrace as the first birds began their song in the trees below the verandah. They were emotionally spent; they had no more words. But they were friends.

Mel left the compound before the rest of the staff had awakened, her notebook full and her heart both joyful and bereft.

WHEN SHE LANDED at Tan Son Nhat, Tien was waiting in the arrivals lounge with a driver and the address she'd been given by the ministry. Mel understood the urgency, and despite her fatigue, didn't object when Tien told her she wanted to go immediately to Anh.

The car headed to the northern outskirts of the city to a district that had been open land when Mel had last been in Saigon. It came to a stop at a tall gate, beyond which Mel and Tien could see what looked like parkland. They were confused and thought the driver had the wrong address, but he pointed out the road sign and the number on the gate.

Mel and Tien climbed out of the car and approached the gate. It was Mel who realized first where they were. She reached out for Tien's hand as a soft moan escaped from her lips. Then, stepping ahead, they passed through the gate and into the cemetery. They followed a path of crushed white rock to the numbered row on the slip of paper that Tien had thought identified an apartment. When they reached the spot they found a polished stone set level with the earth.

Inscribed upon it was Anh's name, the years of her birth and death, and the inscription "Mother of Beloved Daughter Tien."

Tien knelt and touched the stone, tracing her own and her mother's names. Mel knelt beside her and enfolded her daughter close to her heart as Tien's tears began to fall, a curtain of water as steady as the monsoon.

WHEN THEY RETURNED to the hotel, Tien told Mel she wanted to go away for a few days. She had learned of a Buddhist monastery that offered retreats in Da Nang. Before they returned to the States she thought she needed time for solitude and meditation.

"I can leave this afternoon on a bus, if you don't mind."

"I'm fine. I have to write this profile for Sam and then I'm going to sleep for as long as I can. I think it's just what you need."

After she had seen Tien off on the bus, Mel holed up in her hotel room with her notebook, her laptop, and a carafe of tea. She typed nonstop for two hours composing a piece she called Reckoning For A Lifetime: The Costs That Will Not Be Recompensed.

The article began with a list, entitled "Expenditures For A Lifetime."

1. 7 round-trip tickets between Boston and Bangkok
2. 25 Smith-Corona typewriter ribbons
3. 272 cartons of Lucky Strike cigarettes
4. 9 pairs of khaki shirts and shorts
5. 17 pairs of Birkenstock sandals
6. A lung
7. A pediatric practice in Brookline, Massachusetts
8. Anne Marie Reilly, who wrote to him through medical school and residency and the Marines and waited another two years for him to "get Southeast Asia out of his system," but who would not join him when he decided he could not leave and so told Jimmy Lane that she would marry him.
9. 4 pairs of black plastic-framed eyeglasses
10. 7 cases of Glenlivet
11. 12 reams of 24-pound white Strathmore typing paper
12. A fully equipped field operating room
13. An army surplus Jeep
14. A rosary blessed by Father Joe Fallon, S. J., his high school buddy
15. Not being at his mother's bedside when she died of pancreatic cancer
16. 700 doses of penicillin
17. An M-16 rifle and 50 rounds of ammunition

18. A Zippo lighter
19. Galvanized tin to roof the clinic
20. One navy blue suit to wear when he spoke at fundraising dinners
21. Grey's Anatomy, the PDR and a surgery textbook
22. A Douay-Reims Bible
23. Children of his own
24. Lumber to build his mountain clinic
25. The ashes when rebels burned it to the ground

When she finished, she opened the French doors and sat on the balcony. It was dusk, and in contrast to the silence and beauty of the night before, the cacophony of Ho Chi Minh City greeted her just over the hotel's courtyard wall. She contemplated what she had just written and understood that to submit it for publication in the *Post* would be a betrayal of the trust Phil had placed in her.

She went back to the laptop, opened up her Gmail account and attached the article to an e-mail addressed not to Sam but to Phil.

"This is yours," she wrote. "It belongs to no one else."

She'd write another profile for the *Post* in the morning. But first, she desperately needed sleep.

Despite the sounds and lights of the city, she fell into a deep sleep immediately, brought on not only by her physical exhaustion but also by the lightening of a burden. She'd given something back to Phil in return for what he'd given her the night before on his verandah.

In the middle of the night she was awakened by an insistent and disorienting sound. It took her a moment to recognize the ring of her cell phone. It was Phil.

"Where are you?"

She gave him the name of the hotel.

"Stay there."

She mumbled an agreement and then drifted back to sleep. Several hours later, still in bed, she heard the phone again and then a knock on the door.

"I'm here," he said.

She opened the door, the phone still at her ear.

"I've lost enough in my life. Now that I have found you again, letting you go is not a cost I'm willing to bear."

He reached out for her.

All the revelations from the night before flooded back and the emotional connection that had been forged between them suddenly was transformed into a physical one. Her body in its thin cotton nightgown molded itself to the solidity of his. He took her face in his hands and kissed her, his lips hungry and searching. He slid his arms down and slipped them under her, lifting her and carrying her back to the bed.

He saw that the other bed hadn't been slept in.

"Your daughter?"

"Away at a monastery," she murmured.

He sat by her side and she looked up at him.

"No one has ever understood me in the way you do. That article shook me to my core. How did you do that? How did you get me to reveal so much of myself?"

"I took a leap of faith."

"How so?"

"I thought if I offered to peel back a layer of my own, you might reciprocate."

"You were taking a risk."

"I know. But I wanted to know who you were. Not for the article, but for myself. I'd always found you so compelling and that frightened me. I wanted to overcome my fear by understanding who you were."

"And now you know."

"I know *part* of you. There is still more to explore and discover." She smiled as she began to unbutton his shirt.

He stretched out alongside her and kissed her again. Slowly, with great tenderness, they made love. For both of them it had been a long time since they had been with anyone. They savored every stage, holding back while they explored one another, delighting in the contours and hollows of each other's bodies, reveling in the tactile explosion of skin to skin. When they finally came, it was with a deep and vibrant satisfaction. Once again Mel slept, this time wrapped in Phil's arms, his lanky body spooned around her.

Later that day, after Mel had told him about finding Anh's grave, he asked what she and Tien would do next.

"After Tien returns from her retreat, I expect that we'll return to the States."

"How long will she be gone?"

"A few days, perhaps a week."

"So there's nothing to keep you here in Ho Chi Minh City until she returns."

"Only you."

"I can't stay. Even with the staff holding things together, I should return to the mountain. It's where I need to be."

Mel felt her heart constrict. She should have realized how ephemeral and impermanent these last few hours with Phil were. She'd conveniently ignored the reality of their divergent paths in life in the passion and wonder of rediscovering one another. She held back her disappointment that he would leave so soon. No regrets, she told herself. Even knowing that it was only this one night, she'd embrace it once again.

"I have a request," Phil said, stroking the side of her face. "Come back with me while Tien is in Da Nang. You said yourself that I'm the only thing that keeps you here. You can write as easily on my verandah as you can in this room."

Her rational side cautioned her that it would be all the more painful to leave him if she went with him now, only postponing the inevitable. But she had forsaken caution when she opened up her life to him that first night on the mountain.

"I'll come." She took another leap of faith, trusting that whatever happened in the next few days could only enrich their lives, no matter in what direction each turned.

She sent word to the monastery, packed up and left Vietnam, this time with Phil at her side.

The days she spent with him on the mountain deepened the emotional connection between them. In the evenings, she and Phil continued their conversations, delving into what had shaped and challenged them in the thirty years that had separated them. When she remarked that he no longer drank, he offered her the harrowing story of his descent into alcoholism and his subsequent climb to sobriety. In their bed at night their lovemaking captured what they had learned about one another, weaving their stories together in a way that bound them closer.

During the day when Phil was treating patients in the clinic Mel reached out to the Lahu women. Despite the language barrier, she was accepted into their circle, working beside them in the garden and learning to cook a vegetable curry spiced with galangal and chilies. Over the course of her stay she finished the new profile for the *Post*, a piece that she knew captured the complexity of the man and his work.

She wasn't sure if it was the altitude or the clarity of the air or the simplicity of village life, but she felt invigorated, healthier than she had in years. She also felt a satisfaction that she hadn't thought possible.

The end of the week loomed, and with it the pull of all the other threads in her life—her daughter, her work, her close-knit network of friends in Washington. Once again the rational voice intruded and she slipped into a contemplative, distant mood.

That night in bed, as Phil held her, he spoke aloud what neither of them wanted to face.

"When I came to you that night in Ho Chi Minh City, I told you I didn't want to lose you again. This week with you has only reaffirmed for me what you mean to me. I know I am asking something extraordinary of you—to give up the life you've built for yourself. But I cannot bear to let you go this time. Be my wife."

All of the limitations and expectations that had defined her life up until that moment crowded into the darkened room, grasping for her. But she turned inward and listened to the voice that had barely been a whisper in Saigon thirty years before but now was strong and confident.

"Yes," she answered.

They made love, this time with an intensity and passion and understanding strengthened by the choice each had made to be with one another, a choice worth the cost.

The next morning, Tien called to let Mel know she was ready to leave Da Nang.

"Fly to Chiang Mai," Mel told her. "I'll meet you there."

She picked Tien up at the airport and as they drove up the mountain she listened to her daughter's experience at the retreat. She wasn't ready to share with Tien what had happened until she'd had the opportunity to introduce her to Phil in the village. But she was convinced that once Tien knew him, she would understand Mel's decision.

They arrived just before lunch, greeted by the soccer boys who escorted them to the dining room. After introductions, Tien got swept up into the lively conversation around the table and seemed at ease and at peace with herself.

When the meal was over, Phil walked Mel and Tien back to his verandah.

"I have something I want to show you, Tien," he said as he reached for a thick photo album on the table, its cheap plastic cover dry and cracked.

"It's a record of the final days of the orphanage."

"How did you manage to save the photos?" Mel asked, remembering Phil's capture and imprisonment in Cambodia after he left Saigon.

"I'd sent my mother the undeveloped rolls of film before I left Vietnam—a peace offering or a smoke screen, depending on how you look at it. I thought it would comfort her to see the children, knowing she was so worried about my decision to leave Boston. When I was imprisoned, the photos—and your *Newsweek* article—were all she had, so she put together the album. She saved it, and when she passed away my sisters found it and sent it to me."

Tien's eyes grew wide as she moved closer to Phil to view the album. There were photos of the villa and group shots of the different age groups of the children, all of which Tien studied carefully. Then Phil turned the yellowed page and showed her two photos, side by side. In the first, a baby in the arms of a young Vietnamese woman in a pale yellow *ao dai*.

"That is you with your mother, Anh."

Tien bent over the page, gasping.

"She looks like me!"

"This is another photo of you with Anh and Melanie. I took it the day before the evacuation."

"This last item is the *Newsweek* article that sparked the babylift. Your mothers saved your life, Tien. Both of them."

Tien looked across the table at Mel.

"I know that now," she said. She reached out to Mel and Mel embraced her daughter. At that moment Mel felt the same force that had flowed from Anh so many years before, when she had entrusted Mel with her daughter's future, her daughter's life. That force was coming now from Tien, stronger as a result of her journey into the past and her acceptance of who both her mothers were and what they had done for her. Mel knew Tien would flourish; and she could tell from the perceptive, accepting expression in Tien's eyes as she looked at Mel and Phil that Tien would understand Mel's decision to marry Phil and join him in the mountains.

She wiped the tears from her eyes, tears of joy at all that she had regained on this journey—her daughter's understanding and Phil's love.

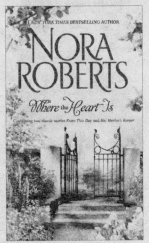
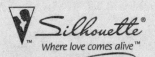

THE FIRST LADY OF THE WEST,
NEW YORK TIMES BESTSELLING AUTHOR
LINDA LAEL MILLER
BRINGS YOU A RIVETING NEW TRILOGY

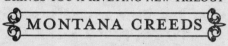

MONTANA CREEDS

Descendants of the legendary McKettrick family,
the Creed brothers couldn't wait to leave small-town
life behind. But now they're back, ready to raise
a little hell—and Stillwater Springs, Montana,
will never be the same.

February 2009   March 2009   April 2009

"Linda Lael Miller creates vibrant characters
and stories I defy you to forget."
—#1 *New York Times* bestselling author
Debbie Macomber

HQN™
We *are* romance™

www.HQNBooks.com

REQUEST YOUR FREE BOOKS!

2 FREE NOVELS
FROM THE ROMANCE/SUSPENSE
COLLECTION PLUS 2 FREE GIFTS!

BOB08R

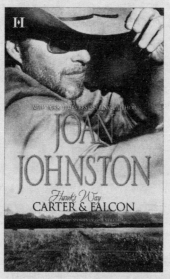

Introducing the Fifth Annual
More Than Words Anthology

Five bestselling authors
Five real-life heroines

A little comfort, caring and compassion go a long way toward making the world a better place. Just ask the dedicated women handpicked from countless worthy nominees across North America to become this year's recipients of Harlequin's More Than Words award. To celebrate their accomplishments, five bestselling authors have honored the winners by writing short stories inspired by these real-life heroines.

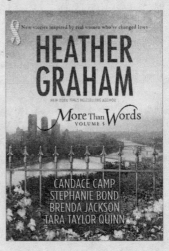

New stories inspired by real women who've changed lives

HEATHER GRAHAM
NEW YORK TIMES BESTSELLING AUTHOR

More Than Words
VOLUME 5

CANDACE CAMP
STEPHANIE BOND
BRENDA JACKSON
TARA TAYLOR QUINN

Visit **www.HarlequinMoreThanWords.com**
to find out more, or to nominate
a real-life heroine in your life.

**Proceeds from the sale of this book will be
reinvested in Harlequin's charitable initiatives.**

Available in April 2009 wherever books are sold.